PENGUIN CLASSICS

CHRISTOPHER MARLOWE
THE COMPLETE PLAYS

CHRISTOPHER MARLOWE (1564–93) was born in Canterbury, the son of a reasonably wealthy shoemaker. He was educated at King's School, Canterbury, and received a scholarship to Corpus Christi, Cambridge, where he obtained his B.A. in 1584. He appears to have been involved in a secret political mission, travelling abroad as a foreign agent. The university authorities suspected him of wishing to enter the English seminary in Rheims as a Catholic convert and it was only through the intervention of the Privy Council that he was awarded his M.A. in 1587.

The exact chronology of Marlowe's work is difficult to determine. At Cambridge he translated parts of Ovid's *Amores* and may also have written the first part of *Tamburlaine*, which was performed in 1587 to great acclaim. He wrote the second part of *Tamburlaine* in the following year. His other great works were written in quick succession, *The Tragical History of Dr Faustus* (*c.* 1588), *The Jew of Malta* (*c.* 1590) and *Edward II* (*c.* 1592). It is interesting to note that Marlowe was the exact contemporary of Shakespeare and some scholars believe that he had a part in the writing of *Henry VI*, *Titus Andronicus* and *Richard III*. There is, however, no direct evidence to support this theory. Marlowe's work went beyond the bounds of traditional dramatic style, he brought a bolder tragic conception to that previously seen on the English stage and displayed the real strength and flexibility of blank verse. The poetry and translations that he produced were also of a very high order: *Hero and Leander*, written in the Italianate Ovidian tradition, is generally considered to be the finest English epyllion of the sixteenth century. Marlowe was arrested in May 1593 on charges of blasphemy arising from evidence given by Kyd. On 1 June 1593 he was stabbed to death by Ingram Friser in a tavern in Deptford and subsequently buried there.

J. B. STEANE was a scholar of Jesus College, Cambridge, where he read English. He is the author of *Marlowe: A Critical Study* (1964) and *Tennyson* (1966). He has also edited several Elizabethan texts, including plays by Dekker and Jonson. His edition of the prose works of Thomas

Nashe, *The Unfortunate Travellers and Other Works*, is also published in the Penguin Classics. For some time now he has been engaged in music criticism, writing reviews for music magazines and periodicals, including *Gramophone*, *The Musical Times* and *Opera Now*; he has also contributed to the *New Grove Dictionary of Opera* and has been a frequent broadcaster on Radio 3. His books on musical subjects include *The Grand Tradition* (1974) and *Voices: Singers and Critics* (1992).

Christopher Marlowe

THE COMPLETE PLAYS

DIDO, QUEEN OF CARTHAGE

TAMBURLAINE THE GREAT

DOCTOR FAUSTUS

THE JEW OF MALTA

EDWARD THE SECOND

THE MASSACRE AT PARIS

Edited with an Introduction by
J. B. Steane

PENGUIN BOOKS

PENGUIN BOOKS

Published by the Penguin Group
Penguin Books Ltd, 27 Wrights Lane, London W8 5TZ, England
Penguin Books USA Inc., 375 Hudson Street, New York, New York 10014, USA
Penguin Books Australia Ltd, Ringwood, Victoria, Australia
Penguin Books Canada Ltd, 10 Alcorn Avenue, Toronto, Ontario, Canada M4V 3B2
Penguin Books (NZ) Ltd, 182–190 Wairau Road, Auckland 10, New Zealand

Penguin Books Ltd, Registered Offices: Harmondsworth, Middlesex, England

This collection published in Penguin English Library 1969
Reprinted in Penguin Classics 1986
9 10

Introduction and Notes copyright © J. B. Sloane, 1969
All rights reserved

Printed in England by Clays Ltd, St Ives plc
Set in Monotype Garamond

To June and Ralph

CONTENTS

INTRODUCTION

THERE was a time not so very long ago when literary gentlemen could meet, say 'Christopher Marlowe' to each other, and be fairly sure that they were going to talk about the same person. Modern scholarship has changed all that, and of course we have to be grateful to it. Thirty years ago Christopher Marlowe was a colourful character certainly, but a relatively simple one, all black and red: a rebel, an atheist, a fiery soul whose works expressed his own heady exuberance, aspirations and despairs; it was also well known that he lacked a sense of humour. Nowadays no one can be so very sure. When modern literary gentlemen start to talk about him it is quite possible that one of them will still have this same Christopher Marlowe in mind, though he would not be accounted very modern by the other if that were so. But this other, better versed in recent criticism, will call to mind, as he says the famous name, somebody quite different: a serious, thoughtful man, a scholar, and a writer deeply concerned with suffering and evil, morality and religion; an ironist and a detached observer; the critical creator of Tamburlaine and Faustus, characters who are no more to be regarded as projections of their author than Macbeth or Hamlet can be counted mouthpieces for Shakespeare. He might indeed go further than this and posit quite decisively a traditionalist; or rather, a Marlowe whose difference from the majority of his fellow-creatures lay simply in his literary ability. This Marlowe could bring new forms, experiences and modes of expression into drama, but in his moral thinking, as revealed by his plays, was Christian, orthodox and devout, holding up before the eyes of his audiences examples of the ways and fates of sinful men from which they could profit as from any sermon or Morality Play.

One may wonder how it is that such divergent views

can be held in the same century about a single author and his not so very numerous works. Two reasons are evident. Much of the change in opinion has come about through the increasing acceptance as a principle of literary criticism that one must not allow biographical matters to influence one's judgement of a piece of writing. If we did not know that Marlowe was reputed to be an atheist, would we find evidence of atheism in his plays? If his play of *Doctor Faustus* were anonymous, would it not be, as Leo Kirschbaum was the first to argue,* clear and unquestionable that 'there is no more obvious Christian document in all Elizabethan drama'? A further cause of change has been the growing insistence of scholars that a work of art should not be seen as an object created in isolation, but as one which reflects aspects of the age in which it was written and involves the traditions of artistic production appropriate to that age: in other words we must try to see Marlowe through Elizabethan eyes and not as though he, like us, had inherited ways of thought and feeling from the nineteenth century. So, it is argued by another American scholar, Roy Battenhouse,† we must interpret Marlowe's *Tamburlaine* as an Elizabethan might, and if we do so we shall find in it, he thinks, not an exaltation of the anti-Christian qualities which Tamburlaine represents, but on the contrary a severe and completely orthodox condemnation of them.

All of these arguments and observations are important, and may lead us to a far fuller understanding of Marlowe than our predecessors had: they will come up for consideration again later on. But it is also true that the facts we know, or think we know, about Marlowe's life are of a kind that makes us very curious to know more; that

* ' Marlowe's Faustus: A Reconsideration', *Review of English Studies*, 19, 1943, 56–67; reprinted in *Christopher Marlowe's Doctor Faustus, Text and Major Criticism*, (ed.) Ribner, Odyssey, New York, 1966.

† *Marlowe's Tamburlaine, A Study in Renaissance Moral Philosophy*, Vanderbilt, Nashville, Tenn., 1941; reprinted 1964.

the connection between 'life' and works *may* be real, and indeed a help to understanding rather than a hindrance; and that we do find recurrent in his writing certain tones that are inescapably personal so that we are from time to time made aware of an author, in a sense that we are not when reading or watching Shakespeare.

So let us recapitulate the main facts about this brief life, if only so that we can try to assess the importance of what we are to forget if we read the works in the modern 'objective' manner.

Marlowe was born in 1564, the same year as Shakespeare, in Canterbury; the son of a cobbler, and a member, it now seems,* of a somewhat turbulent family which had its quarrels with the law and its full share of difficulties, financial and temperamental. He went to the King's School, Canterbury, and from there to Corpus Christi College, Cambridge, which had connections with the school through the benefaction of Archbishop Matthew Parker. It was a Matthew Parker scholarship that Marlowe was awarded for his years at Cambridge and so he must have been expected to take holy orders. At some stage, however, he decided against that, for when he left Cambridge in 1587 it was to go as a playwright to London where the two parts of *Tamburlaine* were produced later that same year. He had also fallen foul of the university authorities for not keeping to regulations about attendance in term time, and because of this they proposed to refuse him his degree; the Queen's Council then intervened on his behalf, saying that he had been serving Her Majesty who recognized his merit and did not wish him to be penalized. They mentioned Rheims, so it seems probable that Marlowe had been employed on some espionage work among the Jesuits there. The minister responsible for security was Francis Walsingham and it was at his brother Thomas's

*See 'Marlowe and Canterbury', William Urry, Times Literary Supplement, 13 February 1964.

house that Marlowe was staying in the early part of 1593 when he was killed, so there are some likely connexions.

His career as a dramatist was notably successful, for *Tamburlaine*, *Doctor Faustus*, *The Jew of Malta* and *The Massacre at Paris* were all exceptionally popular. The chronology of his plays is not certain:* *Dido, Queen of Carthage* may be an early college play, but different critics have argued for it as coming both from the middle of Marlowe's career and from its end; *Doctor Faustus* may come immediately after *Tamburlaine* in the canon, or it may be late, in 1592, that is after *Edward II*. There are also poems: the lyric 'Come live with me and be my love', translations of Ovid's *Amores* and the First Book of Lucan's *Pharsalia*, as well as the two 'Sestiads' of *Hero and Leander*, a poem finished after Marlowe's death by George Chapman.

Of the non-professional side of his life we have no more than glimpses. In 1589 there was a street fight after which Marlowe was arrested; and in 1592 he was bound over to keep the peace. We also know that a week or so before he died he was summoned to report to the Council. These are practically all the direct facts about his life. Thanks to the brilliant and celebrated research of Leslie Hotson† we do, however, possess a detailed account of the alleged manner of his death. The minutes of the Coroner's Inquest tell how on 30 May 1593, four men met at the house of Eleanor Bull, widow, in Deptford; how they spent the afternoon there 'in quiet sort'; and how after supper a dispute arose about the reckoning. Marlowe is said to have suddenly attacked one of them, a man called Ingram Friser, who during the struggle killed him in self-defence. Friser was promptly pardoned and that might appear to be the end of the matter. But two days after Marlowe's death there was handed in to

*In the present edition they are given in a possible, but by no means certain, chronological order.

† *The Death of Christopher Marlowe*, London, 1925.

the authorities a most fascinating document, written by an informer named Richard Baines, and headed 'A note containing the opinion of one Christopher Marly concerning his damnable Judgment of Religion, and scorn of God's word'. Eighteen items are then specified, some of which scoff at the pretensions of the Old and New Testaments, and some at Jesus himself (holding, for example, that 'if the Jews among whom he was born did crucify him they best knew him and whence he came'). Others advance general propositions; one is that 'the first beginning of religion was only to keep men in awe'. But probably most interesting is the final paragraph:

These things, with many other shall by good and honest witness be approved to be his opinions and common speeches, and that this Marlowe doth not only hold them himself, but almost into every company he cometh he persuades men to Atheism, willing them not to be afeared of bugbears and hobgoblins, and utterly scorning both God and his ministers as I Richard Baines will justify and approve both by mine oath and the testimony of many honest men, and almost all men with whom he hath conversed any time will testify the same, and as I think all men in Christianity ought to endeavour that the mouth of so dangerous a member may be stopped, he saith likewise that he hath quoted a number of contrarieties out of the Scripture which he hath given to some great men who in convenient time shall be named. When these things shall be called in question the witness shall be produced. *Richard Baines*

'Some great men', then, were probably to be drawn into what threatened to become a public scandal: so it may be that others beside Richard Baines were interested to see that 'the mouth of so dangerous a member might be stopped'. Possibly Thomas Walsingham feared that he might be implicated in an enquiry (moreover, Ingram Friser was employed by him, and there are certain details about the account given to the Coroner which are not completely convincing). But it is at this point that conjecture inherits the field, and of course conjecture has a fine way of establishing itself as fact. What is fact is that one year later, in March 1594, a Commission of Inquiry was set up at Cerne Abbas, near Sherborne Abbey, the home of Sir Walter Raleigh. Charges of atheism were made, and though nothing was proved there remains a feeling that with so much smoke there must have been some fire. There is also hearsay-evidence for an association between Marlowe and Raleigh, for a certain Richard Chomley, charged with treason and atheism shortly after Marlowe's death, wrote in his testimony that: 'He saieth and verily believeth that one Marlowe is able to show more sound reasons for Atheism than any divine in England is able to give to prove divinity and that Marlowe told him that he hath read the atheist lecture to Sir Walter Raleigh and others'.*

This is not all. When Marlowe was killed, another playwright, Thomas Kyd, was under arrest, and, no doubt in fear of his life, made accusations against Marlowe. 'Marlowe's monstrous opinions' were listed as in the Baines document, and a picture is given of his character. He was 'intemperate and of a cruel heart'; 'in table-talk or otherwise' he would 'jest at the divine Scriptures, gibe at prayers, and strive in argument to frustrate and confute what hath been spoke or writ by prophets and such holy men'; and he also had the disagreeable habit of 'attempting sudden privy injuries to men' for which Kyd says he used to 'reprehend him'. Then there were reports of an unpublished atheistic book, and of course the posthumous tales of a godless life and a brutish death (he 'cursed and blasphemed to his last gasp, and together with his breath an oath flew out of his mouth').†

What weight, then, are we to allow these biographical

---

*On this subject see *The School of Night*, M. C. Bradbrook, Cambridge, 1936, and *Love's Labour's Lost*, revised Arden edition, (ed.) R. David, xliv–xlvi and 109.

† *Theatre of God's Judgments*, Thomas Beard, 1597.

matters? One platitudinous but necessary answer is: no more and no less than the evidence allows. It has to be said because it is not generally what happens. On the one hand, people will talk of 'Kit Marlowe' as though they were on speaking terms and could slap him on the back any day in the Mermaid (and some know him and the 'in' jokes about him even better than that, so that readers of *The Times* on 18 September 1963 were told that 'Marlowe was a well-known homosexual'* – and for that there is no *evidence* at all). On the other hand it seems to me absurd, in the present state of our knowledge, to dismiss all of these Elizabethan rumours and accusations as 'the Marlowe myth'; or to want to discountenance this reputation because it sorts ill with the Marlowe who read Divinity at Cambridge and was praised by his State employers for behaving himself 'orderly and discreetly'; or to hold that even if he did have the unorthodox opinions attributed to him in life, this has nothing to do with his work and that we are sentimental, romantic and reactionary if we entertain any doubts on the matter. And all of these opinions are quite commonly expressed, most forcibly, it appears, in the universities of the United States.

For example, we are told that the plays are essentially the work not of a man 'expressing himself' but of a practitioner of a craft, that of poetic drama. Moreover 'the Renaissance sense' of poetic drama is that 'of an objective discipline to be mastered through the exercise of rhetorical imitation',† and Marlowe must be read in this light. But how do we know that this is '*the* Renaissance sense' of the term? Of course this is what the text-

Historian answers questions about Shakespeare, 2, A. L. Rowse. Baines says that Marlowe said that 'all they that love not tobacco and boys were fools' and homosexuality plays a part in three of his works, in two of them very incidentally: these things are hardly evidence.

† Robert Kimbrough in the *Journal of English and Germanic Philology*, University of Illinois, October 1964.

books taught, and it is what most of Marlowe's precursors did (which is one reason why we don't read them very much). But we do not know that it was *Marlowe's* conception of his craft (we do know that he had a mind of his own); and while he was bound to inherit such a conception as part of his own mind and practice it does not follow that this is the most interesting aspect of his work or that it suggests the best way in which he can be read. It was a very individual mind that created as he created: and what we see as we read is a whole mind involved, not simply or primarily the craftsman's concern with techniques, like a shoemaker's, or a professional rhetorician's. Moreover, Marlowe concerned himself recurrently with certain ideas, feelings and aspects of life: these were what interested him (the man). He also makes his characters speak in tones that have much in common; and that have much in common with the style of Marlowe's non-dramatic poetry, where there is no question of his objectively creating a character. It is not sentimental or romantic to see the man in the work to a greater extent than is true of most artists: it is natural and reasonable. It must also be recognized that it is a possible but not inevitable source of distorted judgement on the works. As for Marlowe the man, atheist and rebel or not, we have to acknowledge that there is no single piece of evidence that is not hearsay – only that there is a good deal of it, that it is reasonably consistent, and that on the other side there is no single fact or piece of hearsay known to us that will rank as evidence against it.

Two of the plays, however, are very directly concerned with God, and these are Marlowe's most famous dramatic works, also perhaps his finest and most important. They are *Tamburlaine* and *Doctor Faustus*, neither of them readily conceivable as the work of an atheist in the modern sense of the word. That sense, of course, is not the Elizabethan: an atheist was not necessarily one who denied the existence of God but one who rejected the churches and orthodox beliefs. In this sense *Tamburlaine* may have been written by an atheist; but a God is present in both parts of the play, felt always as a reality and ultimately as an active force.

Tamburlaine is the play in which Marlowe shows most consistent intensity, most sustained imaginative power and most generously expended poetic resources. It is a quite extraordinarily strong and individual creation, and much of the energy of creativeness is concentrated upon the person of the protagonist. Tamburlaine was the famous Timur who in the fourteenth century ruled in Samarkand, subduing Persians, Tartars, Syrians and Turks, and was prevented only by death from engaging the Chinese. In Marlowe's play he is the Scythian shepherd who rose to greatness by force of character, followed by courageous and strong-spirited men and loved by a beautiful and good woman, and always winning. This may not seem to be the stuff of which great drama is made, for where, one might ask, is the vital element of conflict, unless in the mere confrontations (repeated in many episodes) of one side with another. But conflict in *Tamburlaine* takes a special form, involving reactions and judgements.

> View but his picture in this tragic glass,

says the Prologue

> And then applaud his fortunes as you please.

There is a characteristic note of challenge in that, for the question soon arises, both for the audience and the characters themselves, as to how the fortunes of this conqueror are to be viewed.

> What God, or fiend, or spirit of the earth,
> Or monster turned to a manly shape . . .
> Whether from earth, or hell, or heaven he grow.
> (Pt 1, 2, 6, 15–16, 23)

This is the question posed by Ortygius early in the play, and it firmly directs our attention to a conflict of judgements that is fundamental. For Christian judgement must tell the audience that the fortunes of this man are not to be applauded at all; yet the drama works to counteract this and to compel admiration for one whose values are the antithesis of the Christian's. It works to accomplish this by all the means in its power. First, Tamburlaine is qualitatively established as the superior of all the men around him. He is allowed great dignity, power and beauty of speech: his speech is the characteristic language of the play but that language is most magnificently itself when Tamburlaine speaks it. The first play ends in triumph and glory for him; and though the second brings his death, it too ends on a note of glory, for the epitaph spoken over him is in praise of a man who is the pride of earth and heaven. A dramatist who wanted to discredit this character had plenty of ways open to him: he could have provided some kind of choric commentary (as Marlowe does in *Doctor Faustus*), or he could have lavished less magniloquence and dignity upon Tamburlaine, and allowed a little more to at least some of those who oppose him. Or his opponents could have had a goodness which would show Tamburlaine's wickedness for what it is. But in fact these enemies generally have the same values as Tamburlaine himself: they are simply less attractive in other ways, and have less success. A genuinely contrary set of values is brought into play with the character Mycetes, who says:

> Accurs'd be he that first invented war!
>
> (Pt 1, 2, 4, 1)

But he is a cowardly nincompoop, more ridiculous because the accident of birth has placed a crown on his head; and the speech is there for laughter. Then in the second play another character says:

> I know, sir, what it is to kill a man;
> It works remorse of conscience in me.
>
> (Pt 2, 4, 1, 27–8)

But these admirable sentiments enjoy little respect when spoken as here by a young wastrel, who has no principles in life except to keep his skin whole and enjoy himself with wine, cards and concubines. Tamburlaine's values can only be strengthened in dramatic status by opposition of this kind.

We spoke of a conflict of judgement in the play, however, and it is there. As Cosroe falls through Tamburlaine's double-dealing (Pt 1, 2, 7) his dazed bewilderment evokes some sympathy. When Bajazeth and Zabina imprisoned in their cage express their sorrows (Pt 1, 5, 2) they command first our pity and then that of Tamburlaine's queen, Zenocrate. Zenocrate presents the most potent explicit criticism of Tamburlaine's way of life, and when she laments over 'the Turk and his great emperess' she also recognizes both the claims of those qualities of pity and compassion that Tamburlaine renounces and the power of fortune and death over even the mightiest, including Tamburlaine himself. In Part 2 of the play she brings a touch of moderate good sense and humanity into the household (1, 4) when she asks her husband when he will lead a more peaceful life; and in her death she offers a moving example of patience in suffering as well as a further testimony to the power which no human being can conquer:

> I fare, my lord, as other empresses,
> That, when this frail and transitory flesh
> Hath suck'd the measure of that vital air
> That feeds the body with his dated health,
> Wanes with enforc'd and necessary change.
>
> (Pt 2, 2, 4, 42–6)

The strained quality of Tamburlaine's rant after her death cannot but compare unfavourably. There are also the heroism of Olympia, one of Tamburlaine's victims, and the inevitable repulsion against the increasing excesses of his deeds to tell against him. Then there is the visual side of the play, the very sight of the dead whose suffering is the price of Tamburlaine's 'greatness' (Douglas Cole puts it more strongly: 'the dream of the poetic word is consistently confronted with the reality of the dramatic action'*). Above all there is the death which surely comes to Tamburlaine (though some have denied this) as retribution for hubris and blasphemy. He now has to acknowledge this final reality, and admit to the limitations of even his achievements:

> And shall I die, and this unconquered . . .
> For Tamburlaine, the scourge of God, must die.
>> (Pt 2, 5, 3, 151, repeated 159, and 249)

All of these elements in the play criticize and conflict with the dramatic presentation of Tamburlaine as a man of surpassing worth.

Nevertheless, that worth is what the play predominantly affirms. If one allows oneself to be led by what Marlowe has written, still giving full weight to the opposing elements in the play as well as to all the traditions of thought and dramatic practice that may be involved, one can not, I believe, reasonably doubt that Tamburlaine is predominantly presented for admiration. Nothing confirms this more decisively than the ending, for though Tamburlaine dies, the dramatic presentation of his death changes significantly during the last scenes. At first, when Tamburlaine first feels himself 'distempered', death appears to be retributive (it comes so hard on his greatest boasts and his challenges to the supernatural). And at the opening of the last scene we are still aware of the irony of death asserting mastery over the man he has hitherto served. But the triumph of the dying Tamburlaine over his foes by his mere appearance comes as a last vision of his greatness in action, and it only remains for him then to raise to a new magnificence the

---

* *Suffering and Evil in the Plays of Christopher Marlowe*, Princeton, 1962, p. 259.

greatness of his spirit. He does so by speaking wisely and realistically as well as with vast poetic eloquence. This is not a chastened and defeated Tamburlaine, but a newly exultant one:

> Now, eyes, enjoy your latest benefit,
> And, when my soul hath virtue of your sight,
> Pierce through the coffin and the sheet of gold,
> And glut your longings with a heaven of joy.
>
> (Pt 2, 5, 3, 225–8)

There are some sombre harmonies heard later in the speech, but this is the key-note and it is reaffirmed in the final lines of the play, the Epitaph spoken by Amyras:

> Meet heaven and earth, and here let all things end,
> For earth hath spent the pride of all her fruit,
> And heaven consum'd his choicest living fire!
> Let earth and heaven his timeless death deplore
> For both their worths will equal him no more!

There are so many things Marlowe could have done if his intentions had been anything other than a glorification of this man. He could have had him rage impotently or merely succumb, broken and abject. The captive kings (still, the directions seem to imply, on the stage) could have gloated as Mephostophilis does over Faustus, or pointed a moral as the Chorus does at the end of that other play. But no. Tamburlaine ends as he began, in glory. In him the distinctively Christian virtues are negated: in this sense the play is predominantly and profoundly anti-Christian.

But it is not godless. We are never forgetful for long that there is something beyond, and that whatever it is (Christian or classical or Mohammedan God or simply 'nature'), it is purposive. Tamburlaine sees himself as 'the scourge of God', boasts that 'Jove himself will stretch his hand from heaven . . . and shield me safe from harm,' and that through his death the 'powers' mean to invest him 'in a higher throne':

There is a God, full of revenging wrath,
From whom the thunder and the lightning breaks,
Whose scourge I am, and him will I obey.

(Pt 2, 5, 1, 181–3)

The Mohammedan Orcanes prays in these terms:

That he that sits on high and never sleeps,
Nor in one place is circumscriptible,
But everywhere fills every continent
With strange infusion of his sacred vigour ...

(Pt 2, 2, 2, 49–52)

He is specifically including Christ, or the Christian God, and involved seems to be a conception of a world-spirit above all established religions. This spirit is immanent in creation, infusing it with his *vigour*, and it is in this that Tamburlaine himself seems to carry a religious force: for his vigour is the god within him. He is at one with the Nature, warring, disruptive and all-powerful, that is evoked in the most famous speech of the play:

Nature, that fram'd us of four elements
Warring within our breasts for regiment,
Doth teach us all to have aspiring minds.

(Pt 1, 2, 7, 18–20)

A Nature which 'frames' and 'teaches' is the personal force elsewhere called God: in its strange fashion *Tamburlaine* is also a deeply religious play.

This is one of the ways in which it has kinship with *Doctor Faustus*. What a strange kinship, however, and how continually astonishing that the two works should have come (and so very recognizably) from the same pen. It is perhaps less surprising that critics should be at variance in their interpretations, when Marlowe himself is so diverse.

Doctor Faustus is a predominantly Christian play as surely as *Tamburlaine* is predominantly anti-Christian. In both, however, there are balances, and *Faustus* is not a simple Morality that can be summed up in the last words of the Chorus:

> Faustus is gone. Regard his hellish fall,
> Whose fiendful fortune may exhort the wise
> Only to wonder at unlawful things,
> Whose deepness doth entice such forward wits,
> To practise more than heavenly power permits.

Not even these lines speak with an entirely unambiguous voice. If the 'unlawful things' are for the 'wonder' of the wise and no more than that, even then their interest and attractiveness are still admitted. The 'deepness' of them again testifies to their fascination. The 'forward wits' are the bright young men heading for a fall – or so their elders say: but how adventurous the 'forward wits' sound, and how staid the elders. And when 'heavenly power' is shown as a stern, limiting force which does 'not permit', it too appears greyly negative, working by fear rather than love or attraction.

But the degree of ambivalence one senses in this play depends principally on the extent to which one believes sympathy is created for Faustus. Leo Kirschbaum, in the essay mentioned earlier, finds none at all. For him Faustus is a 'blatant egotist', 'self-deluded, foolishly boastful', 'wholly egocentric', and possessed of 'intellectual pride to an odious degree': this, moreover, is taken to be deliberate characterizing on the part of Marlowe who therefore can have liked his 'hero' little better than does the critic. Perhaps a first qualification of this view is suggested by experience in the theatre, for the present writer at least has never seen a performance where this has been one's basic reaction to the Faustus one is watching (possibly the role should be deliberately played so as to make Faustus odiously conceited – it would be a bold actor who would throw away the opportunities that Marlowe gives him for a warmer characterization).

Instead of this, we are for much of the time too close to this man, his hopes and fears, joys and despairs, to see, summarize and dismiss him in these terms. For example, there is the speech 'Now, Faustus, must thou needs be damn'd?' (1, 5, 1–14), which Kirschbaum quotes and discusses as follows: 'at first all [Faustus'] cocky effrontery is gone. But in a moment he is once more the user of egocentric hyperbole. ... A weakling, he must cover his fears with megalomaniacal fantasy ... (his) conclusion as to the impossibility of God's mercy is the mark of a diseased ego – a lack of humility. And also, we must particularly remark Faustus' self-recognition of his driving passion: "The god thou servest is thine own appetite."' All these strictures have their justice but I am certain that they do not represent the *total* response the lines should evoke. The to-and-fro movement of the speech presents a tormented soul and compels us to feel with him even though there is no question of giving intellectual approval to his thoughts. When he says:

> Away with such vain fancies and despair,
> Despair in God and trust in Belzebub.
> Now go not backward. No, Faustus, be resolute.

he is not being made by Marlowe to speak in a way that allows us simply to observe and judge. Will ('away with such vain fancies') is asserted in a self-addressed imperative: we see the outer self try to control the inner, and so are made to look closely inwards and to realize what wretchedness of yearning and fright is chafing there. 'Despair in God and trust in Belzebub': the symmetrical line stands there, square and strong as on four firmly planted feet; the outer man has won. But with 'Now go not backward' we are brought again to the depths of the inner self, pulling back even in the moment of apparent resolution; the 'voice' of the inner self is left implicit and we are made to supply it with our own inner ear. That is, our minds are drawn in towards Faustus', and in the literal sense of 'feeling-with', we are in sympathy (not agreement) with Faustus. It might be argued that a skilful dramatist will in this way make us enter the scheming mind of the most double-dyed villains, and that this in no way lessens our recognition of their villainy. But there is a basic difference of dramatic context between, say, Richard III or Iago on the one hand and Faustus on the other: their evil hurts others, for whom the drama has taught us to care, but Faustus' evil hurts only himself. It is his own tragedy that we are watching, and there must be times (if not in the soliloquy just discussed then surely in the last great speech and the scene with the students just before it) when we feel not just the mistakenness but also 'the pity of it'.

If pity mixed with condemnation were the only feeling that Marlowe's audience can have for Faustus, then he would still be a poor sort of figure, tragic perhaps but only in a rather weak, pathetic sort of way: an Edward II in fact. But again the experience of reading and seeing the play tells us quite plainly that he is not that. There are also a kind of strength and a kind of attractiveness. Both reside in the quality of his imagination. 'Megalomaniacal fantasy' is Kirschbaum's phrase for this imagination, and it is a fair objective analysis of the 'diseased ego', a 'case' in the psychologist's notebook: but it is also remarkably deaf or blind to the beauty of the lines in which the 'case' expresses himself. Let us take the most famous speech of all, Faustus' address to the spirit-Helen of Troy (there are plenty of other passages which would do, but this has been fixed on by a number of commentators lately). Now this Helen is a succuba, a spirit summoned by Mephostophilis, and when Faustus says 'her lips suck forth my soul' they do in truth do just that. There is a terrible irony of context that places the brightness of the words against a sombre and menacing background. But what is in the foreground is poetry of exceptional radiance and beauty: moreover, a fervour of spirit and responsiveness to the presence of beauty that are powerful and infectious:

> Oh, thou art fairer than the evening's air,
> Clad in the beauty of a thousand stars.
> Brighter art thou than flaming Jupiter,
> When he appeared to hapless Semele:
> More lovely than the monarch of the sky,
> In wanton Arethusa's azure arms,
> And none but thou shalt be my paramour.
>
> (5, 1, 110–16)

I do not believe that any audience, of Marlowe's day or our own, has listened to these lines and been impressed *primarily* by the ironies within them.* The primary reaction in an audience that likes and appreciates poetry (and the Elizabethans did if we do not) is to admire beauty. And this beauty is not a kind of trimming, something external added as an aesthetic luminous irrelevance to the dark realities of the moral drama: it is an essential attribute of the character speaking, and a fundamental way in which the sympathies of the audience can be directed.

Against this, the play carries the deep intellectual and emotional conviction that Faustus is indeed damned. There are some readers who see in the play a bolder cry of protest and a subtler kind of unorthodoxy than I can.† But though I think there is, as in *Tamburlaine*, a

---

*See Kirschbaum (the last page of the essay quoted above) and Cole, *Suffering and Evil*, 222–4. Also R. M. Frye, 'Marlowe's *Doctor Faustus*: The Repudiation of Humanity', *South Atlantic Quarterly*, 55, 1956, 322–8.

†For example, Nicholas Brooke, "Doctor Faustus", *Cambridge Journal*, 5, 2, 1952, and Erich Heller, *The Artist's Journey into the Interior*, Random, New York, 1965, pp. 6–15; Secker & Warburg, 1966. See also some remarks in *Seven Types of Ambiguity* (p. 206 in the Penguin edition) by William Empson who also wrote in *The New Statesman* (2 December 1966): 'It is quite usual now for schools to teach that the Marlowe *Faustus* is simply a Morality Play, so that the author thanks God when the hero goes to Hell. But it seems plain

genuine ambivalence, the play as a whole (its overall design and the force of many details that recent scholars have observed and annotated) is predominantly 'Christian'. Inverted commas seem required, for there is surely very little that is truly Christian in the play's eschatology, or its God, or its concept of sin. Nevertheless, one can only presume that these things reflect Marlowe's own concepts and that in the light of them he saw his Faustus as a soul who being measured is found tragically wanting.

Tamburlaine and *Faustus* are, then, to some extent complementary plays: both are fundamentally religious and philosophical, placing man in relation to his creator and the rest of creation; both focus upon a single person; and both embody a secondary scale of values that works against the primary scale. Both present men of stature placed in a large world-setting. Both give these men fervent and imaginatively powerful lines to speak.

In *The Jew of Malta* and *Edward II*, most of this, most of the time, is not so. The men are smaller, the world is narrower; no world beyond this one is involved, and as we look at the villainy, hypocrisy, pettiness and weakness of life as seen here we can hardly conceive of a reason why heaven should bestow a thought on such a poor and tainted object.

Not that *The Jew of Malta* is a depressing play – the protagonist and the language both have so much life – and perhaps I am wrong in thinking that *Edward II* is. I certainly find it so in reading, and have done in the theatre, but for some people it is the most satisfying play that Marlowe wrote and evidently it can be exciting for

that Marlowe advertised his advanced ideas in pubs, so that the frightened audience were sure he approved of risking all for knowledge: in fact, that the legend meant to him what it did to Goethe and Spengler, and those who live in the age of the Cobalt Bomb. There is evidence enough in the text, but it is only recognized if you grant the initial probability. (I can never see why it is even considered pious to believe that they were all stupid.)'

actors and producer to work on (Toby Robertson, who produced it with the Marlowe Society in 1958 and in London 1965, tells* how he was especially struck by 'the extraordinary speed of events, the way the play leaps from event to event – it is like hurdle jumping'). Certainly it is well constructed. It may not always seem so to the casual viewer (I think, for instance, that when Toby Robertson gives as an example of its 'terrific, pace' one scene which is only four lines long, other people may find a sort of scrappiness, or a sense of over-compression, in such brevity); but a comparison with the chronicle sources leaves one full of admiration for Marlowe's handling. It is true too that there is a wider range of characterization in this play than in the others, and more sense that one is dealing with ordinary rather than extraordinary humanity. But the depressing quality seems to me to be virtually omnipresent and to lie in two pervasive characteristics. One is the almost unredeemed meanness, weakness or wickedness of the people and their actions; the other is the drab thinness of the verse.

Perhaps one exaggerates. Toby Robertson also has something to say about the acting and speaking of the role of Edward. Edward, he says, is 'totally involved as a full physical being ... there is a passionate strength in his despair'; and he quotes:

> Let Pluto's bells ring out my fatal knell,
> And hags howl for my death at Charon's shore.
>
> (4, 6, 89–90)

The reference sends one back to the text, and in this instance it is to be rewarded. The black chasm of the mouth in a grief-stricken face cries with its full force as the 'hags howl', the alliteration catching up 'heaven ... hell ... hence' of the previous lines; and the hoarse noise of the cry as the actor involves himself with his

*In an interview on producing *Edward II*, reprinted in the *Tulane Drama Review* (Marlowe Issue), 8, 4, Summer 1964.

whole physical being will be doubly shocking and moving
after the quiet of the tranquil interlude:

> Father, this life contemplative is heaven:
> O, that I might this life in quiet lead!
>
> (4, 6, 20–21)

But then one reads further, and it is to return to the
desert; for though there are long speeches in this second
part of the play and Marlowe does not seem to feel himself cramped, the poetry is very much a poetry of state-
ment. The abdication scene follows, and it presents a
challenge for the poet's tongue to exercise its power as it
does in, after all, many of Marlowe's great speeches
(Tamburlaine's 'What is beauty saith my sufferings then,'
Aeneas' narrative in *Dido*, Faustus' first and last solilo-
quies, even the principal speeches of Barabas and de
Guise). Edward speaks one hundred and twenty-five lines
out of the scene's one hundred and fifty-five, and of these
four (26–27, 63–64) are imaginative, beautiful and
memorable, but the idiom can be fairly represented by a
passage like this:

> Ah Leicester, weigh how hardly I can brook
> To lose my crown and kingdom without cause;
> To give ambitious Mortimer my right,
> That, like a mountain, overwhelms my bliss;
> In which extreme my mind here murder'd is!
>
> (5, 1, 51–55)

Possibly the deadness of the lines may be held to be
subtly expressive: Edward is blankly deadened, a sucked
orange, and to give him such verse is the only thing to do.
But even if this excuses or explains the poetic barrenness
it does not cancel the fact of it; and it *is* barren (how
stiffly, for instance, the second and third lines scan, how
flatly explicit are these statements about his misery). This
aridity is being illustrated from a passage right in the
heart of the play's more human material, and it suggests,
of course, that a warm compassionate sense of humanity

is not after all going to be achieved by any poetic realization in this play (it is in fact the situation rather than the poetry which does sometimes evoke it). This may not be failure on Marlowe's part: he may be succeeding perfectly in what he is attempting. But the nature of his achievement is none the less depressing. He has written a play about poor, nasty or weak little people; and his poetic achievement has been to clip his own wings, and, with an occasional breakthrough, to create a language in which they can snap and snarl at each other or pity themselves.

Like *Tamburlaine* and *Doctor Faustus*, *The Jew of Malta* and *Edward II* are in some senses complementary plays. The differences are considerable: *The Jew* is a high-spirited entertainment, where *Edward II* presents a sober chronicle; and while the character of Edward is largely weak and passive, Barabas is resourceful and tireless. But both plays show a world that is nasty and brutish; both are secular; both develop a plot rather than unfolding an episodic story, as the other plays do; and neither offers as its characteristic style any sustained poetic intensity by comparison with those others. They are also narrower. If Barabas has something of Tamburlaine's qualities of conqueror and superman, it is in an absurd and ignoble form. Tamburlaine flourishes the sword, Barabas the money-bags; Tamburlaine is a man, Barabas a grotesque (though both have an element of the monster too). Similarly Edward might be compared with Faustus, for both suffer loss through the faults of their own characters. Yet Faustus is outward-looking and active in his aspirations, while Edward is dominated by a single obsession and in his deprivation is impotent and petulant. Eugene Waith puts it well: 'When *Tamburlaine* seems to open up even wider prospects up to the moment of the hero's death, *Edward II* closes down until the focus is upon a prison, a death-bed, a bier.'* Here, then, is further

* 'Edward II: The Shadow of Action', *Tulane Drama Review*, 8, 4, Summer 1964.

diversity in the Christopher Marlowe about whom the literary gentlemen are so much, and so understandably, at variance.

There is more still. A Marlowe who is scarcely to be guessed at from the plays is the poet who translated Ovid's *Amores* and who wrote *Hero and Leander*. It is one of the minor wonders of literature that the author of *Tamburlaine* should have committed himself to sustaining a volume of about 2,400 lines in such a style as this:

> We which were Ovid's five books now are three,
> For these before the rest preferred he.
> If reading five thou plain'st of tediousness,
> Two ta'en away, thy labour will be less.
> With Muse prepar'd I meant to sing of arms,
> Choosing a subject fit for fierce alarms.
> Both verses were alike, till love (men say)
> Began to smile and took one foot away.
>
> (1, 1, 1–8)

We know quite well the Marlowe of 'the mighty line', the man who proudly drew away from the 'jigging vein of rhyming mother-wits' and introduced into the theatre the noble and resonant blank verse that was to be such an expressive instrument. But this other Marlowe, a rhymster himself, both buoyant and sophisticated, and an early practitioner of the closed couplet, still comes as a surprise hardly assimilated into literary history, yet as real as the rest of him. Nor was it just a style adopted for the occasion, for with more assurance and ease he makes it completely his own in *Hero and Leander*:

> It lies not in our power to love or hate,
> For will in us is over-rul'd by fate.
> When two are stripp'd long ere the course begin,
> We wish that one should lose, the other win;
> And one especially do we affect
> Of two gold ingots like in each respect.
> The reason no man knows; let it suffise,

What we behold is censur'd by our eyes.
Where both deliberate, the love is slight:
Who ever lov'd, that lov'd not at first sight?

(1, 167–76)

The closed couplet, neat and antithetical, came to be recognized amongst English verse forms as the best instrument for satire. A good deal of polishing was necessary before the instrument was perfected, and Marlowe, writing about a hundred years before the great age of the couplet, could hardly have brought it to the fine condition it achieved then. But he is on the way:

When in this work's first verse I trod aloft,
Love slack'd my Muse, and made my numbers soft.

(*Ovid*, 1, 1. 21–2)

To give I love, but to be ask'd disdain;
Leave asking, and I'll give what I refrain.

(*Ovid*, 1, 10, 63–4)

A young wench pleaseth, and an old is good;
This for her looks, that for her womanhood.

(*Ovid*, 2, 4, 45–6)

Seeming not won, yet she was won at length:
In such wars women use but half their strength.

(*Hero and Leander*, 2, 295–6)

Thus having swallow'd Cupid's golden hook,
The more she striv'd, the deeper was she strook.

(*Hero and Leander*, 1, 333–4)

Marlowe's inheritors are more numerous than we often think, for if one short and direct line leads to the Elizabethan and Jacobean dramatists of Shakespeare's time and Ben Jonson's, another stretches to the 'Augustan' age of Dryden and Pope.

As we read these poems (and the translations have become essentially English poems), we grow aware also of the sense of humour which earlier critics generally said Marlowe had not got. The tone of the couplet

'Seeming not won . . .' quoted just now is typical: it is wry, knowing, humorous, perhaps cynical. *Hero and Leander* is a complex poem and comedy is one of its elements. Leander's heroic swimming of the Hellespont, for instance, begins with this couplet:

> With that he stripp'd him to the ivory skin,
> And crying 'Love, I come!', leapt lively in.
>
> (2, 153–4)

If we then return to the plays with a more open ear, we shall not find them humourless either. But what is very notable is that the *kind* of humour we find there is repeatedly one of discomfiture. Cupid playing tricks on the old nurse in *Dido*, Mycetes inept and ridiculous in his kingship at the start of *Tamburlaine*, the stabbing and strangling that is nearly always accompanied by a hard, sardonic joke in *The Massacre at Paris*: these are characteristic. Even *Edward II* has its comic moments, cruel little injections of verbal irony, spoken with an unsmiling face and a harsh voice. Looking again at the humour of *Hero and Leander*, we can see that it too is not always (or even characteristically) the pure sunshine humour it might seem to be.

> Thus having swallow'd Cupid's golden hook,
> The more she striv'd, the deeper was she strook.

The neat couplet quoted a page back is a little less pleasant and innocent on a second glance, and it is in key with so much more in the poem:

> Love is not full of pity, as men say,
> But deaf and cruel, where he means to prey.
>
> (2, 287–8)

This poem, where so much is magic and rapture, has also its less comfortable side: a certain ruthlessness, a sophisticated deflation of romantic hyperbole, and a characteristic concern with pride and its humiliation.

But Marlowe *is* also a poet who can create magic and

rapture, and for me (for perhaps at this stage one should declare oneself) this is his most valuable quality. These are vague terms, romantic and subjective too; and probably capable of illustration but not definition:

> Eyes when that Ebena steps to heaven,
> In silence of thy solemn evening's walk,
> Making the mantle of the richest night,
> The moon, the planets, and the meteors, light ...
> > (*Tamburlaine*, Pt 1, 5, 2, 84–7)

> Thus while dum signs their yielding hearts entangled,
> The air with sparks of living fire was spangled,
> And night deep drenched in misty Acheron,
> Heav'd up her head, and half the world upon
> Breath'd darkness forth ...
> > (*Hero and Leander*, 1, 187–91)

> Stand still, you ever-moving spheres of heaven,
> That time may cease and midnight never come.
> Fair nature's eye, rise, rise again, and make
> Perpetual day.
> > (*Doctor Faustus*, 5, 2, 146–9)

I do not mean that his works are things of shreds and patches, some fine lyrical utterances and waste land all round: on the contrary, they are controlled and purposeful, and in them is a considerable intellectual depth. There are also many things that are interesting about them, both as separate works of art and as representing a man's developing work in which one can follow recurrent concerns. But there comes a point where one says 'Yes, but what is it that I fundamentally value in this writer?' The very abundance of the attention he is given itself provokes the question. At least fifteen full-length books on him are still in current use; new editions come out every year; new essays every month. At the present time of writing, the latest study that comes to hand* takes

---

*Siegfried Wyler, 'Marlowe's Technique of Communicating with his Audience, as seen in his Tamburlaine, Part I', *English Studies*, 48, 4, August 1967.

Part I of *Tamburlaine*, selects a particular 'semantic field', lists the 'constituents' (in this case words associated with the idea of conqueror), tabulates their occurence, and works out the average. One feels that with the world in its presently afflicted condition, it must be a very considerable writer indeed whose works justify this kind of activity four hundred years after his birth. And sometimes one is tempted to question whether such an industry (as it has become) is in fact justified, for very often the studies themselves seem to be very little related to any sense of the quality of what is being examined: good lines or bad, third-rate author or genius, it is all grist to the mill. One remembers then that he was a dramatist and that the theatre is perhaps his rightful home. 'Perform him!' cries the blurb on the back-cover of a valuable collection of essays.* But when he is performed it is by no means to an accompaniment of universal enthusiasm (after an unusually successful performance of *The Jew of Malta*, Bernard Levin said that Marlowe should now be shovelled back into his grave, and recent productions of *Faustus* and *Edward II* have drawn a great many lukewarm comments on the plays themselves).

So one is again thrown back to the question 'What is it that I fundamentally value in this writer?' The answer that I find in myself (for such things are bound to be personal) takes two forms. One is a matter of 'interest'. That a man's work should encompass the extremes that *Tamburlaine* and *Edward II* represent remains for me one of the most absorbingly interesting facts of literature; that the range of this small body of work, all written in so few years, should extend to cover also such amazingly unlike pieces as *Doctor Faustus*, *The Jew of Malta* and *Hero and Leander* reinforces the fascination which the artist exercises, and (however warily one approaches this aspect) the man too. But the other answer is outside

* *Marlowe: A Collection of Critical Essays*, (ed.) Leech, Prentice-Hall, New Jersey, 1964.

the sphere of 'interest', and is a simple fact of possession; poetry that is in one's mind, permanently and preciously, as a piece of music or a painting:

Heaven, envious of our joys, is waxen pale;
And when we whisper, then the stars fall down
To be partakers of our honey talk.
(Dido, 4, 4, 52–4)

... the windy country of the clouds
(Dido, 1, 1, 57)

We saw Cassandra sprawling in the streets
(Dido, 2, 1, 274)

And with our sun-bright armour as we march,
We'll chase the stars from heaven ...
(Tamburlaine, Pt 1, 2, 3, 22–3)

See, see, where Christ's blood streams in the firmament.
(Doctor Faustus, 5, 2, 156)

And like a planet, moving several ways
At one self instant, she poor soul assays,
Loving, not to love at all, and every part
Strove to resist the motions of her heart.
(Hero and Leander, 1, 361–4)

Now o'er the sea from her old love comes she ...
(Ovid, 1, 13, 1)

So when this world's compounded union breaks,
Time ends, and to old Chaos all things turn,
Confused stars shall meet ...
(Lucan, 73–5)

Ultimately, it is because Marlowe could write like this that he is now reprinted, and that even at this moment somebody is probably totting up the occurences of words within a certain 'semantic field', while somebody else is working through yet another theological volume in the Corpus Christi library to see if Marlowe read it or at least if someone Marlowe read read it. He himself was one, says Chapman (who knew him)

> ... whose living subject stood
> Up to the chin in the Pierian flood
> *(Hero and Leander*, 3, 189–90)

We can learn a lot about him from the essays and studies, and the debates of scholars; but we can know him only if we venture some little way into the Pierian flood ourselves, and meet him in his own element, which was poetry.

SELECTED FURTHER READING

The Works and Life of Christopher Marlowe General Editor R. H. Case, London, 1930–33, is a detailed edition of the plays and poems in six volumes. *The Revels Plays* and the *New Mermaid* series are both in the process of producing single volume editions, the former having so far printed *Dr Faustus* (1962), edited by John D. Jump, and a particularly valuable edition of *Dido, Queen of Carthage* and *The Massacre at Paris* (1968), by H. J. Oliver. The classic edition of *Doctor Faustus* is still that of W. W. Greg (London, 1950).

For biography, F. S. Boas's *Christopher Marlowe, A Biographical and Critical Study* (Oxford, 1940), is probably the most scholarly and economical book. For criticism, there are two outstanding collections of essays: *Marlowe, A Collection of Critical Essays* (ed. Leech, in the series *Twentieth Century Views*, Prentice Hall, New Jersey, 1964), and the *Tulane Drama Review* (Marlowe Issue, 8, 4, Summer 1964). Single volumes include P. H. Kocher, *Christopher Marlowe: A Study of his Thoughts, Learning and Character* (London, 1946),H. Levin, *The Overreacher* (London, 1954), D. Cole, *Suffering and Evil in the Plays of Christopher Marlowe* (Princeton, 1962), and W. Sanders, *The Dramatist and the Received Idea*, (Cambridge, 1968). The present editor's previous work on Marlowe is to be found in J. B. Steane, *Marlowe: a Critical Study* (Cambridge, 1964).

For background reading the following are recommended:
A. P. Rossiter, *English Drama from Early Times to the Elizabethans* (London, 1950).
I. Ribner, *The English History Play in the Age of Shakespeare* (Princeton, 1957)
D. M. Bevington, *From 'Mankind' to Marlowe* (Harvard, 1962).
Elizabethan Theatre, Stratford-upon-Avon Studies 9 (London, 1966), which contains an important essay on Marlowe by Nicholas Brooke.

THE TRAGEDY OF

Dido, Queen of Carthage

Dramatis Personae

JUPITER
GANYMEDE
MERCURY, *or* HERMES
CUPID
JUNO
VENUS
ÆNEAS
ASCANIUS, *his son*
ACHATES
ILIONEUS
CLOANTHUS
SERGESTUS
OTHER TROJANS
IARBAS
CARTHAGINIAN LORDS
DIDO
ANNA, *her sister*
NURSE

ACT ONE

SCENE ONE

Here the curtains draw; there is discovered JUPITER
dandling GANYMEDE *upon his knee, and* MERCURY
lying asleep.

JUPITER: Come, gentle Ganymede, and play with me.
I love thee well, say Juno what she will.

GANYMEDE: I am much better for your worthless love,
That will not shield me from her shrewish blows!
Today, whenas I fill'd into your cups,
And held the cloth of pleasance whiles you drank,
She reach'd me such a rap for that I spill'd,
As made the blood run down about mine ears.

JUPITER: What, dares she strike the darling of my
thoughts?
By Saturn's soul, and this earth-threatening hair,[1]*   10
That, shaken thrice, makes nature's buildings quake,
I vow, if she but once frown on thee more,
To hang her, meteor like, 'twixt heaven and earth,
And bind her, hand and foot, with golden cords,
As once I did for harming Hercules!

GANYMEDE: Might I but see that pretty sport a-foot,
O, how would I with Helen's brother laugh,
And bring the gods to wonder at the game!
Sweet Jupiter, if e'er I pleas'd thine eye,
Or seemed fair, wall'd-in with eagle's wings,   20
Grace my immortal beauty with this boon,
And I will spend my time in thy bright arms.

JUPITER: What is't, sweet wag, I should deny thy youth?
Whose face reflects such pleasure to mine eyes,
As I, exhal'd with thy fire-darting beams,

17 *Helen's brother*: Castor or Pollux.

*Superior numbers refer to the Additional Notes at the end of the
book.

45

Have oft driven back the horses of the Night,[2]
Whenas they would have hal'd thee from my sight.
Sit on my knee, and call for thy content,
Control proud Fate, and cut the thread of Time.
30 Why, are not all the gods at thy command,
And heaven and earth the bounds of thy delight?
Vulcan[3] shall dance to make thee laughing sport,
And my nine daughters sing when thou art sad;
From Juno's bird I'll pluck her spotted pride,
To make thee fans wherewith to cool thy face;
And Venus' swans shall shed their silver down,
To sweeten out the slumbers of thy bed;
Hermes no more shall show the world his wings,
If that thy fancy in his feathers dwell,
40 But, as this one, I'll tear them all from him,
        Plucks a feather from HERMES' *wings.*
Do thou but say, 'their colour pleaseth me'.
Hold here, my little love; these linked gems
        Gives jewels.
My Juno ware upon her marriage-day,
Put thou about thy neck, my own sweet heart,
And trick thy arms and shoulders with my theft.
GANYMEDE: I would have a jewel for mine ear,
And a fine brooch to put in my hat,
And then I'll hug with you an hundred times.
JUPITER: And shall have, Ganymede, if thou wilt be
        my love.
        Enter VENUS.
50 VENUS: Ay, this is it: you can sit toying there,
And playing with that female wanton boy,
Whiles my Æneas wanders on the seas,
And rests a prey to every billow's pride.
Juno, false Juno, in her chariot's pomp,
Drawn through the heavens by steeds of Boreas' brood,
Made Hebe to direct her airy wheels
Into the windy country of the clouds;

33 *nine daughters*: the Muses.   55 *Boreas*: the north wind.

46

Where, finding Æolus entrench'd with storms,
And guarded with a thousand grisly ghosts,
She humbly did beseech him for our bane,   *60*
And charg'd him drown my son with all his train.
Then gan the winds break ope their brazen doors,
And all Æolia to be up in arms.
Poor Troy must now be sack'd upon the sea,
And Neptune's waves be envious men of war;
Epeus' horse, to Ætna's hill transform'd,
Prepared stands to wrack their wooden walls;
And Æolus, like Agamemnon, sounds
The surges, his fierce soldiers, to the spoil.
See how the night, Ulysses-like, comes forth,   *70*
And intercepts the day, as Dolon erst!
Ay, me! the stars suppris'd, like Rhesus' steeds,
Are drawn by darkness forth Astraeus' tents.
What shall I do to save thee, my sweet boy?
Whenas the waves do threat our crystal world,
And Proteus, raising hills of floods on high,
Intends, ere long, to sport him in the sky.
False Jupiter, reward'st thou virtue so?
What, is not piety exempt from woe?
Then die, Æneas, in thine innocence,   *80*
Since that religion hath no recompense.
JUPITER: Content thee, Cytherea, in thy care,
Since thy Æneas' wandering fate is firm,
Whose weary limbs shall shortly make repose
In those fair walls I promis'd him of yore.
But, first, in blood must his good fortune bud,
Before he be the lord of Turnus' town,
Or force her smile that hitherto hath frown'd.
Three winters shall he with the Rutiles war,

58 *Æolus*: keeper of the winds.
60 *bane*: harm.   63 *Æolia*: the realm of Æolus.
66 *Epeus*: builder of the wooden horse.
71 *Dolon*: Trojan spy, intercepted by Ulysses.
73 *Astraeus*: father of the stars.
87 *Turnus*: king of the Rutilians, slain by Aeneas.

90 And, in the end, subdue them with his sword;
And full three summers likewise shall he waste
In managing those fierce barbarian minds;
Which once perform'd, poor Troy, so long suppress'd.
From forth her ashes shall advance her head,
And flourish once again, that erst was dead.
But bright Ascanius, beauty's better work,
Who with the sun divides one radiant shape,
Shall build his throne amidst those starry towers
That earth-born Atlas, groaning, underprops:
100 No bounds but heaven shall bound his empery,
Whose azur'd gates enchased with his name,
Shall make the morning haste her grey uprise,
To feed her eyes with his engraven fame.
Thus, in stout Hector's race, three hundred years
The Roman sceptre royal shall remain,
Till that a princess-priest conceiv'd by Mars,
Shall yield to dignity a double birth,
Who will eternish Troy in their attempts.
VENUS: How may I credit these thy flattering terms,
110 When yet both sea and sands beset their ships,
And Phoebus, as in Stygian pools, refrains
To taint his tresses in the Tyrrhene main?
JUPITER: I will take order for that presently.
Hermes, awake! and haste to Neptune's realm,
Whereas the Wind-god, warring now with fate,
Beseige[s] th' offspring of our kingly loins.
Charge him from me to turn his stormy powers,
And fetter them in Vulcan's sturdy brass,
That durst thus proudly wrong our kinsman's peace.
        Exit HERMES.
120 Venus, farewell; thy son shall be our care.
Come, Ganymede, we must about this gear.
        Exeunt JUPITER *and* GANYMEDE.
VENUS: Disquiet seas, lay down your swelling looks,

106 *princess-priest*: Rhea Silvia, mother of Romulus and Remus.
112 *Tyrrhene*: The Tyrrhenian Sea.

And court Æneas with your calmy cheer,
Whose beauteous burden well might make you proud,
Had not the heavens, conceiv'd with hell-born clouds,
Veil'd his resplendent glory from your view.
For my sake, pity him, Oceanus,
That erstwhile issu'd from thy watery loins,
And had my being from thy bubbling froth.
Triton, I know, hath fill'd his trump with Troy,   *130*
And therefore will take pity on his toil,
And call both Thetis and Cymothoe
To succour him in this extremity.
 Enter ÆNEAS, ASCANIUS, ACHATES, *and others.*
What, do I see my son now come on shore?
Venus, how art thou compass'd with content,
The while thine eyes attract their sought-for joys!
Great Jupiter, still honour'd may'st thou be
For this so friendly aid in time of need!
Here in this bush disguised will I stand,
Whiles my Æneas spends himself in plaints,   *140*
And heaven and earth with his unrest acquaints.
ÆNEAS: You sons of care, companions of my course,
 Priam's misfortune follows us by sea,
 And Helen's rape doth haunt ye at the heels.
 How many dangers have we overpass'd!
 Both barking Scylla, and the sounding rocks,
 The Cyclops' shelves, and grim Cerania's seat
 Have you o'ergone, and yet remain alive.
 Pluck up your hearts, since Fate still rests our friend,
 And changing heavens may those good days return,   *150*
 Which Pergama did vaunt in all her pride.
ACHATES: Brave prince of Troy, thou only art our god,
 That by thy virtues free'st us from annoy,
 And mak'st our hopes survive to coming joys.
 Do thou but smile, and cloudy heaven will clear,
 Whose night and day descendeth from thy brows.
 Though we be now in extreme misery,

147 *Cerania's seat*: the Ceraunian mountains in Epirus.

And rest the map of weather-beaten woe,
Yet shall the aged sun shed forth his hair,
160 To make us live unto our former heat,
And every beast the forest doth send forth
Bequeath her young ones to our scanted food.
ASCANIUS: Father, I faint; good father, give me meat.
ÆNEAS: Alas, sweet boy, thou must be still a while,
Till we have fire to dress the meat we kill'd!
Gentle Achates, reach the tinder box,
That we may make a fire to warm us with,
And roast our new-found victuals on this shore.
VENUS (*aside*): See, what strange arts necessity finds out!
170 How near, my sweet Æneas, art thou driven!
ÆNEAS: Hold, take this candle, and go light a fire;
You shall have leaves and windfall boughs enow,
Near to these woods, to roast you meat withal.
Ascanius, go and dry thy drenched limbs,
Whiles I with my Achates rove abroad,
To know what coast the wind hath driven us on,
Or whether men or beasts inhabit it.
      Exeunt ASCANIUS *and others.*
ACHATES: The air is pleasant, and the soil most fit
For cities and society's supports;
180 Yet much I marvel that I cannot find
No steps of men imprinted in the earth.
VENUS (*aside*): Now is the time for me to play my part. —
Ho, young men! Saw you, as you came,
Any of all my sisters wandering here,
Having a quiver girded to her side,
And clothed in a spotted leopard's skin?
ÆNEAS: I neither saw nor heard of any such.
But what may I, fair virgin, call your name,
Whose looks set forth no mortal form to view,
190 Nor speech bewrays aught human in thy birth?
Thou art a goddess that delud'st our eyes,
And shroud'st thy beauty in this borrow'd shape;
But whether thou the Sun's bright sister be,

Or one of chaste Diana's fellow nymphs,
Live happy in the height of all content,
And lighten our extremes with this one boon,
As to instruct us under what good heaven
We breathe as now, and what this world is call'd
On which by tempests' fury we are cast.
Tell us, O, tell us, that are ignorant!   *200*
And this right hand shall make thy altars crack
With mountain-heaps of milk-white sacrifice.
VENUS: Such honour, stranger, do I not affect.
It is the use for Turen maids to wear
Their bow and quiver in this modest sort,
And suit themselves in purple for the nonce,
That they may trip more lightly o'er the lawnds,
And overtake the tusked boar in chase.
But for the land whereof thou dost inquire,
It is the Punic kingdom, rich and strong,   *210*
Adjoining on Agenor's stately town,
The kingly seat of Southern Libya,
Whereas Sidonian Dido rules as queen.
But what are you that ask of me these things?
Whence may you come, or whither will you go?
ÆNEAS: Of Troy am I. Æneas is my name,
Who, driven by war from forth my native world,
Put sails to sea to seek out Italy;
And my divine descent from sceptred Jove.
With twice twelve Phrygian ships I plough'd the deep,   *220*
And made that way my mother Venus led;
But of them all scarce seven do anchor safe,
And they so wrack'd and welter'd by the waves,
As every tide tilts 'twixt their oaken sides,
And all of them, unburden'd of their load,
Are ballassed with billows' watery weight.
But hapless I, God wot, poor and unknown,
Do trace these Libyan deserts, all despis'd,
Exil'd forth Europe and wide Asia both,
204 *Turen*: Tyrian.

230 And have not any coverture but heaven.
 VENUS: Fortune hath favour'd thee, whate'er thou be,
  In sending thee unto this courteous coast.
  A' God's name, on! and haste thee to the court,
  Where Dido will receive ye with her smiles.
  And for thy ships, which thou supposest lost,
  Not one of them hath perish'd in the storm,
  But are arrived safe, not far from hence.
  And so I leave thee to thy fortune's lot,
  Wishing good luck unto thy wandering steps.
  Exit.

240 ÆNEAS: Achates, 'tis my mother that is fled;
  I know her by the movings of her feet.
  Stay, gentle Venus, fly not from thy son!
  Too cruel, why wilt thou forsake me thus,
  Or in these shades deceiv'st mine eye so oft?
  Why talk we not together hand in hand,
  And tell our griefs in more familiar terms?
  But thou art gone, and leav'st me here alone
  To dull the air with my discoursive moan.
  Exeunt.

SCENE TWO

Enter IARBAS, *followed by* ILIONEUS, CLOANTHUS,
SERGESTUS, *and others.*

 ILIONEUS: Follow, ye Trojans, follow this brave lord,
  And plain to him the sum of your distress.
 IARBAS: Why, what are you, or wherefore do you sue?
 ILIONEUS: Wretches of Troy, envied of the winds,
  That crave such favour at your honour's feet,
  As poor distressed misery may plead:
  Save, save, O, save our ships from cruel fire,
  That do complain the wounds of thousand waves,
  And spare our lives, whom every spite pursues!
10 We come not, we, to wrong your Libyan gods,

Or steal your household Lares from their shrines.
Our hands are not prepar'd to lawless spoil,
Nor armed to offend in any kind;
Such force is far from our unweapon'd thoughts,
Whose fading weal, of victory forsook,
Forbids all hope to harbour near our hearts.

IARBAS: But tell me, Trojans, Trojans if you be,
Unto what fruitful quarters were ye bound,
Before that Boreas buckled with your sails?

CLOANTHUS: There is a place, Hesperia term'd by us,   20
An ancient empire, famoused for arms,
And fertile in fair Ceres' furrow'd wealth,
Which now we call Italia, of his name
That in such peace long time did rule the same.
Thither made we;
When, suddenly, gloomy Orion rose,
And led our ships into the shallow sands,
Whereas the southern wind with brackish breath,
Dispers'd them all amongst the wrackful rocks.
From thence a few of us escap'd to land;   30
The rest, we fear, are folded in the floods.

IARBAS: Brave men-at-arms, abandon fruitless fears,
Since Carthage knows to entertain distress.

SERGESTUS: Ay, but the barbrous sort do threat our
     ships,
And will not let us lodge upon the sands;
In multitudes they swarm unto the shore,
And from the first earth interdict our feet.

IARBAS: Myself will see they shall not trouble ye:
Your men and you shall banquet in our court,
And every Trojan be as welcome here   40
As Jupiter to silly Baucis' house.
Come in with me; I'll bring you to my queen,
Who shall confirm my words with further deeds.

11 *Lares*: shrines for the spirits of the departed, placed beside the
household hearth.
15 *weal*: fortune.   41 *silly*: simple.

SERGESTUS: Thanks, gentle lord, for such unlook'd-
   for grace:
Might we but once more see Æneas' face,
Then would we hope to quite such friendly turns,
As shall surpass the wonder of our speech.
   Exeunt.

ACT TWO

SCENE ONE

Enter ÆNEAS, ACHATES, ASCANIUS, *and others.*

ÆNEAS: Where am I now? These should be Carthage
   walls.
ACHATES: Why stands my sweet Æneas thus amaz'd?
ÆNEAS: O my Achates, Theban Niobe,
   Who for her sons' death wept out life and breath,
   And, dry with grief, was turn'd into a stone,
   Had not such passions in her head as I!
   Methinks that town there should be Troy, yon Ida's
      hill,
   There Xanthus' stream, because here's Priamus;
   And when I know it is not, then I die.
10 ACHATES: And in this humour is Achates too;
   I cannot choose but fall upon my knees,
   And kiss his hand. O, where is Hecuba?
   Here she was wont to sit; but, saving air,
   Is nothing here; and what is this but stone?
   ÆNEAS: O, yet this stone doth make Æneas weep!
   And would my prayers (as Pygmalion's did)
   Could give it life, that under his conduct
   We might sail back to Troy, and be reveng'd
   On these hard-hearted Grecians which rejoice
20 That nothing now is left of Priamus!
   O, Priamus is left, and this is he!
   Come, come aboard! Pursue the hateful Greeks!
   46 *quite*: requite.

54

ACHATES: What means Æneas?

ÆNEAS: Achates, though mine eyes say this is stone,
Yet thinks my mind that this is Priamus;
And when my grieved heart sighs and says no,
Then would it leap out to give Priam life.
O, were I not at all, so thou mightst be!
Achates, see, King Priam wags his hand!
He is alive; Troy is not overcome!   30

ACHATES: Thy mind, Æneas, that would have it so,
Deludes thy eyesight; Priamus is dead.

ÆNEAS: Ah, Troy is sack'd, and Priamus is dead!
And why should poor Æneas be alive?

ASCANIUS: Sweet father, leave to weep; this is not he,
For were it Priam, he would smile on me.

ACHATES: Æneas, see, here come the citizens.
Leave to lament, lest they laugh at our fears.

    Enter CLOANTHUS, SERGESTUS, ILIONEUS, *and
others.*

ÆNEAS: Lords of this town, or whatsoever style
Belongs unto your name, vouchsafe of ruth   40
To tell us who inhabits this fair town,
What kind of people, and who governs them;
For we are strangers driven on this shore,
And scarcely know within what clime we are.

ILIONEUS: I hear Æneas' voice, but see him not,
For none of these can be our general.

ACHATES: Like Ilioneus speaks this nobleman,
But Ilioneus goes not in such robes.

SERGESTUS: You are Achates, or I deceiv'd.

ACHATES: Æneas, see, Sergestus, or his ghost!   50

ILIONEUS: He names Æneas; let us kiss his feet.

CLOANTHUS: It is our captain; see, Ascanius!

SERGESTUS: Live long Æneas and Ascanius!

ÆNEAS: Achates, speak, for I am overjoy'd.

ACHATES: O Ilioneus, art thou yet alive?

ILIONEUS: Blest be the time I see Achates' face!

   40 *vouchsafe of ruth*: grant for pity.

CLOANTHUS: Why turns Æneas from his trusty friends?

ÆNEAS: Sergestus, Ilioneus, and the rest,
Your sight amaz'd me. O, what destinies
60   Have brought my sweet companions in such plight?
O, tell me, for I long to be resolv'd!

ILIONEUS: Lovely Æneas, these are Carthage walls,
And here Queen Dido wears th' imperial crown,
Who for Troy's sake hath entertain'd us all,
And clad us in these wealthy robes we wear.
Oft hath she ask'd us under whom we serv'd;
And, when we told her, she would weep for grief,
Thinking the sea had swallow'd up thy ships;
And, now she sees thee, how will she rejoice!

70 SERGESTUS: See, where her servitors pass through the
  hall,
Bearing a banquet: Dido is not far.

ILIONEUS: Look, where she comes! Æneas, view her
  well.

ÆNEAS: Well may I view her; but she sees not me.
  Enter DIDO, ANNA, IARBAS, *and* TRAIN.

DIDO: What stranger art thou, that dost eye me thus?

ÆNEAS: Sometime I was a Trojan, mighty queen,
But Troy is not: what shall I say I am?

ILIONEUS: Renowmed Dido, 'tis our general,
Warlike Æneas.

DIDO: Warlike Æneas, and in these base robes!
80   Go fetch the garment which Sichaeus ware.
  Exit an ATTENDANT *who brings in the garment,*
  which ÆNEAS *puts on.*
Brave prince, welcome to Carthage and to me,
Both happy that Æneas is our guest.
Sit in this chair, and banquet with a queen:
Æneas is Æneas, were he clad
In weeds as bad as ever Irus ware.

ÆNEAS: This is no seat for one that's comfortless.

80 *Sichaeus*: Dido's deceased husband.
85 *Irus*: a beggar who fought Ulysses.

May it please your grace to let Æneas wait;
For though my birth be great, my fortune's mean,   *90*
Too mean to be companion to a queen.

DIDO: Thy fortune may be greater than thy birth.
Sit down, Æneas, sit in Dido's place;
And, if this be thy son, as I suppose,
Here let him sit. Be merry, lovely child.

ÆNEAS: This place beseems me not; O pardon me!

DIDO: I'll have it so; Æneas, be content.

ASCANIUS: Madam, you shall be my mother.

DIDO: And so I will, sweet child. Be merry, man:
Here's to thy better fortune and good stars.
Drinks.

ÆNEAS: In all humility, I thank your grace.

DIDO: Remember who thou art; speak like thyself: *100*
Humility belongs to common grooms.

ÆNEAS: And who so miserable as Æneas is?

DIDO: Lies it in Dido's hands to make thee blest,
Then be assur'd thou art not miserable.

ÆNEAS: O Priamus, O Troy, O Hecuba!

DIDO: May I entreat thee to discourse at large,
And truly too, how Troy was overcome?
For many tales go of that city's fall,
And scarcely do agree upon one point.
Some say Antenor did betray the town;   *110*
Others report 'twas Sinon's perjury;
But all in this, that Troy is overcome,
And Priam dead; yet how, we hear no news.

ÆNEAS: A woful tale bids Dido to unfold,
Whose memory, like pale Death's stony mace,
Beats forth my senses from this troubled soul,
And makes Æneas sink at Dido's feet.

DIDO: What, faints Æneas to remember Troy,
In whose defence he fought so valiantly?
Look up, and speak.   *120*

ÆNEAS: Then speak, Æneas, with Achilles' tongue;
And, Dido, and you Carthaginian peers,

57

Hear me; but yet with Myrmidons' harsh ears,
Daily inur'd to broils and massacres,
Lest you be mov'd too much with my sad tale.
The Grecian soldiers, tir'd with ten years' war,
Began to cry, 'Let us unto our ships,
Troy is invincible, why stay we here?'
With whose outcries Atrides being appall'd,
130 Summon'd the captains to his princely tent,
Who, looking on the scars we Trojans gave,
Seeing the number of their men decreas'd,
And the remainder weak and out of heart,
Gave up their voices to dislodge the camp,
And so in troops all march'd to Tenedos;
Where when they came, Ulysses on the sand
Assay'd with honey words to turn them back;
And, as he spoke, to further his intent,
The winds did drive huge billows to the shore,
140 And heaven was darken'd with tempestuous clouds.
Then he alleg'd the gods would have them stay,
And prophesied Troy should be overcome;
And therewithal he call'd false Sinon forth,
A man compact of craft and perjury,
Whose ticing tongue was made of Hermes' pipe,
To force an hundred watchful eyes to sleep;
And him, Epeus having made the horse,
With sacrificing wreaths upon his head,
Ulysses sent to our unhappy town;
150 Who, grovelling in the mire of Xanthus' banks,
His hands bound at his back, and both his eyes
Turn'd up to heaven, as one resolv'd to die,
Our Phrygian shepherd[s] hal'd within the gates,
And brought into the court of Priamus;
To whom he us'd action so pitiful
Looks so remorseful, vows so forcible,
As therewithal the old man, overcome,

123 *Myrmidons*: fought in the Trojan war under Achilles.
129 *Atrides*: the sons of Atreus and their descendants.

Kiss'd him, embrac'd him, and unloos'd his bands:
And then – O Dido, pardon me!
DIDO: Nay, leave not here; resolve me of the rest.   160
ÆNEAS: O, th' enchanting words of that base slave
Made him to think Epeus' pine-tree horse
A sacrifice t' appease Minerva's wrath!
The rather, for that one Laocoon,
Breaking a spear upon his hollow breast,
Was with two winged serpents stung to death.
Whereat aghast, we were commanded straight
With reverence to draw it into Troy,
In which unhappy work was I employ'd.
These hands did help to hale it to the gates,   170
Through which it could not enter, 'twas so huge, –
O, had it never enter'd, Troy had stood!
But Priamus, impatient of delay,
Enforc'd a wide breach in that rampir'd wall
Which thousand battering-rams could never pierce,
And so came in this fatal instrument,
At whose accursed feet, as overjoy'd,
We banqueted, till, overcome with wine,
Some surfeited, and others soundly slept.
Which Sinon viewing, caus'd the Greekish spies   180
To haste to Tenedos and tell the camp.
Then he unlock'd the horse; and suddenly,
From out his entrails, Neoptolemus,
Setting his spear upon the ground, leapt forth,
And, after him, a thousand Grecians more,
In whose stern faces shin'd the quenchless fire
That after burnt the pride of Asia.
By this the camp was come unto the walls,
And through the breach did march into the streets,
Where, meeting with the rest, 'Kill, kill!' they cried.   190
Frighted with this confused noise, I rose,
And looking from a turret, might behold
Young infants swimming in their parents' blood,

183 *Neoptolemus*: Pyrrhus, son of Achilles.

Headless carcasses pil'd up in heaps,
Virgins half-dead, dragg'd by their golden hair,
And with main force flung on a ring of pikes,
Old men with swords thrust through their aged sides,
Kneeling for mercy to a Greekish lad,
Who with steel pole-axes dash'd out their brains.
200 Then buckled I mine armour, drew my sword.
And thinking to go down, came Hector's ghost,
With ashy visage, blueish sulphur eyes,
His arms torn from his shoulders, and his breast
Furrow'd with wounds, and, that which made me
    weep,
Thongs at his heels, by which Achilles' horse
Drew him in triumph through the Greekish camp,
Burst from the earth, crying 'Æneas, fly!
Troy is a-fire, the Grecians have the town!'
DIDO: O Hector, who weeps not to hear thy name?
210 ÆNEAS: Yet flung I forth, and, desperate of my life,
Ran in the thickest throngs, and with this sword
Sent many of their savage ghosts to hell.
At last came Pyrrhus, fell and full of ire,
His harness dropping blood, and on his spear
The mangled head of Priam's youngest son;
And, after him, his band of Myrmidons,
With balls of wild-fire in their murdering paws,
Which made the funeral flame that burnt fair Troy:
All which hemm'd me about, crying, 'This is he!'
220 DIDO: Ah, how could poor Æneas scape their hands?
ÆNEAS: My mother Venus, jealous of my health,
Convey'd me from their crooked nets and bands;
So I escap'd the furious Pyrrhus' wrath,
Who then ran to the palace of the king,
And at Jove's altar finding Priamus,
About whose wither'd neck hung Hecuba,
Folding his hand in hers, and jointly both
Beating their breasts, and falling on the ground,
He, with his falchion's point rais'd up at once,

And with Megaera's eyes, star'd in their face,   230
Threatening a thousand deaths at every glance,
To whom the aged king thus, trembling spoke:
'Achilles' son, remember what I was,
Father of fifty sons, but they are slain;
Lord of my fortune, but my fortune's turn'd;
King of this city, but my Troy is fir'd;
And now am neither father, lord, nor king:
Yet who so wretched but desires to live?
O, let me live, great Neoptolemus!'
Not mov'd at all, but smiling at his tears,   240
This butcher, whilst his hands were yet held up,
Treading upon his breast, strook off his hands.
DIDO: O, end, Æneas! I can hear no more.
ÆNEAS: At which the frantic queen leap'd on his face,
And in his eyelids hanging by the nails,
A little while prolong'd her husband's life.
At last the soldiers pull'd her by the heels,
And swung her howling in the empty air,
Which sent an echo to the wounded king:
Whereat he lifted up his bed-rid limbs,   250
And would have grappled with Achilles' son,
Forgetting both his want of strength and hands;
Which he disdaining, whisk'd his sword about,
And with the wound[4] thereof the king fell down.
Then from the navel to the throat at once
He ripp'd old Priam, at whose latter gasp
Jove's marble statue gan to bend the brow,
As loathing Pyrrhus for this wicked act.
Yet he, undaunted, took his father's flag,
And dipp'd it in the old king's chill-cold blood,   260
And then in triumph ran into the streets,
Through which he could not pass for slaughter'd men;
So, leaning on his sword, he stood stone still,
Viewing the fire wherewith rich Ilion burnt.

230 *Megaera*: one of the Furies, sometimes represented as women
like Gorgons.

By this, I got my father on my back,
This young boy in mine arms, and by the hand
Led fair Creusa, my beloved wife;
When thou, Achates, with thy sword mad'st way,
And we were round environ'd with the Greeks.
270 O, there I lost my wife! And, had not we
Fought manfully, I had not told this tale.
Yet manhood would not serve; of force we fled;
And, as we went unto our ships, thou know'st
We saw Cassandra sprawling in the streets,
Whom Ajax ravish'd in Diana's fane,
Her cheeks swollen with sighs, her hair all rent,
Whom I took up to bear unto our ships;
But suddenly the Grecians follow'd us,
And I, alas, was forc'd to let her lie!
280 Then got we to our ships, and, being aboard,
Polyxena cried out, 'Æneas stay!
The Greeks pursue me; stay, and take me in!'
Mov'd with her voice, I leap'd into the sea,
Thinking to bear her on my back aboard,
For all our ships were launch'd into the deep,
And, as I swom, she, standing on the shore,
Was by the cruel Myrmidons surpris'd
And after by that Pyrrhus sacrific'd.
DIDO: I die with melting ruth; Æneas, leave.
290 ANNA: O, what became of aged Hecuba?
IARBAS: How got Æneas to the fleet again?
DIDO: But how scap'd Helen, she that caus'd this war?
ÆNEAS: Achates, speak; sorrow hath tir'd me quite.
ACHATES: What happen'd to the queen we cannot show;
We hear they led her captive into Greece.
As for Æneas, he swom quickly back;
And Helena betray'd Deiphobus,

275 *Diana's fane*: Diana's temple (but in Virgil and Ovid, Minerva's).
281 *Polyxena*: like Cassandra, a daughter of Priam.
289 *leave*: cease.

Her lover, after Alexander died,
And so was reconcil'd to Menelaus.

DIDO: O, had that ticing strumpet ne'er been born!   *300*
Trojan, thy ruthful tale hath made me sad:
Come, let us think upon some pleasing sport,
To rid me from these melancholy thoughts.

   Exeunt all except ASCANIUS, *whom* VENUS,
   entering with CUPID *at another door, takes by the*
   sleeve as he is going off.

VENUS: Fair child, stay thou with Dido's waiting maid:
I'll give thee sugar-almonds, sweet conserves,
A silver girdle, and a golden purse,
And this young prince shall be thy playfellow.

ASCANIUS: Are you Queen Dido's son?

CUPID: Ay, and my mother gave me this fine bow.

ASCANIUS: Shall I have such a quiver and a bow?   *310*

VENUS: Such bow, such quiver, and such golden shafts,
Will Dido give to sweet Ascanius.
For Dido's sake I take thee in my arms,
And stick these spangled feathers in thy hat.
Eat comfits in mine arms, and I will sing.

   Sings.

Now is he fast asleep; and in this grove,
Amongst green brakes, I'll lay Ascanius,
And strew him with sweet-smelling violets,
Blushing roses, purple hyacinth.
These milk-white doves shall be his centronels,   *320*
Who, if that any seek to do him hurt,
Will quickly fly to Cytherea's⁵ fist.
Now, Cupid, turn thee to Ascanius' shape,
And go to Dido, who instead of him,
Will set thee on her lap, and play with thee.
Then touch her white breast with this arrow head,
That she may dote upon Æneas' love,
And by that means repair his broken ships,
Victual his soldiers, give him wealthy gifts,

298 *Alexander*: Paris of Troy.   320 *centronels*: sentinels.

330   And he, at last, depart to Italy,
Or else in Carthage make his kingly throne.
CUPID: I will, fair mother; and so play my part
As every touch shall wound Queen Dido's heart.
Exit.
VENUS: Sleep, my sweet nephew, in these cooling shades,
Free from the murmur of these running streams,
The cry of beasts, the rattling of the winds,
Or whisking of these leaves: all shall be still,
And nothing interrupt thy quiet sleep,
Till I return, and take thee hence again.
Exit.

ACT THREE

SCENE ONE

Enter CUPID *as* ASCANIUS.

CUPID: Now, Cupid, cause the Carthaginian queen
To be enamour'd of thy brother's looks;
Convey this golden arrow in thy sleeve,
Lest she imagine thou art Venus' son;
And when she strokes thee softly on the head,
Then shall I touch her breast and conquer her.
Enter DIDO, ANNA, *and* IARBAS.
IARBAS: How long, fair Dido, shall I pine for thee?
'Tis not enough that thou dost grant me love,
But that I may enjoy what I desire:
10   That love is childish which consists in words.
DIDO: Iarbas, know, that thou, of all my wooers, –
And yet have I had many mightier kings, –
Hast had the greatest favours I could give.
I fear me, Dido hath been counted light
In being too familiar with Iarbas;
Albeit the gods do know, no wanton thought
Had ever residence in Dido's breast.

64

IARBAS: But Dido is the favour I request.

DIDO: Fear not, Iarbas; Dido may be thine.

ANNA: Look, sister, how Æneas' little son   20
    Plays with your garments and embraceth you.

CUPID: No, Dido will not take me in her arms;
    I shall not be her son, she loves me not.

DIDO: Weep not, sweet boy; thou shalt be Dido's son:
    Sit in my lap, and let me hear thee sing.
        Cupid sings.
    No more, my child; now talk another while,
    And tell me where learn'dst thou this pretty song.

CUPID: My cousin Helen taught it me in Troy.

DIDO: How lovely is Ascanius when he smiles!

CUPID: Will Dido let me hang about her neck?   30

DIDO: Ay, wag, and give thee leave to kiss her too.

CUPID: What will you give me now? I'll have this fan.

DIDO: Take it, Ascanius, for thy father's sake.

IARBAS: Come, Dido, leave Ascanius; let us walk.

DIDO: Go thou away; Ascanius shall stay.

IARBAS: Ungentle queen, is this thy love to me?

DIDO: O stay, Iarbas, and I'll go with thee!

CUPID: And if my mother go, I'll follow her.

DIDO: Why stay'st thou here? Thou art no love of mine.

IARBAS: Iarbas, die, seeing she abandons thee!   40

DIDO: No; live, Iarbas. What hast thou deserv'd,
    That I should say thou art no love of mine?
    Something thou hast deserv'd. — Away, I say!
    Depart from Carthage; come not in my sight.

IARBAS: Am I not king of rich Gaetulia?

DIDO: Iarbas, pardon me, and stay a while.

CUPID: Mother, look here.

DIDO: What tell'st thou me of rich Gaetulia?
    Am not I queen of Libya? Then depart.

IARBAS: I go to feed the humour of my love,   50
    Yet not from Carthage for a thousand worlds.

DIDO: Iarbas!

IARBAS: Doth Dido call me back?

DIDO: No; but I charge thee never look on me.

IARBAS: Then pull out both mine eyes, or let me die.
Exit.

ANNA: Wherefore doth Dido bid Iarbas go?

DIDO: Because his loathsome sight offends mine eye,
And in my thoughts is shrin'd another love.
O Anna, didst thou know how sweet love were,
60   Full soon wouldst thou abjure this single life!

ANNA (*aside*): Poor soul, I know too well the sour of love:
O, that Iarbas could but fancy me!

DIDO: Is not Æneas fair and beautiful?

ANNA: Yes, and Iarbas foul and favourless.

DIDO: Is he not eloquent in all his speech?

ANNA: Yes, and Iarbas rude and rustical.

DIDO: Name not Iarbas: but, sweet Anna, say,
Is not Æneas worthy Dido's love?

ANNA: O sister, were you empress of the world,
70   Æneas well deserves to be your love!
So lovely is he, that, where'er he goes,
The people swarm to gaze him in the face.

DIDO: But tell them, none shall gaze on him but I,
Lest their gross eye-beams taint my lover's cheeks.
Anna, good sister Anna, go for him,
Lest with these sweet thoughts I melt clean away.

ANNA: Then sister, you'll abjure Iarbas' love?

DIDO: Yet must I hear that loathsome name again?
Run for Æneas, or I'll fly to him.
Exit ANNA.

80 CUPID: You shall not hurt my father when he comes.

DIDO: No, for thy sake I'll love thy father well.
O dull-conceited Dido, that till now
Didst never think Æneas beautiful!
But now, for quittance of this oversight,
I'll make me bracelets of his golden hair;
His glistering eyes shall be my looking-glass;
His lips an altar, where I'll offer up

82 *dull-conceited*: dull-witted.

66

As many kisses as the sea hath sands;
Instead of music I will hear him speak;
His looks shall be my only library; *90*
And thou, Æneas, Dido's treasury,
In whose fair bosom I will lock more wealth
Than twenty thousand Indias can afford.
O, here he comes! Love, love, give Dido leave
To be more modest than her thoughts admit,
Lest I be made a wonder to the world.

    Enter ÆNEAS, ACHATES, SERGESTUS, ILIONEUS,
    and CLOANTHUS.

Achates, how doth Carthage please your lord?
ACHATES: That will Æneas show your majesty.
DIDO: Æneas, art thou there?
ÆNEAS: I understand your highness sent for me. *100*
DIDO: No; but now thou art here, tell me, in sooth,
  In what might Dido highly pleasure thee.
ÆNEAS: So much have I receiv'd at Dido's hands,
  As, without blushing, I can ask no more.
  Yet, queen of Afric, are my ships unrigg'd,
  My sails all rent in sunder with the wind,
  My oars broken, and my tackling lost,
  Yea, all my navy split with rocks and shelves;
  Nor stern nor anchor have our maimed fleet;
  Our masts the furious winds strook overboard: *110*
  Which piteous wants if Dido will supply,
  We will account her author of our lives.
DIDO: Æneas, I'll repair thy Trojan ships,
  Conditionally that thou wilt stay with me,
  And let Achates sail to Italy:
  I'll give thee tackling made of rivell'd gold,
  Wound on the barks of odoriferous trees;
  Oars of massy ivory, full of holes,
  Through which the water shall delight to play;
  Thy anchors shall be hew'd from crystal rocks, *120*
  Which, if thou lose, shall shine above the waves;

108 *shelves*: sand-banks.

The masts, whereon thy swelling sails shall hang,
Hollow pyramides of silver plate;
The sails of folded lawn, where shall be wrought
The wars of Troy, – but not Troy's overthrow;
For ballass, empty Dido's treasury:
Take what ye will, but leave Æneas here.
Achates, thou shalt be so newly[6] clad,
As sea-born nymphs shall swarm about thy ships,
130   And wanton mermaids court thee with sweet songs,
Flinging in favours of more sovereign worth
Than Thetis hangs about Apollo's neck,[7]
So that Æneas may but stay with me.
ÆNEAS: Wherefore would Dido have Æneas stay?
DIDO: To war against my bordering enemies.
Æneas, think not Dido is in love;
For, if that man could conquer me,
I had been wedded ere Æneas came.
See where the pictures of my suitors hang;
140   And are not these as fair as fair may be?
ACHATES: I saw this man at Troy, ere Troy was sack'd.
SERGESTUS: I this in Greece, when Paris stole fair
    Helen.
ILIONEUS: This man and I were at Olympia's games.
SERGESTUS: I know this face; he is a Persian born:
    I travell'd with him to Ætolia.
CLOANTHUS: And I in Athens with this gentleman,
    Unless I be deceiv'd, disputed once.
DIDO: But speak, Æneas; know you none of these?
ÆNEAS: No, madam; but it seems that these are kings.
150   DIDO: All these, and others which I never saw,
Have been most urgent suitors for my love;
Some came in person, others sent their legates,
Yet none obtain'd me. I am free from all;
And yet, God knows, entangled unto one.
This was an orator, and thought by words

123 *pyramides*: obelisks or thin spires.
124 *folded lawn*: fine material folded many times.

To compass me, but yet he was deceiv'd;
And this a Spartan courtier, vain and wild:
But his fantastic humours pleas'd not me:
This was Alcion, a musician,
But, play'd he ne'er so sweet, I let him go: *160*
This was the wealthy king of Thessaly;
But I had gold enough, and cast him off:
This, Meleager's son, a warlike prince;
But weapons gree not with my tender years.
The rest are such as all the world well knows:
Yet now[8] I swear, by heaven and him I love,
I was as far from love as they from hate.
ÆNEAS: O, happy shall he be whom Dido loves!
DIDO: Then never say that thou art miserable,
Because, it may be, thou shalt be my love.   *170*
Yet boast not of it, for I love thee not, –
And yet I hate thee not. – O, if I speak,
I shall betray myself! – Æneas, come:
We two will go a-hunting in the woods;
But not so much for thee, – thou art but one, –
As for Achates and his followers.
Exeunt.

SCENE TWO

Enter JUNO *to* ASCANIUS, *who lies asleep.*
JUNO: Here lies my hate, Æneas' cursed brat,
The boy wherein false Destiny delights,
The heir of Fury, the favourite of the Fates,[9]
That ugly imp that shall outwear my wrath,
And wrong my deity with high disgrace.
But I will take another order now,
And raze th' eternal register of Time.
Troy shall no more call him her second hope,
Nor Venus triumph in his tender youth;

164 *gree*: agree, suit.

10 For here, in spite of heaven, I'll murder him,
And feed infection with his let-out[10] life.
Say, Paris, now shall Venus have the ball?
Say, vengeance, now shall her Ascanius die?
O, no! God wot, I cannot watch my time,
Nor quit good turns with double fee down told!
Tut, I am simple, without mind to hurt,
And have no gall at all to grieve my foes!
But lustful Jove and his adulterous child
Shall find it written on confusion's front,
20 That only Juno rules in Rhamnus town.
   Enter VENUS.
VENUS: What should this mean? My doves are back
      return'd,
Who warn me of such danger prest at hand
To harm my sweet Ascanius' lovely life.
Juno, my mortal foe, what make you here?
Avaunt, old witch! and trouble not my wits.
JUNO: Fie, Venus, that such causeless words of wrath
Should e'er defile so fair a mouth as thine!
Are not we both sprung of celestial race,
And banquet, as two sisters, with the gods?
30 Why is it, then, Displeasure should disjoin
Whom kindred and acquaintance co-unites?
VENUS: Out, hateful hag! Thou wouldst have slain my
      son,
Had not my doves discover'd thy intent.
But I will tear thy eyes fro forth thy head,
And feast the birds with their blood-shotten balls,
If thou but lay thy finger on my boy.
JUNO: Is this, then, all the thanks that I shall have
For saving him from snakes' and serpents' stings,
That would have kill'd him, sleeping, as he lay?
40 What, though I was offended with thy son,
And wrought him mickle woe on sea and land,
When, for the hate of Trojan Ganymede,

20 *Rhamnus*: town with the Temple of Nemesis.

That was advanced by my Hebe's shame,[11]
And Paris' judgment of the heavenly ball,
I muster'd all the winds unto his wrack,
And urg'd each element to his annoy?
Yet now I do repent me of his ruth,
And wish that I had never wrong'd him so.
Bootless I saw it was to war with fate
That hath so many unresisted friends: 50
Wherefore I chang'd my counsel with the time,
And planted love where envy erst had sprung.
VENUS: Sister of Jove, if that thy love be such
  As these thy protestations do paint forth,
  We two, as friends, one fortune will divide.
  Cupid shall lay his arrows in thy lap,
  And to a sceptre change his golden shafts;
  Fancy and modesty shall live as mates,
  And thy fair peacocks by my pigeons perch.
  Love my Æneas, and desire is thine;   60
  The day, the night, my swans, my sweets, are thine.
JUNO: More than melodious are these words to me,
  That overcloy my soul with their content.
  Venus, sweet Venus, how may I deserve
  Such amorous favours at thy beauteous hand?
  But, that thou mayst more easily perceive
  How highly I do prize this amity,
  Hark to a motion of eternal league,
  Which I will make in quittance of thy love.
  Thy son, thou know'st, with Dido now remains   70
  And feeds his eyes with favours of her court;
  She, likewise, in admiring spends her time,
  And cannot talk nor think of aught but him;
  Why should not they, then, join in marriage,
  And bring forth mighty kings to Carthage town,
  Whom casualty of sea hath made such friends?
  And, Venus, let there be a match confirm'd
  Betwixt these two, whose loves are so alike;

50 *unresisted*: irresistible.

And both our deities, conjoin'd in one,
80   Shall chain felicity unto their throne.
VENUS: Well could I like this reconcilement's means;
      But much I fear, my son will ne'er consent,
      Whose armed soul, already on the sea,
      Darts forth her light to Lavinia's shore.
JUNO: Fair queen of love, I will divorce these doubts,
      And find the way to weary such fond thoughts.
      This day they both a-hunting forth will ride
      Into the woods adjoining to these walls;
      When, in the midst of all their gamesome sports,
90   I'll make the clouds dissolve their watery works,
      And drench Silvanus' dwellings with their showers.
      Then in one cave the queen and he shall meet,
      And interchangeably discourse their thoughts,
      Whose short conclusion will seal up their hearts
      Unto the purpose which we now propound.
VENUS: Sister, I see you savour of my wiles;
      Be it as you will have for this once.
      Meantime Ascanius shall be my charge;
      Whom I shall bear to Ida in mine arms,
100   And couch him in Adonis' purple down.
      Exeunt.

SCENE THREE

Enter DIDO, ÆNEAS, ANNA, IARBAS, ACHATES,
CUPID *as* ASCANIUS, *and* FOLLOWERS.
DIDO: Æneas, think not but I honour thee,
      That thus in person go with thee to hunt.
      My princely robes, thou see'st, are laid aside,
      Whose glittering pomp Diana's shrouds supplies;
      All fellows now, dispos'd alike to sport;
      The woods are wide, and we have store of game.

91 *Silvanus' dwellings*: the woods.
4 *Diana's shrouds*: hunting costume.

72

Fair Trojan, hold my golden bow a while,
Until I gird my quiver to my side.
Lords, go before; we two must talk alone.

IARBAS (*aside*): Ungentle, can she wrong Iarbas so?　　　10
I'll die before a stranger have that grace.
'We two will talk alone' — what words be these?

DIDO: What makes Iarbas here of all the rest?
We could have gone without your company.

ÆNEAS: But love and duty led him on perhaps
To press beyond acceptance to your sight.

IARBAS: Why, man of Troy, do I offend thine eyes?
Or art thou griev'd thy betters press so nigh?

DIDO: How now, Gaetulian! Are ye grown so brave,
To challenge us with your comparisons?　　　20
Peasant, go seek companions like thyself,
And meddle not with any that I love.
Æneas, be not mov'd at what he says;
For otherwise he will be out of joint.

IARBAS: Women may wrong by privilege of love;
But, should that man of men, Dido except,
Have taunted me in these opprobrious terms,
I would have either drunk his dying blood,
Or else I would have given my life in gage.

DIDO: Huntsmen, why pitch you not your toils apace,　　　30
And rouse the light-foot deer from forth their lair?

ANNA: Sister, see, see Ascanius in his pomp,
Bearing his hunt-spear bravely in his hand!

DIDO: Yea, little son, are you so forward now?

CUPID: Ay, mother; I shall one day be a man,
And better able unto other arms.
Meantime these wanton weapons serve my war,
Which I will break betwixt a lion's jaws.

DIDO: What, dar'st thou look a lion in the face?

CUPID: Ay, and outface him too, do what he can.　　　40

ANNA: How like his father speaketh he in all!

ÆNEAS: And mought I live to see him sack rich Thebes,
And load his spear with Grecian princes' heads,

73

Then would I wish me with Anchises' tomb,
And dead to honour that hath brought me up.

IARBAS (*aside*): And might I live to see thee shipp'd away,
And hoist aloft on Neptune's hideous hills,
Then would I wish me in fair Dido's arms,
And dead to scorn that hath pursu'd me so.

50 ÆNEAS: Stout friend Achates, dost thou know this wood?

ACHATES: As I remember, here you shot the deer
That sav'd your famish'd soldiers' lives from death,
When first you set your foot upon the shore;
And here we met fair Venus, virgin-like,
Bearing her bow and quiver at her back.

ÆNEAS: O, how these irksome labours now delight,
And overjoy my thoughts with their escape!
Who would not undergo all kind of toil,
To be well stor'd with such a winter's tale?

60 DIDO: Æneas, leave these dumps, and let's away,
Some to the mountains, some unto the soil,
You to the valleys, – thou (*to* IARBAS) unto the house.
Exeunt all except IARBAS.

IARBAS: Ay, this it is which wounds me to the death,
To see a Phrygian, far-fet o' the sea,
Preferr'd before a man of majesty.
O love! O hate! O cruel women's hearts,
That imitate the moon in every change,
And, like the planets, ever love to range!
What shall I do, thus wronged with disdain?

70 Revenge me on Æneas or on her?
On her? Fond man, that were to war 'gainst heaven,
And with one shaft provoke ten thousand darts.
This Trojan's end will be thy envy's aim,
Whose blood will reconcile thee to content,
And make love drunken with thy sweet desire.
But Dido, that now holdeth him so dear,

44 *Anchises*: Aeneas' father.   71 *Fond*: foolish.

74

Will die with very tidings of his death:
But time will discontinue her content,
And mould her mind unto new fancy's shapes.
O God of heaven, turn the hand of Fate   *80*
Unto that happy day of my delight!
And then – what then? Iarbas shall but love:
So doth he now, though not with equal gain.
That resteth in the rival of thy pain,
Who ne'er will cease to soar till he be slain.
    Exit.

SCENE FOUR

The storm. Enter ÆNEAS and DIDO in the cave,
at several times.

DIDO: Æneas!
ÆNEAS: Dido!
DIDO: Tell me, dear love, how found you out this cave?
ÆNEAS: By chance, sweet queen, as Mars and Venus
    met.[12]
DIDO: Why, that was in a net, where we are loose;
    And yet I am not free, – O, would I were!
ÆNEAS: Why, what is it that Dido may desire
    And not obtain, be it in human power?
DIDO: The thing that I will die before I ask,
    And yet desire to have before I die.   *10*
ÆNEAS: It is not aught Æneas may achieve?
DIDO: Æneas, no, although his eyes do pierce.
ÆNEAS: What, hath Iarbas anger'd her in aught?
    And will she be avenged on his life?
DIDO: Not anger'd me, except in angering thee.
ÆNEAS: Who, then, of all so cruel may he be
    That should detain thy eye in his defects?
DIDO: The man that I do eye where'er I am,
    Whose amorous face, like Paean, sparkles fire,
    19 *Paean*: Apollo (the sun).

75

20 Whenas he butts his beams on Flora's bed.
Prometheus hath put on Cupid's shape,
And I must perish in his burning arms.
Æneas, O Æneas, quench these flames!
ÆNEAS: What ails my queen? Is she faln sick of late?
DIDO: Not sick, my love; but sick I must conceal
The torment that it boots me not reveal.
And yet I'll speak, – and yet I'll hold my peace.
Do shame her worst, I will disclose my grief:
Æneas, thou art he – what did I say?
30 Something it was that now I have forgot.
ÆNEAS: What means fair Dido by this doubtful speech?
DIDO: Nay, nothing; but Æneas loves me not.
ÆNEAS: Æneas' thoughts dare not ascend so high
As Dido's heart, which monarchs might not scale.
DIDO: It was because I saw no king like thee,
Whose golden crown might balance my content;
But now that I have found what to affect,
I follow one that loveth fame 'fore me,
And rather had seem fair [in] Sirens' eyes,
40 Than to the Carthage queen that dies for him.
ÆNEAS: If that your majesty can look so low
As my despised worths that shun all praise,
With this my hand I give to you my heart,
And vow, by all the gods of hospitality,
By heaven and earth, and my fair brother's bow,
By Paphos, Capys, and the purple sea
From whence my radiant mother did descend,
And by this sword that sav'd me from the Greeks,
Never to leave these new-upreared walls,
50 Whiles Dido lives and rules in Juno's town,
Never to like or love any but her!
DIDO: What more than Delian music do I hear,

21 *Prometheus*: bringer of fire.   37 *affect*: care for.
46 *Paphos*: in Cyprus, near where Aphrodite rose from the waves.
46 *Capys*: father of Anchises.
52 *Delian*: from Delia, festival of Apollo, held at Delos.

That calls my soul from forth his living seat
To move unto the measures of delight?
Kind clouds, that sent forth such a courteous storm
As made disdain to fly to fancy's lap!
Stout love, in mine arms make thy Italy,
Whose crown and kingdom rests at thy command:
Sichaeus, not Æneas, be thou call'd;
The king of Carthage, not Anchises' son: 60
Hold, take these jewels at thy lover's hand,
   Giving jewels, etc.
These golden bracelets, and this wedding-ring,
Wherewith my husband woo'd me yet a maid,
And be thou king of Libya by my gift.
   Exeunt to the cave.

ACT FOUR

SCENE ONE

Enter ACHATES, CUPID *as* ASCANIUS, IARBAS,
  and ANNA.

ACHATES: Did ever men see such a sudden storm,
  Or day so clear so suddenly o'ercast?
IARBAS: I think some fell enchantress dwelleth here,
  That can call them forth whenas she please,
  And dive into black tempest's treasury,
  Whenas she means to mask the world with clouds.
ANNA: In all my life I never knew the like;
  It hailed, it snow'd, it lighten'd, all at once.
ACHATES: I think it was the devils' revelling night,
  There was such hurly-burly in the heavens.   10
  Doubtless Apollo's axle-tree is crack'd,
  Or aged Atlas' shoulder out of joint,
  The motion was so over-violent.

11 *Apollo's axle-tree*: the sun's axis.
12 *Atlas*: who held the world on his shoulders.

IARBAS: In all this coil, where have ye left the queen?
ASCANIUS: Nay, where's my warlike father, can you tell?
ANNA: Behold where both of them come forth the cave.
IARBAS: Come forth the cave? Can heaven endure this
    sight?
  Iarbas, curse that unrevenging Jove,
  Whose flinty darts slept in Typhoeus' den,
20 Whiles these adulterers surfeited with sin.
  Nature, why mad'st me not some poisonous beast,
  That with the sharpness of my edged sting
  I might have stak'd them both unto the earth,
  Whilst they were sporting in this darksome cave?
    Enter, from the cave, ÆNEAS *and* DIDO.
ÆNEAS: The air is clear, and southern winds are whist.
  Come, Dido, let us hasten to the town,
  Since gloomy Æolus doth cease to frown.
DIDO: Achates and Ascanius, well met.
ÆNEAS: Fair Anna, how escap'd you from the shower?
30 ANNA: As others did, by running to the wood.
DIDO: But where were you, Iarbas, all this while?
IARBAS: Not with Æneas in the ugly cave.
DIDO: I see, Æneas sticketh in your mind;
  But I will soon put by that stumbling-block,
  And quell those hopes that thus employ your cares.
    Exeunt.

SCENE TWO

Enter IARBAS *to sacrifice.*
IARBAS: Come, servants, come; bring forth the sacrifice,
  That I may pacify that gloomy Jove,
  Whose empty altars have enlarg'd our ills.
    SERVANTS *bring in the sacrifice, and then exeunt.*

14 *coil*: confusion, uproar.
19 *Typhoeus*: Mt Etna, where Jove's darts were forged.
25 *whist*: quiet.

Eternal Jove, great master of the clouds,
Father of gladness and all frolic thoughts,
That with thy gloomy hand corrects the heaven,
When airy creatures war amongst themselves;
Hear, hear, O, hear Iarbas' plaining prayers,
Whose hideous echoes make the welkin howl,
And all the woods Eliza[13] to resound!   10
The woman that thou will'd us entertain,
Where, staying in our borders up and down,
She crav'd a hide of ground to build a town,
With whom we did divide both laws and land,
And all the fruits that plenty else sends forth,
Scorning our loves and royal marriage-rites,
Yields up her beauty to a stranger's bed;
Who, having wrought her shame, is straightway fled.
Now, if thou be'st a pitying god of power,
On whom ruth and compassion ever waits,   20
Redress these wrongs, and warn him to his ships,
That now afflicts me with his flattering eyes.
    Enter ANNA.
ANNA: How now, Iarbas! At your prayers so hard?
IARBAS: Ay, Anna: is there aught you would with
    me?
ANNA: Nay, no such weighty business of import,
    But may be slack'd until another time:
    Yet, if you would partake with me the cause
    Of this devotion that detaineth you,
    I would be thankful for such courtesy.
IARBAS: Anna, against this Trojan do I pray,   30
    Who seeks to rob me of thy sister's love,
    And dive into her heart by colour'd looks.
ANNA: Alas, poor king, that labours so in vain
    For her that so delighteth in thy pain!
    Be rul'd by me, and seek some other love,
    Whose yielding heart may yield thee more relief.

13 *hide*: measure of land (normally 100 acres).
32 *colour'd*: insincere.

IARBAS: Mine eye is fix'd where fancy cannot start:
O, leave me, leave me to my silent thoughts,
That register the numbers of my ruth,
40   And I will either move the thoughtless flint,
Or drop out both mine eyes in drizzling tears,
Before my sorrow's tide have any stint!

ANNA: I will not leave Iarbas, whom I love,
In this delight of dying pensiveness.
Away with Dido! Anna be thy song;
Anna, that doth admire thee more than heaven.

IARBAS: I may nor will list to such loathsome change,
That intercepts the course of my desire.
Servants, come fetch these empty vessels here;
50   For I will fly from these alluring eyes,
That do pursue my peace where'er it goes.
    Exit. SERVANTS *re-enter, and carry out the
    vessels, etc.*

ANNA: Iarbas, stay! Loving Iarbas, stay!
For I have honey to present thee with.
Hard-hearted, wilt not deign to hear me speak?
I'll follow thee with outcries ne'ertheless,
And strew thy walks with my dishevell'd hair.
    Exit.

SCENE THREE

Enter ÆNEAS.

ÆNEAS: Carthage, my friendly host, adieu!
Since destiny doth call me from the shore:
Hermes this night, descending in a dream,
Hath summon'd me to fruitful Italy.
Jove wills it so; my mother wills it so;
Let my Phoenissa grant, and then I go.
Grant she or no, Æneas must away;

44 *delight*: intense emotion.
6 *Phoenissa*: Dido was Phoenician.

Whose golden fortunes, clogg'd with courtly ease,
Cannot ascend to Fame's immortal house,
Or banquet in bright Honour's burnish'd hall,   *10*
Till he hath furrow'd Neptune's glassy fields,
And cut a passage through his topless hills.
Achates, come forth! Sergestus, Ilioneus,
Cloanthus, haste away! Æneas calls.

    Enter ACHATES, CLOANTHUS, SERGESTUS,
    and ILIONEUS.

ACHATES: What wills our lord, or wherefore did he
    call?

ÆNEAS: The dreams, brave mates, that did beset my
    bed,
When sleep but newly had embrac'd the night,
Commands me leave these unrenowmed reams,
Whereas nobility abhors to stay,
And none but base Æneas will abide.   *20*
Aboard, aboard! since Fates do bid aboard,
And slice the sea with sable-coloured ships,
On whom the nimble winds may all day wait,
And follow them, as footmen, through the deep.
Yet Dido casts her eyes like anchors out
To stay my fleet from loosing forth the bay:
'Come back, come back,' I hear her cry a-far,
'And let me link my body to thy lips,
That, tied together by the striving tongues,
We may, as one, sail into Italy.'   *30*

ACHATES: Banish that ticing dame from forth your
    mouth,
And follow your fore-seeing stars in all:
This is no life for men-at-arms to live,
Where dalliance doth consume a soldier's strength,
And wanton motions of alluring eyes
Effiminate our minds, inur'd to war.

ILIONEUS: Why, let us build a city of our own,
And not stand lingering here for amorous looks.

18 *reams*: realms.

Will Dido raise old Priam forth his grave,
40   And build the town again the Greeks did burn?
No, no; she cares not how we sink or swim,
So she may have Æneas in her arms.
CLOANTHUS: To Italy, sweet friends, to Italy!
We will not stay a minute longer here.
ÆNEAS: Trojans, aboard, and I will follow you.

    Exeunt all except ÆNEAS.

I fain would go, yet beauty calls me back:
To leave her so, and not once say farewell,
Were to transgress against all laws of love.
But, if I use such ceremonious thanks
50   As parting friends accustom on the shore,
Her silver arms will coll me round about,
And tears of pearl cry, 'Stay, Æneas, stay!'
Each word she says will then contain a crown,
And every speech be ended with a kiss:
I may not dure this female drudgery.
To sea, Æneas! find out Italy!

    Exit.

SCENE FOUR

Enter DIDO *and* ANNA.

DIDO: O Anna, run unto the water side!
They say Æneas' men are going aboard;
It may be he will steal away with them.
Stay not to answer me: run, Anna, run!

    Exit ANNA.

O foolish Trojans, that would steal from hence,
And not let Dido understand their drift!
I would have given Achates store of gold,
And Ilioneus gum and Libyan spice;
The common soldiers rich embroider'd coats,
10   And silver whistles to control the winds,

42 *So*: as long as.

Which Circes sent Sichaeus when he liv'd;
Unworthy are they of a queen's reward.
See, where they come: how might I do to chide?

    Re-enter ANNA, *with* ÆNEAS, ACHATES,
    CLOANTHUS, ILIONEUS, SERGESTUS, *and*
    CARTHAGINIAN LORDS.

ANNA: 'Twas time to run. Æneas had been gone;
    The sails were hoising up, and he aboard.

DIDO: Is this thy love to me?

ÆNEAS: O princely Dido, give me leave to speak!
    I went to take my farewell of Achates.

DIDO: How haps Achates bid me not farewell?

ACHATES: Because I fear'd your grace would keep me here.   20

DIDO: To rid thee of that doubt, aboard again:
    I charge thee put to sea, and stay not here.

ACHATES: Then let Æneas go aboard with us.

DIDO: Get you aboard; Æneas means to stay.

ÆNEAS: The sea is rough, the winds blow to the shore.

DIDO: O false Æneas! Now the sea is rough;
    But when you were aboard 'twas calm enough:
    Thou and Achates meant to sail away.

ÆNEAS: Hath not the Carthage queen mine only son?
    Thinks Dido I will go and leave him here?   30

DIDO: Æneas, pardon me; for I forgot
    That young Ascanius lay with me this night.
    Love made me jealous: but, to make amends,
    Wear the imperial crown of Libya,

    Giving him her crown and sceptre.

    Sway thou the Punic sceptre in my stead,
    And punish me, Æneas, for this crime.

ÆNEAS: This kiss shall be fair Dido's punishment.

DIDO: O, how a crown becomes Æneas' head!
    Stay here, Æneas, and command as king.

ÆNEAS: How vain am I to wear this diadem,   40
    And bear this golden sceptre in my hand!
    A burgonet of steel, and not a crown,

42 *burgonet*: helmet.

A sword, and not a sceptre, fits Æneas.

DIDO: O keep them still, and let me gaze my fill!
Now looks Æneas like immortal Jove:
O where is Ganymede, to hold his cup,
And Mercury, to fly for what he calls?
Ten thousand Cupids hover in the air,
And fan it in Æneas' lovely face!

50   O that the clouds were here wherein thou fled'st,
That thou and I unseen might sport ourselves!
Heaven, envious of our joys, is waxen pale;
And when we whisper, then the stars fall down,
To be partakers of our honey talk.

ÆNEAS: O Dido, patroness of all our lives,
When I leave thee, death be my punishment!
Swell, raging seas! frown, wayward Destinies!
Blow, winds! threaten, ye rocks and sandy shelves!
This is the harbour that Æneas seeks:

60   Let's see what tempests can annoy me now.

DIDO: Not all the world can take thee from mine arms.
Æneas may command as many Moors
As in the sea are little water drops.
And now, to make experience of my love,
Fair sister Anna, lead my lover forth,
And, seated on my jennet, let him ride,
As Dido's husband, through the Punic streets;
And will my guard, with Mauritanian darts
To wait upon him as their sovereign lord.

70 ANNA: What if the citizens repine thereat?

DIDO: Those that dislike what Dido gives in charge,
Command my guard to slay for their offence.
Shall vulgar peasants storm at what I do?
The ground is mine that gives them sustenance,
The air wherein they breathe, the water, fire,
All that they have, their lands, their goods, their
  lives,[14]
And I, the goddess of all these, command

70 *repine*: complain, are discontented.

Æneas ride as Carthaginian king.

ACHATES: Æneas, for his parentage, deserves
  As large a kingdom as is Libya. 80

ÆNEAS: Ay, and, unless the Destinies be false,
  I shall be planted in as rich a land.

DIDO: Speak of no other land; this land is thine;
  Dido is thine, henceforth I'll call thee lord.
  Do as I bid thee, sister; lead the way;
  And from a turret I'll behold my love.

ÆNEAS: Then here in me shall flourish Priam's race;
  And thou and I, Achates, for revenge
  For Troy, for Priam, for his fifty sons,
  Our kinsmen's lives and thousand guiltless souls, 90
  Will lead an host against the hateful Greeks,
  And fire proud Lacedaemon o'er their heads.

  Exeunt all except DIDO *and* CARTHAGINIAN
    LORDS.

DIDO: Speaks not Æneas like a conqueror?
  O blessed tempests that did drive him in!
  O happy sand that made him run aground!
  Henceforth you shall be our Carthage gods.
  Ay, but it may be, he will leave my love,
  And seek a foreign land call'd Italy.
  O that I had a charm to keep the winds
  Within the closure of a golden ball; 100
  Or that the Tyrrhene sea were in mine arms,
  That he might suffer shipwrack on my breast,
  As oft as he attempts to hoist up sail!
  I must prevent him; wishing will not serve. —
  Go bid my nurse take young Ascanius,
  And bear him in the country to her house;
  Æneas will not go without his son.
  Yet, lest he should, for I am full of fear,
  Bring me his oars, his tackling, and his sails.

    Exit FIRST LORD.

  What if I sink his ships? O, he'll frown! 110

92 *Lacedaemon*: Sparta.

Better he frown than I should die for grief.
I cannot see him frown; it may not be.
Armies of foes resolv'd to win this town,
Or impious traitors vow'd to have my life,
Affright me not; only Æneas' frown
Is that which terrifies poor Dido's heart.
Not bloody spears, appearing in the air,
Presage the downfall of my empery,
Nor blazing comets threatens Dido's death;
120 It is Æneas' frown that ends my days.
If he forsake me not, I never die;
For in his looks I see eternity,
And he'll make me immortal with a kiss.

> *Re-enter* FIRST LORD, *with* ATTENDANTS *carrying
> tackling, etc.*

FIRST LORD: Your nurse is gone with young Ascanius;
And here's Æneas' tackling, oars, and sails.
DIDO: Are these the sails that, in despite of me,
Pack'd with the winds to bear Æneas hence?
I'll hang ye in the chamber where I lie;
Drive, if you can, my house to Italy.
130 I'll set the casement open, that the winds
May enter in, and once again conspire
Against the life of me, poor Carthage queen.
But, though ye go, he stays in Carthage still;
And let rich Carthage fleet upon the seas,
So I may have Æneas in mine arms.
Is this the wood that grew in Carthage plains,
And would be toiling in the watery billows,
To rob their mistress of her Trojan guest?
O cursed tree, hadst thou but wit or sense,
140 To measure how I prize Æneas' love,
Thou wouldst have leapt from out the sailors' hands,
And told me that Æneas meant to go!
And yet I blame thee not; thou art but wood.
The water, which our poets term a nymph,

127 *Pack'd*: conspired, made agreement with.

86

Why did it suffer thee to touch her breast,
And shrunk not back, knowing my love was there?
The water is an element, no nymph.
Why should I blame Æneas for his flight?
O Dido, blame not him, but break his oars!
These were the instruments that launch'd him forth.   *150*
There's not so much as this base tackling too,
But dares to heap up sorrow to my heart:
Was it not you that hoised up these sails?
Why burst you not, and they fell in the seas?
For this will Dido tie ye full of knots,
And shear ye all asunder with her hands.
Now serve to chastise shipboys for their faults;
Ye shall no more offend the Carthage queen.
Now, let him hang my favours on his masts,
And see if those will serve instead of sails;   *160*
For tackling, let him take the chains of gold
Which I bestow'd upon his followers;
Instead of oars, let him use his hands,
And swim to Italy: I'll keep these sure.
Come, bear them in.
   Exeunt.

SCENE FIVE

Enter NURSE, *with* CUPID *as* ASCANIUS.
NURSE: My Lord Ascanius, ye must go with me.
CUPID: Whither must I go? I'll stay with my mother.
NURSE: No, thou shalt go with me unto my house.
I have an orchard that hath store of plums,
Brown almonds, services, ripe figs, and dates,
Dewberries, apples, yellow oranges;
A garden where are bee-hives full of honey,
Musk-roses, and a thousand sort of flowers;
And in the midst doth run a silver stream,
  5 *services*: pear-shaped fruit.

10   Where thou shalt see the red-gill'd fishes leap,
White swans, and many lovely water-fowls.
Now speak, Ascanius, will you go or no?
CUPID: Come, come, I'll go. How far hence is your
   house?
NURSE: But hereby, child; we shall get thither straight.
CUPID: Nurse, I am weary; will you carry me?
NURSE: Ay, so you'll dwell with me, and call me mother.
CUPID: So you'll love me, I care not if I do.
NURSE: That I might live to see this boy a man!
How prettily he laughs! Go, you wag!
20   You'll be a twigger when you come to age.
Say Dido what she will, I am not old;
I'll be no more a widow; I am young;
I'll have a husband, I, or else a lover.
CUPID: A husband, and no teeth!
NURSE: O what mean I to have such foolish thoughts?
Foolish is love, a toy. – O sacred love!
If there be any heaven in earth, 'tis love,
Especially in women of your years. –
Blush, blush for shame! why shouldst thou think of
   love?
30   A grave, and not a lover, fits thy age. –
A grave! why, I may live a hundred years;
Fourscore is but a girl's age: love is sweet. –
My veins are wither'd, and my sinews dry:
Why do I think of love, now I should die?
CUPID: Come, nurse.
NURSE: Well, if he come a-wooing, he shall speed:
O, how unwise was I to say him nay!
   Exeunt.

20 *twigger*: 'a vigorous, prolific breeder' (*Oxford English Dictionary*).

ACT FIVE

SCENE ONE

Enter ÆNEAS, with a paper in his hand, drawing the platform of the city; ACHATES, SERGESTUS, CLOANTHUS, *and* ILIONEUS.

ÆNEAS: Triumph, my mates! Our travels are at end:
　Here will Æneas build a statelier Troy
　Than that which grim Atrides overthrew.
　Carthage shall vaunt her petty walls no more;
　For I will grace them with a fairer frame,
　And clad her in a crystal livery,
　Wherein the day may evermore delight.
　From golden India Ganges will I fetch,
　Whose wealthy streams may wait upon her towers,
　And triple-wise entrench her round about;　　　　　10
　The sun from Egypt shall rich odours bring,
　Wherewith his burning beams (like labouring bees
　That load their thighs with Hybla's honey's spoils)
　Shall here unburden their exhaled sweets,
　And plant our pleasant suburbs with their fumes.
ACHATES: What length or breadth shall this brave town
　contain?
ÆNEAS: Not past four thousand paces at the most.
ILIONEUS: But what shall it be call'd? Troy, as before?
ÆNEAS: That have I not determin'd with myself.
CLOANTHUS: Let it be term'd Ænea, by your name.　　20
SERGESTUS: Rather Ascania, by your little son.
ÆNEAS: Nay, I will have it called Anchisæon,
　Of my old father's name.
　　　Enter HERMES *with* ASCANIUS.
HERMES: Æneas, stay; Jove's herald bids thee stay.
ÆNEAS: Whom do I see? Jove's winged messenger!
　Welcome to Carthage' new-erected town.

13 *Hybla*: mountain and town in Sicily, famous for honey.

HERMES: Why cousin, stand you building cities here,
And beautifying the empire of this queen,
While Italy is clean out of thy mind?
30 Too-too forgetful of thine own affairs,
Why wilt thou so betray thy son's good hap?
The king of gods sent me from highest heaven,
To sound this angry message in thine ears:
Vain man, what monarchy expect'st thou here?
Or with what thought sleep'st thou in Libya shore?
If that all glory hath forsaken thee,
And thou despise the praise of such attempts,
Yet think upon Ascanius' prophecy,
And young Iulus' more than thousand years,
40 Whom I have brought from Ida, where he slept,
And bore young Cupid unto Cyprus isle.

ÆNEAS: This was my mother that beguil'd the queen,
And made me take my brother for my son.
No marvel, Dido, though thou be in love,
That daily dandlest Cupid in thy arms.
Welcome, sweet child: where hast thou been this long?

ASCANIUS: Eating sweet comfits with Queen Dido's maid,
Who ever since hath lull'd me in her arms.

ÆNEAS: Sergestus, bear him hence unto our ships,
50 Lest Dido, spying him, keep him for a pledge.

Exit SERGESTUS *with* ASCANIUS.

HERMES: Spend'st thou thy time about this little boy,
And giv'st not ear unto the charge I bring?
I tell thee, thou must straight to Italy,
Or else abide the wrath of frowning Jove.

Exit.

ÆNEAS: How should I put into the raging deep,
Who have no sails nor tackling for my ships?
What, would the gods have me, Deucalion-like,[15]
Float up and down where'er the billows drive?
Though she repair'd my fleet and gave me ships,

38 *Ascanius' prophecy*: three-hundred years rule for Aeneas' line, starting with Ascanius.   39 *Iulus*: Ascanius' name in Troy.

90

Yet hath she ta'en away my oars and masts,   *60*
And left me neither sail nor stern aboard.
   Enter IARBAS.
IARBAS: How now, Æneas! Sad? what mean these dumps?
ÆNEAS: Iarbas, I am clean besides myself;
  Jove hath heap'd on me such a desperate charge,
  Which neither art nor reason may achieve,
  Nor I devise by what means to contrive.
IARBAS: As how, I pray? May I entreat you tell?
ÆNEAS: With speed he bids me sail to Italy,
  Whenas I want both rigging for my fleet,
  And also furniture for these my men.   *70*
IARBAS: If that be all, then cheer thy drooping looks,
  For I will furnish thee with such supplies.
  Let some of those thy followers go with me,
  And they shall have what thing soe'er thou need'st.
ÆNEAS: Thanks, good Iarbas, for thy friendly aid.
  Achates and the rest shall wait on thee,
  Whilst I rest thankful for this courtesy.
   Exeunt all except ÆNEAS.
Now will I haste unto Lavinian shore,
And raise a new foundation to old Troy.
Witness the gods, and witness heaven and earth,   *80*
How loath I am to leave these Libyan bounds,
But that eternal Jupiter commands!
   Enter DIDO.
DIDO (*aside*): I fear I saw Æneas' little son
Led by Achates[16] to the Trojan fleet.
If it be so, his father means to fly: —
But here he is; now, Dido, try thy wit. —
Æneas, wherefore go thy men aboard?
Why are thy ships new-rigg'd? or to what end,
Launch'd from the haven, lie they in the road?
Pardon me, though I ask; love makes me ask.   *90*
ÆNEAS: O pardon me, if I resolve thee why!
  Æneas will not feign with his dear love.

70 *furniture*: equipment.   89 *road*: sheltered place near shore.

I must from hence: this day, swift Mercury,
When I was laying a platform for these walls,
Sent from his father Jove, appear'd to me,
And in his name rebuk'd me bitterly
For lingering here, neglecting Italy.
DIDO: But yet Æneas will not leave his love.
ÆNEAS: I am commanded by immortal Jove
100 To leave this town and pass to Italy;
And therefore must of force.
DIDO: These words proceed not from Æneas' heart.
ÆNEAS: Not from my heart, for I can hardly go;
And yet I may not stay. Dido, farewell.
DIDO: Farewell! Is this the 'mends for Dido's love?
Do Trojans use to quit their lovers thus?
Fare well may Dido, so Æneas stay;
I die, if my Æneas say farewell;
ÆNEAS: Then let me go, and never say farewell.
110 DIDO: 'Let me go; farewell; I must from hence.'
These words are poison to poor Dido's soul:
O, speak like my Æneas, like my love!
Why look'st thou toward the sea? The time hath been
When Dido's beauty chain'd thine eyes to her.
Am I less fair than when thou saw'st me first?
O, then, Æneas, 'tis for grief of thee!
Say thou wilt stay in Carthage with thy queen,
And Dido's beauty will return again.
Æneas, say, how canst thou take thy leave?
120 Wilt thou kiss Dido? O, thy lips have sworn
To stay with Dido! Canst thou take her hand?
Thy hand and mine have plighted mutual faith;
Therefore, unkind Æneas, must thou say,
'Then let me go, and never say farewell'?
ÆNEAS: O queen of Carthage, wert thou ugly-black,
Æneas could not choose but hold thee dear!
Yet must he not gainsay the gods' behest.
DIDO: The gods? What gods be those that seek my
death?

Wherein have I offended Jupiter,
That he should take Æneas from mine arms? 130
O, no! the gods weigh not what lovers do:
It is Æneas calls Æneas hence,
And woful Dido, by these blubber'd cheeks,
By this right hand, and by our spousal rites,
Desires Æneas to remain with her.
Si bene quid de te merui, fuit aut tibi quidquam
Dulce meum, miserere domus labentis, et istam,
Oro, si quis adhuc precibus locus, exue mentem.

ÆNEAS: *Desine meque tuis incendere teque querelis;*
Italiam non sponte sequor. 140

DIDO: Hast thou forgot how many neighbour kings
Were up in arms, for making thee my love?
How Carthage did rebel, Iarbas storm,
And all the world calls me a second Helen,
For being entangled by a stranger's looks?
So thou wouldst prove as true as Paris did,
Would, as fair Troy was, Carthage might be sack'd,
And I be call'd a second Helena!
Had I a son by thee, the grief were less,
That I might see Æneas in his face. 150
Now if thou go'st, what canst thou leave behind,
But rather will augment than ease my woe?

ÆNEAS: In vain, my love, thou spend'st thy fainting
breath:
If words might move me, I were overcome.

DIDO: And wilt thou not be mov'd with Dido's words?
Thy mother was no goddess, perjur'd man,
Nor Dardanus the author of thy stock;
But thou art sprung from Scythian Caucasus,

136 *Si bene* . . .: 'If I have deserved well of you in anything, or if anything of mine was dear to you, pity my falling house, and cast from you, I beg, that purpose of yours, if there is still any place for prayers' (*Aeneid*, IV 317–19).
139 *Desine* . . .: 'Cease to inflame me and yourself by your lamentations; it is not of my own will that I make for Italy'. (IV 360–61).

And tigers of Hyrcania gave thee suck.
160   Ah, foolish Dido, to forbear this long!
Wast thou not wrack'd upon this Libyan shore,
And cam'st to Dido like a fisher swain?
Repair'd not I thy ships, made thee a king,
And all thy needy followers noblemen?
O serpent, that came creeping from the shore,
And I for pity harbour'd in my bosom,
Wilt thou now slay me with thy venom'd sting,
And hiss at Dido for preserving thee?
Go, go, and spare not; seek out Italy:
170   I hope that that which love forbids me do,
The rocks and sea-gulfs will perform at large,
And thou shalt perish in the billows' ways,
To whom poor Dido doth bequeath revenge.
Ay, traitor! and the waves shall cast thee up,
Where thou and false Achates first set foot;
Which if it chance, I'll give ye burial,
And weep upon your lifeless carcasses,
Though thou nor he will pity me a whit.
Why star'st thou in my face? If thou wilt stay,
180   Leap in mine arms; mine arms are open wide;
If not, turn from me, and I'll turn from thee;
For though thou hast the heart to say farewell,
I have not power to stay thee.
    Exit ÆNEAS.
                                   Is he gone?
Ay, but he'll come again. He cannot go;
He loves me too-too well to serve me so:
Yet he that in my sight would not relent,
Will, being absent, be obdurate still.
By this is he got to the water-side;
And, see, the sailors take him by the hand;
190   But he shrinks back; and now, remembering me,
Returns amain: welcome, welcome, my love!
But where's Æneas? Ah, he's gone, he's gone!
    Enter ANNA.

ANNA: What means my sister, thus to rave and cry?

DIDO: O Anna, my Æneas is aboard,
  And, leaving me, will sail to Italy!
  Once didst thou go, and he came back again:
  Now bring him back, and thou shalt be a queen,
  And I will live a private life with him.

ANNA: Wicked Æneas!

DIDO: Call him not wicked, sister: speak him fair,   *200*
  And look upon him with a mermaid's eye.
  Tell him, I never vow'd at Aulis' gulf
  The desolation of his native Troy,
  Nor sent a thousand ships unto the walls,
  Nor ever violated faith to him.
  Request him gently, Anna, to return:
  I crave but this, – he stay a tide or two,
  That I may learn to bear it patiently;
  If he depart thus suddenly, I die.
  Run, Anna, run; stay not to answer me.   *210*

ANNA: I go, fair sister: heavens grant good success!
  Exit.
  Enter NURSE.

NURSE: O Dido, your little son Ascanius
  Is gone! He lay with me last night,
  And in the morning he was stoln from me:
  I think, some fairies have beguiled me.

DIDO: O cursed hag and false dissembling wretch,
  That slay'st me with thy harsh and hellish tale!
  Thou for some petty gift hast let him go,
  And I am thus deluded of my boy.
  Away with her to prison presently,   *220*
    Enter ATTENDANTS.
  Trait'ress to kind,[17] and cursed sorceress!

NURSE: I know not what you mean by treason, I;
  I am as true as any one of yours.

DIDO: Away with her! Suffer her not to speak.
  Exit NURSE *with* ATTENDANTS.
  My sister comes: I like not her sad looks.

Re-enter ANNA.

ANNA: Before I came, Æneas was aboard,
 And, spying me, hois'd up the sails amain;
 But I cried out, 'Æneas, false Æneas, stay!'
 Then gan he wag his hand, which, yet held up,
230 Made me suppose he would have heard me speak.
 Then gan they drive into the ocean:
 Which when I view'd, I cried, 'Æneas, stay!
 Dido, fair Dido wills Æneas stay!'
 Yet he, whose heart of adamant or flint,
 My tears nor plaints could mollify a whit –
 Then carelessly I rent my hair for grief:
 Which seen to all, though he beheld me not,
 They gan to move him to redress my ruth,
 And stay a while to hear what I could say;
240 But he, clapp'd under hatches, sail'd away.
DIDO: O Anna, Anna, I will follow him!
ANNA: How can ye go, when he hath all your fleet?
DIDO: I'll frame me wings of wax, like Icarus,
 And, o'er his ships, will soar unto the sun,
 That they may melt, and I fall in his arms;
 Or else I'll make a prayer unto the waves,
 That I may swim to him, like Triton's niece.[18]
 O Anna, fetch Arion's harp,
 That I may tice a dolphin to the shore,
250 And ride upon his back unto my love!
 Look, sister, look! lovely Æneas' ships!
 See, see, the billows heave him up to heaven,
 And now down falls the keels into the deep!
 O sister, sister, take away the rocks!
 They'll break his ships. O Proteus, Neptune, Jove,
 Save, save Æneas, Dido's liefest love!
 Now is he come on shore, safe without hurt:[19]
 But see, Achates wills him put to sea,
 And all the sailors merry-make for joy;
260 But he, remembering me, shrinks back again.
 256 *liefest*: dearest.

See, where he comes! Welcome, welcome, my
    love!

ANNA: Ah, sister, leave these idle fantasies!
    Sweet sister, cease; remember who you are.

DIDO: Dido I am, unless I be deceiv'd:
    And must I rave thus for a runagate?
    Must I make ships for him to sail away?
    Nothing can bear me to him but a ship,
    And he hath all my fleet. – What shall I do,
    But die in fury of this oversight?
    Ay, I must be the murderer of myself: *270*
    No, but I am not; yet I will be straight.
    Anna, be glad; now have I found a mean
    To rid me from these thoughts of lunacy:
    Not far from hence
    There is a woman famoused for arts,
    Daughter unto the nymphs Hesperides,
    Who will'd me sacrifice his ticing relics.
    Go, Anna, bid my servants bring me fire.
       Exit ANNA.
       Enter IARBAS.

IARBAS: How long will Dido mourn a stranger's flight
    That hath dishonour'd her and Carthage both?   *280*
    How long shall I with grief consume my days,
    And reap no guerdon for my truest love?
    Enter ATTENDANTS *with wood and torches.*

DIDO: Iarbas, talk not of Æneas. Let him go!
    Lay to thy hands, and help me make a fire,
    That shall consume all that this stranger left;
    For I intend a private sacrifice,
    To cure my mind, that melts for unkind love.

IARBAS: But, afterwards, will Dido grant me love?

DIDO: Ay, ay, Iarbas; after this is done,
    None in the world shall have my love but thou.   *290*
    They make a fire.
    So, leave me now; let none approach this place.

282 *guerdon:* reward.

Exeunt IARBAS *and* ATTENDANTS.

Now, Dido, with these relics burn thyself,
And make Æneas famous through the world
For perjury and slaughter of a queen.
Here lie the sword that in the darksome cave
He drew, and swore by, to be true to me.
Thou shalt burn first; thy crime is worse than his.
Here lie the garment which I cloth'd him in
When first he came on shore: perish thou too.

300   These letters, lines, and perjur'd papers, all
Shall burn to cinders in this precious flame.
And now, ye gods, that guide the starry frame,
And order all things at your high dispose,
Grant, though the traitors land in Italy,
They may be still tormented with unrest;
And from mine ashes let a conqueror rise,
That may revenge this treason to a queen
By ploughing up his countries with the sword!
Betwixt this land and that be never league;

310   *Litora litoribus contraria, fluctibus undas*
Imprecor, arma armis; pugnent ipsique nepotes!
Live, false Æneas! Truest Dido dies;
Sic, sic juvat ire sub umbras.
> *Throws herself into the flames.*
> *Re-enter* ANNA.

ANNA: O, help, Iarbas! Dido in these flames
Hath burnt herself! Ay me, unhappy me!
> *Re-enter* IARBAS, *running.*

IARBAS: Cursed Iarbas, die to expiate
The grief that tires upon thine inward soul! –
Dido, I come to thee. – Ay me, Æneas!
> *Kills himself.*

---

310 *Litora litoribus* . . .: 'I pray that shoree shall clash with shore,
and wave with billow: let them fight themselves and their
descendants' (*Aeneid*, IV 628–9).
313 *Sic* . . .: 'So, so, it is my choice to go beneath the shades' (to
Hades) (*Aeneid*, IV 660).

ANNA: What can my tears or cries prevail me now?
    Dido is dead!
    Iarbas slain, Iarbas my dear love!
    O sweet Iarbas, Anna's sole delight!
    What fatal Destiny envies me thus,
    To see my sweet Iarbas slay himself?
    But Anna now shall honour thee in death,
    And mix her blood with thine. This shall I do,
    That gods and men may pity this my death,
    And rue our ends, senseless of life or breath:
    Now, sweet Iarbas, stay! I come to thee.
    Kills herself.

THE FIRST PART OF

Tamburlaine the Great

Dramatis Personae

MYCETES, *King of Persia*
COSROE, *his brother*
MEANDER,
THERIDAMAS,
ORTYGIUS, } *Persian lords*
CENEUS,
MENAPHON,
TAMBURLAINE, *a Scythian shepherd*
TECHELLES, } *his followers*
USUMCASANE,
BAJAZETH, *Emperor of the Turks*
KING OF FEZ
KING OF MOROCCO
KING OF ARGIER
KING OF ARABIA
SOLDAN OF EGYPT
GOVERNOR OF DAMASCUS
AGYDAS, } *Median lords*
MAGNETES,
CAPOLIN, *an Egyptian*
PHILEMUS, BASSOES, LORDS, CITIZENS, MOORS,
SOLDIERS, *and* ATTENDANTS
ZENOCRATE, *daughter to the* SOLDAN OF EGYPT
ANIPPE, *her maid*
ZABINA, *wife of* BAJAZETH
EBEA, *her maid*
VIRGINS OF DAMASCUS

THE PROLOGUE

From jigging veins of rhyming mother-wits,
And such conceits as clownage keeps in pay,
We'll lead you to the stately tent of war,
Where you shall hear the Scythian Tamburlaine
Threatening the world with high astounding terms,
And scourging kingdoms with his conquering sword.
View but his picture in this tragic glass,
And then applaud his fortunes as you please.

ACT ONE

SCENE ONE

Enter MYCETES, COSROE, MEANDER, THERIDA-
MAS, ORTYGIUS, CENEUS, MENAPHON, *with others.*

MYCETES: Brother Cosroe, I find myself agriev'd;
  Yet insufficient to express the same,
  For it requires a great and thundering speech.
  Good brother, tell the cause unto my lords;
  I know you have a better wit than I.
COSROE: Unhappy Persia, that in former age
  Hast been the seat of mighty conquerors,
  That, in their prowess and their policies,
  Have triumph'd over Afric and the bounds
  Of Europe where the sun dares scarce appear   10
  For freezing meteors and congealed cold,
  Now to be rul'd and govern'd by a man
  At whose birthday Cynthia with Saturn join'd,
  And Jove, the Sun, and Mercury denied
  To shed their influence in his fickle brain!

13 *Cynthia with Saturn*: the moon, soft, effeminate and change-
able; Saturn, dull and old.

Now Turks and Tartars shake their swords at thee,
Meaning to mangle all thy provinces.

MYCETES: Brother, I see your meaning well enough,
And thorough your planets I perceive you think
20   I am not wise enough to be a king:
But I refer me to my noblemen,
That know my wit, and can be witnesses.
I might command you to be slain for this;
Meander, might I not?

MEANDER: Not for so small a fault, my sovereign
    lord.

MYCETES: I mean it not, but yet I know I might.
Yet live; yea, live; Mycetes wills it so.
Meander, thou, my faithful counsellor,
Declare the cause of my conceived grief,
30   Which is, God knows, about that Tamburlaine,
That, like a fox in midst of harvest-time,
Doth prey upon my flocks of passengers;
And, as I hear, doth mean to pull my plumes.
Therefore 'tis good and meet for to be wise.

MEANDER: Oft have I heard your majesty complain
Of Tamburlaine, that sturdy Scythian thief,
That robs your merchants of Persepolis
Trading by land unto the Western Isles,
And in your confines with his lawless train
40   Daily commits incivil outrages,
Hoping (misled by dreaming prophecies)
To reign in Asia, and with barbarous arms
To make himself the monarch of the East:
But, ere he march in Asia, or display
His vagrant ensign in the Persian fields,
Your grace hath taken order by Theridamas,
Charg'd with a thousand horse, to apprehend
And bring him captive to your highness' throne.

MYCETES: Full true thou speak'st, and like thyself,
    my lord,

37 *Persepolis*: capital of ancient Persia.

Whom I may term a Damon for thy love: *50*
Therefore 'tis best, if so it like you all,
To send my thousand horse incontinent
To apprehend that paltry Scythian.
How like you this, my honourable lords?
Is it not a kingly resolution?

COSROE: It cannot choose, because it comes from
    you.

MYCETES: Then hear thy charge, valiant Theridamas,
    The chiefest captain of Mycetes' host,
    The hope of Persia, and the very legs
    Whereon our state doth lean as on a staff,   *60*
    That holds us up and foils our neighbour foes:
    Thou shalt be leader of this thousand horse,
    Whose foaming gall with rage and high disdain
    Have sworn the death of wicked Tamburlaine.
    Go frowning forth; but come thou smiling home,
    As did Sir Paris with the Grecian dame.
    Return with speed, time passeth swift away,
    Our life is frail, and we may die today.

THERIDAMAS: Before the moon renew her borrow'd
    light,
    Doubt not, my lord and gracious sovereign,   *70*
    But Tamburlaine and that Tartarian rout
    Shall either perish by our warlike hands,
    Or plead for mercy at your highness' feet.

MYCETES: Go, stout Theridamas, thy words are swords,
    And with thy looks thou conquerest all thy foes.
    I long to see thee back return from thence,
    That I may view these milk-white steeds of mine
    All loaden with the heads of killed men,
    And from their knees even to their hoofs below
    Besmear'd with blood that makes a dainty show.   *80*

THERIDAMAS: Then now, my lord, I humbly take my
    leave.

50 *Damon*: a Pythagorean and close friend of Pythias.
52 *incontinent*: immediately.

MYCETES: Theridamas, farewell ten thousand times.
   Exit THERIDAMAS.
  Ah, Menaphon, why stay'st thou thus behind,
  When other men press forward for renown?
  Go, Menaphon, go into Scythia,
  And foot by foot follow Theridamas.
COSROE: Nay, pray you, let him stay; a greater [task]¹*
  Fits Menaphon than warring with a thief.
  Create him pro-rex of all Africa,
90 That he may win the Babylonians' hearts,
  Which will revolt from Persian government,
  Unless they have a wiser king than you.
MYCETES: 'Unless they have a wiser king than you!'
  These are his words; Meander, set them down.
COSROE: And add this to them, – that all Asia
  Lament to see the folly of their king.
MYCETES: Well, here I swear by this my royal
  seat –
COSROE: You may do well to kiss it, then.
MYCETES: Emboss'd with silk as best beseems my state,
100 To be reveng'd for these contemptuous words!
  O where is duty and allegiance now?
  Fled to the Caspian or the Ocean main?
  What, shall I call thee brother? No, a foe;
  Monster of nature, shame unto thy stock,
  That dar'st presume thy sovereign for to mock!
  Meander, come: I am abus'd, Meander.
   Exeunt all except COSROE *and* MENAPHON.
MENAPHON: How now, my lord! What, mated and
  amaz'd
  To hear the king thus threaten like himself?
COSROE: Ah, Menaphon, I pass not for his threats!
110 The plot is laid by Persian noblemen
  And captains of the Median garrisons

---

107 *mated*: numbed, made helpless.   109 *pass*: care.

*Superior numbers refer to the Additional Notes at the end of the book.

To crown me emperor of Asia.
But this it is that doth excruciate
The very substance of my vexed soul,
To see our neighbours, that were wont to quake
And tremble at the Persian monarch's name,
Now sits and laughs our regiment to scorn;
And that which might resolve me into tears,
Men from the farthest equinoctial line
Have swarm'd in troops into the Eastern India,   *120*
Lading their ships with gold and precious stones,
And made their spoils from all our provinces.
MENAPHON: This should entreat your highness to rejoice,
Since Fortune gives you opportunity
To gain the title of a conqueror
By curing of this maimed empery.
Afric and Europe bordering on your land,
And continent to your dominions,
How easily may you, with a mighty host,
Pass into Graecia, as did Cyrus once,   *130*
And cause them to withdraw their forces home,
Lest you subdue the pride of Christendom!
    Trumpets within.
COSROE: But, Menaphon, what means this trumpet's
    sound?
MENAPHON: Behold, my lord, Ortygius and the rest
Bringing the crown to make you emperor!
    Re-enter ORTYGIUS *and* CENEUS, *with others, bearing
    a crown.*
ORTYGIUS: Magnificent and mighty prince Cosroe,
We, in the name of other Persian states
And commons of this mighty monarchy,
Present thee with th' imperial diadem.
CENEUS: The warlike soldiers and the gentlemen,   *140*
That heretofore have fill'd Persepolis
With Afric captains taken in the field,
Whose ransom made them march in coats of gold,

117 *regiment*: government.   128 *continent*: bordering.

With costly jewels hanging at their ears,
And shining stones upon their lofty crests,
Now living idle in the walled towns,
Wanting both pay and martial discipline,
Begin in troops to threaten civil war,
And openly exclaim against the king.
150 Therefore, to stay all sudden mutinies,
We will invest your highness emperor;
Whereat the soldiers will conceive more joy
Than did the Macedonians at the spoil
Of great Darius and his wealthy host.
COSROE: Well, since I see the state of Persia droop
And languish in my brother's government,
I willingly receive th' imperial crown,
And vow to wear it for my country's good,
In spite of them shall malice my estate.
160 ORTYGIUS: And, in assurance of desir'd success,
We here do crown thee monarch of the East,
Emperor of Asia and Persia,
Great lord of Media and Armenia,
Duke of Africa and Albania,
Mesopotamia and of Parthia,
East India and the late-discover'd isles,
Chief lord of all the wide vast Euxine Sea,
And of the ever-raging Caspian Lake.
ALL: Long live Cosroe, mighty emperor!
170 COSROE: And Jove may never let me longer live
Than I may seek to gratify your love,
And cause the soldiers that thus honour me
To triumph over many provinces!
By whose desires of discipline in arms
I doubt not shortly but to reign sole king,
And with the army of Theridamas
(Whither we presently will fly, my lords,)
To rest secure against my brother's force.
ORTYGIUS: We knew, my lord, before we brought the
crown,

Intending your investment so near   *180*
The residence of your despised brother,
The lords would not be too exasperate
To injury or suppress your worthy title;
Or, if they would, there are in readiness
Ten thousand horse to carry you from hence,
In spite of all suspected enemies.

COSROE: I know it well, my lord, and thank you
    all.

ORTYGIUS: Sound up the trumpets, then.
    Trumpets sounded.

ALL: God save the king!
    Exeunt.

SCENE TWO

Enter TAMBURLAINE *leading* ZENOCRATE,
TECHELLES, USUMCASANE, AGYDAS, MAGNETES,
LORDS, *and* SOLDIERS *loaden with treasure.*

TAMBURLAINE: Come, lady, let not this appal your
    thoughts.

The jewels and the treasure we have ta'en
Shall be reserv'd, and you in better state
Than if you were arriv'd in Syria,
Even in the circle of your father's arms,
The mighty Soldan of Egypt.

ZENOCRATE: Ah, shepherd, pity my distressed plight!
(If, as thou seem'st, thou art so mean a man,)
And seek not to enrich thy followers
By lawless rapine from a silly maid,   *10*
Who, travelling with these Median lords
To Memphis, from my uncle's country of Media,
Where all my youth I have been governed,
Have pass'd the army of the mighty Turk,
Bearing his privy-signet and his hand

10 *silly:* helpless.

To safe conduct us thorough Africa.

MAGNETES: And, since we have arrived in Scythia,
    Besides rich presents from the puissant Cham,
    We have his highness' letters to command
20   Aid and assistance, if we stand in need.

TAMBURLAINE: But now you see these letters and
    commands
    Are countermanded by a greater man,
    And through my provinces you must expect
    Letters of conduct from my mightiness,
    If you intend to keep your treasure safe.
    But, since I love to live at liberty
    As easily may you get the Soldan's crown
    As any prizes out of my precinct,
    For they are friends that help to wean my state
30   Till men and kingdoms help to strengthen it,
    And must maintain my life exempt from servitude.
    But, tell me, madam, is your grace betroth'd?

ZENOCRATE: I am, my lord, – for so you do import.

TAMBURLAINE: I am a lord, for so my deeds shall prove,
    And yet a shepherd by my parentage.
    But lady, this fair face and heavenly hue
    Must grace his bed that conquers Asia,
    And means to be a terror to the world,
    Measuring the limits of his empery
40   By east and west, as Phoebus doth his course.
    Lie here, ye weeds that I disdain to wear!
    This complete armour and this curtle-axe
    Are adjuncts more beseeming Tamburlaine.
    And, madam, whatsoever you esteem
    Of this success, and loss unvalued,
    Both may invest you empress of the East.
    And these, that seem but silly country swains,
    May have the leading of so great an host
    As with their weight shall make the mountains quake,
50   Even as when windy exhalations,
    Fighting for passage, tilt within the earth.

TECHELLES: As princely lions, when they rouse them-
 selves,
 Stretching their paws, and threatening herds of beasts,
 So in his armour looketh Tamburlaine.
 Methinks I see kings kneeling at his feet,
 And he with frowning brows and fiery looks
 Spurning their crowns from off their captive heads.

USUMCASANE: And making thee and me, Techelles,
 kings,
 That even to death will follow Tamburlaine.

TAMBURLAINE: Nobly resolv'd, sweet friends and   *60*
 followers!
 These lords perhaps do scorn our estimates,
 And think we prattle with distemper'd spirits:
 But, since they measure our deserts so mean,
 That in conceit bear empires on our spears,
 Affecting thoughts coequal with the clouds,
 They shall be kept our forced followers
 Till with their eyes they view us emperors.

ZENOCRATE: The gods, defenders of the innocent,
 Will never prosper your intended drifts,
 That thus oppress poor friendless passengers.   *70*
 Therefore at least admit us liberty,
 Even as thou hop'st to be eternised
 By living Asia's mighty emperor.

AGYDAS: I hope our lady's treasure and our own
 May serve for ransom to our liberties.
 Return our mules and empty camels back,
 That we may travel into Syria,
 Where her betrothed lord, Alcidamus,
 Expects th' arrival of her highness' person.

MAGNETES: And wheresoever we repose ourselves,   *80*
 We will report but well of Tamburlaine.

TAMBURLAINE: Disdains Zenocrate to live with me?
 Or you, my lord, to be my followers?
 Think you I weigh this treasure more than you?

 64 *conceit*: imagination.

Not all the gold in India's wealthy arms
Shall buy the meanest soldier in my train.
Zenocrate, lovelier than the love of Jove,
Brighter than is the silver Rhodope,
Fairer than whitest snow on Scythian hills,
90   Thy person is more worth to Tamburlaine
Than the possession of the Persian crown,
Which gracious stars have promis'd at my birth.
A hundred Tartars shall attend on thee,
Mounted on steeds swifter than Pegasus;
Thy garments shall be made of Median silk,
Enchas'd with precious jewels of mine own,
More rich and valurous than Zenocrate's;
With milk-white harts upon an ivory sled
Thou shalt be drawn amidst the frozen pools,
100   And scale the icy mountains' lofty tops,
Which with thy beauty will be soon resolv'd.
My martial prizes, with five hundred men,
Won on the fifty-headed Volga's waves,
Shall we all offer to Zenocrate,
And then myself to fair Zenocrate.

TECHELLES: What now! in love?

TAMBURLAINE: Techelles, women must be flattered:
But this is she with whom I am in love.

    Enter a SOLDIER.

SOLDIER: News, news!

110 TAMBURLAINE: How now! What's the matter?

SOLDIER: A thousand Persian horsemen are at hand,
Sent from the king to overcome us all.

TAMBURLAINE: How now, my lords of Egypt and
    Zenocrate!
Now must your jewels be restor'd again,
And I that triumph'd so be overcome?
How say you, lordlings? Is not this your hope?

AGYDAS: We hope yourself will willingly restore them.

88 *Rhodope*: mountain with silver mines in Thrace.
101 *resolved*: melted (Quarto 1605: dissolved).

TAMBURLAINE: Such hope, such fortune, have the
thousand horse.
Soft ye, my lords, and sweet Zenocrate!
You must be forced from me ere you go — *120*
A thousand horsemen! we five hundred foot!
An odds too great for us to stand against.
But are they rich? and is their armour good?
SOLDIER: Their plumed helms are wrought with beaten
gold,
Their swords enamell'd, and about their necks
Hangs massy chains of gold down to the waist;
In every part exceeding brave and rich.
TAMBURLAINE: Then shall we fight courageously with
them?
Or look you I should play the orator?
TECHELLES: No, cowards and faint-hearted runaways *130*
Look for orations when the foe is near:
Our swords shall play the orators for us.
USUMCASANE: Come, let us meet them at the mountain-
foot.
And with a sudden and an hot alarum
Drive all their horses headlong down the hill.
TECHELLES: Come, let us march.
TAMBURLAINE: Stay, Techelles; ask a parley first.
The SOLDIERS *enter.*
Open the mails, yet guard the treasure sure.
Lay out our golden wedges to the view,
That their reflections may amaze the Persians, *140*
And look we friendly on them when they come:
But, if they offer word or violence,
We'll fight, five hundred men-at-arms to one,
Before we part with our possession,
And 'gainst the general we will lift our swords,
And either lance his greedy thirsting throat,
Or take him prisoner, and his chain shall serve
For manacles till he be ransom'd home.
TECHELLES: I hear them come. Shall we encounter them?

150 TAMBURLAINE: Keep all your standings, and not stir a
foot:
Myself will bide the danger of the brunt.
Enter THERIDAMAS, *with others.*

THERIDAMAS: Where is this Scythian Tamburlaine?

TAMBURLAINE: Whom seek'st thou, Persian? I am
Tamburlaine.

THERIDAMAS: Tamburlaine!
A Scythian shepherd so embellished
With nature's pride and richest furniture!
His looks do menace heaven and dare the gods;
His fiery eyes are fix'd upon the earth,
As if he now devis'd some stratagem,
160 Or meant to pierce Avernus' darksome vaults
To pull the triple-headed dog from hell.

TAMBURLAINE: Noble and mild this Persian seems to be,
If outward habit judge the inward man.

TECHELLES: His deep affections make him passionate.

TAMBURLAINE: With what a majesty he rears his looks –
In thee, thou valiant man of Persia,
I see the folly of thy emperor.
Art thou but captain of a thousand horse,
That by characters graven in thy brows,
170 And by thy martial face and stout aspect,
Deserv'st to have the leading of an host?
Forsake thy king, and do but join with me,
And we will triumph over all the world.
I hold the Fates bound fast in iron chains,
And with my hand turn Fortune's wheel about;
And sooner shall the sun fall from his sphere
Than Tamburlaine be slain or overcome.
Draw forth thy sword, thou mighty man-at-arms,
Intending but to raze my charmed skin,
180 And Jove himself will stretch his hand from heaven
To ward the blow, and shield me safe from harm.

160 *Avernus*: hell.
161 *triple-headed dog*: Cerberus, watchdog of Hades.

See, how he rains down heaps of gold in showers,
As if he meant to give my soldiers pay!
And, as a sure and grounded argument
That I shall be the monarch of the East,
He sends this Soldan's daughter rich and brave,
To be my queen and portly emperess.
If thou wilt stay with me, renowmed man,
And lead thy thousand horse with my conduct,
Besides thy share of this Egyptian prize,   *190*
Those thousand horse shall sweat with martial spoil
Of conquer'd kingdoms and of cities sack'd.
Both we will walk upon the lofty cliffs;
And Christian merchants, that with Russian stems
Plough up huge furrows in the Caspian Sea,
Shall vail to us as lords of all the lake.
Both we will reign as consuls of the earth,
And mighty kings shall be our senators.
Jove sometimes masked in a shepherd's weed,
And by those steps that he hath scal'd the heavens   *200*
May we become immortal like the gods.
Join with me now in this my mean estate,
(I call it mean, because, being yet obscure,
The nations far-remov'd admire me not,)
And when my name and honour shall be spread
As far as Boreas claps his brazen wings,
Or fair Boötes sends his cheerful light,
Then shalt thou be competitor with me,
And sit with Tamburlaine in all his majesty.
THERIDAMAS: Not Hermes, prolocutor to the gods,   *210*
    Could use persuasions more pathetical.
TAMBURLAINE: Nor are Apollo's oracles more true
    Than thou shalt find my vaunts substantial.
TECHELLES: We are his friends; and if the Persian king

187 *portly*: stately.   189 *conduct*: leadership.
196 *vail*: doff caps in respect.   206 *Boreas*: the north wind.
207 *Boötes*: the Bear, a northern constellation.
208 *competitor*: companion.

Should offer present dukedoms to our state,
We think it loss to make exchange for that
We are assur'd of by our friend's success.

USUMCASANE: And kingdoms at the least we all expect,
Besides the honour in assured conquests,
220 Where kings shall crouch unto our conquering swords,
And hosts of soldiers stand amaz'd at us,
When with their fearful tongues they shall confess,
These are the men that all the world admires.

THERIDAMAS: What strong enchantments tice my
yielding soul?
Ah, these resolved, noble Scythians!
But shall I prove a traitor to my king?

TAMBURLAINE: No, but the trusty friend of Tamburlaine.

THERIDAMAS: Won with thy words and conquer'd with
thy looks,
I yield myself, my men, and horse to thee,
230 To be partaker of thy good or ill,
As long as life maintains Theridamas.

TAMBURLAINE: Theridamas, my friend, take here my
hand,
Which is as much as if I swore by heaven,
And call'd the gods to witness of my vow.
Thus shall my heart be still combin'd with thine
Until our bodies turn to elements,
And both our souls aspire celestial thrones.
Techelles and Casane, welcome him.

TECHELLES: Welcome, renowmed Persian, to us all!
240 USUMCASANE: Long may Theridamas remain with us!

TAMBURLAINE: These are my friends, in whom I more
rejoice
Than doth the king of Persia in his crown;
And, by the love of Pylades and Orestes,
Whose statues we adore in Scythia,
Thyself and them shall never part from me

224 *tice*: tempt, entice.

Before I crown you kings in Asia.
Make much of them, gentle Theridamas,
And they will never leave thee till the death.

THERIDAMAS: Nor thee nor them, thrice-noble Tamburlaine
Shall want my heart to be with gladness pierc'd,   250
To do you honour and security.

TAMBURLAINE: A thousand thanks, worthy Theridamas.
And now, fair madam, and my noble lords,
If you will willingly remain with me,
You shall have honours as your merits be;
Or else you shall be forc'd with slavery.

AGYDAS: We yield unto thee, happy Tamburlaine.

TAMBURLAINE: For you, then, madam, I am out of doubt.

ZENOCRATE: I must be pleas'd perforce, wretched Zenocrate!
Exeunt.

ACT TWO

SCENE ONE

Enter COSROE, MENAPHON, ORTYGIUS, *and*
CENEUS, *with* SOLDIERS.

COSROE: Thus far are we towards Theridamas,
And valiant Tamburlaine, the man of fame,
The man that in the forehead of his fortune
Bears figures of renown and miracle.
But tell me, that hast seen him, Menaphon,
What stature wields he, and what personage?

MENAPHON: Of stature tall, and straightly fashioned
Like his desire, lift upwards and divine.
So large of limbs, his joints so strongly knit,
Such breadth of shoulders as might mainly bear   10
Old Atlas' burden. 'Twixt his manly pitch,
A pearl more worth than all the world is plac'd,

Wherein by curious sovereignty of art
Are fix'd his piercing instruments of sight,
Whose fiery circles bear encompassed
A heaven of heavenly bodies in their spheres,
That guides his steps and actions to the throne
Where honour sits invested royally.
Pale of complexion, wrought in him with passion,
20   Thirsting with sovereignty and love of arms,
His lofty brows in folds do figure death,
And in their smoothness amity and life.
About them hangs a knot of amber hair,
Wrapped in curls, as fierce Achilles' was,
On which the breath of heaven delights to play,
Making it dance with wanton majesty.
His arms and fingers long and sinewy,[2]
Betokening valour and excess of strength.
In every part proportion'd like the man
30   Should make the world subdu'd to Tamburlaine.
COSROE: Well hast thou pourtray'd in thy terms of life
The face and personage of a wondrous man.
Nature doth strive with Fortune and his stars
To make him famous in accomplish'd worth;
And well his merits shew him to be made
His fortune's master and the king of men,
That could persuade, at such a sudden pinch,
With reasons of his valour and his life,
A thousand sworn and overmatching foes.
40   Then, when our powers in points of swords are join'd,
And clos'd in compass of the killing bullet,
Though strait the passage and the port be made
That leads to palace of my brother's life,
Proud is his fortune if we pierce it not.
And when the princely Persian diadem
Shall overweigh his weary witless head,
And fall, like mellow'd fruit, with shakes of death,
In fair Persia noble Tamburlaine
Shall be my regent, and remain as king.

ORTYGIUS: In happy hour we have set the crown *50*
    Upon your kingly head, that seeks our honour
    In joining with the man ordain'd by heaven
    To further every action to the best.
CENEUS: He that with shepherds and a little spoil
    Durst, in disdain of wrong and tyranny,
    Defend his freedom 'gainst a monarchy,
    What will he do supported by a king,
    Leading a troop of gentlemen and lords,
    And stuff'd with treasure for his highest thoughts!
COSROE: And such shall wait on worthy Tamburlaine. *60*
    Our army will be forty thousand strong,
    When Tamburlaine and brave Theridamas
    Have met us by the river Araris,
    And all conjoin'd to meet the witless king,
    That now is marching near to Parthia,
    And, with unwilling soldiers faintly arm'd,
    To seek revenge on me and Tamburlaine.
    To whom, sweet Menaphon, direct me straight.
MENAPHON: I will, my lord.
    Exeunt.

SCENE TWO

Enter MYCETES, MEANDER, *with other* LORDS;
and SOLDIERS.

MYCETES: Come, my Meander, let us to this gear.
    I tell you true, my heart is swoln with wrath
    On this same thievish villain Tamburlaine,
    And of that false Cosroe, my traitorous brother.
    Would it not grieve a king to be so abus'd,
    And have a thousand horsemen ta'en away?
    And, which is worst, to have his diadem
    Sought for by such scald knaves as love him not?
    I think it would: well, then, by heavens I swear,

1 *gear*: matter, business.   8 *scald*: low.

10 Aurora shall not peep out of her doors,
But I will have Cosroe by the head,
And kill proud Tamburlaine with point of sword.
Tell you the rest, Meander: I have said.

MEANDER: Then, having pass'd Armenian deserts now,
And pitch'd our tents under the Georgian hills,
Whose tops are cover'd with Tartarian thieves,
That lie in ambush, waiting for a prey,
What should we do but bid them battle straight,
And rid the world of those detested troops?

20 Lest, if we let them linger here a while,
They gather strength by power of fresh supplies.
This country swarms with vile outragious men
That live by rapine and by lawless spoil,
Fit soldiers for the wicked Tamburlaine;
And he that could with gifts and promises
Inveigle him that led a thousand horse,
And make him false his faith unto his king,
Will quickly win such as are like himself.
Therefore cheer up your minds; prepare to fight.

30 He that can take or slaughter Tamburlaine,
Shall rule the province of Albania.
Who brings that traitor's head, Theridamas,
Shall have a government in Media,
Beside the spoil of him and all his train:
But, if Cosroe (as our spials say,
And as we know) remains with Tamburlaine,
His highness' pleasure is that he should live,
And be reclaim'd with princely lenity.

Enter a SPY.

SPY: An hundred horsemen of my company,
40 Scouting abroad upon these champion plains,
Have view'd the army of the Scythians;
Which make report it far exceeds the king's.

MEANDER: Suppose they be in number infinite,
Yet being void of martial discipline,

40 *champion*: country.

122

All running headlong after greedy spoils,
And more regarding gain than victory,
Like to the cruel brothers of the earth,
Sprung of the teeth of dragons venomous,
Their careless swords shall lance their fellows' throats
And make us triumph in their overthrow.   50
MYCETES: Was there such brethren, sweet Meander, say,
That sprung of teeth of dragons venomous?
MEANDER: So poets say, my lord.
MYCETES: And 'tis a pretty toy to be a poet.
Well, well, Meander, thou art deeply read;
And having thee, I have a jewel sure.
Go on, my lord, and give your charge, I say;
Thy wit will make us conquerors today.
MEANDER: Then, noble soldiers, to entrap these thieves
That live confounded in disorder'd troops,   60
If wealth or riches may prevail with them,
We have our camels laden all with gold,
Which you that be but common soldiers
Shall fling in every corner of the field;
And, while the base-born Tartars take it up,
You, fighting more for honour than for gold,
Shall massacre those greedy-minded slaves;
And, when their scatter'd army is subdu'd,
And you march on their slaughter'd carcasses,
Share equally the gold that bought their lives,   70
And live like gentlemen in Persia.
Strike up the drum, and march courageously:
Fortune herself doth sit upon our crests.
MYCETES: He tells you true, my masters; so he does.
Drums, why sound ye not when Meander speaks?
    Exeunt, drums sounding.

SCENE THREE

Enter COSROE, TAMBURLAINE, THERIDAMAS,
TECHELLES, USUMCASANE, *and* ORTYGIUS,
with others.

COSROE: Now, worthy Tamburlaine, have I repos'd
  In thy approved fortunes all my hope.
  What think'st thou, man, shall come of our attempts?
  For, even as from assured oracle,
  I take thy doom for satisfaction.
TAMBURLAINE: And so mistake you not a whit, my
    lord;
  For fates and oracles [of] heaven have sworn
  To royalise the deeds of Tamburlaine,
  And make them blest that share in his attempts,
10 And doubt you not but, if you favour me,
  And let my fortunes and my valour sway
  To some direction in your martial deeds,
  The world will strive with hosts of men-at-arms
  To swarm unto the ensign I support.
  The hosts of Xerxes, which by fame is said
  To drink the mighty Parthian Araris,³
  Was but a handful to that we will have.
  Our quivering lances, shaking in the air,
  And bullets, like Jove's dreadful thunderbolts,
20 Enroll'd in flames and fiery smouldering mists,
  Shall threat the gods more than Cyclopian⁴ wars;
  And with our sun-bright armour, as we march,
  We'll chase the stars from heaven, and dim their eyes
  That stand and muse at our admired arms.
THERIDAMAS: You see, my lord, what working words
    he hath;
  But, when you see his actions top his speech,
  Your speech will stay, or so extol his worth
  As I shall be commended and excus'd

5 *doom*: pronouncement.

124

For turning my poor charge to his direction
And these his two renowmed friends, my lord,   *30*
Would make one thrust and strive to be retain'd
In such a great degree of amity.

TECHELLES: With duty and with amity we yield
Our utmost service to the fair Cosroe.

COSROE: Which I esteem as portion of my crown.
Usumcasane and Techelles both,
When she that rules in Rhamnus' golden gates,
And makes a passage for all prosperous arms,
Shall make me solely emperor of Asia,
Then shall your meeds and valours be advanc'd   *40*
To rooms of honour and nobility.

TAMBURLAINE: Then haste, Cosroe, to be king alone,
That I with these my friends and all my men
May triumph in our long-expected fate.
The king your brother is now hard at hand:
Meet with the fool, and rid your royal shoulders
Of such a burden as outweighs the sands
And all the craggy rocks of Caspia.

    Enter a MESSENGER.

MESSENGER: My lord,
We have discovered the enemy   *50*
Ready to charge you with a mighty army.

COSROE: Come, Tamburlaine; now whet thy winged
    sword,
And lift thy lofty arm into the clouds,
That it may reach the king of Persia's crown,
And set it safe on my victorious head.

TAMBURLAINE: See where it is, the keenest
    curtle-axe
That e'er made passage thorough Persian arms!
These are the wings shall make it fly as swift
As doth the lightning or the breath of heaven,
And kill as sure as it swiftly flies.   *60*

COSROE: Thy words assure me of kind success.

37 *Rhamnus*: temple of Nemesis in Attica.

Go, valiant soldier, go before, and charge
The fainting army of that foolish king.
TAMBURLAINE: Usumcasane and Techelles, come:
We are enow to scare the enemy,
And more than needs to make an emperor.
Exeunt to the battle.

SCENE FOUR

Enter MYCETES, *with his crown in his hand.*
MYCETES: Accurs'd be he that first invented war!
They knew not, ah, they knew not, simple men,
How those were hit by pelting cannon-shot
Stand staggering like a quivering aspen-leaf
Fearing the force of Boreas' boisterous blasts!
In what a lamentable case were I,
If nature had not given me wisdom's lore!
For kings are clouts that every man shoots at,
Our crown the pin that thousands seek to cleave.
10 Therefore in policy I think it good
To hide it close; a goodly stratagem,
And far from any man that is a fool.
So shall not I be known; or if I be,
They cannot take away my crown from me.
Here will I hide it in this simple hole.
Enter TAMBURLAINE.
TAMBURLAINE: What, fearful coward, straggling from
the camp,
When kings themselves are present in the field!
MYCETES: Thou liest.
TAMBURLAINE: Base villain, darest thou give me the lie?
20 MYCETES: Away! I am the king. Go, touch me not.
Thou break'st the law of arms, unless thou kneel,
And cry me 'Mercy, noble king!'
TAMBURLAINE: Are you the witty king of Persia?

8 *clouts*: the target in archery; the pin, a peg fixed in its centre.

MYCETES: Ay, marry, am I: have you any suit to me?

TAMBERLAINE: I would entreat you to speak but three
    wise words.

MYCETES: So I can when I see my time.

TAMBURLAINE: Is this your crown?

MYCETES: Ay: didst thou ever see a fairer?

TAMBURLAINE: You will not sell it, will ye?

MYCETES: Such another word, and I will have thee   *30*
    executed. Come, give it me.

TAMBURLAINE: No, I took it prisoner.

MYCETES: You lie; I gave it you.

TAMBURLAINE: Then 'tis mine.

MYCETES: No; I mean I let you keep it.

TAMBURLAINE: Well, I mean you shall have it again.
  Here, take it for a while: I lend it thee,
  Till I may see thee hemm'd with armed men.
  Then shalt thou see me pull it from thy head:
  Thou art no match for mighty Tamburlaine.
    Exit.

MYCETES: O gods, is this Tamburlaine the thief?   *40*
  I marvel much he stole it not away.
    Trumpets within sound to the battle: he runs out.

SCENE FIVE

Enter COSROE, TAMBURLAINE, MENAPHON,
MEANDER, ORTYGIUS, THERIDAMAS,
TECHELLES, USUMCASANE, *with others.*

TAMBURLAINE: Hold thee, Cosroe; wear two imperial
  crowns.
  Think thee invested now as royally,
  Even by the mighty hand of Tamburlaine,
  As if as many kings as could encompass thee
  With greatest pomp had crown'd thee emperor.

COSROE: So do I, thrice-renowmed man-at-arms;
  And none shall keep the crown but Tamburlaine.

Thee do I make my regent of Persia,
And general lieutenant of my armies.
10 Meander, you, that were our brother's guide,
And chiefest counsellor in all his acts,
Since he is yielded to the stroke of war,
On your submission we with thanks excuse,
And give you equal place in our affairs.

MEANDER: Most happy emperor, in humblest terms
I vow my service to your majesty,
With utmost virtue of my faith and duty.

COSROE: Thanks, good Meander. Then, Cosroe, reign,
And govern Persia in her former pomp.
20 Now send embassage to thy neighbour kings,
And let them know the Persian king is chang'd
From one that knew not what a king should do
To one that can command what 'longs thereto.
And now we will to fair Persepolis
With twenty thousand expert soldiers.
The lords and captains of my brother's camp
With little slaughter take Meander's course,
And gladly yield them to my gracious rule.
Ortygius and Menaphon, my trusty friends,
30 Now will I gratify your former good,
And grace your calling with a greater sway.

ORTYGIUS: And as we ever aim'd at your behoof,
And sought your state all honour it deserv'd,
So will we with our powers and our lives
Endeavour to preserve and prosper it.

COSROE: I will not thank thee, sweet Ortygius;
Better replies shall prove my purposes.
And now, Lord Tamburlaine, my brother's camp
I leave to thee and to Theridamas,
40 To follow me to fair Persepolis.
Then will we march to all those Indian mines
My witless brother to the Christians lost,
And ransom them with fame and usury.
And, till thou overtake me, Tamburlaine,

(Staying to order all the scatter'd troops,)
Farewell, lord regent and his happy friends.
I long to sit upon my brother's throne.

MEANDER: Your majesty shall shortly have your wish,
And ride in triumph through Persepolis.

Exeunt all except TAMBURLAINE, THERIDAMAS,
TECHELLES, *and* USUMCASANE.

TAMBURLAINE: And ride in triumph through Perse-   *50*
polis! —
Is it not brave to be a king, Techelles!
Usumcasane and Theridamas,
Is it not passing brave to be a king,
And ride in triumph through Persepolis?

TECHELLES: O, my lord, 'tis sweet and full of pomp!

USUMCASANE: To be a king, is half to be a god.

THERIDAMAS: A god is not so glorious as a king:
I think the pleasure they enjoy in heaven,
Cannot compare with kingly joys in earth; —
To wear a crown enchas'd with pearl and gold,   *60*
Whose virtues carry with it life and death;
To ask and have, command and be obey'd;
When looks breed love, with looks to gain the prize,
Such power attractive shines in princes' eyes.

TAMBURLAINE: Why, say, Theridamas, wilt thou be a
king?

THERIDAMAS: Nay, though I praise it, I can live without it.

TAMBURLAINE: What say my other friends? Will you be
kings?

TECHELLES: Ay, if I could, with all my heart, my lord.

TAMBURLAINE: Why, that's well said, Techelles: so
would I: —
And so would you my masters, would you not?   *70*

USUMCASANE: What then, my lord?

TAMBURLAINE: Why, then, Casane, shall we wish for
aught
The world affords in greatest novelty,

And rest attemptless, faint, and destitute?
Methinks we should not. I am strongly mov'd,
That if I should desire the Persian crown,
I could attain it with a wondrous ease:
And would not all our soldiers soon consent,
If we should aim at such a dignity?

80 THERIDAMAS: I know they would with our persuasions.

TAMBURLAINE: Why, then, Theridamas, I'll first assay
To get the Persian kingdom to myself;
Then thou for Parthia; they for Scythia and Media;
And, if I prosper, all shall be as sure
As if the Turk, the Pope, Afric, and Greece,
Came creeping to us with their crowns a-piece.

TECHELLES: Then shall we send to this triumphing king,
And bid him battle for his novel crown?

USUMCASANE: Nay, quickly, then, before his room be hot.

90 TAMBURLAINE: 'Twill prove a pretty jest, in faith,
my friends.

THERIDAMAS: A jest to charge on twenty thousand men!
I judge the purchase more important far.

TAMBURLAINE: Judge by thyself, Theridamas, not me;
For presently Techelles here shall haste
To bid him battle ere he pass too far,
And lose more labour than the gain will quite.
Then shalt thou see the Scythian Tamburlaine
Make but a jest to win the Persian crown.
Techelles, take a thousand horse with thee,

100 And bid him turn him back to war with us,
That only made him king to make us sport.
We will not steal upon him cowardly,
But give him warning and more warriors.
Haste thee, Techelles; we will follow thee.

Exit TECHELLES.

What saith Theridamas?

THERIDAMAS: Go on, for me.

Exeunt.

96 *quite*: repay.   106 *for me*: as far as I am concerned.

130

SCENE SIX

Enter COSROE, MEANDER, ORTYGIUS, *and*
MENAPHON, *with* SOLDIERS.

COSROE: What means this devilish shepherd, to aspire
    With such a giantly presumption,
    To cast up hills against the face of heaven,
    And dare the force of angry Jupiter?[5]
    But, as he thrust them underneath the hills,
    And press'd out fire from their burning jaws,
    So will I send this monstrous slave to hell,
    Where flames shall ever feed upon his soul.

MEANDER: Some powers divine, or else infernal, mix'd
    Their angry seeds at his conception;   *10*
    For he was never sprung of human race,
    Since with the spirit of his fearful pride,
    He dares so doubtlessly resolve of rule,
    And by profession be ambitious.

ORTYGIUS: What god, or fiend, or spirit of the earth,
    Or monster turned to a manly shape,
    Or of what mould or mettle he be made,
    What star or fate soever govern him,
    Let us put on our meet encountering minds;
    And, in detesting such a devilish thief,   *20*
    In love of honour and defence of right,
    Be arm'd against the hate of such a foe,
    Whether from earth, or hell, or heaven he grow.

COSROE: Nobly resolv'd, my good Ortygius;
    And since we all have suck'd[6] one wholesome air,
    And with the same proportion of elements
    Resolve, I hope we are resembled,
    Vowing our loves to equal death and life.
    Let's cheer our soldiers to encounter him,
    That grievous image of ingratitude,   *30*
    That fiery thirster after sovereignty,
    And burn him in the fury of that flame

That none can quench but blood and empery.
Resolve, my lords and loving soldiers, now
To save your king and country from decay.
Then strike up, drum; and all the stars that make
The loathsome circle of my dated life,
Direct my weapon to his barbarous heart,
That thus opposeth him against the gods,
40 And scorns the powers that govern Persia!
Exeunt, drums sounding.

SCENE SEVEN

Alarms of battle within. Then enter COSROE *wounded,*
TAMBURLAINE, THERIDAMAS, TECHELLES,
USUMCASANE, *with others.*

COSROE: Barbarous and bloody Tamburlaine,
Thus to deprive me of my crown and life!
Treacherous and false Theridamas,
Even at the morning of my happy state,
Scarce being seated in my royal throne,
To work my downfall and untimely end!
An uncouth pain torments my grieved soul
And death arrests the organ of my voice,
Who, entering at the breach thy sword hath made,
10 Sacks every vein and artier of my heart.
Bloody and insatiate Tamburlaine!
TAMBURLAINE: The thirst of reign and sweetness of a
crown,
That caus'd the eldest son of heavenly Ops
To thrust his doting father from his chair,
And place himself in the imperial heaven,
Mov'd me to manage arms against thy state.
What better precedent than mighty Jove?
Nature, that fram'd us of four elements
Warring within our breasts for regiment,
13 *Ops*: Saturn, deposed by Jove.

Doth teach us all to have aspiring minds. *20*
Our souls, whose faculties can comprehend
The wondrous architecture of the world,
And measure every wandering planet's course,
Still climbing after knowledge infinite,
And always moving as the restless spheres,
Wills us to wear ourselves and never rest,
Until we reach the ripest fruit of all,
That perfect bliss and sole felicity,
The sweet fruition of an earthly crown.

THERIDAMAS: And that made me to join with Tam- *30*
 burlaine;
For he is gross and like the massy earth
That moves not upwards, nor by princely deeds
Doth mean to soar above the highest sort.

TECHELLES: And that made us the friends of Tamburlaine,
To lift our swords against the Persian king.

USUMCASANE: For as, when Jove did thrust old Saturn
 down,
Neptune and Dis gain'd each of them a crown,
So do we hope to reign in Asia,
If Tamburlaine be plac'd in Persia.

COSROE: The strangest men that ever nature made! *40*
I know not how to take their tyrannies.
My bloodless body waxeth chill and cold,
And with my blood my life slides through my wound;
My soul begins to take her flight to hell,
And summons all my senses to depart.
The heat and moisture, which did feed each other,
For want of nourishment to feed them both,
Is dry and cold: and now doth ghastly Death
With greedy talents gripe my bleeding heart,
And like a harpy tires on my life. *50*
Theridamas and Tamburlaine, I die:
And fearful vengeance light upon you both!

49 *talents*: talons.   50 *tires*: tear prey (falconry).

Dies. TAMBURLAINE *takes* COSROE'S *crown, and puts it on his own head.*

TAMBURLAINE: Not all the curses which the Furies breathe

Shall make me leave so rich a prize as this.

Theridamas, Techelles, and the rest,

Who think you now is king of Persia?

ALL: Tamburlaine! Tamburlaine!

TAMBURLAINE: Though Mars himself, the angry god of arms,

And all the earthly potentates conspire

60   To dispossess me of this diadem,

Yet will I wear it in despite of them,

As great commander of this eastern world,

If you but say that Tamburlaine shall reign.

ALL: Long live Tamburlaine, and reign in Asia!

TAMBURLAINE: So; now it is more surer on my head

·Than if the gods had held a parliament,

And all pronounc'd me king of Persia.

Exeunt.

ACT THREE

SCENE ONE

Enter BAJAZETH, *the* KINGS OF FEZ, MOROCCO, *and* ARGIER, *with others, in great pomp.*

BAJAZETH: Great kings of Barbary, and my portly¹ bassoes,

We hear the Tartars and the eastern thieves,

Under the conduct of one Tamburlaine,

Presume a bickering with your emperor,

And think to rouse us from our dreadful siege

Of the famous Grecian Constantinople.

You know our army is invincible;

1 *portly*: stately.

As many circumcised Turks we have,
And warlike bands of Christians renied
As hath the ocean or the Terrene sea   *10*
Small drops of water when the moon begins
To join in one her semicircled horns.
Yet would we not be brav'd with foreign power,
Nor raise our siege before the Grecians yield,
Or breathless lie before the city-walls.
KING OF FEZ: Renowmed emperor and mighty general,
What if you sent the bassoes of your guard
To charge him to remain in Asia,
Or else to threaten death and deadly arms
As from the mouth of mighty Bajazeth?   *20*
BAJAZETH: Hie thee, my basso, fast to Persia.
Tell him thy lord, the Turkish emperor,
Dread lord of Afric, Europe and Asia,
Great king and conqueror of Graecia,
The ocean, Terrene, and the Coal-black sea,
The high and highest monarch of the world,
Wills and commands, (for say not I entreat,)
Not once to set his foot in Africa,
Or spread his colours in Graecia,
Lest he incur the fury of my wrath.   *30*
Tell him I am content to take a truce,
Because I hear he bears a valiant mind:
But if, presuming on his silly power,
He be so mad to manage arms with me,
Then stay thou with him; say, I bid thee so.
And if, before the sun have measur'd heaven
With triple circuit, thou regreet us not,
We mean to take his morning's next arise
For messenger he will not be reclaim'd,
And mean to fetch thee in despite of him.   *40*
BASSO: Most great and puissant monarch of the earth,
Your basso will accomplish your behest,
And shew your pleasure to the Persian,

9 *renied*: lapsed, apostate.   10 *Terrene*: Tyrrhenian.

As fits the legate of the stately Turk.
Exit.

KING OF ARGIER: They say he is the king of Persia;
But, if he dare attempt to stir your siege,
'Twere requisite he should be ten times more,
For all flesh quakes at your magnificence.

BAJAZETH: True, Argier; and trembles at my looks.

50 KING OF MOROCCO: The spring is hinder'd by your
smothering host,
For neither rain can fall upon the earth,
Nor sun reflex his virtuous beams thereon,
The ground is mantled with such multitudes.

BAJAZETH: All this is true as holy Mahomet,
And all the trees are blasted with our breaths.

KING OF FEZ: What thinks your greatness best to be
achiev'd
In pursuit of the city's overthrow?

BAJAZETH: I will the captive pioners of Argier
Cut off the water that by leaden pipes
60 Runs to the city from the mountain Carnon;
Two thousand horse shall forage up and down,
That no relief or succour come by land;
And all the sea my galleys countermand.
Then shall our footmen lie within the trench,
And with their cannons, mouth'd like Orcus' gulf,
Batter the walls, and we will enter in;
And thus the Grecians shall be conquered.
Exeunt.

SCENE TWO

Enter ZENOCRATE, AGYDAS, ANIPPE, *with others.*

AGYDAS: Madam Zenocrate, may I presume
To know the cause of these unquiet fits
That work such trouble to your wonted rest?

65 *Orcus' gulf*: the mouth of hell.

'Tis more than pity such a heavenly face
Should by heart's sorrow wax so wan and pale,
When your offensive rape by Tamburlaine
(Which of your whole displeasures should be most)
Hath seem'd to be digested long ago.

ZENOCRATE: Although it be digested long ago,
As his exceeding favours have deserv'd,   *10*
And might content the Queen of Heaven, as well
As it hath chang'd my first-conceiv'd disdain,
Yet since a farther passion feeds my thoughts
With ceaseless and disconsolate conceits,
Which dyes my looks so lifeless as they are,
And might, if my extremes had full events,
Make me the ghastly counterfeit of death.

AGYDAS: Eternal heaven sooner be dissolv'd,
And all that pierceth Phoebe's silver eye,
Before such hap fall to Zenocrate!   *20*

ZENOCRATE: Ah, life and soul, still hover in his breast,
And leave my body senseless as the earth,
Or else unite you to his life and soul,
That I may live and die with Tamburlaine!

Enter, behind, TAMBURLAINE, *with* TECHELLES,
and others.

AGYDAS: With Tamburlaine! Ah, fair Zenocrate,
Let not a man so vile and barbarous,
That holds you from your father in despite,
And keeps you from the honours of a queen,
(Being suppos'd his worthless concubine,)
Be honour'd with your love but for necessity!   *30*
So, now the mighty Soldan hears of you,
Your highness needs not doubt but in short time
He will, with Tamburlaine's destruction,
Redeem you from this deadly servitude.

ZENOCRATE: Leave to wound me with these words,
And speak of Tamburlaine as he deserves.
The entertainment we have had of him

19 *Phoebe*: the moon.

Is far from villany or servitude,
And might in noble minds be counted princely.

40 AGYDAS: How can you fancy one that looks so fierce,
Only dispos'd to martial stratagems?
Who, when he shall embrace you in his arms,
Will tell how many thousand men he slew;
And, when you look for amorous discourse,
Will rattle forth his facts of war and blood,
Too harsh a subject for your dainty ears.

ZENOCRATE: As looks the sun through Nilus' flowing
    stream,
Or when the Morning holds him in her arms,
So looks my lordly love, fair Tamburlaine;
50 His talk much sweeter than the Muses' song
They sung for honour 'gainst Pierides,
Or when Minerva did with Neptune strive:
And higher would I rear my estimate
Than Juno, sister to the highest god,
If I were match'd with mighty Tamburlaine.

AGYDAS: Yet be not so inconstant in your love,
But let the young Arabian live in hope,
After your rescue to enjoy his choice.
You see, though first the king of Persia,
60 Being a shepherd, seem'd to love you much,
Now, in his majesty, he leaves those looks,
Those words of favour, and those comfortings,
And gives no more than common courtesies.

ZENOCRATE: Thence rise the tears that so distain my
    cheeks,
Fearing his love through my unworthiness.

    TAMBURLAINE *goes to her, and takes her away lovingly
    by the hand, looking wrathfully on* AGYDAS, *and says
    nothing. Exeunt all except* AGYDAS.

AGYDAS: Betray'd by fortune and suspicious love,

51 *Pierides*: nine women, defeated in singing contest by the Muses
and turned into birds.
52 *Minerva*: strove with Poseidon for the government of Athens.

Threaten'd with frowning wrath and jealousy,
Surpris'd with fear of hideous revenge,
I stand aghast; but most astonied
To see his choler shut in secret thoughts,   70
And wrapt in silence of his angry soul.
Upon his brows was pourtray'd ugly death;
And in his eyes the fury of his heart,
That shine as comets, menacing revenge,
And casts a pale complexion on his cheeks.
As when the seaman sees the Hyades
Gather an army of Cimmerian clouds,
(Auster and Aquilon with winged steeds,
All sweating, tilt about the watery heavens,
With shivering spears enforcing thunder-claps,   80
And from their shields strike flames of lightning,)
All-fearful folds his sails, and sounds the main,
Lifting his prayers to the heavens for aid
Against the terror of the winds and waves;
So fares Agydas for the late-felt frowns,
That sent a tempest to my daunted thoughts,
And makes my soul divine her overthrow.
    Re-enter TECHELLES *with a naked dagger, and*
    USUMCASANE.
TECHELLES: See you, Agydas, how the king salutes you!
He bids you prophesy what it imports.
AGYDAS: I prophesied before, and now I prove   90
The killing frowns of jealousy and love.
He needed not with words confirm my fear,
For words are vain where working tools present
The naked action of my threaten'd end:
It says, Agydas, thou shalt surely die,
And of extremities elect the least;
More honour and less pain it may procure,
To die by this resolved hand of thine

76 *Hyades*: group of stars, bringing rain if they rose at dawn.
77 *Cimmerian*: black.
78 *Auster and Aquilas*: south-west and north winds.

Than stay the torments he and heaven have sworn.
100 Then haste, Agydas, and prevent the plagues
Which thy prolonged fates may draw on thee.
Go wander free from fear of tyrant's rage,
Removed from the torments and the hell
Wherewith he may excruciate thy soul;
And let Agydas by Agydas die,
And with this stab slumber eternally.
    Stabs himself.
TECHELLES: Usumcasane, see, how right the man
  Hath hit the meaning of my lord the king!
USUMCASANE: Faith, and, Techelles, it was manly done;
110 And, since he was so wise and honourable,
Let us afford him now the bearing hence,
And crave his triple-worthy burial.
TECHELLES: Agreed, Casane; we will honour him.
    Exeunt, bearing out the body.

SCENE THREE

Enter TAMBURLAINE, TECHELLES, USUMCASANE,
THERIDAMAS, *a* BASSO, ZENOCRATE,
ANIPPE, *with others.*
TAMBURLAINE: Basso, by this thy lord and master
  knows
I mean to meet him in Bithynia.
See, how he comes! Tush, Turks are full of brags,
And menace more than they can well perform.
He meet me in the field, and fetch thee hence!
Alas, poor Turk! His fortune is too weak
T' encounter with the strength of Tamburlaine.
View well my camp, and speak indifferently:
Do not my captains and my soldiers look
10 As if they meant to conquer Africa?
BASSO: Your men are valiant, but their number few,

8 *indifferently*: impartially (without fear or favour).

And cannot terrify his mighty host.
My lord, the great commander of the world,
Besides fifteen contributory kings,
Hath now in arms ten thousand janizaries,
Mounted on lusty Mauritanian steeds,
Brought to the war by men of Tripoly;
Two hundred thousand footmen that have serv'd
In two set battles fought in Graecia;
And for the expedition of this war, 20
If he think good, can from his garrisons
Withdraw as many more to follow him.

TECHELLES: The more he brings, the greater is the spoil;
For, when they perish by our warlike hands,
We mean to set our footmen on their steeds,
And rifle all those stately janizars.

TAMBURLAINE: But will those kings accompany your
lord?

BASSO: Such as his highness please: but some must stay
To rule the provinces he late subdu'd.

TAMBURLAINE (*to his officers*): Then fight courageously: 30
their crowns are yours,
This hand shall set them on your conquering heads
That made me emperor of Asia.

USUMCASANE: Let him bring millions infinite of men,
Unpeopling Western Africa and Greece,
Yet we assure us of the victory.

THERIDAMAS: Even he, that in a trice vanquish'd two
kings
More mighty than the Turkish emperor,
Shall rouse him out of Europe, and pursue
His scatter'd army till they yield or die.

TAMBURLAINE: Well said, Theridamas! Speak in that 40
mood,
For *will* and *shall* best fitteth Tamburlaine,
Whose smiling stars give him assured hope
Of martial triumph ere he meet his foes.

15 *janizaries*: Turkish infantry.

I that am term'd the Scourge and Wrath of God,
The only fear and terror of the world,
Will first subdue the Turk, and then enlarge
Those Christian captives which you keep as slaves,
Burdening their bodies with your heavy chains,
And feeding them with thin and slender fare,
50 That naked row about the Terrene sea,
And, when they chance to breathe and rest a space,
Are punish'd with bastones so grievously
That they lie panting on the galleys' side,
And strive for life at every stroke they give.
These are the cruel pirates of Argier,
That damned train, the scum of Africa,
Inhabited with straggling runagates,
That make quick havoc of the Christian blood.
But, as I live, that town shall curse the time
60 That Tamburlaine set foot in Africa.

  Enter BAJAZETH, BASSOES, *the* KINGS OF FEZ,
  MOROCCO, *and* ARGIER; ZABINA *and* EBEA.

BAJAZETH: Bassoes and janizaries of my guard,
 Attend upon the person of your lord,
 The greatest potentate of Africa.
TAMBURLAINE: Techelles and the rest, prepare your
 swords;
 I mean t'encounter with that Bajazeth.
BAJAZETH: Kings of Fez, Morocco, and Argier,
 He calls me Bajazeth, whom you call lord!
 Note the presumption of this Scythian slave!
 I tell thee, villain, those that lead my horse
70 Have to their names titles of dignity;
 And dar'st thou bluntly call me Bajazeth?
TAMBURLAINE: And know thou, Turk, that those which
 lead my horse
 Shall lead thee captive thorough Africa;
 And dar'st thou bluntly call me Tamburlaine?
BAJAZETH: By Mahomet my kinsman's sepulchre,

52 *bastones*: sticks (cf. the bastinado).

And by the holy Alcoran I swear,
He shall be made a chaste and lustless eunuch,
And in my sarell tend my concubines;
And all his captains, that thus stoutly stand,
Shall draw the chariot of my emperess, 80
Whom I have brought to see their overthrow!

TAMBURLAINE: By this my sword that conquer'd Persia,
Thy fall shall make me famous through the world!
I will not tell thee how I'll handle thee,
But every common soldier of my camp
Shall smile to see thy miserable state.

KING OF FEZ: What means the mighty Turkish
emperor,
To talk with one so base as Tamburlaine?

KING OF MOROCCO: Ye Moors and valiant men of
Barbary,
How can ye suffer these indignities? 90

KING OF ARGIER: Leave words, and let them feel your
lances' points,
Which glided through the bowels of the Greeks.

BAJAZETH: Well said, my stout contributory kings!
Your threefold army and my hugy host
Shall swallow up these base-born Persians.

TECHELLES: Puissant, renowm'd, and mighty Tamburlaine,
Why stay we thus prolonging all their lives?

THERIDAMAS: I long to see those crowns won by our
swords,
That we may rule as kings of Africa.

USUMCASANE: What coward would not fight for such a 100
prize?

TAMBURLAINE: Fight all courageously, and be you
kings:
I speak it, and my words are oracles.

BAJAZETH: Zabina, mother of three braver boys
Than Hercules, that in his infancy

78 *sarell*: seraglio.

Did pash the jaws of serpents venomous,
Whose hands are made to gripe a warlike lance,
Their shoulders broad for complete armour fit,
Their limbs more large and of a bigger size
Than all the brats y-sprung from Typhon's loins,
110 Who, when they come unto their father's age,
Will batter turrets with their manly fists; –
Sit here upon this royal chair of state,
And on thy head wear my imperial crown,
Until I bring this sturdy Tamburlaine
And all his captains bound in captive chains.

ZABINA: Such good success happen to Bajazeth!

TAMBURLAINE: Zenocrate, the loveliest maid alive,
Fairer than rocks of pearl and precious stone,
The only paragon of Tamburlaine;
120 Whose eyes are brighter than the lamps of heaven,
And speech more pleasant than sweet harmony;
That with thy looks canst clear the darken'd sky,
And calm the rage of thundering Jupiter;
Sit down by her, adorned with my crown,
As if thou wert the empress of the world.
Stir not, Zenocrate, until thou see
Me march victoriously with all my men,
Triumphing over him and these his kings,
Which I will bring as vassals to thy feet.
130 Till then, take thou my crown, vaunt of my worth,
And manage words with her, as we will arms.

ZENOCRATE: And may my love, the king of Persia,
Return with victory and free from wound!

BAJAZETH: Now shalt thou feel the force of Turkish
arms,
Which lately made all Europe quake for fear.
I have of Turks, Arabians, Moors, and Jews,
Enough to cover all Bithynia.
Let thousands die: their slaughter'd carcasses

109 *Typhon*: father of monsters including the Chimaera, Cerberus
and the Sphinx.

Shall serve for walls and bulwarks to the rest;
And as the heads of Hydra, so my power,   *140*
Subdu'd shall stand as mighty as before.
If they should yield their necks unto the sword,
Thy soldiers' arms could not endure to strike
So many blows as I have heads for thee.
Thou know'st not, foolish-hardy Tamburlaine,
What 'tis to meet me in the open field,
That leave no ground for thee to march upon.

TAMBURLAINE: Our conquering swords shall marshal
    us the way
We use to march upon the slaughter'd foe,
Trampling their bowels with our horses' hoofs,   *150*
Brave horses bred on the white Tartarian hills.
My camp is like to Julius Caesar's host,
That never fought but had the victory;
Nor in Pharsalia was there such hot war
As these my followers willingly would have.
Legions of spirits, fleeting in the air,
Direct our bullets and our weapons' points,
And make your strokes to wound the senseless air;[7]
And when she sees our bloody colours spread,
Then Victory begins to take her flight,   *160*
Resting herself upon my milk-white tent.
But come, my lords, to weapons let us fall;
The field is ours, the Turk, his wife, and all.
    Exit with his followers.

BAJAZETH: Come, kings and bassoes, let us glut our
    swords,
That thirst to drink the feeble Persians' blood.
    Exit with his followers.

ZABINA: Base concubine, must thou be plac'd by me
That am the empress of the mighty Turk?

ZENOCRATE: Disdainful Turkess, and unreverend boss,
Call'st thou me concubine, that am betroth'd
Unto the great and mighty Tamburlaine?   *170*

168 *boss*: perhaps a form of 'basso' (cf. 11).

145

ZABINA: To Tamburlaine, the great Tartarian thief!

ZENOCRATE: Thou wilt repent these lavish words of
thine
When thy great basso-master and thyself
Must plead for mercy at his kingly feet,
And sue to me to be your advocate.

ZABINA: And sue to thee! I tell thee, shameless girl,
Thou shalt be laundress to my waiting-maid.
How lik'st thou her, Ebea? Will she serve?

EBEA: Madam, she thinks perhaps she is too fine;
180 But I shall turn her into other weeds,
And make her dainty fingers fall to work.

ZENOCRATE: Hear'st thou, Anippe, how thy drudge
doth talk?
And how my slave, her mistress, menaceth?
Both for their sauciness shall be employ'd
To dress the common soldiers' meat and drink;
For we will scorn they should come near ourselves.

ANIPPE: Yet sometimes let your highness send for them
To do the work my chambermaid disdains.
They sound to the battle within.

ZENOCRATE: Ye gods and powers that govern Persia,
190 And made my lordly love her worthy king,
Now strengthen him against the Turkish Bajazeth,
And let his foes, like flocks of fearful roes
Pursu'd by hunters, fly his angry looks,
That I may see him issue conqueror!

ZABINA: Now, Mahomet, solicit God himself,
And make him rain down murdering shot from heaven,
To dash the Scythians' brains, and strike them dead,
That dare to manage arms with him
That offer'd jewels to thy sacred shrine
200 When first he warr'd against the Christians!
They sound again to the battle within.

ZENOCRATE: By this the Turks lie weltering in their
blood,

180 *weeds*: clothes.

146

And Tamburlaine is lord of Africa.

ZABINA: Thou art deceiv'd. I heard the trumpets sound
  As when my emperor overthrew the Greeks,
  And led them captive into Africa.
  Straight will I use thee as thy pride deserves;
  Prepare thyself to live and die my slave.

ZENOCRATE: If Mahomet should come from heaven and
  swear
  My royal lord is slain or conquered,
  Yet should he not persuade me otherwise   210
  But that he lives and will be conqueror.

  BAJAZETH *flies and* TAMBURLAINE *pursues him.*
  The battle is short and they enter. BAJAZETH *is*
  overcome.

TAMBURLAINE: Now, king of bassoes, who is conqueror?

BAJAZETH: Thou, by the fortune of this damned foil.[8]

TAMBURLAINE: Where are your stout contributory
  kings?
  Re-enter TECHELLES, THERIDAMAS, *and*
  USUMCASANE.

TECHELLES: We have their crowns; their bodies strow
  the field.

TAMBURLAINE: Each man a crown! Why, kingly
  fought, i'faith!
  Deliver them into my treasury.

ZENOCRATE: Now let me offer to my gracious lord
  His royal crown again so highly won.

TAMBURLAINE: Nay, take the Turkish crown from her,   220
  Zenocrate,
  And crown me Emperor of Africa.

ZABINA: No, Tamburlaine; though now thou gat the
  best,
  Thou shalt not yet be lord of Africa.

THERIDAMAS: Give her the crown, Turkess, you were
  best.
  Takes it from her.

ZABINA: Injurious villains, thieves, runagates,
How dare you thus abuse my majesty?

THERIDAMAS: Here, madam, you are empress; she is
none.
Gives it to ZENOCRATE.

TAMBURLAINE: Not now, Theridamas; her time is past:
The pillars, that have bolster'd up those terms,
230   Are faln in clusters at my conquering feet.

ZABINA: Though he be prisoner, he may be ransom'd.

TAMBURLAINE: Not all the world shall ransom Bajazeth.

BAJAZETH: Ah, fair Zabina! We have lost the field;
And never had the Turkish emperor
So great a foil by any foreign foe.
Now will the Christian miscreants be glad,
Ringing with joy their superstitious bells,
And making bonfires for my overthrow.
But, ere I die, those foul idolaters
240   Shall make me bonfires with their filthy bones;
For, though the glory of this day be lost,
Afric and Greece have garrisons enough
To make me sovereign of the earth again.

TAMBURLAINE: Those walled garrisons will I subdue,
And write myself great lord of Africa.
So from the East unto the furthest West
Shall Tamburlaine extend his puissant arm.
The galleys and those pilling brigandines,
That yearly sail to the Venetian gulf,
250   And hover in the Straits for Christians' wreck,
Shall lie at anchor in the Isle Asant,
Until the Persian fleet and men-of-war,
Sailing along the oriental sea,
Have fetch'd about the Indian continent,
Even from Persepolis to Mexico,
And thence unto the Straits of Jubalter,
Where they shall meet and join their force in one,
Keeping in awe the Bay of Portingale,
And all the ocean by the British shore;

And by this means I'll win the world at last. 260

BAJAZETH: Yet set a ransom on me, Tamburlaine.

TAMBURLAINE: What, think'st thou Tamburlaine
   esteems thy gold?
I'll make the kings of India, ere I die,
Offer their mines to sue for peace to me.
And dig for treasure to appease my wrath.
Come, bind them both, and one lead in the Turk.
The Turkess let my love's maid lead away.
   They bind them.

BAJAZETH: Ah, villains, dare you touch my sacred arms?
O Mahomet! O sleepy Mahomet!

ZABINA: O cursed Mahomet, that mak'st us thus 270
The slaves to Scythians rude and barbarous!

TAMBURLAINE: Come, bring them in; and for this happy
   conquest
Triumph, and solemnise a martial feast.
   Exeunt.

ACT FOUR

SCENE ONE

Enter the SOLDAN OF EGYPT, CAPOLIN, LORDS,
and a MESSENGER.

SOLDAN: Awake, ye men of Memphis! Hear the clang
Of Scythian trumpets; hear the basilisks,
That, roaring, shake Damascus' turrets down!
The rogue of Volga holds Zenocrate,
The Soldan's daughter, for his concubine,
And with a troop of thieves and vagabonds
Hath spread his colours to our high disgrace,
While you, faint-hearted base Egyptians,
Lie slumbering on the flowery banks of Nile,
As crocodiles that unaffrighted rest 10

2 *basilisks*: cannons.

While thundering cannons rattle on their skins.
MESSENGER: Nay, mighty Soldan, did your greatness see
The frowning looks of fiery Tamburlaine,
That with his terror and imperious eyes
Commands the hearts of his associates,
It might amaze your royal majesty.
SOLDAN: Villain, I tell thee, were that Tamburlaine
As monstrous as Gorgon prince of hell,
The Soldan would not start a foot from him.
20 But speak, what power hath he?
MESSENGER: Mighty lord,
Three hundred thousand men in armour clad,
Upon their prancing steeds, disdainfully
With wanton paces trampling on the ground;
Five hundred thousand footmen threatening shot,
Shaking their swords, their spears, and iron bills,
Environing their standard round, that stood
As bristle-pointed as a thorny wood;
Their warlike engines and munition
30 Exceed the forces of their martial men.
SOLDAN: Nay, could their numbers countervail the stars,
Or ever-drizzling drops of April showers,
Or wither'd leaves that autumn shaketh down,
Yet would the Soldan by his conquering power
So scatter and consume them in his rage,
That not a man should live to rue their fall.
CAPOLIN: So might your highness, had you time to sort
Your fighting men, and raise your royal host.
But Tamburlaine by expedition
40 Advantage takes of your unreadiness.
SOLDAN: Let him take all th' advantages he can.
Were all the world conspir'd to fight for him,
Nay, were he devil, as he is no man,
Yet in revenge of fair Zenocrate,
Whom he detaineth in despite of us,
This arm should send him down to Erebus,

18 *Gorgon*: Demogorgon, a devil.

To shroud his shame in darkness of the night.

MESSENGER: Pleaseth your mightiness to understand,
  His resolution far exceedeth all.
  The first day when he pitcheth down his tents,   *50*
  White is their hue, and on his silver crest,
  A snowy feather spangled white he bears,
  To signify the mildness of his mind,
  That, satiate with spoil, refuseth blood.
  But, when Aurora mounts the second time,
  As red as scarlet is his furniture;
  Then must his kindled wrath be quench'd with blood,
  Not sparing any that can manage arms.
  But, if these threats move not submission,
  Black are his colours, black pavilion;   *60*
  His spear, his shield, his horse, his armour, plumes,
  And jetty feathers, menace death and hell;
  Without respect of sex, degree, or age,
  He razeth all his foes with fire and sword.

SOLDAN: Merciless villain, peasant, ignorant
  Of lawful arms or martial discipline!
  Pillage and murder are his usual trades:
  The slave usurps the glorious name of war.
  See, Capolin, the fair Arabian king,
  That hath been disappointed by this slave   *70*
  Of my fair daughter and his princely love,
  May have fresh warning to go war with us,
  And be reveng'd for her disparagement.
  Exeunt.

SCENE TWO

Enter TAMBURLAINE, TECHELLES, THERIDAMAS,
USUMCASANE, ZENOCRATE, ANIPPE, *two* MOORS
drawing BAJAZETH *in a cage, and* ZABINA *following him.*

TAMBURLAINE: Bring out my footstool.
  They take BAJAZETH *out of the cage.*

68 *glorious*: boastful.

BAJAZETH: Ye holy priests of heavenly Mahomet,
That, sacrificing, slice and cut your flesh,
Staining his altars with your purple blood,
Make heaven to frown, and every fixed star
To suck up poison from the moorish fens,
And pour it in this glorious tyrant's throat!

TAMBURLAINE: The chiefest god, first mover of that
sphere
Enchas'd with thousands ever-shining lamps,
10 Will sooner burn the glorious frame of heaven
Than it should so conspire my overthrow.
But, villain, thou that wishest this to me,
Fall prostrate on the low disdainful earth,
And be the footstool of great Tamburlaine,
That I may rise into my royal throne.

BAJAZETH: First shalt thou rip my bowels with thy
sword,
And sacrifice my heart to death and hell,
Before I yield to such a slavery.

TAMBURLAINE: Base villain, vassal, slave to Tambur-
laine,
20 Unworthy to embrace or touch the ground
That bears the honour of my royal weight,
Stoop, villain, stoop! Stoop, for so he bids
That may command thee piecemeal to be torn,
Or scatter'd like the lofty cedar-trees
Struck with the voice of thundering Jupiter.

BAJAZETH: Then, as I look down to the damned fiends,
Fiends, look on me! And thou, dread god of hell,
With ebon sceptre strike this hateful earth,
And make it swallow both of us at once!

TAMBURLAINE *gets up on him into his chair.*

30 TAMBURLAINE: Now clear the triple region⁹ of the air,
And let the Majesty of Heaven behold
Their scourge and terror tread on emperors.
Smile, stars that reign'd at my nativity,
And dim the brightness of their neighbour lamps;

Disdain to borrow light of Cynthia!
For I, the chiefest lamp of all the earth,
First rising in the east with mild aspect,
But fixed now in the meridian line,
Will send up fire to your turning spheres,
And cause the sun to borrow light of you.　　40
My sword struck fire from his coat of steel
Even in Bithynia, when I took this Turk;
As when a fiery exhalation,
Wrapt in the bowels of a freezing cloud,
Fighting for passage, make[s] the welkin crack,
And casts a flash of lightning to the earth.
But ere I march to wealthy Persia,
Or leave Damascus and th' Egyptian fields,
As was the fame of Clymene's brain-sick son[10]
That almost brent the axle-tree of heaven,　　50
So shall our swords, our lances, and our shot
Fill all the air with fiery meteors.
Then, when the sky shall wax as red as blood,
It shall be said I made it red myself,
To make me think of naught but blood and war.

ZABINA: Unworthy king, that by thy cruelty
Unlawfully usurp'st the Persian seat,
Dar'st thou, that never saw an emperor
Before thou met my husband in the field,
Being thy captive, thus abuse his state,　　60
Keeping his kingly body in a cage,
That roofs of gold and sun-bright palaces
Should have prepar'd to entertain his grace?
And treading him beneath thy loathsome feet,
Whose feet the kings of Africa have kiss'd?

TECHELLES: You must devise some torment worse, my
　　lord,
To make these captives rein their lavish tongues.

TAMBURLAINE: Zenocrate, look better to your slave.

ZENOCRATE: She is my handmaid's slave, and she shall
　　look

70 That these abuses flow not from her tongue.
Chide her, Anippe.

ANIPPE: Let these be warnings for you then, my slave,
How you abuse the person of the king;
Or else I swear to have you whipt stark nak'd.

BAJAZETH: Great Tamburlaine, great in my overthrow,
Ambitious pride shall make thee fall as low,
For treading on the back of Bajazeth,
That should be horsed on four mighty kings.

TAMBURLAINE: Thy names and titles and thy dignities
80 Are fled from Bajazeth and remain with me,
That will maintain it 'gainst a world of kings.
Put him in again.
    They put him into the cage.

BAJAZETH: Is this a place for mighty Bajazeth?
Confusion light on him that helps thee thus.

TAMBURLAINE: There, while he lives, shall Bajazeth be
    kept,
And, where I go, be thus in triumph drawn;
And thou, his wife, shall feed him with the scraps
My servitors shall bring thee from my board,
For he that gives him other food than this,
90 Shall sit by him, and starve to death himself:
This is my mind, and I will have it so.
Not all the kings and emperors of the earth,
If they would lay their crowns before my feet,
Shall ransom him, or take him from his cage.
The ages that shall talk of Tamburlaine,
Even from this day to Plato's wondrous year,[11]
Shall talk how I have handled Bajazeth.
These Moors, that drew him from Bithynia
To fair Damascus, where we now remain,
100 Shall lead him with us whereso'er we go.
Techelles, and my loving followers,
Now may we see Damascus' lofty towers,
Like to the shadows of Pyramides
That with their beauties graced the Memphian fields.

The golden stature of their feather'd bird,
That spreads her wings upon the city walls,
Shall not defend it from our battering shot.
The townsmen mask in silk and cloth of gold,
And every house is as a treasury;
The men, the treasure, and the town are ours.   *110*

THERIDAMAS: Your tents of white now pitch'd before
     the gates,
And gentle flags of amity display'd,
I doubt not but the governor will yield,
Offering Damascus to your majesty.

TAMBURLAINE: So shall he have his life, and all the rest.
But, if he stay until the bloody flag
Be once advanc'd on my vermilion tent,
He dies, and those that kept us out so long;
And when they see me march in black array,
With mournful streamers hanging down their heads,   *120*
Were in that city all the world contain'd,
Not one should scape, but perish by our swords.

ZENOCRATE: Yet would you have some pity for my
     sake,
Because it is my country's and my father's.

TAMBURLAINE: Not for the world, Zenocrate, if I have
     sworn.
Come; bring in the Turk.
     Exeunt.

SCENE THREE

Enter SOLDAN, KING OF ARABIA, CAPOLIN,
and SOLDIERS, *with streaming colours.*

SOLDAN: Methinks we march as Meleager[12] did,
Environed with brave Argolian knights,
To chase the savage Calydonian boar,
Or Cephalus,[13] with lusty Theban youths,

105 *feathered bird*: the Ibis, sacred to the Egyptians.

Against the wolf that angry Themis sent
To waste and spoil the sweet Aonian fields.
A monster of five hundred thousand heads,
Compact of rapine, piracy, and spoil,
The scum of men, the hate and scourge of God,
10 Raves in Egyptia, and annoyeth us.
My lord, it is the bloody Tamburlaine,
A sturdy felon, and a base-bred thief,
By murder raised to the Persian crown,
That dares control us in our territories.
To tame the pride of this presumptuous beast,
Join your Arabians with the Soldan's power;
Let us unite our royal bands in one,
And hasten to remove Damascus' siege.
It is a blemish to the majesty
20 And high estate of mighty emperors,
That such a base usurping vagabond
Should brave a king, or wear a princely crown.

KING OF ARABIA: Renowmed Soldan, have ye lately
    heard
The overthrow of mighty Bajazeth
About the confines of Bithynia?
The slavery wherewith he persecutes
The noble Turk and his great emperess?

SOLDAN: I have, and sorrow for his bad success;
But noble lord of great Arabia,
30 Be so persuaded that the Soldan is
No more dismay'd with tidings of his fall,
Than in the haven when the pilot stands,
And views a stranger's ship rent in the winds,
And shivered against a craggy rock:
Yet in compassion of his wretched state,
A sacred vow to heaven and him I make,
Confirming it with Ibis' holy name,
That Tamburlaine shall rue the day, the hour,
Wherein he wrought such ignominious wrong
40 Unto the hallow'd person of a prince,

Or kept the fair Zenocrate so long,
As concubine, I fear, to feed his lust.
KING OF ARABIA: Let grief and fury hasten on revenge;
Let Tamburlaine for his offences feel
Such plagues as heaven and we can pour on him.
I long to break my spear upon his crest,
And prove the weight of his victorious arm;
For fame, I fear, hath been too prodigal
In sounding through the world his partial praise.
SOLDAN: Capolin, hast thou survey'd our powers?   *50*
CAPOLIN: Great emperors of Egypt and Arabia,
The number of your hosts united is,
A hundred and fifty thousand horse,
Two hundred thousand foot, brave men-at-arms,
Courageous and full of hardiness,
As frolic as the hunters in the chase
Of savage beasts amid the desert woods.
KING OF ARABIA: My mind presageth fortunate success;
And, Tamburlaine, my spirit doth foresee
The utter ruin of thy men and thee.   *60*
SOLDAN: Then rear your standards; let your sounding
    drums
Direct our soldiers to Damascus' walls.
Now, Tamburlaine, the mighty Soldan comes,
And leads with him the great Arabian king,
To dim thy baseness and obscurity,
Famous for nothing but for theft and spoil,
To raze and scatter thy inglorious crew
Of Scythians and slavish Persians.
    Exeunt.

SCENE FOUR

A banquet set out; and to it come TAMBURLAINE *all in*
scarlet, ZENOCRATE, THERIDAMAS, TECHELLES,
USUMCASANE, BAJAZETH *drawn in his cage,*
ZABINA, *and others.*

157

TAMBURLAINE: Now hang our bloody colours by
    Damascus,
Reflexing hues of blood upon their heads,
While they walk quivering on their city walls,
Half-dead for fear before they feel my wrath.
Then let us freely banquet, and carouse
Full bowls of wine unto the god of war,
That means to fill your helmets full of gold,
And make Damascus' spoils as rich to you
As was to Jason Colchos' golden fleece.

10   And now, Bajazeth, hast thou any stomach?

BAJAZETH: Ay, such a stomach, cruel Tamburlaine, as I
    could willingly feed upon thy blood-raw heart.

TAMBURLAINE: Nay, thine own is easier to come by:
    pluck out that, and 'twill serve thee and thy wife. Well,
    Zenocrate, Techelles, and the rest, fall to your victuals.

BAJAZETH: Fall to, and never may your meat digest!
Ye Furies, that can mask invisible,
Dive to the bottom of Avernus' pool,
And in your hands bring hellish poison up,

20   And squeeze it in the cup of Tamburlaine!
Or, winged snakes of Lerna, cast your stings,
And leave your venoms in this tyrant's dish!

ZABINA: And may this banquet prove as ominous
As Progne's[14] to th' adulterous Thracian king
That fed upon the substance of his child!

ZENOCRATE: My lord, how can you suffer these
Outrageous curses by these slaves of yours?

TAMBURLAINE: To let them see, divine Zenocrate,
I glory in the curses of my foes,

30   Having the power from the empyreal heaven
To turn them all upon their proper heads.

TECHELLES: I pray you, give them leave, madam; this
    speech is a goodly refreshing for them.

THERIDAMAS: But if his highness would let them be fed
    it would do them more good.

31 *proper*: own.

TAMBURLAINE: Sirrah, why fall you not to? Are you so
daintily brought up, you cannot eat your own flesh?

BAJAZETH: First, legions of devils shall tear thee in
pieces.

USUMCASANE: Villain, knowest thou to whom thou   *40*
speakest?

TAMBURLAINE: O, let him alone. Here; eat, sir; take it
from my sword's point, or I'll thrust it to thy heart.

BAJAZETH *takes the food, and stamps upon it.*

THERIDAMAS: He stamps it under his feet, my lord.

TAMBURLAINE: Take it up, villain, and eat it; or I will
make thee slice the brawn of thy arms into carbonadoes
and eat them.

USUMCASANE: Nay, 'twere better he killed his wife, and
then she shall be sure not to be starved, and he be
provided for a month's victual beforehand.   *50*

TAMBURLAINE: Here is my dagger. Despatch her while
she is fat, for if she live but a while longer she will fall
into a consumption with fretting, and then she will not
be worth the eating.

THERIDAMAS: Dost thou think that Mahomet will suffer
this?

TECHELLES: 'Tis like he will, when he cannot let it.

TAMBURLAINE: Go to; fall to your meat. What, not a
bit! – Belike he hath not been watered today: give him
some drink.   *60*

They give BAJAZETH *water to drink, and he flings it on
the ground.*

Fast, and welcome, sir, while hunger make you eat.
How now, Zenocrate! doth not the Turk and his wife
make a goodly show at a banquet?

ZENOCRATE: Yes, my lord.

THERIDAMAS: Methinks 'tis a great deal better than a
consort of music.

TAMBURLAINE: Yet music would do well to cheer up

46 *carbonadoes*: strips of meat.   57 *let*: prevent.
61 *while*: until.

Zenocrate. Pray thee, tell why art thou so sad? If thou
wilt have a song, the Turk shall strain his voice. But
70   why is it?

ZENOCRATE: My lord, to see my father's town besieg'd,
The country wasted, where myself was born,
How can it but afflict my very soul?
If any love remain in you, my lord,
Or if my love unto your majesty
May merit favour at your highness' hands,
Then raise your siege from fair Damascus' walls,
And with my father take a friendly truce.

TAMBURLAINE: Zenocrate, were Egypt Jove's own
land,
80   Yet would I with my sword make Jove to stoop.
I will confute those blind geographers
That make a triple region in the world,
Excluding regions which I mean to trace,
And with this pen reduce them to a map,
Calling the provinces, cities, and towns,
After my name and thine, Zenocrate.
Here at Damascus will I make the point
That shall begin the perpendicular:
And wouldst thou have me buy thy father's love
90   With such a loss? Tell me, Zenocrate.

ZENOCRATE: Honour still wait on happy Tamburlaine!
Yet give me leave to plead for him, my lord.

TAMBURLAINE: Content thyself: his person shall be safe,
And all the friends of fair Zenocrate,
If with their lives they will be pleas'd to yield,
Or may be forced to make me emperor;
For Egypt and Arabia must be mine.
    Feed, you slave; thou mayst think thyself happy to
be fed from my trencher.

100 BAJAZETH: My empty stomach, full of idle heat,
Draws bloody humours from my feeble parts,
Preserving life by hastening cruel death.

82 *triple region*: Europe and Asia (as one), Africa, and America.

My veins are pale, my sinews hard and dry,
My joints benumb'd; unless I eat, I die.

ZABINA: Eat, Bajazeth. Let us live in spite of them,
looking some happy power will pity and enlarge us.

TAMBURLAINE: Here, Turk, wilt thou have a clean
trencher?

BAJAZETH: Ay, tyrant, and more meat.

TAMBURLAINE: Soft, sir! you must be dieted; too much *110*
eating will make you surfeit.

THERIDAMAS: So it would, my lord, 'specially having so
small a walk and so little exercise.

A second course is brought in of crowns.

TAMBURLAINE: Theridamas, Techelles, and Casane,
here are the cates you desire to finger, are they not?

THERIDAMAS: Ay, my lord: but none save kings must
feed with these.

TECHELLES: 'Tis enough for us to see them, and for
Tamburlaine only to enjoy them.

TAMBURLAINE: Well, here is now to the Soldan of Egypt, *120*
the King of Arabia, and the Governor of Damascus.
Now, take these three crowns, and pledge me, my
contributory kings. I crown you here, Theridamas, king
of Argier; Techelles, king of Fez; and Usumcasane,
king of Moroccus. How say you to this, Turk? These
are not your contributory kings.

BAJAZETH: Nor shall they long be thine, I warrant
them.

TAMBURLAINE: Kings of Argier, Moroccus, and of Fez,
You that have marched with happy Tamburlaine *130*
As far as from the frozen place of heaven
Unto the watery Morning's ruddy bower,
And thence by land unto the torrid zone,
Deserve these titles I endow you with
By valour and by magnanimity.
Your births shall be no blemish to your fame;
For virtue is the fount whence honour springs,

106 *enlarge*: free.　　137 *virtue*: power and ability.

And they are worthy she investeth kings.

THERIDAMAS: And, since your highness hath so well
vouchsaf'd,

140   If we deserve them not with higher meeds
Than erst our states and actions have retained,
Take them away again, and make us slaves.

TAMBURLAINE: Well said, Theridamas: when holy Fates
Shall stablish me in strong Egyptia,
We mean to travel to th' antarctic pole,
Conquering the people underneath our feet,
And be renowm'd as never emperors were.
Zenocrate, I will not crown thee yet,
Until with greater honours I be grac'd.

    Exeunt.

ACT FIVE

SCENE ONE

Enter the GOVERNOR OF DAMASCUS *with three or
four* CITIZENS, *and four* VIRGINS *with branches of
laurel in their hands.*

GOVERNOR: Still doth this man, or rather god of war,
Batter our walls and beat our turrets down;
And to resist with longer stubbornness,
Or hope of rescue from the Soldan's power,
Were but to bring our wilful overthrow,
And make us desperate of our threatened lives.
We see his tents have now been altered
With terrors to the last and cruel'st hue.
His coal-black colours, everywhere advanc'd,

10   Threaten our city with a general spoil;
And, if we should with common rites of arms
Offer our safeties to his clemency,
I fear the custom proper to his sword,
Which he observes as parcel of his fame,

Intending so to terrify the world,
By any innovation or remorse
Will never be dispens'd with till our deaths.
Therefore, for these our harmless virgins' sakes,
Whose honours and whose lives rely on him,
Let us have hope that their unspotted prayers,   20
Their blubber'd cheeks, and hearty humble moans
Will melt his fury into some remorse,
And use us like a loving conqueror.

FIRST VIRGIN: If humble suits or imprecations
    (Utter'd with tears of wretchedness and blood
    Shed from the heads and hearts of all our sex,
    Some made your wives, and some your children,)
    Might have entreated your obdurate breasts
    To entertain some care of our securities
    Whilst only danger beat upon our walls,   30
    These more than dangerous warrants of our death
    Had never been erected as they be,
    Nor you depend on such weak helps as we.

GOVERNOR: Well, lovely virgins, think our country's care,
    Our love of honour, loath to be enthrall'd
    To foreign powers and rough imperious yokes,
    Would not with too much cowardice or fear,
    Before all hope of rescue were denied,
    Submit yourselves and us to servitude.
    Therefore, in that your safeties and our own,   40
    Your honours, liberties, and lives were weigh'd
    In equal care and balance with our own,
    Endure as we the malice of our stars,
    The wrath of Tamburlaine and power of wars;
    Or be the means the overweighing heavens
    Have kept to qualify these hot extremes,
    And bring us pardon in your cheerful looks.

SECOND VIRGIN: Then here, before the Majesty of
    Heaven
    And holy patrons of Egyptia,

24 *imprecations*: prayers.

50   With knees and hearts submissive we entreat
Grace to our words and pity to our looks,
That this device may prove propitious,
And through the eyes and ears of Tamburlaine
Convey events of mercy to his heart;
Grant that these signs of victory we yield
May bind the temples of his conquering head,
To hide the folded furrows of his brows,
And shadow his displeased countenance
With happy looks of ruth and lenity.

60   Leave us, my lord, and loving countrymen:
What simple virgins may persuade, we will.
GOVERNOR: Farewell, sweet virgins, on whose safe return
Depends our city, liberty, and lives.
Exeunt all except the VIRGINS.

SCENE TWO

Enter TAMBURLAINE, *all in black and very melancholy,*
TECHELLES, THERIDAMAS, USUMCASANE,
with others.

TAMBURLAINE: What, are the turtles fray'd out of their
nests?
Alas, poor fools, must you be first shall feel
The sworn destruction of Damascus?
They knew my custom; could they not as well
Have sent ye out when first my milk-white flags,
Through which sweet Mercy threw her gentle beams,
Reflexed them on your disdainful eyes
As now when fury and incensed hate
Flings slaughtering terror from my coal-black tents,
10   And tells for truth submissions comes too late?
FIRST VIRGIN: Most happy king and emperor of the
earth,
Image of honour and nobility,

55 *signs of victory*: laurels.

For whom the powers divine have made the world,
And on whose throne the holy Graces sit;
In whose sweet person is compris'd the sum
Of Nature's skill and heavenly majesty;
Pity our plights! O, pity poor Damascus!
Pity old age, within whose silver hairs
Honour and reverence evermore have reign'd!
Pity the marriage-bed, where many a lord,   20
In prime and glory of his loving joy,
Embraceth now with tears of ruth and blood
The jealous body of his fearful wife,
Whose cheeks and hearts, so punish'd with conceit,
To think thy puissant never-stayed arm
Will part their bodies, and prevent their souls
From heavens of comfort yet their age might bear,
Now wax all pale and wither'd to the death,
As well for grief our ruthless governor
Hath thus refus'd the mercy of thy hand,   30
(Whose sceptre angels kiss and Furies dread,)
As for their liberties, their loves, or lives!
O, then, for these, and such as we ourselves,
For us, for infants, and for all our bloods,
That never nourish'd thought against thy rule,
Pity, O pity, sacred emperor,
The prostrate service of this wretched town;
And take in sign thereof this gilded wreath,
Whereto each man of rule hath given his hand,
And wish'd, as worthy subjects, happy means   40
To be investers of the royal brows
Even with the true Egyptian diadem!
TAMBURLAINE: Virgins, in vain you labour to prevent
   That which mine honour swears shall be perform'd.
   Behold my sword; what see you at the point?
FIRST VIRGIN: Nothing but fear and fatal steel, my lord.
TAMBURLAINE: Your fearful minds are thick and misty,
   then,

24 *conceit*: imagination.

165

For there sits Death; there sits imperious Death,
Keeping his circuit by the slicing edge.
50 But I am pleas'd you shall not see him there;
He now is seated on my horsemen's spears,
And on their points his fleshless body feeds.
Techelles, straight go charge a few of them
To charge these dames, and shew my servant Death,
Sitting in scarlet on their armed spears.

VIRGINS: O, pity us!

TAMBURLAINE: Away with them, I say, and shew them
Death!

The VIRGINS *are taken out by* TECHELLES *and others.*

I will not spare these proud Egyptians,
Nor change my martial observations
60 For all the wealth of Gihon's golden waves,
Or for the love of Venus, would she leave
The angry god of arms and lie with me.
They have refus'd the offer of their lives,
And know my customs are as peremptory
As wrathful planets, death, or destiny.

Re-enter TECHELLES.

What, have your horsemen shown the virgins Death?

TECHELLES: They have, my lord, and on Damascus'
walls
Have hoisted up their slaughtered carcasses.

TAMBURLAINE: A sight as baneful to their souls, I think,
70 As are Thessalian drugs or mithridate.
But go, my lords, put the rest to the sword.

Exeunt all except TAMBURLAINE.

Ah, fair Zenocrate! divine Zenocrate!
Fair is too foul an epithet for thee,
That in thy passion for thy country's love,
And fear to see thy kingly father's harm,
With hair dishevell'd wip'st thy watery cheeks,
And, like to Flora in her morning's pride,

60 *Gihon*: river in Eden.
70 *Thessalia*: land of witchcraft.　　70 *mithridate*: poison.

166

Shaking her silver tresses in the air,
Rain'st on the earth resolved pearl in showers,
And sprinklest sapphires on thy shining face,   80
Where Beauty, mother to the Muses, sits,
And comments volumes with her ivory pen,
Taking instructions from thy flowing eyes;
Eyes, when that Ebena steps to heaven,
In silence of thy solemn evening's walk,
Making the mantle of the richest night,
The moon, the planets, and the meteors, light;
There angels in their crystal armour fight
A doubtful battle with my tempted thoughts
For Egypt's freedom and the Soldan's life,   90
His life that so consumes Zenocrate,
Whose sorrows lay more siege unto my soul
Than all my army to Damascus' walls;
And neither Persia's sovereign nor the Turk
Troubled my senses with conceit of foil
So much by much as doth Zenocrate.
What is beauty, saith my sufferings, then?
If all the pens that ever poets held
Had fed the feeling of their masters' thoughts,
And every sweetness that inspir'd their hearts,   100
Their minds, and muses on admired themes;
If all the heavenly quintessence they still
From their immortal flowers of poesy,
Wherein, as in a mirror, we perceive
The highest reaches of a human wit;
If these had made one poem's period,
And all combin'd in beauty's worthiness,
Yet should there hover in their restless heads
One thought, one grace, one wonder, at the least,
Which into words no virtue can digest.   110
But how unseemly is it for my sex,
My discipline of arms and chivalry,
My nature, and the terror of my name,

101 *admired*: wondrous.

167

To harbour thoughts effeminate and faint![15]
Save only that in beauty's just applause,
With whose instinct the soul of man is touched,
And every warrior that is rapt with love
Of fame, of valour, and of victory,
Must needs have beauty beat on his conceits:
120 I thus conceiving, and subduing both,
That which hath stoop'd the chiefest of the gods,
Even from the fiery-spangled veil of heaven,
To feel the lovely warmth of shepherds' flames,
And march in cottages of strowed reeds,
Shall give the world to note, for all my birth,
That virtue solely in the sum of glory,
And fashions men with true nobility. –
Who's within there?
Enter ATTENDANTS.
Hath Bajazeth been fed today?
130 ATTENDANT: Ay, my lord.
TAMBURLAINE: Bring him forth; and let us know if the
town be ransacked.
Exeunt ATTENDANTS.
Enter TECHELLES, THERIDAMAS, USUMCASANE,
and others.
TECHELLES: The town is ours, my lord, and fresh supply
Of conquest and of spoil is offer'd us.
TAMBURLAINE: That's well, Techelles. What's the news?
TECHELLES: The Soldan and the Arabian king together
March on us with such eager violence
As if there were no way but one with us.
TAMBURLAINE: No more there is not, I warrant thee,
Techelles.
ATTENDANTS *bring in* BAJAZETH *in his cage, follow-
ed by* ZABINA.
Exeunt ATTENDANTS.
140 THERIDAMAS: We know the victory is ours, my lord;
But let us save the reverend Soldan's life
For fair Zenocrate that so laments his state.

TAMBURLAINE: That will we chiefly see unto, Theridamas,
For sweet Zenocrate, whose worthiness
Deserves a conquest over every heart.
And now, my footstool, if I lose the field,
You hope of liberty and restitution?
Here let him stay, my masters, from the tents,
Till we have made us ready for the field.
Pray for us, Bajazeth; we are going.   *150*
    Exeunt all except BAJAZETH *and* ZABINA.
BAJAZETH: Go, never to return with victory!
Millions of men encompass thee about,
And gore thy body with as many wounds!
Sharp forked arrows light upon thy horse!
Furies from the black Cocytus' lake,
Break up the earth, and with their firebrands
Enforce thee run upon the baneful pikes!
Vollies of shot pierce through thy charmed skin,
And every bullet dipt in poison'd drugs!
Or roaring cannons sever all thy joints,   *160*
Making thee mount as high as eagles soar!
ZABINA: Let all the swords and lances in the field
Stick in his breast as in their proper rooms!
At every pore let blood come dropping forth,
That lingering pains may massacre his heart,
And madness send his damned soul to hell!
BAJAZETH: Ah, fair Zabina, we may curse his power,
The heavens may frown, the earth for anger quake;
But such a star hath influence in his sword
As rules the skies and countermands the gods   *170*
More than Cimmerian Styx or Destiny.
And then shall we in this detested guise,
With shame, with hunger, and with horror aye,
Griping our bowels with retorqued thoughts,
And have no hope to end our ecstasies.

155 *Cocytus*: river in Hades.
171 *Cimmerian Styx*: chief river of Hades.
174 *retorqued*: twisted inward.   175 *ecstasies*: delirium.

ZABINA: Then is there left no Mahomet, no God,
No fiend, no fortune, nor no hope of end
To our infamous, monstrous slaveries.
Gape, earth, and let the fiends infernal view
180 A hell as hopeless and as full of fear
As are the blasted banks of Erebus,
Where shaking ghosts with ever-howling groans
Hover about the ugly ferryman,
To get a passage to Elysium!
Why should we live? O, wretches, beggars, slaves!
Why live we, Bajazeth, and build up nests
So high within the region of the air,
By living long in this oppression,
That all the world will see and laugh to scorn
190 The former triumphs of our mightiness
In this obscure infernal servitude?
BAJAZETH: O life, more loathsome to my vexed
thoughts
Than noisome parbreak of the Stygian snakes,
Which fills the nooks of hell with standing air,
Infecting all the ghosts with cureless griefs!
O dreary engines of my loathed sight,
That see my crown, my honour, and my name
Thrust under yoke and thraldom of a thief,
Why feed ye still on day's accursed beams,
200 And sink not quite into my tortur'd soul?
You see my wife, my queen, and emperess,
Brought up and propped by the hand of Fame,
Queen of fifteen contributory queens,
Now thrown to rooms of black abjection,
Smeared with blots of basest drudgery,
And villeiness to shame, disdain, and misery.
Accursed Bajazeth, whose words of ruth,
That would with pity cheer Zabina's heart,
And made our souls resolve in ceaseless tears,
210 Sharp hunger bites upon and gripes the root

193 *parbreak*: vomit.   209 *resolve*: dissolve.

From whence the issue of my thoughts do break!
O poor Zabina! O my queen, my queen!
Fetch me some water for my burning breast,
To cool and comfort me with longer date,
That, in the shorten'd sequel of my life,
I may pour forth my soul into thine arms
With words of love, whose moaning intercourse
Hath hitherto been stay'd with wrath and hate
Of our expressless bann'd inflictions.

ZABINA: Sweet Bajazeth, I will prolong thy life   *220*
   As long as any blood or spark of breath
   Can quench or cool the torments of my grief.
    Exit.

BAJAZETH: Now, Bajazeth, abridge thy baneful days,
   And beat thy brains out of thy conquer'd head,
   Since other means are all forbidden me,
   That may be ministers of my decay.
   O highest lamp of ever-living Jove,
   Accursed day, infected with my griefs,
   Hide now thy stained face in endless night,
   And shut the windows of the lightsome heavens!   *230*
   Let ugly Darkness with her rusty coach,
   Engirt with tempests, wrapt in pitchy clouds,
   Smother the earth with never-fading mists,
   And let her horses from their nostrils breathe
   Rebellious winds and dreadful thunder-claps,
   That in this terror Tamburlaine may live,
   And my pin'd soul, resolv'd in liquid air,
   May still excruciate his tormented thoughts!
   Then let the stony dart of senseless cold
   Pierce through the centre of my wither'd heart,   *24*
   And make a passage for my loathed life!
    He brains himself against the cage.
    Re-enter ZABINA.

ZABINA: What do mine eyes behold? my husband dead!
   His skull all riven in twain! his brains dash'd out,

219 *bann'd*: accursed.

The brains of Bajazeth, my lord and sovereign!
O Bajazeth, my husband and my lord!
O Bajazeth! O Turk! O Emperor!
Give him his liquor? Not I. Bring milk and fire, and
my blood I bring him again. – Tear me in pieces – give
me the sword with a ball of wild-fire upon it. – Down
250 with him! down with him! – Go to my child; away,
away, away! ah, save that infant! save him, save him! –
I, even I, speak to her. – The sun was down – streamers
white, red, black. – Here, here, here! – Fling the meat
in his face – Tamburlaine, Tamburlaine! – Let the
soldiers be buried. – Hell, death, Tamburlaine, hell! –
Make ready my coach, my chair, my jewels. – I come, I
come, I come, I come!
She runs against the cage, and brains herself.
Enter ZENOCRATE *with* ANIPPE.
ZENOCRATE: Wretched Zenocrate! that liv'st to see
Damascus' walls dy'd with Egyptian blood,
260 Thy father's subjects and thy countrymen;
The streets strow'd with dissever'd joints of men,
And wounded bodies gasping yet for life;
But most accurs'd, to see the sun-bright troop
Of heavenly virgins and unspotted maids,
Whose looks might make the angry god of arms
To break his sword and mildly treat of love,
On horsemen's lances to be hoisted up,
And guiltlessly endure a cruel death.
For every fell and stout Tartarian steed,
270 That stamp'd on others with their thundering hoofs,
When all their riders charg'd their quivering spears,
Began to check the ground and rein themselves,
Gazing upon the beauty of their looks.
Ah, Tamburlaine, wert thou the cause of this,
That term'st Zenocrate thy dearest love?
Whose lives were dearer to Zenocrate
Than her own life, or aught save thine own love.
But see, another bloody spectacle!

Ah, wretched eyes, the enemies of my heart,
How are ye glutted with these grievous objects,   *280*
And tell my soul more tales of bleeding ruth!
See, see, Anippe, if they breathe or no.
ANIPPE: No breath, nor sense, nor motion, in them
    both.
Ah, madam, this their slavery hath enforc'd,
And ruthless cruelty of Tamburlaine!
ZENOCRATE: Earth, cast up fountains from thy entrails,
And wet thy cheeks for their untimely deaths;
Shake with their weight in sign of fear and grief!
Blush, heaven, that gave them honour at their birth,
And let them die a death so barbarous!   *290*
Those that are proud of fickle empery
And place their chiefest good in earthly pomp,
Behold the Turk and his great emperess!
Ah, Tamburlaine my love, sweet Tamburlaine,
That fights for sceptres and for slippery crowns,
Behold the Turk and his great emperess!
Thou that, in conduct of thy happy stars,
Sleep'st every night with conquest on thy brows,
And yet wouldst shun the wavering turns of war,
In fear and feeling of the like distress,   *300*
Behold the Turk and his great emperess!
Ah, mighty Jove and holy Mahomet,
Pardon my love! O, pardon his contempt
Of earthly fortune and respect of pity;
And let not conquest, ruthlessly pursu'd,
Be equally against his life incens'd
In this great Turk and hapless emperess!
And pardon me that was not mov'd with ruth
To see them live so long in misery!
Ah, what may chance to thee, Zenocrate?   *310*
ANIPPE: Madam, content yourself, and be resolv'd,
Your love hath Fortune so at his command,
That she shall stay, and turn her wheel no more,
As long as life maintains his mighty arm

That fights for honour to adorn your head.
Enter PHILEMUS.

ZENOCRATE: What other heavy news now brings
Philemus?

PHILEMUS: Madam, your father, and the Arabian king,
The first affecter of your excellence,
Comes now, as Turnus 'gainst Æneas did,
320   Armed with lance into the Egyptian fields,
Ready for battle 'gainst my lord the king.

ZENOCRATE: Now shame and duty, love and fear
presents
A thousand sorrows to my martyr'd soul,
Whom should I wish the fatal victory,
When my poor pleasures are divided thus,
And rack'd by duty from my cursed heart?
My father and my first-betrothed love
Must fight against my life and present love;
Wherein the change I use condemns my faith,
330   And makes my deeds infamous through the world.
But, as the gods, to end the Trojans' toil,
Prevented Turnus of Lavinia,
And fatally enrich'd Æneas' love,
So, for a final issue to my griefs,
To pacify my country and my love,
Must Tamburlaine by their resistless powers,
With virtue of a gentle victory,
Conclude a league of honour to my hope.
Then, as the powers divine have pre-ordain'd,
340   With happy safety of my father's life
Send like defence of fair Arabia.

They sound to the battle within; and TAMBURLAINE
enjoys the victory: after which, the KING OF ARABIA
enters wounded.

KING OF ARABIA: What cursed power guides the
murdering hands
Of this infamous tyrant's soldiers,

319 *Turnus*: betrothed to Lavinia who married Aeneas.

That no escape may save their enemies,
Nor fortune keep themselves from victory?
Lie down, Arabia, wounded to the death,
And let Zenocrate's fair eyes behold,
That, as for her thou bear'st these wretched arms,
Even so for her thou diest in these arms,
Leaving thy blood for witness of thy love.　　　　　350

ZENOCRATE: Too dear a witness for such love, my lord!
Behold Zenocrate, the cursed object
Whose fortunes never mastered her griefs;
Behold her wounded in conceit for thee,
As much as thy fair body is for me!

KING OF ARABIA: Then shall I die with full contented
　　heart,
Having beheld divine Zenocrate,
Whose sight with joy would take away my life
As now it bringeth sweetness to my wound,
If I had not been wounded as I am.　　　　　360
Ah, that the deadly pangs I suffer now
Would lend an hour's licence to my tongue,
To make discourse of some sweet accidents
Have chanc'd thy merits in this worthless bondage,
And that I might be privy to the state
Of thy deserv'd contentment and thy love!
But, making now a virtue of thy sight,
To drive all sorrow from my fainting soul,
Since death denies me further cause of joy,
Depriv'd of care, my heart with comfort dies,　　　　　370
Since thy desired hand shall close mine eyes.
　　Dies.
　　Re-enter TAMBURLAINE, *leading the* SOLDAN;
　　TECHELLES, THERIDAMAS, USUMCASANE, *with*
　　others.

TAMBURLAINE: Come, happy father of Zenocrate,
A title higher than thy Soldan's name.
Though my right hand have thus enthralled thee,
Thy princely daughter here shall set thee free;

She that hath calm'd the fury of my sword,
Which had ere this been bath'd in streams of blood
As vast and deep as Euphrates or Nile.

ZENOCRATE: O sight thrice-welcome to my joyful soul,
380 To see the king, my father, issue safe
From dangerous battle of my conquering love!

SOLDAN: Well met, my only dear Zenocrate,
Though with the loss of Egypt and my crown!

TAMBURLAINE: 'Twas I, my lord, that gat the victory;
And therefore grieve not at your overthrow,
Since I shall render all into your hands,
And add more strength to your dominions
Than ever yet confirm'd th' Egyptian crown.
The god of war resigns his room to me,
390 Meaning to make me general of the world.
Jove, viewing me in arms, looks pale and wan,
Fearing my power should pull him from his throne.
Where'er I come the Fatal Sisters sweat,
And grisly Death, by running to and fro,
To do their ceaseless homage to my sword:
And here in Afric, where it seldom rains,
Since I arriv'd with my triumphant host,
Have swelling clouds, drawn from wide-gasping
    wounds,
Been oft resolv'd in bloody purple showers,
400 A meteor that might terrify the earth,
And make it quake at every drop it drinks.
Millions of souls sit on the banks of Styx,
Waiting the back-return of Charon's boat;
Hell and Elysium swarm with ghosts of men
That I have sent from sundry foughten fields
To spread my fame through hell and up to heaven.
And see, my lord, a sight of strange import, –
Emperors and kings lie breathless at my feet;
The Turk and his great empress, as it seems,
410 Left to themselves while we were at the fight,
Have desperately despatch'd their slavish lives:

With them Arabia, too, hath left his life.
All sights of power to grace my victory;
And such are objects fit for Tamburlaine,
Wherein, as in a mirror, may be seen
His honour, that consists in shedding blood
When men presume to manage arms with him.
SOLDAN: Mighty hath God and Mahomet made thy
 hand,
Renowmed Tamburlaine, to whom all kings
Of force must yield their crowns and emperies;   420
And I am pleas'd with this my overthrow,
If, as beseems a person of thy state,
Thou hast with honour us'd Zenocrate.
TAMBURLAINE: Her state and person want no pomp,
 you see;
And for all blot of foul inchastity,
I record heaven, her heavenly self is clear.
Then let me find no further time to grace
Her princely temples with the Persian crown;
But here these kings that on my fortunes wait,
And have been crowned for proved worthiness   430
Even by this hand that shall establish them,
Shall now, adjoining all their hands with mine,
Invest her here the Queen of Persia.
What saith the noble Soldan, and Zenocrate?
SOLDAN: I yield with thanks and protestations
Of endless honour to thee for her love.
TAMBURLAINE: Then doubt I not but fair Zenocrate
Will soon consent to satisfy us both.
ZENOCRATE: Else should I much forget myself, my lord.
THERIDAMAS: Then let us set the crown upon her head,   440
That long hath linger'd for so high a seat.
TECHELLES: My hand is ready to perform the deed;
For now her marriage-time shall work us rest.
USUMCASANE: And here's the crown, my lord; help set
 it on.
TAMBURLAINE: Then sit thou down, divine Zenocrate;

And here we crown thee Queen of Persia,
And all the kingdoms and dominions
That late the power of Tamburlaine subdu'd.
As Juno, when the giants were suppress'd,
That darted mountains at her brother Jove,
So looks my love, shadowing in her brows
Triumphs and trophies for my victories;
Or at Latona's daughter, bent to arms,
Adding more courage to my conquering mind.
To gratify thee, sweet Zenocrate,
Egyptians, Moors, and men of Asia,
From Barbary unto the Western India,
Shall pay a yearly tribute to thy sire;
And from the bounds of Afric to the banks
Of Ganges shall his mighty arm extend.
And now, my lords and loving followers,
That purchas'd kingdoms by your martial deeds,
Cast off your armour, put on scarlet robes,
Mount up your royal places of estate,
Environed with troops of noblemen,
And there make laws to rule your provinces.
Hang up your weapons on Alcides' post;
For Tamburlaine takes truce with all the world.
Thy first-betrothed love, Arabia,
Shall we with honour, as beseems, entomb
With this great Turk and his fair emperess.
Then, after all these solemn exequies,
We will our rites[16] of marriage solemnise.
    Exeunt.

453 *Latona's daughter*: Artemis, daughter of Leto.

THE SECOND PART OF

Tamburlaine the Great

THE SECOND PART OF THE
BLOODY CONQUESTS OF
MIGHTY TAMBURLAINE.
WITH HIS IMPASSIONATE FURY,
FOR THE DEATH OF
HIS LADY AND LOVE,
FAIR ZENOCRATE:
HIS FORM OF EXHORTATION
AND DISCIPLINE TO
HIS THREE SONS,
AND THE MANNER OF
HIS OWN DEATH.

Dramatis Personae

TAMBURLAINE, *King of Persia*
CALYPHAS,
AMYRAS, } *his sons*
CELEBINUS,
THERIDAMAS, *King of Argier*
TECHELLES, *King of Fez*
USUMCASANE, *King of Morocco*
ORCANES, *King of Natolia*
KING OF TREBIZON
KING OF SORIA
KING OF JERUSALEM
KING OF AMASIA
GAZELLUS, *Viceroy of Byron*
URIBASSA
SIGISMUND, *King of Hungary*
FREDERICK, } *lords of Buda and Bohemia*
BALDWIN,
CALLAPINE, *son to* BAJAZETH, *and prisoner to*
  TAMBURLAINE
ALMEDA, *his keeper*
GOVERNOR OF BABYLON
CAPTAIN OF BALSERA
HIS SON
ANOTHER CAPTAIN
MAXIMUS, PERDICAS, PHYSICIANS, LORDS, CITIZENS,
  MESSENGERS, SOLDIERS, *and* ATTENDANTS
ZENOCRATE, *wife to* TAMBURLAINE
OLYMPIA, *wife to the* CAPTAIN OF BALSERA
TURKISH CONCUBINES

The general welcomes Tamburlaine receiv'd,
When he arrived last upon our stage,
Have made our poet pen his Second Part,
Where death cuts off the progress of his pomp,
And murderous Fates throw all his triumphs down.
But what became of fair Zenocrate,
And with how many cities' sacrifice
He celebrated her sad[1]* funeral,
Himself in presence shall unfold at large.

ACT ONE

SCENE ONE

Enter ORCANES *king of Natolia,* GAZELLUS *viceroy
of Byron,* URIBASSA, *and their* TRAIN, *with drums
and trumpets.*

ORCANES: Egregious viceroys of these eastern parts,
Plac'd by the issue of great Bajazeth,
And sacred lord, the mighty Callapine,
Who lives in Egypt prisoner to that slave
Which kept his father in an iron cage, –
Now have we march'd from fair Natolia
Two hundred leagues, and on Danubius' banks
Our warlike host in complete armour rest,
Where Sigismund, the king of Hungary,
Should meet our person to conclude a truce.   10
What? shall we parley with the Christian?
Or cross the stream, and meet him in the field?
GAZELLUS: King of Natolia, let us treat of peace:
We all are glutted with the Christians' blood,

*Superior numbers refer to the Additional Notes at the end of the
book.

183

And have a greater foe to fight against:
Proud Tamburlaine, that now in Asia,
Near Guyron's head, doth set his conquering feet,
And means to fire Turkey as he goes.
'Gainst him, my lord, you must address your power.

20 URIBASSA: Besides, King Sigismund hath brought from
    Christendom
More than his camp of stout Hungarians, –
Sclavonians, Almains, Rutters,[2] Muffs, and Danes,
That with the halberd, lance, and murdering axe,
Will hazard that we might with surety hold.

ORCANES: Though from the shortest northern parallel,
Vast Grantland, compass'd with the frozen sea,
(Inhabited with tall and sturdy men,
Giants as big as hugy Polypheme,)
Millions of soldiers cut the arctic line,

30 Bringing the strength of Europe to these arms,
Our Turkey blades shall glide through all their throats,
And make this champion mead a bloody fen;
Danubius' stream, that runs to Trebizon,
Shall carry, wrapt within his scarlet waves,
As martial presents to our friends at home,
The slaughter'd bodies of these Christians;
The Terrene main, wherein Danubius falls,
Shall by this battle be the bloody sea;
The wandering sailors of proud Italy

40 Shall meet those Christians fleeting with the tide,
Beating in heaps against their argosies,
And make fair Europe, mounted on her bull,
Trapp'd with the wealth and riches of the world,
Alight, and wear a woeful mourning weed.

GAZELLUS: Yet, stout Orcanes, Prorex of the world,
Since Tamburlaine hath muster'd all his men,

17 *Guyron*: town north-east of Aleppo.
26 *Grantland*: Greenland.   28 *Polypheme*: the Cyclops.
32 *champion*: country, meadow-land.
37 *Terrene*: Mediterranean.   45 *Prorex*: viceroy.

Marching from Cairon northward with his camp,
To Alexandria and the frontier towns,
Meaning to make a conquest of our land,
'Tis requisite to parley for a peace   50
With Sigismund, the king of Hungary,
And save our forces for the hot assaults
Proud Tamburlaine intends Natolia.
ORCANES: Viceroy of Byron, wisely hast thou said.
My realm, the centre of our empery,
Once lost, all Turkey would be overthrown;
And for that cause the Christians shall have peace.
Sclavonians, Almains, Rutters, Muffs, and Danes,
Fear not Orcanes, but great Tamburlaine;
Nor he, but Fortune that hath made him great.   60
We have revolted Grecians, Albanese,
Sicilians, Jews, Arabians, Turks, and Moors,
Natolians, Sorians, black Egyptians,
Illyrians, Thracians, and Bithynians,
Enough to swallow forceless Sigismund,
Yet scarce enough t' encounter Tamburlaine.
He brings a world of people to the field,
From Scythia to the oriental plage
Of India, where ranging Lantchidol
Beats on the regions with his boisterous blows,   70
That never seaman yet discovered.
All Asia is in arms with Tamburlaine,
Even from the midst of fiery Cancer's tropic
To Amazonia under Capricorn;
And thence, as far as Archipelago,
All Afric is in arms with Tamburlaine:
Therefore, viceroys, the Christians must have peace.

69 *Lantchidol*: sea shown on old maps bordering unexplored land
of North West Australia.

SCENE TWO

Enter SIGISMUND, FREDERICK, BALDWIN, *and*
their TRAIN, *with drums and trumpets.*

SIGISMUND: Orcanes, as our legates promis'd thee,
We, with our peers, have cross'd Danubius' stream,
To treat of friendly peace or deadly war.
Take which thou wilt; for, as the Romans us'd,
I here present thee with a naked sword.
Wilt thou have war, then shake this blade at me;
If peace, restore it to my hands again,
And I will sheathe it, to confirm the same.

ORCANES: Stay, Sigismund: forgett'st thou I am he
10   That with the cannon shook Vienna walls,
And made it dance upon the continent,
As when the massy substance of the earth
 Quiver about the axle-tree of heaven?
Forgett'st thou that I sent a shower of darts,
Mingled with powder'd shot and feather'd steel,
So thick upon the blink-ey'd burghers' heads,
That thou thyself, then County Palatine,
The King of Boheme, and the Austric Duke,
Sent heralds out, which basely on their knees,
20   In all your names, desir'd a truce of me?
Forgett'st thou that, to have me raise my siege,
Waggons of gold were set before my tent,
Stampt with the princely fowl that in her wings
Carries the fearful thunderbolt of Jove?
How canst thou think of this, and offer war?

SIGISMUND: Vienna was besieg'd, and I was there,
Then County Palatine, but now a king,
And what we did was in extremity.
But now, Orcanes, view my royal host,
30   That hides these plains, and seems as vast and wide
As doth the desert of Arabia
To those that stand on Badgeth's lofty tower,

32 *Badgeth*: Bagdad.

186

Or as the ocean to the traveller
That rests upon the snowy Appenines;
And tell me whether I should stoop so low,
Or treat of peace with the Natolian king.

GAZELLUS: Kings of Natolia and of Hungary,
We came from Turkey to confirm a league,
And not to dare each other to the field.
A friendly parle might become you both.   *40*

FREDERICK: And we from Europe, to the same intent;
Which if your general refuse or scorn,
Our tents are pitch'd, our men stand in array,
Ready to charge you ere you stir your feet.

ORCANES: So prest are we: but yet, if Sigismund
Speak as a friend, and stand not upon terms,
Here is his sword; let peace be ratified
On these conditions specified before,
Drawn with advice of our ambassadors.

SIGISMUND: Then here I sheathe it, and give thee my   *50*
hand,
Never to draw it out, or manage arms
Against thyself or thy confederates,
But, whilst I live, will be at truce with thee.

ORCANES: But, Sigismund, confirm it with an oath,
And swear in sight of heaven and by thy Christ.

SIGISMUND: By Him that made the world and sav'd my
soul,
The Son of God and issue of a maid,
Sweet Jesus Christ, I solemnly protest
And vow to keep this peace inviolable!

ORCANES: By sacred Mahomet, the friend of God,   *60*
Whose holy Alcoran remains with us,
Whose glorious body, when he left the world,
Clos'd in a coffin mounted up the air,
And hung on stately Mecca's temple roof,
I swear to keep this truce inviolable!
Of whose conditions and our solemn oaths,

45 *prest*: prepared.

187

Sign'd with our hands, each shall retain a scroll,
As memorable witness of our league.
Now, Sigismund, if any Christian king
70 Encroach upon the confines of thy realm,
Send word, Orcanes of Natolia
Confirm'd this league beyond Danubius' stream,
And they will, trembling, sound a quick retreat.
So am I fear'd among all nations.

SIGISMUND: If any heathen potentate or king
Invade Natolia, Sigismund will send
A hundred thousand horse train'd to the war,
And back'd by stout lanciers of Germany,
The strength and sinews of the imperial seat.

80 ORCANES: I thank thee, Sigismund; but when I war,
All Asia Minor, Africa and Greece
Follow my standard and my thundering drums.
Come, let us go and banquet in our tents.
I will despatch chief of my army hence
To fair Natolia and to Trebizon,
To stay my coming 'gainst proud Tamburlaine.
Friend Sigismund, and peers of Hungary,
Come banquet and carouse with us a while,
And then depart we to our territories.
Exeunt.

SCENE THREE

Enter CALLAPINE, *and* ALMEDA *his keeper*.

CALLAPINE: Sweet Almeda, pity the ruthful plight
Of Callapine, the son of Bajazeth,
Born to be monarch of the western world,
Yet here detain'd by cruel Tamburlaine.

ALMEDA: My lord, I pity it, and with my heart
Wish your release; but he whose wrath is death,
My sovereign lord, renowmed Tamburlaine,
Forbids you further liberty than this.

CALLAPINE: Ah, were I now but half so eloquent
  To paint in words what I'll perform in deeds,   *10*
  I know thou wouldst depart from hence with me.
ALMEDA: Not for all Afric: therefore move me not.
CALLAPINE: Yet hear me speak, my gentle Almeda.
ALMEDA: No speech to that end, by your favour, sir.
CALLAPINE: By Cairo runs –
ALMEDA: No talk of running, I tell you, sir.
CALLAPINE: A little further, gentle Almeda.
ALMEDA: Well, sir, what of this?
CALLAPINE: By Cairo runs to Alexandria bay
  Darotes' stream, wherein at anchor lies   *20*
  A Turkish galley of my royal fleet,
  Waiting my coming to the river-side,
  Hoping by some means I shall be releas'd;
  Which, when I come aboard, will hoist up sail,
  And soon put forth into the Terrene sea,
  Where, 'twixt the isles of Cyprus and of Crete,
  We quickly may in Turkish seas arrive.
  Then shalt thou see a hundred kings and more,
  Upon their knees, all bid me welcome home.
  Amongst so many crowns of burnish'd gold,   *30*
  Choose which thou wilt, all are at thy command.
  A thousand galleys, mann'd with Christian slaves,
  I freely give thee, which shall cut the Straits,
  And bring armadoes from the coasts of Spain,
  Fraughted with gold of rich America.
  The Grecian virgins shall attend on thee,
  Skilful in music and in amorous lays,
  As fair as was Pygmalion's ivory girl
  Or lovely Iö metamorphosed.
  With naked negroes shall thy coach be drawn,   *40*
  And, as thou rid'st in triumph through the streets,
  The pavement underneath thy chariot wheels
  With Turkey carpets will be covered,
  And cloth of arras hung about the walls,
  Fit objects for thy princely eye to pierce.

A hundred bassoes, cloth'd in crimson silk,
Shall ride before thee on Barbarian steeds;
And, when thou goest, a golden canopy
Enchas'd with precious stones, which shine as bright
50 As that fair veil that covers all the world,
When Phoebus, leaping from his hemisphere,
Descendeth downward to th' Antipodes:
And more than this, for all I cannot tell.

ALMEDA: How far hence lies the galley, say you?

CALLAPINE: Sweet Almeda, scarce half a league from
hence.

ALMEDA: But need we not be spied going aboard?

CALLAPINE: Betwixt the hollow hanging of a hill,
And crooked bending of a craggy rock,
The sails wrapt up, the mast and tacklings down,
60 She lies so close that none can find her out.

ALMEDA: I like that well. But tell me, my lord, if I
should let you go, would you be as good as your word?
Shall I be made a king for my labour?

CALLAPINE: As I am Callapine the emperor,
And by the hand of Mahomet I swear,
Thou shalt be crown'd a king, and be my mate!

ALMEDA: Then here I swear, as I am Almeda,
Your keeper under Tamburlaine the Great,
(For that's the style and title I have yet,)
70 Although he sent a thousand armed men
To intercept this haughty enterprise,
Yet would I venture to conduct your grace,
And die before I brought you back again!

CALLAPINE: Thanks, gentle Almeda. Then let us haste,
Lest time be past, and lingering let us both.

ALMEDA: When you will, my lord: I am ready.

CALLAPINE: Even straight: and farewell, cursed
Tamburlaine!
Now go I to revenge my father's death.
Exeunt.

75 *let*: prevent.

SCENE FOUR

Enter TAMBURLAINE, ZENOCRATE, *and their*
three sons, CALYPHAS, AMYRAS, *and* CELEBINUS,
with drums and trumpets.

TAMBURLAINE: Now, bright Zenocrate, the world's
    fair eye,
Whose beams illuminate the lamps of heaven,
Whose cheerful looks do clear the cloudy air,
And clothe it in a crystal livery,
Now rest thee here on fair Larissa plains,
Where Egypt and the Turkish empire parts,
Between thy sons, that shall be emperors,
And every one commander of a world.
ZENOCRATE: Sweet Tamburlaine, when wilt thou leave
    these arms,
And save thy sacred person free from scathe,   *10*
And dangerous chances of the wrathful war?
TAMBURLAINE: When heaven shall cease to move on
    both the poles,
And when the ground, whereon my soldiers march,
Shall rise aloft and touch the horned moon,
And not before, my sweet Zenocrate.
Sit up, and rest thee like a lovely queen.
So; now she sits in pomp and majesty,
When these, my sons, more precious in mine eyes
Than all the wealthy kingdoms I subdu'd,
Plac'd by her side, look on their mother's face.   *20*
But yet methinks their looks are amorous,
Not martial as the sons of Tamburlaine.
Water and air, being symbolis'd in one,
Argue their want of courage and of wit;
Their hair as white as milk, and soft as down,
Which should be like the quills of porcupines,
As black as jet, and hard as iron or steel,

5 *Larissa*: coastal town, south of Gaza.

Bewrays they are too dainty for the wars.
Their fingers made to quaver on a lute,
30   Their arms to hang about a lady's neck,
Their legs to dance and caper in the air,
Would make me think them bastards, not my sons,
But that I know they issu'd from thy womb,
That never look'd on man but Tamburlaine.
ZENOCRATE: My gracious lord, they have their mother's
    looks,
But, when they list, their conquering father's heart.
This lovely boy, the youngest of the three,
Not long ago bestrid a Scythian steed,
Trotting the ring, and tilting at a glove,
40   Which when he tainted with his slender rod,
He rein'd him straight, and made him so curvet
As I cried out for fear he should have faln.
TAMBURLAINE: Well done, my boy! Thou shalt have
    shield and lance,
Armour of proof, horse, helm, and curtle-axe,
And I will teach thee how to charge thy foe,
And harmless run among the deadly pikes.
If thou wilt love the wars and follow me,
Thou shalt be made a king and reign with me,
Keeping in iron cages emperors.
50   If thou exceed thy elder brothers' worth,
And shine in complete virtue more than they,
Thou shalt be king before them, and thy seed
Shall issue crowned from their mother's womb.
CELEBINUS: Yes, father; you shall see me, if I live,
Have under me as many kings as you,
And march with such a multitude of men
As all the world shall tremble at their view.
TAMBURLAINE: These words assure me, boy, thou art
    my son.
When I am old and cannot manage arms,

40 *tainted*: struck.
41 *curvet*: leap with all the horse's legs off the ground.

Be thou the scourge and terror of the world.   *60*

AMYRAS: Why may not I, my lord, as well as he,
Be term'd the scourge and terror of the world?

TAMBURLAINE: Be all a scourge and terror to the
world,
Or else you are not sons of Tamburlaine.

CALYPHAS: But while my brothers follow arms, my lord,
Let me accompany my gracious mother.
They are enough to conquer all the world,
And you have won enough for me to keep.

TAMBURLAINE: Bastardly boy, sprung from some
coward's loins,
And not the issue of great Tamburlaine!   *70*
Of all the provinces I have subdu'd
Thou shalt not have a foot, unless thou bear
A mind courageous and invincible.
For he shall wear the crown of Persia
Whose head hath deepest scars, whose breast most
wounds,
Which, being wroth, sends lightning from his eyes,
And in the furrows of his frowning brows
Harbours revenge, war, death, and cruelty;
For in a field, whose superficies
Is cover'd with a liquid purple veil,   *80*
And sprinkled with the brains of slaughter'd men,
My royal chair of state shall be advanc'd;
And he that means to place himself therein,
Must armed wade up to the chin in blood.

ZENOCRATE: My lord, such speeches to our princely
sons
Dismays their minds before they come to prove
The wounding troubles angry war affords.

CELEBINUS: No, madam, these are speeches fit for us;
For, if his chair were in a sea of blood,
I would prepare a ship and sail to it,   *90*
Ere I would lose the title of a king.

79 *superficies*: surface (Octavo editions have 'superfluities').

AMYRAS: And I would strive to swim through pools of blood
Or make a bridge of murder'd carcasses,
Whose arches should be fram'd with bones of Turks,
Ere I would lose the title of a king.

TAMBURLAINE: Well, lovely boys, ye shall be emperors both,
Stretching your conquering arms from east to west.
And, sirrah, if you mean to wear a crown,
When we shall meet the Turkish deputy
100 And all his viceroys, snatch it from his head,
And cleave his pericranion with thy sword.

CALYPHAS: If any man will hold him, I will strike,
And cleave him to the channel with my sword.

TAMBURLAINE: Hold him, and cleave him too, or I'll cleave thee,
For we will march against them presently.
Theridamas, Techelles, and Casane
Promis'd to meet me on Larissa plains,
With hosts a-piece against this Turkish crew;
For I have sworn by sacred Mahomet
110 To make it parcel of my empery.
The trumpets sound; Zenocrate, they come.

SCENE FIVE

Enter THERIDAMAS, *and his* TRAIN, *with drums and trumpets.*

TAMBURLAINE: Welcome Theridamas, king of Argier.

THERIDAMAS: My lord, the great and mighty Tamburlaine,
Arch-monarch of the world, I offer here
My crown, myself, and all the power I have,
In all affection at thy kingly feet.

TAMBURLAINE: Thanks, good Theridamas.

101 *pericranion*: skull.

THERIDAMAS: Under my colours march ten thousand Greeks,
And of Argier and Afric's frontier towns
Twice twenty thousand valiant men-at-arms,
All which have sworn to sack Natolia.   *10*
Five hundred brigandines are under sail,
Meet for your service on the sea, my lord,
That, launching from Argier to Tripoly,
Will quickly ride before Natolia,
And batter down the castles on the shore.

TAMBURLAINE: Well said, Argier! Receive thy crown again.

SCENE SIX

Enter USUMCASANE *and* TECHELLES.

TAMBURLAINE: Kings of Moroccus and of Fesse, welcome.

USUMCASANE: Magnificent and peerless Tamburlaine,
I and my neighbour king of Fesse have brought,
To aid thee in this Turkish expedition,
A hundred thousand expert soldiers.
From Azamor to Tunis near the sea
Is Barbary unpeopled for thy sake,
And all the men, in armour under me,
Which with my crown I gladly offer thee.

TAMBURLAINE: Thanks, king of Moroccus: take your   *10*
crown again.

TECHELLES: And, mighty Tamburlaine, our earthly god,
Whose looks make this inferior world to quake,
I here present thee with the crown of Fesse,
And with an host of Moors train'd to the war,
Whose coal-black faces make their foes retire,
And quake for fear, as if infernal Jove,

16 *infernal Jove*: Pluto.

Meaning to aid thee in these Turkish arms,
Should pierce the black circumference of hell,
With ugly Furies bearing fiery flags,
20 And millions of his strong tormenting spirits:
From strong Tesella unto Biledull
All Barbary is unpeopled for thy sake.

TAMBURLAINE: Thanks, king of Fesse: take here thy
crown again.
Your presence, loving friends and fellow-kings,
Makes me to surfeit in conceiving joy.
If all the crystal gates of Jove's high court
Were open'd wide, and I might enter in
To see the state and majesty of heaven,
It could not more delight me than your sight.
30 Now will we banquet on these plains a while,
And after march to Turkey with our camp,
In number more than are the drops that fall
When Boreas rents a thousand swelling clouds;
And proud Orcanes of Natolia
With all his viceroys shall be so afraid,
That, though the stones, as at Deucalion's flood,[3]
Were turn'd to men, he should be overcome.
Such lavish will I make of Turkish blood,
That Jove shall send his winged messenger
40 To bid me sheathe my sword and leave the field;
The sun, unable to sustain the sight,
Shall hide his head in Thetis' watery lap,
And leave his steeds to fair Boötes' charge;
For half the world shall perish in this fight.
But now, my friends, let me examine ye;
How have ye spent your absent time from me?

USUMCASANE: My lord, our men of Barbary have
march'd
Four hundred miles with armour on their backs,
And lain in leaguer fifteen months and more;
50 For since we left you at the Soldan's court,

49 *leaguer*: camp, besieging cities.

196

We have subdu'd the southern Guallatia,
And all the land unto the coast of Spain.
We kept the narrow Strait of Gibralter,
And made Canaria call us kings and lords.
Yet never did they recreate themselves,
Or cease one day from war and hot alarms;
And therefore let them rest a while, my lord.

TAMBURLAINE: They shall, Casane, and 'tis time, i'faith.

TECHELLES: And I have march'd along the river Nile
 To Machda, where the mighty Christian priest,   *60*
 Call'd John the Great, sits in a milk-white robe,
 Whose triple mitre I did take by force,
 And made him swear obedience to my crown.
 From thence unto Cazates did I march,
 Where Amazonians met me in the field,
 With whom, being women, I vouchsaf'd a league,
 And with my power did march to Zanzibar,
 The western part of Afric, where I view'd
 The Ethiopian sea, rivers and lakes,
 But neither man nor child in all the land.   *70*
 Therefore I took my course to Manico,
 Where, unresisted, I remov'd my camp;
 And, by the coast of Byather, at last
 I came to Cubar, where the negroes dwell,
 And, conquering that, made haste to Nubia;
 There, having sack'd Borno, the kingly seat,
 I took the king and led him bound in chains
 Unto Damasco, where I stay'd before.

TAMBURLAINE: Well done, Techelles! What saith
 Theridamas?

THERIDAMAS: I left the confines and the bounds of   *80*
 Afric,
 And made a voyage into Europe,
 Where, by the river Tyras, I subdu'd
 Stoka, Podolia, and Codemia;
 Then cross'd the sea and came to Oblia,
 And Nigra Silva, where the devils dance,

Which, in despite of them, I set on fire.
From thence I cross'd the gulf call'd by the name
Mare Majore of the inhabitants.
Yet shall my soldiers make no period
90   Until Natolia kneel before your feet.
TAMBURLAINE: Then will we triumph, banquet, and
    carouse;
Cooks shall have pensions to provide us cates,
And glut us with the dainties of the world;
Lachryma Christi and Calabrian wines
Shall common soldiers drink in quaffing bowls,
Ay, liquid gold, when we have conquer'd him,
Mingled with coral and with orient[4] pearl.
Come, let us banquet and carouse the whiles.
   Exeunt.

ACT TWO

SCENE ONE

Enter SIGISMUND, FREDERICK, *and* BALDWIN,
with their TRAIN.

SIGISMUND: Now say, my lords of Buda and Bohemia,
What motion is it that inflames your thoughts,
And stirs your valours to such sudden arms?
FREDERICK: Your majesty remembers, I am sure,
What cruel slaughter of our Christian bloods
These heathenish Turks and pagans lately made
Betwixt the city Zula[5] and Danubius;
How through the midst of Varna and Bulgaria,
And almost to the very walls of Rome,
10   They have, not long since, massacred our camp.
It resteth now, then, that your majesty
Take all advantages of time and power,

89 *period*: stop, end.   7 *Zula*: north of the Danube.
9 *Rome*: Romania, north of Constantinople.

And work revenge upon these infidels.
Your highness knows, for Tamburlaine's repair,
That strikes a terror to all Turkish hearts,
Natolia hath dismiss'd the greatest part
Of all his army, pitch'd against our power
Betwixt Cutheia and Orminius' mount,
And sent them marching up to Belgasar,
Acantha, Antioch, and Caesarea,   20
To aid the kings of Soria and Jerusalem.
Now, then, my lord, advantage take hereof,
And issue suddenly upon the rest,
That, in the fortune of their overthrow,
We may discourage all the pagan troop
That dare attempt to war with Christians.

SIGISMUND: But calls not, then, your grace to memory
The league we lately made with King Orcanes,
Confirm'd by oath and articles of peace,
And calling Christ for record of our truths?   30
This should be treachery and violence
Against the grace of our profession.

BALDWIN: No whit, my lord, for with such infidels,
In whom no faith nor true religion rests,
We are not bound to those accomplishments
The holy laws of Christendom enjoin;
But, as the faith which they profanely plight
Is not by necessary policy
To be esteem'd assurance for ourselves,
So what we vow to them should not infringe   40
Our liberty of arms and victory.

SIGISMUND: Though I confess the oaths they undertake
Breed little strength to our security,
Yet those infirmities that thus defame
Their faiths, their honours, and their religion,
Should not give us presumption to the like.
Our faiths are sound, and must be consummate,[6]
Religious, righteous, and inviolate.

FREDERICK: Assure your grace, 'tis superstition

50   To stand so strictly on dispensive faith,
   And, should we lose the opportunity
   That God hath given to venge our Christians' death,
   And scourge their foul blasphemous paganism,
   As fell to Saul,[7] to Balaam,[8] and the rest,
   That would not kill and curse at God's command,
   So surely will the vengeance of the Highest,
   And jealous anger of his fearful arm,
   Be pour'd with rigour on our sinful heads,
   If we neglect this offer'd victory.

60 SIGISMUND: Then arm, my lords, and issue suddenly,
   Giving commandment to our general host,
   With expedition to assail the pagan,
   And take the victory our God hath given.
     Exeunt.

SCENE TWO

Enter ORCANES, GAZELLUS, *and* URIBASSA,
with their TRAIN.

ORCANES: Gazellus, Uribassa and the rest,
   Now will we march from proud Orminius' mount
   To fair Natolia, where our neighbour kings
   Expect our power and our royal presence,
   T' encounter with the cruel Tamburlaine,
   That nigh Larissa sways a mighty host,
   And with the thunder of his martial tools
   Makes earthquakes in the hearts of men and heaven.

GAZELLUS: And now come we to make his sinews shake
10   With greater power than erst his pride hath felt.
   An hundred kings, by scores, will bid him arms,
   And hundred thousands subjects to each score:
   Which, if a shower of wounding thunderbolts
   Should break out of the bowels of the clouds,
   And fall as thick as hail upon our heads,
   In partial aid to that proud Scythian,

Yet should our courages and steeled crests,
And numbers more than infinite of men,
Be able to withstand and conquer him.

URIBASSA: Methinks I see how glad the Christian king   20
Is made for joy of our admitted truce,
That could not but before be terrified
With unacquainted power of our host.

Enter a MESSENGER.

MESSENGER: Arm, dread sovereign, and my noble lords!
The treacherous army of the Christians,
Taking advantage of your slender power,
Comes marching on us, and determines straight
To bid us battle for our dearest lives.

ORCANES: Traitors, villains, damned Christians!
Have I not here the articles of peace   30
And solemn covenants we have both confirm'd,
He by his Christ, and I by Mahomet?

GAZELLUS: Hell and confusion light upon their heads,
That with such treason seek our overthrow,
And cares so little for their prophet Christ!

ORCANES: Can there be such deceit in Christians,
Or treason in the fleshly heart of man,
Whose shape is figure of the highest God?
Then, if there be a Christ, as Christians say,
But in their deeds deny him for their Christ,   40
If he be son to everliving Jove,
And hath the power of his outstretched arm,
If he be jealous of his name and honour
As is our holy prophet Mahomet,
Take here these papers as our sacrifice
And witness to thy servant's perjury!

He tears to pieces the articles of peace.

Open, thou shining veil of Cynthia,
And make a passage from th' empyreal heaven,
That he that sits on high and never sleeps,
Nor in one place is circumscriptible,   50
But everywhere fills every continent

With strange infusion of his sacred vigour,
May, in his endless power and purity,
Behold and venge this traitor's perjury!
Thou, Christ, that art esteem'd omnipotent,
If thou wilt prove thyself a perfect God,
Worthy the worship of all faithful hearts,
Be now reveng'd upon this traitor's soul,
And make the power I have left behind
60 (Too little to defend our guiltless lives)
Sufficient to discomfit and confound
The trustless force of those false Christians!
To arms, my lords! On Christ still let us cry:
If there be Christ, we shall have victory.
Exeunt.

SCENE THREE

Alarms of battle within. Enter SIGISMUND *wounded.*
SIGISMUND: Discomfited is all the Christian host,
And God hath thunder'd vengeance from on high,
For my accurs'd and hateful perjury.
O just and dreadful punisher of sin,
Let the dishonour of the pains I feel
In this my mortal well-deserved wound
End all my penance in my sudden death!
And let this death, wherein to sin I die,
Conceive a second life in endless mercy!
Dies.

Enter ORCANES, GAZELLUS, URIBASSA, *with others.*
10 ORCANES: Now lie the Christians bathing in their bloods,
And Christ or Mahomet hath been my friend.
GAZELLUS: See here the perjur'd traitor Hungary,
Bloody and breathless for his villainy!
ORCANES: Now shall his barbarous body be a prey
To beasts and fowls, and all the winds shall breathe
Through shady leaves of every senseless tree,

Murmurs and hisses for his heinous sin.
Now scalds his soul in the Tartarian streams,
And feeds upon the baneful tree of hell,
That Zoacum,[9] that fruit of bitterness,   *20*
That in the midst of fire is ingraff'd,
Yet flourisheth as Flora in her pride,
With apples like the heads of damned fiends.
The devils there, in chains of quenchless flame,
Shall lead his soul through Orcus' burning gulf,
From pain to pain, whose change shall never end.
What say'st thou yet, Gazellus, to his foil,
Which we referr'd to justice of his Christ
And to his power, which here appears as full
As rays of Cynthia to the clearest sight?   *30*
GAZELLUS: 'Tis but the fortune of the wars, my lord,
  Whose power is often prov'd a miracle.
ORCANES: Yet in my thoughts shall Christ be honoured,
  Not doing Mahomet an injury,
  Whose power had share in this our victory;
  And since this miscreant hath disgrac'd his faith,
  And died a traitor both to heaven and earth,
  We will both watch and ward shall keep his trunk
  Amidst these plains for fowls to prey upon.
  Go, Uribassa, give it straight in charge.   *40*
URIBASSA: I will, my lord.
    Exit.
ORCANES: And now, Gazellus, let us haste and meet
  Our army, and our brother of Jerusalem,
  Of Soria, Trebizon, and Amasia,
  And happily, with full Natolian bowls
  Of Greekish wine, now let us celebrate
  Our happy conquest and his angry fate.
    Exeunt.

25 *Orcus*: mouth of hell.   27 *foil*: disgrace.

SCENE FOUR

The arras is drawn, and ZENOCRATE *is discovered
lying in her bed of state;* TAMBURLAINE *sitting by her;
three* PHYSICIANS *about her bed, tempering potions;
her three sons* CALYPHAS, AMYRAS, *and* CELEBINUS;
THERIDAMAS, TECHELLES *and* USUMCASANE.

TAMBURLAINE: Black is the beauty of the brightest day;
The golden ball of heaven's eternal fire,
That danc'd with glory on the silver waves,
Now wants the fuel that inflam'd his beams,
And all with faintness and for foul disgrace,
He binds his temples with a frowning cloud,
Ready to darken earth with endless night.
Zenocrate, that gave him light and life,
Whose eyes shot fire from their ivory bowers,
10 And temper'd every soul with lively heat,
Now by the malice of the angry skies,
Whose jealousy admits no second mate,
Draws in the comfort of her latest breath,
All dazzled with the hellish mists of death.
Now walk the angels on the walls of heaven,
As sentinels to warn th' immortal souls
To entertain divine Zenocrate:
Apollo, Cynthia, and the ceaseless lamps
That gently look'd upon this loathsome earth,
20 Shine downwards now no more, but deck the
        heavens
To entertain divine Zenocrate:
The crystal springs, whose taste illuminates
Refined eyes with an eternal sight,
Like tried silver run through Paradise
To entertain divine Zenocrate:
The cherubins and holy seraphins,
That sing and play before the King of Kings,
Use all their voices and their instruments

To entertain divine Zenocrate:
And in this sweet and curious harmony,   *30*
The god that tunes this music to our souls
Holds out his hand in highest majesty
To entertain divine Zenocrate.
Then let some holy trance convey my thoughts
Up to the palace of th' empyreal heaven,
That this my life may be as short to me
As are the days of sweet Zenocrate.
Physicians, will no physic do her good?
FIRST PHYSICIAN: My lord, your majesty shall soon
    perceive,
And if she pass this fit, the worst is past.   *40*
TAMBURLAINE: Tell me, how fares my fair Zenocrate?
ZENOCRATE: I fare, my lord, as other empresses,
    That, when this frail and transitory flesh
    Hath suck'd the measure of that vital air
    That feeds the body with his dated health,
    Wanes with enforc'd and necessary change.
TAMBURLAINE: May never such a change transform my
    love,
    In whose sweet being I repose my life;
    Whose heavenly presence, beautified with health,
    Gives light to Phoebus and the fixed stars;   *50*
    Whose absence makes the sun and moon as dark
    As when, oppos'd in one diameter,
    Their spheres are mounted on the serpent's head,[10]
    Or else descended to his winding train.
    Live still, my love, and so conserve my life,
    Or, dying, be the author of my death.
ZENOCRATE: Live still, my lord! O, let my sovereign
    live!
    And sooner let the fiery element
    Dissolve, and make your kingdom in the sky,
    Than this base earth should shroud your majesty;   *60*
    For, should I but suspect your death by mine,
    The comfort of my future happiness,

And hope to meet your highness in the heavens,
Turn'd to despair, would break my wretched breast,
And fury would confound my present rest.
But let me die, my love; yet, let me die;
With love and patience let your true love die:
Your grief and fury hurts my second life.
Yet let me kiss my lord before I die,
70 And let me die with kissing of my lord.
But, since my life is lengthen'd yet a while,
Let me take leave of these my loving sons,
And of my lords, whose true nobility
Have merited my latest memory.
Sweet sons, farewell! In death resemble me,
And in your lives your father's excellence.
Some music, and my fit will cease, my lord.
> *They call for music.*

TAMBURLAINE: Proud fury, and intolerable fit,
That dares torment the body of my love,
80 And scourge the Scourge of the immortal God!
Now are those spheres, where Cupid us'd to sit,
Wounding the world with wonder and with love,
Sadly supplied with pale and ghastly death,
Whose darts do pierce the centre of my soul.
Her sacred beauty hath enchanted heaven,
And, had she liv'd before the siege of Troy,
Helen, whose beauty summon'd Greece to arms,
And drew a thousand ships to Tenedos,
Had not been nam'd in Homer's Iliads:
90 Her name had been in every line he wrote.
Or, had those wanton poets, for whose birth
Old Rome was proud, but gaz'd a while on her,
Nor Lesbia nor Corinna had been nam'd:
Zenocrate had been the argument
Of every epigram or elegy.
> *The music sounds and* ZENOCRATE *dies.*

What, is she dead? Techelles, draw thy sword,

93 *Lesbia*: celebrated by Catullus, as Corinna by Ovid.

And wound the earth, that it may cleave in twain,
And we descend into th' infernal vaults,
To hale the Fatal Sisters by the hair,
And throw them in the triple moat of hell,   *100*
For taking hence my fair Zenocrate.
Casane and Theridamas, to arms!
Raise cavalieros higher than the clouds,
And with the cannon break the frame of heaven;
Batter the shining palace of the sun,
And shiver all the starry firmament,
For amorous Jove hath snatch'd my love from hence,
Meaning to make her stately queen of heaven.
What god soever holds thee in his arms,
Giving thee nectar and ambrosia,   *110*
Behold me here, divine Zenocrate,
Raving, impatient, desperate and mad,
Breaking my steeled lance, with which I burst
The rusty beams of Janus' temple doors,
Letting out Death and tyrannising War,
To march with me under this bloody flag!
And, if thou pitiest Tamburlaine the Great,
Come down from heaven and live with me again!
THERIDAMAS: Ah, good my lord, be patient! She is dead,
And all this raging cannot make her live.   *120*
If words might serve, our voice hath rent the air;
If tears, our eyes have water'd all the earth;
If grief, our murder'd hearts have strained forth blood.
Nothing prevails, for she is dead, my lord.
TAMBURLAINE: *For she is dead!* Thy words do pierce my
    soul:
Ah, sweet Theridamas, say so no more!
Though she be dead, yet let me think she lives,
And feed my mind that dies for want of her.
Where'er her soul be, thou shalt stay with me,
Embalm'd with cassia, ambergris, and myrrh,   *130*
Not lapt in lead, but in a sheet of gold,

114 *Janus*: the temple doors were shut in peacetime, open in war.

And, till I die, thou shalt not be interr'd.
Then in as rich a tomb as Mausolus'
We both will rest, and have one epitaph
Writ in as many several languages
As I have conquer'd kingdoms with my sword.
This cursed town will I consume with fire,
Because this place bereft me of my love.
The houses, burnt, will look as if they mourn'd;
140 And here will I set up her statua,
And march about it with my mourning camp,
Drooping and pining for Zenocrate.
    The arras is drawn.

ACT THREE

SCENE ONE

Enter the KINGS OF TREBIZON *and* SORIA, *one
bringing a sword and the other a sceptre; next* ORCANES
king of Natolia, and the KING OF JERUSALEM *with
the imperial crown; after,* CALLAPINE; *and, after him,
other* LORDS *and* ALMEDA. ORCANES *and the*
KING OF JERUSALEM *crown* CALLAPINE, *and the
others give him the sceptre.*

ORCANES: Callapinus Cyricelibes, otherwise Cybelius,
son and successive heir to the late mighty emperor
Bajazeth, by the aid of God and his friend Mahomet,
Emperor of Natolia, Jerusalem, Trebizon, Soria,
Amasia, Thracia, Ilyria, Carmonia, and all the hundred
and thirty kingdoms late contributory to his mighty
father, – long live Callapinus, Emperor of Turkey!
CALLAPINE: Thrice-worthy kings of Natolia and the rest,
I will requite your royal gratitudes
10 With all the benefits my empire yields;
And, were the sinews of th' imperial seat
So knit and strengthen'd as when Bajazeth,

My royal lord and father, fill'd the throne,
Whose cursed fate hath so dismember'd it,
Then should you see this thief of Scythia,
This proud usurping king of Persia,
Do us such honour and supremacy,
Bearing the vengeance of our father's wrongs,
As all the world should blot our dignities
Out of the book of base-born infamies.   20
And now I doubt not but your royal cares
Hath so provided for this cursed foe,
That, since the heir of mighty Bajazeth,
An emperor so honour'd for his virtues,
Revives the spirits of true Turkish hearts,
In grievous memory of his father's shame,
We shall not need to nourish any doubt,
But that proud Fortune, who hath follow'd long
The martial sword of mighty Tamburlaine,
Will now retain her old inconstancy,   30
And raise our honour to as high a pitch,
In this our strong and fortunate encounter;
For so hath heaven provided my escape
From all the cruelty my soul sustain'd,
By this my friendly keeper's happy means,
That Jove, surcharg'd with pity of our wrongs,
Will pour it down in showers on our heads,
Scourging the pride of cursed Tamburlaine.
ORCANES. I have a hundred thousand men in arms,
Some that, in conquest of the perjur'd Christian,   40
Being a handful of a mighty host,
Think them in number yet sufficient
To drink the river Nile or Euphrates,
And for their power enow to win the world.
KING OF JERUSALEM: And I as many from Jerusalem,
Judaea, Gaza, and Sclavonia's bounds,
That on Mount Sinai, with their ensigns spread,
Look like the parti-colour'd clouds of heaven
That show fair weather to the neighbour morn.

50 KING OF TREBIZON: And I as many bring from Trebizon,
Chio, Famastro, and Amasia,
All bordering on the Mare-Major sea,
Riso, Sancina, and the bordering towns
That touch the end of famous Euphrates,
Whose courages are kindled with the flames
The cursed Scythian sets on all their towns,
And vow to burn the villain's cruel heart.

KING OF SORIA: From Soria with seventy thousand strong,
Ta'en from Aleppo, Soldino, Tripoly,
60 And so unto my city of Damasco,
I march to meet and aid my neighbour kings;
All which will join against this Tamburlaine,
And bring him captive to your highness' feet.

ORCANES: Our battle, then, in martial manner pitch'd,
According to our ancient use, shall bear
The figure of the semicircled moon,
Whose horns shall sprinkle through the tainted air
The poison'd brains of this proud Scythian.

CALLAPINE: Well then, my noble lords, for this my friend
70 That freed me from the bondage of my foe,
I think it requisite and honourable
To keep my promise and to make him king,
That is a gentleman, I know, at least.

ALMEDA: That's no matter, sir, for being a king; for Tamburlaine came up of nothing.

KING OF JERUSALEM: Your majesty may choose some 'pointed time,
Performing all your promise to the full;
'Tis naught for your majesty to give a kingdom.

CALLAPINE: Then will I shortly keep my promise, Almeda.

ALMEDA: Why, I thank your majesty.
Exeunt.

SCENE TWO

Enter TAMBURLAINE *and his three sons,* CALYPHAS,
AMYRAS, *and* CELEBINUS; USUMCASANE; *four*
ATTENDANTS *bearing the hearse of* ZENOCRATE, *and
the drums sounding a doleful march; the town burning.*

TAMBURLAINE: So burn the turrets of this cursed town,
Flame to the highest region of the air,
And kindle heaps of exhalations,
That, being fiery meteors, may presage
Death and destruction to the inhabitants!
Over my zenith hang a blazing star,
That may endure till heaven be dissolv'd,
Fed with the fresh supply of earthly dregs,
Threatening a death and famine to this land!
Flying dragons, lightning, fearful thunder-claps,   10
Singe these fair plains, and make them seem as black
As is the island where the Furies mask,
Compass'd with Lethe, Styx, and Phlegethon,
Because my dear Zenocrate is dead!
CALYPHAS: This pillar, plac'd in memory of her,
Where in Arabian, Hebrew, Greek, is writ,
*This town, being burnt by Tamburlaine the Great,
Forbids the world to build it up again.*
AMYRAS: And here this mournful streamer shall be
        plac'd,
Wrought with the Persian and Egyptian arms,   20
To signify she was a princess born,
And wife unto the monarch of the East.
CELEBINUS: And here this table as a register
Of all her virtues and perfections.
TAMBURLAINE: And here the picture of Zenocrate,
To show her beauty which the world admir'd;
Sweet picture of divine Zenocrate,
That, hanging here, will draw the gods from heaven,
And cause the stars fix'd in the southern arc,

30   (Whose lovely faces never any view'd
That have not pass'd the centre's latitude,)
As pilgrims travel to our hemisphere,
Only to gaze upon Zenocrate.
Thou shalt not beautify Larissa plains,
But keep within the circle of mine arms.
At every town and castle I besiege,
Thou shalt be set upon my royal tent;
And when I meet an army in the field,
Those looks will shed such influence in my camp,
40   As if Bellona, goddess of the war,
Threw naked swords and sulphur-balls of fire
Upon the heads of all our enemies.
And now, my lords, advance your spears again.
Sorrow no more, my sweet Casane, now.
Boys, leave to mourn; this town shall ever mourn,
Being burnt to cinders for your mother's death.

CALYPHAS: If I had wept a sea of tears for her,
It would not ease the sorrows I sustain.

AMYRAS: As is that town, so is my heart consum'd
50   With grief and sorrow for my mother's death.

CELEBINUS: My mother's death hath mortified my mind,
And sorrow stops the passage of my speech.

TAMBURLAINE: But now, my boys, leave off, and list to
    me,
That mean to teach you rudiments of war.
I'll have you learn to sleep upon the ground,
March in your armour thorough watery fens,
Sustain the scorching heat and freezing cold,
Hunger and thirst, right adjuncts of the war;
And, after this, to scale a castle wall,
60   Besiege a fort, to undermine a town,
And make whole cities caper in the air.
Then next, the way to fortify your men;
In champion grounds what figure serves you best,
For which the quinque-angle form is meet,

63 *champion*: country.

Because the corners there may fall more flat
Whereas the fort may fittest be assail'd,
And sharpest where th' assault is desperate:
The ditches must be deep, the counterscarps
Narrow and steep, the walls made high and broad,
The bulwarks and the rampires large and strong,   70
With cavalieros and thick counterforts,
And room within to lodge six thousand men.
It must have privy ditches, countermines,
And secret issuings to defend the ditch;
It must have high argins and cover'd ways
To keep the bulwark-fronts from battery,
And parapets to hide the musketeers,
Casemates to place the great artillery,
And store of ordnance, that from every flank
May scour the outward curtains of the fort,   80
Dismount the cannon of the adverse part,
Murder the foe, and save the walls from breach.
When this is learn'd for service on the land,
By plain and easy demonstration
I'll teach you how to make the water mount,
That you may dry-foot march through lakes and pools,
Deep rivers, havens, creeks, and little seas,
And make a fortress in the raging waves,
Fenc'd with the concave of a monstrous rock,
Invincible by nature of the place.   90
When this is done, then are ye soldiers,
And worthy sons of Tamburlaine the Great.
CALYPHAS: My lord, but this is dangerous to be done;
We may be slain or wounded ere we learn.
TAMBURLAINE: Villain, art thou the son of Tamburlaine,
And fear'st to die, or with a curtle-axe
To hew thy flesh and make a gaping wound?
Hast thou beheld a peal of ordnance strike
A ring of pikes, mingled with shot and horse,
Whose shatter'd limbs, being toss'd as high as heaven,   100

75 *argins*: earthworks.

213

Hang in the air as thick as sunny motes,
And canst thou, coward, stand in fear of death?
Hast thou not seen my horsemen charge the foe,
Shot through the arms, cut overthwart the hands,
Dying their lances with their streaming blood,
And yet at night carouse within my tent,
Filling their empty veins with airy wine,
That, being concocted, turns to crimson blood,
And wilt thou shun the field for fear of wounds?
110 View me, thy father, that hath conquer'd kings,
And with his host march'd round about the earth,
Quite void of scars and clear from any wound,
That by the wars lost not a dram of blood,
And see him lance his flesh to teach you all.
　　He cuts his arm.
A wound is nothing, be it ne'er so deep;
Blood is the god of war's rich livery.
Now look I like a soldier, and this wound
As great a grace and majesty to me,
As if a chair of gold enamelled,
120 Enchas'd with diamonds, sapphires, rubies,
And fairest pearl of wealthy India,
Were mounted here under a canopy,
And I sat down, cloth'd with the massy robe
That late adorn'd the Afric potentate,
Whom I brought bound unto Damascus' walls.
Come, boys, and with your fingers search my wound,
And in my blood wash all your hands at once,
While I sit smiling to behold the sight.
Now, my boys, what think ye of a wound?
130 CALYPHAS: I know not what I should think of it;
　　methinks 'tis a pitiful sight.
CELEBINUS: 'Tis nothing. Give me a wound, father.
AMYRAS: And me another, my lord.
TAMBURLAINE: Come, sirrah, give me your arm.
CELEBINUS: Here, father, cut it bravely, as you did your
　　own.

TAMBURLAINE: It shall suffice thou dar'st abide a
   wound.
   My boy, thou shalt not lose a drop of blood
   Before we meet the army of the Turk;
   But then run desperate through the thickest throngs,
   Dreadless of blows, of bloody wounds, and death;
   And let the burning of Larissa walls,   140
   My speech of war, and this my wound you see,
   Teach you, my boys, to bear courageous minds,
   Fit for the followers of great Tamburlaine.
   Usumcasane, now come, let us march
   Towards Techelles and Theridamas,
   That we have sent before to fire the towns,
   The towers and cities of these hateful Turks,
   And hunt that coward faint-heart runaway,
   With that accursed traitor Almeda,
   Till fire and sword have found them at a bay.   150
USUMCASANE: I long to pierce his bowels with my
   sword,
   That hath betray'd my gracious sovereign,
   That curs'd and damned traitor Almeda.
TAMBURLAINE: Then let us see if coward Callapine
   Dare levy arms against our puissance,
   That we may tread upon his captive neck,
   And treble all his father's slaveries.
   Exeunt.

SCENE THREE

Enter TECHELLES, THERIDAMAS, *and their* TRAIN.
THERIDAMAS: Thus have we march'd northward from
   Tamburlaine,
   Unto the frontier point of Soria;
   And this is Balsera, their chiefest hold,
   Wherein is all the treasure of the land.
TECHELLES: Then let us bring our light artillery,
   Minions, falc'nets, and sakers, to the trench,
   6 *minions*: small pieces of ordinance.

215

Filling the ditches with the walls' wide breach,
And enter in to seize upon the gold.
How say you, soldiers, shall we not?
10 SOLDIERS: Yes, my lord, yes. Come, let's about it.
THERIDAMAS: But stay a while; summon a parle, drum.
It may be they will yield it quietly,
Knowing two kings, the friends to Tamburlaine,
Stand at the walls with such a mighty power.
      A parley sounded. CAPTAIN *appears on the walls, with*
      OLYMPIA *his wife, and his* SON.
CAPTAIN: What require you, my masters?
THERIDAMAS: Captain, that thou yield up thy hold to
      us.
CAPTAIN: To you! Why, do you think me weary of it?
TECHELLES: Nay, captain, thou art weary of thy life,
If thou withstand the friends of Tamburlaine.
20 THERIDAMAS: These pioners of Argier in Africa,
Even in the cannon's face, shall raise a hill
Of earth and faggots higher than thy fort,
And, over thy argins and cover'd ways,
Shall play upon the bulwarks of thy hold
Volleys of ordnance, till the breach be made
That with his ruin fills up all the trench;
And, when we enter in, not heaven itself
Shall ransom thee, thy wife, and family.
TECHELLES: Captain, these Moors shall cut the leaden
      pipes
30 That bring fresh water to thy men and thee.
And lie in trench before thy castle walls,
That no supply of victual shall come in,
Nor [any] issue forth but they shall die;
And, therefore, captain, yield it quietly.
CAPTAIN: Were you, that are the friends of Tamburlaine,
Brothers of holy Mahomet himself,
I would not yield it. Therefore do your worst:
Raise mounts, batter, intrench, and undermine,
Cut off the water, all convoys that can,

Yet I am resolute: and so farewell.   *40*

CAPTAIN, OLYMPIA, *and* SON, *retire from the walls.*

THERIDAMAS: Pioners, away! And where I stuck the
   stake,
Intrench with those dimensions I prescrib'd.
Cast up the earth towards the castle wall,
Which, till it may defend you, labour low,
And few or none shall perish by their shot.

PIONERS: We will, my lord.

Exeunt PIONERS.

TECHELLES: A hundred horse shall scout about the
   plains,
To spy what force comes to relieve the hold.
Both we, Theridamas, will intrench our men,
And with the Jacob's staff measure the height   *50*
And distance of the castle from the trench,
That we may know if our artillery
Will carry full point-plank unto their walls.

THERIDAMAS: Then see the bringing of our ordnance
Along the trench into the battery,
Where we will have gabions of six foot broad,
To save our cannoneers from musket-shot;
Betwixt which shall our ordnance thunder forth,
And with the breach's fall, smoke, fire and dust,
The crack, the echo and the soldiers' cry,   *60*
Make deaf the air and dim the crystal sky.

TECHELLES: Trumpets and drums, alarum presently!
And, soldiers, play the men! The hold is yours!

Exeunt.

SCENE FOUR

Alarms within. Enter the CAPTAIN, *with* OLYMPIA
and his SON.

OLYMPIA: Come, good my lord, and let us haste from
   hence,

56 *gabions*: cannon-baskets, like sand-bags.

Along the cave that leads beyond the foe:
No hope is left to save this conquer'd hold.
CAPTAIN: A deadly bullet gliding through my side,
Lies heavy on my heart. I cannot live:
I feel my liver pierc'd, and all my veins,
That there begin and nourish every part,
Mangled and torn, and all my entrails bath'd
In blood that staineth from their orifex.
10 Farewell, sweet wife! sweet son, farewell! I die.
Dies.
OLYMPIA: Death, whither art thou gone, that both we live?
Come back again, sweet Death, and strike us both!
One minute end our days, and one sepulchre
Contain our bodies! Death, why com'st thou not?
Well, this must be the messenger for thee:
Drawing a dagger.
Now, ugly Death, stretch out thy sable wings,
And carry both our souls where his remains.
Tell me, sweet boy, art thou content to die?
These barbarous Scythians, full of cruelty,
20 And Moors, in whom was never pity found,
Will hew us piecemeal, put us to the wheel,
Or else invent some torture worse than that;
Therefore die by thy loving mother's hand,
Who gently now will lance thy ivory throat,
And quickly rid thee both of pain and life.
SON: Mother, despatch me, or I'll kill myself,
For think you I can live and see him dead?
Give me your knife, good mother, or strike home:
The Scythians shall not tyrannise on me.
30 Sweet mother, strike, that I may meet my father.
She stabs him, and he dies.
OLYMPIA: Ah, sacred Mahomet, if this be sin,
Entreat a pardon of the God of heaven,
And purge my soul before it come to thee!
*She burns the bodies of her husband and son, and then
attempts to kill herself.*

Enter THERIDAMAS, TECHELLES, *and all their*
TRAIN.

THERIDAMAS: How now, madam! what are you doing?

OLYMPIA: Killing myself, as I have done my son,
  Whose body, with his father's, I have burnt,
  Lest cruel Scythians should dismember him.

TECHELLES: 'Twas bravely done, and like a soldier's
  wife.
  Thou shalt with us to Tamburlaine the Great,
  Who, when he hears how resolute thou wert,   *40*
  Will match thee with a viceroy or a king.

OLYMPIA: My lord deceas'd was dearer unto me
  Than any viceroy, king, or emperor,
  And for his sake here will I end my days.

THERIDAMAS: But, lady, go with us to Tamburlaine,
  And thou shalt see a man greater than Mahomet,
  In whose high looks is much more majesty,
  Than from the concave superficies
  Of Jove's vast palace, the empyreal orb,
  Unto the shining bower where Cynthia sits,   *50*
  Like lovely Thetis, in a crystal robe;
  That treadeth fortune underneath his feet,
  And makes the mighty god of arms his slave;
  On whom Death and the Fatal Sisters wait
  With naked swords and scarlet liveries;
  Before whom, mounted on a lion's back,
  Rhamnusia bears a helmet full of blood,
  And strows the way with brains of slaughter'd men;
  By whose proud side the ugly Furies run,
  Hearkening when he shall bid them plague the world;   *60*
  Over whose zenith, cloth'd in windy air,
  And eagle's wings join'd to her feather'd breast,
  Fame hovereth, sounding of her golden trump,
  That to the adverse poles of that straight line
  Which measureth the glorious frame of heaven

51 *Thetis*: mother of Achilles.
57 *Rhamnusia*: Nemesis, goddess of vengeance.

The name of mighty Tamburlaine is spread;
And him, fair lady, shall thy eyes behold.
Come.

OLYMPIA: Take pity of a lady's ruthful tears,
70   That humbly craves upon her knees to stay,
And cast her body in the burning flame
That feeds upon her son's and husband's flesh.

TECHELLES: Madam, sooner shall fire consume us both
Than scorch a face so beautiful as this,
In frame of which Nature hath show'd more skill
Than when she gave eternal chaos form,
Drawing from it the shining lamps of heaven.

THERIDAMAS: Madam, I am so far in love with you,
That you must go with us: no remedy.

80   OLYMPIA: Then carry me, I care not, where you will,
And let the end of this my fatal journey
Be likewise end to my accursed life.

TECHELLES: No, madam, but the beginning of your joy:
Come willingly, therefore.

THERIDAMAS: Soldiers, now let us meet the general,
Who by this time is at Natolia,
Ready to charge the army of the Turk.
The gold, the silver, and the pearl ye got
Rifling this fort, divide in equal shares.
90   This lady shall have twice so much again
Out of the coffers of our treasury.
Exeunt.

SCENE FIVE

Enter CALLAPINE, ORCANES, *the* KINGS OF
JERUSALEM, TREBIZON, *and* SORIA, *with their*
TRAIN, ALMEDA, *and a* MESSENGER.

MESSENGER: Renowmed emperor, mighty Callapine,
God's great lieutenant over all the world,
Here at Aleppo, with an host of men,

Lies Tamburlaine, this king of Persia,
In number more than are the quivering leaves
Of Ida's forest, where your highness' hounds
With open cry pursue the wounded stag,
Who means to girt Natolia's walls with siege,
Fire the town, and over-run the land.

CALLAPINE: My royal army is as great as his,   10
That, from the bounds of Phrygia to the sea
Which washeth Cyprus with his brinish waves,
Covers the hills, the valleys, and the plains.
Viceroys and peers of Turkey, play the men!
Whet all your swords to mangle Tamburlaine,
His sons, his captains, and his followers:
By Mahomet, not one of them shall live!
The field wherein this battle shall be fought
For ever term the Persians' sepulchre,
In memory of this our victory.   20

ORCANES: Now he that calls himself the scourge of
    Jove,
The emperor of the world, and earthly god,
Shall end the warlike progress he intends,
And travel headlong to the lake of hell,
Where legions of devils knowing he must die
Here in Natolia by your highness' hands,
All brandishing their brands of quenchless fire,
Stretching their monstrous paws, grin with their teeth,
And guard the gates to entertain his soul.

CALLAPINE: Tell me, viceroys, the number of your men,   30
And what our army royal is esteem'd.

KING OF JERUSALEM: From Palestina and Jerusalem,
Of Hebrews three score thousand fighting men
Are come, since last we show'd your majesty.

ORCANES: So from Arabia Desert, and the bounds
Of that sweet land whose brave metropolis
Re-edified the fair Semiramis,

37 *Semiramis*: wife of Ninus, emperor of Nineveh; built the walls
of Babylon.

Came forty thousand warlike foot and horse,
Since last we number'd to your majesty.

40 KING OF TREBIZON: From Trebizon in Asia the Less,
Naturalis'd Turks and stout Bithynians
Came to my bands, full fifty thousand more,
That, fighting, know not what retreat doth mean,
Nor e'er return but with the victory,
Since last we number'd to your majesty.

KING OF SORIA: Of Sorians from Halla is repair'd,
And neighbour cities of your highness' land,
Ten thousand horse, and thirty thousand foot,
Since last we number'd to your majesty;

50 So that the army royal is esteem'd
Six hundred thousand valiant fighting men.

CALLAPINE: Then welcome, Tamburlaine, unto thy
death!
Come, puissant viceroys, let us to the field,
The Persians' sepulchre, and sacrifice
Mountains of breathless men to Mahomet,
Who now, with Jove, opens the firmament
To see the slaughter of our enemies.

Enter TAMBURLAINE *with his three sons,* CALYPHAS,
AMYRAS, *and* CELEBINUS; USUMCASANE,
and others.

TAMBURLAINE: How now, Casane! See, a knot of kings,
Sitting as if they were a-telling riddles!

60 USUMCASANE: My lord, your presence makes them
pale and wan:
Poor souls, they look as if their deaths were near.

TAMBURLAINE: Why, so he is, Casane: I am here.
But yet I'll save their lives, and make them slaves.
Ye petty kings of Turkey, I am come,
As Hector did into the Grecian camp,
To overdare the pride of Graecia,
And set his warlike person to the view
Of fierce Achilles, rival of his fame.
I do you honour in the simile;

For, if I should, as Hector did Achilles,   *70*
(The worthiest knight that ever brandish'd sword,)
Challenge in combat any of you all,
I see how fearfully ye would refuse,
And fly my glove as from a scorpion.

ORCANES: Now thou art fearful of thy army's strength,
Thou wouldst with overmatch of person fight.
But, shepherd's issue, base-born Tamburlaine,
Think of thy end. This sword shall lance thy throat.

TAMBURLAINE: Villain, the shepherd's issue, at whose
    birth
Heaven did afford a gracious aspect,   *80*
And join'd those stars that shall be opposite
Even till the dissolution of the world,
And never meant to make a conqueror
So famous as is mighty Tamburlaine,
Shall so torment thee, and that Callapine,
That, like a roguish runaway, suborn'd
That villain there, that slave, that Turkish dog,
To false his service to his sovereign,
As ye shall curse the birth of Tamburlaine.

CALLAPINE: Rail not, proud Scythian: I shall now   *90*
    revenge
My father's vile abuses and mine own.

KING OF JERUSALEM: By Mahomet, he shall be tied in
    chains,
Rowing with Christians in a brigandine
About the Grecian isles to rob and spoil,
And turn him to his ancient trade again.
Methinks the slave should make a lusty thief.

CALLAPINE: Nay, when the battle ends, all we will meet,
And sit in council to invent some pain
That most may vex his body and his soul.

TAMBURLAINE: Sirrah Callapine, I'll hang a clog about *100*
your neck for running away again: you shall not
trouble me thus to come and fetch you.
But as for you, viceroy, you shall have bits,

And, harness'd like my horses, draw my coach,
And, when ye stay, be lash'd with whips of wire.
I'll have you learn to feed on provender,
And in a stable lie upon the planks.

ORCANES: But, Tamburlaine, first thou shalt kneel to us,
And humbly crave a pardon for thy life.

110 KING OF TREBIZON: The common soldiers of our mighty host
Shall bring thee bound unto the general's tent.

KING OF SORIA: And all have jointly sworn thy cruel death,
Or bind thee in eternal torments' wrath.

TAMBURLAINE: Well, sirs, diet yourselves; you know
I shall have occasion shortly to journey you.

CELEBINUS: See, father, how Almeda the jailor looks upon us!

TAMBURLAINE: Villain, traitor, damned fugitive,
I'll make thee wish the earth had swallow'd thee!
120 Seest thou not death within my wrathful looks?
Go, villain, cast thee headlong from a rock,
Or rip thy bowels, or rend out thy heart,
T' appease my wrath; or else I'll torture thee,
Searing thy hateful flesh with burning irons
And drops of scalding lead, while all thy joints
Be rack'd and beat asunder with the wheel;
For, if thou liv'st, not any element
Shall shroud thee from the wrath of Tamburlaine.

CALLAPINE: Well in despite of thee, he shall be king.
130 Come, Almeda; receive this crown of me.
I here invest thee king of Ariadan,
Bordering on Mare Roso, near to Mecca.

ORCANES: What! take it, man.

ALMEDA (*to Tamburlaine*): Good my lord, let me take it.

CALLAPINE: Dost thou ask him leave? Here, take it.

TAMBURLAINE: Go to, sirrah! Take your crown, and make up the half dozen. So, sirrah, now you are a king, you must give arms.

ORCANES: So he shall, and wear thy head in his scutcheon.   *140*

TAMBURLAINE: No, let him hang a bunch of keys on his standard, to put him in remembrance he was a jailor, that, when I take him, I may knock out his brains with them, and lock you in the stable, when you shall come sweating from my chariot.

KING OF TREBIZON: Away! Let us to the field, that the villain may be slain.

TAMBURLAINE: Sirrah, prepare whips, and bring my chariot to my tent; for, as soon as the battle is done, I'll ride in triumph through the camp.   *150*

   Enter THERIDAMAS, TECHELLES, *and their* TRAIN.
How now, ye petty kings? Lo, here are bugs
Will make the hair stand upright on your heads,
And cast your crowns in slavery at their feet!
Welcome, Theridamas and Techelles, both:
See ye this rout, and know ye this same king?

THERIDAMAS: Ay, my lord; he was Callapine's keeper.

TAMBURLAINE: Well now ye see he is a king. Look to him, Theridamas, when we are fighting, lest he hide his crown as the foolish king of Persia did.

KING OF SORIA: No, Tamburlaine; he shall not be put   *160*
to that exigent, I warrant thee.

TAMBURLAINE: You know not, sir.
But now, my followers and my loving friends,
Fight as you ever did, like conquerors,
The glory of this happy day is yours.
My stern aspect shall make fair Victory,
Hovering betwixt our armies, light on me,
Loaden with laurel-wreaths to crown us all.

TECHELLES: I smile to think how, when this field is fought
And rich Natolia ours, our men shall sweat   *170*
With carrying pearl and treasure on their backs.

TAMBURLAINE: You shall be princes all, immediately.
Come, fight, ye Turks, or yield us victory.

ORCANES: No, we will meet thee, slavish Tamburlaine.
Exeunt severally.

ACT FOUR

SCENE ONE

Alarms within. AMYRAS *and* CELEBINUS *issue from
the tent where* CALYPHAS *sits asleep.*

AMYRAS: Now in their glories shine the golden crowns
  Of these proud Turks, much like so many suns
  That half dismay the majesty of heaven.
  Now, brother, follow we our father's sword,
  That flies with fury swifter than our thoughts,
  And cuts down armies with his conquering wings.
CELEBINUS: Call forth our lazy brother from the tent,
  For, if my father miss him in the field,
  Wrath, kindled in the furnace of his breast,
10 Will send a deadly lightning to his heart.
AMYRAS: Brother, ho! What, given so much to sleep,
  You cannot leave it when our enemies' drums
  And rattling cannons thunder in our ears
  Our proper ruin and our father's foil?
CALYPHAS: Away, ye fools! my father needs not me,
  Nor you, in faith, but that you will be thought
  More childish-valourous than manly-wise.
  If half our camp should sit and sleep with me,
  My father were enough to scare the foe:
20 You do dishonour to his majesty,
  To think our helps will do him any good.
AMYRAS: What, dar'st thou, then, be absent from the fight,
  Knowing my father hates thy cowardice,
  And oft hath warn'd thee to be still in field,
  When he himself amidst the thickest troops
  Beats down our foes, to flesh our taintless swords?

14 *proper*: own.

CALYPHAS: I know, sir, what it is to kill a man;
   It works remorse of conscience in me.
   I take no pleasure to be murderous,
   Nor care for blood when wine will quench my thirst.   *30*
CELEBINUS: O cowardly boy! Fie, for shame, come forth!
   Thou dost dishonour manhood and thy house.
CALYPHAS: Go, go, tall stripling, fight you for us both,
   And take my other toward brother here,
   For person like to prove a second Mars.
   'Twill please my mind as well to hear both you
   Have won a heap of honour in the field,
   And left your slender carcasses behind,
   As if I lay with you for company.
AMYRAS: You will not go then?   *40*
CALYPHAS: You say true.
AMYRAS: Were all the lofty mounts of Zona Mundi
   That fill the midst of farthest Tartary
   Turn'd into pearl and proffer'd for my stay,
   I would not bide the fury of my father,
   When, made a victor in these haughty arms,
   He comes and finds his sons have had no shares
   In all the honours he propos'd for us.
CALYPHAS: Take you the honour, I will take my ease;
   My wisdom shall excuse my cowardice.   *50*
   I go into the field before I need!
     Alarms within. AMYRAS *and* CELEBINUS *run out.*
   The bullets fly at random where they list;
   And, should I go, and kill a thousand men,
   I were as soon rewarded with a shot,
   And sooner far than he that never fights;
   And, should I go, and do nor harm nor good,
   I might have harm, which all the good I have,
   Join'd with my father's crown, would never cure.
   I'll to cards. – Perdicas!
     Enter PERDICAS.
PERDICAS: Here, my lord.   *60*
   34 *toward*: promising.

227

CALYPHAS: Come, thou and I will go to cards to drive away the time.

PERDICAS: Content, my lord: but what shall we play for?

CALYPHAS: Who shall kiss the fairest of the Turks' concubines first, when my father hath conquered them.

PERDICAS: Agreed, i'faith.

They play.

CALYPHAS: They say I am a coward, Perdicas, and I fear as little their taratantaras, their swords, or their cannons as I do a naked lady in a net of gold, and, for
70 fear I should be afraid, would put it off and come to bed with me.

PERDICAS: Such a fear, my lord, would never make ye retire.

CALYPHAS: I would my father would let me be put in the front of such a battle once, to try my valour!
Alarms within.

What a coil they keep! I believe there will be some hurt done anon amongst them.

Enter TAMBURLAINE, THERIDAMAS,
TECHELLES, USUMCASANE; AMYRAS *and*
CELEBINUS *leading in* ORCANES, *and the* KINGS
OF JERUSALEM, TREBIZON, *and* SORIA; *and*
SOLDIERS.

TAMBURLAINE: See now, ye slaves, my children stoops your pride,

And leads your glories sheep-like to the sword!
80 Bring them, my boys, and tell me if the wars
Be not a life that may illustrate gods,
And tickle not your spirits with desire
Still to be train'd in arms and chivalry?

AMYRAS: Shall we let go these kings again, my lord,
To gather greater numbers 'gainst our power,
That they may say, it is not chance doth this,
But matchless strength and magnanimity?

TAMBURLAINE: No, no, Amyras; tempt not Fortune so.
Cherish thy valour still with fresh supplies,

And glut it not with stale and daunted foes.   *90*
But where's this coward villain, not my son,
But traitor to my name and majesty?
   He goes in and brings CALYPHAS *out.*
Image of sloth, and picture of a slave,
The obloquy and scorn of my renown!
How may my heart, thus fired with mine eyes,
Wounded with shame and kill'd with discontent,
Shroud any thought may hold my striving hands
From martial justice on thy wretched soul?

THERIDAMAS: Yet pardon him, I pray your majesty.

TECHELLES *and* USUMCASANE: Let all of us entreat your   *100*
    highness' pardon.

TAMBURLAINE: Stand up, ye base, unworthy soldiers!
    Know ye not yet the argument of arms?

AMYRAS: Good, my lord, let him be forgiven for once,
    And we will force him to the field hereafter.

TAMBURLAINE: Stand up, my boys, and I will teach ye
    arms,
And what the jealousy of wars must do.
O Samarcanda, where I breathed first,
And joy'd the fire of this martial flesh,
Blush, blush, fair city, at thine honour's foil,
And shame of nature, which Jaertis' stream,   *110*
Embracing thee with deepest of his love,
Can never wash from thy distained brows!
Here, Jove, receive his fainting soul again,
A form not meet to give that subject essence
Whose matter is the flesh of Tamburlaine,
Wherein an incorporeal spirit moves,
Made of the mould whereof thyself consists,
Which makes me valiant, proud, ambitious,
Ready to levy power against thy throne,
That I might move the turning spheres of heaven;   *120*
For earth and all this airy region
Cannot contain the state of Tamburlaine.
   Stabs CALYPHAS.

By Mahomet, thy mighty friend, I swear,
In sending to my issue such a soul,
Created of the massy dregs of earth,
The scum and tartar of the elements,
Wherein was neither courage, strength or wit,
But folly, sloth, and damned idleness,
Thou hast procur'd a greater enemy
130   Than he that darted mountains at thy head,
Shaking the burden mighty Atlas bears,
Whereat thou trembling hidd'st thee in the air,
Cloth'd with a pitchy cloud for being seen.
And now, ye canker'd curs of Asia,
That will not see the strength of Tamburlaine,
Although it shine as brightly as the sun,
Now you shall feel the strength of Tamburlaine,
And, by the state of his supremacy,
Approve the difference 'twixt himself and you.
140 ORCANES: Thou show'st the difference 'twixt ourselves
      and thee,
    In this thy barbarous damned tyranny.
  KING OF JERUSALEM: Thy victories are grown so
      violent,
    That shortly heaven, fill'd with the meteors
    Of blood and fire thy tyrannies have made,
    Will pour down blood and fire on thy head,
    Whose scalding drops will pierce thy seething brains,
    And, with our bloods, revenge our bloods on thee.
  TAMBURLAINE: Villains, these terrors and these
      tyrannies
    (If tyrannies war's justice ye repute),
150   I execute, enjoin'd me from above,
To scourge the pride of such as Heaven abhors;
Nor am I made arch-monarch of the world,
Crown'd and invested by the hand of Jove,
For deeds of bounty or nobility;
But, since I exercise a greater name,

126 *tartar*: dregs.

The Scourge of God and terror of the world,
I must apply myself to fit those terms,
In war, in blood, in death, in cruelty,
And plague such peasants as resist in me
The power of Heaven's eternal majesty.   *160*
Theridamas, Techelles, and Casane,
Ransack the tents and the pavilions
Of these proud Turks, and take their concubines,
Making them bury this effeminate brat;
For not a common soldier shall defile
His manly fingers with so faint a boy.
Then bring those Turkish harlots to my tent,
And I'll dispose them as it likes me best.
Meanwhile, take him in.

SOLDIERS: We will, my lord.   *170*
   Exeunt with the body of CALYPHAS.

KING OF JERUSALEM: O damned monster! nay, a fiend
   of hell,
   Whose cruelties are not so harsh as thine,
   Nor yet impos'd with such a bitter hate!

ORCANES: Revenge it, Rhadamanth and Æacus,
   And let your hates, extended in his pains,
   Expel the hate wherein he pains our souls!

KING OF TREBIZON: May never day give virtue to his
   eyes,
   Whose sight, compos'd of fury and of fire,
   Doth send such stern affections to his heart!

KING OF SORIA: May never spirit, vein or artier feed   *180*
   The cursed substance of that cruel heart;
   But, wanting moisture and remorseful blood,
   Dry up with anger, and consume with heat!

TAMBURLAINE: Well, bark, ye dogs: I'll bridle all your
   tongues,
   And bind them close with bits of burnish'd steel,
   Down to the channels of your hateful throats,
   And, with the pains my rigour shall inflict,

174 *Rhadamanth and Æacus*: judges in the underworld.

231

I'll make ye roar, that earth may echo forth
The far-resounding torments ye sustain;
190 As when an herd of lusty Cimbrian bulls
Run mourning round about the females' miss,
And, stung with fury of their following,
Fill all the air with troublous bellowing.
I will, with engines never exercis'd,
Conquer, sack, and utterly consume
Your cities and your golden palaces,
And, with the flames that beat against the clouds,
Incense the heavens and make the stars to melt,
As if they were the tears of Mahomet
200 For hot consumption of his country's pride;
And, till by vision or by speech I hear
Immortal Jove say 'Cease, my Tamburlaine,'
I will persist a terror to the world,
Making the meteors that, like armed men,
Are seen to march upon the towers of heaven,
Run tilting round about the firmament,
And break their burning lances in the air,
For honour of my wondrous victories.
Come, bring them in to our pavilion.
    Exeunt.

SCENE TWO

Enter OLYMPIA.

OLYMPIA: Distress'd Olympia, whose weeping eyes,
Since thy arrival here, beheld no sun,
But, clos'd within the compass of a tent,
Have stain'd thy cheeks and made thee look like death,
Devise some means to rid thee of thy life,
Rather than yield to his detested suit,
Whose drift is only to dishonour thee;
And, since this earth, dew'd with thy brinish tears,
Affords no herbs whose taste may poison thee,

Nor yet this air, beat often with thy sighs,   *10*
Contagious smells and vapours to infect thee,
Nor thy close cave a sword to murder thee,
Let this invention be the instrument.
  Enter THERIDAMAS.

THERIDAMAS: Well met, Olympia. I sought thee in my
    tent,
But, when I saw the place obscure and dark,
Which with thy beauty thou wast wont to light,
Enrag'd, I ran about the fields for thee,
Supposing amorous Jove had sent his son,
The winged Hermes, to convey thee hence.
But now I find thee, and that fear is past,   *20*
Tell me, Olympia, wilt thou grant my suit?

OLYMPIA: My lord and husband's death, with my sweet
    son's,
With whom I buried all affections
Save grief and sorrow, which torment my heart,
Forbids my mind to entertain a thought
That tends to love, but meditate on death,
A fitter subject for a pensive soul.

THERIDAMAS: Olympia, pity him in whom thy looks
Have greater operation and more force
Than Cynthia's in the watery wilderness,   *30*
For with thy view my joys are at the full,
And ebb again as thou depart'st from me.

OLYMPIA: Ah, pity me, my lord, and draw your sword,
Making a passage for my troubled soul,
Which beats against this prison to get out,
And meet my husband and my loving son!

THERIDAMAS: Nothing but still thy husband and thy
    son?
Leave this, my love, and listen more to me:
Thou shalt be stately queen of fair Argier,
And, cloth'd in costly cloth of massy gold,   *40*
Upon the marble turrets of my court

30 *Cynthia*: the moon.

Sit like to Venus in her chair of state,
Commanding all thy princely eye desires;
And I will cast off arms to sit with thee,
Spending my life in sweet discourse of love.

OLYMPIA: No such discourse is pleasant in mine ears,
But that where every period ends with death,
And every line begins with death again.
I cannot love, to be an emperess.

50 THERIDAMAS: Nay, lady, then, if nothing will prevail,
I'll use some other means to make you yield.
Such is the sudden fury of my love,
I must and will be pleas'd, and you shall yield:
Come to the tent again.

OLYMPIA: Stay, good my lord; and, will you save my
honour,
I'll give your grace a present of such price
As all the world can not afford the like.

THERIDAMAS: What is it?

OLYMPIA: An ointment which a cunning alchemist
60 Distilled from the purest balsamum
And simplest extracts of all minerals,
In which the essential form of marble stone,
Temper'd by science metaphysical,
And spells of magic from the mouths of spirits,
With which if you but 'noint your tender skin,
Nor pistol, sword, nor lance, can pierce your flesh.

THERIDAMAS: Why, madam, think ye to mock me thus
palpably?

OLYMPIA: To prove it, I will 'noint my naked throat,
Which when you stab, look on your weapon's point,
70 And you shall see't rebated with the blow.

THERIDAMAS: Why gave you not your husband some
of it,
If you lov'd him, and it so precious?

OLYMPIA: My purpose was, my lord, to spend it so,
But was prevented by his sudden end;

47 *period*: pause, full-stop.

And for a present easy proof hereof,
That I dissemble not, try it on me.
THERIDAMAS: I will, Olympia, and will keep it for
The richest present of this eastern world.
She anoints her throat.
OLYMPIA: Now stab, my lord, and mark your weapon's
point,
That will be blunted if the blow be great.   *80*
THERIDAMAS: Here, then, Olympia.
Stabs her.
What, have I slain her? Villain, stab thyself!
Cut off this arm that murdered my love,
In whom the learned Rabbis of this age
Might find as many wondrous miracles
As in the theoria of the world!
Now hell is fairer than Elysium;
A greater lamp than that bright eye of heaven,
From whence the stars do borrow all their light,
Wanders about the black circumference;   *90*
And now the damned souls are free from pain,
For every Fury gazeth on her looks.
Infernal Dis is courting of my love,
Inventing masques and stately shows for her,
Opening the doors of his rich treasury
To entertain this queen of chastity,
Whose body shall be tomb'd with all the pomp
The treasure of my kingdom may afford.
Exit taking her away.

SCENE THREE

Enter TAMBURLAINE, *drawn in his chariot by the*
KINGS OF TREBIZON *and* SORIA, *with bits in their*
mouths, reins in his left hand, and in his right hand a whip
with which he scourgeth them; AMYRAS, CELEBINUS,

93 *Dis*: the underworld.

TECHELLES, THERIDAMAS, USUMCASANE; ORCANES *king of Natolia, and the* KING OF JERUSALEM, *led by five or six common* SOLDIERS; *and other* SOLDIERS.

TAMBURLAINE: Holla, ye pamper'd jades of Asia!
What, can ye draw but twenty miles a day,
And have so proud a chariot at your heels,
And such a coachman as great Tamburlaine,
But from Asphaltis, where I conquer'd you,
To Byron here, where thus I honour you?
The horse that guide the golden eye of heaven,
And blow the morning from their nostrils,
Making their fiery gait above the clouds,
10 Are not so honour'd in their governor
As you, ye slaves, in mighty Tamburlaine.
The headstrong jades of Thrace Alcides tam'd,
The King Ægeus fed with human flesh,
And made so wanton that they knew their strengths,
Were not subdu'd with valour more divine
Than you by this unconquer'd arm of mine.
To make you fierce, and fit my appetite,
You shall be fed with flesh as raw as blood,
And drink in pails the strongest muscadel.
20 If you can live with it, then live, and draw
My chariot swifter than the racking clouds;
If not, then die like beasts, and fit for naught
But perches for the black and fatal ravens.
Thus am I right the scourge of highest Jove;
And see the figure of my dignity,
By which I hold my name and majesty!

AMYRAS: Let me have coach, my lord, that I may ride,
And thus be drawn by these two idle kings.

TAMBURLAINE: Thy youth forbids such ease, my kingly
boy:
30 They shall tomorrow draw my chariot,
While these their fellow-kings may be refresh'd.

12 *Alcides*: Hercules.

ORCANES: O thou that sway'st the region under earth,
And art a king as absolute as Jove,
Come as thou didst in fruitful Sicily,
Surveying all the glories of the land,
And as thou took'st the fair Proserpina,
Joying the fruit of Ceres' garden-plot,
For love, for honour, and to make her queen,
So, for just hate, for shame, and to subdue
This proud contemner of thy dreadful power,   *40*
Come once in fury and survey his pride,
Haling him headlong to the lowest hell!

THERIDAMAS: Your majesty must get some bits for these,
To bridle their contemptuous cursing tongues,
That, like unruly never-broken jades,
Break through the hedges of their hateful mouths,
And pass their fixed bounds exceedingly.

TECHELLES: Nay, we will break the hedges of their
    mouths,
And pull their kicking colts out of their pastures.

USUMCASANE: Your majesty already hath devis'd   *50*
A mean, as fit as may be, to restrain
These coltish coach-horse tongues from blasphemy.

CELEBINUS: How like you that, sir king? Why speak
    you not?

KING OF JERUSALEM: Ah, cruel brat, sprung from a
    tyrant's loins!
How like his cursed father he begins
To practise taunts and bitter tyrannies!

TAMBURLAINE: Ay, Turk, I tell thee, this same boy is he
That must, advanc'd in higher pomp than this,
Rifle the kingdoms I shall leave unsack'd,
If Jove, esteeming me too good for earth,   *60*
Raise me, to match the fair Aldeboran,
Above the threefold astracism of heaven,
Before I conquer all the triple world.

61 *Aldeboran*: star in the constellation Taurus.
62 *astracism*: constellation.

Now fetch me out the Turkish concubines:
I will prefer them for the funeral
They have bestow'd on my abortive son.
    The CONCUBINES *are brought in.*
Where are my common soldiers now, that fought
So lion-like upon Asphaltis' plains?

SOLDIERS: Here, my lord.

70 TAMBURLAINE: Hold ye, tall soldiers, take ye queens
    a-piece, –
I mean such queens as were kings' concubines.
Take them; divide them, and their jewels too,
And let them equally serve all your turns.

SOLDIERS: We thank your majesty.

TAMBURLAINE: Brawl not, I warn you, for your
    lechery,
For every man that so offends shall die.

ORCANES: Injurious tyrant, wilt thou so defame
The hateful fortunes of thy victory,
To exercise upon such guiltless dames
80 The violence of thy common soldiers' lust?

TAMBURLAINE: Live continent,[11] then, ye slaves, and
    meet not me
With troops of harlots at your slothful heels.

CONCUBINES: O pity us, my lord, and save our honours!

TAMBURLAINE: Are ye not gone, ye villains, with your
    spoils?
    The SOLDIERS *run away with the* CONCUBINES.

KING OF JERUSALEM: O, merciless, infernal cruelty!

TAMBURLAINE: Save your honours! 'twere but time
    indeed,
Lost long before ye knew what honour meant.

THERIDAMAS: It seems they meant to conquer us, my
    lord,
And make us jesting pageants for their trulls.

90 TAMBURLAINE: And now themselves shall make our
    pageant,

    65 *prefer*: promote.

And common soldiers jest with all their trulls.
Let them take pleasure soundly in their spoils,
Till we prepare our march to Babylon,
Whither we next make expedition.
TECHELLES: Let us not be idle, then, my lord,
But presently be prest to conquer it.
TAMBURLAINE: We will, Techelles. Forward, then, ye
   jades!
Now crouch, ye kings of greatest Asia,
And tremble when ye hear this scourge will come
That whips down cities and controlleth crowns,   *100*
Adding their wealth and treasure to my store.
The Euxine sea, north to Natolia;
The Terrene, west; the Caspian, north north-east;
And on the south, Sinus Arabicus;
Shall all be loaded with the martial spoils
We will convey with us to Persia.
Then shall my native city Samarcanda,
And crystal waves of fresh Jaertis' stream,
The pride and beauty of her princely seat,
Be famous through the furthest continents.   *110*
For there my palace royal shall be plac'd,
Whose shining turrets shall dismay the heavens,
And cast the fame of Ilion's tower to hell.
Thorough the streets, with troops of conquer'd kings,
I'll ride in golden armour like the sun;
And in my helm a triple plume shall spring,
Spangled with diamonds, dancing in the air,
To note me emperor of the three-fold world;
Like to an almond tree y-mounted high
Upon the lofty and celestial mount   *120*
Of ever-green Selinus, quaintly deck'd
With blooms more white than Herycina's brows,
Whose tender blossoms tremble every one
At every little breath that thorough heaven is blown.
Then in my coach, like Saturn's royal son

121 *Selinus*: town in Sicily.   122 *Herycina*: Venus.

Mounted his shining chariot gilt with fire,
And drawn with princely eagles through the path
Pav'd with bright crystal and enchas'd with stars
When all the gods stand gazing at his pomp,
130   So will I ride through Samarcanda streets,
Until my soul, dissever'd from this flesh,
Shall mount the milk-white way, and meet him there.
To Babylon, my lords, to Babylon!
    Exeunt.

ACT FIVE

SCENE ONE

Enter the GOVERNOR OF BABYLON, MAXIMUS,
and others, upon the walls.

GOVERNOR: What saith Maximus?
MAXIMUS: My lord, the breach the enemy hath made
  Gives such assurance of our overthrow
  That little hope is left to save our lives,
  Or hold our city from the conqueror's hands.
  Then hang out flags, my lord, of humble truce,
  And satisfy the people's general prayers,
  That Tamburlaine's intolerable wrath
  May be suppressed by our submission.
10 GOVERNOR: Villain, respect'st thou more thy slavish life
  Than honour of thy country or thy name?
  Is not my life and state as dear to me,
  The city and my native country's weal,
  As any thing of price with thy conceit?
  Have we not hope, for all our batter'd walls,
  To live secure and keep his forces out,
  When this our famous lake of Limnasphaltis
  Makes walls afresh with every thing that falls

14 *As . . . conceit*: anything that your mind values.

Into the liquid substance of his stream,
More strong than are the gates of death or hell? 20
What faintness should dismay our courages,
When we are thus defenc'd against our foe,
And have no terror but his threatening looks?
Enter another, kneeling to the GOVERNOR.

CITIZEN: My lord, if ever you did deed of ruth,
And now will work a refuge to our lives,
Offer submission, hang up flags of truce,
That Tamburlaine may pity our distress,
And use us like a loving conqueror.
Though this be held his last day's dreadful siege,
Wherein he spareth neither man nor child, 30
Yet are there Christians of Georgia here,
Whose state he ever pitied and reliev'd,
Will get his pardon, if your grace would send.

GOVERNOR: How is my soul environed!
And this eternis'd city Babylon
Fill'd with a pack of faint-heart fugitives
That thus entreat their shame and servitude!
Enter, above, a SECOND CITIZEN.

SECOND CITIZEN: My lord, if ever you will win our
hearts,
Yield up the town, and save our wives and children;
For I will cast myself from off these walls, 40
Or die some death of quickest violence,
Before I bide the wrath of Tamburlaine.

GOVERNOR: Villains, cowards, traitors to our state!
Fall to the earth, and pierce the pit of hell,
That legions of tormenting spirits may vex
Your slavish bosoms with continual pains!
I care not, nor the town will never yield
As long as any life is in my breast.
Enter THERIDAMAS *and* TECHELLES, *with*
SOLDIERS.

THERIDAMAS: Thou desperate governor of Babylon,
To save thy life, and us a little labour, 50

Yield speedily the city to our hands,
Or else be sure thou shalt be forc'd with pains
More exquisite then ever traitor felt.

GOVERNOR: Tyrant, I turn the traitor in thy throat,
And will defend it in despite of thee.
Call up the soldiers to defend these walls.

TECHELLES: Yield, foolish governor; we offer more
Than ever yet we did to such proud slaves
As durst resist us till our third day's siege.

60 Thou seest us prest to give the last assault,
And that shall bide no more regard of parley.

GOVERNOR: Assault and spare not; we will never yield.
Alarms: and they scale the walls.

Enter TAMBURLAINE, *drawn in his chariot (as before)
by the* KINGS OF TREBIZON *and* SORIA; AMYRAS,
CELEBINUS, USUMCASANE; ORCANES *king of
Natolia, and the* KING OF JERUSALEM, *led by*
SOLDIERS; *and others.*

TAMBURLAINE: The stately buildings of fair Babylon,
Whose lofty pillars, higher than the clouds,
Were wont to guide the seaman in the deep,
Being carried thither by the cannon's force,
Now fill the mouth of Limnasphaltis' lake,
And make a bridge unto the batter'd walls.
Where Belus, Ninus, and great Alexander

70 Have rode in triumph, triumphs Tamburlaine,
Whose chariot wheels have burst th' Assyrians' bones,
Drawn with these kings on heaps of carcasses.
Now in the place, where fair Semiramis,
Courted by kings and peers of Asia,
Hath trod the measures, do my soldiers march,
And in the streets, where brave Assyrian dames
Have rid in pomp like rich Saturnia,
With furious words and frowning visages
My horsemen brandish their unruly blades.

69 *Belus* . . .: the three great kings of Babylon.
77 *Saturnia*: Juno.

Re-enter THERIDAMAS *and* TECHELLES, *bringing*
in the GOVERNOR OF BABYLON.

Who have ye there, my lord?   80

THERIDAMAS: The sturdy governor of Babylon,
That made us all the labour for the town,
And us'd such slender reckoning of your majesty.

TAMBURLAINE: Go, bind the villain. He shall hang in
chains
Upon the ruins of this conquer'd town.
Sirrah, the view of our vermilion tents
Which threaten'd more than if the region
Next underneath the element of fire
Were full of comets and of blazing stars,
Whose flaming trains should reach down to the earth,   90
Could not affright you; no, nor I myself,
The wrathful messenger of mighty Jove,
That with his sword hath quail'd all earthly kings,
Could not persuade you to submission,
But still the ports were shut. Villain, I say,
Should I but touch the rusty gates of hell,
The triple-headed Cerberus would howl,
And wake black Jove to crouch and kneel to me;
But I have sent volleys of shot to you,
Yet could not enter till the breach was made.   100

GOVERNOR: Nor, if my body could have stopt the breach,
Shouldst thou have enter'd, cruel Tamburlaine.
'Tis not thy bloody tents can make me yield,
Nor yet thyself, the anger of the Highest;
For, though thy cannon shook the city-walls,
My heart did never quake, or courage faint.

TAMBURLAINE: Well, now I'll make it quake. Go draw
him up,
Hang him in chains upon the city walls,
And let my soldiers shoot the slave to death.

GOVERNOR: Vile monster, born of some infernal hag,   110
And sent from hell to tyrannise on earth,
Do all thy worst. Nor death, nor Tamburlaine,

Torture, or pain, can daunt my dreadless mind.

TAMBURLAINE: Up with him, then! His body shall be
scarr'd.

GOVERNOR: But, Tamburlaine, in Limnasphaltis' lake
There lies more gold than Babylon is worth,
Which, when the city was besieg'd, I hid:
Save but my life, and I will give it thee.

TAMBURLAINE: Then, for all your valour, you would
save your life?

120 Whereabout lies it?

GOVERNOR: Under a hollow bank, right opposite
Against the western gate of Babylon.

TAMBURLAINE: Go thither, some of you, and take his
gold:
Exeunt some ATTENDANTS.
The rest forward with execution.
Away with him hence, let him speak no more.
I think I make your courage something quail.
Exeunt ATTENDANTS *with the* GOVERNOR OF
BABYLON.
When this is done, we'll march from Babylon,
And make our greatest haste to Persia.
These jades are broken winded and half-tir'd;

130 Unharness them, and let me have fresh horse.
ATTENDANTS *unharness the* KINGS OF TREBIZON
and SORIA.
So, now their best is done to honour me,
Take them and hang them both up presently.

KING OF TREBIZON: Vile tyrant! Barbarous bloody
Tamburlaine!

TAMBURLAINE: Take them away, Theridamas; see them
despatch'd.

THERIDAMAS: I will, my lord.
Exit with the KINGS OF TREBIZON *and* SORIA.

TAMBURLAINE: Come, Asian viceroys; to your tasks a
while,
And take such fortune as your fellows felt.

ORCANES: First let thy Scythian horse tear both our limbs,
Rather than we should draw thy chariot,
And like base slaves abject our princely minds 140
To vile and ignominious servitude.
KING OF JERUSALEM: Rather lend me thy weapon,
Tamburlaine,
That I may sheathe it in this breast of mine.
A thousand deaths could not torment our hearts
More than the thought of this doth vex our souls.
AMYRAS: They will talk still, my lord, if you do not
bridle them.
TAMBURLAINE: Bridle them, and let me to my coach.
ATTENDANTS *bridle* ORCANES *king of Natolia, and
the* KING OF JERUSALEM, *and harness them to the
chariot. The* GOVERNOR OF BABYLON *appears
hanging in chains on the walls. Re-enter* THERIDAMAS.
AMYRAS: See, now, my lord, how brave the captain
hangs!
TAMBURLAINE: 'Tis brave indeed, my boy: well done!
Shoot first, my lord, and then the rest shall follow. 150
THERIDAMAS: Then have at him, to begin withal.
THERIDAMAS *shoots at the* GOVERNOR.
GOVERNOR: Yet save my life, and let this wound appease
The mortal fury of great Tamburlaine!
TAMBURLAINE: No, though Asphaltis' lake were liquid
gold,
And offer'd me as ransom for thy life,
Yet shouldst thou die. Shoot at him all at once.
They shoot.
So, now he hangs like Bagdet's governor,
Having as many bullets in his flesh
As there be breaches in her batter'd wall.
Go now, and bind the burghers hand and foot, 160
And cast them headlong in the city's lake.
Tartars and Persians shall inhabit there;
And, to command the city, I will build
A citadel, that all Africa,

Which hath been subject to the Persian king,
Shall pay me tribute for in Babylon.

TECHELLES: What shall be done with their wives and
children, my lord?

TAMBURLAINE: Techelles, drown them all, man, woman,
and child;
Leave not a Babylonian in the town.

170 TECHELLES: I will about it straight. Come soldiers.
Exit with SOLDIERS.

TAMBURLAINE: Now, Casane, where's the Turkish
Alcoran,
And all the heaps of superstitious books
Found in the temples of that Mahomet
Whom I have thought a god? They shall be burnt.

USUMCASANE: Here they are, my lord.

TAMBURLAINE: Well said! Let there be a fire presently.
They light a fire.
In vain, I see, men worship Mahomet.
My sword hath sent millions of Turks to hell,
Slew all his priests, his kinsmen, and his friends,

180 And yet I live untouch'd by Mahomet.
There is a God, full of revenging wrath,
From whom the thunder and the lightning breaks,
Whose scourge I am, and him will I obey.
So Casane; fling them in the fire.
They burn the books.
Now, Mahomet, if thou have any power,
Come down thyself and work a miracle.
Thou art not worthy to be worshipped
That suffers flames of fire to burn the writ
Wherein the sum of thy religion rests.

190 Why send'st thou not a furious whirlwind down,
To blow thy Alcoran up to thy throne,
Where men report thou sitt'st by God himself?
Or vengeance on the head of Tamburlaine
That shakes his sword against thy majesty,
And spurns the abstracts of thy foolish laws?

Well, soldiers, Mahomet remains in hell;
He cannot hear the voice of Tamburlaine.
Seek out another godhead to adore:
The God that sits in heaven, if any god,
For he is God alone, and none but he.   200

Re-enter TECHELLES.

TECHELLES: I have fulfill'd your highness' will, my lord.
Thousands of men, drown'd in Asphaltis' lake,
Have made the water swell above the banks,
And fishes, fed by human carcasses,
Amaz'd, swim up and down upon the waves,
As when they swallow assafoetida,
Which makes them fleet aloft and gasp for air.

TAMBURLAINE: Well, then, my friendly lords, what now
remains,
But that we leave sufficient garrison,
And presently depart to Persia,   210
To triumph after all our victories?

THERIDAMAS: Ay, good my lord, let us in haste to Persia;
And let this captain be remov'd the walls
To some high hill about the city here.

TAMBURLAINE: Let it be so; about it, soldiers.
But stay: I feel myself distemper'd suddenly.

TECHELLES: What is it dares distemper Tamburlaine?

TAMBURLAINE: Something, Techelles; but I know not
what.
But, forth, ye vassals! Whatsoe'er it be,
Sickness or death can never conquer me.   220

Exeunt.

SCENE TWO

Enter CALLAPINE, KING OF AMASIA, *a* CAPTAIN,
and TRAIN, *with drums and trumpets.*

CALLAPINE: King of Amasia, now our mighty host
Marcheth in Asia Major, where the streams

Of Euphrates and Tigris swiftly runs;
And here may we behold great Babylon,
Circled about with Limnasphaltis' lake,
Where Tamburlaine with all his army lies,
Which being faint and weary with the siege,
We may lie ready to encounter him
Before his host be full from Babylon,
10 And so revenge our latest grievous loss,
If God or Mahomet send any aid.

KING OF AMASIA: Doubt not, my lord, but we shall
   conquer him.
The monster that hath drunk a sea of blood,
And yet gapes still for more to quench his thirst,
Our Turkish swords shall headlong send to hell;
And that vile carcass, drawn by warlike kings,
The fowls shall eat; for never sepulchre
Shall grace this base-born tyrant Tamburlaine.

CALLAPINE: When I record my parents' slavish life,
20 Their cruel death, mine own captivity,
My viceroys' bondage under Tamburlaine,
Methinks I could sustain a thousand deaths,
To be reveng'd of all his villany.
Ah, sacred Mahomet, thou that hast seen
Millions of Turks perish by Tamburlaine,
Kingdoms made waste, brave cities sack'd and burnt,
And but one host is left to honour thee,
Aid thy obedient servant Callapine,
And make him, after all these overthrows,
30 To triumph over cursed Tamburlaine!

KING OF AMASIA: Fear not, my lord: I see great
   Mahomet,
Clothed in purple clouds and on his head
A chaplet brighter than Apollo's crown,
Marching about the air with armed men,
To join with you against this Tamburlaine.

CAPTAIN: Renowmed general, mighty Callapine,
Though God himself and holy Mahomet

Should come in person to resist your power,
Yet might your mighty host encounter all,
And pull proud Tamburlaine upon his knees   *40*
To sue for mercy at your highness' feet.
CALLAPINE: Captain, the force of Tamburlaine is great,
His fortune greater, and the victories
Wherewith he hath so sore dismay'd the world
Are greatest to discourage all our drifts.
Yet, when the pride of Cynthia is at full,
She wanes again; and so shall his, I hope;
For we have here the chief selected men
Of twenty several kingdoms at the least.
Nor ploughman, priest, nor merchant, stays at home;   *50*
All Turkey is in arms with Callapine;
And never will we sunder camps and arms
Before himself or his be conquered.
This is the time that must eternise me
For conquering the tyrant of the world.
Come, soldiers, let us lie in wait for him,
And, if we find him absent from his camp,
Or that it be rejoin'd again at full,
Assail it, and be sure of victory.
   Exeunt.

SCENE THREE

Enter THERIDAMAS, TECHELLES, *and*
USUMCASANE.

THERIDAMAS: Weep, heavens, and vanish into liquid
   tears!
Fall, stars that govern his nativity,
And summon all the shining lamps of heaven
To cast their bootless fires to the earth,
And shed their feeble influence in the air;
Muffle your beauties with eternal clouds,
For Hell and Darkness pitch their pitchy tents,

And Death, with armies of Cimmerian spirits,
Gives battle 'gainst the heart of Tamburlaine.
10 Now, in defiance of that wonted love
Your sacred virtues pour'd upon his throne,
And made his state an honour to the heavens,
These cowards invisibly assail his soul,
And threaten conquest on our sovereign;
But, if he die, your glories are disgrac'd,
Earth droops, and says that hell in heaven is plac'd.
TECHELLES: O, then, ye powers that sway eternal seats,
And guide this massy substance of the earth,
If you retain desert of holiness,
20 As your supreme estates instruct our thoughts,
Be not inconstant, careless of your fame,
Bear not the burden of your enemies' joys,
Triumphing in his fall whom you advanc'd;
But, as his birth, life, health, and majesty
Were strangely blest and governed by heaven,
So honour, heaven (till heaven dissolved be,)
His birth, his life, his health, and majesty!
USUMCASANE: Blush, heaven, to lose the honour of thy
name,
To see thy footstool set upon thy head;
30 And let no baseness in thy haughty breast
Sustain a shame of such inexcellence,
To see the devils mount in angels' thrones,
And angels dive into the pools of hell!
And, though they think their painful date is out,
And that their power is puissant as Jove's,
Which makes them manage arms against thy state,
Yet make them feel the strength of Tamburlaine,
Thy instrument and note of majesty,
Is greater far than they can thus subdue;
40 For, if he die, thy glory is disgrac'd,
Earth droops, and says that hell in heaven is plac'd!
Enter TAMBURLAINE, *drawn in his chariot by*
ORCANES *king of Natolia and the* KING OF

JERUSALEM, *with* AMYRAS, CELEBINUS, *and*
PHYSICIANS.

TAMBURLAINE: What daring god torments my body
thus,
And seeks to conquer mighty Tamburlaine?
Shall sickness prove me now to be a man,
That have been term'd the terror of the world?
Techelles and the rest, come, take your swords,
And threaten him whose hand afflicts my soul.
Come, let us march against the powers of heaven,
And set black streamers in the firmament,
To signify the slaughter of the gods.   *50*
Ah, friends, what shall I do? I cannot stand.
Come, carry me to war against the gods,
That thus envy the health of Tamburlaine.
THERIDAMAS: Ah, good my lord, leave these impatient
words,
Which add much danger to your malady!
TAMBURLAINE: Why, shall I sit and languish in this
pain?
No, strike the drums, and, in revenge of this,
Come, let us charge our spears, and pierce his breast
Whose shoulders bear the axis of the world,
That, if I perish, heaven and earth may fade.   *60*
Theridamas, haste to the court of Jove;
Will him to send Apollo hither straight,
To cure me, or I'll fetch him down myself.
TECHELLES: Sit still, my gracious lord, this grief will
cease,
And cannot last, it is so violent.
TAMBURLAINE: Not last, Techelles! No, for I shall die.
See, where my slave, the ugly monster Death,
Shaking and quivering, pale and wan for fear,
Stands aiming at me with his murdering dart,
Who flies away at every glance I give,   *70*
And, when I look away, comes stealing on!
Villain, away, and hie thee to the field!

I and mine army come to load thy bark
With souls of thousand mangled carcasses.
Look, where he goes! But, see, he comes again,
Because I stay! Techelles, let us march,
And weary Death with bearing souls to hell.

FIRST PHYSICIAN: Pleaseth your majesty to drink this
potion,
Which will abate the fury of your fit,
80 And cause some milder spirits govern you.

TAMBURLAINE: Tell me what think you of my sickness
now?

FIRST PHYSICIAN: I view'd your urine, and the
hypostasis,[12]
Thick and obscure, doth make your danger great.
Your veins are full of accidental heat,
Whereby the moisture of your blood is dried.
The humidum and calor, which some hold
Is not a parcel of the elements,
But of a substance more divine and pure,
Is almost clean extinguished and spent;
90 Which, being the cause of life, imports your death.
Besides, my lord, this day is critical,
Dangerous to those whose crisis is as yours:
Your artiers, which alongst the veins convey
The lively spirits which the heart engenders,
Are parch'd and void of spirit, that the soul,
Wanting those organons by which it moves,
Cannot endure, by argument of art.
Yet, if your majesty may escape this day,
No doubt but you shall soon recover all.

100 TAMBURLAINE: Then will I comfort all my vital parts,
And live, in spite of death, above a day.

Alarms within.

Enter a MESSENGER.

MESSENGER: My lord, young Callapine, that lately fled
from your majesty, hath now gathered a fresh army,

86 *humidum and calor*: moisture and heat.

252

and, hearing your absence in the field, offers to set upon
us presently.

TAMBURLAINE: See, my physicians, now, how Jove hath
sent
A present medicine to recure my pain!
My looks shall make them fly; and, might I follow,
There should not one of all the villain's power
Live to give offer of another fight.   *110*

USUMCASANE: I joy, my lord, your highness is so strong,
That can endure so well your royal presence,
Which only will dismay the enemy.

TAMBURLAINE: I know it will, Casane. Draw, you
slaves!
In spite of death, I will go show my face.
    Alarms. Exit TAMBURLAINE *with all the rest, and
    re-enter presently.*

TAMBURLAINE: Thus are the villains, cowards fled for
fear,
Like summer's vapours vanish'd by the sun;
And, could I but a while pursue the field,
That Callapine should be my slave again.
But I perceive my martial strength is spent: *120*
In vain I strive and rail against those powers
That mean t'invest me in a higher throne,
As much too high for this disdainful earth.
Give me a map; then let me see how much
Is left for me to conquer all the world,
That these, my boys, may finish all my wants.
    One brings a map.
Here I began to march towards Persia,
Along Armenia and the Caspian Sea,
And thence unto Bithynia, where I took
The Turk and his great empress prisoners.   *130*
Then march'd I into Egypt and Arabia;
And here, not far from Alexandria,
Whereas the Terrene and the Red Sea meet,
Being distant less than full a hundred leagues,

I meant to cut a channel to them both,
That men might quickly sail to India.
From thence to Nubia near Borno lake,
And so along the Æthiopian sea,
Cutting the Tropic line of Capricorn,
140   I conquer'd all as far as Zanzibar.
Then, by the northern part of Africa,
I came at last to Graecia, and from thence
To Asia, where I stay against my will;
Which is from Scythia, where I first began,
Backward and forwards near five thousand leagues.
Look here, my boys; see, what a world of ground
Lies westward from the midst of Cancer's line
Unto the rising of this earthly globe,
Whereas the sun, declining from our sight,
150   Begins the day with our Antipodes!
And shall I die, and this unconquered?
Lo, here, my sons, are all the golden mines,
Inestimable drugs and precious stones,
More worth than Asia and the world beside;
And from th'Antarctic Pole eastward behold
As much more land, which never was descried,
Wherein are rocks of pearl that shine as bright
As all the lamps that beautify the sky!
And shall I die, and this unconquered?
160   Here, lovely boys; what death forbids my life,
That let your lives command in spite of death.
AMYRAS: Alas, my lord, how should our bleeding hearts,
Wounded and broken with your highness' grief,
Retain a thought of joy or spark of life?
Your soul gives essence to our wretched subjects,
Whose matter is incorporate in your flesh.
CELEBINUS: Your pains do pierce our souls; no hope
survives,
For by your life we entertain our lives.
TAMBURLAINE: But, sons, this subject, not of force
enough

To hold the fiery spirit it contains,   *170*
Must part, imparting his impressions
By equal portions into both your breasts;
My flesh, divided in your precious shapes,
Shall still retain my spirit, though I die,
And live in all your seeds immortally.
Then now remove me, that I may resign
My place and proper title to my son.
First, take my scourge and my imperial crown,
And mount my royal chariot of estate,
That I may see thee crown'd before I die.   *180*
Help me, my lords, to make my last remove.
        They assist TAMBURLAINE *to descend from the chariot.*
THERIDAMAS: A woeful change, my lord, that daunts
        our thoughts
More than the ruin of our proper souls!
TAMBURLAINE: Sit up, my son, let me see how well
Thou wilt become thy father's majesty.
        They crown him.
AMYRAS: With what a flinty bosom should I joy
The breath of life and burden of my soul,
If not resolv'd into resolved pains,
My body's mortified lineaments
Should exercise the motions of my heart,   *190*
Pierc'd with the joy of any dignity!
O father, if the unrelenting ears
Of Death and Hell be shut against my prayers,
And that the spiteful influence of Heaven
Deny my soul fruition of her joy,
How should I step, or stir my hateful feet
Against the inward powers of my heart,
Leading a life that only strives to die,
And plead in vain unpleasing sovereignty?
TAMBURLAINE: Let not thy love exceed thine honour, son, *200*
Nor bar thy mind that magnanimity

188 *resolv'd into resolved pains*: dissolved into enduring (resolute)
pain.

255

That nobly must admit necessity.
Sit up, my boy, and with these silken reins
Bridle the steeled stomachs of these jades.

THERIDAMAS: My lord, you must obey his majesty,
Since fate commands and proud necessity.

AMYRAS: Heavens witness me with what a broken heart
Mounting the chariot.
And damned spirit I ascend this seat,
And send my soul, before my father die,
210 His anguish and his burning agony!

TAMBURLAINE: Now fetch the hearse of fair
Zenocrate;
Let it be plac'd by this my fatal chair,
And serve as parcel of my funeral.

USUMCASANE: Then feels your majesty no sovereign ease,
Nor may our hearts, all drown'd in tears of blood,
Joy any hope of your recovery?

TAMBURLAINE: Casane, no; the monarch of the earth,
And eyeless monster that torments my soul,
Cannot behold the tears ye shed for me,
220 And therefore still augments his cruelty.

TECHELLES: Then let some god oppose his holy power
Against the wrath and tyranny of Death,
That his tear-thirsty and unquenched hate
May be upon himself reverberate!
They bring in the hearse of Zenocrate.

TAMBURLAINE: Now, eyes, enjoy your latest benefit,
And, when my soul hath virtue of your sight,
Pierce through the coffin and the sheet of gold,
And glut your longings with a heaven of joy.
So, reign, my son; scourge and control those slaves,
230 Guiding thy chariot with thy father's hand.
As precious is the charge thou undertak'st
As that which Clymene's brain-sick son did guide,
When wandering Phœbe's ivory cheeks were
scorch'd,

232 *Clymene's brain-sick son*: Phaethon.

And all the earth, like Ætna, breathing fire.
Be warn'd by him, then; learn with awful eye
To sway a throne as dangerous as his;
For, if thy body thrive not full of thoughts
As pure and fiery as Phyteus' beams,
The nature of these proud rebelling jades
Will take occasion by the slenderest hair,   240
And draw thee piecemeal, like Hippolytus,
Through rocks more steep and sharp than Caspian
    cliffs.
The nature of thy chariot will not bear
A guide of baser temper than myself,
More than heaven's coach the pride of Phaeton.
Farewell, my boys! my dearest friends, farewell!
My body feels, my soul doth weep to see
Your sweet desires depriv'd my company,
For Tamburlaine, the scourge of God, must die.
    Dies.
AMYRAS: Meet heaven and earth, and here let all things   250
    end,
For earth hath spent the pride of all her fruit,
And heaven consum'd his choicest living fire!
Let earth and heaven his timeless death deplore,
For both their worths will equal him no more!
    Exeunt.

238 *Phyteus*: Pythius, Apollo.   253 *timeless*: untimely.

The Tragical History of
Doctor Faustus

DOCTOR FAUSTUS: THE TEXT

THE play survives in two versions: one published in 1604, ten years after Marlowe's death, the other in 1616. The later text is the longer (2121 lines of print, as compared with 1517), and contains several episodes absent from the other. It is not generally thought, however, that these scenes were written by Marlowe himself, and for many years the play was read without any consciousness of there being a 'textual problem' at all: the 1604 text was the earlier and therefore accepted as the more authentic, while the extra material of 1616 was readily accountable as being the additions for which certain other writers were known to have been paid.* But as the twentieth century advanced, more scholars challenged this view, and nowadays it is the 1616 text that is in favour. Consequently this is the version on which the present edition is reluctantly based.

'Reluctantly', because the editor's personal opinion is that the play is artistically stronger in its shorter form. The A text (1604) has everything essential to the presentation of 'the tragical history'; the B text (1616) adds, for the most part, light, simple-minded comedy, innocuous enough except that it distracts the mind from what is serious and valuable in the play; or rather, it fails to occupy the *mind* at all, and so lessens the poetic and dramatic intensity, leaving one feeling something the opposite of the Jew of Malta who had

> Infinite riches in a little room.

Not that the riches were unmixed even in the 'little room' of the A text. There is quite enough knockabout and emptiness in the middle section of this. But at least the balance there is more favourable to the essential, the

*William Birde and Samuel Rowley were paid £4 by Henslowe on 22 November 1602 'for their adicyones in doctor fostes'.

tragic and the poetic: in the B text we are much nearer to the 'set of farces' which we gather *Doctor Faustus* had become in Pope's time.

This is unfortunately a critical rather than an editorial view. The editor has to present the 'best' text, and that does not necessarily mean the version he finds most artistically satisfying. The B text appears to have been working from manuscript that antedates the Quarto of 1604, and that (A) text is most convincingly explained as a shortened version used perhaps on tour, or by a company with fewer resources (B is notably more spectacular). There are places where B is textually inferior to A. Sometimes the censor seems to have been at work, and it may be thanks to him that B's Faustus is not allowed to cry:

See, see where Christ's blood streams in the firmament.

And it is generally in the finest passages rhat the local superiority of A has to be recognized, and so incorporated in a modern edition. But B remains the inevitable basis.

In the present volume, uses of A are recorded in the Additional Notes, pp. 590–95.

Dramatis Personae

CHORUS

FAUSTUS

WAGNER, *servant to* FAUSTUS

GOOD ANGEL AND EVIL ANGEL

VALDES,

CORNELIUS, } *friends to* FAUSTUS

MEPHOSTOPHILIS

LUCIFER

BELZEBUB

THE SEVEN DEADLY SINS

CLOWN/ROBIN

DICK

RAFE

VINTNER

CARTER

HOSTESS

THE POPE

BRUNO

RAYMOND, King of Hungary

CHARLES, the German Emperor

MARTINO

FREDERICK

BENVOLIO

SAXONY

DUKE OF VANHOLT

DUCHESS OF VANHOLT

SPIRITS *in the shapes of* ALEXANDER THE GREAT,
  DARIUS, PARAMOUR *and* HELEN

AN OLD MAN

SCHOLARS, SOLDIERS, DEVILS, COURTIERS,
CARDINALS, MONKS, CUPIDS

Enter CHORUS.

CHORUS: Not marching[1]* in the fields of Thrasimene,
Where Mars did mate[2] the warlike Carthigens,
Nor sporting in the dalliance of love
In courts of kings where state is overturned,
Nor in the pomp of proud audacious deeds,
Intends our muse to vaunt his heavenly verse.
Only this, gentles: we must now perform
The form of Faustus' fortunes, good or bad.
And now to patient judgments we appeal,
And speak for Faustus in his infancy.   10
Now is he born, of parents base of stock,
In Germany, within a town called Rhodes.
At riper years to Wittenberg he went,
Whereas his kinsmen chiefly brought him up.
So much he profits in divinity,
The fruitful plot[3] of scholarism graced,
That shortly he was graced with Doctor's name,
Excelling all; and sweetly can dispute
In th' heavenly matters of theology.
Till swol'n with cunning of a self-conceit,   20
His waxen wings did mount above his reach,
And melting, heavens conspired his overthrow.
For falling to a devilish exercise,
And glutted now with learning's golden gifts,
He surfeits upon cursed necromancy.
Nothing so sweet as magic is to him,
Which he prefers before his chiefest bliss:
And this the man that in his study sits.

*Superior numbers refer to the Additional Notes at the end of the book.

ACT ONE

SCENE ONE

FAUSTUS *in his study.*

FAUSTUS: Settle thy studies, Faustus, and begin
To sound the depth of that thou wilt profess.
Having commenced, be a divine in show,
Yet level at the end of every art
And live and die in Aristotle's works.
Sweet Analytics, 'tis thou hast ravished me.
Bene disserere est finis logices.
Is 'to dispute well logic's chiefest end'?
Affords this art no greater miracle?
10   Then read no more: thou hast attained that end.
A greater subject fitteth Faustus' wit.
Bid *on cai me on*[4] farewell. And Galen,[5] come.
Seeing, *ubi desinit philosophus, ibi incipit medicus.*[6]
Be a physician, Faustus: heap up gold
And be eternized for some wondrous cure.
Summum bonum medicinae sanitas:
'The end of physic is our body's health'.
Why, Faustus, hast thou not attained that end?
Is not thy common talk sound aphorisms?[7]
20   Are not thy bills hung up as monuments,
Whereby whole cities have escaped the plague,
And thousand desperate maladies been cured?
Yet art thou still but Faustus and a man.
Couldst thou make men to live eternally,
Or being dead, raise them to life again,
Then this profession were to be esteemed.
Physic, farewell. Where is Justinian?[8]

12 *on cai me on*: being and non-being (Aristotle).
13 *ubi desinit philosophus* . . .: where the natural philosopher ends,
there the doctor begins (Aristotle).
20 *bills*: prescriptions.

Si una eademque res legatur duobus,
Alter rem, alter valorem rei etc.,
A petty case of paltry legacies!   *30*
Exhaereditare filium non potest pater, nisi —
Such is the subject of the institute
And universal body of the law.
This study fits a mercenary drudge,
Who aims at nothing but external trash,
Too servile and illiberal for me.
When all is done Divinity is best.
Jerome's Bible! Faustus, view it well.
Stipendium peccati mors est.[9] Ha! *Stipendium etc.,*
'The reward of sin is death'. That's hard.   *40*
Si pecasse negamus, fallimur, et nulla est in nobis veritas.[10]
'If we say that we have no sin
We deceive ourselves, and there is no truth in us.'
Why then, belike, we must sin,
And so consequently die.
Ay, we must die, an everlasting death.
What doctrine call you this? *Che sera, sera.*
'What will be, shall be.' Divinity, adieu!
These necromantic books are heavenly,
Lines, circles, scenes, letters and characters: *50*
Ay, these are those that Faustus most desires.
Oh, what a world of profit and delight,
Of power, of honour of, omnipotence,
Is promised to the studious artizan!
All things that move between the quiet poles
Shall be at my command. Emperors and kings
Are but obeyed in their several provinces.
Nor can they raise the wind or rend the clouds.
But his dominion that exceeds in this

28 *Si una eademque res . . .*: If one and the same thing is bequeathed
to two people, one of them should have the thing itself, and
the other the value of it (principle attributed to Justinian).
31 *Exhaereditare filium . . .*: The father may not disinherit the son
(Justinian).

60 Stretcheth as far as doth the mind of man:
A sound magician is a demi-god.
Here, tire my brains to get a deity.
    Enter WAGNER.
Wagner, commend me to my dearest friends,
The German Valdes and Cornelius.
Request them earnestly to visit me.
WAGNER: I will, sir.
    Exit.
FAUSTUS: Their conference will be a greater help to me
Than all my labours, plod I ne'er so fast.
    Enter the GOOD *and* EVIL ANGELS.
GOOD ANGEL: Oh Faustus, lay that damned book aside,
70 And gaze not on it lest it tempt thy soul
And heap God's heavy wrath upon thy head.
Read, read the scriptures: that is blasphemy.
EVIL ANGEL: Go forward, Faustus, in that famous art
Wherein all nature's treasure is contained.
Be thou on earth as Jove is in the sky,
Lord and commander of these elements.
    Exeunt ANGELS.
FAUSTUS: How am I glutted with conceit of this!
Shall I make spirits fetch me what I please,
Resolve me of all ambiguities,
80 Perform what desperate enterprise I will?
I'll have them fly to India for gold,
Ransack the ocean for orient pearl,
And search all corners of the new-found world
For pleasant fruits and princely delicates.
I'll have them read me strange philosophy,
And tell the secrets of all foreign kings.
I'll have them wall all Germany with brass,
And make swift Rhine circle fair Wittenberg.
I'll have them fill the public schools with silk,[11]
90 Wherewith the students shall be bravely clad.
I'll levy soldiers with the coin they bring,

89 *public schools*: lecture rooms of the university faculties.

And chase the Prince of Parma from our land,
And reign sole king of all the provinces.
Yea, stranger engines for the brunt of war
Than was the fiery keel[12] at Antwerp's bridge
I'll make my servile spirits to invent.
Come, German Valdes and Cornelius,
And make me blest with your sage conference.

    Enter VALDES *and* CORNELIUS.

Valdes, sweet Valdes and Cornelius!
Know that your words have won me at the last   *100*
To practise magic and concealed arts.
Yet not your words[13] only but mine own fantasy
That will receive no object for my head,
But ruminates on necromantic skill.
Philosophy is odious and obscure.
Both law and physic are for petty wits.
Divinity is basest of the three,[14]
Unpleasant, harsh, contemptible and vile.
'Tis magic, magic that hath ravished me.
Then, gentle friends, aid me in this attempt,   *110*
And I, that have with subtle syllogisms
Gravelled the pastors of the German Church
And made the flowering pride of Wittenberg
Swarm to my problems as the infernal spirits
On sweet Musaeus[15] when he came to hell,
Will be as cunning as Agrippa[16] was,
Whose shadow made all Europe honour him.
VALDES: Faustus, these books, thy wit and our experience
Shall make all nations to canonize us,
As Indian moors obey their Spanish lords.   *120*
So shall the spirits of every element
Be always serviceable to us three.
Like lions shall they guard us when we please;
Like Almain rutters with their horsemen's staves;

103 *that will receive* . . . : that will let me think of no other subject.
112 *Gravelled*: baffled, defeated.
124 *Almain rutters*: German cavalry-men.

Or Lapland giants trotting by our sides.
Sometimes like women or unwedded maids,
Shadowing more beauty in their airy brows
Than has the white breasts of the queen of love.
From Venice shall they drag huge argosies,
130 And from America the golden fleece
That yearly stuffs old Philip's treasury
If learned Faustus will be resolute.
FAUSTUS: Valdes, as resolute am I in this
As thou to live, therefore object it not.
CORNELIUS: The miracles that magic will perform
Will make thee vow to study nothing else.
He that is grounded in Astrology,
Enriched with tongues, well seen in minerals,
Hath all the principles magic doth require.
140 Then doubt not, Faustus, but to be renowned,
And more frequented for this mystery
Than heretofore the Delphian oracle.
The spirits tell me they can dry the sea,
And fetch the treasure of all foreign wracks.
Yea, all the wealth that our forefathers hid
Within the massy entrails of the earth.
Then tell me, Faustus, what shall we three want?
FAUSTUS: Nothing, Cornelius! Oh, this cheers my soul.
Come, show me some demonstrations magical,
150 That I may conjure in some bushy grove,
And have these joys in full possession.
VALDES: Then haste thee to some solitary grove,
And bear wise Bacon's and Albanus'[17] works,
The Hebrew Psalter and New Testament;
And whatsoever else is requisite
We will inform thee e're our conference cease.
CORNELIUS: Valdes, first let him know the words of art,
And then, all other ceremonies learned,
Faustus may try his cunning by himself.
160 VALDES: First I'll instruct thee in the rudiments,
And then wilt thou be perfecter than I.

FAUSTUS: Then come and dine with me, and after meat
We'll canvass every quiddity thereof,
For ere I sleep, I'll try what I can do.
This night I'll conjure, though I die therefore.
Exeunt.

SCENE TWO

Enter two SCHOLARS.

FIRST SCHOLAR: I wonder what's become of Faustus,
that was wont to make our schools ring with *sic probo.*
Enter WAGNER.

SECOND SCHOLAR: That shall we presently know. Here
comes his boy.

FIRST SCHOLAR: How now, sirrah, where's thy
master?

WAGNER: God in heaven knows.

SECOND SCHOLAR: Why, dost not thou know then?

WAGNER: Yes, I know, but that follows not.

FIRST SCHOLAR: Go to, sirrah. Leave your jesting and   10
tell us where he is.

WAGNER: That follows not by force of argument, which
you, being licentiates, should stand upon. Therefore,
acknowledge your error and be attentive.

SECOND SCHOLAR: Then you will not tell us?

WAGNER: You are deceived, for I will tell you. Yet if you
were not dunces, you would never ask me such a
question. For is he not *Corpus naturale*? And is not that
mobile? Then wherefore should you ask me such a
question? But that I am by nature phlegmatic, slow to   20
wrath and prone to lechery (to love, I would say), it
were not for you to come within forty foot of the place
of execution, although I do not doubt but to see you

163 *canvass every quiddity*: investigate in detail and depth.
2 *sic probo*: 'Thus I prove': triumphant conclusion of scholar's
demonstration.

both hanged the next sessions. Thus, having triumphed
over you, I will set my countenance like a precision, and
begin to speak thus: 'Truly, my dear brethren, my master
is within at dinner with Valdes and Cornelius, as this
wine, if it could speak, would inform your worships.
And so the Lord bless you, preserve you and keep you,
30   my dear brethren.'
    Exit.

FIRST SCHOLAR: Oh Faustus, then I fear that which I
    have long suspected:
That thou art fallen into that damned art
For which they two are infamous through the world.
SECOND SCHOLAR: Were he a stranger, not allied to me,
The danger of his soul would make me mourn.
But come, let us go, and inform the Rector.
It may be his grave counsel may reclaim him.
FIRST SCHOLAR: I fear me nothing will reclaim him
    now.
SECOND SCHOLAR: Yet let us see what we can do.
    Exeunt.

SCENE THREE

Thunder. Enter LUCIFER *and* FOUR DEVILS.
FAUSTUS *to them with this speech.*
FAUSTUS: Now that the gloomy shadow of the night,
Longing to view Orion's drizzling look,
Leaps from th'Antarctick world unto the sky,
And dims the Welkin with her pitchy breath,
Faustus, begin thine incantations
And try if devils will obey thy hest,
Seeing thou hast prayed and sacrificed to them.
Within this circle is Jehova's name
Forward and backward anagrammatised:
10   The abbreviated names of holy saints,
    25 *precisian*: Puritan.

272

Figures of every adjunct to the heavens,
And characters of signs and evening stars,
By which the spirits are enforced to rise.
Then fear not, Faustus, to be resolute
And try the utmost magic can perform.

    Thunder.

Sint mihi dei acherontis propitii, valeat numen triplex Jehovae,
ignei areii, aquatani spiritus salvete: orientis princeps Belze-
bub, inferni ardentis monarcha et demigorgon, propitiamus vos,
ut appareat, et surgat Mephostophilis (Dragon)[18] *quod*
tumeraris: per Jehovam, gehennam, et consecratam aquam   20
quam nunc spargo; signumque crucis quod nunc facio; et per
vota nostra ipse nunc surgat nobis dicatus Mephostophilis.

    Enter a DEVIL.

I charge thee to return and change thy shape.
Thou art too ugly to attend on me.
Go, and return an old Franciscan friar:
That holy shape becomes a devil best.

    Exit DEVIL.

I see there's virtue in my heavenly words.
Who would not be proficient in this art?
How pliant is this Mephostophilis!
Full of obedience and humility,   30
Such is the force of magic and my spells.
Now, Faustus, thou art conjuror laurcate:[19]
Thou canst command great Mephostophilis.
Quin redis Mephostophilis fratris imagine.

    Enter MEPHOSTOPHILIS.

16 *Sint mihi* . . .: May the gods of the underworld (Acheron) be
kind to me; may the triple deity of Jehovah be gone; to the spirits
of fire, air and water, greetings. Prince of the east, Beelzebub,
monarch of the fires below, and Demogorgon, we appeal to you
so that Mephostophilis may appear and rise. Why do you delay
(*Quod tu moraris*)? By Jehovah, hell and the hallowed water which
I now sprinkle, and the sign of the cross, which I now make, and
by our vows, let Mephostophilis himself now arise to serve us.
19 *Dragon*: stage directions see p. 591.
34 *Quin redis* . . .: Why do you not return, Mephostophilis, in the
appearance of a friar? (cf. l. 25 above).

MEPHOSTOPHILIS: Now, Faustus, what wouldst thou
    have me do?

FAUSTUS: I charge thee wait upon me whilst I live,
    To do whatever Faustus shall command,
    Be it to make the moon drop from her sphere,
    Or the ocean to overwhelm the world.

40 MEPHOSTOPHILIS: I am a servant to great Lucifer,
    And may not follow thee without his leave.
    No more than he commands must we perform.

FAUSTUS: Did not he charge thee to appear to me?

MEPHOSTOPHILIS: No, I came now hither of mine
    own accord.

FAUSTUS: Did not my conjuring speeches raise thee?
    Speak.

MEPHOSTOPHILIS: That was the cause, but yet *per accidens*;
    For when we hear one rack the name of God,
    Abjure the scriptures and his saviour Christ,
    We fly in hope to get his glorious soul.

50   Nor will we come unless he use such means
    Whereby he is in danger to be damned.
    Therefore the shortest cut for conjuring
    Is stoutly to abjure all godliness
    And pray devoutly to the prince of hell.

FAUSTUS: So Faustus hath already done, and holds this
    principle:
    There is no chief but only Belzebub,
    To whom Faustus doth dedicate himself.
    This word 'damnation' terrifies not me,
    For I confound hell in elysium.

60   My ghost be with the old philosophers.[20]
    But leaving these vain trifles of men's souls,
    Tell me, what is that Lucifer, thy lord?

MEPHOSTOPHILIS: Arch-regent and commander of all
    spirits.

FAUSTUS: Was not that Lucifer an angel once?

MEPHOSTOPHILIS: Yes, Faustus, and most dearly loved
    of God.

FAUSTUS: How comes it then that he is prince of devils?

MEPHOSTOPHILIS: Oh, by aspiring pride and insolence,
For which God threw him from the face of heaven.

FAUSTUS: And what are you that live with Lucifer?

MEPHOSTOPHILIS: Unhappy spirits that fell with Lucifer,   70
Conspired against our God with Lucifer,
And are for ever damned with Lucifer.

FAUSTUS: Where are you damned?

MEPHOSTOPHILIS: In hell.

FAUSTUS: How comes it then that thou art out of hell?

MEPHOSTOPHILIS: Why, this is hell, nor am I out of it.
Think'st thou that I that saw the face of God
And tasted the eternal joys of heaven,
Am not tormented with ten thousand hells
In being deprived of everlasting bliss?   80
Oh, Faustus, leave these frivolous demands,
Which strike a terror to my fainting soul.

FAUSTUS: What, is great Mephostophilis so passionate
For being deprived of the joys of heaven?
Learn thou of Faustus manly fortitude,
And scorn those joys thou never shalt possess.
Go, bear these tidings to great Lucifer,
Seeing Faustus hath incurred eternal death
By desperate thoughts against Jove's deity.
Say he surrenders up to him his soul,   90
So he will spare him four and twenty years,
Letting him live in all voluptuousness,
Having thee ever to attend on me,
To give me whatsoever I shall ask,
To tell me whatsoever I demand,
To slay mine enemies and to aid my friends
And always be obedient to my will.
Go, and return to mighty Lucifer,
And meet me in my study at midnight,
And then resolve me of thy master's mind.   100

MEPHOSTOPHILIS: I will, Faustus.
  Exit.

FAUSTUS: Had I as many souls as there be stars,
    I'd give them all for Mephostophilis.
    By him I'll be great emperor of the world,
    And make a bridge through the air
    To pass the ocean. With a band of men
    I'll join the hills that bind the Affrick shore,
    And make that country continent to Spain,
    And both contributory to my crown.
110   The Emperor shall not live but by my leave,
    Nor any potentate of Germany.
    Now that I have obtained what I desired,
    I'll live in speculation of this art
    Till Mephostophilis return again.
    Exit.

SCENE FOUR[21]

Enter WAGNER *and the* CLOWN.

WAGNER: Come hither, sirrah boy.

CLOWN: Boy? Oh, disgrace to my person! Zounds!
'Boy' in your face! You have seen many boys with
beards, I am sure.

WAGNER: Sirrah, hast thou no comings in?

CLOWN: Yes, and goings out too, you may see, sir.

WAGNER: Alas, poor slave. See how poverty jests in his
nakedness. I know the villain's out of service and so
hungry that I know he would give his soul to the devil
10   for a shoulder of mutton though it were blood-raw.

CLOWN: Not so neither. I had need to have it well
roasted, and good sauce to it, if I pay so dear, I can tell
you.

WAGNER: Sirrah, wilt thou be my man and wait on me?
And I will make thee go like *Qui mihi discipulus*.

CLOWN: What, in verse?

WAGNER: No, slave, in beaten silk and stavesacre.

15 *Qui mihi discipulus*: One who is my pupil (the opening of a
Latin poem used in schools).
17 *stavesacre*: used for killing vermin.

CLOWN: Stavesacre? That's good to kill vermin. Then
belike, if I serve you I shall be lousy.

WAGNER: Why, so thou shalt be whether thou dost it or   20
no. For, sirrah, if thou dost not presently bind thyself to
me for seven years, I'll turn all the lice about thee into
familiars, and make them tear thee in pieces.

CLOWN: Nay, sir, you may save yourself a labour, for
they are as familiar with me as if they paid for their meat
and drink, I can tell you.

WAGNER: Well, sirrah, leave your jesting and take these
guilders.

CLOWN: Yes, marry, sir, and I thank you too.

WAGNER: So, now thou art to be at an hour's warning,   30
whensoever and wheresoever the devil shall fetch thee.

CLOWN: Here, take your guilders.

WAGNER: Truly, I'll none of them.

CLOWN: Truly but you shall.

WAGNER: Bear witness I gave them him.

CLOWN: Bear witness I give them you again.

WAGNER: Not I. Thou art pressed. Prepare thyself, for I
will presently raise up two devils, to carry thee away:
Banio, Belcher!

CLOWN: Belcher? And Belcher come here, I'll belch   40
him! I am not afraid of a devil.

Enter TWO DEVILS *and the* CLOWN *runs up and
down crying.*

WAGNER: How now, sir, will you serve me now?

CLOWN: Ay, good Wagner. Take away the devil then.

WAGNER: Baliol and Belcher, spirits, away!

Exeunt DEVILS.

CLOWN: What, are they gone? A vengeance on them!
They have vile long nails. There was a he-devil and a
she-devil. I'll tell you how you shall know them: all he-
devils has horns, and all she-devils has clifts and cloven
feet.

WAGNER: Well, sirrah, follow me.   50

23 *familiars*: spirits or devils attendant on a human being.

CLOWN: But, do you hear, if I should serve you, would
you teach me to raise up Banio's and Belcheo's?

WAGNER: I will teach thee to turn thyself to anything, to
a dog, or a cat, or a mouse, or a rat, or anything.

CLOWN: How? A Christian fellow to a dog or a cat, a
mouse or a rat? No, no, sir, if you turn me into anything, let it be in the likeness of a little pretty frisking
flea, that I may be here and there and everywhere. Oh,
I'll tickle the pretty wenches' plackets! I'll be amongst
60   them, i'faith.

WAGNER: Well, sirrah, come.

CLOWN: But do you hear, Wagner?

WAGNER: How? Baliol and Belcher!

CLOWN: Oh Lord, I pray, sir, let Banio and Belcher go
sleep.

WAGNER: Villain, call me Master Wagner, and see that
you walk attentively and let your right eye be always
diametrically fixed upon my left heel, that thou mayest
Quasi vestigias nostras insistere.
Exit.

70   CLOWN: God forgive me, he speaks Dutch fustian! Well,
I'll follow him. I'll serve him, that's flat.
Exit.

SCENE FIVE

Enter FAUSTUS *in his study.*

FAUSTUS: Now, Faustus, must thou needs be damned?[22]
And canst thou not be saved?
What boots it then to think on God or heaven?
Away with such vain fancies and despair,
Despair in God and trust in Belzebub.
Now go not backward. No, Faustus, be resolute.
Why waverest thou? Oh, something soundeth in mine
ears

69 *Quasi vestigias* . . .: as if to tread in our footsteps.

Abjure this magic, turn to God again.
Ay, and Faustus will turn to God again.
To God? He loves thee not. 10
The God thou servest is thine own appetite,
Wherein is fixed the love of Belzebub.
To him I'll build an altar and a church,
And offer lukewarm blood of new-born babes.
Enter the GOOD *and* EVIL ANGELS.

GOOD ANGEL: Sweet Faustus, leave that execrable art.

FAUSTUS: Contrition, prayer, repentance, what of these?

GOOD ANGEL: Oh, they are means to bring thee unto heaven.

EVIL ANGEL: Rather illusions, fruits of lunacy,
That makes men foolish that do trust them most.

GOOD ANGEL: Sweet Faustus, think of heaven and 20 heavenly things.

EVIL ANGEL: No, Faustus, think of honour and of wealth.
Exeunt ANGELS.

FAUSTUS: Of wealth!
Why, the signory of Emden shall be mine!
When Mephostophilis shall stand by me,
What God can hurt thee, Faustus? Thou art safe.
Cast no more doubts. Come, Mephostophilis,
And bring glad tidings from great Lucifer.
Is't not midnight? Come Mephostophilis!
Veni, veni, Mephostophile!
Enter MEPHOSTOPHILIS.
Now tell me, what saith Lucifer, thy lord? 30

MEPHOSTOPHILIS: That I shall wait on Faustus whilst he lives,
So he will buy my service with his soul.

FAUSTUS: Already Faustus hath hazarded that for thee.

MEPHOSTOPHILIS: But now thou must bequeath it solemnly,

23 *signory of Emden*: governorship of the foremost trading town in East Friesland.

And write a deed of gift with thine own blood,
For that security craves great Lucifer.
If thou deny it, I will back to hell.

FAUSTUS: Stay, Mephostophilis, and tell me
What good will my soul do thy lord?

40 MEPHOSTOPHILIS: Enlarge his kingdom.

FAUSTUS: Is that the reason why he tempts us thus?

MEPHOSTOPHILIS: *Solamen miseris, socios habuisse doloris.*

FAUSTUS: Why, have you any pain, that torture others?

MEPHOSTOPHILIS: As great as have the human souls of
men.
But tell me, Faustus, shall I have thy soul?
And I will be thy slave and wait on thee,
And give thee more than thou hast wit to ask.

FAUSTUS: Ay, Mephostophilis, I'll give it thee.

MEPHOSTOPHILIS: Then, Faustus, stab thy arm
courageously,

50 And bind thy soul, that at some certain day
Great Lucifer may claim it as his own,
And then be thou as great as Lucifer.

FAUSTUS: Lo, Mephostophilis, for love of thee
I cut mine arm, and with my proper blood
Assure my soul to be great Lucifer's,
Chief lord and regent of perpetual night.
View here the blood that trickles from mine arm,
And let it be propitious for my wish.

MEPHOSTOPHILIS: But, Faustus, thou must write it in
manner of a deed of gift.

60 FAUSTUS: Ay, so I will. But, Mephostophilis,
My blood congeals and I can write no more!

MEPHOSTOPHILIS: I'll fetch thee fire to dissolve it
straight.
Exit.

FAUSTUS: What might the staying of my blood portend?
Is it unwilling I should write this bill?

42 *Solamen miseris* . . .: It is a comfort in wretchedness to have
companions in woe.

Why streams it not that I may write afresh?
'Faustus gives to thee his soul': ah, there it stayed!
Why shouldst thou not? Is not thy soul thine own?
Then write again: 'Faustus gives to thee his soul'.

Enter MEPHOSTOPHILIS *with a chafer of coals.*

MEPHOSTOPHILIS: Here's fire. Come, Faustus, set it on.

FAUSTUS: So, now my blood begins to clear again.   70
Now will I make an end immediately.

MEPHOSTOPHILIS: Oh what will not I do to obtain his
soul!

FAUSTUS: *Consummatum est*: this bill is ended,
And Faustus hath bequeathed his soul to Lucifer.
But what is this inscription on mine arm?
Homo fuge! Whither should I flie?
If unto heaven, he'll throw me down to hell.
My senses are deceived: here's nothing writ!
Oh, yes, I see it plain. Even here is writ
Homo fuge. Yet shall not Faustus fly.   80

MEPHOSTOPHILIS: I'll fetch him somewhat to delight
his mind.

Exit.

Enter DEVILS, *giving crowns and rich apparel to*
FAUSTUS; *they dance and then depart. Enter*
MEPHOSTOPHILIS.

FAUSTUS: What means this show? Speak, Mephostophilis.

MEPHOSTOPHILIS: Nothing, Faustus, but to delight thy
mind,
And let thee see what magic can perform.

FAUSTUS: But may I raise such spirits when I please?

MEPHOSTOPHILIS: Ay, Faustus, and do greater things
than these.

FAUSTUS: Then there's enough for a thousand souls.[23]
Here, Mephostophilis, receive this scroll,

73 *Consummatum est*: 'It is finished' (the last of Christ's words
from the cross. John, XIX, 30).
76 *Homo fuge*: Fly, oh man.

A deed of gift, of body and of soul:
90   But yet conditionally, that thou perform
All covenants and articles between us both.

MEPHOSTOPHILIS: Faustus, I swear by hell and Lucifer
To effect all promises between us both.

FAUSTUS: Then hear me read it, Mephostophilis.
On these conditions following:

First, that Faustus may be a spirit in form and substance.

Secondly, that Mephostophilis shall be his servant, and be by him commanded.

100   Thirdly, that Mephostophilis shall do for him, and bring him whatsoever.

Fourthly, that he shall be in his chamber or house invisible.

Lastly, that he shall appear to the said John Faustus at all times, in what shape and form soever he please.

I, John Faustus of Wittenberg Doctor, by these presents, do give both body and soul to Lucifer, Prince of the East, and his minister Mephostophilis, and furthermore grant unto them that four and
110   twenty years being expired, and these articles above written being inviolate, full power to fetch or carry the said John Faustus, body and soul, flesh, blood or goods, into their habitation wheresoever.

By me, John Faustus.

MEPHOSTOPHILIS: Speak, Faustus, do you deliver this as your deed?

FAUSTUS: Ay, take it, and the devil give thee good of it.

MEPHOSTOPHILIS: So now, Faustus, ask me what thou wilt.

FAUSTUS: First I will question with thee about hell.
Tell me, where is the place that men call hell?

120 MEPHOSTOPHILIS: Under the heavens.

FAUSTUS: Ay, so are all things else; but whereabouts?

MEPHOSTOPHILIS: Within the bowels of these elements,
Where we are tortured and remain for ever.

Hell hath no limits, nor is circumscribed
In one self place. But where we are is hell,
And where hell is there must we ever be.
And to be short, when all the world dissolves
And every creature shall be purified,
All places shall be hell that is not heaven.

FAUSTUS: Come, I think hell's a fable. 130

MEPHOSTOPHILIS: Ay, think so still, till experience
change thy mind.

FAUSTUS: Why, dost thou think that Faustus shall be
damned?

MEPHOSTOPHILIS: Ay, of necessity, for here's the scroll
In which thou hast given thy soul to Lucifer.

FAUSTUS: Ay, and body too, but what of that?
Think'st thou that Faustus is so fond to imagine
That after this life there is any pain?
Tush, these are trifles and old wives' tales.

MEPHOSTOPHILIS: But Faustus, I am an instance to
prove the contrary,
For I tell thee I am damned, and now in hell. 140

FAUSTUS: How? Now in hell? Nay, and this be hell, I'll
willingly be damned here.
What! Sleeping, eating, walking and disputing?
But leaving this, let me have a wife, the fairest maid in
Germany, for I am wanton and lascivious, and cannot
live without a wife.

MEPHOSTOPHILIS: How, a wife? I prithee, Faustus, talk
not of a wife.

FAUSTUS: Nay, sweet Mephostophilis, fetch me one, for
I will have one.

MEPHOSTOPHILIS: Well, thou wilt have one. Sit there
till I come: I'll fetch thee a wife in the devil's name.

Enter a DEVIL *dressed like a woman, with fireworks.*

FAUSTUS: What sight is this? 150

MEPHOSTOPHILIS: Tell, Faustus, how dost thou like
thy wife?

136 *fond*: foolish.

FAUSTUS: A plague on her for a hot whore.

MEPHOSTOPHILIS: Tut, Faustus, marriage is but a
ceremonial toy.[24]

If thou lovest me, think no more of it.
I'll cull thee out the fairest courtesans
And bring them every morning to thy bed.
She whom thine eye shall like, thy heart shall have,
Be she as chaste as was Penelope,
As wise as Saba, or as beautiful

160   As was bright Lucifer before his fall.
Here, take this book, and peruse it well.
The iterating of these lines brings gold,
The framing of this circle on the ground
Brings thunder, whirlwinds, storm and lightning.
Pronounce this thrice devoutly to thyself
And men in harness shall appear to thee,
Ready to execute what thou commandest.

FAUSTUS: Thanks, Mephostophilis.[25] Yet fain would I
have a book wherein I might behold all spells and

170   incantations, that I might raise up spirits when I please.

MEPHOSTOPHILIS: Here they are in this book.

There turn to them.

FAUSTUS: Now would I have a book where I might see
all characters and planets of the heavens, that I might
know their motions and dispositions.

MEPHOSTOPHILIS: Here they are too.

Turn to them.

FAUSTUS: Nay, let me have one book more, and then I
have done, wherein I might see all plants, herbs and
trees that grow upon the earth.

MEPHOSTOPHILIS: Here they be.

180   FAUSTUS: Oh thou art deceived.

MEPHOSTOPHILIS: Tut, I warrant thee.

Turn to them.

159 *Saba*: the Queen of Sheba (1. Kings).
170 *spirit*: a damned soul.

ACT TWO[26]

SCENE ONE

Enter FAUSTUS *in his study, and* MEPHOSTOPHILIS.

FAUSTUS: When I behold the heavens then I repent,
   And curse thee, wicked Mephostophilis,
   Because thou hast deprived me of those joys.

MEPHOSTOPHILIS: 'Twas thine own seeking, Faustus,
   thank thyself.
   But thinkst thou heaven is such a glorious thing?
   I tell thee, Faustus, it is not half so fair
   As thou or any man that breathes on earth.

FAUSTUS: How prov'st thou that?

MEPHOSTOPHILIS: 'Twas made for man; then he's more
   excellent.

FAUSTUS: If heaven was made for man, 'twas made for   10
   me.
   I will renounce this magic and repent.

   Enter the GOOD *and* EVIL ANGELS.

GOOD ANGEL: Faustus, repent. Yet God will pity thee.

EVIL ANGEL: Thou art a spirit. God cannot pity thee.

FAUSTUS: Who buzzeth in mine ears I am a spirit?
   Be I a devil, yet God may pity me.
   Yea, God will pity me if I repent.

EVIL ANGEL: Ay, but Faustus never shall repent.
   Exeunt.

FAUSTUS: My heart's so hardened I cannot repent.
   Scarce can I name salvation, faith or heaven,
   But fearful echoes thunders in mine ears   20
   'Faustus, thou art damned'. Then swords and knives,
   Poison, guns, halters and envenomed steel
   Are laid before me to dispatch myself.
   And long ere this I should have done the deed,
   Had not sweet pleasure conquered deep despair.
   Have not I made blind Homer sing to me

285

Of Alexander's[27] love and Oenon's[28] death?
And hath not he that built[29] the walls of Thebes
With ravishing sound of his melodious harp
30   Made music with my Mephostophilis?
Why should I die then, or basely despair?
I am resolved, Faustus shall not repent.
Come, Mephostophilis,[30] let us dispute again,
And reason of divine astrology.
Speak, are there many spheres above the moon?
Are all celestial bodies but one globe,
As is the substance of this centric earth?

MEPHOSTOPHILIS: As are the elements, such are the
    heavens,
Even from the moon unto the empyrial orb,
40   Mutually folded in each other's spheres,
And jointly move upon one axle-tree,
Whose termine is termed the world's wide pole.
Nor are the names of Saturn, Mars or Jupiter
Feigned, but are erring stars.

FAUSTUS: But have they all one motion, both *situ et*
    tempore?

MEPHOSTOPHILIS: All move from east to west in four
and twenty hours upon the poles of the world, but
differ in their motions upon the poles of the zodiac.

FAUSTUS: Tush, these slender trifles Wagner can decide.
50   Hath Mephostophilis no greater skill? Who knows not
the double motion of the planets? That the first is
finished in a natural day? The second thus, as Saturn in
thirty years, Jupiter in twelve, Mars in four, the sun,
Venus and Mercury in twenty-eight days. Tush, these
are freshmen's suppositions. But tell me, hath every
sphere a dominion or *intelligentia*?

MEPHOSTOPHILIS: Ay.

42 *termine*: limit.
45 *situ et tempore*: in place (direction of movement) and time (of
revolution round the earth).
56 *intelligentia*: governing angel.

FAUSTUS: How many heavens or spheres are there?

MEPHOSTOPHILIS: Nine, the seven planets, the firmament, and the empyrial heaven. *60*

FAUSTUS: But is there not *coelum igneum et cristallinum*?

MEPHOSTOPHILIS: No, Faustus, they be but fables.

FAUSTUS: Resolve me then in this one question. Why are not conjunctions, oppositions, aspects, eclipses, all at one time, but in some years we have more, in some less?

MEPHOSTOPHILIS: *Per inaequalem motum, respectu totius.*

FAUSTUS: Well, I am answered. Now tell me, who made the world?

MEPHOSTOPHILIS: I will not. *70*

FAUSTUS: Sweet Mephostophilis, tell me.

MEPHOSTOPHILIS: Move me not, Faustus.

FAUSTUS: Villain, have not I bound thee to tell me anything?

MEPHOSTOPHILIS: Ay, that is not against our kingdom, but this is.

Think on hell, Faustus, for thou art damned.

FAUSTUS: Think, Faustus, upon God, that made the world.

MEPHOSTOPHILIS: Remember this —
  Exit.

FAUSTUS: Ay, go, accursed spirit to ugly hell.
  'Tis thou hast damned distressed Faustus' soul. *80*
  Is't not too late?
    Enter the GOOD *and* EVIL ANGELS.

EVIL ANGEL: Too late.

GOOD ANGEL: Never too late, if Faustus will repent.

EVIL ANGEL: If thou repent devils will tear thee in pieces.

---

61 *coelum igneum et cristallinum*: fiery and crystalline heavens beyond God's empyrium.
66 *Per inaequalem ...*: By an unequal movement in respect to the whole (i.e. the planets move at different speeds).
72 *Move*: i.e. to wrath.

GOOD ANGEL: Repent, and they shall never rase thy skin.

Exeunt ANGELS.

FAUSTUS: Ah, Christ my saviour,
Seek to save distressed Faustus' soul.

Enter LUCIFER, BELZEBUB *and*
MEPHOSTOPHILIS.

LUCIFER: Christ cannot save thy soul, for he is just.
There's none but I have interest in the same.

90 FAUSTUS: Oh what art thou that look'st so terribly?

LUCIFER: I am Lucifer, and this is my companion prince in hell.

FAUSTUS: Oh Faustus, they are come to fetch away thy soul.

BELZEBUB: We are come to tell thee thou dost injure us.

LUCIFER: Thou call'st on Christ contrary to thy promise.

BELZEBUB: Thou shouldst not think on God.

LUCIFER: Think on the devil.

BELZEBUB: And his dam too.

FAUSTUS: Nor will I henceforth. Pardon me in this,
And Faustus vows never to look to heaven,

100 Never to name God or to pray to him,
To burn his scriptures, slay his ministers,
And make my spirits pull his churches down.

LUCIFER: Do so, and we will highly gratify thee.[31]

BELZEBUB: Faustus, we are come from hell in person to show thee some pastime. Sit down and thou shalt behold the seven deadly sins appear to thee in their own proper shapes and likeness.

FAUSTUS: That sight will be as pleasant to me as Paradise was to Adam the first day of his creation.

110 LUCIFER: Talk not of Paradise or Creation, but mark this show. Talk of the devil and nothing else. Go, Mephostophilis, fetch them in.

Enter the SEVEN DEADLY SINS.[32]

BELZEBUB: Now, Faustus, question them of their names and dispositions.

288

FAUSTUS: That shall I soon. What art thou, the first?

PRIDE: I am Pride. I disdain to have any parents. I am like to Ovid's flea.[33] I can creep into every corner of a wench. Sometimes like a periwig I sit upon her brow. Next, like a necklace I hang about her neck. Then, like a fan of feathers, I kiss her. And then turning myself to a wrought smock do what I list. But fie, what a smell is here! I'll not speak a word for a king's ransome, unless the ground be perfumed and covered with cloth of Arras.[34]

FAUSTUS: Thou art a proud knave indeed. What art thou, the second?

COVETOUSNESS: I am Covetousness. Begotten of an old churl in a leather bag. And might I now obtain my wish, this house, you and all, should turn to gold, that I might lock you safe into my chest. Oh, my sweet gold!

FAUSTUS: And what art thou, the third?

ENVY: I am envy, begotten of a chimney-sweeper and an oyster-wife. I cannot read and therefore wish all books were burnt. I am lean with seeing others eat. Oh, that there would come a famine over all the world, that all might die, and I live alone, then thou should'st see how fat I'd be. But must thou sit and I stand? Come down, with a vengeance!

FAUSTUS: Out, envious wretch. But what art thou, the fourth?

WRATH: I am Wrath. I had neither father nor mother. I leapt out of a lion's mouth when I was scarce an hour old, and ever since have run up and down the world with this case of rapiers, wounding myself when I could get none to fight withal. I was born in hell, and look to it, for some of you shall be my father.

FAUSTUS: And what art thou, the fifth?

GLUTTONY: I am Gluttony. My parents are all dead, and the devil a penny they have left me, but a small pension and that buys me thirty meals a day and ten bevers: a

150 *bevers*: snacks.

small trifle to suffice nature. I come of a royal pedigree; my father was a gammon of bacon and my mother was a hog's head of claret wine. My godfathers were these: Peter Pickle-herring and Martin Martlemas-beef. But my godmother, oh, she was an ancient gentlewoman, and well-beloved in every good town and city. Her name was Mistress Margery March-beer. Now, Faustus, thou hast heard all my progeny, wilt thou bid me to supper?

160 FAUSTUS: No, I'll see thee hanged. Thou wilt eat up all my victuals.

GLUTTONY: Then the devil choke thee.

FAUSTUS: Choke thyself, Glutton. What art thou, the sixth?

SLOTH: Hey ho, I am Sloth. I was begotten on a sunny bank where I have lain ever since, and you have done me great injury to bring me from thence. Let me be carried thither again by Gluttony and Lechery. I'll not speak another word for a king's ransom.

170 FAUSTUS: And what are you, Mistress Minx, the seventh and last?

LECHERY: Who, I, sir? I am one that loves an inch of raw mutton better than an ell of fried stockfish,[35] and the first letter of my name begins with Lechery.

FAUSTUS: Away to hell! Away, on, piper!

Exeunt the SEVEN DEADLY SINS.

LUCIFER: Now, Faustus, how dost thou like this?

FAUSTUS: Oh, this feeds my soul.

LUCIFER: Tut, Faustus, in hell is all manner of delight.

FAUSTUS: Oh, might I see hell and return again safe, *180* how happy were I then!

LUCIFER: Faustus, thou shalt. At midnight I will send for thee. Meanwhile, peruse this book and view it

154 *Martlemas-beef*: salted for the winter in November (at Martinmas).
157 *March-beer*: a special brew made in March to be drunk two years later.

throughly, and thou shalt turn thyself into what shape thou wilt.

FAUSTUS: Thanks, mighty Lucifer. This will I keep as chary as my life.

LUCIFER: Now, Faustus, farewell, and think on the devil.

FAUSTUS: Farewell, great Lucifer. Come, Mephostophilis.   190

Exeunt omnes, several ways.

SCENE TWO[36]

Enter the CLOWN.

CLOWN: What, Dick, look to the horses there till I come again. I have gotten one of Doctor Faustus' conjuring books, and now we'll have such knavery as't passes.

Enter DICK.

DICK: What, Robin, you must come away and walk the horses.

ROBIN: I walk the horses? I scorn't, faith. I have other matters in hand. Let the horses walk themselves and they will. *A per se a, t.h.e. the: o per se o deny orgon, gorgon.* Keep further from me, o thou illiterate and unlearned hostler.   10

DICK: 'Snails! What hast thou got there? A book? Why, thou canst not tell ne'er a word on't.

ROBIN: That thou shalt see presently. Keep out of the circle, I say, lest I send you into the ostry with a vengeance.

DICK: That's like, faith. You had best leave your foolery, for, an my master come, he'll conjure you, faith!

ROBIN: My master conjure me? I'll tell thee what, an my master come here, I'll clap as fair a pair of horns on's head as e'er thou sawest in thy life.   20

11 *'Snails*: by God's nails.   14 *ostry*: hostry, hostelry.
19 *horns*: sign of a cuckold.

291

DICK: Thou need'st not do that, for my mistress hath done it.

ROBIN: Ay, there be of us here, that have waded as deep into matters as other men, if they were disposed to talk.

DICK: A plague take you! I thought you did not sneak up and down after her for nothing. But I prithee tell me, in good sadness, Robin, is that a conjuring book?

ROBIN: Do but speak what thou't have me to do, and I'll do't. If thou't dance naked, put off thy clothes and I'll conjure thee about presently. Or if thou't go but to the tavern with me, I'll give thee white wine, red wine, claret wine, sack, muskadine, malmesey and whippincrust. Hold, belly, hold; and we'll not pay one penny for it.

DICK: Oh brave! Prithee, let's to it presently, for I am as dry as a dog.

ROBIN: Come, then, let's away.

Exeunt.

ACT THREE

SCENE ONE

Enter the CHORUS.

CHORUS: Learned Faustus,
   To find the secrets of astronomy,
   Graven in the book of Jove's high firmament,
   Did mount him up to scale Olympus top,
   Where sitting in a chariot burning bright,
   Drawn by the strength of yoked dragons' necks,
   He views the clouds,[37] the planets, and the stars,
   The tropic, zones, and quarters of the sky,
   From the bright circle of the horned moon,
   Even to the height of *Primum Mobile*.[38]

27 *sadness*: seriousness.
33 *whippincrust*: hippocras, spiced wine.

And whirling round with this circumference,
Within the concave compass of the pole,
From east to west his dragons swiftly glide,
And in eight days did bring him home again.
Not long he stayed within his quiet house,
To rest his bones after his weary toil,
But new exploits do hale him out again,
And mounted then upon a dragon's back,
That with his wings did part the subtle air,
He now is gone to prove Cosmography,   20
That measures coasts and kingdoms of the earth;
And as I guess will first arrive at Rome,
To see the Pope and manner of his court,
And take some part of holy Peter's feast,
The which this day is highly solemnised.
    Exit.

SCENE TWO

Enter FAUSTUS *and* MEPHOSTOPHILIS.

FAUSTUS: Having now, my good Mephostophilis,
    Passed with delight the stately town of Trier,
    Environed round with airy mountain tops,
    With walls of flint, and deep entrenched lakes,
    Not to be won by any conquering prince,
    From Paris next coasting the realm of France
    We saw the river Main fall into Rhine,
    Whose banks are set with groves of fruitful vines;
    Then up to Naples, rich Campania,
    Whose buildings fair and gorgeous to the eye,   10
    The streets straight forth and paved with finest brick,
    Quarters the town in four equivolence.[39]
    There saw we learned Maro's[40] golden tomb,
    The way he cut an English mile in length,
    Thorough a rock of stone in one night's space.

2 *Trier*: Treves.   13 *Maro*: Virgil.

From thence to Venice, Padua and the rest,
In midst of which a sumptuous temple stands,
That threats the stars with her aspiring top,
Whose frame is paved with sundry coloured stones,
20   And roofed aloft with curious work in gold.
Thus hitherto hath Faustus spent his time.
But tell me now, what resting place is this?
Hast thou, as erst I did command,
Conducted me within the walls of Rome?

MEPHOSTOPHILIS: I have, my Faustus, and for proof
   thereof,
This is the goodly palace of the Pope;
And cause we are no common guests,
I choose his privy chamber for our use.

FAUSTUS: I hope his Holiness will bid us welcome.

30 MEPHOSTOPHILIS: All's one, for we'll be bold with
   his venison.
But now, my Faustus, that thou may'st perceive
What Rome contains for to delight thine eyes,
Know that this city stands upon seven hills,
That underprop the groundwork of the same.
Just through the midst runs flowing Tiber's stream,
With winding banks that cut it in two parts,
Over the which four stately bridges lean,
That make safe passage to each part of Rome.
Upon the bridge called Ponto Angelo
40   Erected is a castle passing strong,
Where thou shalt see such store of ordinance
As that the double cannons forged of brass
Do match the number of the days contained
Within the compass of one complete year.
Beside the gates and high pyramides,[41]
That Julius Caesar brought from Africa.

FAUSTUS: Now by the kingdoms of infernal rule,
Of Styx, or Acheron, and the fiery lake
Of ever-burning Phlegethon, I swear
50   That I do long to see the monuments

And situation of bright splendent Rome.
Come, therefore, let's away.
MEPHOSTOPHILIS: Now, stay, my Faustus. I know
    you'd see the Pope,
And take some part of holy Peter's feast,
The which in state[42] and high solemnity
This day is held through Rome and Italy
In honour of the Pope's triumphant victory.
FAUSTUS: Sweet Mephostophilis, thou pleasest me.
Whilst I am here on earth let me be cloyed
With all things that delight the heart of man.   60
My four and twenty years of liberty
I'll spend in pleasure and in dalliance,
That Faustus' name, whilst this bright frame doth
    stand,
May be admired through the furthest land.
MEPHOSTOPHILIS: 'Tis well said, Faustus. Come then,
    stand by me,
And thou shalt see them come immediately.
FAUSTUS: Nay stay, my gentle Mephostophilis,
And grant me my request, and then I go.
Thou know'st within the compass of eight days
We viewed the face of heaven, of earth and hell.   70
So high our dragons soared into the air,
That looking down, the earth appeared to me
No bigger than my hand in quantity.
There did we view the kingdoms of the world,
And what might please mine eye, I there beheld.
Then in this show let me an actor be,
That this proud Pope may Faustus' cunning see.
MEPHOSTOPHILIS: Let it be so, my Faustus, but first
    stay
And view their triumphs as they pass this way.
And then devise what best contents thy mind   80
By cunning in thine art to cross the Pope,
Or dash the pride of this solemnity,
To make his monks and abbots stand like apes,

And point like antics at his triple crown,
To beat the beads about the friars' pates,
Or clap huge horns upon the cardinals' heads,
Or any villainy thou canst devise,
And I'll perform it, Faustus. Hark, they come!
This day shall make thee be admired in Rome.

Enter the CARDINALS *and* BISHOPS, *some bearing crosiers, some the pillars,* MONKS *and* FRIARS, *singing their procession. Then the* POPE *and* RAYMOND, *King of Hungary with* BRUNO[43] *led in chains.*

90 POPE: Cast down our footstool.

RAYMOND: Saxon Bruno, stoop,
Whilst on thy back his Holiness ascends
Saint Peter's chair and state pontifical.

BRUNO: Proud Lucifer, that state belongs to me:
But thus I fall to Peter, not to thee.

POPE: To me and Peter shalt thou grovelling lie,
And crouch before the papal dignity.
Sounds trumpets then, for thus Saint Peter's heir
From Bruno's back ascends Saint Peter's chair.

A flourish while he ascends.

100 Thus, as the gods creep on with feet of wool
Long ere with iron hands they punish men,
So shall our sleeping vengeance now arise,
And smite with death thy hated enterprise.
Lord cardinals of France and Padua,
Go forthwith to our holy consistory,
And read amongst the statutes decretal,
What by the holy council held at Trent
The sacred synod hath decreed for him
That doth assume the papal government,

110 Without election and a true consent.
Away, and bring us word with speed!

FIRST CARDINAL: We go, my lord.

Exeunt CARDINALS.

POPE: Lord Raymond.

84 *antics*: clowns.

FAUSTUS: Go, haste thee, gentle Mephostophilis,
　Follow the cardinals to the consistory,
　And as they turn their superstitious books,
　Strike them with sloth and drowsy idleness,
　And make them sleep so sound that in their shapes
　Thyself and I may parly with this Pope,
　This proud confronter of the Emperor,　　　　　　　*120*
　And in despite of all his holiness
　Restore this Bruno to his liberty
　And bear him to the states of Germany.
MEPHOSTOPHILIS: Faustus, I go.
FAUSTUS: Dispatch it soon,
　The Pope shall curse that Faustus came to Rome.
　　Exeunt FAUSTUS *and* MEPHOSTOPHILIS.
BRUNO: Pope Adrian, let me have some right of
　law:
　I was elected by the Emperor.
POPE: We will depose the Emperor for that deed,
　And curse the people that submit to him.　　　　　*130*
　Both he and thou shalt stand excommunicate,
　And interdict from Church's privilege
　And all society of holy men.
　He grows too proud in his authority,
　Lifting his lofty head above the clouds
　And like a steeple overpeers the Church.
　But we'll pull down his haughty insolence,
　And, as Pope Alexander, our progenitor,
　Stood on the neck of German Frederick,
　Adding this golden sentence to our praise,　　　　*140*
　That Peter's heirs should tread on emperors
　And walk upon the dreadful adder's back,
　Treading the lion and the dragon down,
　And fearless spurn the killing basilisk,
　So will we quell that haughty schismatic,
　And by authority apostolical
　Depose him from his regal government.
　　144 *basilisk*: a mythical creature who could kill with a glance.

BRUNO: Pope Julius swore to princely Sigismond
 For him and the succeeding popes of Rome,
150 To hold the emperors their lawful lords.
POPE: Pope Julius did abuse the Church's rites,
 And therefore none of his decrees can stand.
 Is not all power on earth bestowed on us?
 And therefore though we would we cannot err.
 Behold this silver belt, whereto is fixed
 Seven golden seals fast sealed with seven seals,
 In token of our seven-fold power from heaven,
 To bind or loose, lock fast, condemn or judge,
 Resign or seal, or what so pleaseth us.
160 Then he and thou, and all the world, shall stoop,
 Or be assured of our dreadful curse,
 To light as heavy as the pains of hell.
  Enter FAUSTUS *and* MEPHOSTOPHILIS, *like the
  cardinals.*
MEPHOSTOPHILIS: Now tell me, Faustus, are we not
 fitted well?
FAUSTUS: Yes, Mephostophilis, and two such cardinals
 Ne'er served a holy Pope as we shall do.
 But whilst they sleep within the consistory,
 Let us salute his reverend fatherhood.
RAYMOND: Behold, my lord, the cardinals are returned.
POPE: Welcome, grave fathers, answer presently
170 What have our holy council there decreed
 Concerning Bruno and the Emperor,
 In quittance of their late conspiracy
 Against our state and papal dignity?
FAUSTUS: Most sacred patron of the Church of Rome,
 By full consent of all the synod
 Of priests and prelates, it is thus decreed:
 That Bruno and the German Emperor
 Be held as lollards and bold schismatics
 And proud disturbers of the Church's peace.
180 And if that Bruno by his own assent,
  178 *lollards*: heretics like the followers of John Wyclif.

Without enforcement of the German peers,
Did seek to wear the triple diadem
And by your death to climb Saint Peter's chair,
The statutes decretal have thus decreed:
He shall be straight condemned of heresy
And on a pile of fagots burnt to death.
POPE: It is enough. Here, take him to your charge,
And bear him straight to Ponto Angelo,
And in the strongest tower enclose him fast.
Tomorrow, sitting in our consistory   *190*
With all our college of grave cardinals,
We will determine of his life or death.
Here, take his triple crown along with you,
And leave it in the Church's treasury.
Make haste again, my good lord cardinals,
And take our blessing apostolical.
MEPHOSTOPHILIS: So, so, was never devil thus blessed
    before.
FAUSTUS: Away, sweet Mephostophilis, be gone:
The cardinals will be plagued for this anon.
    Exeunt FAUSTUS *and* MEPHOSTOPHILIS.
POPE: Go presently, and bring a banquet forth   *200*
That we may solemnise Saint Peter's feast,
And with Lord Raymond, King of Hungary,
Drink to our late and happy victory.
    Exeunt.

SCENE THREE[44]

A sennet while the banquet is brought in, and then enter
FAUSTUS *and* MEPHOSTOPHILIS *in their own shapes.*
MEPHOSTOPHILIS: Now, Faustus, come prepare thyself
    for mirth.
The sleepy cardinals are hard at hand
To censure Bruno that is posted hence,
And on a proud paced steed as swift as thought

Flies o'er the Alps to fruitful Germany,
There to salute the woeful Emperor.
FAUSTUS: The Pope will curse them for their sloth today,
That slept both Bruno and his crown away.
But now, that Faustus may delight his mind,
And by their folly make some merriment,
Sweet Mephostophilis, so charm me here,
That I may walk invisible to all,
And do what e'er I please unseen of any.
MEPHOSTOPHILIS: Faustus, thou shalt. Then kneel
   down presently:
      Whilst on thy head I lay my hand,
      And charm thee with this magic wand.
      First wear this girdle, then appear
      Invisible to all are here.
      The planets seven, the gloomy air,
      Hell and the Furies' forked hair,
      Pluto's blue fire and Hecate's tree,
      With magic spells so compass thee,
      That no eye may thy body see.
So, Faustus, now for all their holiness,
Do what thou wilt, thou shalt not be discerned.
FAUSTUS: Thanks, Mephostophilis. Now, friars, take heed
Lest Faustus make your shaven crowns to bleed.
MEPHOSTOPHILIS: Faustus, no more. See where the
   cardinals come.
      Enter the POPE *and all the* LORDS. *Enter the*
      CARDINALS *with a book.*
POPE: Welcome, lord cardinals. Come, sit down.
Lord Raymond, take your seat. Friars, attend
And see that all things be in readiness
As best beseems this solemn festival.
FIRST CARDINAL: First, may it please your sacred
   Holiness,
To view the sentence of the reverend synod
Concerning Bruno and the Emperor?
POPE: What needs this question? Did I not tell you

Tomorrow we would sit i'the consistory
And there determine of his punishment?
You brought us word even now, it was decreed
That Bruno and the cursed Emperor   *40*
Were by the holy Council both condemned
For loathed lollards and base schismatics.
Then wherefore would you have me view that book?

FIRST CARDINAL: Your Grace mistakes. You gave us
    no such charge.

RAYMOND: Deny it not· We all are witnesses
That Bruno here was late delivered you,
With his rich triple crown to be reserved
And put into the Church's treasury.

BOTH CARDINALS: By holy Paul, we saw them not.

POPE: By Peter, you shall die   *50*
Unless you bring them forth immediately.
Hale them to prison, lade their limbs with gyves!
False prelates, for this hateful treachery,
Cursed be your souls to hellish misery.

FAUSTUS: So, they are safe. Now Faustus, to the feast.
The Pope had never such a frolic guest.

POPE: Lord Archbishop of Rheims, sit down with us.

BISHOP: I thank your Holiness.

FAUSTUS: Fall to, and the devil choke you an you spare.

POPE: Who's that spoke? Friars, look about.   *60*

FRIARS: Here's nobody, if it like your Holiness.

POPE: Lord Raymond, pray fall to. I am beholding
To the Bishop of Milan for this so late a present.

FAUSTUS: I thank you, sir.
    Snatches it.

POPE: How now? Who snatched the meat from me?
Villains, why speak you not?
My good Lord Archbishop, here's a most dainty dish
Was sent me from a cardinal in France.

FAUSTUS: I'll have that too.
    Snatches it.

POPE: What lollards do attend our Holiness   *70*

301

That we receive such great indignity? Fetch me some wine.

FAUSTUS: Ay, pray do, for Faustus is a-dry.

POPE: Lord Raymond, I drink unto your grace.

FAUSTUS: I pledge your grace.

Snatches the glass.

POPE: My wine gone too? Ye lubbers, look about
And find the man that doth this villainy,
Or by our sanctitude you all shall die.
I pray, my lords, have patience at this
Troublesome banquet.

80 BISHOP: Please it your Holiness, I think it be some ghost crept out of Purgatory, and now is come unto your Holiness for his pardon.

POPE: It may be so.
Go, then, command our priests to sing a dirge
To lay the fury of this same troublesome ghost.

The POPE crosseth himself.

FAUSTUS: How now? Must every bit be spiced with a cross?
Nay then, take that.

FAUSTUS *hits him a box of the ear.*

POPE: Oh, I am slain! Help me, my lords.
Oh come, and help to bear my body hence.
90 Damned be this soul for ever for this deed!

Exeunt the POPE and his train.

MEPHOSTOPHILIS: Now, Faustus, what will you do now?
For I can tell you, you'll be cursed with bell, book and candle.

FAUSTUS: Bell, book and candle, candle, book and bell,
Forward and backward, to curse Faustus to hell.

Enter the FRIARS with bell, book and candle, for the dirge.

FIRST FRIAR: Come, brethren, let's about our business with good devotion.

(*sing*) Cursed be he that stole his Holiness' meat from the table. *Maledicat dominus.*

99 *Maledicat dominus*: May God curse him.

Cursed be he that took his Holiness a blow on *100*
the face. *Maledicat dominus.*

Cursed be he that struck Friar Sandelo a blow on
the pate. *Maledicat dominus.*

Cursed be he that disturbeth our holy dirge.
Maledicat dominus.

Cursed be he that took away his Holiness' wine.
Maledicat dominus.

Et omnes sancti. Amen.

FAUSTUS *and* MEPHOSTOPHILIS *beat the* FRIARS,
fling fire-works among them and exeunt.
Enter CHORUS.[45]

CHORUS: When Faustus had with pleasure ta'en the view
Of rarest things and royal courts of kings,   *110*
He stayed his course and so returned home;
Where such as bear his absence but with grief,
I mean his friends and nearest companions,
Did gratulate his safety with kind words,
And in their conference of what befell,
Touching his journey through the world and air,
They put forth questions of astrology,
Which Faustus answered with such learned skill
As they admired and wondered at his wit.
Now is his fame spread forth in every land;   *120*
Amongst the rest, the Emperor is one,
Carolus the Fifth, at whose palace now
Faustus is feasted 'mongst his noblemen.
What there he did in trial of his art,
I leave untold: your eyes shall see performed.

122 *Carolus the Fifth*: The Emperor Charles V (1515–56).

303

SCENE FOUR[46]

Enter ROBIN *the ostler with a book in his hand.*

ROBIN: Oh this is admirable! Here I ha' stol'n one of Doctor Faustus' conjuring books, and, i'faith, I mean to search some circles for my own use. Now will I make all the maidens in our parish dance at my pleasure stark naked before me. And so by that means I shall see more than ere I felt or saw yet.

Enter RAFE *calling* ROBIN.

RAFE: Robin, prithee come away! There's a gentleman tarries to have his horse, and he would have his things rubbed and made clean. He keeps such a chafing with my mistress about it, and she has sent me to look thee out. Prithee, come away!

ROBIN: Keep out, keep out, or else you are blown up. You are dismembered, Rafe, keep out, for I am about a roaring piece of work.

RAFE: Come, what dost thou with that same book? Thou canst not read?

ROBIN: Yes, my master and mistress shall find that I can read, he for his forehead, she for her private study. She's born to bear with me, or else my art fails.

RAFE: Why, Robin, what book is that?

ROBIN: What book? Why, the most intolerable book for conjuring that ere was invented by any brimstone devil.

RAFE: Canst thou conjure with it?

ROBIN: I can do all these things easily with it. First, I can make thee drunk with ippocras at any tavern in Europe, for nothing. That's one of my conjuring works!

RAFE: Our master parson says that's nothing.

ROBIN: True, Rafe. And more, Rafe, if thou hast any mind to Nan Spit, our kitchen maid, then turn her and wind her to thy own use as often as thou wilt, and at midnight.

RAFE: Oh brave Robin! Shall I have Nan Spit, and to

25 *ippocras*: hippocras, spiced wine.

304

mine own use? On that condition, I'll feed thy devil with horsebread as long as he lives, of free cost.

ROBIN: No more, sweet Rafe. Let's go and make clean our boots which lie foul upon our hands, and then to our conjuring, in the devil's name.

Exeunt.

Re-enter ROBIN *and* RAFE *with a silver goblet.*

ROBIN: Come, Rafe, did I not tell thee we were for ever made by this Doctor Faustus' book? *Ecce signum*, here's a simple purchase for horse-keepers. Our horses shall 40 eat no hay as long as this lasts.

Enter the VINTER.

RAFE: But, Robin, here comes the vintner.

ROBIN: Hush, I'll gull him supernaturally. Drawer, I hope all is paid. God be with you. Come, Rafe.

VINTNER: Soft, sir, a word with you. I must yet have a goblet paid from you ere you go.

ROBIN: I, a goblet? Rafe, I a goblet? I scorn you, and you are but a etc. I, a goblet? Search me.

VINTNER: I mean so, sir, with your favour.

ROBIN: How say you now? 50

VINTNER: I must say somewhat to your fellow – you, sir.

RAFE: Me, sir? Me, sir? Search your fill. Now, sir, you may be ashamed to burden honest men with a matter of truth.

VINTNER: Well, t'one of you hath this goblet about you.

ROBIN: You lie, drawer. 'Tis afore me! Sirrah, you! I'll teach ye to impeach honest men. Stand by, I'll scour you for a goblet. Stand aside, you were best. I charge you in the name of Belzebub. Look to the goblet, Rafe.

VINTNER: What mean you, sirrah? 60

ROBIN: I'll tell you what I mean. (*He reads*) *Sanctobolorum Periphrasticon.* Nay, I'll tickle you, vintner – look to the goblet, Rafe. *Polypragmos Belseborams framanto pacostiphos tostu Mephostophilis, Etc.*

39 *Ecce signum*: Behold, the sign (i.e. of the truth).
43 *gull*: fool.   61 *Sanctabolorum . . .*: gibberish.

Enter MEPHOSTOPHILIS, *who sets squibs at their backs.*
They run about.

VINTNER: *O nomine Domine*, what mean'st thou, Robin?
Thou hast no goblet.

RAFE: *Peccatum peccatorum*, here's thy goblet, good vintner.

ROBIN: *Misericordia pro nobis*, what shall I do? Good
70   devil, forgive me now and I'll never rob thy library
more.

    Enter to them MEPHOSTOPHILIS.

MEPHOSTOPHILIS: Vainish villains! Th'one like an
ape, another like a bear, the third an ass, for doing this
enterprise.

Monarch of hell, under whose black survey
Great potentates do kneel with awful fear,
Upon whose altars thousand souls do lie,
How am I vexed with these villains' charms?
From Constantinople am I hither come,
80   Only for pleasure of these damned slaves.

ROBIN: How, from Constantinople? You have had a
great journey. Will you take six pence in your purse to
pay for your supper, and be gone?

MEPHOSTOPHILIS: Well, villains, for your presumption
I transform thee into an ape and thee into a dog, and so
be gone. *Exit.*

ROBIN: How, into an ape? That's brave! I'll have fine
sport with the boys. I'll get nuts and apples enow.

RAFE: And I must be a dog!

90 ROBIN: I'faith thy head will never be out of the potage
pot.

    Exeunt.

ACT FOUR

SCENE ONE[47]

The Emperor's Court.
Enter MARTINO *and* FREDERICK *at several doors.*

MARTINO: What ho, officers, gentlemen!
Hie to the presence to attend the Emperor.
Good Frederick, see the rooms be voided straight.
His Majesty is coming to the hall;
Go back, and see the state in readiness.

FREDERICK: But where is Bruno, our elected Pope,
That on a fury's back came post from Rome?
Will not his grace consort the Emperor?

MARTINO: Oh yes, and with him comes the German
conjuror,
The learned Faustus, fame of Wittenberg,   10
The wonder of the world for magic art.
And he intends to show great Carolus
The race of all his stout progenitors,
And bring in presence of his Majesty
The royal shapes and warlike semblances
Of Alexander and his beauteous paramour.

FREDERICK: Where is Benvolio?

MARTINO: Fast asleep, I warrant you.
He took his rouse with stoups of Rhenish wine
So kindly yesternight to Bruno's health,   20
That all this day the sluggard keeps his bed.

FREDERICK: See, see, his window's ope. We'll call to
him.

MARTINO: What ho, Benvolio?
Enter BENVOLIO *above at a window in his*
nightcap, buttoning.

BENVOLIO: What a devil ail you two?

3 *voided straight*: emptied immediately.
16 *paramour*: his wife, Roxana.
19 *stoups*: flagons, or a measure (cf. pint).

MARTINO: Speak softly, sir, lest the devil hear you;
For Faustus at the court is late arrived,
And at his heels a thousand furies wait
To accomplish whatsoever the Doctor please.

BENVOLIO: What of this?

30 MARTINO: Come, leave thy chamber first, and thou
    shalt see
This conjuror perform such rare exploits
Before the Pope and royal Emperor
As never yet was seen in Germany.

BENVOLIO: Has not the Pope enough of conjuring yet?
He was upon the devil's back late enough,
And if he be so far in love with him,
I would he would post with him to Rome again.

FREDERICK: Speak, wilt thou come and see this sport?

BENVOLIO: Not I.

40 MARTINO: Wilt thou stand in thy window and see it,
    then?

BENVOLIO: Ay, and I fall not asleep i' the meantime.

MARTINO: The Emperor is at hand, who comes to see
What wonders by black spells may compassed be.

BENVOLIO: Well, go you, attend the Emperor. I am content for this once to thrust my head out at a window, for they say if a man be drunk over night the devil cannot hurt him in the morning. If that be true, I have a charm in my head shall control him as well as the conjuror, I warrant you.

Exeunt Martino and *Frederick.*

SCENE TWO[48]

Sennet. CHARLES, *the German Emperor,* BRUNO,
SAXONY, FAUSTUS, MEPHOSTOPHILIS,
FREDERICK, MARTINO, *and* ATTENDANTS.
BENVOLIO *still at the window.*[49]

EMPEROR: Wonder of men, renowned magician,

Thrice-learned Faustus, welcome to our court.
This deed of thine, in setting Bruno free
From his and our professed enemy,
Shall add more excellence unto thine art,
Than if by powerful necromantic spells
Thou couldst command the world's obedience.
For ever be beloved of Carolus;
And if this Bruno thou hast late redeemed,
In peace possess the triple diadem   10
And sit in Peter's chair, despite of chance,
Thou shalt be famous through all Italy,
And honoured of the German Emperor.

FAUSTUS: These gracious words, most royal Carolus,
Shall make poor Faustus to his utmost power
Both love and serve the German Emperor,
And lay his life at holy Bruno's feet.
For proof whereof, if so your Grace be pleased,
The Doctor stands prepared, by power of art,
To cast his magic charms that shall pierce through   20
The ebon gates of ever-burning hell,
And hale the stubborn furies from their caves,
To compass whatsoe'er your Grace commands.

BENVOLIO (*aside*): Blood, he speaks terribly! But for all
that, I do not greatly believe him. He looks as like
a conjuror as the Pope to a coster-monger.

EMPEROR: Then, Faustus, as thou late didst promise us,
We would behold that famous conqueror,
Great Alexander, and his paramour,
In their true shapes and state majestical,   30
That we may wonder at their excellence.

FAUSTUS: Your Majesty shall see them presently.
Mephostophilis, away!
And with a solemn noise of trumpets' sound,
Present before this royal Emperor
Great Alexander and his beauteous paramour.

MEPHOSTOPHILIS: Faustus, I will.

BENVOLIO: Well, Master Doctor, an your devils come

not away quickly, you shall have me asleep presently.
40 Zounds, I could eat myself for anger, to think I have
been such an ass all this while, to stand gaping after the
devil's governor, and can see nothing.

FAUSTUS: I'll make you feel something anon, if my art
fail me not.
My lord, I must forwarn your Majesty
That when my spirits present the royal shapes
Of Alexander and his paramour,
Your Grace demand no questions of the King,
But in dumb silence let them come and go.

EMPEROR: Be it as Faustus please, we are content.

50 BENVOLIO: Ay, ay, and I am content too. And thou bring
Alexander and his paramour before the Emperor, I'll be
Acteon[50] and turn myself to a stag.

FAUSTUS: And I'll play Diana, and send you the horns
presently.

Sennet. Enter at one the EMPEROR ALEXANDER, *at
the other* DARIUS. *They meet.* DARIUS *is thrown down;*
ALEXANDER *kills him, takes off his crown, and, offering
to go out, his* PARAMOUR *meets him. He embraceth
her and sets* DARIUS' *crown upon her head, and coming
back, both salute the* EMPEROR, *who, leaving his state,
offers to embrace them, which* FAUSTUS *seeing, suddenly
stays him. Then trumpets cease and music sounds.*

My gracious lord, you do forget yourself.
These are but shadows, not substantial.

EMPEROR: Oh pardon me, my thoughts are so ravished
With sight of this renowned Emperor,
That in mine arms I would have compassed him.
But, Faustus, since I may not speak to them,
60 To satisfy my longing thoughts at full,
Let me this tell thee: I have heard it said
That this fair lady, whilst she lived on earth,
Had on her neck a little wart or mole.
How may I prove that saying to be true?

FAUSTUS: Your Majesty may boldly go and see.

EMPEROR: Faustus, I see it plain,
  And in this sight thou better pleasest me
  Than if I gained another monarchy.
FAUSTUS: Away, be gone.
  Exit SHOW:
  See, see, my gracious lord, what strange beast is yon,   70
  that thrusts his head out at window?
EMPEROR: Oh, wondrous sight! See, Duke of Saxony,
  Two spreading horns most strangely fastened
  Upon the head of young Benvolio!
SAXONY: What, is he asleep? Or dead?
FAUSTUS: He sleeps, my lord: but dreams not of his
  horns.
EMPEROR: This sport is excellent. We'll call and wake
  him.
  What ho, Benvolio!
BENVOLIO: A plague upon you! Let me sleep awhile.
EMPEROR: I blame thee not to sleep much, having such a   80
  head of thine own.
SAXONY: Look up, Benvolio, 'tis the Emperor calls.
BENVOLIO: The Emperor? Where? Oh, zounds, my
  head!
EMPEROR: Nay, and thy horns hold, 'tis no matter for thy
  head, for that's armed sufficiently.
FAUSTUS: Why, how now, Sir Knight? What, hanged by
  the horns? This most horrible! Fie, fie! Pull in your
  head for shame; let not all the world wonder at you.
BENVOLIO: Zounds, Doctor, is this your villainy?   90
FAUSTUS: Oh, say not so, sir. The Doctor has no skill,
  No art, no cunning, to present these lords
  Or bring before this royal Emperor
  The mighty monarch, warlike Alexander.
  If Faustus do it, you are straight resolved
  In bold Acteon's shape to turn a stag.
  And therefore, my lord, so please your majesty,
  I'll raise a kennel of hounds shall hunt him so
  As all his footmanship shall scarce prevail

100   To keep his carcass from their bloody fangs.
Ho, Belimote, Argiron, Asterote!

BENVOLIO: Hold, hold! Zounds, he'll raise up a kennel
of devils, I think anon. Good my lord, entreat for me.
'Sblood, I am never never able to endure these torments.

EMPEROR: Then, good Master Doctor,
Let me entreat you to remove his horns:
He has done penance now sufficiently.

FAUSTUS: My gracious lord, not so much for injury done
110   to me, as to delight your majesty with some mirth,
hath Faustus justly requited this injurious knight; which
being all I desire, I am content to remove his horns.
Mephostophilis, transform him. And hereafter, sir,
look you speak well of scholars.

BENVOLIO (*aside*): Speak well of ye? 'Sblood, and
scholars be such cuckold-makers to clap horns of
honest men's heads o' this order, I'll ne'er trust smooth
faces and small ruffs more. But an I be not revenged for
this, would I might be turned to a gaping oyster and
120   drink nothing but salt water.

EMPEROR: Come, Faustus, while the Emperor lives,
In recompense of this thy high desert,
Thou shalt command the state of Germany,
And live beloved of mighty Carolus.

    Exeunt omnes.

SCENE THREE

Enter BENVOLIO, MARTINO, FREDERICK *and*
SOLDIERS.

MARTINO: Nay, sweet Benvolio, let us sway thy
thoughts
From this attempt against the conjuror.

BENVOLIO: Away, you love me not, to urge me thus.
Shall I let slip so great an injury,

When every servile groom jests at my wrongs,
And in their rustic gambols proudly say
Benvolio's head was graced with horns today?
Oh, may these eyelids never close again
Till with my sword I have that conjuror slain.
If you will aid me in this enterprise,   10
Then draw your weapons and be resolute.
If not, depart. Here will Benvolio die,
But Faustus' death shall quit my infamy.

FREDERICK: Nay, we will stay with thee, betide what
        may,
And kill that Doctor if he come this way.

BENVOLIO: Then, gentle Frederick, hie thee to the
        grove,
And place our servants and our followers
Close in an ambush there behind the trees.
By this I know the conjuror is near:
I saw him kneel and kiss the Emperor's hand,   20
And take his leave, laden with rich rewards.
Then, soldiers, boldly fight. If Faustus die,
Take you the wealth, leave us the victory.

FREDERICK: Come, soldiers, follow me unto the
        grove.
Who kills him shall have gold and endless love.
        Exit FREDERICK *with the* SOLDIERS.

BENVOLIO: My head is lighter than it was by th'horns,
But yet my heart more ponderous than my head,
And pants until I see that conjuror dead.

MARTINO: Where shall we place ourselves, Benvolio?

BENVOLIO: Here will we stay to bide the first assault.   30
Oh, were that damned hell-hound but in place,
Thou soon shouldst see me quit my foul disgrace.
        Enter FREDERICK.

FREDERICK: Close, close! The conjuror is at hand,
And all alone comes walking in his gown.
Be ready then, and strike the peasant down.

13 *quit*: avenge.

BENVOLIO: Mine be that honour, then. Now sword, strike home.

For horns he gave, I'll have his head anon.

Enter FAUSTUS *with a false head.*

MARTINO: See, see, he comes.

BENVOLIO: No words. This blow ends all.

40   Hell take his soul; his body thus must fall.

Attacks FAUSTUS.

FAUSTUS: Oh!

FREDERICK: Groan you, Master Doctor?

BENVOLIO: Break may his heart with groans! Dear Frederick, see,

Thus will I end his griefs immediately.

Cuts off his head.

MARTINO: Strike with a willing hand: his head is off.

BENVOLIO: The devil's dead! The Furies now may laugh.

FREDERICK: Was this that stern aspect, that awful frown,

Made the grim monarch of infernal spirits

Tremble and quake at his commanding charms?

50 MARTINO: Was this that damned head, whose heart conspired

Benvolio's shame before the Emperor?

BENVOLIO: Ay, that's the head, and here the body lies,

Justly rewarded for his villainies.

FREDERICK: Come, let's devise how we may add more shame

To the black scandal of his hated name.

BENVOLIO: First, on his head, in quittance of my wrongs,

I'll nail huge forked horns, and let them hang

Within the window where he yoked me first,

That all the world may see my just revenge.

60 MARTINO: What use shall we put his beard to?

BENVOLIO: We'll sell it to a chimney-sweeper: it will wear out ten birching brooms, I warrant you.

FREDERICK: What shall eyes do?

BENVOLIO: We'll put out his eyes, and they shall serve
for buttons to his lips, to keep his tongue from catching cold.

MARTINO: An excellent policy! And now, sirs, having
divided him, what shall the body do?

  FAUSTUS *rises.*[51]

BENVOLIO: Zounds, the devil's alive again!

FREDERICK: Give him his head, for God's sake!   *70*

FAUSTUS: Nay, keep it. Faustus will have heads and
  hands.
I call your hearts to recompense this deed.
Knew you not, traitors, I was limited
For four and twenty years to breathe on earth?
And had you cut my body with your swords,
Or hewed this flesh and bones as small as sand,
Yet in a minute had my spirit returned,
And I had breathed a man made free from harm.
But wherefore do I dally my revenge?
Asteroth, Belimoth, Mephostophilis!   *80*
 Enter MEPHOSTOPHILIS *and other* DEVILS.
Go, horse these traitors on your fiery backs,
And mount aloft with them as high as heaven;
Thence pitch them headlong to the lowest hell.
Yet stay, the world shall see their misery,
And hell shall after plague their treachery.
Go, Belimoth, and take this caitiff hence,
And hurl him in some lake of mud and dirt.
Take thou this other: drag him through the woods
Amongst the pricking thorns and sharpest briars,
Whilst with my gentle Mephostophilis,   *90*
This traitor flies unto some steepy rock,
That rolling down may break the villain's bones,
As he intended to dismember me.
Fly hence, dispatch my charge immediately.

FREDERICK: Pity us, gentle Faustus! Save our lives!

FAUSTUS: Away!

FREDERICK: He must needs go that the devil drives.
  Exeunt SPIRITS *with the* KNIGHTS.
  Enter the AMBUSH SOLDIERS.
FIRST SOLDIER: Come, sirs, prepare yourselves in
  readiness.
  Make haste to help these noble gentlemen.
100 I heard them parley with the conjuror.
SECOND SOLDIER: See, where he comes. Dispatch and
  kill the slave.
FAUSTUS: What's here? An ambush to betray my life!
  Then Faustus, try thy skill. Base peasants, stand!
  For lo, these trees remove at my command,
  And stand as bulwarks twixt yourselves and me,
  To shield me from your hated treachery.
  Yet, to encounter this your weak attempt,
  Behold an army comes incontinent.
    FAUSTUS *strikes the door, and enter a devil playing on a
    drum; after him another bearing an ensign; and divers with
    weapons;* MEPHOSTOPHILIS *with fireworks. They set
    upon the soldiers and drive them out.*

SCENE FOUR

Enter at several doors BENVOLIO, FREDERICK *and*
MARTINO, *their heads and faces bloody and besmeared
with mud and dirt, all having horns on their heads.*
MARTINO: What ho, Benvolio!
BENVOLIO: Here! What, Frederick, ho!
FREDERICK: Oh help me, gentle friend. Where is
  Martino?
MARTINO: Dear Frederick, here,
  Half smothered in a lake of mud and dirt,
  Through which the Furies dragged me by the heels.
FREDERICK: Martino, see
  Benvolio's horns again!
MARTINO: Oh misery! How now, Benvolio?

BENVOLIO: Defend me, heaven! Shall I be haunted   *10*
    still?
MARTINO: Nay, fear not, man; we have no power to kill.
BENVOLIO: My friends transformed thus! Oh hellish
    spite!
    Your heads are all set with horns!
FREDERICK: You hit it right:
    It is your own you mean. Feel on your head.
BENVOLIO: Zounds, horns again!
MARTINO: Nay, chafe not, man. We all are sped.
BENVOLIO: What devil attends this damned magician,
    That, spite of spite, our wrongs are doubled?
FREDERICK: What may we do, that we may hide our   *20*
    shames?
BENVOLIO: If we should follow him to work revenge,
    He'd join long asses' ears to these huge horns,
    And make us laughing stocks to all the world.
MARTINO: What shall we then do, dear Benvolio?
BENVOLIO: I have a castle joining near these woods,
    And thither we'll repair and live obscure,
    Till time shall alter these our brutish shapes.
    Sith black disgrace hath thus eclipsed our fame,
    We'll rather die with grief, than live with shame.
    Exeunt omnes.

SCENE FIVE[52]

Enter FAUSTUS *and* MEPHOSTOPHILIS.
FAUSTUS: Now, Mephostophilis, the restless course that
    time doth run with calm and deadly foot,
    Shortening my days and thread of vital life,
    Calls for the payment of my latest years.
    Therefore, sweet Mephostophilis, let us make haste to
    Wittenberg.
MEPHOSTOPHILIS: What, will you go on horseback,
    or on foot?

FAUSTUS: Nay, till I am past this fair and pleasant green
10   I'll walk on foot.

    Enter a HORSE-COURSER.

HORSE-COURSER: I have been all this day seeking one
master Fustian. Mass, see where he is! God save you,
Master Doctor.

FAUSTUS: What, horse-courser! You are well met.

HORSE-COURSER: Do you hear, sir? I have brought you
forty dollars for your horse.

FAUSTUS: I cannot sell him so. If thou likest him for
fifty, take him.

HORSE-COURSER: Alas, sir, I have no more. I pray you,
20   speak for me.

MEPHOSTOPHILIS: I pray you, let him have him. He is
an honest fellow, and he has a great charge, neither
wife nor child.

FAUSTUS: Well, come, give me your money. My boy will
deliver him to you. But I must tell you one thing before
you have him: ride him not into the water at any hand.

HORSE-COURSER: Why, sir, will he not drink of all
waters?

FAUSTUS: Oh yes, he will drink of all waters; but ride
30   him not into the water. Ride him over hedge or ditch or
where thou wilt, but not into the water.

HORSE-COURSER: Well, sir, now I am a made man for
ever. I'll not leave my horse for forty. If he had but the
quality of hey ding ding, hey ding ding, I'd make a brave
living on him. He has a buttock as slick as an eel. Well,
God bye, sir. Your boy will deliver him me. But hark
ye sir: if my horse be sick or ill at ease, if I bring his
water to you, you'll tell me what is?

FAUSTUS: Away, you villain! What, dost think I am a
40   horse-doctor?

    Exit HORSE-COURSER.

What art thou, Faustus, but a man condemned to
die?

34 *hey ding ding*: not a gelding (Greg's conjecture).

Thy fatal time doth draw to final end:
Despair doth drive distrust into my thoughts.
Confound these passions with a quiet sleep.
Tush, Christ did call the thief upon the cross;
Then rest thee, Faustus, quiet in conceit.

Sleeps in his chair.

Enter HORSE-COURSER *all wet, crying.*

HORSE-COURSER: Alas, alas, Doctor Fustian quotha! Mass, Doctor Lopus was never such a doctor. Has given me a purgation has purged me of forty dollars: I shall never see them more. But yet like an ass as I was, I would not be ruled by him, for he bade me I should ride him into no water. Now I, thinking my horse had had some rare quality that he would not have had me known of, I, like a venturous youth, rid him into the deep pond at the town's end. I was no sooner in the middle of the pond but my horse vanished away, and I sat upon a bottle of hay, never so near drowning in my life. But I'll seek out my Doctor and have my forty dollars again, or I'll make it the dearest horse. Oh, yonder is his snipper-snapper. Do you hear? You! Hey-pass, where's your master? 50 60

MEPHOSTOPHILIS: Why, sir, what would you? You cannot speak with him.

HORSE-COURSER: But I *will* speak with him.

MEPHOSTOPHILIS: Why, he's fast asleep. Come some other time.

HORSE-COURSER: I'll speak with him now, or I'll break his glass windows about his ears.

MEPHOSTOPHILIS: I tell thee he has not slept this eight nights. 70

HORSE-COURSER: And he have not slept this eight weeks I'll speak with him.

MEPHOSTOPHILIS: See where he is fast asleep.

46 *conceit*: mind, imagination.
60 *Hey-pass*: here, conjuror (cf. 'your hey-pass and re-pass' 4, 7, 124).

HORSE-COURSER: Ay, this is he. God save ye, Master Doctor. Master Doctor! Master Doctor Fustian! Forty dollars, forty dollars for a bottle of hay!

MEPHOSTOPHILIS: Why, thou seest he hears thee not.

HORSE-COURSER: So, ho, ho! So, ho, ho!

Hollows in his ear.

No, will you not wake? I'll make you wake e'er I go.

He pulls him by the leg, and pulls it away.

80 Alas, I am undone! What shall I do?

FAUSTUS: Oh, my leg, my leg! Help, Mephostophilis. Call the officers. My leg, my leg!

MEPHOSTOPHILIS: Come, villain, to the Constable.

HORSE-COURSER: Oh lord, sir, let me go and I'll give you forty dollars more.

MEPHOSTOPHILIS: Where be they?

HORSE-COURSER: I have none about me. Come to my hostry and I'll give them you.

MEPHOSTOPHILIS: Be gone, quickly!

HORSE-COURSER *runs away.*

90 FAUSTUS: What, is he gone? Farewell he. Faustus has his leg again, and the horse-courser, I take it, a bottle of hay for his labour. Well, this trick shall cost him forty dollars more.

Enter WAGNER.

FAUSTUS: How now, Wagner, what news with thee?

WAGNER: If it please you, the Duke of Vanholt doth earnestly entreat your company, and hath sent some of his men to attend you with provision for your journey.

FAUSTUS: The Duke of Vanholt's an honourable
100 gentleman, and one to whom I must be no niggard of my cunning. Come, away.

Exeunt.

SCENE SIX[54]

Enter CLOWN, DICK, HORSE-COURSER *and a*
CARTER.

CARTER: Come, my masters, I'll bring you to the best
beer in Europe. What ho, hostess. Where be these
whores?
  Enter HOSTESS.

HOSTESS: How now, what lack you? What, my old
guests, welcome!

CLOWN: Sirrah Dick, dost thou know why I stand so
mute?

DICK: No, Robin, why is't?

CLOWN: I am eighteen pence on the score. But say
nothing. See if she have forgotten me.   10

HOSTESS: Who's this, that stands so solemnly by himself? What, my old guest?

CLOWN: Oh, hostess, how do you? I hope my score
stands still.

HOSTESS: Ay, there's no doubt of that, for methinks you
make no haste to wipe it out.

DICK: Why, hostess, I say, fetch us some beer.

HOSTESS: You shall presently. Look up into the hall
there, ho!
  Exit.

DICK: Come, sirs, what shall we do now till mine hostess   20
comes?

CARTER: Marry, sir, I'll tell you the bravest tale how a
conjuror served me. You know Doctor Fauster?

HORSE-COURSER: Ay, a plague take him. Here's some
on's have cause to know him. Did he conjure thee too?

CARTER: I'll tell you how he served me. As I was going
to Wittenberg t'other day, with a load of hay, he met
me and asked me what he should give me for as much
hay as he could eat. Now, sir, I, thinking that a little
would serve his turn, bad him take as much as he would   30

for three-farthings. So he presently gave me my money and fell to eating. And, as I am a cursen man, he never left eating till he had eat up all my load of hay.

ALL: Oh monstrous! Eat a whole load of hay?

CLOWN: Yes, yes, that may be, for I have heard of one that has eat a load of logs.

HORSE-COURSER: Now, sirs, you shall hear how villainously he served me. I went to him yesterday to buy a horse of him, and he would by no means sell him
40 under forty dollars. So, sir, because I knew him to be such a horse as would run over hedge and ditch and never tire, I gave him his money. So when I had my horse, Doctor Fauster bade me ride him night and day and spare him no time. But, quoth he, in any case ride him not into the water. Now, sir, I thinking the horse had some quality that he would not have me know of, what did I but ride him into a great river, and when I came just in the midst, my horse vanished away, and I sat straddling upon a bottle of hay.

50 ALL: Oh brave Doctor!

HORSE-COURSER: But you shall hear how bravely I served him for it: I went me home to his house, and there I found him asleep. I kept a-hallowing and whooping in his ears, but all could not wake him. I, seeing that, took him by the leg and never rested pulling, till I had pulled me his leg quite off, and now 'tis at home in mine hostry.

CLOWN: And has the Doctor but one leg, then? That's excellent, for one of his devils turned me into the like-
60 ness of an ape's face.

CARTER: Some more drink, hostess.

CLOWN: Hark you, we'll into another room and drink a while, and then we'll go seek out the Doctor.

Exeunt omnes.

SCENE SEVEN[55]

Enter the DUKE OF VANHOLT,[56] *his* DUCHESS,
FAUSTUS *and* MEPHOSTOPHILIS.

DUKE: Thanks, Master Doctor, for these pleasant sights.
Nor know I how sufficiently to recompense your great
deserts in erecting that enchanted castle in the air, the
sight whereof so delighted me, as nothing in the world
could please me more.

FAUSTUS: I do think myself, my good lord, highly
recompensed in that it pleaseth your grace to think but
well of that which Faustus hath performed. But,
gracious lady, it may be that you have taken no pleasure
in those sights. Therefore, I pray you tell me, what is   10
the thing you most desire to have. Be it in the world, it
shall be yours. I have heard that great-bellied women
do long for things are rare and dainty.

LADY: True, Master Doctor, and since I find you so kind,
I will make known unto you what my heart desires
to have; and were it now summer, as it is January,
a dead time of the winter, I would request no better
meat than a dish of ripe grapes.

FAUSTUS: This is but a small matter. Go, Mephostophilis,
away.   20

Exit MEPHOSTOPHILIS.

Madame, I will do more than this for your content.

Enter MEPHOSTOPHILIS *again with the grapes.*

Here, now taste ye these. They should be good, for they
come from a far country, I can tell you.

DUKE: This makes me wonder more than all the rest, that
at this time of the year, when every tree is barren of his
fruit, from whence you had these ripe grapes.

FAUSTUS: Please it your grace, the year is divided into
two circles over the whole world, so that when it is
winter with us, in the contrary circle it is likewise
summer with them, as in India, Saba and such countries   30
that lie far East, where they have fruit twice a year. From

whence, by means of a swift spirit that I have, I had
these grapes brought as you see.

LADY: And trust me, they are the sweetest grapes that
e'er I tasted.

The CLOWNS *bounce at the gate within.*

DUKE: What rude disturbers have we at the gate?
Go, pacify their fury. Set it ope,
And then demand of them what they would have.

They knock again and call out to talk with FAUSTUS.

A SERVANT: Why, how now, masters? What a coil is
there?

40   What is the reason you disturb the Duke?

DICK: We have no reason for it, therefore a fig for
him.

SERVANT: Why, saucy varlets, dare you be so bold?

HORSE-COURSER: I hope, sir, we have wit enough to
be more bold than welcome.

SERVANT: It appears so. Pray be bold elsewhere,
And trouble not the Duke.

DUKE: What would they have?

SERVANT: They all cry out to speak with Doctor
Faustus.

50 CARTER: Ay, and we will speak with him.

DUKE: Will you, sir? Commit the rascals.

DICK: Commit with us! He were as good commit with
his father as commit with us.

FAUSTUS: I do beseech your grace let them come in.
They are good subject for a merriment.

DUKE: Do as thou wilt, Faustus; I give thee leave.

FAUSTUS: I thank your grace.

Enter the CLOWN, DICK, CARTER *and*
HORSE-COURSER.

Why, how now, my good friends?
Faith, you are too outrageous, but come near.

60   I have procured your pardons. Welcome all.

CLOWN: Nay, sir, we will be welcome for our money, and

39 *coil*: commotion.   51 *Commit*: arrest.

we will pay for what we take. What ho! Give's half-a-
dozen of beer here, and be hanged.

FAUSTUS: Nay, hark you. Can you tell me where you are?

CARTER: Ay, marry can I. We are under heaven.

SERVANT: Ay, but, sir sauce-box, know you in what
place?

HORSE-COURSER: Ay, ay, the house is good enough to
drink in. Zounds, fill us some beer or we'll break all the
barrels in the house and dash out all your brains with
your bottles. 70

FAUSTUS: Be not so furious. Come, you shall have beer.
My lord, beseech you give me leave awhile.
I'll gage my credit, 'twill content your Grace.

DUKE: With all my heart, kind Doctor; please thyself.
Our servants and our court's at thy command.

FAUSTUS: I humbly thank your Grace. Then fetch some
beer.

HORSE-COURSER: Ay, marry. There spake a doctor indeed, and faith, I'll drink a health to thy wooden leg for
that word.

FAUSTUS: My wooden leg? What dost thou mean by 80
that?

CARTER: Ha, ha, ha! Dost thou hear him, Dick? He has
forgot his leg.

HORSE-COURSER: Ay, ay, he does not stand much upon
that.

FAUSTUS: No, faith. Not much upon a wooden leg.

CARTER: Good lord! That flesh and blood should be so
frail with your worship. Do not you remember a
horse-courser you sold a horse to?

FAUSTUS: Yes, I remember I sold one a horse. 90

CARTER: And do you remember you bid he should not
ride into the water?

FAUSTUS: Yes, I do very well remember that.

CARTER: And do you remember nothing of your leg?

FAUSTUS: No, in good sooth.

73 *gage*: stake.

CARTER: Then I pray remember your courtesy.[57]

FAUSTUS: I thank you, sir.

CARTER: 'Tis not so much worth. I pray you, tell me one thing.

100 FAUSTUS: What's that?

CARTER: Be both your legs bedfellows every night together?

FAUSTUS: Wouldst thou make a colossus of me, that thou askest me such questions?

CARTER: No, truly, sir. I would make nothing of you, but I would fain know that.

Enter HOSTESS *with drink.*

FAUSTUS: Then I assure thee certainly they are.

CARTER: I thank you, I am fully satisfied.

FAUSTUS: But wherefore dost thou ask?

110 CARTER: For nothing, sir: but methinks you should have a wooden bedfellow of one of 'em.

HORSE-COURSER: Why, do you hear, sir? Did not I pull off one of your legs when you were asleep?

FAUSTUS: But I have it again now I am awake. Look you here, sir.

ALL: Oh horrible! Had the Doctor three legs?

CARTER: Do you remember, sir, how you cozened me and eat up my load of –

FAUSTUS *charms him dumb.*

DICK: Do you remember how you made me wear an

120 ape's –

HORSE-COURSER: You whoreson conjuring scab, do you remember how you cozened me with a ho –

CLOWN: Ha'you forgotten me? You think to carry it away with your hey-pass and re-pass. Do you remember the dog's fa –

FAUSTUS *has charmed each dumb in turn;*[58] *exeunt* CLOWNS.

HOSTESS: Who pays for the ale? Hear you, Master

103 *colossus*: statue which spanned Rhodes harbour.
117 *cozened*: tricked.

326

Doctor, now you have sent away my guests, I pray who
shall pay me for my a–?
Exit HOSTESS.

LADY: My lord,
We are much beholding to this learned man.   *130*

DUKE: So are we, madam, which we will recompense
With all the love and kindness that we may.
His artful sport drives all sad thoughts away.
Exeunt.

ACT FIVE

SCENE ONE

Thunder and lightning. Enter devils with covered dishes.
MEPHOSTOPHILIS *leads them into* FAUSTUS' *study.*
Then enter WAGNER.

WAGNER: I think my master means to die shortly.
He hath made his will, and given me his wealth,
His house, his goods, and store of golden plate,
Besides two thousand ducats ready coined.
And yet methinks, if that death were near,
He would not banquet and carouse and swill
Amongst the students, as even now he doth,
Who are at supper with such belly-cheer
As Wagner ne'er beheld in all his life.
See where they come; belike the feast is ended.[59]   *70*
Exit.
Enter FAUSTUS, MEPHOSTOPHILIS *and two or three*
SCHOLARS.

FIRST SCHOLAR: Master Doctor Faustus, since our conference about fair ladies, which was the beautifullest in
all the world, we have determined with ourselves that
Helen of Greece was the admirablest lady that ever
lived. Therefore Master Doctor, if you will do us so
much favour, as to let us see that peerless dame of

Greece, whom all the world admires for majesty, we
should think ourselves much beholding unto you.

FAUSTUS: Gentlemen, for that I know your friendship
is unfeigned,

20 It is not Faustus' custom to deny
The just request of those that wish him well.
You shall behold that peerless dame of Greece,
No otherwise for pomp or majesty,
Than when Sir Paris crossed the seas with her,
And brought the spoils to rich Dardania.
Be silent then, for danger is in words.

Music sounds. MEPHOSTOPHILIS *brings in* HELEN;
she passeth over the stage.

SECOND SCHOLAR: Was this fair Helen, whose admired
worth

Made Greece with ten years wars afflict poor Troy?

THIRD SCHOLAR: Too simple is my wit to tell her
worth

30 Whom all the world admires for majesty.

FIRST SCHOLAR: Now we have seen the pride of
nature's work,
We'll take our leaves, and for this blessed sight
Happy and blest be Faustus evermore.

Enter an OLD MAN.

FAUSTUS: Gentlemen, farewell: the same wish I to you.

Exeunt SCHOLARS.

OLD MAN:[60] Oh gentle Faustus, leave this damned art,
This magic, that will charm thy soul to hell,
And quite bereave thee of salvation.
Though thou hast now offended like a man,
Do not persever in it like a devil.

40 Yet, yet, thou hast an amiable soul,
If sin by custom grow not into nature:
Then, Faustus, will repentance come too late,
Then thou art banished from the sight of heaven;
No mortal can express the pains of hell.
It may be this my exhortation

328

Seems harsh and all unpleasant; let it not,
For, gentle son, I speak it not in wrath,
Or envy of thee, but in tender love,
And pity of thy future misery.
And so have hope, that this my kind rebuke,   *50*
Checking thy body, may amend thy soul.

FAUSTUS: Where art thou, Faustus? Wretch, what hast
    thou done?
Damned art thou, Faustus, damned: despair and die.
Hell claims his right, and with a roaring voice
Says 'Faustus, come, thine hour is almost come'
(MEPHOSTOPHILIS *gives him a dagger*.)
And Faustus now will come to do thee right.

OLD MAN: Oh stay, good Faustus, stay thy desperate
    steps.
I see an angel hover o'er thy head,
And with a vial full of precious grace,   *60*
Offers to pour the same into thy soul.
Then call for mercy and avoid despair.

FAUSTUS: Ah my sweet friend,[61] I feel thy words
To comfort my distressed soul.
Leave me awhile to ponder on my sins.

OLD MAN: I leave thee, but with grief of heart,
Fearing the ruin of thy hopeless soul. *Exit.*

FAUSTUS: Accursed Faustus, wretch, what hast thou
    done?
I do repent, and yet I do despair.
Hell strives with grace for conquest in my breast.   *70*
What shall I do to shun the snares of death?

MEPHOSTOPHILIS: Thou traitor, Faustus, I arrest thy
    soul
For disobedience to my sovereign lord.
Revolt, or I'll in piecemeal tear thy flesh.

FAUSTUS: I do repent I e'er offended him.
Sweet Mephostophilis, entreat thy lord
To pardon my unjust presumption,

74 *Revolt*: turn about (i.e. back to your bargain with the devil).

And with my blood again I will confirm
The former vow I made to Lucifer.

80 MEPHOSTOPHILIS: Do it then, Faustus, with
 unfeigned heart,
Lest greater dangers do attend thy drift.

FAUSTUS: Torment, sweet friend, that base and crooked
 age
That durst dissuade me from thy Lucifer,
With greatest torment that our hell affords.

MEPHOSTOPHILIS: His faith is great: I cannot touch
 his soul.
But what I may afflict his body with
I will attempt, which is but little worth.

FAUSTUS: One thing, good servant, let me crave of
 thee,
To glut the longing of my heart's desire,
90 That I may have unto my paramour
That heavenly Helen which I saw of late,
Whose sweet embraces may extinguish clear
Those thoughts that do dissuade me from my vow,
And keep my vow I made to Lucifer.

MEPHOSTOPHILIS: This, or what else my Faustus shall
 desire,
Shall be performed in twinkling of an eye.

  Enter HELEN *again, passing over between two* CUPIDS.

FAUSTUS: Was this the face that launched a thousand
 ships,
And burnt the topless towers of Ilium?
Sweet Helen, make me immortal with a kiss.
100 Her lips suck forth my soul: see where it flies.
Come, Helen, come, give me my soul again.
Here will I dwell, for heaven is in those lips,
And all is dross that is not Helena.

  Enter ENTER OLD MAN.

I will be Paris, and for love of thee
Instead of Troy shall Wittenberg be sacked,
And I will combat with weak Menelaus,

And wear thy colours on my plumed crest.
Yea, I will wound Achilles in the heel,
And then return to Helen for a kiss.
Oh, thou art fairer than the evening's air,   *110*
Clad in the beauty of a thousand stars.
Brighter art thou than flaming Jupiter,
When he appeared to hapless Semele:
More lovely than the monarch of the sky,[62]
In wanton Arethusa's azure arms,
And none but thou shalt be my paramour.
    Exeunt.

OLD MAN: Accursed Faustus,[63] miserable man,
  That from thy soul exclud'st the grace of heaven,
  And fliest the throne of his tribunal seat.
    Enter the DEVILS.
Satan begins to sift me with his pride,   *120*
As in this furnace God shall try my faith.
My faith, vile hell, shall triumph over thee.
Ambitious fiends, see how the heavens smiles
At your repulse, and laughs your state to scorn.
Hence, hell, for hence I fly unto my God.
    Exeunt.

SCENE TWO[64]

Thunder. Enter LUCIFER, BELZEBUB *and*
MEPHOSTOPHILIS.

LUCIFER: Thus from infernal Dis do we ascend
  To view the subjects of our monarchy,
  Those souls which sin seals the black sons of hell,
  'Mong which as chief, Faustus, we come to thee,
  Bringing with us lasting damnation
  To wait upon thy soul. The time is come
  Which makes it forfeit.

MEPHOSTOPHILIS: And this gloomy night,
  Here in this room will wretched Faustus be.

1 *Dis*: the underworld (Pluto's realm).

10 BELZEBUB: And here we'll stay,
   To mark him how he doth demean himself.

MEPHOSTOPHILIS: How should he, but in desperate
   lunacy?
   Fond worldling, now his heart blood dries with grief.
   His conscience kills it, and his labouring brain
   Begets a world of idle fantasies
   To overreach the devil. But all in vain:
   His store of pleasures must be sauced with pain.
   He and his servant Wagner are at hand.
   Both come from drawing Faustus' latest will.

20 See where they come.
   Enter FAUSTUS *and* WAGNER.

FAUSTUS: Say, Wagner, thou hast perused my will:
   How dost thou like it?

WAGNER: Sir, so wondrous well
   As in all humble duty I do yield
   My life and lasting service for your love.
   Enter the SCHOLARS.

FAUSTUS: Gramercies, Wagner. Welcome, gentlemen.

FIRST SCHOLAR: Now, worthy Faustus, methinks your
   looks are changed.

FAUSTUS: Oh gentlemen!

SECOND SCHOLAR: What ails Faustus?

30 FAUSTUS: Ah, my sweet chamber-fellow, had I lived
   with thee
   Then had I lived still, but now must die eternally.
   Look, sirs, comes he not? Comes he not?

FIRST SCHOLAR: Oh, my dear Faustus, what imports
   this fear?

SECOND SCHOLAR: Is all our pleasure turned to
   melancholy?

THIRD SCHOLAR: He is not well with being over-
   solitary.

SECOND SCHOLAR: If it be so, we'll have physicians,
   and Faustus shall be cured.

13 *Fond*: foolish.

THIRD SCHOLAR: 'Tis but a surfeit, sir; fear nothing.

FAUSTUS: A surfeit of deadly sin, that hath damned
both body and soul.   *40*

SECOND SCHOLAR: Yet Faustus, look up to heaven,
and remember mercy is infinite.

FAUSTUS: But Faustus' offence can ne'er be pardoned,
The serpent that tempted Eve may be saved,
But not Faustus. Oh gentlemen, hear with patience and
tremble not at my speeches. Though my heart pant and
quiver to remember that I have been a student here
these thirty years, oh would I had never seen Wittenberg, never read book. And what wonders I have done
all Germany can witness, yea all the world, for which   *50*
Faustus hath lost both Germany and the world, yea
heaven itself, heaven, the seat of God, the throne of
the blessed, the kingdom of joy, and must remain in
hell for ever. Hell, oh hell for ever. Sweet friends,
what shall become of Faustus, being in hell for ever?

SECOND SCHOLAR: Yet Faustus, call on God.

FAUSTUS: On God, whom Faustus hath abjured? On
God, whom Faustus hath blasphemed? Oh my God, I
would weep, but the devil draws in my tears. Gush
forth blood instead of tears, yea, life and soul. Oh, he   *60*
stays my tongue. I would lift up my hands, but see,
they hold them, they hold them.

ALL: Who, Faustus?

FAUSTUS: Why, Lucifer and Mephostophilis:
Oh gentlemen, I gave them my soul for my cunning.

ALL: Oh, God forbid.

FAUSTUS: God forbade it indeed, but Faustus hath done
it. For vain pleasure of four and twenty years hath
Faustus lost eternal joy and felicity. I writ them a bill
with mine own blood, the date is expired: this is the   *70*
time, and he will fetch me.

FIRST SCHOLAR: Why did not Faustus tell us of this
before, that divines might have prayed for thee?

FAUSTUS: Oft have I thought to have done so, but the

333

devil threatened to tear me in pieces if I named God; to fetch me body and soul if I once gave ear to divinity, and now 'tis too late. Gentlemen, away, lest you perish with me.

SECOND SCHOLAR: Oh what may we do to save Faustus?

80 FAUSTUS: Talk not of me, but save yourselves and depart.

THIRD SCHOLAR: God will strengthen me. I will stay with Faustus.

FIRST SCHOLAR: Tempt not God, sweet friend, but let us into the next room and pray for him.

FAUSTUS: Ay, pray for me, pray for me. And what noise soever you hear, come not unto me, for nothing can rescue me.

90 SECOND SCHOLAR: Pray thou, and we will pray, that God may have mercy upon thee.

FAUSTUS: Gentlemen, farewell. If I live till morning, I'll visit you. If not, Faustus is gone to hell.

ALL: Faustus, farewell.

Exeunt SCHOLARS.

MEPHOSTOPHILIS: Ay, Faustus, now thou hast no hope of heaven,
Therefore despair, think only upon hell,
For that must be thy mansion, there to dwell.

FAUSTUS: Oh, thou bewitching fiend, 'twas thy temptation
Hath robbed me of eternal happiness.

100 MEPHOSTOPHILIS: I do confess it, Faustus, and rejoice.
'Twas I that, when thou were't i' the way to heaven,
Dammed up thy passage; when thou took'st the book
To view the scriptures, then I turned the leaves
And led thine eye.
What, weep'st thou? 'Tis too late, despair.
Farewell.
Fools that will laugh on earth, must weep in hell.
Exit.

Enter the GOOD *and the* EVIL ANGEL *at several doors.*

GOOD ANGEL: Oh Faustus, if thou hadst given ear to me
 Innumerable joys had followed thee.
 But thou didst love the world.

EVIL ANGEL: Gave ear to me,   *110*
 And now must taste hell's pains perpetually.

GOOD ANGEL: Oh, what will all thy riches, pleasures,
 pomps,
 Avail thee now?

EVIL ANGEL: Nothing but vex thee more,
 To want in hell, that had on earth such store.
  Music while the throne descends.

GOOD ANGEL: Oh, thou hast lost celestial happiness,
 Pleasures unspeakable, bliss without end.
 Hadst thou affected sweet divinity,
 Hell, or the devil, had had no power on thee.
 Hadst thou kept on that way, Faustus, behold   *120*
 In what resplendent glory thou hadst sat
 In yonder throne, like those bright shining saints,
 And triumphed over hell. That thou hast lost,
 And now, poor soul, must thy good angel leave
  thee:
 The jaws of hell are open to receive thee.
  Exit.
  Hell is discovered.

EVIL ANGEL: Now, Faustus, let thine eyes with horror
  stare
 Into that vast perpetual torture-house.
 There are the furies tossing damned souls
 On burning forks. Their bodies broil in lead.
 There are live quarters broiling on the coals   *130*
 That ne'er can die. This ever-burning chair
 Is for o'er-tortured souls to rest them in.
 These, that are fed with sops of flaming fire,
 Were gluttons, and loved only delicates,
 And laughed to see the poor starve at their gates.

118 *affected*: pursued, followed.

But yet all these are nothing. Thou shalt see
Ten thousand tortures that more horrid be.

FAUSTUS: Oh, I have seen enough to torture me.

EVIL ANGEL: Nay, thou must feel them, taste the smart
of all:

140   He that loves pleasure must for pleasure fall.
And so I leave thee, Faustus, till anon.
Then wilt thou tumble in confusion.

> *Exit.*
>
> *The clock strikes eleven.*

FAUSTUS: Ah Faustus,[65]
Now hast thou but one bare hour to live,
And then thou must be damned perpetually.
Stand still, you ever-moving spheres of heaven,
That time may cease and midnight never come.
Fair nature's eye, rise, rise again, and make
Perpetual day. Or let this hour be but

150   A year, a month, a week, a natural day,
That Faustus may repent and save his soul.
O lente, lente, currite noctis equi.
The stars move still, time runs, the clock will strike.
The devil will come, and Faustus must be damned.
Oh, I'll leap up to my God: who pulls me down?
See, see, where Christ's blood streams in the
firmament.
One drop would save my soul, half a drop. Ah, my
Christ!
Ah, rend not my heart for naming of my Christ!
Yet will I call on him. Oh, spare me, Lucifer!

160   Where is it now? 'Tis gone:
And see where God stretcheth out his arm,
And bends his ireful brows.
Mountains and hills, come, come, and fall on me,

---

152 *O lente* . . .: 'Stay, night, and run not thus' in Marlowe's own
translation (literally 'O slowly, slowly run, ye horses of night').
In Ovid's poem (*Amores*, 1, 13, 40) the lover wishes that night
would never end so that he could lie with his mistress for ever.

And hide me from the heavy wrath of God.
No, no. Then will I headlong run into the earth.
Earth, gape! Oh no, it will not harbour me.
You stars that reigned at my nativity,
Whose influence hath allotted death and hell,
Now draw up Faustus like a foggy mist   170
Into the entrails of yon labouring cloud,
That when you vomit forth into the air
My limbs may issue from your smoky mouths,
So that my soul may but ascend to heaven.
   The watch strikes.
Ah! half the hour is past,
'Twill all be past anon.
Oh God, if thou wilt not have mercy on my soul,
Yet, for Christ's sake whose blood hath ransomed me,
Impose some end to my incessant pain.
Let Faustus live in hell a thousand years,
A hundred thousand, and at last be saved.   180
Oh, no end is limited to damned souls.
Why wert thou not a creature wanting soul?
Or why is this immortal that thou hast?
Ah, Pythagoras' *metempsychosis*, were that true
This soul should fly from me, and I be changed
Unto some brutish beast.
All beasts are happy, for when they die
Their souls are soon dissolved in elements,
But mine must live still to be plagued in hell.
Cursed be the parents that engendered me!   190
No, Faustus, curse thyself, curse Lucifer,
That hath deprived thee of the joys of heaven.
   The clock strikes twelve.
Oh, it strikes, it strikes! Now body turn to air,
Or Lucifer will bear thee quick to hell.
   Thunder and lightning.

184 *Pythagoras' metempsychosis*: his theory of the transmigration of
souls.
194 *quick*: alive.

337

Oh soul, be changed into little water drops
And fall into the ocean, ne'er be found.
   Thunder. Enter the DEVILS.
My God, my God, look not so fierce on me.
Adders and serpents, let me breathe awhile.
Ugly hell, gape not, come not, Lucifer!

200   I'll burn my books. Ah, Mephostophilis!
   Exeunt with him.

SCENE THREE[66]

Enter the SCHOLARS.

FIRST SCHOLAR: Come, gentlemen, let us go visit
   Faustus,
For such a dreadful night was never seen
Since first the world's creation did begin.
Such fearful shrieks and cries were never heard.
Pray heaven the Doctor have escaped the danger.
SECOND SCHOLAR: Oh help us, heaven! See, here are
   Faustus' limbs,
All torn asunder by the hand of death.
THIRD SCHOLAR: The devils whom Faustus served
   have torn him thus:
For twixt the hours of twelve and one, methought

10   I heard him shriek and call aloud for help,
At which self time the house seemed all on fire
With dreadful horror of these damned fiends.
SECOND SCHOLAR: Well, gentlemen, though Faustus'
   end be such
As every Christian heart laments to think on,
Yet, for he was a scholar once admired
For wondrous knowledge in our German schools,
We'll give his mangled limbs due burial,
And all the students clothed in mourning black
Shall wait upon his heavy funeral.
   Exeunt.

EPILOGUE

Enter the CHORUS.

CHORUS: Cut is the branch that might
straight,
And burned is Apollo's laurel bough,
That sometime grew within this learne
Faustus is gone. Regard his hellish fall,
Whose fiendful fortune may exhort the w
Only to wonder at unlawful things,
Whose deepness doth entice such forward wits,
To practise more than heavenly power permits.

Terminat hora diem, Terminat Author opus.

FINIS.

Final S.D. *Terminat hora* . . . : The hour ends the day, the author
ends his work.

The Jew of Malta

TO MY WORTHY FRIEND, MASTER THOMAS HAMMON, OF GRAYS INN, ETC.

This play, composed by so worthy an author as Mr Marlowe, and the part of the Jew presented by so unimitable an actor as Mr Alleyn, being in this later age commended to the stage; as I ushered it unto the Court, and presented it to the Cock-pit, with these Prologues and Epilogues here inserted, so now being newly brought to the press, I was loath it should be published without the ornament of an Epistle; making choice of you unto whom to devote it; than whom (of all those gentlemen and acquaintance within the compass of my long knowledge) there is none more able to tax ignorance, or attribute right to merit. Sir, you have been pleased to grace some of mine own works with your courteous patronage: I hope this will not be the worse accepted, because commended by me; over whom none can claim more power or privilege than yourself. I had no better a New Year's gift to present you with; receive it therefore as a continuance of the inviolable obligement, by which he rests still engaged; who, as he ever hath, shall always remain,

Tuissimus,

THO. HEYWOOD

3 *Mr Alleyn*: spelt Allin in Quarto. Edward Alleyn (1566–1626), the most famous Elizabethan actor. He also played Tamburlaine and Faustus.
4 *the Court*: theatre in palace of Whitehall.
4 *the Cock-pit*: in Drury Lane; also called the Phoenix.

THE PROLOGUE SPOKEN AT COURT

Gracious and great, that we so boldly dare
('Mongst other plays that now in fashion are)
To present this, writ many years agone,
And in that age thought second unto none,
We humbly crave your pardon. We pursue
The story of a rich and famous Jew
Who liv'd in Malta: you shall find him still,
In all his projects, a sound Machevill,
And that's his character. He that hath passed
So many censures is now come at last   10
To have your princely ears: grace you him; then
You crown the action, and renown the pen.

EPILOGUE SPOKEN AT COURT

It is our fear, dread sovereign, we have bin
Too tedious; neither can't be less than sin
To wrong your princely patience. If we have,
Thus low dejected, we your pardon crave;
And, if aught here offend your ear or sight,
We only act and speak what others write.

*

THE PROLOGUE TO THE STAGE
AT THE COCK-PIT

We know not how our play may pass this stage,
But by the best of *poets in that age   *Marlo.
The Malta-Jew had being and was made;
And he then by the best of †actors play'd: †Allin.
In *Hero and Leander* one did gain
A lasting memory; in *Tamburlaine*,

8 *Machevill*: disciple of Machiavelli.

343

This Jew, with others many, th' other wan
The attribute of peerless, being a man
Whom we may rank with (doing no one wrong)
10   Proteus for shapes, and Roscius for a tongue,
So could he speak, so vary; nor is't hate
To merit in *him who doth personate   *Perkins.
Our Jew this day; nor is it his ambition
To exceed or equal, being of condition
More modest: this is all that he intends,
(And that too at the urgence of some friends,)
To prove his best, and, if none here gainsay it,
The part he hath studied, and intends to play it.

EPILOGUE TO THE STAGE

AT THE COCK-PIT

In graving with Pygmalion to contend,
Or painting with Apelles, doubtless the end
Must be disgrace; our actor did not so:
He only aim'd to go, but not out-go.
Nor think that this day any prize was play'd;
Here were no bets at all, no wagers laid;
All the ambition that his mind doth swell,
Is but to hear from you (by me) 'twas well.

10 *Proteus*: god with special power to change shape.
10 *Roscius*: famous Roman actor.
1 *Pygmalion*: mythological Greek sculptor, whose statue Galatea was given life.
2 *Apelles*: favourite Greek painter of Alexander the Great.
5 *prize*: special contest or exhibition undertaken (as in fencing).

Dramatis Personae

FERNEZE, *governor of Malta*
LODOWICK, *his son*
SELIM CALYMATH, *son to the* GRAND SEIGNIOR
MARTIN DEL BOSCO, *vice-admiral of Spain*
MATHIAS, *a gentleman*
JACOMO,
BARNARDINE, } *friars*
BARABAS, *a wealthy Jew*
ITHAMORE, *a slave*
PILIA-BORZA, *a bully, attendant to* BELLAMIRA
TWO MERCHANTS
THREE JEWS
KNIGHTS, BASSOES, OFFICERS, GUARD, SLAVES,
    MESSENGER, *and* CARPENTERS
KATHARINE, *mother to* MATHIAS
ABIGAIL, *daughter to* BARABAS
BELLAMIRA, *a courtesan*
ABBESS
NUN
MACHEVILL, *the Prologue*

Scene, Malta

Enter MACHEVILL.

MACHEVILL: Albeit the world think Machevill is dead,
Yet was his soul but flown beyond the Alps;
And, now the Guise is dead, is come from France,
To view this land, and frolic with his friends.
To some perhaps my name is odious;
But such as love me, guard me from their tongues,
And let them know that I am Machevill,
And weigh not men, and therefore not men's words.
Admir'd I am of those that hate me most.
Though some speak openly against my books,   10
Yet will they read me, and thereby attain
To Peter's chair; and, when they cast me off,
Are poison'd by my climbing followers.
I count religion but a childish toy,
And hold there is no sin but ignorance.
Birds of the air will tell of murders past.
I am asham'd to hear such fooleries!
Many will talk of title to a crown:
What right had Caesar to the empery?
Might first made kings, and laws were then most sure   20
When, like the Draco's, they were writ in blood.
Hence comes it that a strong built citadel
Commands much more than letters can import:
Which maxim had [but] Phalaris[1]* observ'd,
H'ad never bellow'd in a brazen bull
Of great ones' envy; o' the poor petty wights

3 *Guise*: Duke of Guise, leader of the St Bartholomew massacre
of Huguenots, 1572, died 1588 (cf. Marlowe's *Massacre at Paris*
in which he is the main character).
8 *weigh*: care for.   12 *attain To Peter's chair*: become Pope.
21 *the Draco's*: Draco, Athenian author of inhumane laws (fl. c.
624 BC). Q has 'Drancus'.
26 *wights*: probably meaning 'wits'.

*Superior numbers refer to the Additional Notes at the end of the
book.

347

Let me be envied and not pitied.
But whither am I bound! I come not, I,
To read a lecture here in Britain,
30 But to present the tragedy of a Jew,
Who smiles to see how full his bags are cramm'd;
Which money was not got without my means.
I crave but this, – grace him as he deserves,
And let him not be entertain'd the worse
Because he favours me.
    Exit.

ACT ONE

SCENE ONE

BARABAS *discovered in his counting house, with heaps of gold before him.*
BARABAS: So that of thus much that return was made;
And of the third part of the Persian ships
There was the venture summ'd and satisfied.
As for those Samnites, and the men of Uz,
That bought my Spanish oils and wines of Greece,
Here have I purs'd their paltry silverlings.
Fie, what a trouble 'tis to count this trash!
Well fare the Arabians, who so richly pay
The things they traffic for with wedge of gold,
10 Whereof a man may easily in a day
Tell that which may maintain him all his life.
The needy groom, that never finger'd groat,
Would make a miracle of thus much coin;
But he whose steel-barr'd coffers are cramm'd full,
And all his life-time hath been tired,
Wearying his fingers' ends with telling it,

35 *favours*: resembles.
S.D. *Barabas discovered*: Dyce's stage-direction. Quarto has ' *Enter Barabas*'.
4 *Samnites*: people of Southern Italy.
4 *Uz*: bordering Palestine.   11 *Tell*: count.

Would in his age be loath to labour so,
And for a pound to sweat himself to death.
Give me the merchants of the Indian mines,
That trade in metal of the purest mould;   20
The wealthy Moor, that in the eastern rocks
Without control can pick his riches up,
And in his house heap pearl like pebble stones,
Receive them free, and sell them by the weight!
Bags of fiery opals, sapphires, amethysts,
Jacinths, hard topaz, grass-green emeralds,
Beauteous rubies, sparkling diamonds,
And seld-seen costly stones of so great price,
As one of them, indifferently rated,
And of a carat of this quantity,   30
May serve, in peril of calamity,
To ransom great kings from captivity.
This is the ware wherein consists my wealth;
And thus methinks should men of judgment frame
Their means of traffic from the vulgar trade,
And, as their wealth increaseth, so inclose
Infinite riches in a little room.
But now how stands the wind?
Into what corner peers my halcyon's bill?
Ha! to the east? Yes. See how stands the vanes?   40
East and by south: why, then, I hope my ships
I sent for Egypt and the bordering isles
Are gotten up by Nilus' winding banks;
Mine argosy from Alexandria,
Loaden with spice and silks, now under sail,
Are smoothly gliding down by Candy-shore
To Malta, through our Mediterranean sea –
But who comes here?

Enter a MERCHANT.

29 *indifferently*: fairly, impartially (also I, 2, 190).
39 *halcyon's bill*: a dead kingfisher, suspended, acting as a weather-cock.
46 *Candy-shore*: Crete.

How now!

MERCHANT: Barabas, thy ships are safe,
50   Riding in Malta-road; and all the merchants
With all their merchandise are safe arriv'd,
And have sent me to know whether yourself
Will come and custom them.

BARABAS: The ships are safe thou say'st, and richly
    fraught?

MERCHANT: They are.

BARABAS: Why, then, go bid them come ashore,
And bring with them their bills of entry:
I hope our credit in the custom-house
Will serve as well as I were present there.
60   Go send 'em threescore camels, thirty mules,
And twenty waggons, to bring up the ware.
But art thou master in a ship of mine,
And is thy credit not enough for that?

MERCHANT: The very custom barely comes to more
Than many merchants of the town are worth,
And therefore far exceeds my credit, sir.

BARABAS: Go tell 'em the Jew of Malta sent thee, man:
Tush, who amongst 'em knows not Barabas?

MERCHANT: I go.

70 BARABAS: So, then, there's somewhat come.
Sirrah, which of my ships art thou master of?

MERCHANT: Of the Speranza, sir.

BARABAS: And saw'st thou not
Mine argosy at Alexandria?
Thou couldst not come from Egypt, or by Caire,
But at the entry there into the sea,
Where Nilus pays his tribute to the main,
Thou needs must sail by Alexandria.

MERCHANT: I neither saw them, nor inquir'd of them:
80   But this we heard some of our seamen say,
They wonder'd how you durst with so much wealth
Trust such a crazed vessel, and so far.

50 *Malta-road*: harbour (Quarto: 'Rhode').

BARABAS: Tush, they are wise! I know her and her
    strength.
  But go, go thou thy ways, discharge thy ship,
  And bid my factor bring his loading in.
    Exit MERCHANT.
  And yet I wonder at this argosy.
    Enter a SECOND MERCHANT.
SECOND MERCHANT: Thine argosy from Alexandria,
  Know, Barabas, doth ride in Malta-road,
  Laden with riches, and exceeding store
  Of Persian silks, of gold, and orient pearl.   *90*
BARABAS: How chance you came not with those other
  ships
  That sail'd by Egypt?
SECOND MERCHANT: Sir, we saw 'em not.
BARABAS: Belike they coasted round by Candy-shore
  About their oils or other businesses.
  But 'twas ill done of you to come so far
  Without the aid or conduct of their ships.
SECOND MERCHANT: Sir, we were wafted by a Spanish
  fleet,
  That never left us till within a league,
  That had the galleys of the Turk in chase.   *100*
BARABAS: O, they were going up to Sicily. Well, go
  And bid the merchants and my men despatch,
  And come ashore, and see the fraught discharg'd.
SECOND MERCHANT: I go.
    Exit.
BARABAS: Thus trowls our fortune in by land and sea,
  And thus are we on every side enrich'd.
  These are the blessings promis'd to the Jews,
  And herein was old Abram's happiness:
  What more may heaven do for earthly man
  Than thus to pour out plenty in their laps,   *110*
  Ripping the bowels of the earth for them,
  Making the sea their servant, and the winds

85 *factor*: agent.   105 *trowls*: flowing in abundance.

To drive their substance with successful blasts?
Who hateth me but for my happiness?
Or who is honour'd now but for his wealth?
Rather had I, a Jew, be hated thus,
Than pitied in a Christian poverty;
For I can see no fruits in all their faith,
But malice, falsehood, and excessive pride,
Which methinks fits not their profession.
Haply some hapless man hath conscience,
And for his conscience lives in beggary.
They say we are a scatter'd nation:
I cannot tell; but we have scambled up
More wealth by far than those that brag of faith.
There's Kirriah Jairim, the great Jew of Greece,
Obed in Bairseth, Nones in Portugal,
Myself in Malta, some in Italy,
Many in France, and wealthy every one;
Ay, wealthier far than any Christian.
I must confess we come not to be kings:
That's not our fault: alas, our number's few,
And crowns come either by succession,
Or urg'd by force; and nothing violent,
Oft have I heard tell, can be permanent.
Give us a peaceful rule; make Christian kings,
That thirst so much for principality.
I have no charge, nor many children,
But one sole daughter, whom I hold as dear
As Agamemnon did his Iphigen;[2]
And all I have is hers. But who comes here?

Enter three JEWS.

FIRST JEW: Tush, tell not me! 'Twas done of policy.
SECOND JEW: Come, therefore, let us go to Barabas,
For he can counsel best in these affairs.

---

121 *hapless*: unlucky.
124 *scambled*: scrambled, collected.
142 *policy*: deliberate cunning (word associated with Machiavellian doctrine used repeatedly in the play).

And here he comes.

BARABAS: Why, how now, countrymen?
Why flock you thus to me in multitudes?
What accident's betided to the Jews?

FIRST JEW: A fleet of warlike galleys, Barabas,
Are come from Turkey, and lie in our road: *150*
And they this day sit in the council-house
To entertain them and their embassy.

BARABAS: Why, let 'em come, so they come not to war;
Or let 'em war, so we be conquerors.
(*Aside*) Nay, let 'em combat, conquer, and kill all.
So they spare me, my daughter, and my wealth.

FIRST JEW: Were it for confirmation of a league,
They would not come in warlike manner thus.

SECOND JEW: I fear their coming will afflict us all.

BARABAS: Fond men, what dream you of their   *160*
multitudes?
What need they treat of peace that are in league?
The Turks and those of Malta are in league:
Tut, tut, there is some other matter in't.

FIRST JEW: Why, Barabas, they come for peace or
war.

BARABAS: Haply for neither, but to pass along
Towards Venice, by the Adriatic sea,
With whom they have attempted many times,
But never could effect their stratagem.

THIRD JEW: And very wisely said; it may be so.

SECOND JEW: But there's a meeting in the senate-   *170*
house,
And all the Jews in Malta must be there.

BARABAS: Hum, – all the Jews in Malta must be there?
Ay, like enough: why, then, let every man
Provide him, and be there for fashion-sake.
If anything shall there concern our state,
Assure yourselves I'll look unto (*aside*) myself.

FIRST JEW: I know you will. Well, brethren, let us go.

160 *Fond*: foolish (as in 1, 2, 246).

SECOND JEW: Let's take our leaves. Farewell, good
    Barabas.
BARABAS: Do so. Farewell, Zaareth; farewell, Temainte.
    Exeunt JEWS.

180   And, Barabas, now search this secret out.
    Summon thy senses, call thy wits together:
    These silly men mistake the matter clean.
    Long to the Turk did Malta contribute;
    Which tribute all in policy, I fear,
    The Turk has let increase to such a sum
    As all the wealth of Malta cannot pay;
    And now by that advantage thinks, belike,
    To seize upon the town. Ay, that he seeks.
    Howe'er the world go, I'll make sure for one,
190   And seek in time to intercept the worst,
    Warily guarding that which I ha' got.
    Ego mihimet sum semper proximus.
    Why, let 'em enter. Let 'em take the town.
    Exit.

SCENE TWO

The Senate House.
Enter FERNEZE *governor of Malta,* KNIGHTS, *and*
OFFICERS; *met by* CALYMATH, *and* BASSOES *of*
the Turk.
FERNEZE: Now, bassoes, what demand you at our
    hands?
FIRST BASSO: Know, knights of Malta, that we came
    from Rhodes,
    From Cyprus, Candy, and those other isles
    That lie betwixt the Mediterranean seas.
FERNEZE: What's Cyprus, Candy, and those other isles
    To us or Malta? What at our hands demand ye?

192 *Ego mihimet . . .*: misquoted from Terence's *Andria* ('*Proximus sum egomet mihi*': 'I am my own best friend').

CALYMATH: The ten years' tribute that remains unpaid.

FERNEZE: Alas, my lord, the sum is over-great!
I hope your highness will consider us.

CALYMATH: I wish, grave governor, 'twere in my   *10*
   power
To favour you; but 'tis my father's cause,
Wherein I may not, nay, I dare not dally.

FERNEZE: Then give us leave, great Selim Calymath.

CALYMATH: Stand all aside, and let the knights
   determine,
And send to keep our galleys under sail,
For happily we shall not tarry here.
Now, Governor, how are you resolv'd?

FERNEZE: Thus: since your hard conditions are such
That you will needs have ten years' tribute past,
We may have time to make collection   *20*
Amongst the inhabitants of Malta for't.

FIRST BASSO: That's more than is in our commission.

CALYMATH: What, Callapine! a little courtesy!
Let's know their time; perhaps it is not long.
And 'tis more kingly to obtain by peace
Than to enforce conditions by constraint.
What respite ask you, Governor?

FERNEZE: But a month.

CALYMATH: We grant a month, but see you keep your
   promise.
Now launch our galleys back again to sea,   *30*
Where we'll attend the respite you have ta'en,
And for the money send our messenger.
Farewell, great Governor and brave knights of Malta.

FERNEZE: And all good fortune wait on Calymath!
   Exeunt CALYMATH *and* BASSOES.
Go one and call those Jews of Malta hither:
Were they not summon'd to appear today?

FIRST OFFICER: They were, my lord; and here they
   come.
   Enter BARABAS *and three* JEWS.

FIRST KNIGHT: Have you determin'd what to say to
them?

FERNEZE: Yes; give me leave. And, Hebrews, now come
near.

40 From the Emperor of Turkey is arriv'd
Great Selim Calymath, his highness' son,
To levy of us ten years' tribute past:
Now, then, here know that it concerneth us.

BARABAS: Then, good my lord, to keep your quiet still,
Your lordship shall do well to let them have it.

FERNEZE: Soft, Barabas! There's more 'longs to't than
so.
To what this ten years' tribute will amount,
That we have cast, but cannot compass it
By reason of the wars, that robb'd our store;

50 And therefore are we to request your aid.

BARABAS: Alas, my lord, we are no soldiers!
And what's our aid against so great a prince?

FIRST KNIGHT: Tut, Jew, we know thou art no
soldier:
Thou art a merchant and a money'd man,
And 'tis thy money, Barabas, we seek.

BARABAS: How, my lord! my money!

FERNEZE: Thine and the rest.
For, to be short, amongst you't must be had.

FIRST JEW: Alas, my lord, the most of us are poor!

60 FERNEZE: Then let the rich increase your portions.

BARABAS: Are strangers with your tribute to be tax'd?

SECOND KNIGHT: Have strangers leave with us to get
their wealth?
Then let them with us contribute.

BARABAS: How? Equally?

FERNEZE: No, Jew, like infidels;
For through our sufferance of your hateful lives,

46 *'longs to't than so*: more in it than that.
48 *cast*: calculated.   48 *compass*: obtain, raise.
66 *sufferance*: tolerance.

Who stand accursed in the sight of heaven,
These taxes and afflictions are befall'n,
And therefore thus we are determined.
Read there the articles of our decrees.   70

OFFICER (*reads*): *First, the tribute-money of the Turks shall
all be levied amongst the Jews, and each of them to pay one half
of his estate.*

BARABAS: How! half his estate? (*Aside*) I hope you
mean not mine.

FERNEZE: Read on.

OFFICER (*reads*): *Secondly, he that denies to pay, shall straight
become a Christian.*

BARABAS: How! a Christian! (*Aside*) Hum, – what's
here to do?

OFFICER (*reads*): *Lastly, he that denies this, shall absolutely
lose all he has.*   80

THREE JEWS: O my lord, we will give half!

BARABAS: O earth-metalled villains, and no Hebrews
born!
And will you basely thus submit yourselves
To leave your goods to their arbitrement?

FERNEZE: Why, Barabas! Wilt thou be christened?

BARABAS: No, Governor, I will be no convertite.

FERNEZE: Then pay thy half.

BARABAS: Why, know you what you did by this device?
Half of my substance is a city's wealth.
Governor, it was not got so easily;   90
Nor will I part so slightly therewithal.

FERNEZE: Sir, half is the penalty of our decree.
Either pay that, or we will seize on all.

BARABAS: *Corpo di Dio!* Stay: you shall have half;
Let me be us'd but as my brethren are.

FERNEZE: No, Jew, thou hast denied the articles,
And now it cannot be recall'd.
        Exeunt OFFICERS, *on a sign from* FERNEZE.

BARABAS: Will you, then, steal my goods?
Is theft the ground of your religion?

357

100 FERNEZE: No, Jew; we take particularly thine,
　　　To save the ruin of a multitude.
　　　And better one want for a common good,
　　　Than many perish for a private man.
　　　Yet, Barabas, we will not banish thee,
　　　But here in Malta, where thou gott'st thy wealth,
　　　Live still, and, if thou canst, get more.
　　BARABAS: Christians, what or how can I multiply?
　　　Of naught is nothing made.
　　FIRST KNIGHT: From naught at first thou cam'st to
　　　little wealth,
110　From little unto more, from more to most.
　　　If your first curse fall heavy on thy head,
　　　And make thee poor and scorn'd of all the world,
　　　'Tis not our fault, but thy inherent sin.
　　BARABAS: What, bring you Scripture to confirm your
　　　wrongs?
　　　Preach me not out of my possessions.
　　　Some Jews are wicked, as all Christians are;
　　　But say the tribe that I descended of
　　　Were all in general cast away for sin,
　　　Shall I be tried for their transgression?
120　The man that dealeth righteously shall live;
　　　And which of you can charge me otherwise?
　　FERNEZE: Out, wretched Barabas!
　　　Sham'st thou not thus to justify thyself,
　　　As if we knew not thy profession?
　　　If thou rely upon thy righteousness,
　　　Be patient, and thy riches will increase.
　　　Excess of wealth is cause of covetousness;
　　　And covetousness, O, 'tis a monstrous sin!
　　BARABAS: Ay, but theft is worse. Tush! take not from
　　　me, then,
130　For that is theft; and, if you rob me thus,
　　　I must be forc'd to steal, and compass more.
　　FIRST KNIGHT: Grave Governor, list not to his
　　　exclaims.

Convert his mansion to a nunnery;
His house will harbour many holy nuns.
FERNEZE: It shall be so.
 Re-enter OFFICERS.
      Now, officers, have you done?
FIRST OFFICER: Ay, my lord. We have seiz'd upon
 the goods
And wares of Barabas, which, being valu'd,
Amount to more than all the wealth in Malta;
And of the other we have seized half.
FERNEZE: Then we'll take order for the residue. *140*
BARABAS: Well, then, my lord, say, are you satisfied?
You have my goods, my money, and my wealth,
My ships, my store, and all that I enjoy'd;
And, having all, you can request no more,
Unless your unrelenting flinty hearts
Suppress all pity in your stony breasts,
And now shall move you to bereave my life.
FERNEZE: No, Barabas. To stain our hands with blood
Is far from us and our profession.
BARABAS: Why, I esteem the injury far less, *150*
To take the lives of miserable men
Than be the causers of their misery.
You have my wealth, the labour of my life,
The comfort of mine age, my children's hope;
And therefore ne'er distinguish of the wrong.
FERNEZE: Content thee, Barabas; thou hast naught
 but right.
BARABAS: Your extreme right does me exceeding
 wrong:
But take it to you, i' the devil's name!
FERNEZE: Come, let us in, and gather of these goods
The money for this tribute of the Turk. *160*
FIRST KNIGHT: 'Tis necessary that be look'd unto;
For, if we break our day, we break the league,
And that will prove but simple policy.
 Exeunt all except BARABAS *and the three* JEWS.

BARABAS: Ay, policy! That's their profession,
And not simplicity, as they suggest.
The plagues of Egypt, and the curse of heaven,
Earth's barrenness, and all men's hatred,
Inflict upon them, thou great *Primus Motor*!
And here upon my knees, striking the earth,
170 I ban their souls to everlasting pains,
And extreme tortures of the fiery deep,
That thus have dealt with me in my distress!

FIRST JEW: O, yet be patient, gentle Barabas!

BARABAS: O silly brethren, born to see this day!
Why stand you thus unmov'd with my laments?
Why weep you not to think upon my wrongs?
Why pine not I, and die in this distress?

FIRST JEW: Why, Barabas, as hardly can we brook
The cruel handling of ourselves in this:
180 Thou seest they have taken half our goods.

BARABAS: Why did you yield to their extortion?
You were a multitude, and I but one;
And of me only have they taken all.

FIRST JEW: Yet, brother Barabas, remember Job.

BARABAS: What tell you me of Job? I wot his wealth
Was written thus: he had seven thousand sheep,
Three thousand camels, and two hundred yoke
Of labouring oxen, and five hundred
She asses; but for every one of those,
190 Had they been valu'd at indifferent rate,
I had at home, and in mine argosy,
And other ships that came from Egypt last,
As much as would have bought his beasts and him,
And yet have kept enough to live upon
So that not he, but I, may curse the day,
Thy fatal birthday, forlorn Barabas;
And henceforth wish for an eternal night,
That clouds of darkness may enclose my flesh,
And hide these extreme sorrows from mine eyes.

168 *Primus Motor*: God, the first mover.   170 *ban*: curse.

For only I have toil'd to inherit here   200
The months of vanity, and loss of time,
And painful nights, have been appointed me.
SECOND JEW: Good Barabas, be patient.
BARABAS: Ay, I pray, leave me in my patience. You,
      that
Were ne'er possess'd of wealth, are pleas'd with want.
But give him liberty at least to mourn,
That in a field, amidst his enemies,
Doth see his soldiers slain, himself disarm'd,
And know no means of his recovery.
Ay, let me sorrow for this sudden chance;   210
'Tis in the trouble of my spirit I speak:
Great injuries are not so soon forgot.
FIRST JEW: Come, let us leave him; in his ireful mood
Our words will but increase his ecstasy.
SECOND JEW: On, then: but, trust me, 'tis a misery
To see a man in such affliction. –
Farewell Barabas.
BARABAS: Ay, fare you well.
      Exeunt three JEWS.
See the simplicity of these base slaves,
Who, for the villains have no wit themselves,   220
Think me to be a senseless lump of clay,
That will with every water wash to dirt!
No, Barabas is born to better chance,
And fram'd of finer mould than common men,
That measure naught but by the present time.
A reaching thought will search his deepest wits,
And cast with cunning for the time to come;
For evils are apt to happen every day.
      Enter ABIGAIL, *the Jew's daughter.*
But whither wends my beauteous Abigail?
O, what has made my lovely daughter sad?   230
What, woman! moan not for a little loss;

201 *vanity*: uselessness.   214 *ecstasy*: fury, madness.
220 *for (the villains)*: because . . .   227 *cast*: calculate.

361

Thy father has enough in store for thee.
ABIGAIL: Not for myself, but aged Barabas,
Father, for thee lamenteth Abigail.
But I will learn to leave these fruitless tears,
And, urg'd thereto with my afflictions,
With fierce exclaims run to the senate-house,
And in the senate reprehend them all,
And rent their hearts with tearing of my hair,
240   Till they reduce the wrongs done to my father.
BARABAS: No, Abigail. Things past recovery
Are hardly cur'd with exclamations.
Be silent, daughter; sufferance breeds ease,
And time may yield us an occasion,
Which on the sudden cannot serve the turn.
Besides, my girl, think me not all so fond
As negligently to forego so much
Without provision for thyself and me.
Ten thousand portagues, besides great pearls,
250   Rich costly jewels, and stones infinite,
Fearing the worst of this before it fell,
I closely hid.
ABIGAIL: Where, father?
BARABAS: In my house, my girl.
ABIGAIL: Then shall they ne'er be seen of Barabas;
For they have seiz'd upon thy house and wares.
BARABAS: But they will give me leave once more, I trow,
To go into my house.
ABIGAIL: That may they not,
260   For there I left the Governor placing nuns,
Displacing me; and of thy house they mean
To make a nunnery, where none but their own sect
Must enter in, men generally barr'd.
BARABAS: My gold, my gold, and all my wealth is gone!

245 *which on the sudden . . .*: which just at present will not work the trick.
249 *portagues*: gold coins.

You partial heavens, have I deserv'd this plague?
What, will you thus oppose me, luckless stars,
To make me desperate in my poverty?
And, knowing me impatient in distress,
Think me so mad as I will hang myself,
That I may vanish o'er the earth in air,   *270*
And leave no memory that e'er I was?
No, I will live! Nor loathe I this my life:
And since you leave me in the ocean thus
To sink or swim, and put me to my shifts,
I'll rouse my senses, and awake myself.
Daughter, I have it: thou perceiv'st the plight
Wherein these Christians have oppressed me:
Be rul'd by me, for in extremity
We ought to make bar of no policy.
ABIGAIL: Father, whate'er it be, to injure them   *280*
That have so manifestly wronged us,
What will not Abigail attempt?
BARABAS: Why, so.
Then thus: thou told'st me they have turn'd my house
Into a nunnery, and some nuns are there?
ABIGAIL: I did.
BARABAS: Then, Abigail, there must my girl
Entreat the abbess to be entertain'd.
ABIGAIL: How! as a nun?
BARABAS: Ay, daughter; for religion   *290*
Hides many mischiefs from suspicion.
ABIGAIL: Ay, but, father, they will suspect me there.
BARABAS: Let 'em suspect, but be thou so precise
As they may think it done of holiness.
Entreat 'em fair, and give them friendly speech,
And seem to them as if thy sins were great,
Till thou hast gotten to be entertain'd.
ABIGAIL: Thus, father, shall I much dissemble.
BARABAS: Tush!

293 *precise*: puritanical in manner.
297 *entertain'd*: admitted (also l. 297 below).

300 As good dissemble that thou never mean'st
As first mean truth and then dissemble it:
A counterfeit profession is better
Than unseen hypocrisy.

ABIGAIL: Well, father, say I be entertain'd,
What then shall follow?

BARABAS: This shall follow then.
There have I hid, close underneath the plank
That runs along the upper-chamber floor,
The gold and jewels which I kept for thee.

310 But here they come: be cunning, Abigail.

ABIGAIL: Then, father, go with me.

BARABAS: No, Abigail, in this
It is not necessary I be seen;
For I will seem offended with thee for't.
Be close, my girl, for this must fetch my gold.

> *They retire.*
> *Enter* FRIAR JACOMO, FRIAR BARNARDINE,
> ABBESS, *and a* NUN.

FRIAR JACOMO: Sisters,
We now are almost at the new-made nunnery.

ABBESS: The better; for we love not to be seen.
'Tis thirty winters long since some of us

320 Did stray so far amongst the multitude.

FRIAR JACOMO: But, madam, this house
And waters of this new-made nunnery
Will much delight you.

ABBESS: It may be so. – But who comes here?

> ABIGAIL *comes forward.*

ABIGAIL: Grave abbess, and you happy virgins' guide,
Pity the state of a distressed maid!

ABBESS: What art thou, daughter?

ABIGAIL: The hopeless daughter of a hapless Jew,
The Jew of Malta, wretched Barabas,

330 Sometime the owner of a goodly house,
Which they have now turn'd to a nunnery.

302 *profession*: i.e. of religious faith. 315 *close*: secretive.

364

ABBESS: Well, daughter, say, what is thy suit with us?

ABIGAIL: Fearing the afflictions which my father feels
Proceed from sin or want of faith in us,
I'd pass away my life in penitence,
And be a novice in your nunnery,
To make atonement for my labouring soul.

FRIAR JACOMO: No doubt, brother, but this
proceedeth of the spirit.

FRIAR DARNARDINE: Ay, and of a moving spirit too,
brother: but come,
Let us entreat she may be entertain'd.   340

ABBESS: Well, daughter, we admit you for a nun.

ABIGAIL: First let me as a novice learn to frame
My solitary life to your strait laws,
And let me lodge where I was wont to lie.
I do not doubt, by your divine precepts
And mine own industry, but to profit much.

BARABAS (aside): As much, I hope, as all I hid is worth.

ABBESS: Come, daughter, follow us.

BARABAS (coming forward): Why, how now, Abigail!
What mak'st thou 'mongst these hateful Christians?   350

FRIAR JACOMO: Hinder her not, thou man of little
faith,
For she has mortified herself.

BARABAS: How! Mortified?

FRIAR JACOMO: And is admitted to the sisterhood.

BARABAS: Child of perdition, and thy father's shame!
What wilt thou do among these hateful fiends?
I charge thee on my blessing that thou leave
These devils and their damned heresy!

ABIGAIL: Father, give me –

BARABAS: Nay, back, Abigail –   360
    Aside to ABIGAIL *in a whisper:*
And think upon the jewels and the gold;
The board is marked thus that covers it. –
(*Aloud*) Away, accursed, from thy father's sight!

352 *mortified herself*: is dead to the things of this world.

FRIAR JACOMO: Barabas, although thou art in
    misbelief,
And wilt not see thine own afflictions,
Yet let thy daughter be no longer blind.
BARABAS: Blind friar, I reck not thy persuasions, –
    (*Aside to* ABIGAIL *in a whisper*): The board is marked
    thus † that covers it –
    (*Aloud*) For I had rather die than see her thus. –
370 Wilt thou forsake me too in my distress,
Seduced daughter? (*Aside to her in a whisper*) Go,
    forget not. –
    (*Aloud*) Becomes it Jews to be so credulous? –
    (*Aside to her in a whisper*) Tomorrow early I'll be at
    the door. –
    (*Aloud*) No, come not at me! If thou wilt be damn'd,
Forget me, see me not! And so, be gone! –
    (*Aside to her in a whisper*) Farewell. Remember
    tomorrow morning. –
    (*Aloud*) Out, out, thou wretch!
    Exit, on one side, BARABAS. *Exeunt, on the other side,*
    FRIARS, ABBESS, NUN, *and* ABIGAIL: *and, as they*
    are going out,
    enter MATHIAS.
MATHIAS: Who's this? Fair Abigail, the rich Jew's
    daughter,
Become a nun! Her father's sudden fall
380 Has humbled her, and brought her down to this.
Tut, she were fitter for a tale of love,
Than to be tired out with orisons;
And better would she far become a bed,
Embraced in a friendly lover's arms,
Than rise at midnight to a solemn mass.
    Enter LODOWICK.

367 *reck*: care for.
368 †: mark in Quarto indicating the gesture Barabas is to make.
372 *Becomes it*: does it do credit to.
382 *orisons*: prayers.

LODOWICK: Why, how now, Don Mathias! in a dump?

MATHIAS: Believe me, noble Lodowick, I have seen
 The strangest sight, in my opinion,
 That ever I beheld.

LODOWICK: What was't, I prithee? 390

MATHIAS: A fair young maid, scarce fourteen years of
  age,
 The sweetest flower in Cytherea's field,
 Cropt from the pleasures of the fruitful earth,
 And strangely metamorphos'd nun.

LODOWICK: But say, what was she?

MATHIAS: Why, the rich Jew's daughter.

LODOWICK: What, Barabas, whose goods were lately
  seiz'd?
 Is she so fair?

MATHIAS: And matchless beautiful.
 As, had you seen her, 'twould have mov'd your heart, 400
 Though countermur'd with walls of brass, to love,
 Or, at the least, to pity.

LODOWICK: An if she be so fair as you report,
 'Twere time well spent to go and visit her.
 How say you? Shall we?

MATHIAS: I must and will, sir, there's no remedy.

LODOWICK: And so will I too, or it shall go hard.
 Farewell, Mathias.

MATHIAS: Farewell, Lodowick.
 Exeunt severally.

386 *in a dump*: in a fit of depression, pensive.
392 *Cytherea*: Venus.
401 *countermur'd*: Collier's conjecture (i.e. having a second wall built round the city for defence). Quarto has 'countermin'd'.

ACT TWO

SCENE ONE

A street outside the Nunnery.
Enter BARABAS, *with a light.*

BARABAS: Thus like the sad presaging raven that tolls
  The sick man's passport in her hollow beak,
  And in the shadow of the silent night
  Doth shake contagion from her sable wings,
  Vex'd and tormented runs poor Barabas
  With fatal curses towards these Christians.
  The incertain pleasures of swift-footed time
  Have ta'en their flight, and left me in despair;
  And of my former riches rests no more
10 But bare remembrance, like a soldier's scar,
  That has no further comfort for his maim.
  O Thou, that with a fiery pillar ledd'st
  The sons of Israel through the dismal shades,
  Light Abraham's offspring, and direct the hand
  Of Abigail this night! Or let the day
  Turn to eternal darkness after this!
  No sleep can fasten on my watchful eyes,
  Nor quiet enter my distemper'd thoughts,
  Till I have answer of my Abigail.

Enter ABIGAIL *above.*

20 ABIGAIL: Now have I happily espied a time
  To search the plank my father did appoint;
  And here, behold, unseen, where I have found
  The gold, the pearls, and jewels, which he hid.

BARABAS: Now I remember those old women's words,
  Who in my wealth would tell me winter's tales,
  And speak of spirits and ghosts that glide by night
  About the place where treasure hath been hid.
  And now methinks that I am one of those;
  For, whilst I live, here lives my soul's sole hope,

And, when I die, here shall my spirit walk.   *30*

ABIGAIL: Now that my father's fortune were so good
  As but to be about this happy place!
  'Tis not so happy: yet, when we parted last,
  He said he would attend me in the morn.
  Then, gentle Sleep, where'er his body rests,
  Give charge to Morpheus that he may dream
  A golden dream, and of the sudden walk,
  Come and receive the treasure I have found.

BARABAS: *Bueno para todos mi ganado no era:*
  As good go on, as sit so sadly thus.   *40*
  But stay: what star shines yonder in the east?
  The loadstar of my life, if Abigail.
  Who's there?

ABIGAIL: Who's that?

BARABAS: Peace, Abigail! 'tis I.

ABIGAIL: Then, father, here receive thy happiness.

BARABAS: Hast thou't?

ABIGAIL: Here. (*Throws down bags.*) Hast thou't?
  There's more, and more, and more.

BARABAS: O my girl!   *50*
  My gold, my fortune, my felicity,
  Strength to my soul, death to mine enemy!
  Welcome the first beginner of my bliss!
  O Abigail, Abigail, that I had thee here too!
  Then my desires were fully satisfied:
  But I will practise thy enlargement thence:
  O girl! O gold! O beauty! O my bliss!
  Hugs the bags.

ABIGAIL: Father, it draweth towards midnight now,
  And 'bout this time the nuns begin to wake.

---

30 *walk*: usually emended to 'wake'.
39 *Bueno para todos* . . .: Literally 'My flock was not good for all'.
Possible meanings: (a) the wealth is not always available or all-
powerful; (b) Barabas doesn't mean it to be used by anybody else.
42 *loadstar*: pole-star, guiding light.
56 *practise thy enlargement*: work for your release.

60   To shun suspicion, therefore, let us part.

BARABAS: Farewell, my joy, and by my fingers take
          A kiss from him that sends it from his soul.
              Exit ABIGAIL *above.*
          Now, Phoebus, ope the eye-lids of the day,
          And, for the raven, wake the morning lark,
          That I may hover with her in the air,
          Singing o'er these, as she does o'er her young.
              Hermoso placer de los dineros.[3]
              Exit.

SCENE TWO

The Senate House.
Enter FERNEZE, MARTIN DEL BOSCO, KNIGHTS,
and OFFICERS.

FERNEZE: Now, Captain, tell us whither thou art
          bound.
          Whence is thy ship that anchors in our road?
          And why thou cam'st ashore without our leave?

MARTIN DEL BOSCO: Governor of Malta, hither am I
          bound;
          My ship, the Flying Dragon, is of Spain,
          And so am I. Del Bosco is my name,
          Vice-admiral unto the Catholic King.

FIRST KNIGHT: 'Tis true, my lord; therefore entreat
          him well.

MARTIN DEL BOSCO: Our fraught is Grecians, Turks,
          and Afric Moors;

10   For late upon the coast of Corsica,
          Because we vail'd not to the Turkish fleet,
          Their creeping galleys had us in the chase:
          But suddenly the wind began to rise,

67 *Hermoso placer* . . .: 'beautiful pleasure of money'.
9 *fraught*: freight.
11 *vail'd*: lowered topsails in sign of respect.
11 *Turkish*: Gilchrist's conjecture. Quarto has 'Spanish'.

And then we luff'd and tack'd, and fought at ease.
Some have we fir'd, and many have we sunk;
But one amongst the rest became our prize:
The captain's slain; the rest remain our slaves,
Of whom we would make sale in Malta here.

FERNEZE: Martin del Bosco, I have heard of thee.
Welcome to Malta, and to all of us!   20
But to admit a sale of these thy Turks,
We may not, nay, we dare not give consent,
By reason of a tributary league.

FIRST KNIGHT: Del Bosco, as thou lov'st and
honour'st us,
Persuade our Governor against the Turk.
This truce we have is but in hope of gold,
And with that sum he craves might we wage war.

MARTIN DEL BOSCO: Will knights of Malta be in
league with Turks,
And buy it basely too for sums of gold?
My lord, remember that, to Europe's shame,   30
The Christian Isle of Rhodes, from whence you came,
Was lately lost, and you were stated here
To be at deadly enmity with Turks.

FERNEZE: Captain, we know it; but our force is small.

MARTIN DEL BOSCO: What is the sum that Calymath
requires?

FERNEZE: A hundred thousand crowns.

MARTIN DEL BOSCO: My lord and king hath title to
this isle,
And he means quickly to expel you hence.
Therefore be rul'd by me, and keep the gold:
I'll write unto his majesty for aid,   40
And not depart until I see you free.

FERNEZE: On this condition shall thy Turks be sold.

14 *luff'd and tack'd*: Dyce conjecture (Quarto has 'left and took')
i.e. sailed into the wind to change course.
23 *tributary league*: alliance based on the payment of tribute-money.
32 *stated*: stationed.

Go, officers, and set them straight in show.
Exeunt OFFICERS.
Bosco, thou shalt be Malta's general;
We and our warlike knights will follow thee
Against these barbarous misbelieving Turks.
MARTIN DEL BOSCO: So shall you imitate those you
    succeed;
For, when their hideous force environ'd Rhodes,
Small though the number was that kept the town,
50 They fought it out, and not a man surviv'd
To bring the hapless news to Christendom.
FERNEZE: So will we fight it out. Come, let's away.
Proud daring Calymath: instead of gold,
We'll send thee bullets wrapt in smoke and fire.
Claim tribute where thou wilt, we are resolv'd—
Honour is bought with blood, and not with gold.
Exeunt.

SCENE THREE

The Market-place.
Enter OFFICERS, *with* ITHAMORE *and other*
SLAVES.
FIRST OFFICER: This is the market-place. Here let 'em
    stand:
Fear not their sale, for they'll be quickly bought.
SECOND OFFICER: Every one's price is written on his
    back,
And so much must they yield, or not be sold.
FIRST OFFICER: Here comes the Jew. Had not his
    goods been seiz'd,
He'd give us present money for them all.
Enter BARABAS.
BARABAS: In spite of these swine-eating Christians,
(Unchosen nation, never circumcis'd,
Such as, poor villains, were ne'er thought upon

Till Titus and Vespasian conquer'd us,)   *10*
Am I become as wealthy as I was.
They hop'd my daughter would ha' been a nun;
But she's at home, and I have bought a house
As great and fair as is the governor's;
And there, in spite of Malta, will I dwell,
Having Ferneze's hand, whose heart I'll have,
Ay, and his son's too, or it shall go hard.
I am not of the tribe of Levi, I,
That can so soon forget an injury.
We Jews can fawn like spaniels when we please,   *20*
And when we grin we bite; yet are our looks
As innocent and harmless as a lamb's.
I learn'd in Florence how to kiss my hand,
Heave up my shoulders when they call me dog,
And duck as low as any bare-foot friar,
Hoping to see them starve upon a stall,
Or else be gather'd for in our synagogue,
That, when the offering-basin comes to me,
Even for charity I may spit into't. –
Here comes Don Lodowick, the Governor's son,   *30*
One that I love for his good father's sake.
          Enter LODOWICK.
LODOWICK: I hear the wealthy Jew walked this way.
    I'll seek him out, and so insinuate,
    That I may have a sight of Abigail,
    For Don Mathias tells me she is fair.
BARABAS (*aside*): Now will I show myself to have more
    of the serpent than the dove; that is, more knave than
    fool.
LODOWICK: Yond' walks the Jew: now for fair
    Abigail.
BARABAS (*aside*): Ay, ay, no doubt but she's at your   *40*
    command.
LODOWICK: Barabas, thou know'st I am the Governor's
    son.
BARABAS: I would you were his father too, sir! that's all

the harm I wish you. (*Aside*) The slave looks like a
hog's cheek new singed.

LODOWICK: Whither walk'st thou, Barabas?

BARABAS: No further. 'Tis a custom held with us,
That when we speak with Gentiles like to you,
We turn into the air to purge ourselves;
For unto us the promise doth belong.

50 LODOWICK: Well, Barabas, canst help me to a
diamond?

BARABAS: O, sir, your father had my diamonds.
Yet I have one left that will serve your turn. –
(*Aside*) I mean my daughter; but, ere he shall have her,
I'll sacrifice her on a pile of wood:
I ha' the poison of the city for him,
And the white leprosy.

LODOWICK: What sparkle does it give without a foil?

BARABAS: The diamond that I talk of ne'er was foil'd.
(*Aside*) But, when he touches it, it will be foil'd. –

60 (*Aloud*) Lord Lodowick, it sparkles bright and fair.

LODOWICK: Is it square or pointed, pray, let me know.

BARABAS: Pointed it is, good sir, (*aside*) but not for
you.

LODOWICK: I like it much the better.

BARABAS: So do I too.

LODOWICK: How shows it by night?

BARABAS: Outshines Cynthia's rays: –
You'll like it better far o' nights than days.

LODOWICK: And what's the price?

BARABAS (*aside*): Your life, an if you have it. (*Aloud*)
O my lord,

70 We will not jar about the price: come to my house,
And I will give't your honour (*aside*) with a
vengeance.

LODOWICK: No, Barabas, I will deserve it first.

---

57 *foil*: thin metal placed under a jewel to heighten its brilliance.
'Foil'd' (l. 58) continues this meaning; but in l. 59 means
'defiled'.

BARABAS: Good sir,
　Your father has deserv'd it at my hands,
　Who, of mere charity and Christian ruth,
　To bring me to religious purity,
　And, as it were, in catechising sort,
　To make me mindful of my mortal sins,
　Against my will, and whether I would or no,
　Seiz'd all I had, and thrust me out-a-doors,　　　　　*80*
　And made my house a place for nuns most chaste.
LODOWICK: No doubt your soul shall reap the fruit
　of it.
BARABAS: Ay, but, my lord, the harvest is far off.
　And yet I know the prayers of those nuns
　And holy friars, having money for their pains,
　Are wondrous; (*aside*) and indeed do no man good; –
　And, seeing they are not idle, but still doing,
　'Tis likely they in time may reap some fruit, –
　I mean, in fullness of perfection.
LODOWICK: Good Barabas, glance not at our holy nuns.　*90*
BARABAS: No, but I do it through a burning zeal, –
　(*aside*) Hoping ere long to set the house a-fire;
　For, though they do a while increase and multiply,
　I'll have a saying to that nunnery. –
　(*Aloud*) As for the diamond, sir, I told you of,
　Come home, and there's no price shall make us part,
　Even for your honourable father's sake, –
　(*aside*) It shall go hard but I will see your death. –
　(*Aloud*) But now I must be gone to buy a slave.
LODOWICK: And, Barabas, I'll bear thee company.　　*100*
BARABAS: Come, then; here's the market-place.
　What's the price of this slave? two hundred crowns?
　Do the Turks weigh so much?
FIRST OFFICER: Sir, that's his price.
BARABAS: What, can he steal, that you demand so
　much?
　Belike he has some new trick for a purse;

75 *ruth*: pity.　　90. *glance*: slander, seek to discredit.

An if he has, he is worth three hundred plates,[4]
So that, being bought, the town seal might be got
To keep him for his life-time from the gallows.

110 The sessions-day is critical to thieves,
And few or none escape but by being purg'd.

LODOWICK: Rat'st thou this Moor but at two hundred
plates?

FIRST OFFICER: No more, my lord.

BARABAS: Why should this Turk be dearer than that
Moor?

FIRST OFFICER: Because he is young, and has more
qualities.

BARABAS: What, hast the philosopher's stone? An thou
hast, break my head with it; I'll forgive thee.

SLAVE: No, sir. I can cut and shave.

BARABAS: Let me see, sirrah, are you not an old shaver?

120 SLAVE: Alas, sir, I am a very youth!

BARABAS: A youth! I'll buy you, and marry you to Lady
Vanity, if you do well.

SLAVE: I will serve you, sir.

BARABAS: Some wicked trick or other. It may be, under
colour of shaving, thou'lt cut my throat for my goods.
Tell me, hast thou thy health well?

SLAVE: Ay, passing well.

BARABAS: So much the worse: I must have one that's
sickly, an't be but for sparing victuals. 'Tis not a stone
130 of beef a day will maintain you in these chops. – Let
me see one that's somewhat leaner.

FIRST OFFICER: Here's a leaner; how like you him?

BARABAS: Where wast thou born?

ITHAMORE: In Thrace; brought up in Arabia.

BARABAS: So much the better; thou art for my turn.

119 *shaver*: cheat (slang).
121 *youth ... Lady Vanity*: reference to characters in Morality
Plays.
125 *colour*: pretence, excuse.
129 *an't be but for ...*: if only for economizing over food.

An hundred crowns? I'll have him; there's the coin.
Gives money.

FIRST OFFICER: Then mark him, sir, and take him
hence.

BARABAS (*aside*): Ay, mark him, you were best; for
this is he
That by my help shall do much villany. —
(*Aloud*) My lord, farewell. — Come, sirrah; you are   *140*
mine. —
(*To* LODOWICK) As for the diamond, it shall be yours.
I pray, sir, be no stranger at my house;
All that I have shall be at your command.
Enter MATHIAS *and* KATHARINE, *his mother.*

MATHIAS (*aside*): What make the Jew and Lodowick
so private?
I fear me 'tis about fair Abigail.

BARABAS (*to* LODOWICK): Yonder comes Don
Mathias; let us stay:
He loves my daughter, and she holds him dear;
But I have sworn to frustrate both their hopes,
And be reveng'd upon the (*aside*) Governor.
Exit LODOWICK.

KATHARINE: This Moor is comeliest, is he not? Speak,   *150*
son.

MATHIAS: No, this is the better, mother, view this well.

BARABAS (*to* MATHIAS): Seem not to know me here
before your mother,
Lest she mistrust the match that is in hand.
When you have brought her home, come to my
house;
Think of me as thy father. Son, farewell.

MATHIAS: But wherefore talk'd Don Lodowick with
you?

BARABAS: Tush, man! We talk'd of diamonds, not of
Abigail.

KATHARINE: Tell me, Mathias, is not that the Jew?

146 *stay*: stop talking.

BARABAS: As for the comment on the Maccabees,
160   I have it, sir, and 'tis at your command.

MATHIAS: Yes, madam, and my talk with him was
About the borrowing of a book or two.

KATHARINE: Converse not with him; he is cast off
from heaven. –
Thou hast thy crowns, fellow. – Come, let's away.

MATHIAS: Sirrah Jew, remember the book.

BARABAS: Marry, will I, sir.

Exeunt KATHARINE *and* MATHIAS.

FIRST OFFICER: Come, I have made a reasonable
market; let's away.

Exeunt OFFICERS *with* SLAVES.

BARABAS: Now let me know thy name, and therewithal
Thy birth, condition, and profession.

170 ITHAMORE: Faith, sir, my birth is but mean, my name's
Ithamore, my profession what you please.

BARABAS: Hast thou no trade? Then listen to my
words,
And I will teach [thee] that shall stick by thee.
First, be thou void of these affections:
Compassion, love, vain hope, and heartless fear;
Be mov'd at nothing, see thou pity none,
But to thyself smile when the Christians moan.

ITHAMORE: O, brave, master! I worship your nose for this.

BARABAS: As for myself, I walk abroad a-nights,
180   And kill sick people groaning under walls.
Sometimes I go about and poison wells;
And now and then, to cherish Christian thieves,
I am content to lose some of my crowns,
That I may, walking in my gallery,
See 'em go pinion'd along by my door.
Being young, I studied physic, and began
To practise first upon the Italian;
There I enrich'd the priests with burials,
And always kept the sexton's arms in ure

189 *ure*: use.

378

With digging graves and ringing dead men's knells.   *190*
And, after that, was I an engineer,
And in the wars 'twixt France and Germany,
Under the pretence of helping Charles the Fifth,
Slew friend and enemy with my stratagems:
Then after that was I an usurer,
And with extorting, cozening, forfeiting,
And tricks belonging unto brokery,
I fill'd the gaols with bankrupts in a year,
And with young orphans planted hospitals;
And every moon made some or other mad,   *200*
And now and then one hang himself for grief,
Pinning upon his breast a long great scroll
How I with interest tormented him.
But mark how I am blest for plaguing them:
I have as much coin as will buy the town.
But tell me now, how hast thou spent thy time?
ITHAMORE: Faith, master.
In setting Christian villages on fire,
Chaining of eunuchs, binding galley slaves.
One time I was an hostler in an inn,   *210*
And in the night time secretly would I steal
To travellers' chambers, and there cut their throats.
Once at Jerusalem, where the pilgrims kneel'd,
I strewed powder on the marble stones,
And therewithal their knees would rankle so,
That I have laugh'd a-good to see the cripples
Go limping home to Christendom on stilts.
BARABAS: Why, this is something: make account of me
As of thy fellow. We are villains both,
Both circumcised. We hate Christians both,   *220*
Be true and secret; thou shalt want no gold.
But stand aside; here comes Don Lodowick.
   Enter LODOWICK.
LODOWICK: O, Barabas, well met.

196 *cozening*: cheating.   199 *hospitals*: alms-houses.
217 *stilts*: crutches.

Where is the diamond you told me of?

BARABAS: I have it for you, sir: please you walk in
with me –
What, ho, Abigail! Open the door, I say!
Enter ABIGAIL, *with letters.*

ABIGAIL: In good time, father; here are letters come
From Ormus, and the post stays here within.

BARABAS: Give me the letters. Daughter, do you hear?
230   Entertain Lodowick, the Governor's son,
With all the courtesy you can afford,
Provided that you keep your maidenhead –
(*Aside to her*) Use him as if he were a Philistine;
Dissemble, swear, protest, vow to love him:
He is not of the seed of Abraham. –
(*Aloud*) I am a little busy, sir; pray pardon me. –
Abigail, bid him welcome for my sake.

ABIGAIL: For your sake and his own he's welcome
hither.

BARABAS: Daughter, a word more: (*aside to her*) kiss
him, speak him fair,
240   And like a cunning Jew so cast about,
That ye be both made sure ere you come out.

ABIGAIL (*aside to him*): O father, Don Mathias is my
love!

BARABAS (*aside to her*): I know it: yet, I say, make love
to him;
Do, it is requisite it should be so. –
(*Aloud*) Nay, on my life, it is my factor's hand;
But go you in, I'll think upon the account.
Exeunt ABIGAIL *and* LODOWICK *into the house.*
The account is made, for Lodowick dies.
My factor sends me word that a merchant's fled
That owes me for a hundred tun of wine:
250   I weigh it thus much (*snapping his fingers*)! I have
wealth enough;

228 *Ormus*: trading city on the Persian Gulf.
241 *made sure*: betrothed.   245 *factor*: agent.

For now by this has he kiss'd Abigail,
And she vows love to him, and he to her.
And sure as heaven rain'd manna for the Jews,
So sure shall he and Don Mathias die:
His father was my chiefest enemy.
  Enter MATHIAS.
Whither goes Don Mathias? Stay a while.
MATHIAS: Whither but to my fair love Abigail?
BARABAS: Thou know'st and heaven can witness it is
    true,
  That I intend my daughter shall be thine.
MATHIAS: Ay, Barabas, or else thou wrong'st me much. *260*
BARADAS: O, heaven forbid I should have such a
    thought!
  Pardon me though I weep: the Governor's son
  Will, whether I will or no, have Abigail;
  He sends her letters, bracelets, jewels, rings.
MATHIAS: Does she receive them?
BARABAS: She! No, Mathias, no, but sends them back,
  And, when he comes, she locks herself up fast;
  Yet through the key-hole will he talk to her,
  While she runs to the window looking out
  When you should come and hale him from the door. *270*
MATHIAS: O treacherous Lodowick!
BARABAS: Even now, as I came home, he slipt me in,
  And I am sure he is with Abigail.
MATHIAS: I'll rouse him thence.
BARABAS: Not for all Malta; therefore sheathe your
    sword.
  If you love me, no quarrels in my house;
  But steal you in, and seem to see him not:
  I'll give him such a warning ere he goes,
  As he shall have small hopes of Abigail.
  Away, for here they come. *280*
    Re-enter LODOWICK *and* ABIGAIL.

274 *rouse him thence*: hunting term: drive him like an animal from
his lair.

MATHIAS: What, hand in hand! I cannot suffer this.

BARABAS: Mathias, as thou lov'st me, not a word.

MATHIAS: Well, let it pass. Another time shall serve.
Exit into the house.

LODOWICK: Barabas, is not that the widow's son?

BARABAS: Ay, and take heed, for he hath sworn your death.

LODOWICK: My death! What, is the base-born peasant mad?

BARABAS: No, no; but happily he stands in fear
Of that which you, I think, ne'er dream upon,
My daughter here, a paltry silly girl.

290 LODOWICK: Why, loves she Don Mathias?

BARABAS: Doth she not with her smiling answer you?

ABIGAIL (*aside*): He has my heart; I smile against my will.

LODOWICK: Barabas, thou know'st I have lov'd thy daughter long.

BARABAS: And so has she done you, even from a child.

LODOWICK: And now I can no longer hold my mind.

BARABAS: Nor I the affection that I bear to you.

LODOWICK: This is thy diamond. Tell me, shall I have it?

BARABAS: Win it, and wear it; it is yet unsoil'd.
O, but I know your lordship would disdain
300 To marry with the daughter of a Jew:
And yet I'll give her many a golden cross,
With Christian posies round about the ring.

LODOWICK: 'Tis not thy wealth, but her that I esteem;
Yet crave I thy consent.

BARABAS: And mine you have; yet let me talk to her.
(*Aside to her*) This offspring of Cain, this Jebusite,
That never tasted of the Passover,
Nor e'er shall see the land of Canaan,

281 *suffer*: allow (l. 345 below).
302 *posies*: mottoes written round the coin's edge.
306 *Jebusite*: Canaanite tribe dispossessed by King David.

Nor our Messias that is yet to come,
This gentle maggot Lodowick I mean,   *310*
Must be deluded. Let him have thy hand,
But keep thy heart till Don Mathias comes.

ABIGAIL: What, shall I be betroth'd to Lodowick?

BARABAS: It's no sin to deceive a Christian;
For they themselves hold it a principle,
Faith is not to be held with heretics.
But all are heretics that are not Jews;
This follows well, and therefore, daughter, fear not.
(*To* LODOWICK) I have entreated her, and she will
grant.

LODOWICK: Then, gentle Abigail, plight thy faith to me. *320*

ABIGAIL: I cannot choose, seeing my father bids:
Nothing but death shall part my love and me.

LODOWICK: Now have I that for which my soul hath
long'd.

BARABAS (*aside*): So have not I; but yet I hope I shall.

ABIGAIL (*aside*): O wretched Abigail, what hast thou
done?

LODOWICK: Why on the sudden is your colour chang'd?

ABIGAIL: I know not: but farewell, I must be gone.

BARABAS: Stay her, but let her not speak one word more.

LODOWICK: Mute o' the sudden! Here's a sudden
change.

BARABAS: O, muse not at it; 'tis the Hebrews' guise,   *330*
That maidens new-betrothed should weep a while.
Trouble her not; sweet Lodowick, depart.
She is thy wife, and thou shalt be mine heir.

LODOWICK: O, is't the custom? Then I am resolv'd:
But rather let the brightsome heavens be dim,
And nature's beauty choke with stifling clouds,
Than my fair Abigail should frown on me. –
There comes the villain; now I'll be reveng'd.

Re-enter MATHIAS.

BARABAS: Be quiet, Lodowick; it is enough
That I have made thee sure to Abigail.   *340*

LODOWICK: Well, let him go.

Exit.

BARABAS: Well, but for me, as you went in at doors
You had been stabb'd: but not a word on't now.
Here must no speeches pass, nor swords be drawn.

MATHIAS: Suffer me, Barabas, but to follow him.

BARABAS: No; so shall I, if any hurt be done,
Be made an accessary of your deeds.
Revenge it on him when you meet him next.

MATHIAS: For this I'll have his heart.

350 BARABAS: Do so. Lo, here I give thee Abigail!

MATHIAS: What greater gift can poor Mathias have?
Shall Lodowick rob me of so fair a love?
My life is not so dear as Abigail.

BARABAS: My heart misgives me, that, to cross your love,
He's with your mother; therefore after him.

MATHIAS: What, is he gone unto my mother?

BARABAS: Nay, if you will, stay till she comes herself.

MATHIAS: I cannot stay; for, if my mother come,
She'll die with grief.

Exit.

360 ABIGAIL: I cannot take my leave of him for tears.
Father, why have you thus incens'd them both?

BARABAS: What's that to thee?

ABIGAIL: I'll make 'em friends again.

BARABAS: You'll make 'em friends! Are there not Jews
enow in Malta,
But thou must dote upon a Christian?

ABIGAIL: I will have Don Mathias; he is my love.

BARABAS: Yes, you shall have him. – Go, put her in.

ITHAMORE: Ay, I'll put her in.

Puts in ABIGAIL.

BARABAS: Now tell me, Ithamore, how lik'st thou this?

370 ITHAMORE: Faith, master, I think by this
You purchase both their lives: is it not so?

BARABAS: True, and it shall be cunningly perform'd.

ITHAMORE: O, master, that I might have a hand in this!

BARABAS: Ay, so thou shalt: 'tis thou must do the deed.
Take this, and bear it to Mathias straight.
Giving a letter.
And tell him that it comes from Lodowick.
ITHAMORE: 'Tis poison'd, is it not?
BARABAS: No, no; and yet it might be done that way:
It is a challenge feign'd from Lodowick.
ITHAMORE: Fear not; I will so set his heart a-fire,   380
That he shall verily think it comes from him.
BARABAS: I cannot choose but like thy readiness.
Yet be not rash, but do it cunningly.
ITHAMORE: As I behave myself in this, employ me
hereafter.
BARABAS: Away, then!
Exit ITHAMORE.
So, now will I go in to Lodowick,
And, like a cunning spirit, feign some lie,
Till I have set 'em both at enmity.
Exit.

ACT THREE

SCENE ONE

Enter BELLAMIRA, *a courtesan.*
BELLAMIRA: Since this town was besieg'd, my gain
grows cold.
The time has been, that but for one bare night
A hundred ducats have been freely given.
But now against my will I must be chaste:
And yet I know my beauty doth not fail.
From Venice merchants, and from Padua
Were wont to come rare-witted gentlemen,
Scholars I mean, learned and liberal;
And now, save Pilia-Borza, comes there none,

1 *my gain grows cold*: business has been bad.
9 *Pilia-Borza*: literally 'Pick-purse'.

10 And he is very seldom from my house;
And here he comes.
Enter PILIA-BORZA.

PILIA-BORZA: Hold thee, wench, there's something for
thee to spend.
Showing a bag of silver.

BELLAMIRA: 'Tis silver; I disdain it.

PILIA-BORZA: Ay, but the Jew has gold,
And I will have it, or it shall go hard.

BELLAMIRA: Tell me, how cam'st thou by this?

PILIA-BORZA: Faith, walking the back-lanes, through
the gardens, I chanced to cast mine eye up to the Jew's
20 counting-house, where I saw some bags of money, and
in the night I clambered up with my hooks; and, as I
was taking my choice, I heard a rumbling in the house;
so I took only this, and run my way. – But here's the
Jew's man.

BELLAMIRA: Hide the bag.
Enter ITHAMORE.

PILIA-BORZA: Look not towards him, let's away. Zoons,
what a looking thou keepest! Thou'lt betray's anon.
Exeunt BELLAMIRA *and* PILIA-BORZA.

ITHAMORE: O, the sweetest face that ever I beheld! I
know she is a courtesan by her attire: now would I give
30 a hundred of the Jew's crowns that I had such a
concubine.
Well, I have deliver'd the challenge in such sort,
As meet they will, and fighting die, – brave sport!
Exit.

SCENE TWO

Enter MATHIAS.

MATHIAS: This is the place: now Abigail shall see
Whether Mathias holds her dear or no.
Enter LODOWICK.[5]

26 *Zoons*: Zounds (God's wounds).

LODOWICK: What, dares the villain write in such base
terms?
Looking at a letter.

MATHIAS: Thou villain, durst thou court my Abigail?

LODOWICK: I did it; and revenge it, if thou dar'st!
They fight.
Enter BARABAS *above.*

BARABAS: O, bravely fought! and yet they thrust not
home.
Now Lodowick! now Mathias! – So!
Both fall.
So, now they have show'd themselves to be tall
fellows.

CRIES WITHIN: Part 'em, part 'em!

BARABAS: Ay, part 'em now they are dead. Farewell,   *10*
farewell!
Exit above.
Enter FERNEZE, KATHARINE, *and* ATTENDANTS.

FERNEZE: What sight is this? My Lodowick slain!
These arms of mine shall be thy sepulchre.

KATHARINE: Who is this? My son Mathias slain!

FERNEZE: O Lodowick, hadst thou perish'd by the Turk,
Wretched Ferneze might have veng'd thy death!

KATHARINE: Thy son slew mine, and I'll revenge his
death.

FERNEZE: Look, Katharine, look! Thy son gave mine
these wounds.

KATHARINE: O, leave to grieve me! I am griev'd enough.

FERNEZE: O, that my sighs could turn to lively breath,
And these my tears to blood, that he might live!   *20*

KATHARINE: Who made them enemies?

FERNEZE: I know not, and that grieves me most of all.

KATHARINE: My son lov'd thine.

FERNEZE: And so did Lodowick him.

KATHARINE: Lend me that weapon that did kill my son,
And it shall murder me.

18 *leave*: cease.

FERNEZE: Nay, madam, stay; that weapon was my son's,
 And on that rather should Ferneze die.
KATHARINE: Hold, let's inquire the causers of their
 deaths,
30 That we may venge their blood upon their heads.
FERNEZE: Then take them up, and let them be interr'd
 Within one sacred monument of stone,
 Upon which altar I will offer up
 My daily sacrifice of sighs and tears,
 And with my prayers pierce impartial heavens,
 Till they [disclose] the causers of our smarts,
 Which forc'd their hands divide united hearts.
 Come, Katharine; our losses equal are;
 Then of true grief let us take equal share.
  Exeunt with the bodies.

SCENE THREE

Enter ITHAMORE.

ITHAMORE: Why, was there ever seen such villany,
 So neatly plotted, and so well perform'd?
 Both held in hand, and flatly both beguil'd.
  Enter ABIGAIL.
ABIGAIL: Why, how now, Ithamore! Why laugh'st
 thou so?
ITHAMORE: O mistress! ha, ha, ha!
ABIGAIL: Why, what ail'st thou?
ITHAMORE: O, my master!
ABIGAIL: Ha!
ITHAMORE: O mistress, I have the bravest, gravest,
10 secret, subtle, bottle-nosed knave to my master, that
 ever gentleman had!
ABIGAIL: Say, knave, why rail'st upon my father thus?
ITHAMORE: O, my master has the bravest policy!
ABIGAIL: Wherein?

36 *disclose*: conjecture Collier (Quarto has no verb).

ITHAMORE: Why, know you not?

ABIGAIL: Why, no.

ITHAMORE: Know you not of Mathia[s'] and Don Lodowick['s] disaster?

ABIGAIL: No, what was it?

ITHAMORE: Why, the devil invented a challenge, my   *20*
master writ it, and I carried it, first to Lodowick, and
imprimis to Mathia[s];
And then they met, [and,] as the story says,
In doleful wise they ended both their days.

ABIGAIL: And was my father furtherer of their deaths?

ITHAMORE: Am I Ithamore?

ABIGAIL: Yes.

ITHAMORE: So sure did your father write, and I carry
the challenge.

ABIGAIL: Well, Ithamore, let me request thee this: *30*
Go to the new-made nunnery, and inquire
For any of the friars of Saint Jaques,
And say, I pray them come and speak with me.

ITHAMORE: I pray, mistress, will you answer me to one
question?

ABIGAIL: Well, sirrah, what is't?

ITHAMORE: A very feeling one: have not the nuns fine
sport with the friars now and then?

ABIGAIL: Go to, Sirrah Sauce! Is this your question?
Get ye gone.   *40*

ITHAMORE: I will, forsooth, mistress.
    Exit.

ABIGAIL: Hard-hearted father, unkind Barabas!
Was this the pursuit of thy policy,
To make me show them favour severally,
That by my favour they should both be slain?
Admit thou lov'dst not Lodowick for his sire,
Yet Don Mathias ne'er offended thee.
But thou wert set upon extreme revenge,

22 *imprimis*: first (but Ithamore misunderstands).
44 *severally*: separately.

389

Because the Governor[6] dispossess'd thee once,
50 And couldst not venge it but upon his son;
Nor on his son but by Mathias' means;
Nor on Mathias but by murdering me.
But I perceive there is no love on earth,
Pity in Jews, nor piety in Turks.
But here comes cursed Ithamore with the friar.

Re-enter ITHAMORE *with* FRIAR JACOMO.

FRIAR JACOMO: *Virgo, salve.*

ITHAMORE: When, duck you?

ABIGAIL: Welcome, grave friar. Ithamore, be gone.

Exit ITHAMORE.

Know, holy sir, I am bold to solicit thee.

60 FRIAR JACOMO: Wherein?

ABIGAIL: To get me be admitted for a nun.

FRIAR JACOMO: Why, Abigail, it is not yet long since
That I did labour thy admission,
And then thou didst not like that holy life.

ABIGAIL: Then were my thoughts so frail and
unconfirm'd
As I was chain'd to follies of the world;
But now experience, purchased with grief,
Has made me see the difference of things.
My sinful soul, alas, hath pac'd too long
70 The fatal labyrinth of misbelief,
Far from the sun that gives eternal life!

FRIAR JACOMO: Who taught thee this?

ABIGAIL: The abbess of the house,
Whose zealous admonition I embrace.
O, therefore, Jacomo, let me be one,
Although unworthy, of that sisterhood!

FRIAR JACOMO: Abigail, I will: but see thou change
no more,
For that will be most heavy to thy soul.

ABIGAIL: That was my father's fault.

57 *When, duck you:* exclamation provoked by the sanctimonious
bowing of the Friar.

FRIAR JACOMO: Thy father's! How? 80

ABIGAIL: Nay, you shall pardon me. (*Aside*) O Barabas,
 Though thou deservest hardly at my hands,
 Yet never shall these lips bewray thy life!

FRIAR JACOMO: Come, shall we go?

ABIGAIL: My duty waits on you.

 Exeunt.

SCENE FOUR

Enter BARABAS, *reading a letter.*

BARABAS: What, Abigail become a nun again!
 False and unkind! What, hast thou lost thy father?
 And, all unknown and unconstrain'd of me,
 Art thou again got to the nunnery?
 Now here she writes, and wills me to repent:
 Repentance! *Spurca!* what pretendeth this?
 I fear she knows — 'tis so — of my device
 In Don Mathias' and Lodovico's deaths:
 If so, 'tis time that it be seen into;
 For she that varies from me in belief, 10
 Gives great presumption that she loves me not,
 Or, loving, doth dislike of something done.
 But who comes here?

  Enter ITHAMORE.

       O Ithamore, come near.
 Come near, my love; come near, thy master's life,
 My trusty servant, nay, my second self;[7]
 For I have now no hope but even in thee,
 And on that hope my happiness is built.
 When saw'st thou Abigail?

ITHAMORE: Today.

BARABAS: With whom? 20

ITHAMORE: A friar.

BARABAS: A friar! False villain, he hath done the deed.

 6 *Spurca*: Base, filthy!

ITHAMORE: How, sir!

BARABAS: Why, made mine Abigail a nun.

ITHAMORE: That's no lie, for she sent me for him.

BARABAS: O unhappy day!
False, credulous, inconstant Abigail!
But let 'em go: and, Ithamore, from hence
Ne'er shall she grieve me more with her disgrace;
30   Ne'er shall she live to inherit aught of mine,
Be bless'd of me, nor come within my gates,
But perish underneath my bitter curse,
Like Cain by Adam for his brother's death.

ITHAMORE: O master –

BARABAS: Ithamore, entreat not for her. I am mov'd,
And she is hateful to my soul and me:
And, 'less[8] thou yield to this that I entreat,
I cannot think but that thou hat'st my life.

ITHAMORE: Who, I, master? Why, I'll run to some rock,
40   And throw myself headlong into the sea;
Why, I'll do anything for your sweet sake.

BARABAS: O trusty Ithamore! No servant, but my friend!
I here adopt thee for mine only heir:
All that I have is thine when I am dead;
And, whilst I live, use half; spend as myself.
Here, take my keys, – I'll give 'em thee anon.
Go buy thee garments; but thou shalt not want.
Only know this, that thus thou art to do –
But first go fetch me in the pot of rice
50   That for our supper stands upon the fire.

ITHAMORE (aside): I hold my head, my master's hungry – I go, sir.
    Exit.

BARABAS: Thus every villain ambles after wealth,
Although he ne'er be richer than in hope.
But, husht!
    Re-enter ITHAMORE *with the pot.*

ITHAMORE: Here 'tis, master.

BARABAS: Well said, Ithamore! What, hast thou brought
The ladle with thee too?

ITHAMORE: Yes, sir. The proverb says, he that eats with
the devil had need of a long spoon; I have brought you
a ladle.   60

BARABAS: Very well, Ithamore; then now be secret;
And for thy sake, whom I so dearly love,
Now shalt thou see the death of Abigail,
That thou mayst freely live to be my heir.

ITHAMORE: Why, master, will you poison her with a
mess of rice-porridge that will preserve life, make her
round and plump, and batten more than you are aware?

BARABAS: Ay, but Ithamore, seest thou this?
It is a precious powder that I bought
Of an Italian in Ancona once,   70
Whose operation is to bind, infect,
And poison deeply, yet not appear
In forty hours after it is ta'en.

ITHAMORE: How, master?

BARABAS: Thus, Ithamore:
This even they use in Malta here, – 'tis call'd
Saint Jaques' Even, and then, I say, they use
To send their alms unto the nunneries:
Among the rest, bear this, and set it there:
There's a dark entry where they take it in,   80
Where they must neither see the messenger,
Nor make inquiry who hath sent it them.

ITHAMORE: How so?

BARABAS: Belike there is some ceremony in't.
There, Ithamore, must thou go place this pot:
Stay, let me spice it first.

ITHAMORE: Pray, do, and let me help you, master.
Pray, let me taste first.

67 *batten*: grow fat.

BARABAS: Prithee, do.

ITHAMORE *tastes.*

90   What say'st thou now?

ITHAMORE: Troth, master, I'm loath such a pot of
pottage should be spoiled.

BARABAS: Peace, Ithamore! 'tis better so than spar'd.

Puts the powder into the pot.

Assure thyself thou shalt have broth by the eye.

My purse, my coffer, and myself is thine.

ITHAMORE: Well, master, I go.

BARABAS: Stay, first let me stir it, Ithamore.

As fatal be it to her as the draught

Of which great Alexander drunk and died;

And with her let it work like Borgia's wine,

100   Whereof his sire the Pope was poisoned!

In few, the blood of Hydra, Lerna's bane,

The juice of hebon, and Cocytus' breath,

And all the poisons of the Stygian pool,

Break from the fiery kingdom, and in this

Vomit your venom, and envenom her

That, like a fiend, hath left her father thus!

ITHAMORE (*aside*): What a blessing has he given't! Was
ever pot of rice-porridge so sauced? – What shall I do
with it?

110 BARABAS: O my sweet Ithamore, go set it down;

And come again as soon as thou hast done,

For I have other business for thee.

ITHAMORE: Here's a drench to poison a whole stable of
Flanders mares: I'll carry't to the nuns with a powder.

BARABAS: And the horse-pestilence to boot. Away!

98 *Alexander*: said to have caught a fever after heavy drinking.

100 *the Pope*: Alexander VI (1431–1503), thought to have been
poisoned by his son Cesare Borgia.

101 *blood of Hydra*: serpent with nine heads which terrorized (was
the 'bane' of) the countryside of Lerna.

102 *juice of hebon*: henbane, poisonous plant.

102 *Cocytus*: river in Hades.

103 *Stygian pool*: waters of the Styx, regarded as poisonou

ITHAMORE: I am gone:
　Pay me my wages, for my work is done.
　　Exit with the pot.
BARABAS: I'll pay thee with a vengeance, Ithamore!
　Exit.

SCENE FIVE

Enter FERNEZE, MARTIN DEL BOSCO, KNIGHTS,
and BASSO.[9]

FERNEZE: Welcome, great Basso: how fares Calymath?
　What wind drives you thus into Malta-road?
BASSO: The wind that bloweth all the world besides,
　Desire of gold.
FERNEZE: Desire of gold, great sir!
　That's to be gotten in the Western Inde:
　In Malta are no golden minerals.
BASSO: To you of Malta thus saith Calymath:
　The time you took for respite is at hand
　For the performance of your promise pass'd,　　　　　10
　And for the tribute money I am sent.
FERNEZE: Basso, in brief, shalt have no tribute here,
　Nor shall the heathens live upon our spoil:
　First will we raze the city-walls ourselves,
　Lay waste the island, hew the temples down,
　And, shipping off our goods to Sicily,
　Open an entrance for the wasteful sea,
　Whose billows, beating the resistless banks,
　Shall overflow it with their refluence.
BASSO: Well, Governor, since thou hast broke the league　20
　By flat denial of the promis'd tribute,
　Talk not of razing down your city-walls.
　You shall not need trouble yourselves so far,
　For Selim Calymath shall come himself,
　And with brass bullets batter down your towers,

19 *refluence*: flowing back.

And turn proud Malta to a wilderness,
For these intolerable wrongs of yours:
And so farewell.

FERNEZE: Farewell.

Exit BASSO.

30 And now, you men of Malta, look about,
And let's provide to welcome Calymath.
Close your port-cullis, charge your basilisks,
And, as you profitably take up arms,
So now courageously encounter them,
For by this answer broken is the league,
And naught is to be look'd for now but wars,
And naught to us more welcome is than wars.

Exeunt.

SCENE SIX

Enter FRIAR JACOMO *and* FRIAR BARNARDINE.

FRIAR JACOMO: O brother, brother, all the nuns are
sick,
And physic will not help them! They must die.

FRIAR BARNARDINE: The abbess sent for me to be
confess'd.
O, what a sad confession will there be!

FRIAR JACOMO: And so did fair Maria send for me.
I'll to her lodging; hereabouts she lies.

Exit.

Enter ABIGAIL.

FRIAR BARNARDINE: What, all dead, save only
Abigail!

ABIGAIL: And I shall die too, for I feel death coming.
Where is the friar that convers'd with me?

10 FRIAR BARNARDINE: O, he is gone to see the other
nuns.

ABIGAIL: I sent for him; but, seeing you are come,

32 *basilisks*: large cannons.

Be you my ghostly father: and first know,
That in this house I liv'd religiously,
Chaste, and devout, much sorrowing for my sins;
But, ere I came –
FRIAR BARNARDINE: What then?
ABIGAIL: I did offend high heaven so grievously
As I am almost desperate for my sins,
And one offence torments me more than all.
You knew Mathias and Don Lodowick?   20
FRIAR BARNARDINE: Yes, what of them?
ABIGAIL: My father did contract me to 'em both;
First to Don Lodowick: him I never lov'd;
Mathias was the man that I held dear,
And for his sake did I become a nun.
FRIAR BARNARDINE: So: say how was their end?
ABIGAIL: Both, jealous of my love, envied each other;
And by my father's practice, which is there
     Gives writing.
Set down at large, the gallants were both slain.
FRIAR BARNARDINE: O, monstrous villany!   30
ABIGAIL: To work my peace, this I confess to thee.
Reveal it not; for then my father dies.
FRIAR BARNARDINE: Know that confession must not
     be reveal'd;
The canon-law forbids it, and the priest
That makes it known, being degraded first,
Shall be condemn'd, and then sent to the fire.
ABIGAIL: So I have heard; pray, therefore, keep it
     close.
Death seizeth on my heart: ah, gentle friar,
Convert my father that he may be sav'd,
And witness that I die a Christian!   40
     Dies.
FRIAR BARNARDINE: Ay, and a virgin too; that
     grieves me most.
But I must to the Jew, and exclaim on him,
28 *practice*: cunning.

And make him stand in fear of me.

Re-enter FRIAR JACOMO.

FRIAR JACOMO: O brother, all the nuns are dead! Let's
bury them.

FRIAR BARNARDINE: First help to bury this; then go
with me,

And help me to exclaim against the Jew.

FRIAR JACOMO: Why, what has he done?

FRIAR BARNARDINE: A thing that makes me tremble
to unfold.

FRIAR JACOMO: What, has he crucified a child?

50 FRIAR BARNARDINE: No, but a worse thing: 'twas
told me in shrift.

Thou know'st 'tis death, an if it be reveal'd.

Come, let's away.

Exeunt.

ACT FOUR

SCENE ONE

Enter BARABAS *and* ITHAMORE. *Bells within.*

BARABAS: There is no music to a Christian knell!
How sweet the bells ring now the nuns are dead,
That sound at other times like tinkers' pans!
I was afraid the poison had not wrought,
Or, though it wrought, it would have done no good,
For every year they swell, and yet they live:
Now all are dead, not one remains alive.

ITHAMORE: That's brave, master: but think you it will
not be known?

10 BARABAS: How can it, if we two be secret?

ITHAMORE: For my part, fear you not.

BARABAS: I'd cut thy throat, if I did.

ITHAMORE: And reason too.

1 *no music to*: none to compare with.

398

But here's a royal monastery hard by;
Good master, let me poison all the monks.

BARABAS: Thou shalt not need; for, now the nuns are dead,

They'll die with grief.

ITHAMORE: Do you not sorrow for your daughter's death?

BARABAS: No, but I grieve because she liv'd so long,
An Hebrew born, and would become a Christian: 20
Cazzo, diabolo![10]

ITHAMORE: Look, look, master; here come two religious caterpillars.

Enter FRIAR JACOMO *and* FRIAR BARNARDINE.

BARABAS: I smelt 'em ere they came.

ITHAMORE: God-a-mercy, nose! Come, let's begone.

FRIAR BARNARDINE: Stay, wicked Jew; repent, I say, and stay.

FRIAR JACOMO: Thou hast offended, therefore must be damn'd.

BARABAS: I fear they know we sent the poison'd broth.

ITHAMORE: And so do I, master; therefore speak 'em fair.

FRIAR BARNARDINE: Barabas, thou hast —   30

FRIAR JACOMO: Ay, not what thou hast —

BARABAS: True, I have money; what though I have?

FRIAR BARNARDINE: Thou art a —

FRIAR JACOMO: Ay, that thou art, a —

BARABAS: What needs all this? I know I am a Jew.

FRIAR BARNARDINE: Thy daughter —

FRIAR JACOMO: Ay, thy daughter —

BARABAS: O, speak not of her! Then I die with grief.

FRIAR BARNARDINE: Remember that —

FRIAR JACOMO: Ay, remember that —   40

BARABAS: I must needs say that I have been a great usurer.

FRIAR BARNARDINE: Thou hast committed —

BARABAS: Fornication: but that was in another country,

And besides the wench is dead.

FRIAR BARNARDINE: Ay, but, Barabas,
Remember Mathias and Don Lodowick.

BARABAS: Why, what of them?

FRIAR BARNARDINE: I will not say that by a forged
challenge they met.

BARABAS (*aside to* ITHAMORE): She has confess'd, and
we are both undone,

50   My bosom inmate![11] but I must dissemble.
(*Aloud*) O holy friars, the burden of my sins
Lie heavy on my soul! Then, pray you, tell me,
Is't not too late now to turn Christian?
I have been zealous in the Jewish faith,
Hard-hearted to the poor, a covetous wretch,
That would for lucre's sake have sold my soul.
A hundred for a hundred I have ta'en;
And now for store of wealth may I compare
With all the Jews in Malta: but what is wealth?

60   I am a Jew, and therefore am I lost.
Would penance serve for this my sin,
I could afford to whip myself to death.

ITHAMORE: And so could I; but penance will not
serve.

BARABAS: To fast, to pray, and wear a shirt of hair,
And on my knees creep to Jerusalem.
Cellars of wine, and sollars full of wheat,
Warehouses stuff'd with spices and with drugs,
Whole chests of gold in bullion and in coin,
Besides I know not how much weight in pearl,

70   Orient and round, have I within my house;
At Alexandria merchandise, unsold;
But yesterday two ships went from this town,
Their voyage will be worth ten thousand crowns.
In Florence, Venice, Antwerp, London, Seville,
Frankfort, Lubeck, Moscow, and where not,

---

57 *hundred for a hundred*: usury at rate of 100 per cent interest.
66 *sollars*: lofts, used as store-rooms.

Have I debts owing; and in most of these
Great sums of money lying in the banco.
All this I'll give to some religious house,
So I may be baptiz'd, and live therein.

FRIAR JACOMO: O good Barabas, come to our house! *80*

FRIAR BARNARDINE: O, no, good Barabas, come to
our house!
And Barabas, you know –

BARABAS: I know that I have highly sinn'd:
You shall convert me, you shall have all my wealth.

FRIAR JACOMO: O Barabas, their laws are strict!

BARABAS: I know they are; and I will be with you.

FRIAR JACOMO: They wear no shirts, and they go
barefoot too.

BARABAS: Then 'tis not for me; and I am resolv'd
You shall confess me, and have all my goods.

FRIAR JACOMO: Good Barabas, come to me. *90*

BARABAS: You see I answer him, and yet he stays;
Rid him away, and go you home with me.

FRIAR JACOMO: I'll be with you tonight.

BARABAS: Come to my house at one o'clock this night.

FRIAR JACOMO: You hear your answer, and you may
be gone.

FRIAR BARNARDINE: Why, go, get you away.

FRIAR JACOMO: I will not go for thee.

FRIAR BARNARDINE: Not! Then I'll make thee, rogue.

FRIAR JACOMO: How! dost call me rogue?[12]
They fight.

ITHAMORE: Part 'em, master, part 'em. *100*

BARABAS: This is mere frailty! Brethren, be content.
Friar Barnardine, go you with Ithamore.
You know my mind; let me alone with him.[13]

FRIAR JACOMO: Why does he go to thy house? Let
him be gone.

BARABAS: I'll give him something, and so stop his
mouth.
Exit ITHAMORE *with* FRIAR BARNARDINE.

401

I never heard of any man but he
Malign'd the order of the Jacobins;
But do you think that I believe his words?
Why, brother, you converted Abigail;
110   And I am bound in charity to requite it,
And so I will. O Jacomo, fail not, but come.
FRIAR JACOMO: But Barabas, who shall be your
    godfathers?
For presently you shall be shriv'd.
BARABAS: Marry, the Turk shall be one of my
    godfathers,
But not a word to any of your covent.
FRIAR JACOMO: I warrant thee, Barabas.
    Exit.
BARABAS: So, now the fear is past, and I am safe;
For he that shriv'd her is within my house.
What if I murder'd him ere Jacomo comes?
120   Now I have such a plot for both their lives,
As never Jew nor Christian knew the like:
One turn'd my daughter, therefore he shall die;
The other knows enough to have my life,
Therefore 'tis not requisite he should live.
But are not both these wise men, to suppose
That I will leave my house, my goods, and all,
To fast and be well whipt? I'll none of that.
Now, Friar Barnardine, I come to you:
I'll feast you, lodge you, give you fair words,
130   And, after that, I and my trusty Turk –
No more, but so: it must and shall be done.
    Enter ITHAMORE.
Ithamore, tell me, is the friar asleep?
ITHAMORE: Yes; and I know not what the reason is,
Do what I can, he will not strip himself,
Nor go to bed, but sleeps in his own clothes.

107 *Jacobins*: the Dominican (black)friars originally of Rue St
Jacques in Paris.
115 *covent*: convent.

I fear me he mistrusts what we intend.

BARABAS: No, 'tis an order which the friars use:
Yet, if he knew our meanings, could he scape?

ITHAMORE: No, none can hear him, cry he ne'er so loud.

BARABAS: Why, true; therefore did I place him there.   *140*
The other chambers open towards the street.

ITHAMORE: You loiter, master; wherefore stay we thus?
O, how I long to see him shake his heels!

BARABAS: Come on, sirrah:
Off with your girdle; make a handsome noose. –
  ITHAMORE *takes off his girdle, and ties a noose on it.*
Friar, awake!
  They put the noose round the FRIAR'S *neck.*

FRIAR BARNARDINE: What, do you mean to strangle me?

ITHAMORE: Yes, 'cause you use to confess.

BARABAS: Blame not us, but the proverb, – Confess
and be hanged. – Pull hard!   *150*

FRIAR BARNARDINE: What, will you have my life?

BARABAS: Pull hard, I say. – You would have had my
goods.

ITHAMORE: Ay, and our lives too. – Therefore pull
amain!
  They strangle the FRIAR.
'Tis neatly done, sir; here's no print at all.

BARABAS: Then is it as it should be. Take him up.

ITHAMORE: Nay, master, be ruled by me a little.
  *Takes the body, sets it upright against the wall, and
  puts a staff in its hand.*
So, let him lean upon his staff. Excellent! He stands as
if he were begging of bacon.

BARABAS: Who would not think but that this friar liv'd?
What time o' night is't now, sweet Ithamore?   *160*

ITHAMORE: Towards one.

BARABAS: Then will not Jacomo be long from hence.
  Exeunt.
  Enter FRIAR JACOMO.

143 *shake his heels*: i.e. on the gallows.

FRIAR JACOMO: This is the hour wherein I shall
    proceed.
    O happy hour, wherein I shall convert
    An infidel, and bring his gold into our treasury!
    But soft! is not this Barnardine? It is;
    And, understanding I should come this way,
    Stands here o' purpose, meaning me some wrong,
    And intercept my going to the Jew.

170   Barnardine!
    Wilt thou not speak? Thou think'st I see thee not.
    Away, I'd wish thee, and let me go by:
    No, wilt thou not? Nay, then, I'll force my way;
    And see, a staff stands ready for the purpose.
    As thou lik'st that, stop me another time!
        Strikes him and he falls.
        Enter BARABAS *and* ITHAMORE.

BARABAS: Why, how now, Jacomo! What hast thou
    done?

FRIAR JACOMO: Why, stricken him that would have
    struck at me.

BARABAS: Who is it? Barnardine! Now, out, alas, he
    is slain!

ITHAMORE: Ay, master, he's slain. Look how his brains
180   drop out on's nose.

FRIAR JACOMO: Good sirs, I have done't: but nobody
    knows it but you two; I may escape.

BARABAS: So might my man and I hang with you for
    company.

ITHAMORE: No, let us bear him to the magistrates.

FRIAR JACOMO: Good Barabas, let me go.

BARABAS: No, pardon me; the law must have his
    course.
    I must be forc'd to give in evidence,
    That, being importun'd by this Barnardine

190   To be a Christian, I shut him out,
    And there he sate. Now I, to keep my word,
    180 *on's:* of his.

And give my goods and substance to your house,
Was up thus early, with intent to go
Unto your friary, because you stay'd.

ITHAMORE: Fie upon 'em! master, will you turn
Christian, when holy friars turn devils and murder one
another?

BARABAS: No, for this example I'll remain a Jew.
Heaven bless me! What, a friar a murderer!
When shall you see a Jew commit the like?   200

ITHAMORE: Why, a Turk could ha' done no more.

BARABAS: Tomorrow is the sessions; you shall to it.
Come Ithamore, let's help to take him hence.

FRIAR JACOMO: Villains, I am a sacred person; touch
me not.

BARABAS: The law shall touch you, we'll but lead you,
we.
'Las, I could weep at your calamity!
Take in the staff too, for that must be shown:
Law wills that each particular be known.

    Exeunt.

SCENE TWO

Enter BELLAMIRA *and* PILIA-BORZA.

BELLAMIRA: Pilia-Borza, didst thou meet with Ithamore?

PILIA-BORZA: I did.

BELLAMIRA: And didst thou deliver my letter?

PILIA-BORZA: I did.

BELLAMIRA: And what think'st thou? Will he come?

PILIA-BORZA: I think so: and yet I cannot tell; for, at
the reading of the letter, he looked like a man of
another world.

BELLAMIRA: Why so?   10

PILIA-BORZA: That such a base slave as he should be

194 *stay'd*: were late.

saluted by such a tall man as I am, from such a beautiful dame as you.

BELLAMIRA: And what said he?

PILIA-BORZA: Not a wise word; only gave me a nod, as who should say, 'Is it even so?' and so I left him, being driven to a non-plus at the critical aspect of my terrible countenance.

BELLAMIRA: And where didst meet him?

20 PILIA-BORZA: Upon mine own free-hold, within forty foot of the gallows, conning his neck-verse, I take it, looking of a friar's execution; whom I saluted with an old hempen proverb, *Hodie tibi, cras mihi*, and so I left him to the mercy of the hangman; but, the exercise being done, see where he comes.

Enter ITHAMORE.

ITHAMORE: I never knew a man take his death so patiently as this friar. He was ready to leap off ere the halter was about his neck; and, when the hangman had put on his hempen tippet, he made such haste to his prayers, as 30 if he had had another cure to serve. Well, go whither he will, I'll be none of his followers in haste. And now I think on't, going to the execution, a fellow met me with a muschatoes like a raven's wing, and a dagger with a hilt like a warming pan; and he gave me a letter from one Madam Bellamira, saluting me in such sort as if he had meant to make clean my boots with his lips. The effect was, that I should come to her house. I wonder what the reason is; it may be she sees more in me than I can find in myself; for she writes further, that she loves 40 me ever since she saw me, and who would not requite such love? Here's her house; and here she comes. And now would I were gone! I am not worthy to look upon her.

12 *tall man*: fine fellow.
20 *free-hold*: the 'legitimate' territory of the pick-pocket.
23 *Hodie tibi* ...: Today you, tomorrow me.
29 *hempen tippet*: noose of hangman's rope.   30 *cure*: parish.
33 *muschatoes*: moustache.

PILIA-BORZA: This is the gentleman you writ to.

ITHAMORE (*aside*): Gentleman! he flouts me: what gentry can be in a poor Turk of tenpence? I'll be gone.

BELLAMIRA: Is't not a sweet-faced youth, Pilia?

ITHAMORE (*aside*): Again, sweet youth! (*Aloud*) Did not you, sir, bring the sweet youth a letter?

PILIA-BORZA: I did, sir, and from this gentlewoman,   50
who, as myself and the rest of the family, stand or fall at your service.

BELLAMIRA: Though woman's modesty should hale me back,

I can withhold no longer; welcome, sweet love.

ITHAMORE (*aside*): Now am I clean, or rather foully, out of the way.

BELLAMIRA: Whither so soon?

ITHAMORE (*aside*): I'll go steal some money from my master to make me handsome. (*Aloud*) Pray, pardon me; I must go see a ship discharged.   60

BELLAMIRA: Canst thou be so unkind to leave me thus?

PILIA-BORZA: An ye did but know how she loves you, sir!

ITHAMORE: Nay, I care not how much she loves me. – Sweet Allamira, would I had my master's wealth for thy sake!

PILIA-BORZA: And you can have it, sir, an if you please.

ITHAMORE: If 'twere above ground, I could, and would have it; but he hides and buries it up, as partridges do   70
their eggs, under the earth.

PILIA-BORZA: And is't not possible to find it out?

ITHAMORE: By no means possible.

BELLAMIRA (*aside to* PILIA-BORZA): What shall we do with this base villain, then?

46 *Turk of tenpence*: common derogatory expression (cf. 'ten-penny infidel').
60 *discharged*: unloaded.
65 *Allamira*: thus Quarto (Ithamore gets the name wrong).

PILIA-BORZA (*aside to her*): Let me alone; do but you
speak him fair.
(*Aloud*) But you know some secrets of the Jew,
Which, if they were reveal'd, would do him harm.

80 ITHAMORE: Ay, and such as – go to, no more! I'll make
him send me half he has, and glad he scapes so too.
Pen and ink: I'll write unto him; we'll have money
straight.

PILIA-BORZA: Send for a hundred crowns at least.

ITHAMORE: Ten hundred thousand crowns. – (*Writing*)
Master Barabas, –

PILIA-BORZA: Write not so submissively, but threatening him.

ITHAMORE (*writing*): *Sirrah Barabas, send me a hundred*
90 *crowns.*

PILIA-BORZA: Put in two hundred at least.

ITHAMORE (*writing*): *I charge thee send me three hundred*
by this bearer, and this shall be your warrant: if you do not –
no more, but so.

PILIA-BORZA: Tell him you will confess.

ITHAMORE (*writing*): *Otherwise I'll confess all.* – Vanish,
and return in a twinkle.

PILIA-BORZA: Let me alone; I'll use him in his kind.

ITHAMORE: Hang him, Jew!

Exit PILIA-BORZA *with the letter.*

100 BELLAMIRA: Now, gentle Ithamore, lie in my lap.
Where are my maids? Provide a running banquet;
Send to the merchant, bid him bring me silks;
Shall Ithamore my love go in such rags?

ITHAMORE: And bid the jeweller come hither too.

BELLAMIRA: I have no husband, sweet; I'll marry thee.

ITHAMORE: Content: but we will leave this paltry land,
And sail from hence to Greece, to lovely Greece.
I'll be thy Jason, thou my golden fleece;
Where painted carpets o'er the meads are hurl'd,
110 And Bacchus' vineyards overspread the world;
Where woods and forests go in goodly green;

I'll be Adonis, thou shalt be Love's Queen;
The meads, the orchards, and the primrose-lanes,
Instead of sedge and reed, bear sugar-canes:
Thou in those groves, by Dis above,
Shalt live with me, and be my love.

BELLAMIRA: Whither will I not go with gentle Ithamore?

    Re-enter PILIA-BORZA.

ITHAMORE: How now? Hast thou the gold?

PILIA-BORZA: Yes.   *120*

ITHAMORE: But came it freely? Did the cow give down her milk freely?

PILIA-BORZA: At reading of the letter, he stared and stamped, and turned aside. I took him by the beard, and looked upon him thus; told him he were best to send it. Then he hugged and embraced me.

ITHAMORE: Rather for fear than love.

PILIA-BORZA: Then, like a Jew, he laughed and jeered, and told me he loved me for your sake, and said what a faithful servant you had been.   *130*

ITHAMORE: The more villain he to keep me thus: here's goodly 'parel, is there not?

PILIA-BORZA: To conclude, he gave me ten crowns.

    Delivers the money to ITHAMORE.

ITHAMORE: But ten? I'll not leave him worth a grey groat. Give me a ream of paper: we'll have a kingdom of gold for't.

PILIA-BORZA: Write for five hundred crowns.

ITHAMORE (*writing*): *Sirrah Jew, as you love your life, send me five hundred crowns, and give the bearer a hundred.* – Tell him I must have't.   *140*

PILIA-BORZA: I warrant your worship shall have't.

ITHAMORE: And, if he ask why I demand so much, tell him I scorn to write a line under a hundred crowns.

PILIA-BORZA: You'd make a rich poet, sir. I am gone.

    Exit with the letter.

  115 *Dis*: Pluto, lord of the Underworld.

ITHAMORE: Take thou the money; spend it for my sake.

BELLAMIRA: 'Tis not thy money, but thyself I weigh.
  Thus Bellamira esteems of gold;
    Throws it aside.
  But thus of thee.
    Kisses him.

ITHAMORE: That kiss again! – (*Aside*) She runs
  division of my lips.

150 What an eye she casts on me! it twinkles like a star.

BELLAMIRA: Come, my dear love, let's in and sleep
  together.

ITHAMORE: O, that ten thousand nights were put in one,
  that we might sleep seven years together afore we
  wake!

BELLAMIRA: Come, amorous wag, first banquet, and
  then sleep.
    Exeunt.

SCENE THREE

Enter BARABAS, *reading a letter.*

BARABAS: *Barabas, send me three hundred crowns –*
  Plain Barabas! O, that wicked courtesan!
  He was not wont to call me Barabas –
  Or else I will confess – ay, there it goes:
  But, if I get him, *coupe de gorge* for that.
  He sent a shaggy, totter'd, staring slave,
  That, when he speaks, draws out his grisly beard,
  And winds it twice or thrice about his ear;
  Whose face has been a grind-stone for men's swords;
10 His hands are hack'd, some fingers cut quite off,
  Who, when he speaks, grunts like a hog, and looks
  Like one that is employ'd in catzery

149 *runs divisions of*: like rapid and varied playing upon a musical
instrument.
5 *coupe de gorge*: cut his throat.
12 *catzery*: involved with prostitutes.

And cross-biting; such a rogue
As is the husband to a hundred whores.
And I by him must send three hundred crowns!
Well, my hope is, he will not stay there still;
And, when he comes – O, that he were but here!
   Enter PILIA-BORZA.

PILIA-BORZA: Jew, I must ha' more gold.

BARABAS: Why, want'st thou any of thy tale?

PILIA-BORZA: No, but three hundred will not serve his   *20*
turn.

BARABAS: Not serve his turn, sir!

PILIA-BORZA: No, sir; and therefore I must have five
hundred more.

BARABAS: I'll rather –

PILIA-BORZA: O, good words, sir, and send it you
were best! See, there's his letter.
   Gives letter.

BARABAS: Might he not as well come as send? Pray, bid
him come and fetch it: what he writes for you, ye shall
have straight.   *30*

PILIA-BORZA: Ay, and the rest too, or else –

BARABAS (*aside*): I must make this villain away – (*Aloud*)
Please you dine with me, sir, (*aside*) and you shall be
most heartily poisoned.

PILIA-BORZA: No, God-a-mercy. Shall I have these
crowns?

BARABAS: I cannot do it; I have lost my keys.

PILIA-BORZA: O, if that be all, I can pick ope your
locks.

BARABAS: Or climb up to my counting-house window: *40*
you know my meaning.

PILIA-BORZA: I know enough, and therefore talk not
to me of your counting-house. The gold! Or know,
Jew, it is in my power to hang thee.

BARABAS: (*aside*) I am betray'd. –
   (*Aloud*) 'Tis not five hundred crowns that I esteem;

13 *cross-biting*: swindling.   19 *tale*: sum of money.

I am not mov'd at that: this angers me,
That he, who knows I love him as myself,
Should write in this imperious vein. Why sir,
50   You know I have no child, and unto whom
Should I leave all, but unto Ithamore?

PILIA-BORZA: Here's many words, but no crowns: the crowns!

BARABAS: Commend me to him, sir, most humbly,
And unto your good mistress as unknown.

PILIA-BORZA: Speak, shall I have 'em, sir?

BARABAS: Sir, here they are. —
   Gives money.
(*Aside*) O, that I should part with so much gold! —
Here, take 'em, fellow, with as good a will —
60   (*Aside*) As I would see thee hang'd! (*Aloud*) O, love
stops my breath!
Never lov'd man servant as I do Ithamore.

PILIA-BORZA: I know it, sir.

BARABAS: Pray, when, sir, shall I see you at my house?

PILIA-BORZA: Soon enough to your cost, sir. Fare you well.
   Exit.

BARABAS: Nay, to thine own cost, villain, if thou com'st!
Was ever Jew tormented as I am?
To have a shag-rag knave to come [force from me]¹⁴
Three hundred crowns, and then five hundred crowns!
Well, I must seek a means to rid 'em all,
70   And presently; for in his villany
He will tell all he knows, and I shall die for't.
I have it:
I will in some disguise go see the slave,
And how the villain revels with my gold.
   Exit.

SCENE FOUR

Enter BELLAMIRA, ITHAMORE, *and* PILIA-BORZA.

BELLAMIRA: I'll pledge thee, love, and therefore drink it off.

ITHAMORE: Say'st thou me so? Have at it! And, do you hear . . .
Whispers to her.

BELLAMIRA: Go to, it shall be so.

ITHAMORE: Of that condition I will drink it up:
Here's to thee.

BELLAMIRA: Nay, I'll have all or none.

ITHAMORE: There, if thou lov'st me, do not leave a drop.   10

BELLAMIRA: Love thee! Fill me three glasses.

ITHAMORE: Three and fifty dozen: I'll pledge thee.

PILIA-BORZA: Knavely spoke, and like a knight-at-arms.

ITHAMORE: Hey, *Rivo Castiliano!*[15] a man's a man.

BELLAMIRA: Now to the Jew.

ITHAMORE: Ha! To the Jew; and send me money you were best.

PILIA-BORZA: What wouldst thou do, if he should send thee none?   20

ITHAMORE: Do nothing. But I know what I know: he's a murderer.

BELLAMIRA: I had not thought he had been so brave a man.

ITHAMORE: You knew Mathias and the Governor's son. He and I killed 'em both, and yet never touched 'em.

PILIA-BORZA: O, bravely done!

ITHAMORE: I carried the broth that poisoned the nuns; And he and I — snicle! hand to! fast![16] — strangled a friar.

BELLAMIRA: You two alone?   30

ITHAMORE: We two; and 'twas never known, nor never shall be for me.

413

PILIA-BORZA (*aside to* BELLAMIRA): This shall with me
unto the Governor.

BELLAMIRA (*aside to* PILIA-BORZA): And fit it should:
but first let's ha' more gold. –

(*Aloud*) Come, gentle Ithamore, lie in my lap.

ITHAMORE: Love me little, love me long: let music
rumble,

Whilst I in thy incony lap do tumble.

 Enter BARABAS, *disguised as a French musician, with a
lute, and a nosegay in his hat.*

40 BELLAMIRA: A French musician! – Come, let's hear
your skill.

BARABAS: Must tuna my lute for sound, twang twang
first.

ITHAMORE: Wilt drink, Frenchman? here's to thee with
a – Pox on this drunken hiccup!

BARABAS: Gramercy, monsieur.

BELLAMIRA: Prithee, Pilia-Borza, bid the fiddler give me
the posy in his hat there.

PILIA-BORZA: Sirrah, you must give my mistress your
50 posy.

BARABAS: *A votre commandement, madame.*

 Giving nosegay.

BELLAMIRA: How sweet, my Ithamore, the flowers
smell!

ITHAMORE: Like thy breath, sweetheart; no violet like
'em.

PILIA-BORZA: Foh! Methinks they stink like a hollyhock.

BARABAS (*aside*): So, now I am reveng'd upon 'em all.
60 The scent thereof was death; I poison'd it.

ITHAMORE: Play, fiddler, or I'll cut your cat's guts into
chitterlings.

BARABAS: *Pardonnez moi,* be no in tune yet: so, now,
now all be in.

39 *incony*: sweet (also involving slang meaning of 'cony' for a
woman's private parts).
61 *chitterlings*: pig's intestines used for sausages.

ITHAMORE: Give him a crown, and fill me out more
wine.

PILIA-BORZA: There's two crowns for thee: play.
Giving money.

BARABAS (*aside*): How liberally the villain gives me mine
own gold!
He plays.

PILIA-BORZA: Methinks he fingers very well.   70

BARABAS (*aside*): So did you when you stole my gold.

PILIA-BORZA: How swiftly he runs!

BARABAS (*aside*): You run swifter when you threw my
gold out of my window.

BELLAMIRA: Musician, hast been in Malta long?

BARABAS: Two, three, four month, madam.

ITHAMORE: Dost not know a Jew, one Barabas?

BARABAS: Very mush: monsieur, you no be his man?

PILIA-BORZA: His man?

ITHAMORE: I scorn the peasant: tell him so.   80

BARABAS (*aside*): He knows it already.

ITHAMORE: 'Tis a strange thing of that Jew: he lives
upon pickled grasshoppers and sauced mushrooms.

BARABAS (*aside*): What a slave's this! The Governor
feeds not as I do.

ITHAMORE: He never put on clean shirt since he was
circumcised.

BARABAS (*aside*): O rascal! I change myself twice a-day.

ITHAMORE: The hat he wears, Judas left under the
elder when he hanged himself.   90

BARABAS (*aside*): 'Twas sent me for a present from the
Great Cham.

PILIA-BORZA: A nasty slave he is. — Whither now,
fiddler?

BARABAS: *Pardonnez moi, monsieur*; me be no well.

PILIA-BORZA: Farewell, fiddler.
Exit BARABAS.

One letter more to the Jew.

91 *Grand Cham*: Emperor of Tartary.

BELLAMIRA: Prithee, sweet love, one more, and write
it sharp.

100 ITHAMORE: No, I'll send by word of mouth now. Bid
him deliver thee a thousand crowns, by the same token
that the nuns loved rice, that Friar Barnardine slept in
his own clothes; any of 'em will do it.

PILIA-BORZA: Let me alone to urge it, now I know the
meaning.

ITHAMORE: The meaning has a meaning. Come, let's in:
To undo a Jew is charity, and not sin.

Exeunt.

ACT FIVE

SCENE ONE

An open place near the city walls.
Enter FERNEZE, KNIGHTS, MARTIN DEL BOSCO,
and OFFICERS.

FERNEZE: Now, gentlemen, betake you to your arms,
And see that Malta be well fortified;
And it behoves you to be resolute,
For Calymath, having hover'd here so long,
Will win the town, or die before the walls.

FIRST KNIGHT: And die he shall: for we will never
yield.

Enter BELLAMIRA *and* PILIA-BORZA.

BELLAMIRA: O, bring us to the Governor!

FERNEZE: Away with her! She is a courtesan.

BELLAMIRA: What'er I am, yet, Governor, hear me speak.
10   I bring thee news by whom thy son was slain:
Mathias did it not; it was the Jew.

PILIA-BORZA: Who, besides the slaughter of these
gentlemen,
Poison'd his own daughter and the nuns,

Strangled a friar, and I know not what
Mischief beside.

FERNEZE: Had we but proof of this –

BELLAMIRA: Strong proof, my lord: his man's now at my lodging
That was his agent; he'll confess it all.

FERNEZE: Go fetch him straight.

    Exeunt OFFICERS.

                            I always fear'd that Jew.　*20*

Re-enter OFFICERS *with* BARABAS *and* ITHAMORE.

BARABAS: I'll go alone; dogs, do not hale me thus.

ITHAMORE: Nor me neither; I cannot out-run you, constable. – O, my belly!

BARABAS (*aside*): One dram of powder more had made all sure:
What a damn'd slave was I!

FERNEZE: Make fires, heat irons, let the rack be fetched.

FIRST KNIGHT: Nay, stay, my lord; 't may be he will confess.

BARABAS: Confess! What mean you, lords? Who should confess?

FERNEZE: Thou and thy Turk; 'twas you that slew my son.

ITHAMORE: Guilty, my lord, I confess. Your son and　*30*
Mathias were both contracted unto Abigail: [he] forged a counterfeit challenge.

BARABAS: Who carried that challenge?

ITHAMORE: I carried it, I confess; but who writ it?
Marry, even he that strangled Barnardine, poisoned the nuns and his own daughter.

FERNEZE: Away with him! His sight is death to me.

BARABAS: For what? You men of Malta, hear me speak.
She is a courtesan, and he a thief,
And he my bondman; let me have law,
For none of this can prejudice my life.　*40*

FERNEZE: Once more, away with him! – You shall have law.

BARABAS: Devils, do your worst! – (*Aside*) I['ll] live in
    spite of you. –
    (*Aloud*) As these have spoke, so be it to their souls! –
    (*Aside*) I hope the poison'd flowers will work anon.
    Exeunt OFFICERS *with* BARABAS *and* ITHAMORE;
    BELLAMIRA, *and* PILIA-BORZA.
    Enter KATHARINE.

KATHARINE: Was my Mathias murder'd by the Jew?
    Ferneze, 'twas thy son that murder'd him.

FERNEZE: Be patient, gentle madam; it was he;
    He forg'd the daring challenge made them fight.

KATHARINE: Where is the Jew? Where is that murderer?

50 FERNEZE: In prison, till the law has pass'd on him.
    Re-enter FIRST OFFICER.

FIRST OFFICER: My lord, the courtesan and her man
    are dead;
    So is the Turk and Barabas the Jew.

FERNEZE: Dead?

FIRST OFFICER: Dead, my lord, and here they bring
    his body.

BOSCO: This sudden death of his is very strange.
    Re-enter OFFICERS, *carrying* BARABAS *as dead*.

FERNEZE: Wonder not at it, sir; the heavens are just.
    Their deaths were liket heir lives; then think not of 'em.
    Since they are dead, let them be buried.
    For the Jew's body, throw that o'er the walls,
    To be a prey for vultures and wild beasts.

60   So, now away and fortify the town.
    Exeunt all, leaving BARABAS *on the floor*.

BARABAS (*rising*): What, all alone? Well fare, sleepy
    drink!
    I'll be reveng'd on this accursed town;
    For by my means Calymath shall enter in.
    I'll help to slay their children and their wives,
    To fire the churches, pull their houses down,
    Take my goods too, and seize upon my lands.
    I hope to see the Governor a slave,

And, rowing in a galley, whipt to death.

Enter CALYMATH, BASSOES, *and* TURKS.

CALYMATH: Whom have we there? A spy? 70

BARABAS: Yes, my good lord, one that can spy a place
Where you may enter, and surprise the town.
My name is Barabas; I am a Jew.

CALYMATH: Art thou that Jew whose goods we heard
were sold
For tribute money?

BARABAS: The very same, my lord:
And since that time they have hir'd a slave, my man,
To accuse me of a thousand villanies.
I was imprisoned, but scap'd their hands,

CALYMATH: Didst break prison?

BARABAS: No, no: 80
I drank of poppy and cold mandrake juice;
And being asleep, belike they thought me dead,
And threw me o'er the walls: so, or how else,
The Jew is here, and rests at your command.

CALYMATH: 'Twas bravely done. But tell me, Barabas,
Canst thou, as thou report'st, make Malta ours?

BARABAS: Fear not, my lord, for here, against the
trench,[17]
The rock is hollow, and of purpose digg'd,
To make a passage for the running streams
And common channels of the city. 90
Now, whilst you give assault unto the walls,
I'll lead five hundred soldiers through the vault,
And rise with them i' the middle of the town,
Open the gates for you to enter in,
And by this means the city is your own.

CALYMATH: If this be true, I'll make thee Governor.

BARABAS: And if it be not true, then let me die.

CALYMATH: Thou'st doom'd thyself. — Assault it
presently.

Exeunt.

98 *presently*: immediately.

SCENE TWO

Alarums within. Enter CALYMATH, BASSOES,
TURKS, *and* BARABAS; *with* FERNEZE *and*
KNIGHTS *prisoners.*

CALYMATH: Now vail your pride, you captive
    Christians,
And kneel for mercy to your conquering foe.
Now where's the hope you had of haughty Spain?
Ferneze, speak; had it not been much better
To keep[18] thy promise than be thus surpris'd?

FERNEZE: What should I say? We are captives, and must
    yield.

CALYMATH: Ay, villains, you must yield, and under
    Turkish yokes
Shall groaning bear the burden of our ire.
And, Barabas, as erst we promis'd thee,

10 For thy desert we make thee Governor;
Use them at thy discretion.

BARABAS: Thanks, my lord.

FERNEZE: O fatal day, to fall into the hands
Of such a traitor and unhallow'd Jew!
What greater misery could heaven inflict?

CALYMATH: 'Tis our command; and, Barabas, we give,
To guard thy person, these our Janizaries:
Entreat them well, as we have used thee.
And now, brave Bassoes, come; we'll walk about

20 The ruin'd town, and see the wrack we made.
Farewell, brave Jew, farewell, great Barabas!

BARABAS: May all good fortune follow Calymath!
    Exeunt CALYMATH *and* BASSOES.
And now, as entrance to our safety,
To prison with the Governor and these
Captains, his consorts and confederates.

1 *vail*: lower, humble.   17 *Janizaries*: Turkish infantry.
18 *Entreat*: treat.

FERNEZE: O villain! heaven will be reveng'd on thee.

BARABAS: Away! no more; let him not trouble me.

Exeunt TURKS *with* FERNEZE *and* KNIGHTS.

Thus hast thou gotten, by thy policy,
No simple place, no small authority.
I now am Governor of Malta; true, —   30
But Malta hates me, and, in hating me,
My life's in danger; and what boots it thee,
Poor Barabas, to be the Governor,
Whenas thy life shall be at their command?
No, Barabas, this must be look'd into;
And, since by wrong thou gott'st authority,
Maintain it bravely by firm policy;
At least, unprofitably lose it not.
For he that liveth in authority,
And neither gets him friends nor fills his bags,   40
Lives like the ass that Æsop speaketh of,
That labours with a load of bread and wine,
And leaves it off to snap on thistle tops.
But Barabas will be more circumspect.
Begin betimes; Occasion's bald behind:
Slip not thine opportunity, for fear too late
Thou seek'st for much, but canst not compass it.
Within here!

Enter FERNEZE, *with a* GUARD.

FERNEZE: My lord?

BARABAS: Ay, *lord*; thus slaves will learn.   50
Now, Governor, — stand by there, wait within, —

Exeunt GUARD.

This is the reason that I sent for thee:
Thou seest thy life and Malta's happiness
Are at my arbitrement; and Barabas
At his discretion may dispose of both.
Now tell me, Governor, and plainly too,
What think'st thou shall become of it and thee?

FERNEZE: This, Barabas: since things are in thy power,
I see no reason but of Malta's wrack,

60 Nor hope of thee but extreme cruelty.
Nor fear I death, nor will I flatter thee.
BARABAS: Governor, good words! Be not so furious.
'Tis not thy life which can avail me aught;
Yet you do live, and live for me you shall.
And as for Malta's ruin, think you not
'Twas slender policy for Barabas
To dispossess himself of such a place?
For sith, as once you said, within this isle,
In Malta here, that I have got my goods,
70 And in this city still have had success,
And now at length am grown your Governor,
Yourself shall see it shall not be forgot;
For, as a friend not known but in distress,
I'll rear up Malta, now remediless.
FERNEZE: Will Barabas recover Malta's loss?
Will Barabas be good to Christians?
BARABAS: What wilt thou give me, Governor, to
procure
A dissolution of the slavish bands
Wherein the Turk hath yok'd your land and you?
80 What will you give me if I render you
The life of Calymath, surprise his men,
And in an out-house of the city shut
His soldiers, till I have consum'd 'em all with fire?
What will you give him that procureth this?
FERNEZE: Do but bring this to pass which thou
pretendest,
Deal truly with us as thou intimatest,
And I will send amongst the citizens,
And by my letters privately procure
Great sums of money for thy recompense:
90 Nay, more, do this, and live thou Governor still.
BARABAS: Nay, do thou this, Ferneze, and be free.
Governor, I enlarge thee. Live with me;
Go walk about the city, see thy friends.

85 *pretendest*: hold out, offer.

Tush, send not letters to 'em; go thy self,
And let me see what money thou canst make.
Here is my hand that I'll set Malta free.
And thus we cast it: to a solemn feast
I will invite young Selim Calymath,
Where be thou present, only to perform
One stratagem that I'll impart to thee,   *100*
Wherein no danger shall betide thy life,
And I will warrant Malta free for ever.

FERNEZE: Here is my hand; believe me, Barabas,
I will be there, and do as thou desirest.
When is the time?

BARABAS: Governor, presently.
For Calymath, when he hath view'd the town,
Will take his leave, and sail toward Ottoman.

FERNEZE: Then will I, Barabas, about this coin,
And bring it with me to thee in the evening.   *110*

BARABAS: Do so, but fail not. Now farewell, Ferneze.
  Exit FERNEZE.
And thus far roundly goes the business:
Thus, loving neither, will I live with both,
Making a profit of my policy;
And he from whom my most advantage comes,
Shall be my friend.
This is the life we Jews are us'd to lead;
And reason too, for Christians do the like.
Well, now about effecting this device.
First, to surprise great Selim's soldiers,   *120*
And then to make provision for the feast,
That at one instant all things may be done.
My policy detests prevention.
To what event my secret purpose drives,
I know; and they shall witness with their lives.
  Exeunt.

112 *roundly*: with full success.

SCENE THREE

Enter CALYMATH *and* BASSOES.

CALYMATH: Thus have we view'd the city, seen the sack,
And caus'd the ruins to be new-repair'd,
Which with our bombards' shot and basilisk[s]
We rent in sunder at our entry:
Two lofty turrets[19] that command the town,
And, now I see the situation,
And how secure this conquer'd island stands,
Environ'd with the Mediterranean sea,
Strong countermin'd[20] with other petty isles,
10   And, toward Calabria, back'd by Sicily
Where Syracusian Dionysius reign'd.
I wonder how it could be conquered thus.

    Enter a MESSENGER.

MESSENGER: From Barabas, Malta's Governor, I bring
A message unto mighty Calymath.
Hearing his sovereign was bound for sea,
To sail to Turkey, to great Ottoman,
He humbly would entreat your majesty
To come and see his homely citadel,
And banquet with him ere thou leav'st the isle.

20   CALYMATH: To banquet with him in his citadel?
I fear me, messenger, to feast my train
Within a town of war so lately pillag'd
Will be too costly and too troublesome.
Yet would I gladly visit Barabas,
For well has Barabas deserv'd of us.

MESSENGER: Selim, for that, thus saith the Governor:
That he hath in store a pearl so big,
So precious, and withal so orient,
As, be it valu'd but indifferently,
30   The price thereof will serve to entertain

11 *Syracusian Dionysius*: the elder Dionysius, tyrant of Syracuse, from 405 to 367 B.C.
29 *indifferently*: at a modest rate.

Selim and all his soldiers for a month.
Therefore he humbly would entreat your highness
Not to depart till he has feasted you.
CALYMATH: I cannot feast my men in Malta walls,
Except he place his tables in the streets.
MESSENGER: Know, Selim, that there is a monastery
Which standeth as an out-house to the town.
There will he banquet them; but thee at home,
With all thy bassoes and brave followers.
CALYMATH: Well, tell the Governor we grant his suit.   *40*
We'll in this summer evening feast with him.
MESSENGER: I shall, my lord.
    Exit.
CALYMATH: And now, bold bassoes, let us to our tents,
And meditate how we may grace us best,
To solemnise our Governor's great feast.
    Exeunt.

SCENE FOUR

Enter FERNEZE, KNIGHTS, *and* MARTIN DEL
BOSCO.

FERNEZE: In this, my countrymen, be rul'd by me:
Have special care that no man sally forth
Till you shall hear a culverin discharg'd
By him that bears the linstock, kindled thus;
Then issue out and come to rescue me,
For happily I shall be in distress,
Or you released of this servitude.
FIRST KNIGHT: Rather than thus to live as Turkish
    thralls,
What will we not adventure?
FERNEZE: On, then; be gone.   *10*
KNIGHTS: Farewell, grave Governor.
    Exeunt, on one side, KNIGHTS *and* MARTIN DEL
    BOSCO; *on the other,* FERNEZE.

3 *culverin*: a long cannon.   6 *happily*: possibly.

SCENE FIVE

Enter, above, BARABAS, *with a hammer, very busy;
and* CARPENTERS.

BARABAS: How stand the cords? How hang these
   hinges? Fast?
Are all the cranes and pulleys sure?
FIRST CARPENTER: All fast.
BARABAS: Leave nothing loose, all levell'd to my mind.
Why, now I see that you have art indeed.
There, carpenters, divide that gold amongst you.
   Giving money.
Go, swill in bowls of sack and muscadine;
Down to the cellar, taste of all my wines.
FIRST CARPENTER: We shall, my lord, and thank
   you.
   Exeunt CARPENTERS.
10 BARABAS: And, if you like them, drink your fill and
   die;
For, so I live, perish may all the world!
Now, Selim Calymath, return me word
That thou wilt come, and I am satisfied.
   Enter MESSENGER.
Now, sirrah; what, will he come?
MESSENGER: He will; and has commanded all his men
To come ashore, and march through Malta streets,
That thou mayst feast them in thy citadel.
BARABAS: Then now are all things as my wish would
   have 'em;
There wanteth nothing but the Governor's pelf;
20 And see, he brings it.
   Enter FERNEZE.
                              Now, Governor, the sum.
FERNEZE: With free consent, a hundred thousand
   pounds.

4 *levell'd to my mind*: according to my plan.

BARABAS: Pounds say'st thou, Governor? Well, since
   it is no more,
I'll satisfy myself with that; nay, keep it still,
For, if I keep not promise, trust not me.
And, Governor, now partake my policy,
First, for his army, they are sent before,
Enter'd the monastery, and underneath
In several places are field-pieces pitch'd,
Bombards, whole barrels full of gunpowder,   *30*
That on the sudden shall dissever it,
And batter all the stones about their ears,
Whence none can possibly escape alive.
Now, as for Calymath and his consorts,
Here have I made a dainty gallery,
The floor whereof, this cable being cut,
Doth fall asunder, so that it doth sink
Into a deep pit past recovery.
Here, hold that knife; and, when thou seest he comes,
   Throws down a knife.
And with his bassoes shall be blithely set,   *40*
A warning-piece shall be shot off from the tower,
To give thee knowledge when to cut the cord,
And fire the house. Say, will not this be brave?
FERNEZE: O, excellent! Here, hold thee, Barabas;
   I trust thy word; take what I promis'd thee.
BARABAS: No, Governor, I'll satisfy thee first.
Thou shalt not live in doubt of anything.
Stand close, for here they come.
       FERNEZE *retires.*
                      Why, is not this
A kingly kind of trade, to purchase towns   *50*
By treachery, and sell 'em by deceit?
Now, tell me worldlings, underneath the sun
If greater falsehood ever has been done?
   Enter CALYMATH *and* BASSOES.
CALYMATH: Come, my companion bassoes: see, I pray,
How busy Barabas is there above

To entertain us in his gallery.
Let us salute him. – Save thee, Barabas!
BARABAS: Welcome, great Calymath!
FERNEZE (*aside*): How the slave jeers at him!
60 BARABAS: Will't please thee, mighty Selim Calymath,
To ascend our homely stairs?
CALYMATH: Ay, Barabas.
Come, bassoes, ascend.
FERNEZE (*coming forward*): Stay, Calymath;
For I will show thee greater courtesy
Than Barabas would have afforded thee.
KNIGHT (*within*): Sound a charge there!

> *A charge sounded within:* FERNEZE *cuts the cord; the
> floor of the gallery gives way, and* BARABAS *falls into
> a cauldron placed in a pit.*

> *Enter* KNIGHTS *and* MARTIN DEL BOSCO.

CALYMATH: How now! what means this?
BARABAS: Help, help me, Christians, help!
70 FERNEZE: See, Calymath! This was devis'd for thee.
CALYMATH: Treason, treason! Bassoes, fly!
FERNEZE: No, Selim, do not fly.
See his end first, and fly then if thou canst.
BARABAS: O, help me, Selim! Help me, Christians!
Governor, why stand you all so pitiless?
FERNEZE: Should I in pity of thy plaints or thee,
Accursed Barabas, base Jew, relent?
No, thus I'll see thy treachery repaid,
But wish thou hadst behav'd thee otherwise.
80 BARABAS: You will not help me, then?
FERNEZE: No, villain, no.
BARABAS: And, villains, know you cannot help me
now.
Then, Barabas, breathe forth thy latest fate,
And in the fury of thy torments strive
To end thy life with resolution.
Know, Governor, 'twas I that slew thy son,
I fram'd the challenge that did make them meet.

Know, Calymath, I aim'd thy overthrow:
And, had I but escap'd this stratagem,
I would have brought confusion on you all,⁣   *90*
Damn'd Christians, dogs, and Turkish infidels!
But now begins the extremity of heat
To pinch me with intolerable pangs.
Die, life! fly, soul! tongue, curse thy fill, and die!
Dies.

CALYMATH: Tell me, you Christians, what doth this
    portend?

FERNEZE: This train he laid to have entrapp'd thy life.
Now, Selim, note the unhallow'd deeds of Jews:
Thus he determin'd to have handled thee,
But I have rather chose to save thy life.

CALYMATH: Was this the banquet he prepar'd for us?⁣   *100*
Let's hence, lest further mischief be pretended.

FERNEZE: Nay, Selim, stay, for, since we have thee
    here,
We will not let thee part so suddenly.
Besides, if we should let thee go, all's one,
For with thy galleys couldst thou not get hence,
Without fresh men to rig and furnish them.

CALYMATH: Tush, Governor, take thou no care for
    that.
My men are all aboard,
And do attend my coming there by this.

FERNEZE: Why, heard'st thou not the trumpet sound⁣   *110*
    a charge?

CALYMATH: Yes, what of that?

FERNEZE: Why, then the house was fir'd,
Blown up, and all thy soldiers massacred.

CALYMATH: O, monstrous treason!

FERNEZE: A Jew's courtesy.
For he that did by treason work our fall,
By treason hath deliver'd thee to us.
Know, therefore, till thy father hath made good
The ruins done to Malta and to us,

120   Thou canst not part; for Malta shall be freed,
        Or Selim ne'er return to Ottoman.
     CALYMATH: Nay, rather, Christians, let me go to
        Turkey,
        In person there to mediate[21] your peace.
        To keep me here will naught advantage you.
     FERNEZE: Content thee, Calymath, here thou must stay,
        And live in Malta prisoner; for come all the world
        To rescue thee, so will we guard us now,
        As sooner shall they drink the ocean dry,
        Than conquer Malta, or endanger us.
130   So, march away; and let due praise be given,
        Neither to Fate nor Fortune, but to Heaven.
        Exeunt.

Edward the Second

Dramatis Personae

KING EDWARD THE SECOND
PRINCE EDWARD, *his son, afterwards* KING EDWARD
  THE THIRD
EARL OF KENT, *brother of* KING EDWARD THE
  SECOND
GAVESTON
ARCHBISHOP OF CANTERBURY
BISHOP OF COVENTRY
BISHOP OF WINCHESTER
EARL OF WARWICK
EARL OF LANCASTER
EARL OF PEMBROKE
EARL OF ARUNDEL
EARL OF LEICESTER
SIR THOMAS BERKELEY
MORTIMER *the elder*
MORTIMER *the younger, his nephew*
SPENSER *the elder*
SPENSER *the younger, his son*
BALDOCK
BEAUMONT
SIR WILLIAM TRUSSEL
THOMAS GURNEY
SIR JOHN MATREVIS
LIGHTBORN
SIR JOHN OF HAINAULT
LEVUNE
RICE AP HOWEL
ABBOT
MONKS
HERALD
LORDS, POOR MEN, JAMES, MOWER, CHAMPION,
  MESSENGERS, SOLDIERS, *and* ATTENDANTS
QUEEN ISABELLA, *wife to* KING EDWARD THE SECOND
NIECE *to* KING EDWARD THE SECOND, *daughter to the*
  DUKE OF GLOUCESTER
LADIES

ACT ONE

SCENE ONE

A street in London.
Enter GAVESTON, *reading a letter.*

GAVESTON: *My father is deceas'd. Come, Gaveston,*
And share the kingdom with thy dearest friend.
Ah, words that make me surfeit with delight!
What greater bliss can hap to Gaveston
Than live and be the favourite of a king!
Sweet prince, I come! these, these thy amorous lines
Might have enforc'd me to have swum from France,
And, like Leander, gasp'd upon the sand,
So thou wouldst smile, and take me in thine arms.
The sight of London to my exil'd eyes   10
Is as Elysium to a new-come soul:
Not that I love the city or the men,
But that it harbours him I hold so dear, –
The king, upon whose bosom let me die,
And with the world be still at enmity.
What need the arctic people love star-light,
To whom the sun shines both by day and night?
Farewell base stooping to the lordly peers!
My knee shall bow to none but to the king.
As for the multitude, that are but sparks,   20
Rak'd up in embers of their poverty.
Tanti, – I'll fawn first on the wind,
That glanceth at my lips, and flieth away.

    Enter three POOR MEN.

But how now! what are these?

POOR MEN: Such as desire your worship's service.

GAVESTON: What canst thou do?

FIRST POOR MAN: I can ride.

GAVESTON: But I have no horses. What art thou?

SECOND POOR MAN: A traveller.

  22 *Tanti*: So much for that.

30   GAVESTON: Let me see; thou wouldst do well
      To wait at my trencher and tell me lies at dinnertime,
      And as I like your discoursing, I'll have you.
      And what art thou?
    THIRD POOR MAN: A soldier, that hath serv'd against
      the Scot.
    GAVESTON: Why, there are hospitals for such as you:
      I have no war, and therefore, sir, be gone.
    THIRD POOR MAN: Farewell, and perish by a soldier's
      hand,
      That wouldst reward them with an hospital!
    GAVESTON (*aside*): Ay, ay, these words of his move me
      as much
40   As if a goose should play the porpintine
      And dart her plumes, thinking to pierce my breast.
      But yet it is no pain to speak men fair;
      I'll flatter these, and make them live in hope.
      (*To the men*) You know that I came lately out of France,
      And yet I have not view'd my lord the king:
      If I speed well, I'll entertain you all.
    ALL: We thank your worship.
    GAVESTON: I have some business: leave me to myself.
    ALL: We will wait here about the court.
50   GAVESTON: Do.
        Exeunt POOR MEN.
                    These are not men for me.
      I must have wanton poets, pleasant wits,
      Musicians, that with touching of a string
      May draw the pliant king which way I please:
      Music and poetry is his delight;
      Therefore I'll have Italian masques[1]* by night,
      Sweet speeches, comedies, and pleasing shows;
      And in the day, when he shall walk abroad,
      Like sylvan nymphs my pages shall be clad;

31 *trencher*: plate at table.   40 *porpintine*: porcupine.

*Superior numbers refer to the Additional Notes at the end of the book.

My men, like satyrs grazing on the lawns,
Shall with their goat-feet dance an antic hay;   *60*
Sometime a lovely boy in Dian's shape,
With hair that gilds the water as it glides,
Crownets of pearl about his naked arms,
And in his sportful hands an olive-tree,
To hide those parts which men delight to see,
Shall bathe him in a spring; and there, hard by,
One like Actaeon,[2] peeping through the grove,
Shall by the angry goddess be transform'd,
And running in the likeness of an hart,
By yelping hounds pull'd down, and seem to die: *70*
Such things as these best please his majesty.
Here comes my lord! the king and the nobles
From the parliament. I'll stand aside.

    Retires.

    Enter KING EDWARD, KENT, LANCASTER, *the*
    ELDER MORTIMER, *the* YOUNGER MORTIMER,
    WARWICK, PEMBROKE, *and* ATTENDANTS.

KING EDWARD: Lancaster!
LANCASTER: My lord?
GAVESTON (*aside*): That Earl of Lancaster do I abhor.
KING EDWARD: Will you not grant me this? (*Aside*)
    In spite of them
  I'll have my will; and these two Mortimers,
  That cross me thus, shall know I am displeased.
ELDER MORTIMER: If you love us, my lord, hate   *80*
    Gaveston.
GAVESTON (*aside*): That villain Mortimer! I'll be his death.
YOUNGER MORTIMER: Mine uncle here, this earl, and I
    myself,
  Were sworn to your father at his death,
  That he should ne'er return into the realm:
  And know, my lord, ere I will break my oath,
  This sword of mine, that should offend your foes,
  Shall sleep within the scabbard at thy need,

  60 *antic hay*: an old (antique) country dance.

437

And underneath thy banners march who will,
For Mortimer will hang his armour up.
90 GAVESTON (*aside*): *Mort dieu!*
KING EDWARD: Well, Mortimer, I'll make thee rue
these words.
Beseems it thee to contradict thy king?
Frown'st thou thereat, aspiring Lancaster?
The sword shall plane the furrows of thy brows,
And hew these knees that now are grown so stiff.
I will have Gaveston; and you shall know
What danger 'tis to stand against your king.
GAVESTON (*aside*): Well done, Ned!
LANCASTER: My lord, why do you thus incense your
peers,
100 That naturally would love and honour you,
But for that base and obscure Gaveston?
Four earldoms have I, besides Lancaster, –
Derby, Salisbury, Lincoln, Leicester;
These will I sell, to give my soldiers pay,
Ere Gaveston shall stay within the realm.
Therefore, if he be come, expel him straight.
KENT: Barons and earls, your pride hath made me mute;
But now I'll speak, and to the proof, I hope.
I do remember, in my father's days,
110 Lord Percy of the North, being highly mov'd,
Brav'd Mowberay in presence of the king;
For which, had not his highness lov'd him well,
He should have lost his head; but with his look
Th' undaunted spirit of Percy was appeas'd,
And Mowberay and he were reconcil'd:
Yet dare you brave the king unto his face.
Brother, revenge it! And let these their heads
Preach upon poles, for trespass of their tongues!
WARWICK: O, our heads!
120 KING EDWARD: Ay, yours! And therefore I would
wish you grant . . .
111 *Brav'd*: challenged.

WARWICK: Bridle thy anger, gentle Mortimer.

YOUNGER MORTIMER: I cannot, nor I will not! I
    must speak.

Cousin, our hands I hope shall fence our heads,
And strike off his that makes you threaten us.
Come, let us leave the brain-sick king,
And henceforth parley with our naked swords.

ELDER MORTIMER: Wiltshire hath men enough to save
    our heads.

WARWICK: All Warwickshire will love him for my sake.³

LANCASTER: And northward Gaveston hath many
    friends.

Adieu, my lord; and either change your mind,   *130*
Or look to see the throne, where you should sit,
To float in blood, and at thy wanton head
The glozing head of thy base minion thrown.

    Exeunt all except KING EDWARD, KENT,
    GAVESTON, *and* ATTENDANTS.

KING EDWARD: I cannot brook these haughty
    menaces:

Am I a king, and must be over-rul'd?
Brother, display my ensigns in the field:
I'll bandy with the barons and the earls,
And either die, or live with Gaveston.

GAVESTON: I can no longer keep me from my lord.
    Comes forward.

KING EDWARD: What, Gaveston! Welcome! Kiss not   *140*
    my hand:

Embrace me, Gaveston, as I do thee.
Why shouldst thou kneel? know'st thou not who I
    am?
Thy friend, thyself, another Gaveston!
Not Hylas⁴ was more mourned of Hercules
Than thou hast been of me since thy exile.

GAVESTON: And since I went from hence, no soul in hell
Hath felt more torment than poor Gaveston.

  133 *glozing*: flattering.

KING EDWARD: I know it. Brother, welcome home my
friend.
Now let the treacherous Mortimers conspire,
150 And that high-minded Earl of Lancaster:
I have my wish, in that I joy thy sight;
And sooner shall the sea o'erwhelm my land
Than bear the ship that shall transport thee hence.
I here create thee Lord High Chamberlain,
Chief Secretary to the state and me,
Earl of Cornwall, King and Lord of Man.
GAVESTON: My lord, these titles far exceed my worth.
KENT: Brother, the least of these may well suffice
For one of greater birth than Gaveston.
160 KING EDWARD: Cease, brother, for I cannot brook
these words.
Thy worth, sweet friend, is far above my gifts:
Therefore, to equal it, receive my heart.
If for these dignities thou be envied,
I'll give thee more; for, but to honour thee,
Is Edward pleas'd with kingly regiment.
Fear'st thou thy person? thou shalt have a guard:
Wantest thou gold? go to my treasury:
Wouldst thou be lov'd and fear'd? receive my seal.
Save or condemn, and in our name command
170 What so thy mind affects, or fancy likes.
GAVESTON: It shall suffice me to enjoy your love;
Which whiles I have, I think myself as great
As Caesar riding in the Roman street,
With captive kings at his triumphant car.
Enter the BISHOP OF COVENTRY.
KING EDWARD: Whither goes my Lord of Coventry
so fast?
BISHOP OF COVENTRY: To celebrate your father's
exequies.
But is that wicked Gaveston return'd?
KING EDWARD: Ay, priest, and lives to be reveng'd
on thee,

That wert the only cause of his exile.

GAVESTON: 'Tis true; and, but for reverence of these   *180*
    robes,
Thou shouldst not plod one foot beyond this place.

BISHOP OF COVENTRY: I did no more than I was
    bound to do:
And, Gaveston, unless thou be reclaim'd,
As then I did incense the parliament,
So will I now, and thou shalt back to France.

GAVESTON: Saving your reverence, you must pardon me.
    Laying hands on the BISHOP.

KING EDWARD: Throw off his golden mitre, rend his
    stole,
And in the channel christen him anew!

KENT: Ah, brother, lay not violent hands on him!
For he'll complain unto the see of Rome.   *190*

GAVESTON: Let him complain unto the see of hell:
I'll be reveng'd on him for my exile.

KING EDWARD: No, spare his life, but seize upon his
    goods:
Be thou lord bishop, and receive his rents,
And make him serve thee as thy chaplain.
I give him thee; here, use him as thou wilt.

GAVESTON: He shall to prison, and there die in bolts.

KING EDWARD: Ay, to the Tower, the Fleet, or where
    thou wilt.

BISHOP OF COVENTRY: For this offence be thou
    accurs'd of God!

KING EDWARD: Who's there? Convey this priest to the   *200*
    Tower.

BISHOP OF COVENTRY: True, true.

KING EDWARD: But, in the meantime, Gaveston, away,
And take possession of his house and goods.

188 *channel*: gutter.
198 *the Fleet*: prison near Fleet Street.
201 *True, true*: sarcasm, recognizing the double meaning of
'convey', Elizabethan slang for 'steal'.

Come, follow me, and thou shalt have my guard
To see it done, and bring thee safe again.

GAVESTON: What should a priest do with so fair a
house?
A prison may beseem his holiness.
Exeunt.

SCENE TWO

Near the King's Palace.
Enter, on one side, the ELDER *and the* YOUNGER
MORTIMER; *on the other,* WARWICK, *and*
LANCASTER.

WARWICK: 'Tis true, the bishop is in the Tower,
And goods and body given to Gaveston.

LANCASTER: What, will they tyrannize upon the
Church?
Ah, wicked king! accursed Gaveston!
This ground, which is corrupted with their steps,
Shall be their timeless sepulchre or mine.

YOUNGER MORTIMER: Well, let that peevish
Frenchman guard him sure:
Unless his breast be sword-proof, he shall die.

ELDER MORTIMER: How now! why droops the Earl of
Lancaster?

10 YOUNGER MORTIMER: Wherefore is Guy of Warwick
discontent?

LANCASTER: That villain Gaveston is made an earl.

ELDER MORTIMER: An earl!

WARWICK: Ay, and besides Lord Chamberlain of the
realm,
And Secretary too, and Lord of Man.

ELDER MORTIMER: We may not nor we will not suffer
this.

YOUNGER MORTIMER: Why post we not from hence to
levy men?

LANCASTER: 'My Lord of Cornwall' now at every word!
And happy is the man whom he vouchsafes,
For vailing of his bonnet, one good look.
Thus, arm in arm, the king and he doth march: 20
Nay, more, the guard upon his lordship waits,
And all the court begins to flatter him.

WARWICK: Thus leaning on the shoulder of the king,
He nods, and scorns, and smiles at those that pass.

ELDER MORTIMER: Doth no man take exceptions at the
slave?

LANCASTER: All stomach him, but none dare speak a
word.

YOUNGER MORTIMER: Ah, that bewrays their baseness,
Lancaster!
Were all the earls and barons of my mind,
We'll hale him from the bosom of the king,
And at the court-gate hang the peasant up,   30
Who, swoln with venom of ambitious pride,
Will be the ruin of the realm and us.

WARWICK: Here comes my Lord of Canterbury's grace.

LANCASTER: His countenance bewrays he is displeas'd.

Enter the ARCHBISHOP OF CANTERBURY, *and an*
ATTENDANT.

ARCHBISHOP OF CANTERBURY: First were his sacred
garments rent and torn;
Then laid they violent hands upon him; next,
Himself imprison'd, and his goods asseiz'd.
This certify the Pope: away, take horse.

Exit ATTENDANT.

LANCASTER: My lord, will you take arms against the
king?

ARCHBISHOP OF CANTERBURY: What need I? God   40
himself is up in arms
When violence is offer'd to the Church.

YOUNGER MORTIMER: Then will you join with us, that
be his peers,

19 *vailing*: taking off.

To banish or behead that Gaveston?

ARCHBISHOP OF CANTERBURY: What else, my lords?
for it concerns me near;
The bishopric of Coventry is his.
Enter QUEEN ISABELLA.

YOUNGER MORTIMER: Madam, whither walks your
majesty so fast?

QUEEN ISABELLA: Unto the forest, gentle Mortimer,
To live in grief and baleful discontent;
For now my lord the king regards me not,
50 But dotes upon the love of Gaveston.
He claps his cheeks, and hangs about his neck,
Smiles in his face, and whispers in his ears;
And, when I come, he frowns, as who should say,
'Go whither thou wilt, seeing I have Gaveston.'

ELDER MORTIMER: Is it not strange that he is thus
bewitch'd?

YOUNGER MORTIMER: Madam, return unto the court
again:
That sly inveigling Frenchman we'll exile,
Or lose our lives; and yet, ere that day come,
The king shall lose his crown; for we have power,
60 And courage too, to be reveng'd at full.

ARCHBISHOP OF CANTERBURY: But yet lift not your
swords against the king.

LANCASTER: No; but we'll lift Gaveston from hence.

WARWICK: And war must be the means, or he'll stay still.

QUEEN ISABELLA: Then let him stay; for, rather than
my lord
Shall be oppress'd by civil mutinies,
I will endure a melancholy life,
And let him frolic with his minion.

ARCHBISHOP OF CANTERBURY: My lords, to ease all
this, but hear me speak:
We and the rest, that are his counsellors,
70 Will meet, and with a general consent
Confirm his banishment with our hands and seals.

LANCASTER: What we confirm the king will frustrate.

YOUNGER MORTIMER: Then may we lawfully revolt
from him.

WARWICK: But say, my lord, where shall this meeting
be?

ARCHBISHOP OF CANTERBURY: At the New Temple.[5]

YOUNGER MORTIMER: Content.

ARCHBISHOP OF CANTERBURY: And, in the
meantime, I'll entreat you all
To cross to Lambeth, and there stay with me.

LANCASTER: Come, then, let's away.

YOUNGER MORTIMER: Madam, farewell.   80

QUEEN ISABELLA: Farewell, sweet Mortimer; and, for
my sake,
Forbear to levy arms against the king.

YOUNGER MORTIMER: Ay, if words will serve; if not,
I must.
Exeunt.

SCENE THREE

A street in London.
Enter GAVESTON *and* KENT.

GAVESTON: Edmund, the mighty prince of Lancaster,
That hath more earldoms than an ass can bear,
And both the Mortimers, two goodly men,
With Guy of Warwick, that redoubted knight,
Are gone towards Lambeth: there let them remain.
Exeunt.

SCENE FOUR

The New Temple.
Enter LANCASTER, WARWICK, PEMBROKE,
the ELDER MORTIMER, *the* YOUNGER
MORTIMER, *the* ARCHBISHOP OF CANTERBURY,
and ATTENDANTS.

LANCASTER: Here is the form of Gaveston's exile.
May it please your lordship to subscribe your name.

ARCHBISHOP OF CANTERBURY: Give me the paper.

He subscribes, as the others do after him.

LANCASTER: Quick, quick, my lord; I long to write my name.

WARWICK: But I long more to see him banish'd hence.

YOUNGER MORTIMER: The name of Mortimer shall fright the king,
Unless he be declin'd from that base peasant.

Enter KING EDWARD, GAVESTON, *and* KENT.

KING EDWARD: What, are you mov'd that Gaveston sits here?
It is our pleasure; we will have it so.

10 LANCASTER: Your grace doth well to place him by your side,
For nowhere else the new earl is so safe.

ELDER MORTIMER: What man of noble birth can brook this sight?
Quam male conveniunt!
See what a scornful look the peasant casts!

PEMBROKE: Can kingly lions fawn on creeping ants?

WARWICK: Ignoble vassal, that, like Phaeton,
Aspir'st unto the guidance of the sun!

YOUNGER MORTIMER: Their downfall is at hand, their forces down:
We will not thus be fac'd and over-peer'd.

20 KING EDWARD: Lay hands on that traitor Mortimer!

ELDER MORTIMER: Lay hands on that traitor Gaveston!

KENT: Is this the duty that you owe your king?

WARWICK: We know our duties, let him know his peers.

KING EDWARD: Whither will you bear him? Stay, or ye shall die!

ELDER MORTIMER: We are no traitors, therefore threaten not.

13 *Quam male conveniunt!*: How ill-matched they are!

GAVESTON: No, threaten not, my lord, but pay them
    home!
  Were I a king –

YOUNGER MORTIMER: Thou, villain! wherefore talk'st
    of a king,
  That hardly art a gentleman by birth?

KING EDWARD: Were he a peasant, being my minion,   *30*
  I'll make the proudest of you stoop to him.

LANCASTER: My lord, you may not thus disparage us.
  Away, I say, with hateful Gaveston!

ELDER MORTIMER: And with the Earl of Kent that
    favours him.

    ATTENDANTS *remove* GAVESTON *and* KENT.

KING EDWARD: Nay, then, lay violent hands upon
    your king!
  Here, Mortimer, sit thou in Edward's throne;
  Warwick and Lancaster, wear you my crown.
  Was ever king thus over-rul'd as I?

LANCASTER: Learn, then, to rule us better, and the
    realm.

YOUNGER MORTIMER: What we have done, our heart-   *40*
    blood shall maintain.

WARWICK: Think you that we can brook this upstart
    pride?

KING EDWARD: Anger and wrathful fury stops my
    speech.

ARCHBISHOP OF CANTERBURY: Why are you mov'd?
    Be patient, my lord,
  And see what we your counsellors have done.

YOUNGER MORTIMER: My lords, now let us all be
    resolute,
  And either have our wills, or lose our lives.

KING EDWARD: Meet you for this, proud over-daring
    peers?
  Ere my sweet Gaveston shall part from me,
  This isle shall fleet upon the ocean,
  And wander to the unfrequented Inde.   *50*

ARCHBISHOP OF CANTERBURY: You know that I am
    legate to the Pope:
On your allegiance to the see of Rome,
Subscribe, as we have done, to his exile.

YOUNGER MORTIMER: Curse him, if he refuse; and
    then may we
Depose him, and elect another king.

KING EDWARD: Ay, there it goes! But yet I will not yield:
Curse me! Depose me! Do the worst you can!

LANCASTER: Then linger not, my lord, but do it
    straight.

ARCHBISHOP OF CANTERBURY: Remember how the
    bishop was abus'd:

60   Either banish him that was the cause thereof,
Or I will presently discharge these lords
Of duty and allegiance due to thee.

KING EDWARD (*aside*): It boots me not to threat; I
    must speak fair:
The legate of the Pope will be obey'd.
(*Aloud*) My lord, you shall be Chancellor of the realm;
Thou, Lancaster, High Admiral of our fleet;
Young Mortimer and his uncle shall be earls;
And you, Lord Warwick, President of the North;
And thou of Wales. If this content you not,

70   Make several kingdoms of this monarchy,
And share it equally amongst you all,
So I may have some nook or corner left,
To frolic with my dearest Gaveston.

ARCHBISHOP OF CANTERBURY: Nothing shall alter
    us; we are resolv'd.

LANCASTER: Come, come, subscribe.

YOUNGER MORTIMER: Why should you love him whom
    the world hates so?

KING EDWARD: Because he loves me more than all the
    world.
Ah, none but rude and savage-minded men
Would seek the ruin of my Gaveston!

You that be noble-born should pity him.   *80*

WARWICK: You that are princely-born should shake
    him off:

For shame, subscribe, and let the lown depart.

ELDER MORTIMER: Urge him, my lord.

ARCHBISHOP OF CANTERBURY: Are you content to
    banish him the realm?

KING EDWARD: I see I must, and therefore am
    content:

Instead of ink, I'll write it with my tears.
    Subscribes.

YOUNGER MORTIMER: The king is love-sick for his
    minion.

KING EDWARD: 'Tis done: and now, accursed hand,
    fall off!

LANCASTER: Give it me: I'll have it publish'd in the
    streets.

YOUNGER MORTIMER: I'll see him presently despatch'd   *90*
    away.

ARCHBISHOP OF CANTERBURY: Now is my heart at
    ease.

WARWICK: And so is mine.

PEMBROKE: This will be good news to the common sort.

ELDER MORTIMER: Be it or no, he shall not linger here.
    Exeunt all except KING EDWARD.

KING EDWARD: How fast they run to banish him I
    love!

They would not stir, were it to do me good.

Why should a king be subject to a priest?

Proud Rome, that hatchest such imperial grooms,

For these thy superstitious taper-lights,

Wherewith thy antichristian churches blaze,   *100*

I'll fire thy crazed buildings, and enforce

The papal towers to kiss the lowly ground,

With slaughter'd priests make Tiber's channel swell,

And banks rais'd higher with their sepulchres!

82 *lown*: peasant, clod.

As for the peers, that back the clergy thus,
If I be king, not one of them shall live.
   Re-enter GAVESTON.

GAVESTON: My lord, I hear it whisper'd everywhere,
That I am banish'd and must fly the land.

KING EDWARD: 'Tis true, sweet Gaveston: O, were
   it false!
110 The legate of the Pope will have it so,
And thou must hence, or I shall be depos'd.
But I will reign to be reveng'd of them;
And therefore, sweet friend, take it patiently.
Live where thou wilt, I'll send thee gold enough;
And long thou shalt not stay, or, if thou dost,
I'll come to thee; my love shall ne'er decline.

GAVESTON: Is all my hope turn'd to this hell of grief?

KING EDWARD: Rend not my heart with thy too-
   piercing words.
Thou from this land, I from myself am banish'd.

120 GAVESTON: To go from hence grieves not poor
   Gaveston;
But to forsake you, in whose gracious looks
The blessedness of Gaveston remains;
For nowhere else seeks he felicity.

KING EDWARD: And only this torments my wretched
   soul,
That, whether I will or no, thou must depart.
Be Governor of Ireland in my stead,
And there abide till fortune call thee home.
Here, take my picture, and let me wear thine:
   They exchange pictures.
O, might I keep thee here, as I do this,
130 Happy were I! but now most miserable.

GAVESTON: 'Tis something to be pitied of a king.

KING EDWARD: Thou shalt not hence; I'll hide thee,
   Gaveston.

GAVESTON: I shall be found, and then 'twill grieve me
   more.

KING EDWARD: Kind words and mutual talk makes
    our grief greater:
Therefore, with dumb embracement, let us part.
Stay, Gaveston; I cannot leave thee thus.
GAVESTON: For every look, my lord, drops down a
    tear.
Seeing I must go, do not renew my sorrow.
KING EDWARD: The time is little that thou hast to stay,
And, therefore, give me leave to look my fill.   *140*
But, come, sweet friend; I'll bear thee on thy way.
GAVESTON: The peers will frown.
KING EDWARD: I pass not for their anger. Come, let's
    go:
O, that we might as well return as go!
    Enter QUEEN ISABELLA.
QUEEN ISABELLA: Whither goes my lord?
KING EDWARD: Fawn not on me, French strumpet; get
    thee gone!
QUEEN ISABELLA: On whom but on my husband
    should I fawn?
GAVESTON: On Mortimer; with whom, ungentle
    queen, –
I say no more – judge you the rest, my lord.
QUEEN ISABELLA: In saying this, thou wrong'st me,   *150*
    Gaveston.
Is't not enough that thou corrupt'st my lord,
And art a bawd to his affections,
But thou must call mine honour thus in question?
GAVESTON: I mean not so; your grace must pardon me.
KING EDWARD: Thou art too familiar with that
    Mortimer,
And by thy means is Gaveston exil'd.
But I would wish thee reconcile the lords,
Or thou shalt ne'er be reconcil'd to me.
QUEEN ISABELLA: Your highness knows, it lies not in
    my power.
    143 *pass*: care.

451

160   KING EDWARD: Away, then! touch me not. – Come,
     Gaveston.

  QUEEN ISABELLA: Villain, 'tis thou that robb'st me of
     my lord.

  GAVESTON: Madam, 'tis you that rob me of my lord.

  KING EDWARD: Speak not unto her: let her droop and
     pine.

  QUEEN ISABELLA: Wherein, my lord, have I deserv'd
     these words?

     Witness the tears that Isabella sheds,

     Witness this heart, that, sighing for thee, breaks,

     How dear my lord is to poor Isabel!

  KING EDWARD: And witness heaven how dear thou
     art to me.

     There weep; for, till my Gaveston be repeal'd,

170   Assure thyself thou com'st not in my sight.

     Exeunt KING EDWARD *and* GAVESTON.

  QUEEN ISABELLA: O miserable and distressed queen!

     Would, when I left sweet France, and was embarked,

     That charming Circe, walking on the waves,

     Had chang'd my shape! or at the marriage-day

     The cup of Hymen had been full of poison!

     Or with those arms, that twin'd about my neck,

     I had been stifled, and not liv'd to see

     The king my lord thus abandon me!

     Like frantic Juno will I fill the earth

180   With ghastly murmur of my sighs and cries;

     For never doted Jove on Ganymede

     So much as he on cursed Gaveston.

     But that will more exasperate his wrath;

     I must entreat him, I must speak him fair,

     And be a means to call home Gaveston.

     And yet he'll ever dote on Gaveston;

     And so am I for ever miserable.

     Re-enter LANCASTER, WARWICK, PEMBROKE,
     the ELDER *and the* YOUNGER MORTIMER.

  LANCASTER: Look, where the sister of the king of France

Sits wringing of her hands and beats her breast!

WARWICK: The king, I fear, hath ill entreated her. 190

PEMBROKE: Hard is the heart that injures such a saint.

YOUNGER MORTIMER: I know 'tis 'long of Gaveston
she weeps.

ELDER MORTIMER: Why? He is gone.

YOUNGER MORTIMER: Madam, how fares your grace?

QUEEN ISABELLA: Ah, Mortimer, now breaks the
king's hate forth,
And he confesseth that he loves me not!

YOUNGER MORTIMER: Cry quittance, madam, then,
and love not him.

QUEEN ISABELLA: No, rather will I die a thousand
deaths.
And yet I love in vain; he'll ne'er love me.

LANCASTER: Fear ye not, madam; now his minion's 200
gone,
His wanton humour will be quickly left.

QUEEN ISABELLA: O, never, Lancaster! I am enjoin'd
To sue unto you all for his repeal:
This wills my lord, and this must I perform,
Or else be banish'd from his highness' presence.

LANCASTER: For his repeal, madam? He comes not
back,
Unless the sea cast up his shipwrack'd body.

WARWICK: And to behold so sweet a sight as that,
There's none here but would run his horse to death.

YOUNGER MORTIMER: But, madam, would you have us 210
call him home?

QUEEN ISABELLA: Ay, Mortimer, for, till he be restor'd,
The angry king hath banish'd me the court;
And, therefore, as thou lov'st and tender'st me,
Be thou my advocate unto these peers.

YOUNGER MORTIMER: What, would you have me plead
for Gaveston?

ELDER MORTIMER: Plead for him he that will, I am
resolv'd.

LANCASTER: And so am I, my lord: dissuade the queen.

QUEEN ISABELLA: O, Lancaster, let him dissuade the king!

For 'tis against my will he should return.

220 WARWICK: Then speak not for him; let the peasant go.

QUEEN ISABELLA: 'Tis for myself I speak, and not for him.

PEMBROKE: No speaking will prevail, and therefore cease.

YOUNGER MORTIMER: Fair queen, forbear to angle for the fish

Which, being caught, strikes him that takes it dead;

I mean that vile torpedo, Gaveston,

That now, I hope, floats on the Irish seas.

QUEEN ISABELLA: Sweet Mortimer, sit down by me a while,

And I will tell thee reasons of such weight

As thou wilt soon subscribe to his repeal.

230 YOUNGER MORTIMER: It is impossible: but speak your mind.

QUEEN ISABELLA: Then thus; – but none shall hear it but ourselves.

Talks to YOUNGER MORTIMER *apart.*

LANCASTER: My lords, albeit the queen win Mortimer,

Will you be resolute and hold with me?

ELDER MORTIMER: Not I, against my nephew.

PEMBROKE: Fear not; the queen's words cannot alter him.

WARWICK: No? Do but mark how earnestly she pleads!

LANCASTER: And see how coldly his looks make denial!

WARWICK: She smiles. Now, for my life, his mind is chang'd!

LANCASTER: I'll rather lose his friendship, I, than grant.

240 YOUNGER MORTIMER: Well, of necessity it must be so.

My lords, that I abhor base Gaveston

I hope your honours make no question,

225: *torpedo*: electric ray fish.

And therefore, though I plead for his repeal,
'Tis not for his sake, but for our avail,
Nay, for the realm's behoof, and for the king's.

LANCASTER: Fie, Mortimer, dishonour not thyself!
Can this be true, 'twas good to banish him?
And is this true, to call him home again?
Such reasons make white black, and dark night day.

YOUNGER MORTIMER: My lord of Lancaster, mark the   250
respect.

LANCASTER: In no respect can contraries be true.

QUEEN ISABELLA: Yet, good my lord, hear what he can
allege.

WARWICK: All that he speaks is nothing. We are
resolv'd.

YOUNGER MORTIMER: Do you not wish that Gaveston
were dead?

PEMBROKE: I would he were!

YOUNGER MORTIMER: Why, then, my lord, give me
but leave to speak.

ELDER MORTIMER: But, nephew, do not play the
sophister.

YOUNGER MORTIMER: This which I urge is of a
burning zeal
To mend the king and do our country good.
Know you not Gaveston hath store of gold,   260
Which may in Ireland purchase him such friends
As he will front the mightiest of us all?
And whereas he shall live and be belov'd,
'Tis hard for us to work his overthrow.

WARWICK: Mark you but that, my lord of Lancaster.

YOUNGER MORTIMER: But, were he here, detested as
he is,
How easily might some base slave be suborn'd
To greet his lordship with a poniard,
And none so much as blame the murderer,
But rather praise him for that brave attempt,   270
And in the chronicle enrol his name

455

For purging of the realm of such a plague!

PEMBROKE: He saith true.

LANCASTER: Ay, but how chance this was not done
before?

YOUNGER MORTIMER: Because, my lords, it was not
thought upon.
Nay, more, when he shall know it lies in us
To banish him, and then to call him home,
'Twill make him vail the top-flag of his pride,
And fear to offend the meanest nobleman.

280 ELDER MORTIMER: But how if he do not, nephew?

YOUNGER MORTIMER: Then may we with some colour
rise in arms;
For, howsoever we have borne it out,
'Tis treason to be up against the king;
So shall we have the people of our side,
Which, for his father's sake, lean to the king,
But cannot brook a night-grown mushrump,
Such a one as my Lord of Cornwall is,
Should bear us down of the nobility.
And, when the commons and the nobles join,

290 'Tis not the king can buckler Gaveston;
We'll pull him from the strongest hold he hath.
My lords, if to perform this I be slack,
Think me as base a groom as Gaveston.

LANCASTER: On that condition, Lancaster will grant.

WARWICK: And so will Pembroke and I.

ELDER MORTIMER: And I.

YOUNGER MORTIMER: In this I count me highly
gratified,
And Mortimer will rest at your command.

QUEEN ISABELLA: And when this favour Isabel
forgets,

300 Then let her live abandon'd and forlorn.
But see, in happy time, my lord the king,
Having brought the Earl of Cornwall on his way,

281 *colour*: reason, excuse.   290 *buckler*: protect.

Is new return'd. This news will glad him much:
Yet not so much as me; I love him more
Than he can Gaveston. Would he lov'd me
But half so much! Then were I treble-blest.
      Re-enter KING EDWARD, *mourning.*

KING EDWARD: He's gone, and for his absence thus I
      mourn:
Did never sorrow go so near my heart
As doth the want of my sweet Gaveston;
And, could my crown's revenue bring him back,   310
I would freely give it to his enemies,
And think I gain'd, having bought so dear a friend.

QUEEN ISABELLA: Hark, how he harps upon his
      minion!

KING EDWARD: My heart is as an anvil unto sorrow,
Which beats upon it like the Cyclops' hammers,[6]
And with the noise turns up my giddy brain.
And makes me frantic for my Gaveston.
Ah, had some bloodless Fury rose from hell,
And with my kingly sceptre struck me dead,
When I was forc'd to leave my Gaveston!   320

LANCASTER: *Diablo*, what passions call you these?

QUEEN ISABELLA: My gracious lord, I come to bring
      you news.

KING EDWARD: That you have parled with your
      Mortimer?

QUEEN ISABELLA: That Gaveston, my lord, shall be
      repeal'd.

KING EDWARD: Repeal'd! The news is too sweet to be
      true.

QUEEN ISABELLA: But will you love me, if you find it so?

KING EDWARD: If it be so, what will not Edward do?

QUEEN ISABELLA: For Gaveston, but not for Isabel.

KING EDWARD: For thee, fair queen, if thou lov'st
      Gaveston,
I'll hang a golden tongue about thy neck,   330
Seeing thou hast pleaded with so good success.

QUEEN ISABELLA: No jewels hang about my neck
   Than these, my lord; nor let me have more wealth
   Than I may fetch from this rich treasury.
   O, how a kiss revives poor Isabel!

KING EDWARD: Once more receive my hand, and let
   this be
   A second marriage 'twixt thyself and me.

QUEEN ISABELLA: And may it prove more happy
   than the first!
   My gentle lord, bespeak these nobles fair,
340   That wait attendance for a gracious look,
   And on their knees salute your majesty.

KING EDWARD: Courageous Lancaster, embrace thy
   king;
   And, as gross vapours perish by the sun,
   Even so let hatred with thy sovereign's smile:
   Live thou with me as my companion.

LANCASTER: This salutation overjoys my heart.

KING EDWARD: Warwick shall be my chiefest
   counsellor:
   These silver hairs will more adorn my court
   Than gaudy silks or rich embroidery.
350   Chide me, sweet Warwick, if I go astray.

WARWICK: Slay me, my lord, when I offend your grace.

KING EDWARD: In solemn triumphs and in public
   shows
   Pembroke shall bear the sword before the king.

PEMBROKE: And with this sword Pembroke will fight
   for you.

KING EDWARD: But wherefore walks young Mortimer
   aside?
   Be thou commander of our royal fleet;
   Or, if that lofty office like thee not,
   I make thee here Lord Marshal of the realm.

YOUNGER MORTIMER: My lord, I'll marshal so your
   enemies,
360   As England shall be quiet, and you safe.

KING EDWARD: And as for you, Lord Mortimer of
    Chirke,
  Whose great achievements in our foreign war
  Deserve no common place nor mean reward,
  Be you the general of the levied troops
  That now are ready to assail the Scots.

ELDER MORTIMER: In this your grace hath highly
    honour'd me,
  For with my nature war doth best agree.

QUEEN ISABELLA: Now is the king of England rich
    and strong,
  Having the love of his renowned peers.

KING EDWARD: Ay, Isabel, ne'er was my heart so light.   *370*
  Clerk of the crown, direct our warrant forth,
  For Gaveston, to Ireland!
    Enter BEAUMONT *with warrant.*
                          Beaumont, fly
  As fast as Iris or Jove's Mercury.

BEAUMONT: It shall be done, my gracious lord.
    Exit.

KING EDWARD: Lord Mortimer, we leave you to your
    charge.
  Now let us in, and feast it royally.
  Against our friend the Earl of Cornwall comes
  We'll have a general tilt and tournament,
  And then his marriage shall be solemnis'd;
  For wot you not that I have made him sure   *380*
  Unto our cousin, the Earl of Gloucester's heir?

LANCASTER: Such news we hear, my lord.

KING EDWARD: That day, if not for him, yet for my
    sake,
  Who in the triumph will be challenger,
  Spare for no cost. We will requite your love.

WARWICK: In this or aught your highness shall command
    us.

373 *Iris*: Juno's messenger.
377 *Against*: until, in preparation for.

KING EDWARD: Thanks, gentle Warwick. Come, let's in
and revel.
Exeunt all except the ELDER *and the* YOUNGER
MORTIMER.

ELDER MORTIMER: Nephew, I must to Scotland; thou
stay'st here.

Leave now to oppose thyself against the king.

390 Thou seest by nature he is mild and calm;
And, seeing his mind so dotes on Gaveston,
Let him without controlment have his will.
The mightiest kings have had their minions;
Great Alexander lov'd Hephaestion,
The conquering Hercules[7] for Hylas wept,
And for Patroclus stern Achilles droop'd.
And not kings only, but the wisest men;
The Roman Tully lov'd Octavius,
Grave Socrates wild Alcibiades.

400 Then let his grace, whose youth is flexible,
And promiseth as much as we can wish,
Freely enjoy that vain light-headed earl,
For riper years will wean him from such toys.

YOUNGER MORTIMER: Uncle, his wanton humour
grieves not me;
But this I scorn, that one so basely born
Should by his sovereign's favour grow so pert,
And riot it with the treasure of the realm,
While soldiers mutiny for want of pay.
He wears a lord's revenue on his back,

410 And, Midas-like, he jets it in the court,
With base outlandish cullions at his heels,
Whose proud fantastic liveries make such show
As if that Proteus, god of shapes, appear'd.
I have not seen a dapper Jack so brisk.
He wears a short Italian hooded cloak,
Larded with pearl, and in his Tuscan cap
A jewel of more value than the crown.

410 *jets*: struts.   411 *outlandish*: foreign.

Whiles other walk below, the king and he
From out a window laugh at such as we,
And flout our train, and jest at our attire.   420
Uncle, 'tis this that makes me impatient.
ELDER MORTIMER: But, nephew, now you see the king
    is chang'd.
YOUNGER MORTIMER: Then so am I, and live to do
    him service.
But, whiles I have a sword, a hand, a heart,
I will not yield to any such upstart.
You know my mind: come, uncle, let's away.
    Exeunt.

ACT TWO

SCENE ONE

A hall in Gloucester's house.
Enter the YOUNGER SPENSER *and* BALDOCK.
BALDOCK: Spenser,
    Seeing that our lord the Earl of Gloucester's dead,
    Which of the nobles dost thou mean to serve?
YOUNGER SPENSER: Not Mortimer, nor any of his
    side,
Because the king and he are enemies.
Baldock, learn this of me: a factious lord
Shall hardly do himself good, much less us;
But he that hath the favour of a king
May with one word advance us while we live.
The liberal Earl of Cornwall is the man
On whose good fortune Spenser's hope depends.   10
BALDOCK: What, mean you then to be his follower?
YOUNGER SPENSER: No, his companion; for he loves
    me well,
And would have once preferr'd me to the king.
13 *preferr'd*: recommended.

BALDOCK: But he is banish'd; there's small hope of him.

YOUNGER SPENSER: Ay, for a while, but, Baldock,
    mark the end.
A friend of mine told me in secrecy
That he's repeal'd and sent for back again;
And even now a post came from the court
With letters to our lady from the king,
20   And, as she read, she smil'd; which makes me think
It is about her lover Gaveston.

BALDOCK: 'Tis like enough; for, since he was exil'd,
She neither walks abroad nor comes in sight.
But I had thought the match had been broke off,
And that his banishment had chang'd her mind.

YOUNGER SPENSER: Our lady's first love is not
    wavering.
My life for thine, she will have Gaveston.

BALDOCK: Then hope I by her means to be preferr'd,
Having read unto her since she was a child.

30 YOUNGER SPENSER: Then, Baldock, you must cast the
    scholar off,
And learn to court it like a gentleman.
'Tis not a black coat and a little band,
A velvet-cap'd cloak, fac'd before with serge,
And smelling to a nosegay all the day,
Or holding of a napkin in your hand,
Or saying a long grace at a table's end,
Or making low legs to a nobleman,
Or looking downward, with your eyelids close,
And saying, 'Truly, an't may please your honour,'
40   Can get you any favour with great men.
You must be proud, bold, pleasant, resolute,
And now and then stab, as occasion serves.

BALDOCK: Spenser, thou know'st I hate such formal
    toys,
And use them but of mere hypocrisy.
Mine old lord, whiles he liv'd, was so precise,
That he would take exceptions at my buttons,

And, being like pins' heads, blame me for the bigness;
Which made me curate-like in mine attire,
Though inwardly licentious enough,
And apt for any kind of villainy.   *10*
I am none of these common pedants, I,
That cannot speak without *propterea quod.*[8]

YOUNGER SPENSER: But one of those that saith
   qua doquidem,
And hath a special gift to form a verb.

BALDOCK: Leave off this jesting; here my lady comes.
   Enter KING EDWARD'S NIECE.

NIECE: The grief for his exile was not so much
As is the joy of his returning home.
This letter came from my sweet Gaveston:
What need'st thou, love, thus to excuse thyself?
I know thou couldst not come and visit me.   *60*
(*Reads*) *I will not long be from thee, though I die;* –
This argues the entire love of my lord; –
(*Reads*) *When I forsake thee, death seize on my heart!*
But rest thee here where Gaveston shall sleep.
   Puts the letter into her bosom.
Now to the letter of my lord the king:
He wills me to repair unto the court,
And meet my Gaveston. Why do I stay,
Seeing that he talks thus of my marriage day?
Who's there? Baldock!
See that my coach be ready; I must hence.   *70*

BALDOCK: It shall be done, madam.

NIECE: And meet me at the park-pale presently.
   Exit BALDOCK.
Spenser, stay you, and bear me company,
For I have joyful news to tell thee of.
My lord of Cornwall is a-coming over,
And will be at the court as soon as we.

YOUNGER SPENSER: I knew the king would have him
   home again.

NIECE: If all things sort out, as I hope they will,

Thy service, Spenser, shall be thought upon.

80 YOUNGER SPENSER: I humbly thank your ladyship.

NIECE: Come, lead the way: I long till I am there.

Exeunt.

SCENE TWO

Before Tynemouth Castle.

Enter KING EDWARD, QUEEN ISABELLA, KENT,
LANCASTER, *the* YOUNGER MORTIMER,
WARWICK, PEMBROKE, *and* ATTENDANTS.

KING EDWARD: The wind is good; I wonder why he stays:

I fear me he is wrack'd upon the sea.

QUEEN ISABELLA: Look, Lancaster, how passionate he is,

And still his mind runs on his minion!

LANCASTER: My lord, –

KING EDWARD: How now! what news? Is Gaveston arriv'd?

YOUNGER MORTIMER: Nothing but Gaveston! What m ans our grace?

You have matt rs of more weight to think upon:

The King of France sets foot in Normandy.

10 KING EDWARD: A trifle! We'll expel him when we please.

But tell me, Mortimer, what's thy device

Against the stately triumph we decreed?

YOUNGER MORTIMER: A homely one, my lord, not worth the telling.

KING EDWARD: Prithee, let me know it.

YOUNGER MORTIMER: But, seeing you are so desirous, thus it is:

A lofty cedar tree, fair flourishing,

11 *device*: symbolic design or text painted on a shield.
12 *Against*: for the occasion of.

On whose top branches kingly eagles perch,
And by the bark a canker creeps me up,
And gets unto the highest bough of all;
The motto, *Æque tandem*.   20

KING EDWARD: And what is yours, my Lord of
    Lancaster?

LANCASTER: My lord, mine's more obscure than
    Mortimer's.
Pliny reports, there is a flying-fish
Which all the other fishes deadly hate,
And therefore, being pursu'd, it takes the air.
No sooner is it up, but there's a fowl
That seizeth it: this fish, my lord, I bear.
The motto this, *Undique mors est*.

KENT: Proud Mortimer! Ungentle Lancaster!
Is this the love you bear your sovereign?   30
Is this the fruit your reconcilement bears?
Can you in words make show of amity,
And in your shields display your rancorous minds?
What call you this but private libelling
Against the Earl of Cornwall and my brother?

QUEEN ISABELLA: Sweet husband, be content; they all
    love you.

KING EDWARD: They love me not that hate my
    Gaveston.
I am that cedar; shake me not too much;
And you the eagles, soar ye ne'er so high,
I have the jesses that will pull you down;   40
And *Æque tandem* shall that canker cry
Unto the proudest peer of Britainy.
Thou that compar'st him to a flying-fish,
And threaten'st death whether he rise or fall,
'Tis not the hugest monster of the sea,

20 *Aeque tandem*: equally at length (the parasite is as high as the tree itself).
28 *Undique mors est*: death is everywhere.
40 *jesses*: straps attached to a trained hawk.

Nor foulest harpy, that shall swallow him.

YOUNGER MORTIMER: If in his absence thus he
favours him,
What will he do whenas he shall be present?

LANCASTER: That shall we see: look, where his lordship
comes!

Enter GAVESTON.

50 KING EDWARD: My Gaveston!
Welcome to Tynemouth! Welcome to thy friend!
Thy absence made me droop and pine away,
For, as the lovers of fair Danaë,
When she was lock'd up in a brazen tower,
Desir'd her more, and wax'd outrageous,
So did it sure with me; and now thy sight
Is sweeter far than was thy parting hence
Bitter and irksome to my sobbing heart.

GAVESTON: Sweet lord and king, your speech
preventeth mine;
60 Yet have I words left to express my joy.
The shepherd, nipt with biting winter's rage,
Frolics not more to see the painted spring
Than I do to behold your majesty.

KING EDWARD: Will none of you salute my Gaveston?

LANCASTER: Salute him! Yes. Welcome, Lord Chamberlain!

YOUNGER MORTIMER: Welcome is the good Earl of
Cornwall!

WARWICK: Welcome, Lord Governor of the Isle of
Man!

PEMBROKE: Welcome, Master Secretary!

KENT: Brother, do you hear them?

70 KING EDWARD: Still will these earls and barons use me
thus?

GAVESTON: My lord, I cannot brook these injuries.

QUEEN ISABELLA (*aside*): Ay me, poor soul, when these
begin to jar!

59 *preventeth*: anticipates.

466

KING EDWARD: Return it to their throats; I'll be thy
warrant.

GAVESTON: Base, leaden earls, that glory in your birth,
Go sit at home, and eat your tenants' beef,
And come not here to scoff at Gaveston,
Whose mounting thoughts did never creep so low
As to bestow a look on such as you.

LANCASTER: Yet I disdain not to do this for you.
Draws his sword.

KING EDWARD: Treason! treason! where's the traitor? *80*

PEMBROKE: Here, here!

KING EDWARD: Convey hence Gaveston; they'll
murder him.

GAVESTON: The life of thee shall salve this foul disgrace.

YOUNGER MORTIMER: Villain, thy life! unless I miss
mine aim.
Wounds GAVESTON.

QUEEN ISABELLA: Ah, furious Mortimer, what hast
thou done?

YOUNGER MORTIMER: No more than I would answer,
were he slain.
Exit GAVESTON *with* ATTENDANTS.

KING EDWARD: Yes, more than thou canst answer,
though he live!
Dear shall you both aby this riotous deed:
Out of my presence! Come not near the court.

YOUNGER MORTIMER: I'll not be barr'd the court for *90*
Gaveston.

LANCASTER: We'll hale him by the ears unto the block.

KING EDWARD: Look to your own heads; his is sure
enough.

WARWICK: Look to your own crown, if you back him
thus.

KENT: Warwick, these words do ill beseem thy years.

KING EDWARD: Nay, all of them conspire to cross
me thus:

88 *aby*: 'abide', pay for.

But, if I live, I'll tread upon their heads
That think with high looks thus to tread me down.
Come, Edmund, let's away and levy men.
'Tis war that must abate these barons' pride.

Exeunt KING EDWARD, QUEEN ISABELLA, *and*
KENT.

100 WARWICK: Let's to our castles, for the king is mov'd.

YOUNGER MORTIMER: Mov'd may he be, and perish in
his wrath!

LANCASTER: Cousin, it is no dealing with him now;
He means to make us stoop by force of arms.
And therefore let us jointly here protest
To prosecute that Gaveston to the death.

YOUNGER MORTIMER: By heaven, the abject villain
shall not live!

WARWICK: I'll have his blood, or die in seeking it.

PEMBROKE: The like oath Pembroke takes.

LANCASTER: And so doth Lancaster.

110 Now send our heralds to defy the king,
And make the people swear to put him down.

Enter a MESSENGER.

YOUNGER MORTIMER: Letters! From whence?

MESSENGER: From Scotland, my lord.

Giving letters to MORTIMER.

LANCASTER: Why, how now, cousin! How fares all our
friends?

YOUNGER MORTIMER: My uncle's taken prisoner by
the Scots.

LANCASTER: We'll have him ransom'd, man: be of good
cheer.

YOUNGER MORTIMER: They rate his ransom at five
thousand pound.
Who should defray the money but the king,
Seeing he is taken prisoner in his wars?

120 I'll to the king.

LANCASTER: Do, cousin, and I'll bear thee company.

WARWICK: Meantime my Lord Pembroke and myself

Will to Newcastle here, and gather head.

YOUNGER MORTIMER: About it, then, and we will
follow you.

LANCASTER: Be resolute and full of secrecy.

WARWICK: I warrant you.

Exit with PEMBROKE.

YOUNGER MORTIMER: Cousin, an if he will not
ransom him,

I'll thunder such a peal into his ears

As never subject did unto his king.

LANCASTER: Content; I'll bear my part. Holla! who's   *130*
there?

Enter GUARD.

YOUNGER MORTIMER: Ay, marry, such a guard as this
doth well.

LANCASTER: Lead on the way.

GUARD: Whither will your lordships?

YOUNGER MORTIMER: Whither else but to the king?

GUARD: His highness is dispos'd to be alone.

LANCASTER: Why, so he may, but we will speak to him.

GUARD: You may not in, my lord.

YOUNGER MORTIMER: May we not?

Enter KING EDWARD *and* KENT.

KING EDWARD: How now!

What noise is this? Who have we there? Is't you?   *140*
Going.

YOUNGER MORTIMER: Nay, stay, my lord; I come to
bring you news.

Mine uncle's taken prisoner by the Scots.

KING EDWARD: Then ransom him.

LANCASTER: 'Twas in your wars; you should ransom
him.

YOUNGER MORTIMER: And you shall ransom him, or
else –

KENT: What, Mortimer, you will not threaten him?

---

123 gather head: collect our troops.

KING EDWARD: Quiet yourself, you shall have the
    broad seal,
To gather for him th[o]roughout the realm.
LANCASTER: Your minion Gaveston hath taught you
    this.
150 YOUNGER MORTIMER: My lord, the family of the
    Mortimers
Are not so poor, but, would they sell their land,
'Twould levy men enough to anger you.
We never beg, but use such prayers as these.
    Laying hold of his sword.
KING EDWARD: Shall I still be haunted thus?
YOUNGER MORTIMER: Nay, now you are here alone,
    I'll speak my mind.
LANCASTER: And so will I, and then, my lord, farewell.
YOUNGER MORTIMER: The idle triumphs, masques,
    lascivious shows,
And prodigal gifts bestow'd on Gaveston,
Have drawn thy treasury dry, and made thee weak;
160 The murmuring commons, overstretched, break.
LANCASTER: Look for rebellion, look to be depos'd.
Thy garrisons are beaten out of France,
And lame and poor lie groaning at the gates.
The wild O'Neill, with swarms of Irish kerns,
Lives uncontroll'd within the English pale.
Unto the walls of York the Scots make road,
And, unresisted, drive away rich spoils.
YOUNGER MORTIMER: The haughty Dane commands
    the narrow seas,
While in the harbour ride thy ships unrigg'd.
170 LANCASTER: What foreign prince sends thee ambassa-
    dors?
YOUNGER MORTIMER: Who loves thee, but a sort of
    flatterers?
LANCASTER: Thy gentle queen, sole sister of Valois,

164 *kerns*: light-armed foot soldiers.
165 *pale*: the part round Dublin colonized by the English.

Complains that thou hast left her all forlorn.

YOUNGER MORTIMER: Thy court is naked, being
    bereft of those
That make a king seem glorious to the world,
I mean the peers, whom thou shouldst dearly love.
Libels are cast again thee in the street;
Ballads and rhymes made of thy overthrow.

LANCASTER: The northern borderers, seeing their
    houses burnt,
Their wives and children slain, run up and down,   *180*
Cursing the name of thee and Gaveston.

YOUNGER MORTIMER: When wert thou in the field
    with banner spread?
But once, and then thy soldiers march'd like players,
With garish robes, not armour; and thyself,
Bedaub'd with gold, rode laughing at the rest,
Nodding and shaking of thy spangled crest,
Where women's favours hung like labels down.

LANCASTER: And thereof came it that the fleering
    Scots,
To England's high disgrace, have made this jig:
Maids of England, sore may you mourn,   *190*
For your lemans you have lost at Bannocksbourn,
With a heave and a ho!
What weeneth the king of England
So soon to have won Scotland!
With a rombelow!

YOUNGER MORTIMER: Wigmore shall fly to set my
    uncle free.

LANCASTER: And when 'tis gone our swords shall
    purchase more.
If you be mov'd, revenge it as you can:
Look next to see us with our ensigns spread.
    Exit with YOUNGER MORTIMER.

KING EDWARD: My swelling heart for very anger   *200*
    breaks:

191 *lemans*: lovers.

471

How oft have I been baited by these peers,
And dare not be reveng'd, for their power is great!
Yet, shall the crowing of these cockerels
Affright a lion? Edward, unfold thy paws,
And let their lives' blood slake thy fury's hunger.
If I be cruel and grow tyrannous,
Now let them thank themselves, and rue too late.

KENT: My lord, I see your love to Gaveston
Will be the ruin of the realm and you,
210 For now the wrathful nobles threaten wars,
And therefore, brother, banish him for ever.

KING EDWARD: Art thou an enemy to my Gaveston?

KENT: Ay, and it grieves me that I favour'd him.

KING EDWARD: Traitor, be gone! Whine thou with
Mortimer.

KENT: So will I, rather than with Gaveston.

KING EDWARD: Out of my sight, and trouble me no
more!

KENT: No marvel though thou scorn thy noble peers,
When I thy brother am rejected thus.

KING EDWARD: Away!

Exit KENT.

220 Poor Gaveston, that hast no friend but me!
Do what they can, we'll live in Tynemouth here,
And so I walk with him about the walls,
What care I though the earls begirt us round?
Here comes she that is cause of all these jars.

Enter QUEEN ISABELLA, *with* EDWARD'S
NIECE, *two* LADIES, GAVESTON, BALDOCK,
and the YOUNGER SPENSER.

QUEEN ISABELLA: My lord, 'tis thought the earls are up
in arms.

KING EDWARD: Ay, and 'tis likewise thought you
favour him.

QUEEN ISABELLA: Thus do you still suspect me without
cause?

NIECE: Sweet uncle, speak more kindly to the queen.

GAVESTON: My lord, dissemble with her; speak her fair.

KING EDWARD: Pardon me, sweet; I forgot myself.   *230*

QUEEN ISABELLA: Your pardon is quickly got of Isabel.

KING EDWARD: The younger Mortimer is grown so
brave,
That to my face he threatens civil wars.

GAVESTON: Why do you not commit him to the Tower?

KING EDWARD: I dare not, for the people love him
well.

GAVESTON: Why, then, we'll have him privily made
away.

KING EDWARD: Would Lancaster and he had both
carous'd
A bowl of poison to each other's health!
But let them go, and tell me what are these.

NIECE: Two of my father's servants whilst he liv'd: *240*
May't please your grace to entertain them now.

KING EDWARD: Tell me, where wast thou born? What
is thine arms?

BALDOCK: My name is Baldock, and my gentry
I fetch'd from Oxford, not from heraldry.

KING EDWARD: The fitter art thou, Baldock, for my
turn.
Wait on me, and I'll see thou shalt not want.

BALDOCK: I humbly thank your majesty.

KING EDWARD: Knowest thou him, Gaveston?

GAVESTON: Ay, my lord.
His name is Spenser; he is well allied;   *250*
For my sake let him wait upon your grace.
Scarce shall you find a man of more desert.

KING EDWARD: Then, Spenser, wait upon me; for his
sake
I'll grace thee with a higher style ere long.

YOUNGER SPENSER: No greater titles happen unto me
Than to be favour'd of your majesty!

KING EDWARD: Cousin, this day shall be your
marriage feast.

And, Gaveston, think that I love thee well,
To wed thee to our niece, the only heir
260   Unto the Earl of Gloucester late deceas'd.
GAVESTON: I know, my lord, many will stomach me,
But I respect neither their love nor hate.
KING EDWARD: The headstrong barons shall not limit me;
He that I list to favour shall be great.
Come, let's away, and, when the marriage ends,
Have at the rebels and their complices!
    Exeunt.

SCENE THREE

Near Tynemouth Castle.
Enter KENT, LANCASTER, *the* YOUNGER
MORTIMER, WARWICK, PEMBROKE, *and others.*
KENT: My lords, of love to this our native land,
I come to join with you, and leave the king;
And in your quarrel, and the realm's behoof,
Will be the first that shall adventure life.
LANCASTER: I fear me you are sent of policy,
To undermine us with a show of love.
WARWICK: He is your brother, therefore have we cause
To cast the worst, and doubt of your revolt.
KENT: Mine honour shall be hostage of my truth:
10   If that will not suffice, farewell, my lords.
YOUNGER MORTIMER: Stay, Edmund: never was Plantagenet
False of his word, and therefore trust we thee.
PEMBROKE: But what's the reason you should leave him now?
KENT: I have inform'd the Earl of Lancaster.
LANCASTER: And it sufficeth. Now, my lords, know this,
That Gaveston is secretly arriv'd,

And here in Tynemouth frolics with the king.
Let us with these our followers scale the walls,
And suddenly surprise them unawares.

YOUNGER MORTIMER: I'll give the onset. 20

WARWICK: And I'll follow thee.

YOUNGER MORTIMER: This totter'd ensign of my
    ancestors,
Which swept the desert shore of that Dead Sea
Whereof we got the name of Mortimer,
Will I advance upon this castle walls —
Drums, strike alarum, raise them from their sport,
And ring aloud the knell of Gaveston!

LANCASTER: None be so hardy as to touch the king;
But neither spare you Gaveston nor his friends.
    Exeunt.

SCENE FOUR

In Tynemouth Castle.
Enter, severally, KING EDWARD *and the* YOUNGER
SPENSER.

KING EDWARD: O, tell me, Spenser, where is Gaveston?

YOUNGER SPENSER: I fear me he is slain, my gracious
    lord.

KING EDWARD: No, here he comes; now let them spoil
    and kill.
    Enter QUEEN ISABELLA, KING EDWARD'S
    NIECE, GAVESTON, *and* NOBLES.
Fly, fly, my lords! The earls have got the hold.
Take shipping, and away to Scarborough.
Spenser and I will post away by land.

GAVESTON: O, stay, my lord! They will not injure you.

KING EDWARD: I will not trust them, Gaveston; away!

GAVESTON: Farewell, my lord.

KING EDWARD: Lady, farewell. 10

NIECE: Farewell, sweet uncle, till we meet again.

KING EDWARD: Farewell, sweet Gaveston; and farewell, niece.

QUEEN ISABELLA: No farewell to poor Isabel thy queen?

KING EDWARD: Yes, yes, for Mortimer your lover's sake.

QUEEN ISABELLA: Heavens can witness, I love none but you.

Exeunt all except QUEEN ISABELLA.

From my embracements thus he breaks away.
O, that mine arms could close this isle about,
That I might pull him to me where I would!
Or that these tears, that drizzle from mine eyes,
20 Had power to mollify his stony heart,
That, when I had him, we might never part!

Enter LANCASTER, WARWICK, *the* YOUNGER
MORTIMER, *and others. Alarums within.*

LANCASTER: I wonder how he scap'd.

YOUNGER MORTIMER: Who's this? The queen!

QUEEN ISABELLA: Ay, Mortimer, the miserable queen,
Whose pining heart her inward sighs have blasted,
And body with continual mourning wasted.
These hands are tir'd with haling of my lord
From Gaveston, from wicked Gaveston;
And all in vain, for, when I speak him fair,
30 He turns away and smiles upon his minion.

YOUNGER MORTIMER: Cease to lament, and tell us where's the king?

QUEEN ISABELLA: What would you with the king? Is't him you seek?

LANCASTER: No, madam, but that cursed Gaveston.
Far be it from the thought of Lancaster
To offer violence to his sovereign!
We would but rid the realm of Gaveston:
Tell us where he remains, and he shall die.

QUEEN ISABELLA: He's gone by water unto Scarborough.

Pursue him quickly, and he cannot scape;
The king hath left him, and his train is small. *40*

WARWICK: Forslow no time, sweet Lancaster; let's
march.

YOUNGER MORTIMER: How comes it that the king and
he is parted?

QUEEN ISABELLA: That this your army, going several
ways,
Might be of lesser force, and with the power
That he intendeth presently to raise,
Be easily suppress'd: and therefore be gone.

YOUNGER MORTIMER: Here in the river rides a
Flemish hoy:
Let's all aboard, and follow him amain.

LANCASTER: The wind that bears him hence will fill
our sails.
Come, come, aboard! 'Tis but an hour's sailing. *50*

YOUNGER MORTIMER: Madam, stay you within this
castle here.

QUEEN ISABELLA: No, Mortimer, I'll to my lord the
king.

YOUNGER MORTIMER: Nay, rather sail with us to
Scarborough.

QUEEN ISABELLA: You know the king is so suspicious
As, if he hear I have but talk'd with you,
Mine honour will be call'd in question;
And therefore, gentle Mortimer, be gone.

YOUNGER MORTIMER: Madam, I cannot stay to answer
you,
But think of Mortimer as he deserves.
Exeunt all except QUEEN ISABELLA.

QUEEN ISABELLA: So well hast thou deserv'd, sweet *60*
Mortimer,
As Isabel could live with thee for ever.
In vain I look for love at Edward's hand,
Whose eyes are fix'd on none but Gaveston.
Yet once more I'll importune him with prayers:

If he be strange, and not regard my words,
My son and I will over into France,
And to the king my brother there complain
How Gaveston hath robb'd me of his love.
But yet, I hope, my sorrows will have end,
70   And Gaveston this blessed day be slain.
    Exit.

SCENE FIVE

The open country.
Enter GAVESTON, *pursued.*

GAVESTON: Yet, lusty lords, I have escap'd your hands,
    Your threats, your 'larums, and your hot pursuits;
    And, though divorced from King Edward's eyes,
    Yet liveth Pierce of Gaveston unsurpris'd,
    Breathing in hope (malgrado all your beards,
    That muster rebels thus against your king)
    To see his royal sovereign once again.

    Enter WARWICK, LANCASTER, PEMBROKE, *the*
    YOUNGER MORTIMER, SOLDIERS, JAMES *and*
    other ATTENDANTS OF PEMBROKE.

WARWICK: Upon him, soldiers! Take away his weapons!
YOUNGER MORTIMER: Thou proud disturber of thy
    country's peace,
10   Corrupter of thy king, cause of these broils,
    Base flatterer, yield! And, were it not for shame,
    Shame and dishonour to a soldier's name,
    Upon my weapon's point here shouldst thou fall,
    And welter in thy gore.
LANCASTER: Monster of men,
    That, like the Greekish strumpet, train'd to arms
    And bloody wars so many valiant knights,
    Look for no other fortune, wretch, than death!
    King Edward is not here to buckler thee.

5 *malgrado*: in spite of.

478

WARWICK: Lancaster, why talk'st thou to the slave?   *20*
  Go, soldiers, take him hence; for, by my sword,
  His head shall off. Gaveston, short warning
  Shall serve thy turn: it is our country's cause
  That here severely we will execute
  Upon thy person. Hang him at a bough.
GAVESTON: My lord! –
WARWICK: Soldiers, have him away.
  But, for thou wert the favourite of a king,
  Thou shalt have so much honour at our hands.
GAVESTON: I thank you all, my lords. Then I perceive   *30*
  That heading is one, and hanging is the other,
  And death is all.
   Enter ARUNDEL.
LANCASTER: How now, my Lord of Arundel!
ARUNDEL: My lords, King Edward greets you all by me.
WARWICK: Arundel, say your message.
ARUNDEL: His majesty, hearing that you had taken
    Gaveston,
  Entreateth you by me, yet but he may
  See him before he dies; for why, he says,
  And sends you word, he knows that die he shall;
  And, if you gratify his grace so far,   *40*
  He will be mindful of the courtesy.
WARWICK: How now!
GAVESTON: Renowmed Edward, how thy name
  Revives poor Gaveston!
WARWICK: No, it needeth not:
  Arundel, we will gratify the king
  In other matters; he must pardon us in this.
  Soldiers, away with him!
GAVESTON: Why, my Lord of Warwick,
  Will not these delays beget my hopes?   *50*
  I know it, lords, it is this life you aim at,
  Yet grant King Edward this.
YOUNGER MORTIMER: Shalt thou appoint
  What we shall grant? Soldiers, away with him!

Thus we'll gratify the king:
We'll send his head by thee. Let him bestow
His tears on that, for that is all he gets
Of Gaveston, or else his senseless trunk.

LANCASTER: Not so, my lord, lest he bestow more cost
60   In burying him than he hath ever earn'd.

ARUNDEL: My lords, it is his majesty's request,
And in the honour of a king he swears,
He will but talk with him, and send him back.

WARWICK: When, can you tell? Arundel, no; we wot,
He that the care of his realm remits,
And drives his nobles to these exigents
For Gaveston, will, if he seize him once,
Violate any promise to possess him.

ARUNDEL: Then, if you will not trust his grace in keep,
70   My lords, I will be pledge for his return.

YOUNGER MORTIMER: 'Tis honourable in thee to offer
  this;
But, for we know thou art a noble gentleman,
We will not wrong thee so,
To make away a true man for a thief.

GAVESTON: How mean'st thou, Mortimer? That is
  over-base.

YOUNGER MORTIMER: Away, base groom, robber of
  kings' renown!
Question with thy companions and thy mates.

PEMBROKE: My Lord Mortimer, and you, my lords,
  each one,
To gratify the king's request therein,
80   Touching the sending of this Gaveston,
Because his majesty so earnestly
Desires to see the man before his death,
I will upon mine honour undertake
To carry him, and bring him back again,
Provided this, that you, my Lord of Arundel,
Will join with me.

WARWICK: Pembroke, what wilt thou do?

Cause yet more bloodshed? Is it not enough
That we have taken him, but must we now
Leave him on 'Had I wist,' and let him go?   *90*

PEMBROKE: My lords, I will not over-woo your
      honours,
But, if you dare trust Pembroke with the prisoner,
Upon mine oath, I will return him back.

ARUNDEL: My Lord of Lancaster, what say you in this?

LANCASTER: Why, I say, let him go on Pembroke's
      word.

PEMBROKE: And you, Lord Mortimer?

YOUNGER MORTIMER: How say you, my Lord of
      Warwick?

WARWICK: Nay, do your pleasures: I know how 'twill
      prove.

PEMBROKE: Then give him me.

GAVESTON: Sweet sovereign, yet I come   *100*
To see thee ere I die!

WARWICK (*aside*): Yet not perhaps,
If Warwick's wit and policy prevail.

YOUNGER MORTIMER: My Lord of Pembroke, we
      deliver him you:
Return him on your honour. Sound, away!

      Exeunt all except PEMBROKE, ARUNDEL,
      GAVESTON, JAMES *and other* ATTENDANTS
      OF PEMBROKE.

PEMBROKE: My lord, you shall go with me.
My house is not far hence, out of the way
A little, but our men shall go along.
We that have pretty wenches to our wives,
Sir, must not come so near and balk their lips.   *110*

ARUNDEL: 'Tis very kindly spoke, my Lord of
      Pembroke:
Your honour hath an adamant of power
To draw a prince.

PEMBROKE: So, my lord. Come, hither, James:

112 *adamant*: magnet, loadstone.

I do commit this Gaveston to thee;
Be thou this night his keeper; in the morning
We will discharge thee of thy charge. Be gone.

GAVESTON: Unhappy Gaveston, whither go'st thou
now?

Exit with JAMES *and other* ATTENDANTS OF
PEMBROKE.

HORSE-BOY: My lord, we'll quickly be at Cobham.
Exeunt.

ACT THREE

SCENE ONE

The open country.
Enter GAVESTON *mourning,* JAMES *and other*
ATTENDANTS OF PEMBROKE.

GAVESTON: O treacherous Warwick, thus to wrong thy
friend!

JAMES: I see it is your life these arms pursue.

GAVESTON: Weaponless must I fall, and die in bands?
O, must this day be period of my life,
Centre of all my bliss? And ye be men,
Speed to the king.

Enter WARWICK *and* SOLDIERS.

WARWICK: My Lord of Pembroke's men,
Strive you no longer: I will have that Gaveston.

JAMES: Your lordship doth dishonour to yourself,
10   And wrong our lord, your honourable friend.

WARWICK: No, James, it is my country's cause I
follow.
Go, take the villain! Soldiers, come away;
We'll make quick work. Commend me to your
master,
My friend, and tell him that I watch'd it well.

4 *period*: end, full-stop.

482

Come, let thy shadow parley with King Edward.

GAVESTON: Treacherous earl, shall not I see the king?

WARWICK: The king of heaven perhaps, no other king.
Away!

Exeunt WARWICK *and* SOLDIERS *with*
GAVESTON.

JAMES: Come, fellows: it booted not for us to strive:
We will in haste go certify our lord.   20
Exeunt.

SCENE TWO

Near Boroughbridge in Yorkshire.
Enter KING EDWARD, *the* YOUNGER SPENSER,
BALDOCK, NOBLEMEN *of the king's side, and*
SOLDIERS *with drums and fifes.*

KING EDWARD: I long to hear an answer from the
barons
Touching my friend, my dearest Gaveston.
Ah, Spenser, not the riches of my realm
Can ransom him! Ah, he is mark'd to die!
I know the malice of the younger Mortimer.
Warwick I know is rough, and Lancaster
Inexorable; and I shall never see
My lovely Pierce, my Gaveston again.
The barons overbear me with their pride.

YOUNGER SPENSER: Were I King Edward, England's   10
sovereign,
Son to the lovely Eleanor of Spain,
Great Edward Longshanks' issue, would I bear
These braves, this rage, and suffer uncontroll'd
These barons thus to beard me in my land,
In mine own realm? My lord, pardon my speech:
Did you retain your father's magnanimity,

15 *shadow*: ghost, shade.
12 *Longshanks*: Edward I (1272–1307).

Did you regard the honour of your name,
You would not suffer thus your majesty
Be counterbuff'd of your nobility.

20 Strike off their heads, and let them preach on poles.
No doubt, such lessons they will teach the rest,
As by their preachments they will profit much,
And learn obedience to their lawful king.

KING EDWARD: Yea, gentle Spenser, we have been
    too mild,
Too kind to them; but now have drawn our sword,
And, if they send me not my Gaveston,
We'll steel it on their crest, and poll their tops.

BALDOCK: This haught resolve becomes your majesty,
Not to be tied to their affection,
30 As though your highness were a school-boy still.
And must be aw'd and govern'd like a child.

Enter the ELDER SPENSER *with his truncheon, and*
SOLDIERS.

ELDER SPENSER: Long live my sovereign, the noble
    Edward,
In peace triumphant, fortunate in wars!

KING EDWARD: Welcome, old man. Com'st thou in
    Edward's aid?
Then tell thy prince of whence and what thou art.

ELDER SPENSER: Lo, with a band of bowmen and of
    pikes,
Brown bills and targeteers, four hundred strong,
Sworn to defend King Edward's royal right,
I come in person to your majesty;
40 Spenser, the father of Hugh Spenser there,
Bound to your highness everlastingly
For favours done, in him, unto us all.

KING EDWARD: Thy father, Spenser?

YOUNGER SPENSER: True, an it like your grace,
That pours, in lieu of all your goodness shown,
His life, my lord, before your princely feet.

28 *haught*: noble, high.

484

KING EDWARD: Welcome ten thousand times, old man,
    again!
  Spenser, this love, this kindness to thy king,
  Argues thy noble mind and disposition.
  Spenser, I here create thee Earl of Wiltshire,   *50*
  And daily will enrich thee with our favour,
  That, as the sunshine, shall reflect o'er thee.
  Beside, the more to manifest our love,
  Because we hear Lord Bruce doth sell his land,
  And that the Mortimers are in hand withal,
  Thou shalt have crowns of us t'outbid the barons;
  And, Spenser, spare them not, but lay it on.
  Soldiers, a largess, and thrice-welcome all!
YOUNGER SPENSER: My lord, here comes the queen.
    Enter QUEEN ISABELLA, PRINCE EDWARD,
    and LEVUNE, *a Frenchman.*
KING EDWARD: Madam, what news?   *60*
QUEEN ISABELLA: News of dishonour, lord, and
    discontent.
  · Our friend Levune, faithful and full of trust,
  Informeth us, by letters and by words,
  That Lord Valois our brother, King of France,
  Because your highness hath been slack in homage,
  Hath seized Normandy into his hands.
  These be the letters, this the messenger.
KING EDWARD: Welcome, Levune. Tush, Sib, if this
    be all,
  Valois and I will soon be friends again.
  But to my Gaveston: shall I never see,   *70*
  Never behold thee now! Madam, in this matter
  We will employ you and your little son;
  You shall go parley with the King of France.
  Boy, see you bear you bravely to the king,
  And do your message with a majesty.
PRINCE EDWARD: Commit not to my youth things of
  more weight

68 *Sib*: wife.

Than fits a prince so young as I to bear.
And fear not, lord and father, heaven's great beams
On Atlas' shoulder shall not lie more safe
80   Than shall your charge committed to my trust.

QUEEN ISABELLA: Ay, boy, this towardness makes
    thy mother fear
Thou are not mark'd to many days on earth!

KING EDWARD: Madam, we will that you with speed
    be shipp'd,
And this our son; Levune shall follow you
With all the haste we can despatch him hence.
Choose of our lords to bear you company,
And go in peace; leave us in wars at home.

QUEEN ISABELLA: Unnatural wars, where subjects
    brave their king:
God end them once! My lord, I take my leave,
90   To make my preparation for France.
    Exit with PRINCE EDWARD.
    Enter ARUNDEL.

KING EDWARD: What, Lord Arundel, dost thou come
    alone?

ARUNDEL: Yea, my good lord, for Gaveston is dead.

KING EDWARD: Ah, traitors, have they put my friend to
    death?
Tell me, Arundel, died he ere thou cam'st,
Or didst thou see my friend to take his death?

ARUNDEL: Neither, my lord, for, as he was surpris'd,
Begirt with weapons and with enemies round,
I did your highness' message to them all,
Demanding him of them, entreating rather,
100   And said, upon the honour of my name,
That I would undertake to carry him
Unto your highness, and to bring him back.

KING EDWARD: And, tell me, would the rebels deny
    me that?

YOUNGER SPENSER: Proud recreants!

KING EDWARD: Yea, Spenser, traitors all!

ARUNDEL: I found them at the first inexorable.
 The Earl of Warwick would not bide the hearing,
 Mortimer hardly; Pembroke and Lancaster
 Spake least; and when they flatly had denied,
 Refusing to receive me pledge for him,   *110*
 The Earl of Pembroke mildly thus bespake:
 'My lords, because our sovereign sends for him,
 And promiseth he shall be safe return'd,
 I will this undertake, to have him hence,
 And see him re-deliver'd to your hands.'

KING EDWARD: Well, and how fortunes that he came
 not?

YOUNGER SPENSER: Some treason or some villainy was
 cause.

ARUNDEL: The Earl of Warwick seiz'd him on his way;
 For, being deliver'd unto Pembroke's men,
 Their lord rode home, thinking his prisoner safe, *120*
 But, ere he came, Warwick in ambush lay,
 And bare him to his death, and in a trench
 Strake off his head, and march'd unto the camp.

YOUNGER SPENSER: A bloody part, flatly 'gainst law of
 arms!

KING EDWARD: O, shall I speak, or shall I sigh and die!

YOUNGER SPENSER: My lord, refer your vengeance to
 the sword
 Upon these barons! Hearten up your men;
 Let them not unreveng'd murder your friends!
 Advance your standard, Edward, in the field,
 And march to fire them from their starting-holes. *130*

KING EDWARD (*kneeling*): By earth, the common
 mother of us all,
 By heaven, and all the moving orbs thereof,
 By this right hand, and by my father's sword,
 And all the honours 'longing to my crown,
 I will have heads and lives for him as many
 As I have manors, castles, towns, and towers!
 Rises.

Treacherous Warwick! traitorous Mortimer!
If I be England's king, in lakes of gore
Your headless trunks, your bodies will I trail,
140   That you may drink your fill, and quaff in blood,
And stain my royal standard with the same,
That so my bloody colours may suggest
Remembrance of revenge immortally
On your accursed traitorous progeny,
You villains that have slain my Gaveston!
And in this place of honour and of trust,
Spenser, sweet Spenser, I adopt thee here;
And merely of our love we do create thee
Earl of Gloucester and Lord Chamberlain,
150   Despite of times, despite of enemies.

YOUNGER SPENSER: My lord, here's in a messenger
    from the barons
Desires access unto your majesty.

KING EDWARD: Admit him near.

    Enter HERALD *with his coat of arms.*

HERALD: Long live King Edward, England's lawful lord!

KING EDWARD: So wish not they, I wis, that sent thee
    hither.
Thou com'st from Mortimer and his complices:
A ranker rout of rebels never was.
Well, say thy message.

HERALD: The barons, up in arms, by me salute
160   Your highness with long life and happiness;
And bid me say, as plainer to your grace,
That if without effusion of blood
You will this grief have ease and remedy,
That from your princely person you remove
This Spenser, as a putrifying branch
That deads the royal vine, whose golden leaves
Empale your princely head, your diadem,
Whose brightness such pernicious upstarts dim,
Say they, and lovingly advise your grace
170   To cherish virtue and nobility,

And have old servitors in high esteem,
And shake off smooth dissembling flatterers.
This granted, they, their honours, and their lives,
Are to your highness vow'd and consecrate.

YOUNGER SPENSER: Ah, traitors! Will they still display
their pride?

KING EDWARD: Away! Tarry no answer, but be gone!
Rebels, will they appoint their sovereign
His sports, his pleasures, and his company?
Yet, ere thou go, see how I do divorce
  Embraces YOUNGER SPENSER.
Spenser from me. Now get thee to thy lords,   *180*
And tell them I will come to chastise them
For murdering Gaveston: hie thee, get thee gone!
Edward, with fire and sword, follows at thy heels.
  Exit HERALD.
My lord, perceive you how these rebels swell?
Soldiers, good hearts! Defend your sovereign's right,
For now, even now, we march to make them stoop.
Away!
  *Exeunt. Alarums, excursions, a great fight, and a
  retreat sounded, within.*

SCENE THREE

The battlefield, Boroughbridge.
Re-enter KING EDWARD, *the* ELDER SPENSER, *the*
YOUNGER SPENSER, BALDOCK, *and* NOBLEMEN
of the king's side.

KING EDWARD: Why do we sound retreat? Upon
them, lords!
This day I shall pour vengeance with my sword
On those proud rebels that are up in arms,
And do confront and countermand their king.

YOUNGER SPENSER: I doubt it not, my lord; right will
prevail.

ELDER SPENSER: 'Tis not amiss, my liege, for either part
  To breathe a while. Our men, with sweat and dust
  All chok'd well near, begin to faint for heat,
  And this retire refresheth horse and man.

10 YOUNGER SPENSER: Here come the rebels.

  Enter the YOUNGER MORTIMER, LANCASTER,
  WARWICK, PEMBROKE, *and others.*

YOUNGER MORTIMER: Look, Lancaster, yonder is
  Edward
Among his flatterers.

LANCASTER: And there let him be,
  Till he pay dearly for their company.

WARWICK: And shall, or Warwick's sword shall smite
  in vain.

KING EDWARD: What, rebels, do you shrink and sound
  retreat?

YOUNGER MORTIMER: No, Edward, no; thy flatterers
  faint and fly.

LANCASTER: Thou'd best betimes forsake them and
  their trains,
  For they'll betray thee, traitors as they are.

20 YOUNGER SPENSER: Traitor on thy face, rebellious
  Lancaster!

PEMBROKE: Away, base upstart! Brav'st thou nobles
  thus?

ELDER SPENSER: A noble attempt and honourable deed,
  Is it not, trow ye, to assemble aid
  And levy arms against your lawful king?

KING EDWARD: For which, ere long, their heads shall
  satisfy
  T' appease the wrath of their offended king.

YOUNGER MORTIMER: Then, Edward, thou wilt fight
  it to the last,
  And rather bathe thy sword in subjects' blood
  Than banish that pernicious company?

30 KING EDWARD: Ay, traitors all, rather than thus be
  brav'd,

Make England's civil towns huge heaps of stones,
And ploughs to go about our palace-gates.

WARWICK: A desperate and unnatural resolution!
Alarum! To the fight!
Saint George for England, and the barons' right!

KING EDWARD: Saint George for England, and King
    Edward's right!

Alarums. Exeunt the two parties severally.
Re-enter KING EDWARD *and his* FOLLOWERS,
with the BARONS *and* KENT *captive.*

KING EDWARD: Now, lusty lords, now not by
    chance of war,
But justice of the quarrel and the cause,
Vail'd is your pride. Methinks you hang the heads;
But we'll advance them, traitors. Now 'tis time   40
To be aveng'd on you for all your braves,
And for the murder of my dearest friend,
To whom right well you knew our soul was knit,
Good Pierce of Gaveston, my sweet favourite.
Ah, rebels, recreants, you made him away!

KENT: Brother, in regard to thee and of thy land,
Did they remove that flatterer from thy throne.

KING EDWARD: So, sir, you have spoke: away, avoid
    our presence!

Exit KENT.

Accursed wretches, was't in regard of us,
When we had sent our messenger to request   50
He might be spar'd to come to speak with us,
And Pembroke undertook for his return,
That thou, proud Warwick, watch'd the prisoner,
Poor Pierce, and headed him 'gainst law of arms?
For which thy head shall overlook the rest
As much as thou in rage outwent'st the rest.

WARWICK: Tyrant, I scorn thy threats and menaces;
'Tis but temporal that thou canst inflict.

LANCASTER: The worst is death; and better die to live
Than live in infamy under such a king.   60

491

KING EDWARD: Away with them, my lord of
    Winchester!
  These lusty leaders, Warwick and Lancaster,
  I charge you roundly, off with both their heads!
  Away!

WARWICK: Farewell, vain world!

LANCASTER: Sweet Mortimer, farewell!

YOUNGER MORTIMER: England, unkind to thy
    nobility,
  Groan for this grief! Behold how thou art maim'd!

KING EDWARD: Go, take that haughty Mortimer to
    the Tower,
70 There see him safe bestow'd; and, for the rest,
  Do speedy execution on them all.
  Be gone!

YOUNGER MORTIMER: What, Mortimer! Can ragged
    stony walls
  Immure thy virtue that aspires to heaven?
  No, Edward, England's scourge, it may not be;
  Mortimer's hope surmounts his fortune far.
    The CAPTIVE BARONS *are led off.*

KING EDWARD: Sound drums and trumpets! March
    with me, my friends.
  Edward this day hath crown'd him king anew.
    Exeunt all except the YOUNGER SPENSER,
    LEVUNE, *and* BALDOCK.

YOUNGER SPENSER: Levune, the trust that we repose
    in thee
80 Begets the quiet of King Edward's land.
  Therefore be gone in haste, and with advice
  Bestow that treasure on the lords of France,
  That, therewith all enchanted, like the guard
  That suffer'd Jove to pass in showers of gold
  To Danaë,[9] all aid may be denied
  To Isabel the queen, that now in France
  Makes friends, to cross the seas with her young son,
  And step into his father's regiment.

LEVUNE: That's it these barons and the subtle queen
  Long levell'd at.   *90*
BALDOCK: Yea, but, Levune, thou seest
  These barons lay their heads on blocks together:
  What they intend, the hangman frustrates clean.
LEVUNE: Have you no doubts, my lords. I'll clap so
  close
  Among the lords of France with England's gold,
  That Isabel shall make her plaints in vain,
  And France shall be obdurate with her tears.
YOUNGER SPENSER: Then make for France amain;
  Levune, away!
  Proclaim King Edward's wars and victories.
  Exeunt.

ACT FOUR

SCENE ONE

Near the Tower of London.
Enter KENT.

KENT: Fair blows the wind for France: blow, gentle
  gale,
  Till Edmund be arriv'd for England's good!
  Nature, yield to my country's cause in this!
  A brother? no, a butcher of thy friends!
  Proud Edward, dost thou banish me thy presence?
  But I'll to France, and cheer the wronged queen,
  And certify what Edward's looseness is.
  Unnatural king, to slaughter noble men
  And cherish flatterers! Mortimer, I stay
  Thy sweet escape. Stand gracious, gloomy night,   *10*
  To his device!
  Enter the YOUNGER MORTIMER *disguised.*

90 *levell'd*: aimed.   98 *amain*: without delay.
9 *stay*: await.   11 *device*: plan.

YOUNGER MORTIMER: Holla! Who walketh there?
    Is't you, my lord?
KENT: Mortimer, 'tis I.
    But hath thy potion wrought so happily?
YOUNGER MORTIMER: It hath, my lord: the warders
    all asleep,
    I thank them, gave me leave to pass in peace.
    But hath your grace got shipping unto France?
KENT: Fear it not.
    Exeunt.

SCENE TWO

Paris.
Enter QUEEN ISABELLA *and* PRINCE EDWARD.
QUEEN ISABELLA: Ah, boy, our friends do fail us all
    in France!
    The lords are cruel, and the king unkind.
    What shall we do?
PRINCE EDWARD: Madam, return to England,
    And please my father well, and then a fig
    For all my uncle's friendship here in France!
    I warrant you, I'll win his highness quickly;
    'A loves me better than a thousand Spensers.
QUEEN ISABELLA: Ah, boy, thou art deceiv'd, at
    least in this,
10   To think that we can yet be tun'd together!
    No, no, we jar too far. Unkind Valois!
    Unhappy Isabel! When France rejects,
    Whither, O, whither dost thou bend thy steps?
    Enter SIR JOHN OF HAINAULT.
SIR JOHN: Madam, what cheer?
QUEEN ISABELLA: Ah, good Sir John of Hainault,
    Never so cheerless nor so far distrest!
SIR JOHN: I hear, sweet lady, of the king's unkindness.
    But droop not, madam; noble minds contemn

Despair. Will your grace with me to Hainault,
And there stay time's advantage with your son?   *20*
How say you, my lord? Will you go with your
   friends,
And shake off all our fortunes equally?

PRINCE EDWARD: So pleaseth the queen my mother,
   me it likes.
The king of England, nor the court of France,
Shall have me from my gracious mother's side,
Till I be strong enough to break a staff;
And then have at the proudest Spenser's head!

SIR JOHN: Well said, my lord!

QUEEN ISABELLA: O my sweet heart, how do I moan
   thy wrongs,
Yet triumph in the hope of thee, my joy!   *30*
Ah, sweet Sir John, even to the utmost verge
Of Europe, or the shore of Tanais
Will we with thee, to Hainault so, we will.
The marquis is a noble gentleman;
His grace, I dare presume, will welcome me.
But who are these?

   Enter KENT *and the* YOUNGER MORTIMER.

KENT: Madam, long may you live
Much happier than your friends in England do!

QUEEN ISABELLA: Lord Edmund and Lord
   Mortimer alive!
Welcome to France! The news was here, my lord,   *40*
That you were dead, or very near your death.

YOUNGER MORTIMER: Lady, the last was truest of the
   twain.
But Mortimer, reserv'd for better hap,
Hath shaken off the thraldom of the Tower,
And lives t' advance your standard, good my lord.

PRINCE EDWARD: How mean you? And the king my
   father lives?
No, my Lord Mortimer, not I, I trow.

32 *Tanais*: the River Don.

QUEEN ISABELLA: Not, son! Why not? I would it
    were no worse!
But, gentle lords, friendless we are in France.

50 YOUNGER MORTIMER: Monsieur Le Grand, a noble
    friend of yours,
Told us at our arrival all the news, —
How hard the nobles, how unkind the king
Hath show'd himself: but, madam, right makes room
Where weapons want, and, though a many friends
Are made away, as Warwick, Lancaster,
And others of our party and faction,
Yet have we friends, assure your grace, in England,
Would cast up caps, and clap their hands for joy,
To see us there, appointed for our foes.

60 KENT: Would all were well, and Edward well reclaim'd,
For England's honour, peace, and quietness!

YOUNGER MORTIMER: But by the sword, my lord,
    't must be deserv'd.
The king will ne'er forsake his flatterers.

SIR JOHN: My lords of England, sith th'ungentle king
Of France refuseth to give aid of arms
To this distressed queen, his sister, here,
Go you with her to Hainault. Doubt ye not
We will find comfort, money, men, and friends,
Ere long to bid the English king a base.[10]

70 How say, young prince, what think you of the
    match?

PRINCE EDWARD: I think King Edward will outrun us
    all.

QUEEN ISABELLA: Nay, son, not so; and you must not
    discourage
Your friends that are so forward in your aid.

KENT: Sir John of Hainault, pardon us, I pray.
These comforts that you give our woeful queen
Bind us in kindness all at your command.

QUEEN ISABELLA: Yea, gentle brother: and the God
    of heaven

Prosper your happy motion, good Sir John!

YOUNGER MORTIMER: This noble gentleman, forward
    in arms,
    Was born, I see, to be our anchor-hold.   *80*
    Sir John of Hainault, be it thy renown,
    That England's queen and nobles in distress
    Have been by thee restor'd and comforted.

SIR JOHN: Madam, along; and you, my lord, with me,
    That England's peers may Hainault's welcome see.
    Exeunt.

SCENE THREE

The Royal Palace, London.
Enter KING EDWARD, ARUNDEL, *the* ELDER
SPENSER, *the* YOUNGER SPENSER, *and others.*

KING EDWARD: Thus, after many threats of wrathful
    war,
    Triumpheth England's Edward with his friends,
    And triumph Edward with his friends uncontroll'd!
    My Lord of Gloucester, do you hear the news?

YOUNGER SPENSER: What news, my lord?

KING EDWARD: Why, man, they say there is great
    execution
    Done through the realm. My Lord of Arundel,
    You have the note, have you not?

ARUNDEL: From the Lieutenant of the Tower, my lord.

KING EDWARD: I pray, let us see it.   *10*
    Takes the note from ARUNDEL.
    What have we there?
    Read it, Spenser.
    Gives the note to YOUNGER SPENSER, *who reads*
    their names.
    Why, so: they bark'd apace a month ago;
    Now, on my life, they'll neither bark nor bite.
    Now, sirs, the news from France? Gloucester, I trow

The lords of France love England's gold so well
As Isabella gets no aid from thence.
What now remains? Have you proclaim'd, my lord,
Reward for them can bring in Mortimer?

20 YOUNGER SPENSER: My lord, we have, and, if he be
in England,
'A will be had ere long, I doubt it not.

KING EDWARD: If, dost thou say? Spenser, as true as
death,
He is in England's ground: our port-masters
Are not so careless of their king's command.
Enter a MESSENGER.
How now! What news with thee? From whence come
these?

MESSENGER: Letters, my lord, and tidings forth of
France:
To you, my Lord of Gloucester, from Levune.
Gives letters to YOUNGER SPENSER.

KING EDWARD: Read.

YOUNGER SPENSER (*reading*): *My duty to your honour*
30 *promised, etc., I have, according to instructions in that*
behalf, dealt with the King of France his lords, and effected
that the queen, all discontented and discomforted, is gone:
whither, if you ask, with Sir John of Hainault, brother to
the marquis, into Flanders. With them are gone Lord
Edmund and the Lord Mortimer, having in their company
divers of your nation, and others; and, as constant report
goeth, they intend to give King Edward battle in England,
sooner than he can look for them. This is all the news of
import.

40 *Your honour's in all service, Levune.*

KING EDWARD: Ah, villains, hath that Mortimer
escap'd?
With him is Edmund gone associate?
And will Sir John of Hainault lead the round?

43 *round*: dance.

498

Welcome, o' God's name, madam, and your son!
England shall welcome you and all your rout.
Gallop apace, bright Phoebus, through the sky;
And, dusky Night, in rusty iron car,
Between you both shorten the time, I pray,
That I may see that most desired day,
When we may meet these traitors in the field!   10
Ah, nothing grieves me, but my little boy
Is thus misled to countenance their ills!
Come, friends, to Bristow, there to make us strong:
And, winds, as equal be to bring them in,
As you injurious were to bear them forth!
    Exeunt.

SCENE FOUR

Near Harwich.
Enter QUEEN ISABELLA, PRINCE EDWARD,
KENT, *the* YOUNGER MORTIMER, *and* SIR JOHN
OF HAINAULT.
QUEEN ISABELLA: Now, lords, our loving friends
    and countrymen,
Welcome to England all, with prosperous winds!
Our kindest friends in Belgia have we left,
To cope with friends at home; a heavy case
When force to force is knit, and sword and glaive
In civil broils makes kin and countrymen
Slaughter themselves in others, and their sides
With their own weapons gor'd! But what's the help?
Misgovern'd kings are cause of all this wrack;
And, Edward, thou art one among them all,   10
Whose looseness hath betray'd thy land to spoil,
And made the channels overflow with blood
Of thine own people. Patron shouldst thou be,
But thou –

46 *Phoebus*: the sun.   5 *glaive*: lance.

YOUNGER MORTIMER: Nay, madam, if you be a warrior,
   You must not grow so passionate in speeches.
   Lords, sith that we are, by sufferance of heaven,
   Arriv'd and armed in this prince's right,
   Here for our country's cause swear we to him
20   All homage, fealty, and forwardness;
   And for the open wrongs and injuries
   Edward hath done to us, his queen, and land,
   We come in arms to wreck it with the sword,
   That England's queen in peace may repossess
   Her dignities and honours, and withal
   We may remove these flatterers from the king
   That havock England's wealth and treasury.
SIR JOHN: Sound trumpets, my lord, and forward let
   us march.
   Edward will think we come to flatter him.
30   KENT: I would he never had been flatter'd more!
   Exeunt.

SCENE FIVE

Near Bristol.
Enter KING EDWARD, BALDOCK, *and the*
YOUNGER SPENSER *in flight.*
YOUNGER SPENSER: Fly, fly, my lord! The queen is
   overstrong!
   Her friends do multiply, and yours do fail.
   Shape we our course to Ireland, there to breathe.
KING EDWARD: What, was I born to fly and run away,
   And leave the Mortimers conquerors behind?
   Give me my horse, and let's reinforce our troops.
   And in this bed of honours die with fame.
BALDOCK: O, no, my lord! This princely resolution
   Fits not the time: away! we are pursu'd.
   Exeunt.
   Enter KENT, *with a sword and target.*
10   KENT: This way he fled; but I am come too late.

Edward, alas, my heart relents for thee!
Proud traitor, Mortimer, why dost thou chase
Thy lawful king, thy sovereign, with thy sword?
Vile wretch, and why hast thou, of all unkind,
Borne arms against thy brother and thy king?
Rain showers of vengeance on my cursed head,
Thou God, to whom in justice it belongs
To punish this unnatural revolt!
Edward, this Mortimer aims at thy life:
O, fly him then! But, Edmund, calm this rage;   20
Dissemble, or thou diest; for Mortimer
And Isabel do kiss, while they conspire.
And yet she bears a face of love, forsooth!
Fie on that love that hatcheth death and hate!
Edmund, away! Bristow to Longshanks' blood
Is false; be not found single for suspect.
Proud Mortimer pries near into thy walks.

> *Enter* QUEEN ISABELLA, PRINCE EDWARD, *the*
> YOUNGER MORTIMER, *and* SIR JOHN OF
> HAINAULT.

QUEEN ISABELLA: Successful battles gives the God of
    kings
To them that fight in right, and fear his wrath.
Since, then, successfully we have prevail'd,   30
Thanked be heaven's great architect and you!
Ere farther we proceed, my noble lords,
We here create our well-beloved son,
Of love and care unto his royal person,
Lord Warden of the realm; and, sith the Fates
Have made his father so infortunate,
Deal you, my lords, in this, my loving lords,
As to your wisdoms fittest seems in all.

KENT: Madam, without offence if I may ask
How will you deal with Edward in his fall?   40

PRINCE EDWARD: Tell me, good uncle, what Edward
    do you mean?

KENT: Nephew, your father; I dare not call him king.

YOUNGER MORTIMER: My Lord of Kent, what needs
    these questions?
'Tis not in her controlment nor in ours;
But as the realm and parliament shall please,
So shall your brother be disposed of.
(*Aside to the* QUEEN) I like not this relenting mood
    in Edmund:
Madam, 'tis good to look to him betimes.
QUEEN ISABELLA: My lord, the Mayor of Bristow
    knows our mind.
50 YOUNGER MORTIMER: Yea, madam, and they scape
    not easily
That fled the field.
QUEEN ISABELLA: Baldock is with the king:
A goodly chancellor, is he not, my lord?
SIR JOHN: So are the Spensers, the father and the son.
KENT: This Edward is the ruin of the realm.[11]
    Enter RICE AP HOWEL *with the* ELDER
    SPENSER *prisoner, and* ATTENDANTS.
RICE AP HOWEL: God save Queen Isabel and her
    princely son!
Madam, the Mayor and citizens of Bristow,
In sign of love and duty to this presence,
Present by me this traitor to the state,
60 Spenser, the father to that wanton Spenser,
That, like the lawless Catiline[12] of Rome,
Revell'd in England's wealth and treasury.
QUEEN ISABELLA: We thank you all.
YOUNGER MORTIMER: Your loving care in this
Deserveth princely favours and rewards.
But where's the king and the other Spenser fled?
RICE AP HOWEL: Spenser the son, created Earl of
    Gloucester,
Is with that smooth-tongu'd scholar Baldock gone,
And shipp'd but late for Ireland with the king.
70 YOUNGER MORTIMER (*aside*): Some whirlwind fetch
    them back, or sink them all!

They shall be started thence, I doubt it not.

PRINCE EDWARD: Shall I not see the king my father yet?

KENT (*aside*): Unhappy is Edward, chas'd from England's
    bounds!

SIR JOHN: Madam, what resteth? Why stand you in a
    muse?

QUEEN ISABELLA: I rue my lord's ill-fortune: but, alas,
    Care of my country call'd me to this war!

YOUNGER MORTIMER: Madam, have done with care
    and sad complaint.
Your king hath wrong'd your country and himself,
And we must seek to right it as we may.
Meanwhile have hence this rebel to the block: *80*
Your lordship cannot privilege your head.

ELDER SPENSER: Rebel is he that fights against his
    prince:
So fought not they that fought in Edward's right.

YOUNGER MORTIMER: Take him away; he prates.
    Exeunt ATTENDANTS *with the* ELDER SPENSER.
                      You, Rice ap Howel,
Shall do good service to her majesty,
Being of countenance in your country here,
To follow these rebellious runagates.
We in meanwhile, madam, must take advice.
How Baldock, Spenser, and their complices,
May in their fall be follow'd to their end.   *90*
    Exeunt.

SCENE SIX

The Abbey of Neath, Glamorganshire.
Enter the ABBOT, MONKS, KING EDWARD, *the*
YOUNGER SPENSER, *and* BALDOCK (*the three latter
disguised*).

ABBOT: Have you no doubt, my lord; have you no fear.
As silent and as careful we will be
To keep your royal person safe with us,

71 *started*: forced out.   86 *of countenance*: of authority, in favour.

Free from suspect, and fell invasion
Of such as have your majesty in chase,
Yourself, and those your chosen company,
As danger of this stormy time requires.

KING EDWARD: Father, thy face should harbour no
    deceit.

O, hadst thou ever been a king, thy heart,
10 Pierc'd deeply with the sense of my distress,
Could not but take compassion of my state!
Stately and proud in riches and in train,
Whilom I was, powerful and full of pomp.
But what is he whom rule and empery
Have not in life or death made miserable?
Come, Spenser, come, Baldock, come, sit down by
    me;
Make trial now of that philosophy
That in our famous nurseries of arts
Thou suck'dst from Plato and from Aristotle.
20 Father, this life contemplative is heaven:
O, that I might this life in quiet lead!
But we, alas, are chas'd! – and you, my friends,
Your lives and my dishonour they pursue.
Yet, gentle monks, for treasure, gold, nor fee,
Do you betray us and our company.

FIRST MONK: Your grace may sit secure, if none but we
Do wot of your abode.

YOUNGER SPENSER: Not one alive: but shrewdly I
    suspect
A gloomy fellow in a mead below;
30 'A gave a long look after us, my lord;
And all the land, I know, is up in arms,
Arms that pursue our lives with deadly hate.

BALDOCK: We were embark'd for Ireland, wretched we,
With awkward winds and with sore tempests driven,
To fall on shore, and here to pine in fear
Of Mortimer and his confederates.

4 *fell*: foul.   13 *Whilom*: formerly.

KING EDWARD: Mortimer! Who talks of Mortimer?
Who wounds me with the name of Mortimer,
That bloody man? Good father, on thy lap
Lay I this head, laden with mickle care.   *40*
O, might I never ope these eyes again,
Never again lift up this drooping head,
O, never more lift up this dying heart!

YOUNGER SPENSER: Look up, my lord. Baldock, this
    drowsiness
Betides no good. Here even we are betray'd!
    Enter, with Welsh hooks, RICE AP HOWEL, *a*
    MOWER, *and* LEICESTER.

MOWER: Upon my life, these be the men ye seek.

RICE AP HOWEL: Fellow, enough. My lord, I pray,
    be short;
A fair commission warrants what we do.

LEICESTER: The queen's commission, urg'd by
    Mortimer:
What cannot gallant Mortimer with the queen?   *50*
Alas, see where he sits, and hopes unseen
T'escape their hands that seek to reave his life!
Too true it is, *Quem dies vidit veniens superbum,
Hunc dies vidit fugiens jacentem.*
But, Leicester, leave to grow so passionate.
Spenser and Baldock, by no other names,
I arrest you of high treason here.
Stand not on titles, but obey th' arrest:
'Tis in the name of Isabel the queen.
My lord, why droop you thus?   *60*

KING EDWARD: O day, the last of all my bliss on earth!
Centre of all misfortune! O my stars,
Why do you lour unkindly on a king?
Comes Leicester, then, in Isabella's name,
To take my life, my company from me?

52 *reave*: take away.
53 *Quem dies* . . .: The man whom the new day sees in his pride, is by
the closing day seen prostrate.

Here, man, rip up this panting breast of mine,
And take my heart in rescue of my friends!

RICE AP HOWEL: Away with them!

YOUNGER SPENSER: It may become thee yet
70 To let us take our farewell of his grace.

ABBOT: My heart with pity earns to see this sight;
A king to bear these words and proud commands!

KING EDWARD: Spenser, ah, sweet Spenser, thus, then,
must we part.

YOUNGER SPENSER: We must, my lord; so will the
angry heavens.

KING EDWARD: Nay, so will hell and cruel Mortimer:
The gentle heavens have not to do in this.

BALDOCK: My lord, it is in vain to grieve or storm.
Here humbly of your grace we take our leaves.
Our lots are cast; I fear me, so is thine.

80 KING EDWARD: In heaven we may, in earth ne'er shall
we meet.
And, Leicester, say, what shall become of us?

LEICESTER: Your majesty must go to Killingworth.

KING EDWARD: Must! it is somewhat hard when kings
must go.

LEICESTER: Here is a litter ready for your grace,
That waits your pleasure, and the day grows old.

RICE AP HOWEL: As good be gone, as stay and be be-
nighted.

KING EDWARD: A litter hast thou? Lay me in a hearse,
And to the gates of hell convey me hence.
Let Pluto's bells ring out my fatal knell,
90 And hags howl for my death at Charon's shore;
For friends hath Edward none but these and these,
And these must die under a tyrant's sword.

RICE AP HOWEL: My lord, be going: care not for these,
For we shall see them shorter by the heads.

KING EDWARD: Well, that shall be shall be: part we
must;

71 *earns*: grieves.   82 *Killingworth*: Kenilworth.

Sweet Spenser, gentle Baldock, part we must.
Hence, feigned weeds! unfeigned are my woes.
Throwing off his disguise.
Father, farewell. Leicester, thou stay'st for me;
And go I must. Life, farewell, with my friends!
Exeunt KING EDWARD *and* LEICESTER.

YOUNGER SPENSER: O, is he gone? is noble Edward 100
gone?
Parted from hence, never to see us more!
Rend, sphere of heaven! and, fire, forsake thy orb!
Earth, melt to air! Gone is my sovereign,
Gone, gone, alas, never to make return!

BALDOCK: Spenser, I see our souls are fleeted hence;
We are depriv'd the sunshine of our life.
Make for a new life, man; throw up thy eyes
And heart and hand to heaven's immortal throne;
Pay nature's debt with cheerful countenance,
Reduce we all our lessons unto this: 110
To die, sweet Spenser, therefore live we all;
Spenser, all live to die, and rise to fall.

RICE AP HOWEL: Come, come, keep these preachments
till you come to the place appointed. You, and such as
you are, have made wise work in England. Will your
lordships away?

MOWER: Your worship I trust will remember me?

RICE AP HOWEL: Remember thee, fellow! What else?
Follow me to the town.
Exeunt.

ACT FIVE

SCENE ONE

Kenilworth Castle.
Enter KING EDWARD, LEICESTER, *the* BISHOP
OF WINCHESTER, *and* TRUSSEL.

LEICESTER: Be patient, good my lord, cease to lament;

Imagine Killingworth Castle were your court,
And that you lay for pleasure here a space,
Not of compulsion or necessity.
KING EDWARD: Leicester, if gentle words might
    comfort me,
Thy speeches long ago had eas'd my sorrows,
For kind and loving hast thou always been.
The griefs of private men are soon allay'd;
But not of kings. The forest deer, being struck,
10   Runs to an herb that closeth up the wounds;
But when the imperial lion's flesh is gor'd,
He rends and tears it with his wrathful paw,
[And], highly scorning that the lowly earth
Should drink his blood, mounts up into the air.
And so it fares with me, whose dauntless mind
Th' ambitious Mortimer would seek to curb,
And that unnatural queen, false Isabel,
That thus hath pent and mew'd me in a prison;
For such outrageous passions cloy my soul,
20   As with the wings of rancour and disdain
Full often am I soaring up to heaven,
To plain me to the gods against them both.
But when I call to mind I am a king,
Methinks I should revenge me of the wrongs
That Mortimer and Isabel have done.
But what are kings, when regiment is gone,
But perfect shadows in a sunshine day?
My nobles rule; I bear the name of king;
I wear the crown; but am controll'd by them,
30   By Mortimer, and my unconstant queen,
Who spots my nuptial bed with infamy;
Whilst I am lodg'd within this cave of care,
Where sorrow at my elbow still attends,
To company my heart with sad laments,
That bleeds within me for this strange exchange.
But tell me, must I now resign my crown,
To make usurping Mortimer a king?

BISHOP OF WINCHESTER: Your grace mistakes; it is
  for England's good
  And princely Edward's right we crave the crown.
KING EDWARD: No, 'tis for Mortimer, not Edward's   *40*
  head
  For he's a lamb, encompassed by wolves,
  Which in a moment will abridge his life.
  But, if proud Mortimer do wear this crown,
  Heavens turn it to a blaze of quenchless fire!
  Or, like the snaky wreath of Tisiphon,
  Engirt the temples of his hateful head!
  So shall not England's vine be perished,
  But Edward's name survive, though Edward dies.
LEICESTER: My lord, why waste you thus the time away?
  They stay your answer: will you yield your crown?   *50*
KING EDWARD: Ah, Leicester, weigh how hardly I can
  brook
  To lose my crown and kingdom without cause;
  To give ambitious Mortimer my right,
  That, like a mountain, overwhelms my bliss;
  In which extreme my mind here murder'd is!
  But what the heavens appoint I must obey.
  Here, take my crown; the life of Edward too:
    Taking off the crown.
  Two kings in England cannot reign at once.
  But stay a while. Let me be king till night,
  That I may gaze upon this glittering crown;   *60*
  So shall my eyes receive their last content,
  My head, the latest honour due to it,
  And jointly both yield up their wished right.
  Continue ever, thou celestial sun;
  Let never silent night possess this clime;
  Stand still, you watches of the element;
  All times and seasons, rest you at a stay,
  That Edward may be still fair England's king!
  But day's bright beams doth vanish fast away,

45 *Tisiphon*: one of the Furies, whose hair was of serpents.

70　And needs I must resign my wished crown.
　　Inhuman creatures, nurs'd with tiger's milk,
　　Why gape you for your sovereign's overthrow?
　　My diadem, I mean, and guiltless life.
　　See, monsters, see! I'll wear my crown again.
　　　Putting on the crown.
　　What, fear you not the fury of your king?
　　But, hapless Edward, thou art fondly led;
　　They pass not for thy frowns as late they did,
　　But seek to make a new-elected king;
　　Which fills my mind with strange despairing thoughts,
80　Which thoughts are martyred with endless torments;
　　And in this torment comfort find I none,
　　But that I feel the crown upon my head;
　　And therefore let me wear it yet a while.
TRUSSEL: My lord, the parliament must have present
　　news;
　　And therefore say, will you resign or no?
　　　The KING *rageth.*
KING EDWARD: I'll not resign, but, whilst I live,
　　[be king].
　　Traitors, be gone, and join you with Mortimer!
　　Elect, conspire, install, do what you will:
　　Their blood and yours shall seal these treacheries!
90　BISHOP OF WINCHESTER: This answer we'll return;
　　and so, farewell.
　　　Going with TRUSSEL.
LEICESTER: Call them again, my lord, and speak them
　　fair,
　　For, if they go, the prince shall lose his right.
KING EDWARD: Call thou them back; I have no
　　power to speak.
LEICESTER: My lord, the king is willing to resign.
BISHOP OF WINCHESTER: If he be not, let him choose.
KING EDWARD: O, would I might! But heavens and
　　earth conspire

76 *fondly*: foolishly.　　77 *pass*: care.

510

To make me miserable. Here, receive my crown.
Receive it? No, these innocent hands of mine
Shall not be guilty of so foul a crime;
He of you all that most desires my blood,   *100*
And will be call'd the murderer of a king,
Take it. What, are you mov'd? Pity you me?
Then send for unrelenting Mortimer,
And Isabel, whose eyes being turn'd to steel
Will sooner sparkle fire than shed a tear.
Yet stay, for rather than I'll look on them,
Here, here! (*Gives the crown*) Now, sweet God of
    heaven,
Make me despise this transitory pomp,
And sit for aye enthronised in heaven!
Come, death, and with thy fingers close my eyes,   *110*
Or, if I live, let me forget myself!
BISHOP OF WINCHESTER: My lord, –
KING EDWARD: Call me not lord. Away, out of my
    sight!
Ah, pardon me! Grief makes me lunatic.
Let not that Mortimer protect my son;
More safety is there in a tiger's jaws
Than his embracements. Bear this to the queen,
Wet with my tears, and dried again with sighs:
    Gives a handkerchief.
If with the sight thereof she be not mov'd,
Return it back, and dip it in my blood.   *120*
Commend me to my son, and bid him rule
Better than I: yet how have I transgress'd,
Unless it be with too much clemency?
TRUSSEL: And thus, most humbly do we take our leave.
KING EDWARD: Farewell.
    Exeunt the BISHOP OF WINCHESTER *and*
    TRUSSEL *with the crown.*
I know the next news that they bring
Will be my death; and welcome shall it be:
To wretched men death is felicity.

LEICESTER: Another post! What news brings he?
Enter BERKELEY, *who gives a paper to* LEICESTER.
KING EDWARD: Such news as I expect. Come,
Berkeley, come,
130   And tell thy message to my naked breast.
BERKELEY: My lord, think not a thought so villainous
Can harbour in a man of noble birth.
To do your highness service and devoir,
And save you from your foes, Berkeley would die.
LEICESTER: My lord, the council of the queen
commands
That I resign my charge.
KING EDWARD: And who must keep me now? Must
you, my lord?
BERKELEY: Ay, my most gracious lord; so 'tis decreed.
KING EDWARD (*taking the paper*): By Mortimer, whose
name is written here!
140   Well may I rent his name that rends my heart.
Tears it.
This poor revenge hath something eas'd my mind:
So may his limbs be torn as is this paper!
Hear me, immortal Jove, and grant it too!
BERKELEY: Your grace must hence with me to Berkeley
straight.
KING EDWARD: Whither you will: all places are alike,
And every earth is fit for burial.
LEICESTER: Favour him, my lord, as much as lieth inyou.
BERKELEY: Even so betide my soul as I use him!
KING EDWARD: Mine enemies hath pitied my estate,
150   And that's the cause that I am now remov'd.
BERKELEY: And thinks your grace that Berkeley will be
cruel?
KING EDWARD: I know not; but of this am I assur'd,
That death ends all, and I can die but once.
Leicester, farewell.
LEICESTER: Not yet, my lord; I'll bear you on your way.
Exeunt.

SCENE TWO

The Royal Palace, London.
Enter QUEEN ISABELLA *and the* YOUNGER
MORTIMER.

YOUNGER MORTIMER: Fair Isabel, now have we our
  desire;
  The proud corrupters of the light-brain'd king
  Have done their homage to the lofty gallows,
  And he himself lies in captivity.
  Be rul'd by me, and we will rule the realm:
  In any case take heed of childish fear,
  For now we hold an old wolf by the ears,
  That, if he slip, will seize upon us both,
  And gripe the sorer, being grip'd himself.
  Think therefore, madam, it imports us much   10
  To erect your son with all the speed we may,
  And that I be protector over him:
  For our behoof will bear the greater sway
  Whenas a king's name shall be under-writ.
QUEEN ISABELLA: Sweet Mortimer, the life of Isabel,
  Be thou persuaded that I love thee well;
  And therefore, so the prince, my son be safe,
  Whom I esteem as dear as these mine eyes,
  Conclude against his father what thou wilt,
  And I myself will willingly subscribe.   20
YOUNGER MORTIMER: First would I hear news he were
  depos'd,
  And then let me alone to handle him.
   Enter MESSENGER.
  Letters! from whence?
MESSENGER: From Killingworth, my lord.
QUEEN ISABELLA: How fares my lord the king?
MESSENGER: In health, madam, but full of pensiveness.
QUEEN ISABELLA: Alas, poor soul, would I could ease
  his grief!

Enter the BISHOP OF WINCHESTER *with the crown.*

Thanks, gentle Winchester. – Sirrah, be gone.

Exit MESSENGER.

BISHOP OF WINCHESTER: The king hath willingly resign'd his crown.

30 QUEEN ISABELLA: O, happy news! Send for the prince my son.

BISHOP OF WINCHESTER: Further, or this letter was seal'd, Lord Berkeley came,

So that he now is gone from Killingworth;

And we have heard that Edmund laid a plot

To set his brother free; no more but so.

The Lord of Berkeley is so pitiful

As Leicester that had charge of him before.

QUEEN ISABELLA: Then let some other be his guardian.

YOUNGER MORTIMER: Let me alone; here is the privy-seal, –

Exit the BISHOP OF WINCHESTER.

Who's there? (*To* ATTENDANTS *within*) Call hither Gurney and Matrevis. –

40 To dash the heavy-headed Edmund's drift,

Berkeley shall be discharg'd, the king remov'd,

And none but we shall know where he lieth.

QUEEN ISABELLA: But, Mortimer, as long as he survives,

What safety rests for us or for my son?

YOUNGER MORTIMER: Speak, shall he presently be despatch'd and die?

QUEEN ISABELLA: I would he were, so 'twere not by my means!

Enter MATREVIS *and* GURNEY.

YOUNGER MORTIMER: Enough. Matrevis, write a letter presently

Unto the Lord of Berkeley from ourself,

That he resign the king to thee and Gurney;

50 And, when 'tis done, we will subscribe our name.

31 *or*: ere, before.

514

MATREVIS: It shall be done, my lord.
Writes.
YOUNGER MORTIMER: Gurney, –
GURNEY: My lord?
YOUNGER MORTIMER: As thou intend'st to rise by
Mortimer,
Who now makes Fortune's wheel turn as he please,
Seek all the means thou canst to make him droop,
And neither give him kind word nor good look.
GURNEY: I warrant you, my lord.
YOUNGER MORTIMER: And this above the rest:
because we hear
That Edmund casts to work his liberty,   *60*
Remove him still from place to place by night,
Till at the last he come to Killingworth,
And then from thence to Berkeley back again;
And by the way, to make him fret the more,
Speak curstly to him; and in any case
Let no man comfort him, if he chance to weep,
But amplify his grief with bitter words.
MATREVIS: Fear not, my lord; we'll do as you command.
YOUNGER MORTIMER: So, now away! Post thither-
wards amain.
QUEEN ISABELLA: Whither goes this letter? to my lord   *70*
the king?
Commend me humbly to his majesty,
And tell him that I labour all in vain
To ease his grief and work his liberty;
And bear him this as witness of my love.
Gives ring.
MATREVIS: I will, madam.
Exit with GURNEY.
YOUNGER MORTIMER: Finely dissembled! Do so still,
sweet queen.
Here comes the young prince with the Earl of Kent.

65 *curstly*: harshly.

QUEEN ISABELLA: Something he whispers in his childish ears.

YOUNGER MORTIMER: If he have such access unto the prince,

80   Our plots and stratagems will soon be dash'd.

QUEEN ISABELLA: Use Edmund friendly, as if all were well.

Enter PRINCE EDWARD, *and* KENT *talking with him.*

YOUNGER MORTIMER: How fares my honourable Lord of Kent?

KENT: In health, sweet Mortimer. How fares your grace?

QUEEN ISABELLA: Well, if my lord your brother were enlarg'd.

KENT: I hear of late he hath depos'd himself.

QUEEN ISABELLA: The more my grief.

YOUNGER MORTIMER: And mine.

KENT (*aside*): Ah, they do dissemble!

QUEEN ISABELLA: Sweet son, come hither; I must talk with thee.

90   YOUNGER MORTIMER: You, being his uncle and the next of blood,

Do look to be protector o'er the prince.

KENT: Not I, my lord: who should protect the son,

But she that gave him life? I mean the queen.

PRINCE EDWARD: Mother, persuade me not to wear the crown.

Let him be king; I am too young to reign.

QUEEN ISABELLA: But be content, seeing it his highness' pleasure.

PRINCE EDWARD: Let me but see him first, and then I will.

KENT: Ay, do, sweet nephew.

QUEEN ISABELLA: Brother, you know it is impossible.

100 PRINCE EDWARD: Why, is he dead?

QUEEN ISABELLA: No, God forbid!

KENT: I would those words proceeded from your heart!

YOUNGER MORTIMER: Inconstant Edmund, dost thou favour him,
That wast a cause of his imprisonment?

KENT: The more cause have I now to make amends.

YOUNGER MORTIMER (*aside to* QUEEN ISABELLA): I tell thee, 'tis not meet that one so false
Should come about the person of a prince.
My lord, he hath betray'd the king his brother,
And therefore trust him not.

PRINCE EDWARD: But he repents, and sorrows for it *110* now.

QUEEN ISABELLA: Come, son, and go with this gentle lord and me.

PRINCE EDWARD: With you I will, but not with Mortimer.

YOUNGER MORTIMER: Why, youngling, 'sdain'st thou so of Mortimer?
Then I will carry thee by force away.

PRINCE EDWARD: Help, uncle Kent! Mortimer will wrong me.

QUEEN ISABELLA: Brother Edmund, strive not; we are his friends.
Isabel is nearer than the Earl of Kent.

KENT: Sister, Edward is my charge; redeem him.

QUEEN ISABELLA: Edward is my son, and I will keep him.

KENT (*aside*): Mortimer shall know that he hath wronged *120* me.
Hence will I haste to Killingworth Castle,
And rescue aged Edward from his foes,
To be reveng'd on Mortimer and thee.

Exeunt, on one side, QUEEN ISABELLA, PRINCE EDWARD, *and the* YOUNGER MORTIMER; *on the other,* KENT.

118 *redeem*: release him and honour the agreement.

SCENE THREE

Near Kenilworth Castle.
Enter MATREVIS, GURNEY, *and* SOLDIERS, *with*
KING EDWARD.

MATREVIS: My lord, be not pensive; we are your friends.
Men are ordain'd to live in misery;
Therefore, come; dalliance dangereth our lives.

KING EDWARD: Friends, whither must unhappy
    Edward go?
Will hateful Mortimer appoint no rest?
Must I be vexed like the nightly bird,
Whose sight is loathsome to all winged fowls?
When will the fury of his mind assuage?
When will his heart be satisfied with blood?
10   If mine will serve, unbowel straight this breast,
And give my heart to Isabel and him:
It is the chiefest mark they level at.

GURNEY: Not so, my liege: the queen hath given this
    charge,
To keep your grace in safety.
Your passions make your dolours to increase.

KING EDWARD: This usage makes my misery increase.
But can my air of life continue long,
When all my senses are annoy'd with stench?
Within a dungeon England's king is kept,
20   Where I am starv'd for want of sustenance.
My daily diet is heart-breaking sobs,
That almost rents the closet of my heart:
Thus lives old Edward not reliev'd by any,
And so must die, though pitied by many.
O, water, gentle friends, to cool my thirst,
And clear my body from foul excrements!

MATREVIS: Here's channel-water, as our charge is
    given:
Sit down, for we'll be barbers to your grace.

KING EDWARD: Traitors, away! What, will you
   murder me,
Or choke your sovereign with puddle-water?   *30*
GURNEY: No, but wash your face, and shave away
   your beard,
Lest you be known, and so be rescued.
MATREVIS: Why strive you thus? Your labour is in vain.
KING EDWARD: The wren may strive against the
   lion's strength,
But all in vain: so vainly do I strive
To seek for mercy at a tyrant's hand.
   They wash him with puddle-water, and shave his
   beard away.
Immortal powers, that know the painful cares
That wait upon my poor distressed soul,
O, level all your looks upon these daring men
That wrong their liege and sovereign, England's   *40*
   king!
O Gaveston, it is for thee that I am wrong'd!
For me both thou and both the Spensers died!
And for your sakes a thousand wrongs I'll take.
The Spensers' ghosts, wherever they remain,
Wish well to mine; then, tush, for them I'll die.
MATREVIS: 'Twixt theirs and yours shall be no enmity.
Come, come, away! Now put the torches out:
We'll enter in by darkness to Killingworth.
GURNEY: How now! Who comes there?
   Enter KENT.
MATREVIS: Guard the king sure. It is the Earl of Kent.   *50*
KING EDWARD: O gentle brother, help to rescue me!
MATREVIS: Keep them asunder. Thrust in the king!
KENT: Soldiers, let me but talk to him one word.
GURNEY: Lay hands upon the earl for this assault.
KENT: Lay down your weapons, traitors! Yield the king!
MATREVIS: Edmund, yield thou thyself, or thou shalt
   die.
KENT: Base villains, wherefore do you gripe me thus?

GURNEY: Bind him, and so convey him to the court.

KENT: Where is the court but here? Here is the king

60 And I will visit him: why stay you me?

MATREVIS: The court is where Lord Mortimer
remains:

Thither shall your honour go; and so, farewell.

Exeunt MATREVIS *and* GURNEY *with*
KING EDWARD.

KENT: O, miserable is that common-weal,

Where lords keep courts, and kings are lock'd in
prison!

FIRST SOLDIER: Wherefore stay we? On, sirs, to the
court!

KENT: Ay, lead me whither you will, even to my death,

Seeing that my brother cannot be releas'd.

Exeunt.

SCENE FOUR

The Royal Palace, London.

Enter the YOUNGER MORTIMER.

YOUNGER MORTIMER: The king must die, or
Mortimer goes down.

The commons now begin to pity him:

Yet he that is the cause of Edward's death,

Is sure to pay for it when his son's of age;

And therefore will I do it cunningly.

This letter, written by a friend of ours,

Contains his death, yet bids them save his life:

(*Reads*) *Edwardum occidere nolite timere bonum est,*

Fear not to kill the king, 'tis good he die.

10 But read it thus, and that's another sense:

Edwardum occidere nolite timere bonum est,

Kill not the king, 'tis good to fear the worst.

Unpointed as it is, thus shall it go.

13 *unpointed:* unpunctuated.

That, being dead, if it chance to be found,
Matrevis and the rest may bear the blame,
And we be quit that caus'd it to be done.
Within this room is lock'd the messenger
That shall convey it, and perform the rest;
And, by a secret token that he bears,
Shall he be murder'd when the deed is done.   20
Lightborn, come forth!

  Enter LIGHTBORN.

       Art thou as resolute as thou wast?

LIGHTBORN: What else, my lord? And far more
 resolute.

YOUNGER MORTIMER: And hast thou cast how to
 accomplish it?

LIGHTBORN: Ay, ay; and none shall know which way
 he died.

YOUNGER MORTIMER: But at his looks, Lightborn,
 thou wilt relent.

LIGHTBORN: Relent! Ha, ha! I use much to relent.

YOUNGER MORTIMER: Well, do it bravely, and be secret.

LIGHTBORN: You shall not need to give instructions;
 'Tis not the first time I have kill'd a man.
 I learn'd in Naples how to poison flowers,   30
 To strangle with a lawn thrust down the throat,
 To pierce the wind pipe with a needle's point,
 Or, whilst one is asleep, to take a quill,
 And blow a little powder in his ears,
 Or open his mouth, and pour quick-silver down.
 But yet I have a braver way than these.

YOUNGER MORTIMER: What's that?

LIGHTBORN: Nay, you shall pardon me; none shall know
 my tricks.

YOUNGER MORTIMER: I care not how it is, so it be not
 spied.
 Deliver this to Gurney and Matrevis.   40

  Gives letter.

27 *bravely*: in fine style (similarly 'braver' l. 36).

521

At every ten miles' end thou hast a horse.

Take this (*gives money*): away, and never see me more!

LIGHTBORN: No?

YOUNGER MORTIMER: No, unless thou bring me news
of Edward's death.

LIGHTBORN: That will I quickly do. Farewell, my lord.
Exit.

YOUNGER MORTIMER: The prince I rule, the queen
do I command,

And with a lowly congé to the ground

The proudest lords salute me as I pass;

I seal, I cancel, I do what I will.

50   Fear'd am I more than lov'd; – let me be fear'd,

And, when I frown, make all the court look pale.

I view the prince with Aristarchus' eyes,

Whose looks were as a breeching to a boy.

They thrust upon me the protectorship,

And sue to me for that that I desire;

While at the council-table, grave enough,

And not unlike a bashful puritan,

First I complain of imbecility,

Saying it is *onus quam gravissimum*;

60   Till, being interrupted by my friends,

Suscepi that *provinciam*, as they term it;

And, to conclude, I am Protector now.

Now is all sure: the queen and Mortimer

Shall rule the realm, the king; and none rule us.

Mine enemies will I plague, my friends advance;

And what I list command who dare control?

Major sum quàm cui possit fortuna nocere.

47 *congé*: bow.

52 *Aristarchus*: a severe scholar and teacher of the second century
B.C.

59 *onus quam gravissimus*: a most heavy burden.

61 *Suscepi . . . provinciam*: I accepted the province (i.e. the re-
sponsibility).

67 *Major sum . . .*: I am too great for fortune to harm.

And that this be the coronation-day,
It pleaseth me and Isabel the queen.
Trumpets within.
The trumpets sound; I must go take my place. 70
  Enter KING EDWARD THE THIRD, QUEEN
  ISABELLA, *the* ARCHBISHOP OF CANTERBURY,
  CHAMPION, *and* NOBLES.
ARCHBISHOP OF CANTERBURY: Long live King
  Edward, by the grace of God
King of England and Lord of Ireland!
CHAMPION: If any Christian, Heathen, Turk, or Jew,
Dares but affirm that Edward's not true king,
And will avouch his saying with the sword,
I am the Champion that will combat him.
YOUNGER MORTIMER: None comes: sound, trumpets!
  Trumpets.
KING EDWARD THE THIRD: Champion, here's to thee.
  Gives purse.
QUEEN ISABELLA: Lord Mortimer, now take him to
  your charge.
  Enter SOLDIERS *with* KENT *prisoner.*
YOUNGER MORTIMER: What traitor have we there with 80
  blades and bills?
FIRST SOLDIER: Edmund the Earl of Kent.
KING EDWARD THE THIRD: What hath he done?
FIRST SOLDIER: 'A would have taken the king away
  perforce,
As we were bringing him to Killingworth.
YOUNGER MORTIMER: Did you attempt his rescue,
  Edmund? Speak.
KENT: Mortimer, I did: he is our king,
And thou compell'st this prince to wear the crown.
YOUNGER MORTIMER: Strike off his head: he shall have
  martial law.
KENT: Strike off my head! Base traitor, I defy thee!
KING EDWARD THE THIRD: My lord, he is my uncle, 90
  and shall live.

523

YOUNGER MORTIMER: My lord, he is your enemy, and
    shall die.

KENT: Stay, villains!

KING EDWARD THE THIRD: Sweet mother, if I
    cannot pardon him

Entreat my Lord Protector for his life.

QUEEN ISABELLA: Son, be content: I dare not speak a
    word.

KING EDWARD THE THIRD: Nor I; and yet methinks
    I should command:

But, seeing I cannot, I'll entreat for him.

My lord, if you will let my uncle live,

I will requite it when I come to age.

100 YOUNGER MORTIMER: 'Tis for your highness' good
    and for the realm's.

How often shall I bid you bear him hence?

KENT: Art thou king? Must I die at thy command?

YOUNGER MORTIMER: At our command. Once more,
    away with him!

KENT: Let me but stay and speak. I will not go:

Either my brother or his son is king,

And none of both them thirst for Edmund's blood:

And therefore, soldiers, whither will you hale me?

    Soldiers hale KENT *away, and carry him to be beheaded.*

KING EDWARD THE THIRD: What safety may I look
    for at his hands,

If that my uncle shall be murder'd thus?

110 QUEEN ISABELLA: Fear not, sweet boy; I'll guard thee
    from thy foes.

Had Edmund liv'd, he would have sought thy death.

Come son, we'll ride a-hunting in the park.

KING EDWARD THE THIRD: And shall my uncle
    Edmund ride with us?

QUEEN ISABELLA: He is a traitor; think not on him.
    Come.

    Exeunt.

SCENE FIVE

Berkeley Castle.
Enter MATREVIS *and* GURNEY.

MATREVIS: Gurney, I wonder the king dies not,
Being in a vault up to the knees in water,
To which the channels of the castle run,
From whence a damp continually ariseth
That were enough to poison any man,
Much more a king, brought up so tenderly.

GURNEY: And so do I, Matrevis. Yesternight
I open'd but the door to throw him meat,
And I was almost stifled with the savour.

MATREVIS: He hath a body able to endure   10
More than we can inflict, and therefore now
Let us assail his mind another while.

GURNEY: Send for him out thence, and I will anger him.

MATREVIS: But stay; who's this?
    Enter LIGHTBORN.

LIGHTBORN: My Lord Protector greets you.
    Gives letter.

GURNEY: What's here? I know not how to conster it.

MATREVIS: Gurney, it was left unpointed for the nonce:
Edwardum occidere nolite timere,
That's his meaning.

LIGHTBORN: Know you this token? I must have the   20
    king.
    Gives token.

MATREVIS: Ay, stay a while; thou shalt have answer
    straight.
This villain s sent to make away the king.

GURNEY: I thought as much.

MATREVIS: And, when the murder's done,
See how he must be handled for his labour,
    Pereat iste! Let him have the king;

16 *conster*: construe.   26 *Pereat iste*: Let him die himself.

525

What else? Here is the keys, this is the lake.
Do as you are commanded by my lord.

LIGHTBORN: I know what I must do. Get you away:
30   Yet be not far off, I shall need your help.
See that in the next room I have a fire,
And get me a spit, and let it be red-hot.

MATREVIS: Very well.

GURNEY: Need you anything besides?

LIGHTBORN: What else? A table and a feather-bed.

GURNEY: That's all?

LIGHTBORN: Ay, ay: so, when I call you, bring it in.

MATREVIS: Fear not you that.

GURNEY: Here's a light to go into the dungeon.

    Gives light to LIGHTBORN, *and then exit with*
    MATREVIS.

40 LIGHTBORN: So, now
Must I about this gear: ne'er was there any
So finely handled as this king shall be.
Foh, here's a place indeed, with all my heart!

KING EDWARD: Who's there? What light is that?
    Wherefore comes thou?

LIGHTBORN: To comfort you, and bring you joyful
    news.

KING EDWARD: Small comfort finds poor Edward in
    thy looks.
Villain, I know thou com'st to murder me.

LIGHTBORN: To murder you, my most gracious lord?
Far is it from my heart to do you harm.
50   The queen sent me to see how you were us'd,
For she relents at this your misery:
And what eye can refrain from shedding tears,
To see a king in this most piteous state?

KING EDWARD: Weep'st thou already? List a while
    to me,
And when thy heart, were it as Gurney's is,
Or as Matrevis', hewn from the Caucasus,
Yet will it melt ere I have done my tale.

This dungeon where they keep me is the sink
Wherein the filth of all the castle falls.

LIGHTBORN: O villains!   60

KING EDWARD: And there, in mire and puddle, have
    I stood
This ten days' space; and, lest that I should sleep,
One plays continually upon a drum.
They give me bread and water, being a king;
So that, for want of sleep and sustenance,
My mind's distemper'd and my body's numb'd,
And whether I have limbs or no I know not.
O, would my blood dropp'd out from every vein,
As doth this water from my tatter'd robes!
Tell Isabel the queen, I look'd not thus,   70
When for her sake I ran at tilt in France,
And there unhors'd the Duke of Cleremont.

LIGHTBORN: O, speak no more my lord! This breaks
    my heart.
Lie on this bed, and rest yourself a while.

KING EDWARD: These looks of thine can harbour
    naught but death;
I see my tragedy written in thy brows.
Yet stay a while; forbear thy bloody hand,
And let me see the stroke before it comes,
That even then when I shall lose my life,
My mind may be more steadfast on my God.   80

LIGHTBORN: What means your highness to mistrust me
    thus?

KING EDWARD: What mean'st thou to dissemble with
    me thus?

LIGHTBORN: These hands were never stain'd with
    innocent blood,
Nor shall they now be tainted with a king's.

KING EDWARD: Forgive my thought for having such
    a thought.
One jewel have I left; receive thou this.
    Giving jewel.

Still fear I, and I know not what's the cause,
But every joint shakes as I give it thee.
O, if thou harbour'st murder in thy heart,
90   Let this gift change thy mind, and save thy soul!
Know that I am a king: O, at that name
I feel a hell of grief! Where is my crown?
Gone, gone! And do I remain alive?

LIGHTBORN: You're overwatch'd, my lord: lie down
    and rest.

KING EDWARD: But that grief keeps me waking, I
    should sleep;
For not these ten days have these eyes' lids clos'd.
Now, as I speak, they fall; and yet with fear
Open again. O, wherefore sitt'st thou here?

LIGHTBORN: If you mistrust me, I'll be gone, my lord.

100 KING EDWARD: No, no; for, if thou mean'st to murder
    me,
Thou wilt return again; and therefore stay.
    Sleeps.

LIGHTBORN: He sleeps.

KING EDWARD (*waking*): O, let me not die yet! Stay, O,
    stay a while!

LIGHTBORN: How now, my lord!

KING EDWARD: Something still buzzeth in mine ears,
And tells me, if I sleep, I never wake.
This fear is that which makes me tremble thus;
And therefore tell me, wherefore art thou come?

LIGHTBORN: To rid thee of thy life. Matrevis, come!
    Enter MATREVIS *and* GURNEY.

110 KING EDWARD: I am too weak and feeble to resist.
Assist me, sweet God, and receive my soul!

LIGHTBORN: Run for the table.

KING EDWARD: O, spare me, or despatch me in a trice!
    MATREVIS *brings in a table.*

LIGHTBORN: So, lay the table down, and stamp on it,
But not too hard, lest that you bruise his body.
    KING EDWARD *is murdered.*

MATREVIS: I fear me that this cry will raise the town,
  And therefore let us take horse and away.
LIGHTBORN: Tell me, sirs, was it not bravely done?
GURNEY: Excellent well: take this for thy reward.
  Stabs LIGHTBORN, *who dies.*
  Come, let us cast the body in the moat,   *120*
  And bear the king's to Mortimer our lord:
  Away!
  Exeunt with the bodies.

SCENE SIX

The Royal Palace, London.
Enter the YOUNGER MORTIMER *and* MATREVIS.
YOUNGER MORTIMER: Is't done, Matrevis, and the
  murderer dead?
MATREVIS: Ay, my good lord: I would it were undone!
YOUNGER MORTIMER: Matrevis, if thou now grow'st
  penitent,
  I'll be thy ghostly father; therefore choose,
  Whether thou wilt be secret in this,
  Or else die by the hand of Mortimer.
MATREVIS: Gurney, my lord, is fled, and will, I fear,
  Betray us both; therefore let me fly.
YOUNGER MORTIMER: Fly to the savages!
MATREVIS: I humbly thank your honour.   *10*
  Exit.
YOUNGER MORTIMER: As for myself, I stand as Jove's
  huge tree,
  And others are but shrubs compar'd to me.
  All tremble at my name, and I fear none:
  Let's see who dare impeach me for his death!
  Enter QUEEN ISABELLA.
  QUEEN ISABELLA: Ah, Mortimer, the king my son
    hath news

4 *ghostly father*: confessor, priest.

His father's dead, and we have murder'd him!

YOUNGER MORTIMER: What if he have? The king is
yet a child.

QUEEN ISABELLA: Ay, but he tears his hair and wrings
his hands,

And vows to be reveng'd upon us both.

20 Into the council-chamber he is gone,

To crave the aid and succour of his peers.

Ay me, see where he comes, and they with him!

Now, Mortimer, begins our tragedy.

Enter KING EDWARD THE THIRD, LORDS, *and*
ATTENDANTS.

FIRST LORD: Fear not, my lord; know that you are a king.

KING EDWARD THE THIRD: Villain! –

YOUNGER MORTIMER: Ho, now, my lord!

KING EDWARD THE THIRD: Think not that I am
frighted with thy words.

My father's murder'd through thy treachery;

And thou shalt die, and on his mournful hearse

30 Thy hateful and accursed head shall lie,

To witness to the world that by thy means

His kingly body was too soon interr'd.

QUEEN ISABELLA: Weep not, sweet son.

KING EDWARD THE THIRD: Forbid not me to weep;
he was my father,

And had you lov'd him half so well as I,

You could not bear his death thus patiently.

But you, I fear, conspir'd with Mortimer.

FIRST LORD: Why speak you not unto my lord the king?

YOUNGER MORTIMER: Because I think scorn to be
accus'd.

40 Who is the man dare say I murder'd him?

KING EDWARD THE THIRD: Traitor, in me my
loving father speaks,

And plainly saith, 'twas thou that murder'dst him.

YOUNGER MORTIMER: But hath your grace no other
proof than this?

KING EDWARD THE THIRD: Yes, if this be the hand
of Mortimer.
Showing letter.

YOUNGER MORTIMER (*aside to* QUEEN ISABELLA):
False Gurney hath betray'd me and himself.

QUEEN ISABELLA: I fear'd as much: murder can not be
hid.

YOUNGER MORTIMER: 'Tis my hand; what gather you
by this?

KING EDWARD THE THIRD: That thither thou didst
send a murderer.

YOUNGER MORTIMER: What murderer? Bring forth the
man I sent.

KING EDWARD THE THIRD: Ah, Mortimer, thou   *50*
know'st that he is slain!
And so shalt thou be too. Why stays he here?
Bring him unto a hurdle, drag him forth;
Hang him, I say, and set his quarters up,
But bring his head back presently to me.

QUEEN ISABELLA: For my sake, sweet son, pity
Mortimer!

YOUNGER MORTIMER: Madam, entreat not: I will
rather die
Than sue for life unto a paltry boy.

KING EDWARD THE THIRD: Hence with the traitor,
with the murderer!

YOUNGER MORTIMER: Base Fortune, now I see, that
in thy wheel
There is a point, to which when men aspire,   *60*
They tumble headlong down: that point I touch'd,
And, seeing there was no place to mount up higher,
Why shall I grieve at my declining fall?
Farewell, fair queen. Weep not for Mortimer,
That scorns the world, and, as a traveller,
Goes to discover countries yet unknown.

KING EDWARD THE THIRD: What, suffer you the
traitor to delay?

Exit the YOUNGER MORTIMER *with* FIRST
LORD *and some of the* ATTENDANTS.

QUEEN ISABELLA: As thou receivedst thy life from me,
Spill not the blood of gentle Mortimer!

70 KING EDWARD THE THIRD: This argues that you
spilt my father's blood,
Else would you not entreat for Mortimer.

QUEEN ISABELLA: I spill his blood! No.

KING EDWARD THE THIRD: Ay, madam, you; for so
the rumour runs.

QUEEN ISABELLA: That rumour is untrue! for loving
thee,
Is this report rais'd on poor Isabel.

KING EDWARD THE THIRD: I do not think her so
unnatural.

SECOND LORD: My lord, I fear me it will prove too true.

KING EDWARD THE THIRD: Mother, you are
suspected for his death,
And therefore we commit you to the Tower,
80 Till further trial may be made thereof.
If you be guilty, though I be your son,
Think not to find me slack or pitiful.

QUEEN ISABELLA: Nay, to my death; for too long have
I liv'd,
Whenas my son thinks to abridge my days.

KING EDWARD THE THIRD: Away with her! Her
words enforce these tears,
And I shall pity her, if she speak again.

QUEEN ISABELLA: Shall I not mourn for my beloved
lord,
And with the rest accompany him to his grave?

SECOND LORD: Thus, madam, 'tis the king's will you
shall hence.

90 QUEEN ISABELLA: He hath forgotten me. Stay, I am
his mother.

SECOND LORD: That boots not; therefore, gentle
madam, go.

QUEEN ISABELLA: Then come, sweet death, and rid me
of this grief!

Exit with SECOND LORD *and some of the*
ATTENDANTS.

Re-enter FIRST LORD, *with the head of the* YOUNGER
MORTIMER.

FIRST LORD: My lord, here is the head of Mortimer.

KING EDWARD THE THIRD: Go fetch my father's
hearse, where it shall lie;

And bring my funeral robes.

Exeunt ATTENDANTS.

          Accursed head,

Could I have rul'd thee then, as I do now,

Thou hadst not hatch'd this monstrous treachery!

Here comes the hearse: help me to mourn, my lords.

Re-enter ATTENDANTS, *with the hearse and funeral
robes.*

Sweet father, here unto thy murder'd ghost

I offer up this wicked traitor's head;   *100*

And let these tears, distilling from mine eyes,

Be witness of my grief and innocency.

Exeunt.

     FINIS

The Massacre at Paris

Dramatis Personae

CHARLES THE NINTH, *King of France*
DUKE OF ANJOU, *his brother, afterwards* KING HENRY
  THE THIRD
KING OF NAVARRE
PRINCE OF CONDÉ, *his cousin*
DUKE OF GUISE,
CARDINAL OF LORRAINE, } *brothers*
DUKE DUMAINE,
SON TO THE DUKE OF GUISE, *a boy*
THE LORD HIGH ADMIRAL
DUKE JOYEUX
EPERNOUN
PLESHÉ
BARTUS
TWO LORDS OF POLAND
GONZAGO
RETES
MOUNTSORRELL
MUGEROUN
THE CUTPURSE
LOREINE, *a preacher*
SEROUNE
RAMUS
TALAEUS
FRIAR
SURGEON
ENGLISH AGENT
APOTHECARY
CAPTAIN OF THE GUARD, PROTESTANTS,
  SCHOOLMASTERS, SOLDIERS, MURDERERS,
  ATTENDANTS, *etc.*
CATHERINE, *the Queen-Mother of France*
MARGARET, *her daughter, wife to the* KING OF NAVARRE
THE OLD QUEEN OF NAVARRE
DUCHESS OF GUISE
WIFE *to* SEROUNE
MAID *to the* DUCHESS OF GUISE

ACT ONE

SCENE ONE

Enter CHARLES, *the French king;* CATHERINE, *the Queen-Mother; the* KING OF NAVARRE; MARGARET, *Queen of Navarre; the* PRINCE OF CONDÉ; *the* LORD HIGH ADMIRAL; *the* OLD QUEEN OF NAVARRE; *with others.*

CHARLES: Prince of Navarre, my honourable brother,
  Prince Condé, and my good Lord Admiral,
  I wish this union[1]* and religious league,
  Knit in these hands, thus join'd in nuptial rites,
  May not dissolve till death dissolve our lives;
  And that the native sparks of princely love,
  That kindled first this motion in our hearts,
  May still be fuell'd in our progeny.
NAVARRE: The many favours which your grace hath
  shown,
  From time to time, but specially in this,   10
  Shall bind me ever to your highness' will,
  In what Queen-Mother or your grace commands.
CATHERINE: Thanks, son Navarre. You see we love
  you well,
  That link you in marriage with our daughter here;
  And, as you know, our difference in religion
  Might be a means to cross you in your love.
CHARLES: Well, madam, let that rest.
  And now, my lords, the marriage-rites perform'd,
  We think it good to go and consummate
  The rest with hearing of a holy mass.   20
  Sister, I think yourself will bear us company.
MARGARET: I will, my good lord.
CHARLES: The rest that will not go, my lords, may
  stay.

*Superior numbers refer to the Additional Notes at the end of the book.

539

Come, mother,
Let us go to honour this solemnity.

CATHERINE (*aside*): Which I'll dissolve with blood and
    cruelty.

    Exeunt all except the KING OF NAVARRE,
    CONDÉ, *and the* ADMIRAL.

NAVARRE: Prince Condé, and my good Lord Admiral,
Now Guise may storm, but do us little hurt,
Having the king, Queen Mother on our sides
30   To stop the malice of his envious heart,
That seeks to murder all the protestants.
Have you not heard of late how he decreed
(If that the king had given consent thereto)
That all the protestants that are in Paris
Should have been murdered the other night?

ADMIRAL: My lord, I marvel that th' aspiring Guise
Dares once adventure, without the king's consent,
To meddle or attempt such dangerous things.

CONDÉ: My lord, you need not marvel at the Guise,
40   For what he doth, the Pope will ratify,
In murder, mischief, or in tyranny.

NAVARRE: But He that sits and rules above the clouds
Doth hear and see the prayers of the just,
And will revenge the blood of innocents,
That Guise hath slain by treason of his heart,
And brought by murder to their timeless ends.

ADMIRAL: My lord, but did you mark the Cardinal,
The Guise's brother, and the Duke Dumaine,
How they did storm at these your nuptial rites,
50   Because the house of Bourbon now comes in,
And joins your lineage to the crown of France?

NAVARRE: And that's the cause that Guise so frowns
    at us,
And beats his brains to catch us in his trap,
Which he hath pitch'd within his deadly toil.

46 *timeless*: untimely.   54 *pitched*: cast his nets.
54 *toil*: trap.

Come, my lords, let's go to the church, and pray
That God may still defend the right of France,
And make his Gospel flourish in this land.
Exeunt.

SCENE TWO

Enter the DUKE OF GUISE.

GUISE: If ever Hymen lour'd at marriage-rites,
And had his altars deck'd with dusky lights;
If ever sun stain'd heaven with bloody clouds,
And made it look with terror on the world;
If ever day were turn'd to ugly night,
And night made semblance of the hue of hell;
This day, this hour, this fatal night,
Shall fully show the fury of them all.
Apothecary!
Enter APOTHECARY.

APOTHECARY: My lord? 10
GUISE: Now shall I prove, and guerdon to the full,
The love thou bear'st unto the house of Guise.
Where are those perfum'd gloves which I sent
To be poison'd? Hast thou done them? Speak;
Will every savour breed a pang of death?
APOTHECARY: See where they be, my good lord; and
he that smells
But to them, dies.
GUISE: Then thou remainest resolute?
APOTHECARY: I am, my lord, in what your grace
commands,
Till death. 20
GUISE: Thanks, my good friend: I will requite thy love.
Go, then, present them to the Queen Navarre;
For she is that huge blemish in our eye,
That makes these upstart heresies in France.
11 *guerdon*: reward.

Be gone, my friend, present them to her straight.
Exit APOTHECARY.
Soldier!
Enter a SOLDIER.

SOLDIER: My lord?

GUISE: Now come thou forth, and play thy tragic part.
Stand in some window, opening near the street,
30   And when thou see'st the Admiral ride by,
Discharge thy musket, and perform his death,
And then I'll guerdon thee with store of crowns.

SOLDIER: I will, my lord.
Exit.

GUISE: Now, Guise, begins those deep-engender'd
thoughts
To burst abroad those never-dying flames
Which cannot be extinguish'd but by blood.
Oft have I levell'd, and at last have learn'd
That peril is the chiefest way to happiness,
And resolution honour's fairest aim.
40   What glory is there in a common good,
That hangs for every peasant to achieve?
That like I best that flies beyond my reach.
Set me to scale the high Pyramides,
And thereon set the diadem of France;
I'll either rend it with my nails to naught,
Or mount the top with my aspiring wings,
Although my downfall be the deepest hell.
For this I wake, when others think I sleep;
For this I wait, that scorn attendance else.
50   For this, my quenchless thirst, whereon I build,
Hath often pleaded kindred to the king;
For this, this head, this heart, this hand, and sword,
Contrives, imagines, and fully executes,
Matters of import aimed at by many,
Yet understood by none.
For this, hath heaven engender'd me of earth;

49 *attendance*: waiting.

For this, this earth sustains my body's weight,
And with this weight I'll counterpoise a crown,
Or with seditions weary all the world.
For this, from Spain the stately Catholics   60
Sends Indian gold to coin me French ecues;
For this, have I a largess from the Pope,
A pension, and a dispensation too;
And by that privilege to work upon,
My policy hath fram'd religion.
Religion! *O Diabole!*
Fie, I am asham'd, however that I seem,
To think a word of such a simple sound,
Of so great matter should be made the ground!
The gentle king, whose pleasure uncontroll'd   70
Weakeneth his body, and will waste his realm,
If I repair not what he ruinates.
Him, as a child, I daily win with words,
So that for proof he barely bears the name;
I execute, and he sustains the blame.
The Mother Queen works wonders for my sake,
And in my love entombs the hope of France,
Rifling the bowels of her treasury,
To supply my wants and necessity.
Paris hath full five hundred colleges,   80
As monasteries, priories, abbeys, and halls,
Wherein are thirty thousand able men,
Besides a thousand sturdy student Catholics;
And more, – of my knowledge, in one cloister keeps
Five hundred fat Franciscan friars and priests.
All this, and more, if more may be compris'd,
To bring the will of our desires to end.
Then, Guise,
Since thou hast all the cards within thy hands,
To shuffle or cut, take this as surest thing,   90
That, right or wrong, thou deal thyself a king.
Ay, but, Navarre, Navarre, – 'tis but a nook of France,

61 *ecues*: crowns.   65 *policy*: Machiavellian cunning.

Sufficient yet for such a petty king,
That, with a rabblement of his heretics,
Blinds Europe's eyes, and troubleth our estate.
Him will we – (*pointing to his sword*) but first let's
    follow those in France
That hinder our possession to the crown.
As Caesar to his soldiers, so say I:
Those that hate me will I learn to loathe.
Give me a look, that, when I bend the brows,
Pale death may walk in furrows of my face;
A hand, that with a grasp may gripe the world;
An ear to hear what my detractors say;
A royal seat, a sceptre, and a crown;
That those which do behold, they may become
As men that stand and gaze against the sun.
The plot is laid, and things shall come to pass
Where resolution strives for victory.
    Exit.

100

SCENE THREE

Enter the KING OF NAVARRE, QUEEN MARGARET,
the OLD QUEEN OF NAVARRE, *the* PRINCE OF
CONDÉ, *and the* ADMIRAL; *they are met by the*
APOTHECARY *with the gloves, which he gives to the*
OLD QUEEN.

APOTHECARY: Madam,
I beseech your grace to accept this simple gift.
OLD QUEEN OF NAVARRE: Thanks, my good friend.
    Hold, take thou this reward.
    Gives a purse.
APOTHECARY: I humbly thank your majesty.
    Exit.
OLD QUEEN OF NAVARRE: Methinks the gloves have
    a very strong perfume,
The scent whereof doth make my head to ache.

NAVARRE: Doth not your grace know the man that gave
    them you?

OLD QUEEN OF NAVARRE: Not well, but do remember
    such a man.

ADMIRAL: Your grace was ill-advis'd to take them, then,
    Considering of these dangerous times.   *10*

OLD QUEEN OF NAVARRE: Help, son Navarre! I am
    poison'd!

MARGARET: The heavens forbid your highness such
    mishap!

NAVARRE: The late suspicion of the Duke of Guise
    Might well have mov'd your highness to beware
    How you did meddle with such dangerous gifts.

MARGARET: Too late it is, my lord, if that be true,
    To blame her highness; but I hope it be
    Only some natural passion makes her sick.

OLD QUEEN OF NAVARRE: O, no, sweet Margaret!
    The fatal poison
    Works within my head; my brain-pan breaks;   *20*
    My heart doth faint; I die!
    Dies.

NAVARRE: My mother poison'd here before my face!
    O gracious God, what times are these!
    O, grant, sweet God, my days may end with hers,
    That I with her may die and live again!

MARGARET: Let not this heavy chance, my dearest lord,
    (For whose effects my soul is massacred),
    Infect thy gracious breast with fresh supply
    To aggravate our sudden misery.

ADMIRAL: Come, my lords, let us bear her body hence, *30*
    And see it honoured with just solemnity.
    As they are going out, the SOLDIER *dischargeth his*
    musket at the ADMIRAL.

CONDÉ: What, are you hurt, my Lord High Admiral?

ADMIRAL: Ay, my good lord, shot through the arm.

NAVARRE: We are betray'd![2] Come, my lords,

    18 *natural passion*: natural bodily discomfort.

And let us go tell the king of this.

ADMIRAL: These are
The cursed Guisians, that do seek our death.
O, fatal was this marriage to us all.

Exeunt, bearing out the body of the OLD QUEEN OF
NAVARRE.

SCENE FOUR

Enter KING CHARLES, CATHERINE *the*
Queen-Mother, GUISE, ANJOU, *and* DUMAINE.

CATHERINE: My noble son, and princely Duke of
Guise,
Now have we got the fatal, straggling deer
Within the compass of a deadly toil,
And, as we late decreed, we may perform.

CHARLES: Madam, it will be noted through the world
An action bloody and tyrannical;
Chiefly, since under safety of our word
They justly challenge their protection.
Besides, my heart relents that noble men,
10   Only corrupted in religion,
Ladies of honour, knights, and gentlemen,
Should, for their conscience, taste such ruthless ends.

ANJOU: Though gentle minds should pity others' pains,
Yet will the wisest note their proper griefs,
And rather seek to scourge their enemies
Than be themselves base subjects to the whip.

GUISE: Methinks, my Lord, Anjou hath well advis'd
Your highness to consider of the thing,
And rather choose to seek your country's good
20   Than pity or relieve these upstart heretics.

CATHERINE: I hope these reasons may serve my
princely son
To have some care for fear of enemies.

3 *toil*: trap.   14 *proper*: own.

CHARLES: Well, madam, I refer it to your majesty,
  And to my nephew here, the Duke of Guise.
  What you determine, I will ratify.
CATHERINE: Thanks to my princely son. Then tell
    me, Guise,
  What order will you set down for the massacre?
GUISE: Thus, madam. They
  That shall be actors in this massacre
  Shall wear white crosses on their burgonets,   30
  And tie white linen scarfs about their arms;
  He that wants these, and is suspected of heresy,
  Shall die, be he king or emperor. Then I'll have
  A peal of ordnance shot from the tower, at which
  They all shall issue out, and set the streets,
  And then,
  The watchword being given, a bell shall ring,
  Which when they hear, they shall begin to kill,
  And never cease until that bell shall cease;
  Then breathe a while.   40
    Enter the ADMIRAL'S SERVING-MAN.
CHARLES: How now, fellow! What news?
SERVING-MAN: And it please your grace, the Lord
    High Admiral,
  Riding the streets, was traitorously shot;
  And most humbly entreats your majesty
  To visit him, sick in his bed.
CHARLES: Messenger, tell him I will see him straight.
    Exit SERVING-MAN.
  What shall we do now with the Admiral?
CATHERINE: Your majesty were best go visit him,
  And make a show as if all were well.
CHARLES: Content; I will go visit the Admiral.   50
GUISE: And I will go take order for his death.
    Exeunt CATHERINE *and* GUISE.
    The ADMIRAL *discovered in bed.*
CHARLES: How fares it with my Lord High Admiral?
  Hath he been hurt with villains in the street?

I vow and swear, as I am King of France,
To find and to repay the man with death,
With death delay'd and torments never us'd,
That durst presume, for hope of any gain,
To hurt the noble man their sovereign loves.

ADMIRAL: Ah, my good lord, these are the Guisians,
60   That seek to massacre our guiltless lives!

CHARLES: Assure yourself, my good Lord Admiral,
I deeply sorrow for your treacherous wrong;
And that I am not more secure myself
Than I am careful you should be preserv'd.
Cousin, take twenty of our strongest guard,
And, under your direction, see they keep
All treacherous violence from our noble friend;
Repaying all attempts with present death
Upon the cursed breakers of our peace.
70   And so be patient, good Lord Admiral,
And every hour I will visit you.

ADMIRAL: I humbly thank your royal majesty.

Exeunt omnes.

SCENE FIVE

Enter GUISE, ANJOU, DUMAINE, GONZAGO,
RETES, MOUNTSORRELL, *and* SOLDIERS, *to the
massacre.*

GUISE: Anjou, Dumaine, Gonzago, Retes, swear,
By the argent crosses in your burgonets,
To kill all that you suspect of heresy.

DUMAINE: I swear by this, to be unmerciful.

ANJOU: I am disguis'd, and none knows who I am,
And therefore mean to murder all I meet.

GONZAGO: And so will I.

RETES: And I.

GUISE: Away, then! Break into the Admiral's house.

10 RETES: Ay, let the Admiral be first despatch'd.

GUISE: The Admiral,

Chief standard-bearer to the Lutherans,
Shall in the entrance of this massacre
Be murder'd in his bed.
Gonzago, conduct them thither; and then
Beset his house, that not a man may live.

ANJOU: That charge is mine. Switzers, keep you the
    streets;
And at each corner shall the king's guard stand.

GONZAGO: Come, sirs, follow me.
    Exit GONZAGO *with others.*

ANJOU: Cousin, the captain of the Admiral's guard,   *20*
Plac'd by my brother, will betray his lord.
Now, Guise, shall Catholics flourish once again;
The head being off, the members cannot stand.

RETES: But look, my lord, there's some in the Admiral's
    house.
    The ADMIRAL *discovered in bed;* GONZAGO *and others
    in the house.*

ANJOU: In lucky time: come, let us keep this lane,
And slay his servants that shall issue out.

GONZAGO: Where is the Admiral?

ADMIRAL: O, let me pray before I die!

GONZAGO: Then pray unto our Lady; kiss this cross.
    Stabs him.

ADMIRAL: O God, forgive my sins!   *30*
    Dies.

GUISE: Gonzago, what, is he dead?

GONZAGO: Ay, my lord.

GUISE: Then throw him down.
    The body of the ADMIRAL *is thrown down.*

ANJOU: Now, cousin, view him well:
It may be 'tis some other, and he escap'd.

GUISE: Cousin, 'tis he; I know him by his look.
See where my soldier shot him through the arm;
He miss'd him near, but we have struck him now.
    Ah, base Chatillon and degenerate,

17 *Switzers*: Swiss mercenaries.

40 Chief standard-bearer to the Lutherans,
Thus, in despite of thy religion,
The Duke of Guise stamps on thy lifeless bulk!
ANJOU: Away with him! Cut off his head and hands,
And send them for a present to the Pope;
And, when this just revenge is finished,
Unto Mount Faucon will we drag his corse;
And he, that living hated so the Cross,
Shall, being dead, be hang'd thereon in chains.
GUISE: Anjou, Gonzago, Retes, if that you three
50 Will be as resolute as I and Dumaine,
There shall not a Huguenot breathe in France.
ANJOU: I swear by this cross, we'll not be partial,
But slay as many as we can come near.
GUISE: Mountsorrell, go shoot the ordnance off,
That they, which have already set the street,
May know their watchword; then toll the bell,
And so let's forward to the massacre.
MOUNTSORRELL: I will, my lord.
        Exit.
GUISE: And now, my lords, let's closely to our business.
60 ANJOU: Anjou will follow thee.
DUMAINE: And so will Dumaine.
        The ordnance being shot off, the bell tolls.
GUISE: Come, then, let's away.
        Exeunt.

SCENE SIX

Enter GUISE, *and the rest, with their swords drawn,
chasing the Protestants.*
GUISE: *Tue, tue, tue!*
Let none escape! Murder the Huguenots!
ANJOU: Kill them! kill them!
        Exeunt.
        Enter LOREINE, *running;* GUISE *and the rest
        pursuing him.*

550

GUISE: Loreine, Loreine! follow Loreine! – Sirrah,
  Are you a preacher of these heresies?
LOREINE: I am a preacher of the word of God;
  And thou a traitor to thy soul and him.
GUISE: 'Dearly beloved brother,' – thus 'tis written.
  Stabs LOREINE, *who dies.*
ANJOU: Stay, my lord, let me begin the psalm.
GUISE: Come, drag him away, and throw him in a ditch. *10*
  Exeunt with the body.
  Enter MOUNTSORRELL, *and knocks at* SEROUNE'S
  door.
SEROUNE'S WIFE (*within*): Who is that which knocks
  there?
MOUNTSORRELL: Mountsorrell, from the Duke of
  Guise.
SEROUNE'S WIFE (*within*): Husband, come down; here's
  one would speak with you.
From the Duke of Guise.
  Enter SEROUNE *from the house.*
SEROUNE: To speak with me, from such a man as he?
MOUNTSORRELL: Ay, ay, for this, Seroune; and thou
  shalt ha't.
  Showing his dagger.
SEROUNE: O, let me pray, before I take my death!
MOUNTSORRELL: Despatch, then, quickly.
SEROUNE: O Christ, my Saviour!
MOUNTSORRELL: Christ, villain! *20*
  Why, darest thou to presume to call on Christ,
  Without the intercession of some saint?
  Sanctus Jacobus, he's my saint; pray to him.
SEROUNE: O, let me pray unto my God!
MOUNTSORRELL: Then take this with you.
  Stabs SEROUNE, *who dies, and then exit.*

SCENE SEVEN

Enter RAMUS,[3] *in his study.*

RAMUS: What fearful cries comes from the river Seine,
That fright poor Ramus sitting at his book!
I fear the Guisians have pass'd the bridge,
And mean once more to menace me.
    Enter TALAEUS.[4]

TALAEUS: Fly, Ramus, fly, if thou wilt save thy life!
RAMUS: Tell me, Talaeus, wherefore should I fly?
TALAEUS: The Guisians are
Hard at thy door, and mean to murder us.
Hark, hark, they come! I'll leap out at the window.
10 RAMUS: Sweet Talaeus, stay.
    Enter GONZAGO *and* RETES.
GONZAGO: Who goes there?
RETES: 'Tis Talaeus, Ramus' bedfellow.
GONZAGO: What art thou?
TALAEUS: I am, as Ramus is, a Christian.
RETES: O, let him go; he is a Catholic.
    Exit TALAEUS.
GONZAGO: Come, Ramus, more gold, or thou shalt
have the stab.
RAMUS: Alas, I am a scholar! How should I have gold?
All that I have is but my stipend from the king,
Which is no sooner receiv'd but it is spent.
    Enter GUISE, ANJOU, DUMAINE,
    MOUNTSORRELL, *and* SOLDIERS.
20 ANJOU: Who have you there?
RETES: 'Tis Ramus, the king's Professor of Logic.
GUISE: Stab him.
RAMUS: O, good my lord,
Wherein hath Ramus been so offensious?
GUISE: Marry, sir, in having a smack in all,
And yet didst never sound anything to the depth.
Was it not thou that scoff'st the *Organon,*

27 *Organon*: Aristotle's books on logic.

552

And said it was a heap of vanities?
He that will be a flat dichotomist,
And seen in nothing but epitomes,   30
Is in your judgment thought a learned man;
And he, forsooth, must go and preach in Germany,
Excepting against doctors' axioms,
And *ipse dixi* with this quiddity,
Argumentum testimonii est inartificiale.
To contradict which, I say, Ramus shall die:
How answer you that? Your *nego argumentum*
Cannot serve, sirrah. – Kill him.
RAMUS: O, good my lord, let me but speak a word!
ANJOU: Well, say on.   40
RAMUS: Not for my life do I desire this pause;
But in my latter hour to purge myself,
In that I know the things that I have wrote,
Which, as I hear, one Scheckius takes it ill,
Because my places, being three, contains all his.
I knew the *Organon* to be confus'd,
And I reduc'd it into better form:
And this for Aristotle will I say,
That he that despiseth him can ne'er
Be good in logic or philosophy;   50
And that's because the blockish Sorbonnists
Attribute as much unto their works
As to the service of the eternal God.
GUISE: Why suffer you that peasant to declaim?
Stab him, I say, and send him to his friends in hell.
ANJOU: Ne'er was there collier's son so full of pride.
     Stabs RAMUS, *who dies.*
GUISE: My Lord of Anjou, there are a hundred
     Protestants,

30 *seen in*: versed in.   34 *quiddity*: quibble.
35 *Argumentum* . . .: literally, 'The argument of the evidence is
inartificial'.
37 *nego argumentum*: 'I refuse the argument'.
45 *places*: proofs.
51 *Sorbonnists*: theologians at the Sorbonne.

Which we have chas'd into the river Seine,
That swim about, and so preserve their lives.

60   How may we do? I fear me they will live.

DUMAINE: Go place some men upon the bridge,
With bows and darts, to shoot at them they see,
And sink them in the river as they swim.

GUISE: 'Tis well advis'd, Dumaine; go see it straight be
done.

Exit DUMAINE.

And in the meantime, my lord, could we devise
To get those pedants from the King Navarre,
That are tutors to him and the Prince of Condé —

ANJOU: For that, let me alone: cousin, stay you here
And when you see me in, then follow hard.

    ANJOU *knocketh at the door; and enter the* KING OF
    NAVARRE *and the* PRINCE OF CONDÉ, *with their*
    two SCHOOLMASTERS.

70   How now, my lords! How fare you?

NAVARRE: My lord, they say
That all the Protestants are massacred.

ANJOU: Ay, so they are; but yet, what remedy?
I have done what I could to stay this broil.

NAVARRE: But yet, my lord, the report doth run,
That you were one that made this massacre.

ANJOU: Who I? you are deceiv'd; I rose but now.

    GUISE, GONZAGO, RETES, MOUNTSORRELL, *and*
    SOLDIERS, *come forward.*

GUISE: Murder the Huguenots! Take those pedants
hence!

NAVARRE: Thou traitor, Guise, lay off thy bloody
hands!

80 CONDÉ: Come, let us go tell the king.

Exit with the KING OF NAVARRE.

GUISE: Come sirs,
I'll whip you to death with my poniard's point.

Stabs the SCHOOLMASTERS, *who die.*

ANJOU: Away with them both!

Exeunt ANJOU *and* SOLDIERS *with the bodies.*

GUISE: And now, sirs, for this night let our fury stay.
Yet will we not that the massacre shall end.
Gonzago, post you to Orleans,
Retes to Dieppe, Mountsorrell unto Rouen,
And spare not one that you suspect of heresy.
And now stay
That bell, that to the devil's matins rings.   *90*
Now every man put off his burgonet,
And so convey him closely to his bed.

    Exeunt.

ACT TWO

SCENE ONE

Enter ANJOU, *with two* LORDS OF POLAND.

ANJOU: My lords of Poland, I must needs confess,
The offer of your Prince Electors far
Beyond the reach of my deserts;
For Poland is, as I have been inform'd,
A martial people, worthy such a king
As hath sufficient counsel in himself
To lighten doubts, and frustrate subtle foes;
And such a king, whom practice long hath taught
To please himself with manage of the wars,
The greatest wars within our Christian bounds, –   *10*
I mean our wars against the Muscovites,
And, on the other side, against the Turk,
Rich princes both, and mighty emperors.
Yet, by my brother Charles, our king of France,
And by his grace's council, it is thought
That, if I undertake to wear the crown
Of Poland, it may prejudice their hope
Of my inheritance to the crown of France;
For, if th' Almighty take my brother hence,

20 By due descent the regal seat is mine.
With Poland, therefore, must I covenant thus:
That if, by death of Charles, the diadem
Of France be cast on me, then, with your leaves,
I may retire me to my native home.
If your commission serve to warrant this,
I thankfully shall undertake the charge
Of you and yours, and carefully maintain
The wealth and safety of your kingdom's right.
FIRST LORD: All this, and more, your highness shall
command,
30 For Poland's crown and kingly diadem.
ANJOU: Then, come, my lords, let's go.
Exeunt.

SCENE TWO

Enter two MEN, *with the* ADMIRAL'S *body.*

FIRST MAN: Now, sirrah, what shall we do with the
Admiral?
SECOND MAN: Why, let us burn him for an heretic.
FIRST MAN: O, no! his body will infect the fire, and the
fire the air, and so we shall be poisoned with him.
SECOND MAN: What shall we do, then?
FIRST MAN: Let's throw him into the river.
SECOND MAN: O, 'twill corrupt the water, and the water
the fish, and by the fish ourselves, when we eat them!
10 FIRST MAN: Then throw him into the ditch.
SECOND MAN: No, no. To decide all doubts, be ruled by
me: let's hang him here upon this tree.
FIRST MAN: Agreed.
They hang up the body on a tree, and then exeunt.
Enter GUISE, CATHERINE *the Queen-Mother, and*
the CARDINAL OF LORRAINE, *with*
ATTENDANTS.
GUISE: Now, madam, how like you our lusty Admiral?

CATHERINE: Believe me, Guise, he becomes the place
    so well
  As I could long ere this have wish'd him there.
  But come,
  Let's walk aside; the air's not very sweet.
GUISE: No, by my faith, madam.
  Sirs, take him away, and throw him in some ditch.   20
    The ATTENDANTS *bear off the* ADMIRAL'S *body.*
  And now, madam, as I understand,
  There are a hundred Huguenots and more,
  Which in the woods do hold their synagogue,
  And meet daily about this time of day;
  And thither will I, to put them to the sword.
CATHERINE: Do so, sweet Guise; let us delay no time;
  For, if these stragglers gather head again,
  And disperse themselves throughout the realm of
    France,
  It will be hard for us to work their deaths.
  Be gone; delay no time, sweet Guise.   30
GUISE: Madam,
  I go as whirlwinds rage before a storm.
  Exit.
CATHERINE: My Lord of Lorraine, have you mark'd
  of late,
  How Charles our son begins for to lament
  For the late night's work which my lord of Guise
  Did make in Paris amongst the Huguenots?
CARDINAL OF LORRAINE: Madam, I have heard him
  solemnly vow,
  With the rebellious King of Navarre,
  For to revenge their deaths upon us all.
CATHERINE: Ay, but, my lord, let me alone for that;   40
  For Catherine must have her will in France.
  As I do live, so surely shall he die,
  And Henry then shall wear the diadem;
  And, if he grudge or cross his mother's will,
  40 *let me alone*: leave that to me.

I'll disinherit him and all the rest;
For I'll rule France, but they shall wear the crown,
And, if they storm, I then may pull them down.
Come, my lord, let us go.
Exeunt.

SCENE THREE

Enter five or six PROTESTANTS, *with books, and kneel
together. Then enter* GUISE *and others.*

GUISE: Down with the Huguenots! Murder them!

FIRST PROTESTANT: O Monsieur de Guise, hear me
but speak!

GUISE: No, villain; that tongue of thine,
That hath blasphem'd the holy Church of Rome,
Shall drive no plaints into the Guise's ears,
To make the justice of my heart relent.
Tue, tue, tue! let none escape.
They kill the Protestants.
So, drag them away.
Exeunt with the bodies.

ACT THREE

SCENE ONE

Enter KING CHARLES, *supported by the* KING OF
NAVARRE *and* EPERNOUN; CATHERINE *the
Queen-Mother, the* CARDINAL OF LORRAINE,
PLESHÉ, *and* ATTENDANTS.

CHARLES: O, let me stay, and rest me here a while!
A griping pain hath seiz'd upon my heart;
A sudden pang, the messenger of death.

CATHERINE: O, say not so! Thou kill'st thy mother's
heart.

CHARLES: I must say so; pain forceth me complain.

NAVARRE: Comfort yourself, my lord, and have no
    doubt
But God will sure restore you to your health.

CHARLES: O, no, my loving brother of Navarre!
I have deserv'd a scourge, I must confess;
Yet is there patience of another sort   10
Than to misdo the welfare of their king:
God grant my nearest friends may prove no worse!
O, hold me up! my sight begins to fail,
My sinews shrink, my brains turn upside down;
My heart doth break: I faint and die.[5]
    Dies.

CATHERINE: What, art thou dead? Sweet son, speak
    to thy mother!
O, no, his soul is fled from out his breast,
And he nor hears nor sees us what we do!
My lords, what resteth there now for to be done,
But that we presently despatch ambassadors   20
To Poland, to call Henry back again,
To wear his brother's crown and dignity?
Epernoun, go see it presently be done,
And bid him come without delay to us.

EPERNOUN: Madam, I will.
    Exit.

CATHERINE: And now, my lords, after these funerals
    done,
We will, with all the speed we can, provide
For Henry's coronation from Polony.
Come, let us take his body hence.
    The body of KING CHARLES *is borne out; and exeunt
    all except the* KING OF NAVARRE *and* PLESHÉ.

NAVARRE: And now, Navarre whilst that these broils   30
    do last,
My opportunity may serve me fit
To steal from France, and hie me to my home,
For here's no safety in the realm for me:

And now that Henry is recall'd from Poland,
It is my due, by just succession;
And therefore, as speedily as I can perform,
I'll muster up an army secretly,
For fear that Guise, join'd with the king of Spain,
Might seek to cross me in mine enterprise.

40 But God, that always doth defend the right,
Will show his mercy, and preserve us still.

PLESHÉ: The virtues of our true religion
Cannot but march, with many graces more,
Whose army shall discomfit all your foes,
And, at the length, in Pampelonia crown
(In spite of Spain, and all the popish power,
That holds it from your highness wrongfully)
Your majesty her rightful lord and sovereign.

NAVARRE: Truth, Pleshé; and God so prosper me in all,

50 As I intend to labour for the truth,
And true profession of His holy word!
Come, Pleshé, let's away whilst time doth serve.
  Exeunt.

SCENE TWO

*Trumpets sounded within, and a cry of 'Vive le Roi,' two
or three times. Enter* ANJOU *crowned as King Henry
the Third;* CATHERINE *the Queen-Mother, the*
CARDINAL OF LORRAINE, GUISE, EPERNOUN,
MUGEROUN, *the* CUTPURSE, *and others.*

ALL: *Vive le Roi, Vive le Roi!*
  A flourish of trumpets.

CATHERINE: Welcome from Poland, Henry, once
  again!
Welcome to France, thy father's royal seat!
Here hast thou a country void of fears,

45 *Pampelonia*: Pampeluna, capital of Navarre.

A warlike people to maintain thy right,
A watchful senate for ordaining laws,
A loving mother to preserve thy state,
And all things that a king may wish besides;
All this, and more, hath Henry with his crown.

CARDINAL OF LORRAINE: And long may Henry   *10*
   enjoy all this, and more!

ALL: *Vive le Roi, Vive le Roi!*
   A flourish of trumpets.

HENRY: Thanks to you all. The guider of all crowns
   Grant that our deeds may well deserve your loves!
   And so they shall, if fortune speed my will,
   And yield your thoughts to height of my deserts.
   What say our minions? Think they Henry's heart
   Will not both harbour love and majesty?
   Put off that fear, they are already join'd:
   No person, place, or time, or circumstance,
   Shall slack my love's affection from his bent.   *20*
   As now you are, so shall you still persist,
   Removeless from the favours of your king.

MUGEROUN: We know that noble minds change not
   their thoughts
   For wearing of a crown, in that your grace
   Hath worn the Poland diadem before
   You were invested in the crown of France.

HENRY: I tell thee, Mugeroun, we will be friends,
   And fellows too, whatever storms arise.

MUGEROUN: Then may it please your majesty to give
   me leave
   To punish those that do profane this holy feast.   *30*
     MUGEROUN *cuts off the* CUTPURSE'S *ear, for
     cutting the gold buttons off his cloak.*

HENRY: How mean'st thou that?

CUTPURSE: O Lord, mine ear!

MUGEROUN: Come, sir, give me my buttons, and here's
   your ear.

GUISE: Sirrah, take him away.

HENRY: Hands off, good fellow; I will be his bail
For this offence. – Go, sirrah, work no more
Till this our coronation-day be past. –
And now,
Our solemn rites of coronation done,
40   What now remains but for a while to feast,
And spend some days in barriers, tourney, tilt,
And like disports, such as do fit the court?
Let's go, my lords; our dinner stays for us.
> *Exeunt all except* CATHERINE *the Queen-Mother and*
> *the* CARDINAL OF LORRAINE.

CATHERINE: My Lord Cardinal of Lorraine, tell me,
How likes your grace my son's pleasantness?
His mind, you see, runs on his minions,
And all his heaven is to delight himself;
And, whilst he sleeps securely thus in ease,
Thy brother Guise and we may now provide
50   To plant ourselves with such authority
As not a man may live without our leaves.
Then shall the Catholic faith of Rome
Flourish in France, and none deny the same.

CARDINAL OF LORRAINE: Madam, as in secrecy I
    was told,
My brother Guise hath gather'd a power of men,
Which are, he saith, to kill the Puritans;
But 'tis the house of Bourbon that he means.
Now, madam, must you insinuate with the king,
And tell him that 'tis for his country's good,
60   And common profit of religion.

CATHERINE: Tush, man, let me alone with him,
To work the way to bring this thing to pass;
And, if he do deny what I do say,
I'll despatch him with his brother presently,
And then shall Monsieur wear the diadem.
Tush, all shall die unless I have my will;
For, while she lives, Catherine will be queen.

65 *Monsieur*: the Duc d'Alençon.

Come, my lord, let us go seek the Guise,
And then determine of this enterprise.
Exeunt.

ACT FOUR

SCENE ONE

Enter the DUCHESS OF GUISE *and her* MAID.

DUCHESS OF GUISE: Go fetch me pen and ink, –
MAID: I will, madam.
DUCHESS OF GUISE: That I may write unto my
    dearest lord.
    Exit MAID.
Sweet Mugeroun, 'tis he that hath my heart,
And Guise usurps it 'cause I am his wife.
Fain would I find some means to speak with him,
But cannot, and therefore am enforc'd to write,
That he may come and meet me in some place,
Where we may one enjoy the other's sight.
    Re-enter the MAID, *with pen, ink, and paper.*
So, set it down, and leave me to myself.   *10*
    Exit MAID. *The* DUCHESS *writes.*
O, would to God this quill that here doth write,
Had late been pluck'd from out fair Cupid's wing,
That it might print these lines within his heart!
    Enter GUISE.
GUISE: What, all alone, my love? and writing too?
I prithee, say to whom thou writes.
DUCHESS OF GUISE: To such
A one, my lord, as when she reads my lines
Will laugh, I fear me, at their good array.
GUISE: I pray thee, let me see.
DUCHESS OF GUISE: O, no, my lord; a woman only   *20*
    must
Partake the secrets of my heart.

563

GUISE: But, madam, I must see.

> *Seizes the paper.*

Are these your secrets that no man must know?

DUCHESS OF GUISE: O, pardon me, my lord!

GUISE: Thou trothless and unjust! What lines are these?
Am I grown old, or is thy lust grown young?
Or hath my love been so obscur'd in thee,
That others need to comment on my text?
Is all my love forgot, which held thee dear,

30   Ay, dearer than the apple of mine eye?
Is Guise's glory but a cloudy mist,
In sight and judgment of thy lustful eye?
Mort Dieu! wert not the fruit within thy womb,
Of whose increase I set some longing hope,
This wrathful hand should strike thee to the heart.
Hence, strumpet! hide thy head for shame,
And fly my presence, if thou look to live!

> *Exit* DUCHESS.

O wicked sex, perjured and unjust!
Now do I see that from the very first

40   Her eyes and looks sow'd seeds of perjury.
But villain, he, to whom these lines should go,
Shall buy her love even with his dearest blood.

> *Exit.*

SCENE TWO

> *Enter the* KING OF NAVARRE, PLESHÉ, BARTUS,
> *and* TRAIN, *with drums and trumpets.*

NAVARRE: My lords, sith in a quarrel just and right
We undertake to manage these our wars
Against the proud disturbers of the faith,
(I mean the Guise, the Pope, and king of Spain,
Who set themselves to tread us under foot,
And rent our true religion from this land;

25 *trothless*: disloyal.

But for you know our quarrel is no more
But to defend their strange inventions,
Which they will put us to with sword and fire,)
We must with resolute minds resolve to fight,　　　　*10*
In honour of our God, and country's good.
Spain is the council-chamber of the Pope,
Spain is the place where he makes peace and war;
And Guise for Spain hath now incens'd the king
To send his power to meet us in the field.

BARTUS: Then in this bloody brunt they may behold
The sole endeavour of your princely care,
To plant the true succession of the faith,
In spite of Spain and all his heresies.

NAVARRE: The power of vengeance now encamps itself　*20*
Upon the haughty mountains of my breast;
Plays with her gory colours of revenge,
Whom I respect as leaves of boasting green,
That change their colour when the winter comes,
When I shall vaunt as victor in revenge.

　　　Enter a MESSENGER.

How now, sirrah! what news?

MESSENGER: My lord, as by our scouts we understand,
A mighty army comes from France with speed;
Which are already muster'd in the land,
And means to meet your highness in the field.　　　*30*

NAVARRE: In God's name, let them come!
This is the Guise that hath incens'd the king
To levy arms, and make these civil broils.
But canst thou tell who is their general?

MESSENGER: Not yet, my lord, for thereon do they
　　stay;
But, as report doth go, the Duke of Joyeux
Hath made great suit unto the king therefore.

NAVARRE: It will not countervail his plans, I hope.
I would the Guise in his stead might have come!

8 *defend*: repel.　　8 *inventions*: plots.
35 *thereon do they stay*: that is what they wait for.

40 But he doth lurk within his drowsy couch,
And makes his footstool on security:
So he be safe, he cares not what becomes
Of king or country; no, not for them both.
But come, my lords, let us away with speed,
And place ourselves in order for the fight.
Exeunt.

SCENE THREE

Enter KING HENRY, GUISE, EPERNOUN, *and*
JOYEUX.

HENRY: My sweet Joyeux, I make thee general
Of all my army, now in readiness
To march against the rebellious King Navarre.
At thy request I am content thou go,
Although my love to thee can hardly suffer't,
Regarding still the danger of thy life.

JOYEUX: Thanks to your majesty: and so, I take my
leave.
Farewell to my Lord of Guise, and Epernoun.

GUISE: Health and hearty farewell to my Lord Joyeux.
Exit JOYEUX.

10 HENRY: So kindly, cousin of Guise, you and your wife
Do both salute our lovely minions.
Remember you the letter, gentle sir,
Which your wife writ
To my dear minion, and her chosen friend?
Makes horns at GUISE.

GUISE: How now, my lord! Faith, this is more than
need.
Am I thus to be jested at and scorn'd?
'Tis more than kingly or emperious:
And, sure, if all the proudest kings
In Christendom should bear me such derision,

s.d. after 14 *makes horns*: meaning he is a cuckold.

They should know how I scorn'd them and their   *20*
  mocks.
I love your minions! Dote on them yourself;
I know none else but holds them in disgrace;
And here, by all the saints in heaven, I swear,
That villain for whom I bear this deep disgrace,
Even for your words that have incens'd me so,
Shall buy that strumpet's favour with his blood!
Whether he have dishonour'd me or no,
Par la mort Dieu, il mourra!
  Exit.

HENRY: Believe me, this jest bites sore.

EPERNOUN: My lord, 'twere good to make them   *30*
  friends,
For his oaths are seldom spent in vain.
  Enter MUGEROUN.

HENRY: How now, Mugeroun! Met'st thou not the
  Guise at the door?

MUGEROUN: Not I, my lord. What if I had?

HENRY: Marry, if thou hadst, thou mightst have had
  the stab.
For he hath solemnly sworn thy death.

MUGEROUN: I may be stabb'd, and live till he be dead.
But wherefore bears he me such deadly hate?

HENRY: Because his wife bears thee such kindly love.

MUGEROUN: If that be all, the next time that I meet her
I'll make her shake off love with her heels.   *40*
But which way is he gone? I'll go take a walk
On purpose from the court to meet with him.
  Exit.

HENRY: I like not this. Come Epernoun,
Let's go seek the duke, and make them friends.
  Exeunt.

SCENE FOUR

*Alarums, within, and a cry – 'The Duke Joyeux
is slain.' Enter the* KING OF NAVARRE, BARTUS,
and TRAIN.

NAVARRE: The duke is slain, and all his power
    dispers'd,
  And we are grac'd with wreaths of victory.
  Thus God, we see, doth ever guide the right,
  To make his glory great upon the earth.
BARTUS: The terror of this happy victory,
  I hope, will make the king surcease his hate,
  And either never manage army more,
  Or else employ them in some better cause.
NAVARRE: How many noblemen have lost their lives
10 In prosecution of these cruel arms,
  Is ruth and almost death to call to mind.
  But God we know will always put them down
  That lift themselves against the perfect truth;
  Which I'll maintain so long as life doth last,
  And with the Queen of England join my force
  To beat the papal monarch from our lands,
  And keep those relics from our countries' coasts.
  Come, my lords; now that this storm is overpast,
  Let us away with triumph to our tents.
  Exeunt.

SCENE FIVE

Enter a SOLDIER.

SOLDIER: Sir, to you, sir, that dares make the duke a
cuckold, and use a counterfeit key to his privy-chamber-
door; and although you take out nothing but your own,
yet you put in that which displeaseth him, and so
forestall his market, and set up your standing where you

6 *surcease*: relinquish.   17 *relics*: forces of superstition.

should not; and whereas he is your landlord, you will
take upon you to be his, and till the ground that he
himself should occupy, which is his own free land; if it
be not too free – there's the question; and though I
come not to take possession (as I would I might!) yet I   10
mean to keep you out; which I will, if this gear hold.

Enter MUGEROUN.

What, are ye come so soon? Have at ye, sir!

Shoots at MUGEROUN *and kills him.*

Enter GUISE *and* ATTENDANTS.

GUISE (*giving a purse*): Hold thee,[6] tall soldier, take thee
this and fly.

Exit SOLDIER.

Lie there, the king's delight, and Guise's scorn!
Revenge it, Henry, as thou list or dare;
I did it only in despite of thee.

ATTENDANTS *bear off* MUGEROUN'S *body.*

Enter KING HENRY *and* EPERNOUN.

HENRY: My Lord of Guise, we understand
That you have gathered a power of men:
What your intent is yet we cannot learn,
But we presume it is not for our good.   20

GUISE: Why, I am no traitor to the crown of France;
What I have done, 'tis for the Gospel sake.

EPERNOUN: Nay, for the Pope's sake, and thine own
benefit.
What peer in France but thou, aspiring Guise,
Durst be in arms without the king's consent?
I challenge thee for treason in the cause.

GUISE: Ah, base Epernoun! were not his highness here,
Thou shouldst perceive the Duke of Guise is mov'd.

HENRY: Be patient, Guise, and threat not Epernoun,
Lest thou perceive the king of France be mov'd.   30

GUISE: Why, I am a prince of the Valoyses line,
Therefore an enemy of the Bourbonites.
I am a juror in the holy league,
And therefore hated of the Protestants.

What should I do but stand upon my guard?
And, being able, I'll keep an host in pay.

EPERNOUN: Thou able to maintain an host in pay,
That liv'st by foreign exhibition!
The Pope and King of Spain are thy good friends;
40   Else all France knows how poor a duke thou art.

HENRY: Ay, those are they that feed him with their
gold,
To countermand our will, and check our friends.

GUISE: My lord, to speak more plainly, thus it is:
Being animated by religious zeal,
I mean to muster all the power I can,
To overthrow those factious Puritans.
And know, my lord, the Pope will sell his triple
crown,
Ay, and the Catholic Philip, king of Spain,
Ere I shall want, will cause his Indians
50   To rip the golden bowels of America.
Navarre, that cloaks them underneath his wings,
Shall feel the house of Lorraine is his foe.
Your highness needs not fear mine army's force;
'Tis for your safety, and your enemies' wrack.

HENRY: Guise, wear our crown, and be thou king of
France,
And, as dictator, make or war or peace,
Whilst I cry *placet*, like a senator!
I cannot brook thy haughty insolence.
Dismiss thy camp, or else by our edict
60   Be thou proclaim'd a traitor throughout France.

GUISE (*aside*): The choice is hard; I must dissemble.
(*Aloud*) My lord, in token of my true humility,
And simple meaning to your majesty,
I kiss your grace's hand, and take my leave,
Intending to dislodge my camp with speed.

HENRY: Then farewell, Guise; the king and thou are
friends.

38 *exhibition*: support.   57 *placet*: 'It pleases' ('Ay' in a vote).

Exit GUISE.

EPERNOUN: But trust him not, my lord; for, had your
    highness
    Seen with what a pomp he enter'd Paris,
    And how the citizens with gifts and shows
    Did entertain him,   70
    And promised to be at his command –
    Nay, they fear'd not to speak in the streets,
    That the Guise durst stand in arms against the king,
    For not effecting of his holiness' will.
HENRY: Did they of Paris entertain him so?
    Then means he present treason to our state.
    Well, let me alone. Who's within there?
    Enter ATTENDANT *with a pen and ink.*
    Make a discharge of all my council straight,
    And I'll subscribe my name, and seal it straight.
    ATTENDANT *writes.*
    My head shall be my council; they are false;   80
    And, Epernoun, I will be rul'd by thee.
EPERNOUN: My lord,
    I think, for safety of your royal person,
    It would be good the Guise were made away,
    And so to quite your grace of all suspect.
HENRY: First let us set our hand and seal to this,
    And then I'll tell thee what I mean to do.
    Writes.
    So, convey this to the council presently.
    Exit ATTENDANT.
    And, Epernoun, though I seem mild and calm,
    Think not but I am tragical within.   90
    I'll secretly convey me unto Blois;
    For, now that Paris takes the Guise's part,
    Here is no staying for the king of France,
    Unless he mean to be betray'd and die.
    But, as I live, so sure the Guise shall die.
    Exeunt.

ACT FIVE

SCENE ONE

Enter the KING OF NAVARRE, *reading a letter, and*
BARTUS.

NAVARRE: My lord, I am advertised from France
That the Guise hath taken arms against the king,
And that Paris is revolted from his grace.
BARTUS: Then hath your grace fit opportunity
To show your love unto the king of France,
Offering him aid against his enemies,
Which cannot but be thankfully receiv'd.
NAVARRE: Bartus, it shall be so. Post then to France,
And there salute his highness in our name;
10   Assure him all the aid we can provide
Against the Guisians and their complices.
Bartus, be gone: commend me to his grace,
And tell him, ere it be long, I'll visit him.
BARTUS: I will, my lord.
    Exit.
NAVARRE: Pleshé!
    Enter PLESHÉ.
PLESHÉ: My lord!
NAVARRE: Pleshé, go muster up our men with speed,
And let them march away to France amain,
For we must aid the king against the Guise.
20   Be gone, I say; 'tis time that we were there.
PLESHÉ: I go, my lord.
    Exit.
NAVARRE: That wicked Guise, I fear me much will be
The ruin of that famous realm of France,
For his aspiring thoughts aim at the crown,
And takes his vantage on religion,
To plant the Pope and Popelings in the realm,
And bind it wholly to the see of Rome.

25 *vantage*: opportunity.

But, if that God do prosper mine attempts,
And send us safely to arrive in France,
We'll beat him back, and drive him to his death   *30*
That basely seeks the ruin of his realm.
   Exit.

SCENE TWO

Enter the CAPTAIN OF THE GUARD, *and three*
MURDERERS.

CAPTAIN: Come on, sirs. What, are you resolutely bent,
  Hating the life and honour of the Guise?
  What, will you not fear, when you see him come?
FIRST MURDERER: Fear him, said you? Tush, were he
  here, we would kill him presently.
SECOND MURDERER: O, that his heart were leaping in
  my hand!
THIRD MURDERER: But when will he come, that we
  may murder him?
CAPTAIN: Well, then, I see you are resolute.   *10*
FIRST MURDERER: Let us alone; I warrant you.
CAPTAIN: Then, sirs, take your standings within this
  chamber;
  For anon the Guise will come.
ALL THREE MURDERERS: You will give us our money?
CAPTAIN: Ay, ay, fear not. Stand close: so; be resolute.
  Exeunt MURDERERS.
  Now falls the star whose influence governs France,
  Whose light was deadly to the Protestants:
  Now must he fall, and perish in his height.
  Enter KING HENRY *and* EPERNOUN.
HENRY: Now, captain of my guard, are these murderers
  ready?
CAPTAIN: They be, my good lord.   *20*
HENRY: But are they resolute, and arm'd to kill,
  Hating the life and honour of the Guise?

CAPTAIN: I warrant ye, my lord.

Exit.

HENRY: Then come, proud Guise, and here disgorge
    thy breast,
Surcharg'd with surfeit of ambitious thoughts.
Breathe out that life wherein my death was hid,
And end thy endless treasons with thy death.

Enter the GUISE *and knocketh.*

GUISE: *Holà, varlet, hé!* Epernoun, where is the king?

EPERNOUN: Mounted his royal cabinet.

30   GUISE: I prithee, tell him that the Guise is here.

EPERNOUN: An please your grace, the Duke of Guise
    doth crave
Access unto your highness.

HENRY: Let him come in.
Come, Guise, and see thy traitorous guile outreach'd,
And perish in the pit thou mad'st for me.

The GUISE *comes to the* KING.

GUISE: Good morrow to your majesty.

HENRY: Good morrow to my loving cousin of Guise.
How fares it this morning with your excellence?

GUISE: I heard your majesty was scarcely pleas'd,

40   That in the court I bare so great a train.

HENRY: They were to blame that said I was displeas'd;
And you, good cousin, to imagine it.
'Twere hard with me, if I should doubt my kin,
Or be suspicious of my dearest friends.
Cousin, assure you I am resolute,
Whatsoever any whisper in mine ears,
Not to suspect disloyalty in thee:
And so, sweet coz, farewell.

Exit with EPERNOUN.

GUISE: So;

50   Now sues the king for favour to the Guise,
And all his minions stoop when I command.
Why, this 'tis to have an army in the field.
Now, by the holy sacrament, I swear,

As ancient Romans o'er their captive lords,
So will I triumph o'er this wanton king;
And he shall follow my proud chariot's wheels.
Now do I but begin to look about,
And all my former time was spent in vain.
Hold, sword,
For in thee is the Duke of Guise's hope.   **60**

   Re-enter THIRD MURDERER.

Villain, why dost thou look so ghastly? Speak.

THIRD MURDERER: O, pardon me, my Lord of
   Guise!

GUISE: Pardon thee! Why, what hast thou done?

THIRD MURDERER: O my lord, I am one of them that
   is set to murder you!

GUISE: To murder me, villain?

THIRD MURDERER: Ay, my lord: the rest have ta'en
   their standings in the next room; therefore, good my
   lord, go not forth.   **70**

GUISE: Yet Caesar shall go forth.[7]
   Let mean conceits and baser men fear death:
   Tut, they are peasants. I am Duke of Guise;
   And princes with their looks engender fear.

FIRST MURDERER (*within*): Stand close; he is coming;
   I know him by his voice.

GUISE: As pale as ashes! Nay, then, 'tis time
   To look about.

   Enter FIRST *and* SECOND MURDERERS.

FIRST AND SECOND MURDERERS: Down with him,
   down with him!   **80**

   They stab GUISE.

GUISE: O, I have my death's wound! Give me leave to
   speak.

SECOND MURDERER: Then pray to God, and ask
   forgiveness of the king.

GUISE: Trouble me not. I ne'er offended him,
   Nor will I ask forgiveness of the king.
   O, that I have not power to stay my life,

Nor immortality to be reveng'd!
To die by peasants, what a grief is this!
Ah, Sixtus, be reveng'd upon the king!
90   Philip and Parma, I am slain for you!
Pope, excommunicate! Philip depose,
The wicked branch of curs'd Valois his line!
Vive la messe! perish Huguenots!
Thus Caesar did go forth, and thus he died.[8]
    Dies.
    Enter the CAPTAIN OF THE GUARD.
CAPTAIN: What, have you done?
Then stay a while, and I'll go call the king.
But see, where he comes.
    Enter KING HENRY, EPERNOUN, *and*
    ATTENDANTS.
My lord, see, where the Guise is slain.
HENRY: Ah, this sweet sight is physic to my soul!
100   Go fetch his son for to behold his death.
    Exit an ATTENDANT.
Surcharg'd with guilt of thousand massacres,
Monsieur of Lorraine, sink away to hell!
And, in remembrance of those bloody broils,
To which thou didst allure me, being alive;
And here in presence of you all, I swear,
I ne'er was king of France until this hour.
This is the traitor that hath spent my gold
In making foreign wars and civil broils.
Did he not draw a sort of English priests
110   From Douai to the seminary at Rheims,
To hatch forth treason 'gainst their natural queen?
Did he not cause the king of Spain's huge fleet
To threaten England, and to menace me?

89 *Sixtus*: Pope Sixtus V (1521–90).
90 *Philip*: Philip II of Spain.
90 *Parma*: Duke of Parma (1545–92).
102 *Monsieur of Lorraine*: Guise was Henry of Lorraine.
111 *treason*: the Babington Plot of 1586.

Did he not injure Monsieur that's deceas'd?
Hath he not made me, in the Pope's defence,
To spend the treasure, that should strength my
    land,
In civil broils between Navarre and me?
Tush, to be short, he meant to make me monk,
Or else to murder me, and so be king.
Let Christian princes, that shall hear of this,   120
(As all the world shall know our Guise is dead),
Rest satisfied with this: that here I swear,
Ne'er was there king of France so yok'd as I.
EPERNOUN: My lord, here is his son.
    Enter GUISE'S SON.
HENRY: Boy, look, where your father lies.
GUISE'S SON: My father slain! Who hath done this
    deed?
HENRY: Sirrah, 'twas I that slew him; and will slay
Thee too, and thou prove such a traitor.
GUISE'S SON: Art thou king, and hast done this
    bloody deed?
I'll be reveng'd.   130
    Offers to throw his dagger.
HENRY: Away to prison with him! I'll clip his wings
Or e'er he pass my hands. Away with him.
    Some of the ATTENDANTS *bear off* GUISE'S SON.
But what availeth that this traitor's dead,
When Duke Dumaine, his brother, is alive,
And that young cardinal that is grown so proud?
    To the CAPTAIN OF THE GUARD.
Go to the governor of Orleans,
And will him, in my name, to kill the duke.
    To the MURDERERS.
Get you away, and strangle the cardinal.
    Exeunt CAPTAIN OF THE GUARD *and*
    MURDERERS.
These two will make one entire Duke of Guise,
Especially with our old mother's help.   140

EPERNOUN: My lord, see where she comes, as if she
    droop'd
  To hear these news.
HENRY: And let her droop; my heart is light enough.
    Enter CATHERINE *the Queen-Mother.*
  Mother, how like you this device of mine?
  I slew the Guise, because I would be king.
CATHERINE: King! Why, so thou wert before:
  Pray God thou be a king now this is done!
HENRY: Nay, he was king, and countermanded me:
  But now I will be king, and rule myself,
150   And make the Guisians stoop that are alive.
CATHERINE: I cannot speak for grief. When thou wast
    born,
  I would that I had murder'd thee, my son!
  My son! Thou art a changeling, not my son;
  I curse thee, and exclaim thee miscreant,
  Traitor to God and to the realm of France!
HENRY: Cry out, exclaim, howl till thy throat be hoarse!
  The Guise is slain, and I rejoice therefore:
  And now will I to arms. Come, Epernoun,
  And let her grieve her heart out, if she will.
    Exit with EPERNOUN.
160 CATHERINE: Away! leave me alone to meditate.
    Exeunt ATTENDANTS.
  Sweet Guise, would he had died, so thou wert here!
  To whom shall I bewray my secrets now,
  Or who will help to build religion?
  The Protestants will glory and insult;
  Wicked Navarre will get the crown of France;
  The Popedom cannot stand; all goes to wrack;
  And all for thee, my Guise! What may I do?
  But sorrow seize upon my toiling soul!
  For, since the Guise is dead, I will not live.[9]
    Exit.

SCENE THREE

Enter two MURDERERS, *dragging in the* CARDINAL.

CARDINAL: Murder me not; I am a cardinal.

FIRST MURDERER: Wert thou the Pope, thou mightst not 'scape from us.

CARDINAL: What, will you file your hands with churchmen's blood?

SECOND MURDERER: Shed your blood! O Lord, no! for we intend to strangle you.

CARDINAL: Then there is no remedy, but I must die?

FIRST MURDERER: No remedy; therefore prepare yourself.

CARDINAL: Yet lives my brother Duke Dumaine, and many more,
  To revenge our death upon that cursed king,
  Upon whose heart may all the Furies gripe,
  And with their paws drench his black soul in hell!   *10*

FIRST MURDERER: Yours, my Lord Cardinal, you should have said.
  Now they strangle him.
  So, pluck amain.
  He is hard-hearted; therefore pull with violence.
  Come, take him away.
  Exeunt with the body.

SCENE FOUR

Enter DUMAINE, *reading a letter, with others.*

DUMAINE: My noble brother murder'd by the king!
  O, what may I do for to revenge thy death?
  The king's alone, it cannot satisfy.
  Sweet Duke of Guise, our prop to lean upon,
  Now thou art dead, here is no stay for us.
  I am thy brother, and I'll revenge thy death,

  3 *file*: stain.

And root Valoys his line from forth of France,
And beat proud Bourbon to his native home,
That basely seeks to join with such a king,
10 Whose murderous thoughts will be his overthrow.
He will'd the governor of Orleans, in his name,
That I with speed should have been put to death;
But that's prevented, for to end his life,
And all those traitors to the Church of Rome
That durst attempt to murder noble Guise.
    Enter FRIAR.
FRIAR: My lord, I come to bring you news that your
    brother the Cardinal of Lorraine, by the king's consent,
    is lately strangled unto death.
DUMAINE: My brother Cardinal slain, and I alive?
20 O words of power to kill a thousand men!
Come, let us away, and levy men;
'Tis war that must assuage this tyrant's pride.
FRIAR: My lord, hear me but speak.
I am a friar of the order of the Jacobins,
That for my conscience' sake will kill the king.
DUMAINE: But what doth move thee, above the rest, to
    do the deed?
FRIAR: O my lord, I have been a great sinner in my
    days, and the deed is meritorious.
DUMAINE: But how wilt thou get opportunity?
30 FRIAR: Tush, my lord, let me alone for that.
DUMAINE: Friar, come with me;
We will go talk more of this within.
    Exeunt.

SCENE FIVE

Drums and trumpets. Enter KING HENRY, *the*
KING OF NAVARRE, EPERNOUN, BARTUS,
PLESHÉ, SOLDIERS, *and* ATTENDANTS.
HENRY: Brother of Navarre, I sorrow much

That ever I was prov'd your enemy,
And that the sweet and princely mind you bear
Was ever troubled with injurious wars.
I vow, as I am lawful King of France,
To recompense your reconciled love
With all the honours and affections
That ever I vouchsaf'd my dearest friends.

NAVARRE: It is enough if that Navarre may be
Esteemed faithful to the King of France,   *10*
Whose service he may still command till death.

HENRY: Thanks to my kingly brother of Navarre.
Then here we'll lie before Lutetia walls,
Girting this strumpet city with our siege,
Till, surfeiting with our afflicting arms,
She cast her hateful stomach to the earth.

    Enter a MESSENGER.

MESSENGER: An it please your majesty, here is a friar
of the order of the Jacobins, sent from the President
of Paris, that craves access unto your grace.

HENRY: Let him come in.   *20*

    Exit MESSENGER.
    Enter FRIAR, *with a letter.*

EPERNOUN: I like not this friar's look:
'Twere not amiss, my lord, if he were search'd.

HENRY: Sweet Epernoun, our friars are holy men,
And will not offer violence to their king,
For all the wealth and treasure of the world.
Friar, thou dost acknowledge me thy king?

FRIAR: Ay, my good lord, and will die therein.

HENRY: Then come thou near, and tell what news thou
    bring'st.

FRIAR: My lord,
The President of Paris greets your grace   *30*
And sends his duty by these speedy lines,
Humbly craving your gracious reply.

    Gives letter.

13 *Lutetia*: Paris.

HENRY: I'll read them, friar, and then I'll answer thee.

FRIAR: *Sancte Jacobe,* now have mercy upon me!
Stabs the KING *with a knife, as he reads the letter;*
and then the KING *gets the knife, and kills him.*

EPERNOUN: O, my lord, let him live a while!

HENRY: No let the villain die, and feel in hell
Just torments for his treachery.

NAVARRE: What, is your highness hurt?

HENRY: Yes, Navarre; but not to death, I hope.

40 NAVARRE: God shield your grace from such a sudden death!
Go call a surgeon hither straight.
Exit an ATTENDANT.

HENRY: What irreligious pagans' parts be these,
Of such as hold them of the holy church!
Take hence that damned villain from my sight.
ATTENDANTS *carry out the* FRIAR'S *body.*

EPERNOUN: Ah, had your highness let him live,
We might have punish'd him to his deserts!

HENRY: Sweet Epernoun, all rebels under heaven
Shall take example by his punishment,
How they bear arms against their sovereign.

50 Go call the English agent hither straight:
Exit an ATTENDANT.
I'll send my sister England news of this,
And give her warning of her treacherous foes.
Enter a SURGEON.

NAVARRE: Pleaseth your grace to let the surgeon search your wound?

HENRY: The wound, I warrant ye, is deep, my lord.
Search, surgeon, and resolve me what thou see'st.
The SURGEON *searches the wound.*
Enter the ENGLISH AGENT.
Agent for England, send thy mistress word
What this detested Jacobin hath done.
Tell her, for all this, that I hope to live;
Which if I do, the papal monarch goes

To wrack, and [th'] antichristian kingdom falls.   **60**
These bloody hands shall tear his triple crown,
And fire accursed Rome about his ears;
I'll fire his crazed buildings, and enforce
The papal towers to kiss the lowly earth.
Navarre, give me thy hand: I here do swear
To ruinate that wicked Church of Rome,
That hatcheth up such bloody practices;
And here protest eternal love to thee,
And to the Queen of England specially,
Whom God hath bless'd for hating papistry.   **70**

NAVARRE: These words revive my thoughts, and
    comforts me.
To see your highness in this virtuous mind.

HENRY: Tell me, surgeon, shall I live?

SURGEON: Alas, my lord, the wound is dangerous,
For you are stricken with a poison'd knife!

HENRY: A poison'd knife! What, shall the French
    king die,
Wounded and poison'd both at once?

EPERNOUN: O, that
    That damned villain were alive again,
    That we might torture him with some new-found   **80**
    death!

BARTUS: He died a death too good:
The devil of hell torture his wicked soul!

HENRY: Ah, curse him not, sith he is dead!
O, the fatal poison works within my breast!
Tell me, surgeon, and flatter not – may I live?

SURGEON: Alas, my lord, your highness cannot live!

NAVARRE: Surgeon, why say'st thou so? The king may
    live.

HENRY: O, no, Navarre! Thou must be king of France!

NAVARRE: Long may you live, and still be King of
    France.

EPERNOUN: Or else die Epernoun!   **90**

HENRY: Sweet Epernoun, thy king must die. My lords,

Fight in the quarrel of this valiant prince,
For he's your lawful king, and my next heir;
Valoyses line ends in my tragedy.
Now let the house of Bourbon wear the crown;
And may it never end in blood, as mine hath done!
Weep not, sweet Navarre, but revenge my death.
Ah, Epernoun, is this thy love to me?
Henry, thy king, wipes off these childish tears,
100 And bids thee whet thy sword on Sixtus' bones,
That it may keenly slice the Catholics.
He loves me not that sheds most tears,
But he that makes most lavish of his blood.
Fire Paris, where these treacherous rebels lurk.
I die, Navarre; come bear me to my sepulchre.
Salute the Queen of England in my name,
And tell her, Henry dies her faithful friend.[10]
    Dies.
NAVARRE: Come, lords, take up the body of the king,
That we may see it honourably interr'd:
110 And then I vow for to revenge his death
As Rome, and all those popish prelates there,
Shall curse the time that e'er Navarre was king,
And rul'd in France by Henry's fatal death.
    They march out, with the body of KING HENRY *lying
    on four men's shoulders, with a dead march, drawing
    weapons on the ground.*

ADDITIONAL NOTES

DIDO, QUEEN OF CARTHAGE

The title page of the 1594 Quarto couples the name of Thomas Nashe with Marlowe's; but there is very little internal evidence of Nashe's hand, and the most commonly accepted explanation is that he prepared the play for performance by the Children of Her Majesty's Chapel, and perhaps for subsequent publication.

The play is based on Virgil, *Aeneid*, Books I, II, and IV. Of the 1,736 lines, 194 are straight translations, 420 are re-expressed (T. M. Pearce, University of New Mexico thesis, 1930). Perhaps it should be added (for the figures might suggest that Marlowe is overmuch dependent on Virgil) that (in this editor's opinion) comparison only emphasizes Marlowe's creative involvement with his material: it would be quite wrong to assume that he was only doing a piece of hackwork in translating and adapting. For sources for Aeneas' narrative (2, 2) see Ethel Seaton, 'Marlowe's Light Reading', *Elizabethan and Jacobean Studies Presented to F. P. Wilson in Honour of his Seventieth Birthday*, Oxford, 1959.

1. *hair*: Dyce's conjecture. Quarto has 'air' (cf. also l. 159 below).
2. *driven back the horses of the Night*: from Ovid, *Amores* I, xiii, 40 ('O lente, lente currite noctis equi' as quoted in *Doctor Faustus*, 5, 2, 152).
3. *Vulcan*: His limp set the gods laughing in the *Iliad* (I, 599–600).
4. *wound*: This is the Quarto reading, usually emended, after Collier's suggestion, to 'wind', by analogy with the lines from *Hamlet*:

> Pyrrhus at Priam drives; in rage strikes wide;
> But with the whiff and wind of his fell sword
> Th' unnerved father falls. (2, 2, 466–8)

For some discussion of the relationship between the Player King's speech in *Hamlet* and Aeneas' in this play see Tucker

Brooke's edition of Marlowe, Methuen, 1930, pp. 160–61; and Steane, *Marlowe: A Critical Study*, Cambridge, 1964, pp. 55–6.

5. *Cytherea*: Quarto has Citheides.

6. *newly*: Collier's conjecture. Quarto has 'meanly'.

7. *Thetis . . . neck*: the sun (Apollo) embraced by Thetis as he sinks in the sea.

8. *now*: Dyce's conjecture. Quarto has 'how'.

9. *Fates*: Hurst's conjecture. Quarto has 'face'.

10. *let-out*: Hurst's conjecture. Quarto has 'left out'.

11. *my Hebe's shame*: Juno's daughter, Hebe, was cup-bearer to the gods before Ganymede.

12. *Mars and Venus met*: trapped in a net by Vulcan (Ovid, *Metamorphoses*, IV, 170–84).

13. *Eliza*: suggests a tribute to Queen Elizabeth, but Elissa is also Dido's name, and the two forms were interchangeable.

14. *lives*: Dyce's conjecture. Quarto has 'loves'.

15. *Deucalion-like*: In the Greek myth of the flood, Deucalion and his wife were the sole survivors.

16. *Achates*: Tucker Brooke (ed. cit., p. 219) points out that it was Sergestus whom Aeneas ordered to take Ascanius aboard (l. 49 above): probably a slip on the writer's part.

17. *to kind*: to nature. Collier's conjecture. Quarto has 'too keend'.

18. *Triton's niece*: 'I can only suppose that Scylla, the daughter of Nisus, King of Megara, is meant (see Ovid, *Metamorphoses*, VIII, 143–4). She had nothing to do with Triton, but the other Scylla, the sea-monster who is often confused with her, is represented, as either his daughter or sister' (McKerrow).

19. *Now is he come . . .*: very close to lines 189–93 above. Tucker Brooke conjectures that the lines were originally an alternative version of the same passage.

TAMBURLAINE; PART ONE

For the place-names which come so frequently in the plays, readers are referred to an invaluable essay by Ethel Seaton, called *Marlowe's Map*, published first in *Essays and Studies by Members of the English Association*, 1924, and reprinted in *Marlowe: A Collection of Critical Essays*, (ed.) Clifford Leech, in the series *Twentieth Century Views*, Prentice Hall, New Jersey, 1964. Miss Seaton shows how mistaken was the idea that Marlowe threw the names around with fine poetic abandon and little care for accuracy. On the contrary, he followed Abraham Ortelius' *Theatrum Orbis Terrarum* closely and was familiar with the work of other authorities too. The essay is useful as a guide to this aspect of the *Tamburlaine* plays and also because it shows us Marlowe at work: Clifford Leech points out that it was one of the first studies to show him as a scholar and a craftsman rather than as a wild, subjective genius.

The Octavo and Quarto editions of 1590 onwards were prefaced by an address 'To the Gentlemen Readers' by the printer, Richard Jones:

> *To the Gentlemen Readers: and others*
> *that take pleasure in reading*
> *Histories*

Gentlemen, and courteous readers whosoever: I have here published in print for your sakes, the two tragical discourses of the Scythian shepherd Tamburlaine, that became so great a conqueror and so mighty a monarch. My hope is that they will be now no less acceptable unto you to read after your serious affairs and studies than they have been lately delightful for many of you to see when the same were shewed in London upon stages. I have purposely omitted and left out some fond and frivolous gestures, digressing (and in my poor opinion) far unmeet for the matter, which I thought might seem more tedious unto the wise than any way else to be regarded, though haply they have been of some vain conceited fondlings greatly gaped at, what times they were shewed upon the stage in their graced deformities. Nevertheless, now, to be mixtured in print with such matter of worth, it would prove a great disgrace to so honourable and stately a history. Great folly were it in me to commend unto your wisdoms either the eloquence of the author that writ them, or the worthiness of the matter itself. I therefore leave unto your learned censures both the one and the other, and myself, the poor printer of them, unto your most courteous and favourable protection, which, I you vouchsafe to accept, you shall evermore bind me to employ what travail and service I can, to the advancing and pleasuring of your excellent degree.

Yours, most humble at commandment,

R. I. Printer

1. task : Robinson's conjecture (ed. 1826).

2. *sinewy*: Dyce's conjecture (ed. 1850). Octavos 1590, 1593, 1597 have 'snowy'. 1605 reads 'His arms long, his fingers snowy-white'.

3. *Xerxes . . . Parthian Araris*: Xerxes, with a huge army, fought unsuccessfully against the Greeks in 480 B.C. By the 'Araris' here and elsewhere (cf. 2, 1, 63) Marlowe probably means the Araxes, though the legend appears to refer to a different river altogether (cf. 'While they were encamped here, all the rivers I have mentioned supplied enough water for their needs except the Echeidorus, which was drunk dry.' Heredotus, *The Histories*, VII, 21; translated by Selincourt, Penguin, 1954 p. 455).

4. *Cyclopian*: the Titans, and not the Cyclops, rebelled against Jove, but the confusion was common in Marlowe's time.

5. *angry Jupiter*: Jove punished Typhoeus by burying him under Etna, but the analogous rebellion against his power was that of the Titans.

6. *And since we all have sucked*: 'Since we have so much in common (we breathe the same air, and are composed of much the same natural elements in a similar proportion) I hope we are also alike in determination to honour the bond of love between us by taking equal chances of death or survival.'

7. *air*: Dyce's conjecture. Octavos have 'lure' and 'lute'.

8. *foil*: Dyce's conjecture. Octavos have 'soil'.

9. *triple region*: The air was thought to be divided into upper, middle and lower regions.

10. *Clymene's brain-sick son*: Phaethon, who tried to ride the chariot of the sun. The axle-tree is the axis on which the spheres were supposed to turn.

11. *Plato's wondrous year*: when the major heavenly bodies begin and end the year in the same relative positions (Plato, *Timaeus*, 39 D).

12. *Meleager . . .*: led the chase of the Calydonian boar in company with famous heroes (some of them Argonauts). Recorded in Ovid's *Metamophoses*, VIII, 260–546.

13. *Cephalus*: This chase is described in Ovid's *Metamorphoses*, VII, 759–93.

14. *Progne*: Procne tricked Philomela and Tereus, King of

Thrace, into eating their child Itys (Ovid, *Metamorphoses*, VI, 565).

15. *But how unseemly . . .*: The meaning of this sentence is clear, but what follows is difficult and almost certainly involves some textual corruption. A non-literal paraphrase may be found useful, bearing in mind, of course, that interpretations of the passage are bound to be partly personal. Tamburlaine is saying that any kind of softness in a man is an effeminate degeneracy. He goes on: 'The single qualification to this is the proper recognition or praise with which a man is rewarded by beauty; for the sense of beauty is instinctive in man, and every soldier who is inspired by desire for fame, valour and victory must have the stimulus of beauty playing on his imagination. I both possess and keep in check this imaginative power, which has in its time been strong enough to make the greatest of the gods forsake his heavenly splendours to live for a while the lowly life of a shepherd. And I, who was born in such humble, limiting conditions myself, now say this to all the world: it is virtue that is the sole source of a man's greatness, and it is virtue that makes a man truly noble.' The emphasis on 'virtue' is presumably at the expense of such considerations as antiquity or distinction of lineage. And the connotation of virtue is probably not essentially goodness, but rather of power and strength of character. There are many textual differences and editorial emendations. 'Stoop'd' (l. 121) is Dyce's conjecture: the octavos have 'stop'd'. 'Fiery spangled' (l. 122) is the reading in the first two octavos; the others have 'spangled fiery'. For 'lovely' (l. 123) Collier suggested 'lowly'; for 'march' (l. 124) Broughton suggested 'mask'.

16. *rites*: Octavos have 'celebrated rites'. The omission of 'celebrated' was first proposed by Mitford (*Gentleman's Magazine*, January 1841) and has been accepted by most subsequent editors.

TAMBURLAINE: PART TWO

1. *sad*: Robinson's conjecture. Octavos have 'said'.
2. *Almains*, *Rutters*: Collier suggested 'Almain Rutters' by analogy with *Doctor Faustus*, I, 1, 124.

3. *Deucalion's flood*: The story is told in Ovid's *Metamorphoses*, I, 318–437 (the story of the stones, 381–415).

4. *orient*: Robinson's conjecture. Octavos have 'oriental'.

5. *Zula . . . Rome*: 'Zula, which has vanished from the average modern map, appears in the *Europe* of Ortelius to the north of the Danube, in the province of Rascia; the same map offers a possible explanation of that puzzling *Rome*, which cannot mean Rome though it may mean Constantinople: the word may have been suggested by ROMA in large type just north of Constantinople, violently and ludicrously separated from its NIA.' (Ethel Seaton, *Marlowe's Map*.)

6. *consummate*: Dyce's conjecture. Octavos have 'consinuate'.

7. *Saul*: I. Samuel, XV.

8. *Balaam*: Numbers, XXII and XXIII. Una Ellis-Fermor notes: 'But Marlowe's scriptural knowledge is not so sound as his knowledge of Ovid, for Balaam's position is the converse of Sigismond's' (*Tamburlaine*, (ed.) Ellis-Fermor, Methuen, 1930).

9. *Zoacum*: The source of the lines, identified by Seaton (*Revue of English Studies*) October 1929: *Fresh Sources for Marlowe*), is *Chronicum Turcorum Tomi Duo* by Philippus Lonicerus (Frankfurt, 1578, 1584). Marlowe follows the passage closely.

10. *serpent's head*: Scorpio to be in line with the earth, the sun and moon (in eclipse).

11. *continent*: Robinson's conjecture. Octavos have 'content'.

12. *hypostasis*: Robinson's conjecture. Octavos have 'hipostates'.

DOCTOR FAUSTUS

1. *Not marching . . . audacious deeds*: reference to earlier plays performed by the company, possibly by Marlowe himself. No extant play is suggested by the first two lines, but ll. 3 and 4 could describe *Edward II*, and l. 5, *Tamburlaine*.

2. *mate*: usually taken to mean defeat (as in 'checkmate') but in fact the Carthaginians under Hannibal *won* the battle of Lake Trasymenus. Mars 'mated' the Carthaginians, then, in the sense that he entered into them: he was on their side and with his spirit in them they won (cf. Lady Constance

on Fortune: 'Sh'adulterates hourly with thine uncle John'. *King John*, 3, 1, 56).

3. *The fruitful plot*: line omitted in B text (1616).

4. *on cai me on*: Oncaymaeon in 1604 text. Printed as Oeconomy in subsequent editions till Bullen's (1885).

5. *Galen*: (130–200 A.D.), most famous of ancient physicians.

6. *Seeing, Ubi desinit . . .*: line omitted in B.

7. *Is not thy common talk . . .*: line omitted in B.

8. *Justinian*: Justinian I (c. 482–565), codifier of Roman law.

9. *Stipendium pdccati . . .*: Romans, VI, 23.

10. *Si peccasse negamus . . .*: I. John, I, 8.

11. *with silk*: Bullen's emendation: all quartos have 'skill'.

12. *the fiery keel*: a fire-ship used to destroy the Duke of Parma's bridge across the Scheldt in 1585.

13. *Yet not your words . . . skill*: lines omitted in B.

14. *Divinity is basest . . . vile*: lines omitted in B.

15. *Musaeus*: legendary Greek poet, perhaps here confused with Orpheus, to whom the spirits thronged in Hades (Virgil, *Georgics*, IV, 453–527).

16. *Agrippa*: Cornelius Agrippa, famous early 16th century German magician. The 'shadows' are the shades or spirits he invoked.

17. *Bacon's and Albanus' works*: Roger Bacon, 13th century philosopher, reputedly practising black magic. Albanus, perhaps Pietro d'Abano (?1250–1316), a supposed sorcerer, burnt by the Inquisition in effigy after his death.

18. *Dragon*: formerly taken as part of the invocation, now seen as an inserted stage-direction. The Admiral's men, who performed the play, had 'j dragon in fostes' (included in a list of props drawn up probably by Henslowe in 1598). Leo Kirschbaum (*Revue of English Studies*, 18, 1942) suggests that this was a warning to stage hands to prepare for the dragon's appearance at the end of the invocation.

19. *Now, Faustus, thou art . . .*: line omitted in B.

20. *My ghost be . . .*: those who disbelieved in the doctrine of punishment after death.

21. *Scene four*: B version till S.D. (*Enter two devils . . .*), then from A text to end of scene.

22. *Now, Faustus, must thou needs . . .*: A text used for this speech.

23. *Then there's enough . . .*: line omitted in B.

24. *How, a wife? . . . ceremonial toy*: except for l. 150 ('What sight is this?') the A version is followed here.

25. *Thanks, Mephostophilis . . .*: the A version to the end of scene.

26. Prefacing this scene, the quartos interpolate here a speech given to Wagner, that appears again, properly placed, as the first six and last five lines of the second chorus at the beginning of Act three.

27. *Alexander*: Paris of Troy.

28. *Oenon*: a nymph loved by Paris before he met Helen, and who killed herself for love of him.

29. *he that built . . .*: Amphion, whose music charmed the stones so that they rose and built the Theban walls of their own accord.

30. *Come, Mephostophilis . . .*: see F. R. Johnson: 'Marlowe's Astronomy and Renaissance Skepticism' (*Journal of English Literary History*, 13, 1946).

31. *Never to name God . . . gratify thee*: lines omitted in B.

32. *the Seven Deadly Sins*: The authorship of this passage is much disputed. Kocher ('Nashe's Authorship of the Prose Scenes in *Faustus*' (*Modern Language Quarterly*, 3, 1942) argues that it is by Nashe; Greg ('Marlowe's *Doctor Fautus* 1604–1616', pp. 138–9) tables it as probably among Samuel Rowley's contributions to the play.

33. *Ovid's flea: Carmine de Pulice*, a mediaeval poem attributed to Ovid.

34. *cloth of Arras*: Flemish cloth for tapestries.

35. *ell of fried stockfish*: 'Lechery is saying in effect that she prefers a small quantity of virility to a large extent of impotence' (Gill).

36. *Scene two*: omitted in A, which, however, has a similar scene, between Robin and Rafe, which is not in B.

37. *He views the clouds . . . subtle air*: thirteen lines missing in A. Also l. 21 ('That measures coasts and kingdoms of the earth').

38. *Primum mobile*: beyond the planets, the first sphere to move and hence to start motion in the others.

39. *Scene two*: ll. 12, 19–20, 26, 53–6 are not in A. There are other slight differences. From l. 55 to the end of the scene there is nothing corresponding in A.

40. *Maro*: Virgil (Publius Virgilius Maro) was regarded in the

Middle Ages as a sorcerer, and it was suppos ed that he had cut the tunnel running through Mount Posilippo from Naples to Baie by magic.

41. *pyramides*: obelisk before the gates of St Peter's, Rome, brought from Heliopolis by Caligula.

42. *The which in state* . . .: A has here:

> Where thou shalt see a troupe of bald-pate friars,
> Whose *summum bonum* is in belly-cheer.

43. *Saxon Bruno*: No historical identification is possible. The episode is not in the *English Faustbook*, and may have been developed out of hints in Foxe's *Book of Martyrs*. Greg (p. 351) points out that whereas Hadrian VI (1522–3) was contemporary with the historical Faustus, the Pope who opposed the Emperor Frederick Barbarossa was Hadrian IV (1154–9). Barbarossa was forced by Hadrian's successor, Alexander III (1159–81) to acknowledge the Pope's supremacy.

History is again confused in line 148 for there was no Pope called Julian in the time of the Emperor Sigismond (1368–1437).

44. *Scene three*: There is nothing in the A text concerning Bruno; instead the Cardinal of Lorraine is introduced as the guest of honour. The food-snatching and the ceremony of anathema are substantially as in B.

45. *Enter Chorus*: speech taken from A; nothing corresponding in B. Probably misplaced and intended to appear as preface to Act four.

46. *Scene four*: from A. The corresponding scene in B gives only the episode with the Vintner, the earlier section having been partly anticipated in 2, 3 (not in A). The two entrances of Mephostophilis (S.D. '*Enter Meph. who sets squibs etc.*,' and a few lines later '*Enter to them Mephostophilis*') suggests that they were alternative ways of ending the scene; but there is no reason why both should not be played, with Mephostophilis standing aside during the fireworks episode, and confronting them face to face at his speech.

47. *Act four, scene one*: scene not in A. The Chorus speech (p. 303) is probably misplaced in the quartos and should introduce this scene.

48. *Scene two*: A's version is similar, though with fewer acting

parts, less elaborate stage direction and a higher proportion of prose to verse. Benvolio is simply called 'A Knight' and although he is given the horns as a punishment for jibing at Faustus, he does not swear to gain revenge, so there is no sequel as in B (4, 3, and 4).

49. *Benvolio still at window*: S.D. added.

50. *Acteon*: Acteon saw Diana bathing. In revenge she turned him into a stag and his own hounds killed him.

51. *Faustus rises*: S.D. added.

52. *Scene five*: text from A. B has a shorter version, omitting notably the dialogue between Faustus and Mephostophilis, ll. 1–7, the Horse-courser's speech after 'Well sir, now I am a made man for ever' (l. 32), and the dialogue between Mephostophilis and the horse-courser (ll. 62–89).

53. *Doctor Lopus*: Dr Lopez, the Queen's physician, executed in 1594 for alleged complicity in attempt to murder the Queen. Marlowe died in 1593, and this reference is the one indisputable addition to whatever Marlowe originally wrote.

54. *Scene six*: omitted in A. Readily dispensible in that it tells the tale of the horse in the water over again, but preparing for the entrance of the clowns in the next scene, episodes also absent from A.

55. *Scene seven*: much shorter in A, the clowns not introduced.

56. *Vanholt*: the Duchy of Anholt or Anhalt in Central Germany.

57. *courtesy*: pun on curtsy, continuing the punning joke about the leg ('He has forgot his leg' (l. 82) means both that he has forgotten about the wooden leg and that he has not bowed – 'he does not stand much upon that' i.e. ceremony or good manners).

58. *Faustus has charmed each dumb in turn* S.D. added.

59. *And yet methinks . . . ended*: following A text.

60. *Old Man*: A's version of this speech:

> Ah, Doctor Faustus, that I might prevail
> To guide thy steps unto the way of life
> By which sweet path thou mayest attain the goal
> That shall conduct thee to celestial rest.
> Break heart, drop blood, and mingle it with tears,
> Tears falling from repentant heaviness
> Of thy most vild and loathsome filthiness,
> The stench whereof corrupts the inward soul

With such flagitious crimes of heinous sins
As no commiseration may expel,
But mercy, Faustus, of thy saviour sweet,
Whose blood alone must wash away thy guilt.

61. *Ah, my sweet friend*: from A. B has 'Oh, friend'.
62. *More lovely than the monarch* . . .: There is no extant myth corresponding with this. Roma Gill notes: 'perhaps Marlowe is referring to the reflection of the sun in blue waters'.
63. *Accursed Faustus*: to the end of scene, from A. Nothing in B.
64. *Scene two*: The A version omits the devils and the short dialogue with Wagner, beginning with Faustus and the scholars. Then with the departure of the scholars it moves straight into Faustus' last speech.
65. *Ah, Faustus*: following A text for this. A is superior in several ways (e.g. B omits the line 'See, see where Christ's blood streams in the firmament').
68. *Scene three*: not in A.

THE JEW OF MALTA

The earliest surviving text of the play is the Quarto of 1633, printed rather more than forty years after the play was written. The date of composition is uncertain, but 1589 or 1590 is generally accepted as most likely. The gap in time raises questions about the reliability of the text as we have it, and it used to be confidently asserted that while the first two acts were Marlowe's own, the rest was either the work of early collaborators or the result of a degeneration suffered by the text in successive performances up to the Court revival which led to the surviving quartos being printed. The Prologues and Epilogues written for these performances are by Thomas Heywood, a prolific writer and one who confesses to having had a hand in many plays other than his own. Nothing, however, is demonstrably of his workmanship in this play, and the tendency among modern scholars has been more and more to discountenance the idea that Heywood altered the text in any significant way. In fact opinion is nowadays much more inclined to believe that the play survives substantially as it was originally written, and that there is no need to suppose that anybody other than Marlowe wrote any part of it.

There is no single source for the tale, though various episodes have their origins in English and Italian popular literature. The career of the Jew may have been based on the lives of several people. One of the most likely to have come to Marlowe's knowledge is the Portuguese Jew, Juan Miques: the claims of the various candidates are summarized by A. Freeman in an essay called 'A Source for the Jew of Malta' *Notes and Queries*, April 1962, pp. 139–41) where further possible sources are also suggested.

Among a good deal that has been written recently about the play, two studies might be found particularly interesting: the chapter in Donald Bevington's *From Mankind to Marlowe*, Harvard, 1962 (reprinted in the collection of essays on Marlowe edited by Clifford Leech, Prentice Hall 1964); and an essay called 'Innocent Barabas' by Alfred Harbage (*Tulane Drama Review*, Summer 1964).

1. *Phalaris*: a cruel Sicilian ruler of the 6th Century B.C., who roasted his enemies in a 'brazen bull', and was eventually burned to death in it himself. 'Had' means 'if he had' (i.e. 'if Phalaris had simply relied on the exercise of power instead of trying persuasion, he would have won').
2. *As Agamemnon . . .*: 'The most notable aspect of the relationship of Agamemnon to his daughter was never his affection for her but his willingness to sacrifice her for his own ends' (Douglas Cole, op. cit. p. 128).
3. *Hermoso placer . . .*: The Quarto usually misprints the foreign expressions, and here has 'Hermoso Piarer, de les Denirch'. The emended version is Dyce's.
4. *An if he has . . .*: 'If he has (some new way of stealing) he is worth a great deal (plates were pieces of silver), as long as his owner can obtain the town-seal to guarantee his pardon from the gallows; for the days of the assizes are crucial times in the life of a thief, and there is hardly any way of escape except in as far as the purgation of death itself is a way out'. For 'plates' Quarto has 'plats'.
5. *Enter Lodowick*: There is a confusion in the text here. Quarto has '*Enter Lodowick reading*' yet Mathias has the

line 'What, dares the villain write in such base terms?'.
Bennett suggests that something has fallen out of the text
here. I follow Craik's conjectural solution, giving Lodowick
the line 'What . . . terms' and adding a line for Mathias.

6. *Governor*: Cunningham's conjecture. Quarto has 'prior'.

7. *self*: Dyce's conjecture. Quarto has 'life' (probably trans-
cribed by the printer from line above).

8. *'less*: Collier's conjecture. Quarto has 'least'.

9. *basso*: Here and in some other places Quarto has 'bashaws'.

10. *Cazzo, diabolo*: literally 'Penis! The devil' (Quarto has
'*Catho diabola*'). Gifford (Jonson 2, 48) glosses '*cazzo*': 'a
petty oath, a cant exclamation, generally expressive, among
the Italian populace, who have it constantly on their mouth,
of defiance and contempt'.

11. *inmate*: Quarto has 'inmates'. Brooke and others emend
to 'intimates'.

12. *rogue*: Collier's conjecture. Quarto has 'go'.

13. *You know my mind . . .*: Quarto allocates this and the next
line to Ithamore.

14. [*force from me*]: Dyce's conjecture. Quarto has no verb.
Some suggest 'convey'.

15. *Rivo Castellano*: perhaps meaning 'let the drink flow' (cf.
'And *Rivo* will he cry, and *Castile* too', Hazlitt's Dodsley,
7, 505, quoted by Bennett, p. 142).

16. *snicle . . .*: Craik's conjecture who quotes Kittredge's
paraphrase: 'Snare him! lay your hand to it! Firmly now!'.
Quarto has 'I snicle hand too fast'.

17. *trench*: Dyce's conjecture. Quarto has 'truce'; others read
'sluice'.

18. *to keep*: Wagner's conjecture. Quarto has 'to kept'.

19. *Two lofty turrets*: as l. 10 in Quarto. Editors after Robinson
seeing it as misplaced transposed it with the line following
('Where Syracusian Dionysius reign'd'). Craik moves it
forward to l. 5, and the present edition follows this.

20. *countermin'd*: Craik suggests 'countermur'd' by analogy
with 1, 3, 399.

21. *mediate*: Robinson's conjecture. Quarto has 'meditate'.

EDWARD II

Edward II reigned from 1307 to 1327. His friend Gaveston had been exiled by Edward I in 1305 for encouraging the Prince to break into the grounds of the Bishop of Coventry; Edward recalled him and imprisoned the Bishop in the first year of his own reign, as in the play. The troubles which followed led to Gaveston's execution in 1312. At this point in the Chronicle Marlowe handles his material very boldly and makes Edward's anger over Gaveston's death the immediate cause of his renewed wars against the barons, whereas in fact there was a gap of nine years; his victory (3, 3) which seems to follow hard on the death of Gaveston was in fact not gained till 1322. Again it seems in the play to be a matter of months between this success and its reversal (4, 5), whereas the Chronicle tells of Edward's defeat as coming four years later, in 1326. His abdication and murder followed in the next year. Kent and Mortimer both survived till 1330, and here again the play compresses historical time, so that all these events are linked in a chain of immediate cause and effect.

Allowing for this telescoping of history, Marlowe follows his main source, Holinshed's *Chronicles* (1577 and 1587), fairly closely. His Edward is less dignified in his abdication speech than Holinshed's; and his Gaveston is not exactly the 'goodly gentleman and stout' who braves the barons in the Chronicle, though his influence on the King and court is described in much the same way. Some important features of the reign are omitted, and the importance of Young Mortimer is increased (Mortimer had no part in the action against Gaveston, for instance, and, according to Holinshed, was not responsible for the King's death). Occasionally Marlowe takes his material from another source: the forcible shaving of Edward, for example, is found not in Holinshed but in Stow's *Annals of England*, 1580. Further detailed comparisons are made in the edition of the play by Charlton and Waller (Methuen, 1933, new edition, 1955). Generally the impression accords with that of the historian Stubbs who wrote of Edward's reign: 'There is a miserable level of political selfishness, which marks without exception every public man; there is an sbsence of sincere feeling except in the shape of hatred and revenge . . . and there is no great triumph of good or evil to add a moral or inspire a sympathy'.

1. *Italian masques*: an anachronism. The Court Masque, familiar in Tudor times, had its hey-day in the reign of James I, and Italy was generally considered the land of its origin.

2. *Actaeon*: Actaeon, while out hunting, found the goddess Diana and her nymphs bathing, and, because he watched them, was punished by being changed into a stag.

3. *all Warwickshire will love him*: A common emendation substitutes 'leave' for 'love', and 'Gaveston' for 'Lancaster', but this misses the sarcasm of both sentences.

4. *Hylas*: a handsome youth who joined Hercules' Argonauts although Hercules had killed his father. For love, the Naids enticed him into the water: Hercules searched passionately but found only the echo of his voice.

5. *the New Temple*: founded by Knights Templars, 1184; later known as the Outer, Middle and Inner Temple (the 'old' Temple was in Holborn).

6. *Cyclops hammers*: Virgil (*Georgics*, IV, 170ff. and *Aeneid*, VIII, 418ff.) refers to the Cyclops as working for Vulcan in his smithy under Mt Etna.

7. *Hercules*: early editions have 'Hector' (but cf. note to Scene one, l. 144).

8. *propterea quod*: Both this and '*quandoquidem*' mean 'because', but presumably one was regarded as ponderous, the other as elegant. Baldock means he is no mere pedant, using old-fashioned constructions; Spenser adds that he has the scholarly graces and perhaps those of the gallant as well ('form a verb' suggesting a play on the meanings of 'conjugate').

9. *Jove . . . Danaë*: Danaë's father imprisoned her in a brazen tower because of a prophecy that her son would cause his death. Jove penetrated the tower in a shower of gold and she bore him a son, Perseus.

10. *bid . . . a base*: In the boys' game called prisoner's base, the one who leaves his base is pursued by the other player who tries to take him captive. To bid a base is to dare your opponent.

11. *Kent: This Edward . . .*: The line has given trouble because the opinion expressed comes oddly from Kent who is now sympathetic to Edward. Some editors give the speech to Young Mortimer, but without textual authority. Others interpret it as an aside made to the young prince, 'Edward' then becoming a vocative. Or it can be seen as a deceptive speech, designed to measure the Queen's party that he is on their side (earlier in the scene he has said that he will have to 'dissemble' while in their presence).

12. *Catiline*: an ambitious and unscrupulous Roman soldier and politician who died in 62 B.C.

THE MASSACRE AT PARIS

The play survives in a much maimed and abbreviated form: it is only 1,263 lines long (compared with the 2,316 of *Tamburlaine* Pt 1 or the 2,670 of *Edward II*), and the verse has been badly mangled by publisher and printer. One possible indication of what has been lost is provided by the 'Collier leaf' (see p. 601), comparison between the lines given there and the text as printed in the play suggesting that the passages omitted were precisely the more thoughtful ones and therefore, to us, potentially the most interesting.

The act and scene divisions have been added by the present editor.

1. *this union*: the marriage between Henry of Navarre and Margaret of Valois in 1572.

2. *we are betrayed*: The last four lines of the scene are given as prose in the octavo. This happens frequently and is generally taken as another sign of the text's bad condition. Further examples will not be noted in this edition.

3. *Ramus*: famous and controversial French logician and philosopher (1515–72).

4. *Taleus*: Omer Talon (c. 1510–1610), professor of rhetoric and friend of Ramus.

5. *Scene one*: Charles IX died 30 May 1574.

6. *Hold thee . . .*: There exists another version of this speech. This is in the so-called 'Collier leaf', a sheet of paper that

came into the possession of J. P. Collier who printed a transcription of it in 1831. It is still in existence and has been carefully examined, for Collier was a notorious forger. Modern opinion generally credits it as authentic, and the handwriting could well, in that case, be Marlowe's own (see F. S. Boas, *Christopher Marlowe*, Oxford University Press, 1940, pp. 168–71). The manuscript contains the speech of the Soldier, Mugeroun's death, and, most interestingly, the Guise's speech, sixteen lines long, as opposed to the mere four lines of the octavo:

> Hold thee, tall soldier. Take thee this and fly.
> Thus fall, imperfect exhalation,
> Which our great sun of France could not effect,
> A fiery meteor in the firmament!
> Lie there, the King's delight, and Guise's scorn!
> Revenge it, Henry, if thou list, or dar'st.
> I did it only in despite of thee.
> Fondly hast thou incens'd the Guise's soul,
> That of itself was hot enough to work
> Thy just digestion with extremest shame!
> The army I have gathered now shall aim
> More at thy end than exterpation;
> And when thou think'st I have forgotten this,
> And that thou most reposest on my faith,
> Then will I wake thee from thy foolish dream
> And let thee see thyself my prisoner.

7. *Yet Caesar . . .*: identical with Shakespeare's *Julius Caesar*, 2, 2, 28.
8. *Death of Guise*: December 23 1588.
9. *I will not live*: She died 5 January 1589.
10. *Death of Henry III*: 2 August 1589.

Discover more about our forthcoming books through Penguin's FREE newspaper...

Penguin
Quarterly

It's packed with:

- exciting features
- author interviews
- previews & reviews
- books from your favourite films & TV series
- exclusive competitions & much, much more...

Write off for your free copy today to:
Dept JC
Penguin Books Ltd
FREEPOST
West Drayton
Middlesex
UB7 0BR
NO STAMP REQUIRED

READ MORE IN PENGUIN

In every corner of the world, on every subject under the sun, Penguin represents quality and variety – the very best in publishing today.

For complete information about books available from Penguin – including Puffins, Penguin Classics and Arkana – and how to order them, write to us at the appropriate address below. Please note that for copyright reasons the selection of books varies from country to country.

In the United Kingdom: Please write to *Dept. JC, Penguin Books Ltd, FREEPOST, West Drayton, Middlesex UB7 OBR*

If you have any difficulty in obtaining a title, please send your order with the correct money, plus ten per cent for postage and packaging, to *PO Box No. 11, West Drayton, Middlesex UB7 OBR*

In the United States: Please write to *Penguin USA Inc., 375 Hudson Street, New York, NY 10014*

In Canada: Please write to *Penguin Books Canada Ltd, 10 Alcorn Avenue, Suite 300, Toronto, Ontario M4V 3B2*

In Australia: Please write to *Penguin Books Australia Ltd, 487 Maroondah Highway, Ringwood, Victoria 3134*

In New Zealand: Please write to *Penguin Books (NZ) Ltd, 182–190 Wairau Road, Private Bag, Takapuna, Auckland 9*

In India: Please write to *Penguin Books India Pvt Ltd, 706 Eros Apartments, 56 Nehru Place, New Delhi 110 019*

In the Netherlands: Please write to *Penguin Books Netherlands B.V., Keizersgracht 231 NL–1016 DV Amsterdam*

In Germany: Please write to *Penguin Books Deutschland GmbH, Friedrichstrasse 10–12, W–6000 Frankfurt/Main 1*

In Spain: Please write to *Penguin Books S. A., C. San Bernardo 117 6°, E–28015 Madrid*

In Italy: Please write to *Penguin Italia s.r.l., Via Felice Casati 20, 1–20124 Milano*

In France: Please write to *Penguin France S. A., 17 rue Lejeune, F–31000 Toulouse*

In Japan: Please write to *Penguin Books Japan, Ishikiribashi Building, 2–5–4, Suido, Tokyo 112*

In Greece: Please write to *Penguin Hellas Ltd, Dimocritou 3, GR–106 71 Athens*

In South Africa: Please write to *Longman Penguin Southern Africa (Pty) Ltd, Private Bag X08, Bertsham 2013*

READ MORE IN PENGUIN

A CHOICE OF CLASSICS

St Anselm	**The Prayers and Meditations**
St Augustine	**The Confessions**
Bede	**Ecclesiastical History of the English People**
Geoffrey Chaucer	**The Canterbury Tales**
	Love Visions
	Troilus and Criseyde
Marie de France	**The Lais of Marie de France**
Jean Froissart	**The Chronicles**
Geoffrey of Monmouth	**The History of the Kings of Britain**
Gerald of Wales	**History and Topography of Ireland**
	The Journey through Wales and
	The Description of Wales
Gregory of Tours	**The History of the Franks**
Robert Henryson	**The Testament of Cresseid and Other Poems**
Walter Hilton	**The Ladder of Perfection**
Julian of Norwich	**Revelations of Divine Love**
Thomas à Kempis	**The Imitation of Christ**
William Langland	**Piers the Ploughman**
Sir John Mandeville	**The Travels of Sir John Mandeville**
Marguerite de Navarre	**The Heptameron**
Christine de Pisan	**The Treasure of the City of Ladies**
Chrétien de Troyes	**Arthurian Romances**
Marco Polo	**The Travels**
Richard Rolle	**The Fire of Love**
François Villon	**Selected Poems**

READ MORE IN PENGUIN

A CHOICE OF CLASSICS

John Aubrey	**Brief Lives**
Francis Bacon	**The Essays**
George Berkeley	**Principles of Human Knowledge** and **Three Dialogues between Hylas and Philonous**
James Boswell	**The Life of Johnson**
Sir Thomas Browne	**The Major Works**
John Bunyan	**The Pilgrim's Progress**
Edmund Burke	**Reflections on the Revolution in France**
Thomas de Quincey	**Confessions of an English Opium Eater**
	Recollections of the Lakes and the Lake Poets
Daniel Defoe	**A Journal of the Plague Year**
	Moll Flanders
	Robinson Crusoe
	Roxana
	A Tour through the Whole Island of Great Britain
Henry Fielding	**Amelia**
	Jonathan Wild
	Joseph Andrews
	Tom Jones
Oliver Goldsmith	**The Vicar of Wakefield**

READ MORE IN PENGUIN

A CHOICE OF CLASSICS